CELESTINA

broadview editions
series editor: L.W. Conolly

"On some rude fragment of the rocky shore": Thomas Stothard's illustration of Smith's Sonnet 12, *Elegiac Sonnets*, Jan. 1st, 1789.

CELESTINA

Charlotte Smith

edited by Loraine Fletcher

broadview editions

Library and Archives Canada Cataloguing in Publication

Smith, Charlotte, 1749–1806
  Celestina / Charlotte Smith ; edited by Loraine Fletcher.

(Broadview editions)
Includes bibliographical references.
ISBN 1-55111-458-5

  I. Fletcher, Loraine. II. Title. III. Series.

PR3688.S4C44 2004   823′.6   C2004-904295-5

Broadview Press Ltd. is an independent, international publishing house, incorporated in 1985. Broadview believes in shared ownership, both with its employees and with the general public; since the year 2000 Broadview shares have traded publicly on the Toronto Venture Exchange under the symbol BDP.

The Broadview Editions series represents the ever-changing canon of literature by bringing together texts long regarded as classics with valuable lesser-known works.

We welcome comments and suggestions regarding any aspect of our publications – please feel free to contact us at the addresses below or at broadview@broadviewpress.com.

North America
Post Office Box 1243, Peterborough, Ontario, Canada K9J 7H5
3576 California Road, Orchard Park, NY, USA 14127
Tel: (705) 743-8990   Fax: (705) 743-8353
e-mail: customerservice@broadviewpress.com

UK, Ireland, and continental Europe
NBN Plymbridge, Estover Road, Plymouth PL6 7PY UK
Tel: 44 (0) 1752 202301   Fax: 44 (0) 1752 202331
Fax Order Line: 44 (0) 1752 202333
Customer Service: cservs@nbnplymbridge.com Orders: orders@nbnplymbridge.com

Australia and New Zealand
UNIREPS, University of New South Wales
Sydney, NSW, 2052
Tel: 61 2 9664 0999   Fax: 61 2 9664 5420
email: info.press@unsw.edu.au

www.broadviewpress.com

Advisory editor for this volume: Colleen Franklin

Typesetting and assembly: True to Type Inc., Mississauga, Canada.

PRINTED IN CANADA

Contents

Acknowledgements

I am very grateful to the Leverhulme Trust for the Fellowship that has given me time to work both on Smith's first novel, *Emmeline*, and on this edition of her third, *Celestina*, which has not been reissued since the 1790s. Like everyone interested in Charlotte Smith, I am greatly indebted to Judith Phillips Stanton for her achievement in collecting and annotating Smith's letters; she has generously allowed me to use them before their publication. They are now published by Indiana University Press, augmented by recent discoveries during the renovations at Petworth House. Many thanks to Peter Mendes for the first edition of *Celestina*, from which I have worked, to Barbara Conolly, Leonard Conolly and Jennifer Bingham, my Broadview editors, and to Colleen Franklin, my copy editor, who have been most patient and helpful. Thanks also to Mary Bryden, Michela Calore, Robin Howells, Chris MacLeod, Nik Macleod, Tony Simons, Adam Smyth, Maurice Slawinski and Carolyn Williams for their kindness in sharing IT skills and tracing fugitive quotations and allusions. Barbara Morris and the staff at Reading University Library have been, as ever, very helpful. I am especially grateful to Pam Brain of Brains Typography, Reading, for her patience and efficiency in typing in the text from the original with its cursive "s." Citation from Shakespeare is from the Norton edition.

Loraine Fletcher, University of Reading.

Introduction

Celestina and the Courtship Novel

Charlotte Smith's third novel is a story about the search for love and identity by an orphan whose adoptive mother dies when she is in her teens. The courtship novel, which centres on a young girl's entrance into adult society and her choice among competing suitors, was the most popular narrative pattern for fiction of its day, and allowed great flexibility. Its tone is often satiric: the narrator and the heroine use their wit to discriminate among varied characters and customs. Often the heroine is herself the object of narrative irony, only at the end learning to judge like the narrator. Samuel Richardson's *Pamela* (1740), Frances Burney's *Cecilia* (1782), Mary Wollstonecraft's *Mary, A Fiction* (1789), all bear some relation to the courtship-novel pattern, though all interrogate marriage. But genre is flexible: "courtship story," "novel of sensibility" and "Gothic tale" are interchangeable terms for much of the fiction of the later eighteenth century.

By then, the novel had become for many as compulsive a medium as television is now. It mapped emotion or "sensibility," alerting readers to the hidden springs of motive, encouraging debate on what makes a good society. The novelists' sense of the dark side of marriage and the family created Gothic plot-developments in confining houses or states of isolation and insanity: subversion was built into the courtship genre from the start and remained there, independent of social change. The "simple" story[1] of a young woman's marriage choice, or ultimate refusal of marriage, could be made to carry a huge freight of authorial comment on manners, fashions, morals, changing social patterns, economics, genetics, and sexual and national politics. In the next century, Charles Dickens, George Eliot and Henry James would retain a large courtship element for many of their plots.

Eighteenth-century courtship-novelists are often as ambiguous about rank as they are about marriage. An orphaned or deprived hero or heroine shows up the false values of more socially secure characters, who are disconcerted, and the reader's sense of fitness gratified, when the virtuous victim turns out to be very rich or a legitimate

---

1 Elizabeth Inchbald was ironic in her choice of title—*A Simple Story*—for her 1791 novel analysing the complexities of power-relations between the sexes.

aristocrat, outranking the snobs. Such Cinderella patterns where the author has it both ways may seem intellectually dishonest now. However, despite the popularity of Richardson's tragic *Clarissa*, readers usually preferred happy endings and saw neat closure as part of the genre, not necessarily deleting the impact of earlier scenes.

Smith found original ways to develop the form in each of her first three novels; *Celestina*, published in 1791, was preceded by *Emmeline* (1788) and *Ethelinde* (1789). But they have much in common: self-possessed, reflective heroines, conflicting family relationships, acerbic radical satire, acceptance that marriage is a woman's goal but that great caution is necessary in achieving it, a more tolerant attitude to extramarital sex and the "fallen" woman than is usually found in English novels of the eighteenth and nineteenth centuries, threatening castles emblematic of gender and national hierarchies, and contrasting locations including sublime mountain landscape. *Emmeline* questions contemporary patterns of family-arranged and teenage marriage. *Ethelinde* shows more concern with the "strange disposition of the goods of fortune";[1] it is mainly about money. *Celestina* satirises definition of nobility as inherited rank and celebrates what seemed the beginning of a fairer system.

In her third novel Smith explores the limited possibilities in the 1780s for a young woman without known family, though with an income just adequate for a "merely negative life" (129), as the heroine calls it: a few books, a few clothes, a small rented cottage in Devonshire. Celestina makes uneasy visits to other people's houses and an enterprising journey to the Hebrides. Obstacles to her marriage are raised in the form of a potentially incestuous relationship: she may be the daughter rather than the adopted daughter of her patroness, the mother of the man she has loved from childhood. Her questionable identity encodes the "illegitimacy," the lack of human rights of many women less obviously and romantically singular. Apparent marginality and obstacles set in the path of true love, however, are conventional ingredients for any eighteenth-century novel.

Two original developments in narrative fiction found in *Celestina* will be considered in more detail later, but should be briefly noted here. Firstly, the heroine's wide reading and talent as a poet associate her closely with the author, who was more than twice her age at the time of writing. Celestina's mind is older from the start than that of a naïve heroine who learns from her mistakes, a more common central character in this genre. Though passing from seventeen to twenty, the standard heroine's age, through the main part of the action, she

---

1 *Ethelinde*, Vol. 5, 109.

has a habit of spontaneous literary composition and a knowledge of English, Italian and French poetry and prose that contemporary readers might more readily expect to find in the author of *Elegiac Sonnets*, Smith's volume of poems published in 1784 and constantly reissued and updated. And Celestina's satiric perceptions of English society too are hard to distinguish from the narrator's.

Secondly, *Celestina*'s concluding episodes lock onto the beginnings of the French Revolution. The narrative was evidently designed to shift into political observation in its last volume. Still chronically hard up after the publication of *Ethelinde*, Smith was starting to think about a third novel as early as August, 1789,[1] five weeks after the storming of the Bastille, when events in France, and English attitudes to those events, were confused and changing rapidly. By beginning with a heroine abandoned at birth in a Celestine convent in the south of France, she left herself the option of taking English characters to France at some stage, letting them learn about French suffering under the tyranny of the *ancien régime*—the old constitution before the Revolution, in which monarch and feudal nobility governed with absolute power—and finding that they have some connection with these historic events.

This novel follows the pattern of Smith's previous two, with a poor and vulnerable heroine, a powerful network of cruel or careless aristocrats, and a good selection of "cats and tiffany Misses,"[2] matchmakers and fortune hunters. It is more derivative than *Emmeline* or *Ethelinde*: the duel and Celestina's alarms at Ranelagh resemble a dramatic scene at Vauxhall in Burney's *Cecilia*. But it embodies a wider range of social and political ideas than Smith's earlier work.

On 8 September 1790, Smith wrote confidently to her publisher, Thomas Cadell,[3] of "having no doubt of putting the whole upon

1 On 22 August she wrote to Dr. Thomas Shirly about her need to take a break from looking after her children in Brighton and start a new novel at her friend Henrietta O'Neill's home at Shanes' Castle near Dublin.

2 *Ethelinde*, Vol. 4, 6.

3 Thomas Cadell's firm in the Strand was long-established and respected: he had published, for example, Samuel Johnson's *Lives of the Poets* and Edward Gibbon's *The Decline and Fall of the Roman Empire*. He became Smith's friend and mentor while publishing her early work, including her translations, *Manon Lescaut* and *The Romance of Real Life*, her first three courtship novels, and the continually expanded volumes of her *Elegiac Sonnets*. But he disliked her pro-revolutionary tendency, first observable in *Celestina*, and refused her next two novels, *Desmond* and *The Old Manor House*. From the mid-1790s the firm was run by his son, also Thomas, and William Davies, with neither of whom she got on so well, though they published her last novel, *The Young Philosopher*. See the Chronology.

paper (since it is already settled in my head)." And the integrity of the satiric point of view over four volumes bears her out. Rank and inheritance are her targets from the start. Her observation is dry, as in the description of Philip Molyneux, "the calm coldness of [whose] manner gave an idea of latent powers, which he was supposed to be too indolent to exert" (69). But the subjects of her satire are allowed some depth, even some pathos. Matilda Willoughby, who marries Molyneux mainly for his prospective baronetcy, is left to contemplate her beautiful long Chinese eyes before her mirror at night alone, as her husband goes off to his own room. The most interesting and ambiguous of the "bad" characters, Miss Fitz-Hayman, has intelligence and some honesty, but still falls victim to her own uncontrolled feelings, her erotic sensibility, when the marriage her parents have arranged for her fails to materialise. High rank, whether acquired by effort or conferred by birth, makes nobody happy except Lord Castlenorth, who is senile.

He embodies what Smith most despises and hopes to see reformed in England. In his obsession with heraldry, that is, with the coats of arms that from early-medieval times recorded the land-grabbing and intermarriage of powerful families, he functions as the microcosm of an England imploding under the weight of dead tradition. Castlenorth's constitution and the body politic are equally diseased, in a metaphor which goes back to classical times[1] but which Smith revives with some subtlety. She allows little sense of an old chivalric ideal betrayed by contemporary aristocracy. On the contrary, those who acquired honours and land by the Norman Conquest were merely the greatest thieves, though with an energy their descendants lack. Celestina's and her two closest friends' experience of the inequity of the English social system, developed in the first three volumes, prepares the way for the fourth, where we see the aristocratic order dismantled in France, and are left expecting similar emancipation from the weak remnant of feudalism in England, now Castlenorth is dead. The novel's radical politics are diffused through the story rather than attached opportunistically at the end, showing how closely Smith could relate her own political perceptions to the changes taking place in France after the summer of 1789.

One danger of the courtship-novel plot is the risk of losing narrative suspense: the outcome is often too easy to see at the beginning. The hero, the suitor who will win the heroine from one or more

---

1   It is found, for example, in Plutarch's life of Coriolanus in *Parallel Lives*.

competitors, is usually easy to spot from his moral eminence and facility as a rescuer. *Celestina* does not quite avoid predictability in its marriage-ending, but Smith does her best to keep up suspense. Willoughby lacks moral eminence and behaves badly enough to allow the possibility that one of Celestina's two other suitors, or a third making a late appearance, will emerge from the hierarchy of characters to marry her. And though the narrator is always reliable, the villainous Lady Castlenorth's claim that Celestina is Willoughby's half-sister is supported by narrative coincidence from page one onwards. The misleading clues are not too obvious, and readers may be drawn as detectives into thinking that their independent perceptions are preparing for a surprise denouement.

To the modern reader, Montague Thorold is an unlikely replacement hero. His constantly pestering Celestina in Devonshire, his secretly following her to Skye, would invite a harassment suit now. He is odd by eighteenth-century standards too, as is clear from the response of other characters to him. Smith's psychoanalytic case-study is brought up by a respected clerical father to lead an unusually moral life for a young man of the 1780s; his sexual repression emerges at times as dementia. The narrator's characterisation is ambiguous: she shows what a nuisance he is to Celestina, but his presence is useful following the death of her friend's husband, and she feels more kindly towards him by the last volume. His portrayal provides a measure of how greatly manners and courtship customs have changed since the late eighteenth century. Stalking and the pilfering of fetishistic personal items have not vanished, but they are at least subject to legal sanctions, not something for which the victim needs to thank the persecutor. Smith dramatises vividly how close romantic devotion and intrusive obsession can be on the spectrum of "love."

Vavasour, the libertine suitor, is perhaps no more likely than Thorold to displace Willoughby in Celestina's or the contemporary reader's esteem. Smith gives him an agreeably racy tone in conversation, and he is not a seducer, though he maintains Emily generously as his mistress when her reputation is irretrievable. The distinction was important to Smith's contemporaries. But his virtues, like his vices, stem from unexamined upper class assumptions of superiority that the novel finds increasingly inadequate: he degenerates rapidly, while the moral—as distinct from the romantic—hero of *Celestina* is the hard-working secretary Cathcart, though he is allowed only a background presence most of the time. In the previous generation, Celestina's father and uncle are each configured as both romantic and moral heroes.

Vavasour and Willoughby are friends, and at one point, when he is particularly jealous, Willoughby is described as "speaking less like himself than like Vavasour, whose vehemence he seemed to adopt" (370). Smith practised this ideological doubling of traits in paralleled characters throughout her career, here to suggest how prevalent are Vavasour's jealousy and domineering assumptions, how disturbing his likeness to Willoughby. In *Emmeline*, Smith had broken novelistic codes to produce a new hero half-way through the action, and first readers of *Celestina* could not be sure she would not do something unexpected again. Thus Smith keeps an element of suspense alive in a young-girl's-courtship formula which she perhaps felt constricting the third time in succession, but which had always allowed expansion into areas beyond the domestic.

Multiple narrative, a characteristic of Smith's previous fiction, also helps to sustain interest in a four-decker. Celestina becomes a patroness and friend to two other women. Jessy Woodburn, a farmer's daughter who goes into service in a London household, tells her story towards the end of volume one. Sophy Elphinstone, whose connections are in the City among middle-class merchant families, tells her story at the end of volume two. Their lives exemplify, respectively, the drift to the cities that was following industrialisation, and the expansion of colonial trade which marked the last quarter of the eighteenth and the first half of the nineteenth centuries. Celestina's parents turn out to be scions of French and English nobility who have rebelled against their families, so a sisterhood forms from across the social spectrum, validating sorority. Fraternity was the third of the pledges, after liberty and equality, of the recently established French National Assembly.

A strong sense of pattern emerges, which continues into the third and fourth volumes. Gary Kelly's general comment on technique in reformist novels of the 1790s is especially relevant to Smith:

> Their unity of design had reference to a certain observance of decorum in fashioning the novel's parts—'design' in the sense of plan, disposition of elements to make up a whole which has an artistic harmony. But they also aimed for unity of intent, a design in which their various 'designs' on the reader were integrated with one another, with the autobiographical impulse, and with the novel's artistic character.[1]

---

1 Gary Kelly, *The English Jacobin Novel, 1780-1805*, 19.

The first two volumes' embedded narratives have intersected before Jessy or Sophy meet Celestina. Each story is elicited by Celestina's sympathetic encouragement. Cutting across social circumstance and education, each sub-heroine pools her experience of family problems and bereavements, love, poverty and isolation, with Celestina and with the reader. We are positioned to acknowledge the truth of feeling as the only valid and useful bond of society.

Jessy, Sophy and Celestina, like all Smith's heroes and heroines, display sensibility, a capacious term and difficult to define. Characters of sensibility are lovers of literature, reflective observers of their times, and poets, or at least capable of poetic expression. Artistic or musical, with a love of nature, they find it hard to adapt to society's demands, rejecting the security of a convenient marriage, or work that would contaminate them. As S.R. Martin says,

> the heroine must rely on her own resources or those of a friend or two because Charlotte Smith sees society misorganised on vicious principles: there is no coherent established system of social norms fit for an intelligent, sensitive being to discover and adapt to.[1]

As sufferers themselves, her "sensible" or feeling characters are sympathetic to the grief of others. Strong feelings take effect on their bodies in sleeplessness, tears or faintness. The language of sensibility derived partly from medicine, which linked susceptibility to nervous illness with the moral life of sympathetic feeling. As John Mullan argues:

> Discussions of nervous disorder, hypochondria, and melancholy are, for most of the [eighteenth] century, shadowed by images of the pleasures and privileges that might come with such supposed afflictions. The pleasures and privileges are typically associated with kinds of retreat, variously rendered as evidence of 'Indolence' or of 'Sensibility', from worldly ambition and commercial activity.[2]

Though Cathcart works hard for a City firm, his efforts are sustained only for his sister and her children, and bring him close to breakdown. Sensibility, essential for a lover or a friend, is incompatible

---

1   S.R. Martin, "Charlotte Smith, 1749-1806, A Critical Survey of her Works and Place in Literary History." Ph.D. Thesis, University of Sheffield, 1980, 235.
2   John Mullan, *Sentiment and Sociability*, 215.

with worldly success, though a lucky but clearly fictional last minute legacy, kind patron or revelation of noble birth can make way for the happy ending.

Willoughby's version of sensibility and acute feeling is more extreme than in any of the female characters; emotion drives him, like Montague Thorold and Vavasour, close to madness at times. Gender difference is reversed from its "norm" in *Celestina*, with the women showing more fortitude than the men, many of the men more emotionalism or vulnerability than the women. But "norms" are always in a state of flux, and there was conscious blurring of gender boundaries in the Age of Sensibility in many aspects of the culture, as we can see in some of the portraiture of the time. Willoughby refers to a projected loveless marriage with Miss Fitz-Hayman as prostituting himself, a concept elsewhere only just coming into use to analyse the female marriage-market.

Physical sensitivity to experience is a liability, since it is inseparable from sexual responsiveness. Hence the dangerous sexuality usually associated with artistic traits in this type of novel. Smith's central characters embody feeling as an eroticism which may, if uncontrolled, tilt towards physical or mental breakdown, as with Willoughby, or towards a reckless disregard for decency, as with Miss Fitz-Hayman, who commits incest with her mother's lover. Sense and reason untempered by strong emotion are the qualities of contrasted characters like the Molyneux, who are cool, self-interested and materially successful.

But the capacity to feel and to suffer is a precondition of humanitarianism. It is the one real value Smith has to set against her satiric pictures of aristocratic and mercantile society. The sympathising hero and heroine and their friends, though threatened, bear witness that the heart is capable of benevolence and human nature innately good, as the Swiss philosopher Jean-Jacques Rousseau believed. The narrator's sympathy for the victims of society, if communicated to the reader, implies the possibility of reform and progress. Many of the reforms that took place in the next century, prison reform, the cutting of the number of crimes that carried the death penalty, the abolition of slavery in the British Empire and North America, the provision of medical care for the army, the reform of the Anglican clergy, the gradual emancipation of women and the Reform Bill of 1832 itself, all had their roots in the previous century and especially in the 1790s. Discussing the literature of the time, Marilyn Butler says, "Humanitarian feeling for the real-life underdog is a strong vein from the 1760s to the 1790s, often echoing real-life campaigns for reform."[1] Smith's courtship novels, like others of the late eighteenth century, linked sensibility, satire and a reformist agenda.

As well as telling a suspenseful story, taking the reader on an imaginary tour abroad or commenting openly or in code on the condition of England, courtship novels presented models of behaviour and lifestyle guides. At intervals throughout *Celestina*, the narrator pauses to update the hero's and heroine's emotional dilemmas, moving into and out of their consciousness to analyse and judge. Here the "agony aunt" side of the narrator's persona emerges. For instance, when Celestina considers her options after long suspense about Willoughby's feelings for her, and as her consciousness moves between past, present and future, the reader is drawn into a sense of the contingency and problematic nature of all relationships. The zigzags of the heroine's mind are tentative at first, acting out her difficult choices through syntactically balanced sentences, or registering indecision in concessive or conditional clauses. But as the passage continues, her train of thought emerges into confidence with:

> if Celestina had any fault, it was a sort of latent pride, the child of conscious worth and elevated understanding; which, though she was certainly obscurely, and possibly dishonourably born, she never could subdue and, perhaps, never seriously tried to subdue it. She felt, that in point of intellect she was superior to almost every body she conversed with; she could not look into the glass without seeing the reflection of a form, worthy of so fair an inhabitant as an enlightened human soul....(350)

Her supposed illegitimacy, at the time of writing arguably shameful, and certainly a social disadvantage, is contrasted with a pride imaged as a free and newborn "child of conscious worth." Her frank approval of her body and mind is evident as she gazes in the glass; her worth is self-engendered and self-validated, confident to meet the judgement of the rest of the world. Smith creates a heroine who, in spite of lost status, has it in her power to make herself anew, to look in her mirror and like herself without reference to artificial standards. The word "enlightened" shows where this ideal is coming from. It

---

1 Marilyn Butler, *Romantics, Rebels and Reactionaries* (Oxford: Oxford UP, 1981) 31.

was beginning to connote a freedom from prejudice acquired through reading authors who, like Rousseau or Voltaire, questioned religious and social orthodoxies. The first dictionary-registered use of "enlightenment" to indicate a historical period of increasing secularisation and equality of opportunity was in the 1790s, just after the usage here. Both "enlightened," in this context, and "enlightenment," imply a reliance on reason, a break with the customs and superstitions of the past. Through her heroine, Smith asserts the value of the small individual life and its right to the pursuit of happiness. Even when rehearsing standard love-problems in a courtship novel, Smith's range of diction constantly carries her reader towards the philosophical debates of her time and offers plenty of intellectual challenge.

Where the novel is focused on its heroine, narrative passes easily into free indirect speech, where Celestina's authority is indistinguishable from the narrator's. When she receives an invitation to stay with Lady Horatia in London, Vavasour foresees that he will acquire dangerous rivals; he

> would very gladly have persuaded her against accepting it, had he any pretence to offer for his objections: but having none, and not daring to invent any, he had confined himself to mutterings about prudish old cats, and representing to Celestina, that she was going to confine herself as an humble companion, to bear all the caprices of a superannuated woman of quality. Celestina heard him at first with concern, from an idea that he had heard Lady Horatia misrepresented; but when, on his afterwards repeating this conversation, she found that he knew nothing of her character even from report, and only described her in so unpleasant a light from his wish to deter Celestina from finding a refuge in her house, anger conquered her concern, and even her complaisance, and she besought him in very strong terms never again to name Lady Horatia Howard to her, unless he could prevail upon himself to remember that she deserved, from her character rather than her rank, the respect of every man, and particularly of every *gentleman*. (351)

Observation of the social world passes into general rules of conduct, eliding the roles of narrator and heroine. Smith's narrative style is typically one of long, latinate sentences and aphoristic pronouncements, belonging both to heroine and narrator, and offering a style of female virtue which is confident and socially-assured. By some standards of the time, Celestina is arrogant. But Smith's assertion of her heroine's right to self-esteem must have given pleasure to a lot of woman readers struggling with more repressive notions of humility, self-examination and self-blame as the particular duties of their sex.

Although the narrator occasionally remembers to commend Celestina's silence in company, we always see her as articulate and decisive. She is never persuaded to adopt Lady Horatia's view of her suitors, and except when taunted with her illegitimacy is unaffected by Lady Castlenorth's disapproval. Though grieving for Willoughby, she initiates adventurous new plans for herself when she goes to Skye with Sophy Elphinstone. In volume four, she was evidently intended to cross to France on her own to seek her parentage, though Smith, as often happened, had too much material for the length Cadell had specified, four volumes in this case, and was forced to jettison that plan. Smith's feminine model is as independent as possible for an unmarried young woman in the middle or upper class who wished to remain socially acceptable. But in the final reconciliation with Willoughby she goes well beyond generally acceptable heroine's behaviour, embracing him when she thinks he is married to Miss Fitz-Hayman: Smith crosses orthodox boundaries here, but the reader is so close to the end that the transgression is hardly noticeable.

As Jane Spencer shows,[1] Eliza Haywood's *The History of Miss Betsy Thoughtless* (1751), initiated a form of novel, generally female-authored, that centred on a changing female consciousness and had its roots in the conduct books. However inadequate, for different reasons, they found the conduct books of their own times, Burney, Smith, Ann Radcliffe and Jane Austen were all engaged in a form of moral guidance, though the guidance is subtle and sometimes oppositionist, challenging accepted custom and opinion.

In Emily, for instance, Smith creates a character morally superior to Celestina. As one might expect in a novel supporting innovation in national politics, *Celestina* is daring in its attitude to established sexual morality and society's treatment of the "fallen" woman. Emily is seduced at fifteen on a promise of marriage, then taken into "keeping," maintenance as a mistress, by Vavasour. She gives money she makes from him to a doctor in a vain attempt to save her nephew's life. Later, when she is dying, she tries to persuade Celestina to marry him, as she is convinced this will make him happy. Her death late in the novel, her story of defeat in the battle of the sexes, undermines the happy ending of the main plot. Emily's position on the margins

---

1 In *The Rise of the Woman Novelist*, 142.

of everyone else's story formally enacts the annual fate of hundreds of such women. They are "ruined" and drop out of society, unforgotten perhaps, but seldom spoken of afterwards. Before she first appears, Vavasour has said that his acquaintance has lain, with one exception, amongst women not likely to be "sent broken-hearted to Bristol,"[1] not likely to be much affected by men's ill-treatment of them. The reader thinks at the time that the exception is Celestina, but realises later that he meant Emily. Such "ruined" or "fallen" women remain in their friends' or lovers' consciousnesses, but hidden from the rest of society. When Celestina eventually meets her, Emily is dying, and

> [t]he blood might almost be seen to circulate in her veins, so plainly did they appear; and her eyes had the dazzling radiance of ethereal fire.... A few locks of her fine light hair had escaped from her head-dress, and played like broken rays from a receding planet, round a face, which only those who had hearts unhappily rigid, could behold, without feeling the sense of her errors suspended or overwhelmed by strong emotions of the tenderest pity. (523)

She is pictured almost as a saint. Her seducer, Beresford, never suffers for his deception or for an act which would now be considered the rape of a minor. Extramarital sexual experience in men carried little social stigma, while women were often rejected by their families and forced to turn to prostitution to survive. Emily assumes the position and iconography of suffering, violated women initiated in *Clarissa*. The images of "ethereal fire" and "receding planet" suggest that the double standard of sexual morality is a disaster on a cosmic scale. Emily's concealed life and late appearance are a better handling of the "fallen woman" narrative than Smith had managed in *Emmeline*. At a time when novels were becoming more and more cross-referential, naming could be programmatic. Emily's name directed the contemporary reader to compare a sympathetic treatment here with patriarchal constructions of fallen women, both Emilys, in Henry Mackenzie's *The Man of Feeling* (1771) and William Hayley's *The Young Widow* (1789).

---

1 See p. 202 and note.

Self-Representation

From Smith's first publication, *Elegiac Sonnets* (1784), she included in her work autobiographical material intended to be recognised as such; to this shrewd strategy she owed her success, creating a loyal readership who bought her books because they wanted to hear of developments in her own story. In *Elegiac Sonnets*, which came out in edition after edition, accruing new verse sometimes first published in the novels, the sonnet speaker looks forward to death but must continue to tread her rugged path of deprivation and solitude for her children's sake. The London literary world, the world of the all-powerful reviews and magazines, was smaller then than it is now. It was not difficult for reviewers, or ordinary readers, to connect the desolate maternal speaker of the poems with a real author trying to provide for eight children because their father was too irresponsible to work. Smith included a satiric portrait of her husband Benjamin as Mr. Stafford in *Emmeline*, and in *Ethelinde* drew on memories of serving time with him in the grim King's Bench Prison, London, when he was imprisoned for debt in 1783.

In her poems, novels, play, children's books and letters, Smith presented a saga of her own marital unhappiness, poverty and anxiety about her children as what Sarah Zimmerman calls a "serialised auto-biographical narrative."[1] In her third novel, she put some of her own biographical experience, recognisable to readers of the Sonnets, into the secondary narratives of Jessy and Sophy, and gave her poetic sensibility to Celestina, who is imagined on Skye as a lonely figure on a rocky seashore. Smith inserted the digressive journey to the Hebrides to introduce a sublime landscape as appropriate setting for her bleaker poetry, and allow a unique and imaginative way of linking author and heroine. As Celestina sits beside the sea, jots down phrases for a sonnet or watches as her friend's husband is shipwrecked in a storm, she enacts the pictured emblem of the author's sensibility created by Thomas Stothard, which had appeared as an illustration in the fifth, subscription edition of Smith's *Elegiac Sonnets*, published while Smith was planning *Celestina* (see Frontispiece).

The edition was a triumph for Smith. Cadell had taken over as her publisher from Richard Dodsley, who reluctantly published her first volume of sonnets in 1784. This fifth edition was beautifully produced by Cadell and issued on New Year's Day, 1789. There are 815

---

1 Sarah Zimmerman, "Charlotte Smith's Letters," 60.

subscribers listed at the beginning, including the Duchess of Cumberland, the Archbishop of Canterbury, her friends the Honourable John and Henrietta O'Neill, the writers Frances Burney, Elizabeth Carter, and Mary Delany, and the tragic actress Sarah Siddons. Of the volume's five illustrations, two are by Stothard, except for William Blake the greatest illustrator of his time, adept at catching the mood of a text. Beginning as a designer for women's and literary magazines, he had already contributed to editions of Fielding, Smollett, Richardson, Sterne, Defoe and Swift; by the end of his career he would have illustrated Shakespeare and most of the major English authors with sympathy and inventiveness. By 1789 he was exhibiting at the Royal Academy.

Whether Smith's friend and mentor William Hayley[1] or Cadell secured him for *Elegiac Sonnets* is unknown, but he produced one of his best designs for Smith in the figure of Sensibility. His second illustration in this volume, for Smith's Sonnet 26, "To the River Arun," is of the poet Otway as an infant. This is as sweet as a Victorian, Kate Greenaway illustration, too much so for most modern tastes. Both pictures were engraved by James Neagle, who also gained a lasting reputation for his illustrations of Shakespeare and *The Arabian Nights Entertainments*.

The female emblem of Sensibility faces Sonnet 12, "Written on the Seashore.—October, 1784," perhaps the most plaintive and characteristic of all Smith's sonnets; it admirably captures this poem's and the whole volume's construction of the concept. Given the importance of the picture to *Celestina*, it is worth quoting the whole sonnet here:

On some rude fragment of the rocky shore,
Where on the fractured cliff, the billows break,
Musing, my solitary seat I take,
And listen to the deep and solemn roar.

O'er the dark waves the winds tempestuous howl;
The screaming sea-bird quits the troubled sea:
But the wild gloomy scene has charms for me,
And suits the mournful temper of my soul.

---

1 Hayley was then a well-known poet, playwright, biographer and essayist, to whom Smith dedicated *Elegiac Sonnets*.

Already shipwreck'd by the storms of Fate,
Like the poor mariner methinks I stand,
Cast on a rock; who sees the distant land
From whence no succour comes—or comes too late.
Faint and more faint are heard his feeble cries,
'Till in the rising tide, th' exhausted sufferer dies.[1]

In Stothard's drawing an elegantly dressed young woman is sitting on a rocky shore, while in the distance a ship is driven towards cliffs by a storm. The sky is overcast, but there are lights flashing behind her. The drapery is reminiscent of drawings by Blake, with whom Stothard had worked in the early 1780s; Blake, indeed, claimed he had taught Stothard "how to see."[2] The pictured woman is holding pages of manuscript in her hand, linking her to Smith, since she is the visual representation of the speaker of *Elegiac Sonnets*, and linking her also to the reader, who is holding the published poems. The woman's gaze is turned inward rather than on the manuscript or the imminent wreck. It is a drawing of exquisite grace. As a tribute to and illustration of her writing, it must have given Smith great pleasure, and incited her to re-inscribe the figure into her current narrative as the Celestina of volume three.

To do this, she had to place her heroine on a desolate shore where she composes poetry and where Northern Lights flash, and invent the unlikely circumstance of a heroine's friend with a husband engaged in the Skye herring industry to provide the necessary background shipwreck. It is some measure of the priority she gave to her poetry over her novels, and to her self-representation over her plot, that she was prepared to include such a bizarre narrative digression to fit the picture. But for many readers this will be the most interesting volume.

In *Emmeline*, the hero and the "fallen" Lady Adelina are the poets. Reviewers had regretted the absence of poetry in *Ethelinde*. Here, Celestina is the only poet, contributing five sonnets and one short verse narrative, "The Peasant of the Alps," all of which Smith had written before she began her novel,[3] though each is integrated dramatically. The poems are written in contemplation of the natural

1 *The Poems of Charlotte Smith*, ed. Curran, 20.
2 "I found them [Stothard and John Flaxman] blind, I taught them how to see / And now they know neither themselves nor me." Cited by Mona Wilson in *The Life of William Blake* (London: Nonesuch Press, 1927) 13.
3 See Smith's letter of 8 September 1790, to Cadell.

world. All but one, "On this lone island, whose unfruitful breast," are about the loss of love and the speaker's consequent desolation. The first, "Oh Thou! who sleeps't where hazle-bands entwine," and the second, "Farewel ye lawns!—by fond remembrance blest," are placed in an English landscape, the first in a country churchyard, though without the grim effects often found in the "Graveyard"[1] school of poetry, the second in the grounds of a great estate.

These two are typical of Smith's earlier elegiac sonnets, with a melancholy speaker set against a harmonising landscape. "Oh Thou! who sleeps't" is a good example of Smith's aural and metrical delicacy. Onomatopoeic language creates a sense of tranquillity. The sentiments are familiar classical ones, and there is no "turn" or change of subject at the end of the octave:

Though canst not now thy fondest hopes resign
Even in the hour that should have made thee blest.
Light lies the turf upon thy virgin breast [....]

The plangency of the run-on rhyme-scheme with its couplet at the hinge of octave and sestet enacts the lingering of speaker and village lover beside the grave: there can be no "moving on." As in Thomas Gray's "Elegy in a Country Churchyard," published in 1750, the speaker stands a little apart both from the village world of love and grief and from the indifferent outside world.

In some of Smith's sonnets, the sestet is banal, a moral predictably extracted from the emblem invoked in the octave: "The Pilgrim" and "The Laplander," the fourth and fifth sonnets in this volume and the second and third supposedly written on Skye, are inert in their sestets. But even these less successful examples are interesting in their contrast of light and shade. Smith was working towards—and eventually achieved in some passages of *Beachy Head*—a romantic inscription of coloured light, effects of radiance, something her contemporary J.M.W. Turner put dazzlingly into paint. A chiaroscuro forms from light reflected against darkness or storm in land or seascapes; she aims for the same painterly effect in prose in the passages where Celestina watches the approaching storm and the Aurora Borealis, the Northern Lights.

The Lights, which suggest the flashes of illumination of the

---

1 The "Graveyard School" was a term applied to Robert Blair (1699-1746), Edward Young (1683-1765), and their imitators.

Romantic poet, are visible behind the figure in the Stothard picture, though not very clearly. In reinscribing Stothard's emblem of her sensibility as Celestina, backlit against the desolate Hebridean landscape and the sea, Smith again dramatises her own poetic persona and invites the reader to contemplate her own artistic talent and isolation. Volume three is particularly dense in authorial self-representation. The portrayal of Benjamin Smith as Elphinstone makes some amends for the wholly unlikeable Stafford version in *Emmeline*, while Elphinstone's death by shipwreck off the coast of Skye draws the reader's attention to Smith's quasi-widowhood and marital wreckage. The passage where Celestina takes Sophy to visit Elphinstone's grave in the cold church at night among human bones extends the limits of Gothic horror and self-revelation. The phrasing of Coral Howells' definition of Gothic is interesting here:

> There is nothing confident or optimistic about Gothic fiction: its main areas of feeling treat of melancholy, anxiety-ridden sentimental love and horror; it is a shadowy world of ruins and twilit scenery lit up from time to time by lurid flashes of passion and violence.[1]

Smith creates that concept of Romantic authorship in the Skye passages. The Stothard picture was her own emblem, the visible sign of her hard-won achievement. As well as its primary meaning, "achievement" signified a coat of arms: Smith uses the word in that sense for the armorial bearings in stained glass in the chapel at Rochemarte. Castlenorth's only claim to respect, his entitlement to the outdated medieval devices of heraldry, is contrasted in volume three with the reworking in prose narrative of Smith's own authorial blazon, drawn with all Stothard's skill and imagination to illustrate her achievement in *Elegiac Sonnets*. In the picture and in *Celestina*, the poet's sensibility is defined as emerging partly, perhaps, from sublime landscape or remembered verse, but more from female interiority and sadness.

Celestina then is Smith's self-representative poet within the novel, though as a nineteen-year-old deserted on her wedding day, she is an *alter ego* more passionate than Smith felt she could be outside a fictional persona. The first of her sonnets on Skye, "On this lone island," contrasts the unfruitful breast of the Hebridean rock, just able to

---

1   Coral Howells, *Love, Mystery and Misery*, 5.

maintain a few sheep, with imagined happiness if she were "of thy tenderness and love possesst," in the summers or finding a refuge from the dark, "Elysium in thy sheltering arms," in the winters on Skye. Imagination is linked to erotic feeling here, as it often was in the 1790s, and the *Critical Review* thought the language, "though beautiful and elegant rather too warm" (Appendix A.3).

The short narrative poem placed later, "The Peasant of the Alps,"[1] also has its tactile and sensuous images of

> The chamois' velvet spoil that forms the bed,
> Where in her arms he finds repose.[2]

This poem is about the cruelty of the natural world; the peasant's love is crushed with his home and garden beneath an avalanche. Celestina goes nowhere near the Alps; this could as easily and more credibly have been set in the Pyrenees and given to Willoughby to compose during his explorations there. But Smith clearly wanted a woman speaker to voice a range of attitudes to love, loss and death which are more erotic and desolate than those usually expressed by woman poets of her time. For Celestina, literature is talismanic, her greatest help in times of trouble, as Smith's letters suggest it was for her. Celestina reads and writes in an attempt to make sense of the world, and can quote from memory Petrarch, Metastasio, Guarini, Bertaut and Rousseau, as well as Shakespeare, Cowper, Thomson, Sterne and Gray, among many others.

But minor characters carry more of Smith's actual biographical experience. Celestina meets Jessy on a stagecoach where both are pestered by an overbearing grocer. A coach journey, which forced a temporary physical intimacy on passengers of different tastes and backgrounds, was a useful eighteenth-century novelistic device. Here Celestina first feels the consequence of a loss of status: there is no social barrier now to prevent John Jedwyn harassing her, perhaps even assaulting her. But she acts decisively to avoid the danger and shield Jessy too, and from this journey comes the first real friend she makes. Jessy's tale of isolation, exhaustion, and longing for the country, though mediated in prose and coming from a social register different from Smith's sonnet-speaker, is another version of that speak-

---

1   Ann Radcliffe imitated this narrative of disaster among sublime land-scapes in her "Storied Sonnet" in Emily's crossing the Alps in *The Mysteries of Udolpho*. See Appendix A.4.
2   *The Poems of Charlotte Smith*, ed. Curran, 90.

er's elegiac regret. Jessy tells Celestina about her life as housemaid to a family in business in the City, in the same area of London as Smith had once lived as a newly-married, newly-unhappy woman above her father-in-law's warehouse. Jessy says:

> Ah! Madam! Often of a Sunday in the summer I have gone up into our dining room, because the street was so close and narrow that below we hardly saw day light from one end of the year to the other; and I have opened the sash, and looked against the black walls and shut windows of the houses opposite, and have thought how dismal it was! Ah! I remembered too well the beautiful green hills, the meadows and woods, where I so often used to ramble with my sister when we were children, in our own country,[1] before we were old enough to know that my poor mother was unhappy, and had learned to weep with her! How often have I wished those days would come again, and how often have I shut my eyes and tried to fancy that I saw once more all the dear objects that were then so charming. Alas! The dream would not last long! Or if it did it served only to make me feel more unhappy, when, instead of being able to indulge it, I was obliged to go back to hard, and what was worse, to dirty work in our dismal kitchen. In Devonshire I had been used to work hard enough; but I had always fresh air to breathe, and could now and then of an evening sit at our cottage window, and look at the moon, and fancy that my mother might be there with my sister, and that they saw and pitied their unfortunate Jessy. (115)

The passage of more than two hundred years has put some obstacles in the way of appreciation of Smith's work. "Charming," for instance, is not a word a modern writer would use in this context: some might say "magical." In the West, few women now have to cope with the daily, dirty struggle to keep a house in the urban smoke clean enough to pass the rigorous inspection of a mistress who could easily replace them, or put elaborate meals on their employer's table that have to be prepared by roasting, and cleaned away by boiling water at an open fire, stifling in the summer and always dangerous. Many servants lived a life we would find unbearable, however hardworking we think ourselves. So we may feel that Jessy is complaining about very little, because Smith does not show us the details:

---

1   County.

everyone then would know them. An effort of historical imagination is needed to feel the effect of the Jessy and Sophy sub-narratives.

Smith's "To the Moon," Sonnet 4 of *Elegiac Sonnets*, published in the first edition of 1784, prefigures Jessy's conceit of an inhabited moon where the speaker longs to be. The speaker, like Jessy, longs for rest there:

And oft I think—fair planet of the night,
That in thy orb, the wretched may have rest:
The sufferers of the earth perhaps may go,
Released by death—to thy benignant sphere;
And the sad children of Despair and Woe
Forget, in thee, their cup of sorrow here.[1]

A moon inhabited by the souls of the dead is not an original thought of Smith's, but it serves to link Jessy to the speaker of *Elegiac Sonnets*, and therefore to the author. Several sonnets in that first volume, typical of the literary cult of sensibility, dismiss the labouring classes' sensitivity to mental pain. But here Smith constructs her working girl as suffering great distress with equal fortitude to her heroine and to her own received persona in the sonnets. Yet as Chris Jones says, "Despite this extension of sympathy, granting to the lowly their rights of sensibility, there is still often an irritating sense of elitism among some predominantly liberal writers,"[2] and this is certainly true of *Celestina*. But such constructions of sisterhood show both an originality that later writers developed, and Smith's capacity to change and grow as she adapted for her novels—the word recovers its original meaning—the new ideas coming out of France in 1789 and 1790.

Sophy Elphinstone's biography has much in common with Smith's. She prepares to tell her story in a way that reminds the reader of the constructedness of all narratives, whether they are "history," "biography," or "fiction." She and Celestina, enclosed in a coach and travelling north, are, she says,

"[....] something like the personages with whom we are presented in old romances, and who meet in forests and among rocks and recount their adventures; but do you know, my dear Miss de Mor-

---

1   *The Poems of Charlotte Smith*, ed. Curran, 15.
2   Chris Jones, *Radical Sensibility: Literature and Ideas in the 1790s*, 67.

nay, that I feel very much disposed to enact such a personage, and though it is but a painful subject, to relate to you my past life?"

"And do you know, my dear Madam," replied Celestina, "that no wandering lady in romance had ever more inclination to lose her own reflections in listening to the history of some friend who had by chance met her, lost in the thorny labyrinth of uneasy thoughts, than I have to listen to you."(255)

By reference to an earlier form of fiction,[1] Smith keeps us conscious that this too is "story," that women's painful lives which are the subject of such stories change little from one generation to another, that Celestina, Sophy, the author and the reader will find much in common. Both Wollstonecraft (Appendix A.1) and the writer in the *Critical Review* (Appendix A.3) knew or guessed that Sophy's marriage was based on Smith's marriage to Benjamin Smith, the son of a wealthy City merchant and West Indiaman, as the traders in sugar, rum and slaves were called. In Sophy's dislike of the City, with its spectacular bankruptcies and undeserved successes, in her sufferings as a mother, losing her eldest two sons, she resembles Smith. Both *Emmeline* and the sonnets had shown self-representative figures as anxious and devoted mothers. Sophy's account of her son's death, her recourse to opiates and her sense of the City merchants' ingratitude when she is desperate for money, are based on Smith's personal experience, as many contemporary readers knew. She would soon begin to acknowledge her anxiety about her children and her financial desperation in her prefaces.

Recognising an author's self-representation within a poem or novel is very different from "biographical criticism." In the former, we respond to an effect carefully created by the author. In the latter, we use whatever we know or guess of the biography as a quick way to "explain" the work. The first approach is valid, in fact essential to full understanding. The second is reductive of both the work and the life. Smith was creating one meaning for what we now call Romanticism, its heroizing of the author-narrator, its sense of danger on foreign shores of the mind. That meaning was evolving in the 1790s, and in the redeployment of Stothard's emblem and in the creation of intra-textual female poets, Smith was gendering it female. Self-

---

1   French heroic romances, for instance Madeleine de Scudéry's *Artamène* (1633), were translated and still available in England in the eighteenth century. However, Mrs. Elphinstone could be referring to Ariosto's or Spenser's epics, *Orlando Furioso* or *The Faerie Queene*.

representation is open to the charge of self-absorption and muted in its effects. But it is always political in its effort to encourage the reader, through identification with the author's suffering as depicted in the work, to change perception, to see that the story does not stop when the book does, to understand that things in the real world need changing, whether relations between the sexes or "things as they are,"[1] the decrees of law and custom.

Girondin Romance

When Smith left her husband in 1787, she moved with the seven children still at home from a large house in Woolbeding, Sussex to a smaller one in the village of Wyke, near Aldershot in the adjoining county, Surrey. At Wyke she wrote remarkably fast, producing her first two novels, adding poems for inclusion in new editions of *Elegiac Sonnets*, and writing at least one play, though she could not find a manager willing to stage it. When she moved to Brighton, or Brighthelmstone as it was then called, there were more distractions, and whether a third courtship novel was hard to write, or whether her social life was more extensive, *Celestina* took longer to complete.

On the South coast fifty-five miles from London, Brighton had grown rapidly in the 1780s from a fishing village to a popular holiday resort, with good libraries and shops exciting enough to attract wealthy visitors, many there for the sea bathing. From early on the town had a fast and politically radical tone. Smith remembered holidays at Brighton before her marriage when she was "a gay dancer at Balls, and a light-hearted Equestrian on the Hills."[2] Later she had brought children there to convalesce, and negotiated with her husband's creditors when he was in hiding in Normandy. By the late 1780s, the Prince of Wales had lavishly restored the Marine Pavilion, bringing new work and new money into the town. Estranged from his father George III, and his antithesis in character, his presence attracted Oppositionists like Charles James Fox and other Whig politicians, and wits and writers like Richard Sheridan, Edward Gibbon and Hayley. Since Brighton was on a direct route from London to Paris, most influential or successful people were likely to pass

---

1   "*Things As They Are, or Caleb Williams*" is the title of William Godwin's novel about the war between a master and a servant, written at the height of the Terror, 1794, and exploring class conflict.

2   In a letter to Sarah Rose, 10 September 1805.

through at some point, staying at The Ship or one of the other great inns that served the daily packet-boats to France.

When political unrest erupted in Paris and other French provincial cities in 1788 and 1789, Brighton people were often the first to get the news from returning travellers bringing pamphlets and newspapers straight from the patriot presses, and were among those who argued most passionately about unfolding events. Later, Catherine Dorset would suggest in her memoir that Brighton society with its radical ferment had influenced her sister's political thinking.

The meeting at Versailles of the three "Estates," the clergy, nobility and bourgeoisie, in May 1789, ended in a unilateral decision by the Third to claim power in the French constitution. In July, further rioting ended in the release of the Bastille's prisoners and its Governor's murder. The implications of all this in France and at home were discussed at every level of English society. Not just the national papers but even Smith's local *West Sussex Advertiser* soon had its man in Paris, who reported the unfolding events fully and at first sympathetically. The France of the *ancien régime* was England's hereditary enemy, so English feeling was perhaps the quicker to support change and maintain that the French aristocracy had brought their troubles on themselves.

Some important architects of the new regime came from the region of the Gironde, and were known as Girondins, their leader the temperate and humane Jean-Pierre Brissot, who ran and largely wrote a newspaper, the *Patriote Français*. The Girondins wanted change by legal and gradual means; for almost three years they succeeded in restraining the extreme element in the revolutionary party, the Jacobins. The latter acquired their name because they first met to debate in the dining room of a Dominican order of monks, themselves called Jacobins because their first house in France was in the Rue St. Jacques. English sympathisers with the revolution like Smith, Wollstonecraft, William Godwin, Helen Maria Williams, Mary Robinson, Robert Bage, Thomas Holcroft, Elizabeth Inchbald and Mary Hays were really Girondins, favouring reform by peaceful means, though they were called Jacobins by those who disapproved of them, and the contemptuous term has stuck.

Smith, who had grown up as a privileged daughter of the landed gentry, now found herself, an Oppositionist by temperament and by personal experience of poverty and legal injustice, on the side of the underprivileged and dispossessed. The extent to which English liberal thinking in the late 1780s tied in with the aims of the Girondins is evident in the seamless way the last part of *Celestina* follows from all that has gone before.

From the beginning, domestic history is linked to political and economic events. An initial brief history of the Willoughby family goes back as far as the Civil Wars of the 1640s. The heroine is born in 1770, but the main part of the action is limited to three years. Celestina's adoptive mother Mrs. Willoughby dies early in 1787, her adoptive sister Matilda marries Molyneux in the late spring, and Celestina spends that summer on a tour with them in the West Country, returning to London in the autumn where she meets the Castlenorths and learns that Willoughby still wants to marry her despite his mother's dying wishes. She moves to a cottage near Exeter in mid-winter, where he follows her, and their marriage is planned for the end of March 1788, but never takes place because he hears that she is his half sister rather than his adoptive sister. She stays with the Thorolds, visits Skye in the summer of 1788, and spends the winter and part of the following summer in London with her friend Lady Horatia. By late August or early September she is at Exeter. Willoughby spends most of 1788 abroad looking for the truth of her parentage and in a state of indecision. He becomes engaged to Miss Fitz-Hayman in the spring of 1789, but follows her to Paris and breaks the engagement. Hearing only distantly of the great changes taking place in the capital, he spends the late summer in the Pyrenees, where he meets the Chevalier de Bellegarde, Celestina's uncle, learns who her parents were and how they died, and hurries back to England in September 1789. After a brief return to France, the narrative ends in the spring of 1790.

Within this time-frame, as already noted, are embedded first-person reminiscences that take the reader back several generations. Sophy Elphinstone's narrative goes back as far as the Seven Years' War, as it came to be called. Victory for England in 1763 lays the foundation of her father-in-law's business success. She crosses to America for the second time after the American War of Independence. Jessy's first-person narrative is about leaving home to go into service in the City where she meets Sophy's brother, Cathcart, but her family history goes back two generations to her grandparents' marriage. Sophy's and Jessy's stories, from their different social strata, endorse Celestina's experience of the individual life entirely at the mercy of war, economic depression or the malignity of entrenched power.

These perceptions are summed up in volume four's embedded narrative of the Chevalier de Bellegarde, Celestina's uncle, but his story finally introduces the possibility of change through rebellion and blood sacrifice. Before it begins, Willoughby's observations of Castle Rochemarte and its surroundings invoke history back to the

French Renaissance and the superstitious, violent days of the religious wars of the League. The Chevalier de Bellegarde's memories of his tyrannical father again return to the Seven Years' War, when the old Count de Bellegarde lost favour at court on the fall of Québec to the English.[1] After that he grew more inflexible towards his two sons and his daughter, Genevieve. They all defy him, Genevieve marrying an English Protestant, Mr. Ormond, in secret while the Chevalier, the younger de Bellegarde brother, marries Jacquelina, who is of bourgeois parentage. The two young couples hide in a remote part of Castle Rochemarte, where Celestina and her cousin Anzoletta are conceived. When the old Count de Bellegarde discovers them, the young men are wounded, forcibly evicted from the castle, and imprisoned for several years. Genevieve dies shortly after Celestina's birth, killed by her father's harsh treatment, and Jacquelina is forced to enter a convent.

In this retrospective narrative about Celestina's mother, the novel is at its most Gothic, with a heroine crushed by the weight of patriarchal cruelty, symbolised by the dark castle in which she dies. Eventually the de Bellegarde brothers fight on the American side in the War of Independence, while Ormond, because he is in the British army when war breaks out, fights and dies for a cause he does not believe in. The elder de Bellegarde brother dies in some of the war's heaviest fighting, leaving the Chevalier, the narrator of these events, as the inheritor of Castle Rochemarte, though he chooses to renounce the title. The family history of rebellion against the old Count de Bellegarde has formed a French Revolution in miniature.

The American Revolution, the Chevalier says, "awakened in my mind the spirit of freedom," (517) and many of his real-life contemporaries, like Marie-Joseph, Marquis de Lafayette, were experiencing that same awakening as Smith wrote. Historians have tried to identify the localities to which clusters of French soldiers came back from America as sites of the first outbreaks of Revolution. There is probably no exact correlation, but the colonists' overthrow of the British, with French aid, and the establishment of electoral representation in America—though it disregarded the black population—seemed like a new age of enlightenment, and admitted the tantalising possibility of change in France. Their part in the American War allowed the French to think of revolution as a patriotic rather than as a treasonable act. That connection was more difficult to make in England.

---

1   As a child of nine or ten, Smith had written an elegy, now lost, on the death of James Wolfe, the English general who captured Québec.

Smith, writing mainly in the latter part of 1790, could see how the American Revolution and the establishment of a Republic became a model for the French, and she embodies that perception in her plot. The victory in America heartens the Chevalier in his efforts to defy authority and recover his wife, daughter and niece, though it is too late to save his sister or brother-in-law. His service for the new American Republic encourages his enthusiasm for the reforms initiated all over France as the novel ends. The old power of the feudal order seems over. The King and Queen are to be the servants of their people. The King's unlimited power, of which one hated consequence was the *lettre de cachet*, the right to imprison without term or trial, a right deputed to the feudal aristocracy in the provinces, ended symbolically with the fall of the Bastille. Titles were abolished on 19 June 1790, so de Bellegarde's reversion to his family name of Montignac anticipates the law.

The Girondins planned to curb the power of the church also. Monastic vows were abolished on 13 February 1790, when the time-span covered by the novel ends. After that, monks and nuns were free to leave their monasteries and convents. Tithes had been abolished, and severe limitation of the numbers and kinds of clergy to be recognised by the state was then being debated: a decree on the Civil Constitution of the Clergy was issued on 12 July, 1790. After 27 November 1790, clergy were required to take an oath of loyalty to the new regime (Appendix B.5). For some, this was not a problem, but for many Catholic clergy it was the last straw, and clerical emigration or imprisonment for refusal increased. Many of the prisoners killed by the mob in the September massacres of 1792 were clergy who had refused to take the oath. By then, some men and women in closed orders were being evicted into the outside world whether they wished it or not; often they did not, many having freely chosen a monastic life.

But Smith, a quiet sceptic in religious matters, welcomed the reorganisation of the clergy and the subordination of religion to an enlightened government, and worked that ideology into her plot. A corrupt priest, one among many who keep a lavish summer house close to the Castle and their own Benedictine house for liaison with their female parishioners, is the co-villain of this episode, along with the old Count de Bellegarde. The priest tries to seduce Genevieve while controlling her father. For Smith, established religion disregards the teaching of the Gospels, merely buttressing the power of the state and the nobility. Once the church is subordinated to the new regime, Jacquelina can leave her convent and return to her husband and child.

Castle Rochemarte itself owes its construction to Smith's reading of Edmund Burke's *Reflections on the Revolution in France*, published on 1 November 1790. Burke was a lawyer and politician, in his youth a liberal who had defended the action of the American rebels and attacked the slave trade. But he reacted against the Revolution, angered by the destruction of ancient institutions and the imprisonment of the French royal family. Though *Reflections* appeared before their attempted escape to Austria, they were in effect prisoners already. In *Reflections*, Burke analysed the state through the metaphor of an old castle. He was not the first to use this metaphor: Smith's admired William Cowper, for instance, in his long meditative poem *The Task*, writes of "the old castle of the state."[1] But Burke extended the metaphor throughout his book. The extract in this edition, for instance, describes a building whose foundations and walls remain, but where renovation is needed. He implies that France before the Revolution was basically sound in its constitution, though some reform might have been desirable. There was no need for the complete overthrow of the social order that he now deplores (Appendix B.2). Wollstonecraft replied to him by the end of the month (Appendix B.3), and many other writers took part in the "Great Debate" in England that the Revolution inevitably produced.

Celestina, or at least its fourth volume, is one such response. Smith, like most literate and politically-minded English people at the time, read Burke. Castlenorth seems a parodic incarnation of his traditionalism. And she re-deployed his castle image in her creation of Rochemarte, built during the brutal, feudal Middle Ages, but now fallen partially into decay. Willoughby learns about the de Bellegarde family and their castle, hidden in the Pyrenees close to a Benedictine convent (the word could mean a closed order of monks as well as of nuns). The close proximity of castle and religious establishment is always found in Smith's Gothic castles: state religion and government buttress each other, crushing individual liberty. By the time of Willoughby's visit, September 1789, the Benedictines have abandoned or been evicted from their convent. As he approaches Rochmarte for the first time, he sees that

the ground was rugged and uneven, scattered with masses of ruined buildings, that had formerly been part of the outward fortifications, but of which some were fallen into the fosse,[2] and

---

1 Cowper, *The Task*, book 5, 525.
2 Moat or trench fortification.

others overgrown with alder, ash and arbeal. The gate of the castle, and all beyond the moat, however, was yet entire, as were the walls within its circumference, bearing every where the marks of great antiquity, but of such ponderous strength, as time alone had not been able to destroy.—Where breaches had been made by cannon, the walls had been repaired; but this work being of less durability than the original structure, had gone to decay; and the depradations of war were still very visible. The whole was composed of grey stone; the towers, at each end, rose in frowning grandeur, above the rest of the building; and having only loops, and no windows, impressed ideas of darkness and imprisonment, while the moss and wall flowers filled the interstices of the broken stones; and an infinite number of birds made their nests among the shattered cornices, and half-fallen battlements, filling the air with their shrill cries. (486–87)

Rochemarte is a relic of medieval times, showing the scars of old sieges, but still habitable. Now it is burgeoning with new life, with plants in its mortar and birds in its turrets. The images of darkness, stasis and confinement contrast with the greenery between the stones and in the moat to suggest the country's renewal, achieved by the Revolution. The broken stones and shattered cornices improve the castle, since they give space for birds to perch and nest and for flowers to grow. Nature is beginning to triumph over established power: Rochemarte is greening over, no longer the gloomy prison where Genevieve died. Some rooms are habitable, and de Bellegarde is creating a space for his daughter and her governess. The ideas of Rousseau, who considered the old European hierarchies to be contrary to nature, are apparent here, and his philosophy was becoming increasingly important to Smith. Every phrase of Smith's house-descriptions can be read metaphorically; even the birds filling the air with their shrill cries as they take over the building might be compared to the invaders of the Bastille in the previous July.

A little later, as Willoughby, inside Rochemarte, prepares to listen to de Bellegarde tell his story of youthful rebellion against authority, he fixes his eyes on a scene outside one of the windows where again architecture and landscape imaginatively symbolise political movement. Willoughby looks towards

a wood of fir and cypress, fringing the abrupt ascent of the mountain, which rose almost perpendicularly from the plain. As this acclivity commanded the castle, two strong redoubts were built on it, where, in hostile times, parties were stationed to keep the enemy from possessing posts, whence the castle might be annoyed. In the port-holes of these fortresses, now fast approaching to decay, the cannon yet remained, though rusty and useless— and the strong buttresses, and circular towers, were seen to aspire above the dark trees, on every side encompassing them—while, a little to the west, from a fractured rock, of yellow granite, which started out amid the trees, a boiling and rapid stream rushed with violence, and pouring down among the trees, was seen only at intervals, as they either crowded over it, or, receding, left its foaming current to flash in the rays of the sun. (491-92)

Again we are reminded of the violent history of France, and though some elements of the *ancien régime* are weakened, some are still dangerously aspiring. The remains of the old castle seem indestructible, suggesting the difficulties in the way of complete political renovation. More than in the previous passage, there is a suggestion here of the violence as well as the natural beauty and energy of revolutionary force: the woods are dark, perhaps threatening, as well as the towers; the stream is boiling, with the power to fracture even granite, and its course remains frighteningly hidden at times by the "crowded" trees. It flashes in the rays of the sun like knives. At first the Revolution was not associated in English minds with an urban mob, as it became later. The people in charge just before July 1789 were broadly speaking the people who were in charge just afterwards. But one can see here that Smith had misgivings. These Rochemarte descriptions show her novelistic strategies at their most innovative; they work on the reader through subtle implication, not through polemics. Smith herself does not predict or advocate a total demolition of the castle-state; but she imagines the old order comprehensively renovated and made habitable. At a time of great political excitement, she grasped the connection of domestic to civic and seized Burke's castle image to conclude *Celestina*. Her reflections on the Revolution are profound and imaginative.

Towards the end of volume four the punctuation of the original becomes careless, with dashes substituting for most of the usual punctuation points. This may be due to Smith's or Cadell's pressure on the compositor to put the book into print while the revolution debate was still current and while her house image could be picked up and understood. She, or Cadell, need not have worried, as the house metaphor was to become a commonplace of political thinking and a permanent, reliable novelistic code for suggesting the national through the domestic. Even at such an innovative time as the early 1790s, the minting of that metaphor could have come only from an astute and imaginative political thinker.

Consonant with the Revolution's ideals too, a spirit of internationalism prevails towards the close. When Celestina thinks of travelling to France to find her parentage for herself, she considers that "the whole World was her country" (460), and the Genevieve-Ormond, Celestina-Willoughby, Anzolletta-Thorold pairings suggest that the best marriages are made across national boundaries. There is of course naiveté in Smith's fable: it seems unlikely that a Chevalier de Bellegarde, with or without his title, would cheerfully marry his daughter to an English country clergyman; and Jacquelina, who might have allowed Smith an opportunity to construct imaginatively a marriage of noble and commoner, scarcely exists as a character. The manuscript of the fourth volume was already far too long, and Smith had no space to develop the new ideas sketched in at the end. She saved them for her next two novels.

Celestina and *Sense and Sensibility*

Smith's first novel, *Emmeline*, appeared when Jane Austen was only thirteen, but she was fascinated by it, especially by its hero-villain Delamere. There is conclusive evidence that she continued to read Smith's novels as they came out.[1] In the early 1790s she was already writing an epistolary narrative provisionally called "Elinor and Marianne" which eventually became *Sense and Sensibility*. This is a critique of the cult of sensibility, though of much else besides. The lines of demarcation and balance of sympathy between self-control and impulse in Austen's first published novel will always be matters of debate. But in general, as noted, novels of sensibility privileged feeling over reason and restraint, rejecting the rules and customs of an older generation. And in general, Austen's novel is understood to reassert reason and a traditional Christian self-control. Her choice of the name Willoughby alone for a central character proves nothing: it was a popular name with novelists. Burney's attractive villain in *Evelina* (1778) is an early use, which carries the necessary *Burke's Peerage*

---

1 See "Charlotte Smith and Jane Austen," and throughout, in my *Charlotte Smith: A Critical Biography*.

ring; a Willoughby fought at Agincourt. But the relationship between *Sense and Sensibility* and *Celestina* is closer than that between Austen's novel and any that preceded it.

Willoughby's contemptuous pity for his uncle, Lord Castlenorth, while expecting to inherit his money, his frequent rudeness excused by self-absorption, and the lack of principle that allows him to court Miss Fitz-Hayman though he dislikes her, set him up for Smith's own satiric judgement at times; still more did they set him up for a judgement less tolerant of the political and cultural attitudes he exemplifies. In her teens Austen was already writing parodies of fashionable novelistic heroes, spoilt young men who assert radical politics and proclaim the rights of man while rejecting the rights of their closest relations. "Love and Freindship" with its egomaniac, light-fingered heroines and vacuous, unemployed heroes is the most ebullient and best-known of her teenage parodies.

But the disparate pastiches of novels of sensibility in "A Collection of Letters" are equally sophisticated. In "Letter the fifth From a young Lady very much in love to her Friend," the heroine's self-delusion is on the parodic side of satire; but the excess language is not so far from some straight novels of sensibility of the 1780s and 1790s, including some passages by Smith when off form. Austen's conniving Lady Scudamore, who has an interest in encouraging the heiress Henrietta Halton into marriage with a fortune-hunter, Musgrove, describes his modesty and merit to her victim:

"In short my Love it was the work of some hours for me to persuade the poor despairing Youth that you had really a preference for him; but when at last he could no longer deny the force of my arguments, or discredit what I told him, his transports, his Raptures, his Extasies are beyond my power to describe."

"Oh! the dear Creature," cried I, "how passionately he loves me! But, dear Lady Scudamore, did you tell him that I was totally dependent on my Uncle and Aunt?"

Yes, I told him everything."

"And what did he say?"

"He exclaimed with virulence against Uncles and Aunts; Accused the Laws of England for allowing them to possess their Estates when wanted by their Nephews or Nieces, and wished he were in the House of Commons, that he might reform the Legislature, and rectify all its abuses."

"Oh! The sweet Man! What a spirit he has," said I.[1]

Austen, then fifteen or so, is close to Burke though much funnier on vapid liberal ideology; Musgrove is a parodic version of a hero of sensibility like George Willoughby, who gains an inheritance by the lucky circumstance that his uncle Castlenorth never discovers that he has broken off his engagement to his cousin, Castlenorth's daughter. Austen mocks or relegates to a sub-plot the typical happy ending of the Jacobin or reformist anti-authority novel, which results from the fortunate death of a rich old relation. Not only the Willoughby-Celestina narrative is happily resolved by a death: Cathcart and Jessy conceal their marriage while waiting unashamedly for her grandfather to die and leave them his money; the grandfather has no point of view at all. Smith's ethics in *Celestina* invited sustained attack by Austen.

Sense and Sensibility, like *Celestina*, is set between Devonshire and London, though Austen avoids Smith's excursions into foreign and sublime landscapes. Austen's London scenes are especially close to their counterparts in the earlier novel. Marianne writes rashly to John Willoughby when she first arrives in London with Elinor and Mrs. Jennings, and receives no answer. Her agitation while she waits for a reply is similar to what is felt by Celestina as she waits in Lady Horatia's drawing-room for George Willoughby's reply to her pleading letter. Marianne meets her Willoughby by chance at a party (Appendix A.5), as Celestina does in Volume III, Chapter 9.

The party scenes are so similar it is fair to assume that Austen initially intended a recognisable critique of Smith's. Elinor takes the protective role to Marianne that Montague Thorold takes to Celestina. In Smith's novel, the distress of hero and heroine is equal. Each thinks the other is engaged, and each is wrong. In Austen's novel, John Willoughby has recently become engaged to Sophy Grey, needing her fortune to repair his own now that his relation, a Mrs. Smith, has cast him off on finding that he seduced a fifteen-year-old girl. Marianne, who tends to think in literary stereotypes, tries to convince herself that her lover's estrangement is the result of slander or misunderstandings, as is the case in Smith's novel. Only after John Willoughby's brutal letter to her is she convinced of the real, and mercenary, explanation. Both novels are interested in the amount of money needed for marriage; Marianne learns after long suffering to

---

1 *The Novels of Jane Austen*, ed. R.W. Chapman, Vol. 6, *Minor Works*, 169.

understand that her lover would have regretted the loss of income if he married her, something Celestina understands much earlier in her narrative.

Smith's Willoughby is absolved from any real blame by the way she develops her plot. Miss Fitz-Hayman turns out to have a lover already, so he is justified in breaking their engagement, and neither narrator nor hero are embarrassed about his accepting Castlenorth's legacy. For Smith, all money is tainted by the injustice of its distribution and also, as she was just beginning to see, by the means of its production, so there is no logical reason for her why Willoughby, or anyone else who can get it, should not inherit Castlenorth's. His moodiness and abuse of hospitality, attributed to his passion or his misery, are at times amusing to the narrator, and expected traits of the spirited hero of sensibility. Austen's Willoughby has similar traits, but they come with a warning, and erotic love that recognises no value greater than itself, though attractive, is rejected by the later novel.

George Willoughby's race down to Devonshire at the end of *Celestina*, fearing to find the heroine married, is repeated in the later novel by John Willoughby's race down to Devonshire near the end of *Sense and Sensibility*, fearing to find Marianne dead. But though Austen's Willoughby almost exculpates himself, he can never quite do so. A reader's consciousness of the duplication of the earlier ride and explanation merely emphasises Austen's rejection of the cluster of qualities that make up the hero of sensibility.

There are less obvious resemblances: Lady Horatia and Mrs. Jennings are both guardian-figures speaking for sense, neither convincingly. The false reports to Celestina and Willoughby that the other is married make for an exciting conclusion—Smith was pleased with her ending (Appendix C.1). Austen adopted the strategy of false report, but instead of using it in the narrative of Marianne's relations with Willoughby, she gives a tense, emotional close to her sober Elinor-Edward plot, an edge which would be lacking if Elinor merely learned from a third party or in a letter that after all Edward had not married Lucy. If the reader is aware of the resemblance, the effect is to help define Elinor and Edward as the "romantic" couple after all.

Sense and Sensibility is of course entirely free-standing. By 1811, when it was published, *Celestina* would be unknown to most novel readers or at best a memory. We do not need to read *Celestina* to see that Austen's first novel analyses the egotism that drove the cult of sensibility, its assumption that the finer feelings would always be funded and served by somebody else. But while a knowledge of the earlier novel is certainly not essential to an appreciation of Austen's,

it will show more clearly what Austen found interesting and dangerous in the radical feeling of the 1790s, what incited her to opposition as a satirist. The Marianne-Willoughby plot has always tended to
engage more readers than the Elinor-Edward one, and some have
seen its end as anti-climactic. To read *Sense and Sensibility* in relation
to *Celestina* is to see more clearly what Austen's narrator rejects, and
regrets rejecting.

Comparison between the two novelists will almost always end in
Austen's favour. At her best a graceful and inventive stylist, often a
wit, Smith was however under constant pressure to write too much
too fast, never revised and so seldom entirely did herself justice.

Achievement and Influence

Smith's originality amounts to genius in her embodiment of political and social tension in castles and houses, and in landscapes. She and
Mary Wollstonecraft were the first writers to see that the personal is
the political, but Smith was quicker than Wollstonecraft to convey
that perception into the plots and domestic settings of the novel. Two
years later she was to use an ancient and extensive building as an
emblem of the condition of England in *The Old Manor House*. Wollstonecraft quickly adopted the strategy. More importantly, so did
Austen, who deployed it most fully in *Mansfield Park* but also in her
other novels; later novelists have drawn on the metaphor ever since.
It admits infinite variation and subtlety, from *Mansfield Park* and
Charles Dickens' *Bleak House* to E.M. Forster's *Howard's End*, Evelyn
Waugh's *A Handful of Dust* and Kazuo Ishiguro's *The Remains of the
Day*. Grasping the potential for fiction in Burke's metaphor was a
major and permanent achievement, leaving a profound impression
on the subsequent course of literary history.

But Smith's influence on contemporary poets and especially on
Wordsworth is also important. On his way to Paris to see the effects
of the Revolution for himself (Appendix C.2) Wordsworth stopped
in Brighton to visit Smith. She was a distant relation by marriage, but
more importantly she was a poet he had admired since he was sixteen and at school at Hawkshead, when the first volume of her sonnets appeared. On this visit she showed him work in manuscript, perhaps including passages of *Celestina*. He was then twenty-one,
unpublished and unknown. Her Jessy story anticipates the manner
and subject matter of some of his Lyrical Ballads. His "Poor Susan,"
especially, with its triumph of a young prostitute's creative imagina-

tion over the bitter circumstances of her life, is close to Jessy's narrative of her time as a servant. On her way home in the early morning, at the corner of Wood Street, Poor Susan sees:

> A mountain ascending, a vision of trees....
> Green pastures she views in the midst of the dale....

As well as in her novels, Smith attempted to register the inner vision of the poor and outcast in some of the narrative verse of her 1797 volume. "The Forest Boy," for instance, the story of a country boy, William, forced into the navy, who never returns to his mother and sweetheart, is close to the subject matter of *Lyrical Ballads*, published a year later. As Phoebe waits for her dead William:

> Her senses are injured; her eyes dim with tears
> By the river she ponders; and weaves
> Reed garlands, against her dear William appears....[1]

The *faux-naïf* tone and anti-war polemic just predates Wordsworth. In a footnote to "Stanzas Suggested in a Steamboat off St. Bees' Heads," composed on a walking tour in the summer of 1833, he referred to Smith as

> a lady to whom English verse is under greater obligations than are likely to be either acknowledged or remembered. She wrote little, and that little unambitiously, but with true feeling for rural nature, at a time when nature was not much regarded by English Poets; for in point of time her earlier writings preceded, I believe, those of Cowper and Burns.[2]

The amiably vague tone covers inaccuracies. Cowper's first publication just preceded Smith's first edition of *Elegiac Sonnets*, though Burns' Kilmarnock volume came three years later. Far from writing little, poverty forced her, as Wordsworth must have known, to write much more, much faster than she wished, and she produced a staggering sixty-three volumes, often long volumes, of poetry, novels and children's books in twenty-three years, inevitably with frequent

---

1 *The Poems of Charlotte Smith*, ed. Curran, 116.
2 William Wordsworth, *The Poetical Works*, ed. de Selincourt (Oxford: Oxford UP, 1959), Vol. 4, 403.

detriment to her artistry at its best. But at its best, her art is highly ambitious, analysing England's economic and political ills in the sugar-coating of romantic fiction, and offering domestic, specifically female struggles as fit subjects for that elitist form, the sonnet. Her career trajectory of enthusiasm for the Revolution followed by disillusion and retreat into a green world anticipated Wordsworth's own. Close study of both poets might suggest that this late tribute to her in a footnote hardly clears his debt.

As in the verse for *Celestina*, Smith continued to use personification, the characteristic figure of speech of earlier eighteenth century poetry. Gentle concepts named Love, Sorrow, Nature, Happiness or Friendship, husked from the intense concatenation of ideas that inform personification in Pope or Johnson, are left as frail survivors of the great age of wit. But in the early 1790s Smith was already attentive to accurate botanical and zoological detail, rendering the competitive cruelty as well as the beauty in nature and adopting scientific naming in the notes, strategies developed later in her career that would take her poetry in a different direction from the Romantics. She admired and learned from Erasmus Darwin, whose *Loves of the Plants* (1789) celebrated plant reproduction and the battle between species.

Despite her obvious haste and padding, the ideals of a generation of writers wanting reform are registered in her novels with forcefulness and originality. In her poetry she was developing a distinctive manner that by the time of *Beachy Head* (1807) would span chiaroscuro land and seascapes, meditation on fossil shells and evolution, and the recognition that her own long struggle to bring up her children is ceaselessly replicated in the natural world. An early Romantic, she also anticipates some preoccupations of the mid-nineteenth century.

Loraine Fletcher
University of Reading, UK

Charlotte Smith: A Brief Chronology

1749   4 May: Charlotte Turner born in King Street, London, first child of Nicholas and Anna (née Towers) Turner.

1752   Anna Turner dies after the births of two more children, Catherine Anna and Nicholas. Nicholas Turner (father) travels in Europe leaving his children in the care of their aunt, Lucy Towers, mainly at Bignor Park, Sussex.

1755   At school in Chichester, Sussex.

1758   At school in Kensington, London; (?) her father returns.

1760   25 Oct: Accession of George III.

1761   Leaves school, "comes out" into London society; Nicholas Turner, in financial difficulties, sells Stoke Place, near Guildford.

1763   Seven Years' War ends, securing British holdings in North America, India and the West Indies.

1764   30 Aug: Nicholas Turner (father) marries Henrietta Meriton.

1765   23 Feb: After an eight-month engagement, Charlotte Turner marries Benjamin Smith, second son of Richard Smith, West Indies planter and a director in the East India Company. CS lives over family warehouse in Cheapside, East London.

1766   Spring: First son born, name unknown.

1767   Spring: Second son, Benjamin Berney, born, first child dies; Richard Smith marries Lucy Towers; CS and family move to Southgate.

1768   Third child, William Towers, born.

1769   10 May: Fourth child, Charlotte Mary, born.

1770   Fifth child, Braithwaite, born.

1771   Smiths move to Tottenham, London; sixth child, Nicholas Hankey, born. CS occasionally works as a writer for her father-in-law's firm. Catherine Turner (sister) marries Michael Dorset (army captain).

1773   Seventh child, Charles Dyer, born.

1774   Eighth child, Anna Augusta, born.

1775   Smiths move to Lys Farm, Hampshire, formerly centre of firm's cattle-breeding enterprise.
        American War of Independence.

1776   Ninth child, Lucy Elenore, born.
        13 Oct: Richard Smith dies leaving about £36,000 and

property in an ambiguous will which attempts to hold money in a trust for his many grandchildren but results in years of litigation.

1777   May: Benjamin Berney dies.
9 Oct: Tenth child, Lionel, born.

1781   Benjamin Smith appointed High Sheriff for Hampshire.

1782   Eleventh child, Harriet Amelia, born.

1783   Peace of Versailles; Britain recognises American States' independence.
Dec: Benjamin arrested for debt and embezzlement of his father's trust fund, sent to the King's Bench Prison, London; CS spends part of his time there with him.

1784   15 May: *Elegiac Sonnets and Other Essays* (J. Dodsley), reprinted with additional poems in ten editions in CS's lifetime, including subscription editions with illustrations in 1789 and 1797, the fifth and subsequent editions published first by Thomas Cadell, then by Thomas Cadell, Junior and William Davies.
2 July: Benjamin released after CS negotiates with Trustees; he goes to France to escape his creditors.
Oct: CS meets William Hayley, her patron and dedicatee of *Elegiac Sonnets*; she joins Benjamin in Normandy.

1785   Winter: Twelfth child, George Augustus Frederick, born.
Spring: CS returns to Sussex with the children.
Summer: *Manon Lescaut, or, The Fatal Attachment* (Thomas Cadell), a translation of Prevost d'Exiles: withdrawn but reissued anonymously next year.
CS living at Woolbeding, Sussex.

1786   William Smith goes to Bengal with East India Company.
18 June: Braithwaite dies.

1787   *The Romance of Real Life* (Thomas Cadell), a translation of selected tales from Gayot de Pitaval's *Les Causes Celèbres*.
15 April: CS leaves Benjamin and moves to Wyhe (now Wyke) near Guildford with the children; Benjamin lives in Scotland to avoid his creditors.

1788   April: *Emmeline, the Orphan of the Castle* (Thomas Cadell), sells out and is quickly reprinted.

1789   *Ethelinde, or The Recluse of the Lake* (Thomas Cadell). CS moves to Brighton.
1 May: Meeting of the Estates-General at Versailles.
14 July: Storming of Bastille.

1790   Nicolas Hankey goes to Calcutta with East India Company.
        CS increasingly pro-Revolutionary.
1791   *Celestina* (Thomas Cadell).
        June: Attempted escape of French royal family.
1792   July: *Desmond* (G.G.J. & J. Robinson).
        10 Aug: Massacre of Swiss Guard.
        (?) Aug. to 1 Sept: CS spends 2-3 weeks at William Hayley's
        house, Eartham in Sussex, with William Cowper and
        George Romney, who makes pastel drawings of her and
        Cowper. CS writes first volume of *The Old Manor House*.
        2-3 Sept: September Massacres.
        31 Oct: Girondin leaders executed.
1793   Jan: *The Old Manor House* (J. Bell).
        21 Jan: Louis XVI executed; Britain at war with France.
        CS moves to Storrington, Sussex.
        July: *The Emigrants, a poem, in two books* (Thomas Cadell).
        Anna Augusta marries Alexandre de Foville, French émigré.
        Lionel expelled from Winchester College.
        6 Sept: Charles Dyer Smith's (CS's son) leg amputated at
        siege of Dunkirk.
        10 Sept: CS's friend Henrietta O'Neill dies at Lisbon.
        Reign of Terror.
1794   *The Wanderings of Warwick* (J. Bell), a sequel to *The Old
        Manor House*; *The Banished Man* (Cadell and Davies).
        CS arrested for debt but friends assist her; she moves to
        Bath for medical reasons; the de Fovilles evade detention by
        Storrington tradespeople to join her there.
        24 July: Anna Augusta gives birth to a son who dies on 27
        July.
        (?) Lucy Towers dies.
        Oct: Bailiffs threaten to seize CS's books, but Egremont's
        agent removes them to Petworth House.
1795   Jan: De Foville and Lionel challenge Thomas Dyer, one of
        the Trust lawyers, to a duel for his unwillingness to help
        Augusta financially; they are arrested but the case is
        dropped.
        Rural Walks: in dialogues intended for the use of young persons
        (Cadell and Davies); *Montalbert* (Sampson Low).
        23 April: Anna Augusta dies.
        CS moves to Exmouth, then Weymouth, with the younger
        children.

1796　*Rambles Farther: a Continuation of Rural Walks, in dialogues intended for the use of young persons* (Sampson Low); *A Narrative of the Loss of the Catharine, Venus and Piedmont Transports, and the Thomas, Golden Grove and Aeolus Merchant-ships near Weymouth, on Wednesday the 18ᵗʰ November last. Drawn up from information taken on the spot by Charlotte Smith, and published for the Benefit of an unfortunate Survivor from one of the wrecks, and her infant child* (Sampson Low); *Marchmont* (Sampson Low).

　　　　CS moves to Oxford.

1797　Seventh edition of *Elegiac Sonnets*, in 2 vols.

1798　*Minor Morals, interspersed with sketches of natural history, historical anecdotes, and original stories* (Sampson Low); *The Young Philosopher* (Cadell and Davies).

　　　　12 June: Lucy Elenore marries Thomas Newhouse.

　　　　William on leave; Harriet goes back to Bengal with him; CS living in London; George Wyndham, Earl of Egremont pays off Thomas Dyer (Benjamin Smith's brother-in-law) and takes over administration of Smith Trust.

　　　　Irish rebellion.

1799　27 April: *What is She? A Comedy* opens and runs for six nights at the Theatre Royal, Covent Garden.

　　　　Strained relations with Nicholas Turner and Egremont.

1800　CS living at Bignor; she negotiates the sale of Gays' Plantation in Barbados over next four years.

　　　　23 Sept: Harriet returns from Bengal.

1801　*The Letters of a Solitary Wanderer* (Sampson Low), vols. 1-3.

　　　　Charles dies in Barbados on Trust business; Lucy Newhouse leaves her husband and returns to CS pregnant and with two children; CS living at Frant.

　　　　Mary Hays' critique and life of CS in *British Public Characters*.

1802　*The Letters of a Solitary Wanderer* (Longman & Rees), vols. 4 & 5.

　　　　April: Lionel promoted to major.

　　　　CS living between London and Frant; Nicholas Hankey sends his daughter Lucena to her from India.

1804　(with Catherine Dorset) *Conversations, Introducing Poetry; chiefly on subjects of natural history, for the use of children and young persons* (Joseph Johnson).

　　　　CS living at Elstead; in ill health and destitute, she negotiates the sale of her books.

　　　　Sept: She meets Benjamin again at Petworth House.

1803   *A History of England, from the earliest records, to the peace of Amiens in a series of letters to a young lady at school* (Richard Phillips), vols. 1 & 2 by CS, vol. 3 by Mary Hays.

1804   23 Feb: Benjamin Smith dies in prison for debt at Berwick-on-Tweed.
16 Sept: George dies in Surinam.
28 Oct: CS dies at Tilford, Surrey, and is buried near her mother at St John's, Stoke-next-Guildford.

1807   *Beachy Head, Fables and Other Poems* (Joseph Johnson); *A Natural History of Birds, intended chiefly for young persons* (Joseph Johnson).

1813   22 April: Settlement of Richard Smith's estate.

1832   3 Dec: Lionel knighted.

1833   27 April: Lionel made governor of Barbados, afterwards of Jamaica; his commitment to Emancipation and a humane prison system makes him unpopular with the planters, and he is removed, but in 1837 made Colonel of the 40th Regiment, and a baronet on Victoria's coronation.

A Note on the Text

Celestina. A Novel in Four Volumes was published in 1791 by the long-established and respected firm of Thomas Cadell. He was already the publisher of Smith's *Elegiac Sonnets and Other Essays*, of *Manon Lescaut* (originally withdrawn but re-bound as one volume and issued anonymously the next year, 1785), of *The Romance of Real Life*, her collection of short stories translated from the French, and of her first two courtship novels, *Emmeline* and *Ethelinde*.

A second edition of *Celestina* was published in 1791. A Dublin edition was issued by R. Cross, P. Wogan et al. in three volumes, also in 1791: such "pirated" publications earned no royalties for the author but were then legal. Cadell issued a third edition in 1792 and a fourth in 1794. As with most of Smith's novels there was a French edition, and *Celestine, ou la Victime des Préjugés*, translated by the pseudonymous "Madame de Rome," appeared in 1795, or Year Three of the new regime.

I have taken the first edition of *Celestina* as copy text. I have kept Smith's spelling (even when it is inconsistent) except where that might be confusing or distracting; I have changed the spelling of Skie to Skye. I have also retained her use of the semi-colon where modern usage would have a comma, establishing the necessary breaks in her typically multi-claused and weighty sentences. But I have made changes in her use of the apostrophe, which she added to "its" as a possessive, and in the original's inverted commas around quotations, her own interpolated poems, and letters, where they are sometimes repeated at the beginning of every line in the original. She seems to have quoted—at least from English authors—from memory, and I have allowed her version to stand, noting any large disparity.

I have silently supplied some dropped question marks and inverted commas, and corrected obvious typographical errors. Volume Four of the original is haphazardly punctuated, especially towards the end, with dashes where one might from the earlier volumes expect commas or semi-colons. This may well be evidence that Smith was in a hurry to get the book out before the debate surrounding Edmund Burke's *Reflections on the Revolution in France* had a chance to die down, and should perhaps be retained as evidence of her working conditions. However, the punctuation is so distracting I decided to suppress some dashes silently and supply punctuation to bring the last volume into line with the earlier ones.

This is, I believe, the first time the novel has appeared in an English version since 1794.

CELESTINA

A NOVEL

IN FOUR VOLUMES

By CHARLOTTE SMITH

VOLUME I

Chapter I

Mrs. Willoughby was, at the age of thirty, left a widow, with a son and a daughter, of whom she was extremely fond, and to whose education she entirely devoted herself. George Willoughby, her son, had been placed at Eton[1] by his father, but attended by a private tutor,[2] a man of sense and learning, who was distantly related to their family. When he was about thirteen, a fever, from which he narrowly escaped, so injured his constitution, that his mother was directed by his physicians to take him to the South of Europe. Thither she and her daughter, with Mr. Everard, accompanied him. A few months completely restored his health; and they then went all together to Geneva; where, after a short residence, she left her son to pursue his studies under the care of Mr. Everard; and with her daughter Matilda, then near eight years old, she fixed herself for some time at Hières, on the coast of Provence; a town with whose beauty she had been much struck four or five years before, when to divert her concern for the loss of her husband, she had made a tour of some months through France and Italy.

Matilda was placed in a convent, for the purpose of instruction; and there she became the playfellow of a little girl almost three years younger, who was known among the Nuns by the name of *la petite Celestine*.[3] The fondness which soon subsisted between her and Matilda introduced her of course to Mrs. Willoughby, who was at first sight charmed with her beauty, and after a few interviews, so delighted with her infantine caresses, that she became as anxious to see her every day as she was to see her own child. Her countenance, with that blooming delicacy which the French distinguish by calling it '*le vrai teint Anglois*,'[4] had all that animation which is more usually

---

1 Eton College, on the Thames near Windsor, is one of the oldest English public schools, founded by Henry VI in 1440. Education there in Smith's time was still entirely in the classics, in Greek and Latin.

2 Some public schools allowed pupils to be accompanied by their private tutors, who would otherwise be unemployed in term-time.

3 The little Celestine. Celestina takes her name from the order of nuns she lives with, the Celestines, who in turn take their name from the saint and Pope (422-32), Celestine I.

4 The real English complexion.

found among the natives of the South of Europe; yet this spirited expression often melted into softness so insinuating, that it was difficult to say whether pensive tenderness or sparkling vivacity was the most predominant; or whether it was the loveliness of her little form and face, or the enchantment of her manners, which made her so very attractive, that the very servants who saw her with Matilda became so fond of her, as never to carry her back to the convent, after a visit to their lady, but with reluctance and regret.

The Nuns, however, with whom she lived, seemed, either from seeing her constantly, or for want of taste, to be quite insensible of perfections which won every other heart. They treated her sometimes with harshness, and always with indifference; so that to be with Mrs. Willoughby soon became the greatest happiness the little Celestina could enjoy. Mrs. Willoughby found an equal pleasure in returning her affection; and was sometimes moved even to tears, when happening to caress Matilda, the other amiable child would approach as if to share her tenderness, take her hand, look innocently in her face, and say with a sigh, "*Helas! que n'ai je aussi une Maman!*"[1]

These artless expressions, and the coldness with which the sisterhood treated their infant pensioner,[2] raised in Mrs. Willoughby a great desire to know to whom the child belonged: but every attempt to gain information was at first repressed by so much reserve, that she almost despaired of being gratified. At length however she received a hint, that by the skilful application of means equally potent in Courts or Convents, she might learn all the Nuns knew; and in consequence of pursuing this hint, she was informed, that the last Superior of the house, who had been dead two years, had received Celestina into it when only a few months old, as a child whose birth it was of the utmost consequence to conceal: that only the Superior herself, and her Confessor, who was also dead, had ever known to whom she belonged; every trace of which secret had by them been so carefully obliterated, that after the decease of both, every attempt at discovery had been ineffectual. It was believed a considerable sum of money had been received as the price of secrecy, and as a provision for the child; but it had never been carried to account,[3] or any part of it appropriated to the use of the community in general, who

---

1 Smith's note: Alas! that I don't have a mother too!
2 Boarder.
3 Openly recorded as the convent's property.

now consequently murmured at the necessity they were under, as they said, *par charité, et pour l'amour de Dieu*,[1] to support *la petite Celestine* for life: but they added, that as soon as she was old enough to take the vows, she must became a Nun, and fill one of the inferior offices[2] of the convent, since she had no friends[3] or money to pay for being on a higher footing.

The pity excited by this account, added to the sensibility[4] with which, infant as she was, she felt her own situation; her tender attachment to her benefactress, and to Matilda, and the sense and sweetness visible in all she said and did, procured for her, in the tender and generous heart of Mrs. Willoughby, an interest little short of what she felt for Matilda herself. Every hour increased this interest; till after a stay of eighteen months at Hières, during which she had seen her almost every day, she found, in reflecting on her departure, that she should be really unhappy the rest of her life, if she returned to England, and left this amiable child to a fate so melancholy in itself, and so unworthy of the promise of perfection given by her infancy. Having once entertained the idea of taking her to England, it soon became too pleasing to be relinquished. There were however great difficulties in the way. Though the community complained of Celestina as a burden to them, they made, as they declared, a point of conscience, not to part with her to an heretic;[5] and the more solicitous Mrs. Willoughby became, the more they declaimed against the sin it would be to hazard the soul of *la petite Celestine* for the sake of any worldly advantage. While the matter was yet in debate, George Willoughby and Mr. Everard, who had been sent for that the whole family might return to England together, arrived; and the latter finding how much Mrs. Willoughby desired to become the sole protectress of the little orphan, prevailed with Father Angelo, the present confessor, to remove at once all the scruples he had been instrumental in raising: in a word, Mr. Everard used the argument to which Monks, in despite of their professions of poverty, are not more

---

1 Smith's note: in charity, and for the love of God.
2   Jobs.
3 Relations, a common eighteenth-century usage.
4 Feeling, sympathy, sensitivity. Like its adjective "sensible," the word had acquired a range of meanings.
5 Mrs. Willoughby, like most eighteenth-century English people, is Protestant and Anglican (Church of England), and so a heretic, that is, someone with a false view of religion, in the judgement of many Roman Catholics.

insensible than the rest of mankind; and Mrs. Willoughby having left a certificate of her having taken Celestina out of the convent, a promise to educate her without influencing her to change her religion, and to provide for her, together with a direction where she might, in case of enquiry, be found, was permitted to carry with her, from Hières, the lovely little French girl, who was from that hour put on an equal footing with her own daughter, and whom she seemed as tenderly to love.

After an absence of between three and four years, Mrs. Willoughby and her family returned to England; where to all her friends, who were generally struck with the beauty and elegance of her adopted child, she related, without reserve, the little history of their accidental attachment.

George Willoughby, now in his seventeenth year, was sent to Cambridge;[1] his tutor retired to a small living,[2] which had fallen[3] near his estate in the West of England, since his absence, and to which his mother, as patroness in his minority,[4] had presented this excellent and amiable man.

Mrs. Willoughby usually passed the winters in London; where masters of music, drawing, dancing, and languages, attended her two girls, for so she equally termed Matilda and her little friend:—their summers were divided between public places and Alstone (or Alvestone, as it was spelt), an estate between Sidmouth and Exeter,[5] of which her husband had been so fond, that he had hurt his fortune by the large sums he had expended on its improvement. This attachment George seemed to inherit; and in compliment to him, his mother always passed the vacations there: Willoughby himself having no pleasure so great as in talking and thinking of the happiness he should enjoy, when he should have become master of Alvestone, and see his mother and sister, of whom he was extremely fond, settled there with him for the greatest part of every year. Mrs. Willoughby, whose love for him might have been said to border on weakness, if it had been possible to discover any excess in the attachment of a

---

1 To university. Oxford, Cambridge, Edinburgh and Trinity College, Dublin were then the only universities in Britain.
2 Mr Everard, a clergyman, is given a small Church of England "living," a parish to run by Mrs. Willoughby, who as the patroness of a great estate would have several such livings in her gift.
3 Fallen vacant because of the death of the previous clergyman.
4 The time up to his twenty-first birthday, when he becomes legally adult.
5 Towns on the south-west coast of England.

mother to a son so uncommonly deserving, had always encouraged the inclination he had from his infancy betrayed for this his paternal seat: though his little projects often gave her pain; for she knew what she had with more tenderness than prudence studiously concealed from him, that his father's affairs were at his death so much embarrassed, as to render it doubtful whether a minority of near thirteen years would so far clear his estates, as to enable him at the end of that period to reside in this favourite place, with the splendour and hospitality for which his ancestors had for centuries been eminent. The last Mr. Willoughby had indeed continued the same line of conduct in the country; but his manner of living in town had been quite unlike that of his prudent and plainer ancestors; who had but just recovered his estate, when it was transmitted to him, from the injuries it had received by their adherence to Charles the First; during whose unfortunate reign they had sold some part of their extensive possessions, and had been plundered of more.[1] His grandfather and great-grandfather had nearly retrieved the whole of the estate round Alvestone, where they piqued themselves on losing none of the family consequence; but the manners of the times in which he lived, and a disposition extremely gay and volatile, had led the last possessor into expenses, which, if they did not oblige him to sell, had obliged him to mortgage great part of this, as well as all his other estates; and being charged at his death with twelve hundred a year to his widow, and the interest of ten thousand pounds given to his daughter,[2] they slowly and with difficulty produced, under the management of very careful executors, little more than sufficient to pay such charges, and the interest of the money for which they were mortgaged.

Mrs. Willoughby however was unwilling to interrupt the felicity of her son's happiest hours, by representing to him a dreary prospect of the future; especially as she thought that future might, as it advanced, become brighter; and that it was possible all his gay visions might be realized. He had a great-uncle, far advanced in life, and

---

1 Willoughby's ancestors were Royalists or Cavaliers, on King Charles I's side against the Parliamentarian forces under Oliver Cromwell. They have lost lands and money in the Civil Wars preceding Charles' execution in 1649, and afterwards during the Republic.
2 Many young women were provided with a dowry or "fortune" according to their family's means. Matilda's father has left her a dowry of £10,000 in his will, to be paid to her husband on her marriage, with the interest accruing since her father's death.

very rich, who, though the late Mr. Willoughby had disobliged him, might, she thought, through mere family pride, give to the son, what he had often declared the father should never possess. Her brother, Lord Castlenorth, was the last male of his illustrious race: he had only a daughter; and an increase of his family becoming every day more improbable, he had concerted with his sister, even while George (who was younger than his daughter) was yet a child, how the family might be restored by a union of its two remaining branches.

The good sense of Mrs. Willoughby had not entirely saved her from family pride; and this project, which the situation of her son's fortune rendered doubly desirable, had by degrees taken such possession of her mind, that nothing would have made her more unhappy, than suspecting it might not take effect. After her return with her family from France, she had an interview with her brother, Lord Castlenorth, who was then in England (though his health occasioned him for the most part to reside abroad), and it was then agreed with him, or rather with Lady Castlenorth, whose will was his law, that if the young people liked each other, of which they hardly suffered themselves to doubt, the match should take place as soon as young Willoughby became of age, who was then to assume the name of Fitz-Hayman, and in whose favour, when united with the sole heiress of the family, there was little doubt of procuring the succession to the title.[1] Willoughby, who was yet ignorant of this proposed arrangement, had accompanied his mother in her visit: but far from feeling any partiality for his cousin, he had hardly taken any notice of her, and had passed all those hours when common civility did not oblige him to attend the family, in wandering with his tutor over the extensive domain belonging to his Lordship's magnificent seat. He seemed indeed much more sensible of the charms of Castlenorth, which was the name of his uncle's house, from whence the title was derived, than pleased with either its present or its future possessor. Mr. Everard, who anxiously watched every emotion of his mind, saw this, and he saw too that his pupil was of a temper which would ill bear to be dictated to in a point so nearly connected with his own happiness. He prevailed therefore, with some difficulty, on Mrs. Willoughby, not to explain her views till nearer the period when she

---

1 Since the Castlenorths have no son, the title "Lord Castlenorth" would probably be allowed to pass to Willoughby on his uncle's death, as he would be both Castlenorth's nephew and son-in-law. The marriage of cousins has been always legal and sometimes encouraged in England.

meant they should be perfected; and they left Castlenorth without Willoughby's having the smallest suspicion of them, or carrying away any other idea of his cousin, than that she was a tall, fat, formal brown girl, whom he soon forgot and never desired to remember. His uncle's complaints and quack[1] medicines—his long lectures on genealogy[2] and heraldry[3]—had tired him; and Lady Castlenorth's dictatorial manner offended and disgusted him. He told Mr. Everard, that the only hour in which he had felt any pleasure during his abode at their house, was that in which his mother fixed the time of departing for her own. Thither he returned with redoubled delight, after the restraint he had felt himself under at Castlenorth; for there lay all his plans of future felicity, and there were Matilda and Celestina, his two sisters, as he always called them, who seemed equally dear to him.

In a few months he went to Cambridge; and Mr. Everard, who afterwards saw him only for a few days in the year, had no longer the same opportunities of judging of his sentiments. He still however had interest enough with Mrs. Willoughby, to prevail on her to delay any intimation of the intended alliance. Lord Castlenorth, his lady, and daughter, were now in Italy, and were to remain there till within six months of the time fixed among themselves for the marriage of the latter: but above a twelvemonth before the arrival of the former period, Mr. Everard died. Mrs. Willoughby and her family lost in him the sincerest and most capable monitor: a loss which greatly affected Willoughby, as well as his mother, who sent for her son from Cambridge on that melancholy occasion. Thither he had hardly

---

1 Medicines prescribed by a "quack," a pretender to medical knowledge.
2 The study of the family tree, status and inter-relationships of individuals and families.
3 Heraldry, a complex subject developing from the early Middle Ages in Europe, is the study of armorial bearings, that is, of coats of arms on shields, flags, clothing and escutcheons (representations of shields), of the history and derivation of these arms and of the families who have been granted the titles which they represent. Titles and honours indicated by armorial bearings were usually granted originally by a monarch for service in battle. The intricate system of signs or emblems meant that the status and probable family loyalties of the bearer were often clear at first sight even to a stranger, which was useful on a battlefield, on the road, or at court. Soldiers or servants of the bearer would wear the emblems and colours of their master, an early form of army uniform or servants' livery. The narrator implies, however, that by the 1790s the study of heraldry is old-fashioned and pointless.

returned, before the uncle of his father, on whom he had great dependence, and who had not long before taken him into his favour, and promised to make him his heir, died without having altered his will, and endowed an hospital with the estate which he had really meant to give his nephew, had not death overtaken him before he could conquer his habitual indolence, aggravated by the feebleness and imbecility of eighty-seven.

This disappointment was severely felt by Mrs. Willoughby, who apprehended that not only the immediate but the contingent interest of her son might be deeply affected by it: she doubted whether it would not change the intention of her brother in his favor; but after some weeks of uneasy suspense, she received assurances from Italy that those his intentions and wishes were still the same.

Mrs. Willoughby, though reassured in this respect, was still in very low spirits, and felt every hour, with increasing severity, the loss she had sustained in such a friend as Mr. Everard, whom she lamented indeed publicly, but still more bitterly in private. Her constitution, naturally very delicate, began to decline under the sorrow which oppressed her. Matilda, then about sixteen, was the only person about her who seemed insensible of the alteration which now made a slow but very evident progress in her looks and manner. Her countenance was still pleasing and interesting, but very languid; her eyes had lost their fire; and she grew very thin. Her amiable manners remained; but all her vivacity in conversation was fled. She no longer enjoyed society, of which she had been so fond: but she still went into company, because Matilda, now of an age to enter into all the gaieties of high life, did indeed engage in them with an avidity which her mother was too indulgent to repress, though she could not approve it. Sometimes however she suffered so much from crowded rooms and late hours, that though she did not even then complain, her physicians insisted on her forbearing so continually to hazard her health. Matilda, who was very uneasy if long kept from company, was then put under the care of some of her mother's friends, and the task of attending on her beloved benefactress fell entirely to the lot of Celestina, who was never so happy as when employed in it, and who now having just completed her fourteenth year, surpassed, in the perfections both of person and mind, all that Mrs. Willoughby, partial as she had always been to her, had ever supposed she would attain.

Above two years passed away: Willoughby pursuing very regularly his studies at Cambridge; Matilda pursuing as regularly every amusement that offered itself; and Celestina, careless of all that has usually attractions for youth, devoting her whole time and thoughts to Mrs. Willoughby, who without saying any thing of what she felt to be inevitable, was gradually sinking into the grave.

This conviction made her determine to disclose to her son, when she next saw him, her purpose in regard to Miss Fitz-Hayman; but it was a resolution she could not bring herself to make, without infinite regret; for in giving her reasons for wishing this alliance, it was necessary for her to open to him the real state of his fortune; of which her tenderness, in this instance perhaps injudicious, had hitherto kept him in ignorance. The longer this affectionate mother thought of the pain she should inflict on her son, the less she found herself able to undertake it: she therefore determined that Mr. Dawson, who had been employed many years by his father as steward and manager of the estates, should, under the pretence of consulting him on his affairs, now that he was of an age to direct in them, disclose to him their real situation. For this purpose he went to Cambridge; and there this unpleasant explanation was made to Willoughby: who learned, that his father, towards the latter end of his life, had mortgaged above a third of his property for nearly its value; that what remained was not only encumbered by heavy debts, which were to be discharged out of it, but had a charge of twelve hundred a year, his mother's jointure,[1] and was to pay his sister ten thousand pounds, with interest till she married—burdens which so diminished the income, as to make it impossible to save any thing during his minority, and left him no prospect of ever enjoying his paternal estate unembarrassed, but by an opulent marriage. Though Mr. Dawson had, with as much caution and tenderness as possible, opened to Willoughby the real condition of his affairs, the young man, of warm passions and keen feelings, could not hear such a mortifying account but with the extremest pain and humiliation. Unable to remain tranquilly at Cambridge, he immediately set out for London, and asked of his mother a farther explanation; as if unwilling to receive from any hand but hers a blow so cruel, which seemed to destroy for ever all his favourite hopes.

Mrs. Willoughby had ever been so far from suspecting that her son loved money, that tendency to carelessness in that respect had sometimes alarmed her: she was therefore extremely surprized at the eagerness of his enquiries, and the evident anxiety and concern he

---

1   The sum agreed by premarital settlement to be paid to a widow out of her husband's estate.

expressed at his disappointment. But having convinced him that all he had heard was but too true, and recovered from the agitation into which the necessity of giving him so much pain had thrown her, she seized the opportunity, while his mind seemed to turn with uneasy solicitude towards the means of redeeming his patrimony, to suggest to him the plan she had so long considered as infallible— "My dear George," said she, "there is one way by which all this may be repaired; and your estate, devolving to you from a long line of ancestors, of whom any man might be proud, may not only be repaired but encreased, by an alliance of which an ambitious man may be still prouder. My brother, Lord Castlenorth, is the last male of a line distinguished since the Conquest;[1] your cousin, his only daughter, will inherit his fortune; the titles die with him. It is equally natural therefore for him and for me, to wish that you, my son, in becoming the husband of my niece, may possess the estates and honours of my family, which on such a union would be easily obtained; and that in you may be revived, or rather perpetuated, the family of Fitz-Hayman. I did not intend to have named this to you till your farther acquaintance with your cousin, who returns to England in the course of the next summer, should have made it on your part a measure of inclination; for from all the accounts I have had of her, she is very amiable and highly accomplished: but my uncertain health, and the near approach of that period when you become master of yourself, have at length determined me to tell you my thoughts in a matter, on which the prosperity of your future life depends. I need not say, George, that seeing it in that light, there is nothing in this world so near my heart as its completion."

Willoughby, whose mind was contending with the various emotions this discourse of his mother's had raised, remained silent and confused. He changed colour; he sighed, as if to throw off the unexpected pressure on his heart; and Mrs. Willoughby, who saw with concern that he entered not into the project with the alacrity she had expected, began again to describe to him not only the numerous advantages which must follow the marriage, but to repeat all she had heard, and more that she had imagined, of the perfections of Miss Fitz-Hayman.

Willoughby however appeared rather to be musing than attending to almost the only conversation from his mother that he had ever

---

1 The conquest of England by the Norman duke who became William I, defeating the English King Harold at Hastings in 1066.

thought tedious. When she seemed to have exhausted the subject, he still paused a moment; then taking his hand from his forehead, he asked his mother—whether she thought Miss Fitz-Hayman as lovely as Celestina?

"As lovely as Celestina!" replied Mrs. Willoughby in great and apparently painful surprize—"how came Celestina to occur to you?"

"Nay," answered her son, attempting to appear indifferent— "I know not how, unless because she is the prettiest young woman I have lately seen."

"Surely you do not think of Celestina," reassumed Mrs. Willoughby with encreased emotion—"surely you are not imprudent enough to entertain an idea of her otherwise than as a sister. There are objections—insuperable objections. For God's sake, George, let me be assured that you will never again think of her."

"Dear Madam," returned Willoughby with some quickness, "that is really more than I can promise. How is it possible for me to assure you, with any hope of my being able to keep my word, that I will not think of a beautiful and interesting object, which, whenever I am with you, is continually before my eyes?"

"Well then," said his mother with yet more chagrin, "since it is so, you will compel me to remove her where...."

"Surely," cried the young man, eagerly interrupting her, "that would be very cruel—very cruel as it would affect Celestina, and very unnecessary as it relates to me; for I shall now be very seldom at home; and I can, without any danger of breaking my word, assure you, that nothing will ever make your son forget the duty he owes you, or hazard giving you pain. I am very sorry I named Celestina, since you seem so uneasy at it. Think of it no more I beseech you; and continue to love, as you used to do, my adopted sister, or I shall never forgive myself for any inadvertence."

Willoughby then, without staying to talk over farther the proposed alliance with Miss Fitz-Hayman, hurried away; and that he might avoid all farther conversation with his mother, he staid out to supper that night, and immediately after breakfast the following morning returned to Cambridge; telling her, as he took leave, that it would be time enough to talk over the business she had opened to him when the parties to whom it related were in England, but that she might assure herself that *her* happiness was always nearer his heart than his own.

This was the first time in his life that he parted from Matilda and

Celestina without saluting[1] them both. When breakfast was over, and he had taken leave of his mother, he kissed his sister as usual, and was approaching Celestina, who already held out her hand to him, when catching his mother's eye, who seemed to look at him reproachingly, he blushed, and only bowing and wishing Celestina her health till he saw her again, he hastened to the door, and without venturing even to look at her, as she followed him thither with his mother and sister, he mounted his horse and disappeared.

Hurt cruelly at this behaviour, (which from the very different judgment she had formed of it, had yet more alarmed his mother,) Celestina could not repress the tears which she felt rising to her eyes. Mrs. Willoughby stood at the door till her son turned into another street; and was then going to her own room, when Celestina, from an emotion she could not command, caught her hand and burst into tears: and for the first time in her life, her benefactress, instead of soothing her, received her mournful caresses with repulsive coldness, and almost without speaking to her left her. Matilda was as usual engaged to a morning concert, and had neither time nor inclination to attend to the concern of Celestina or the displeasure of her mother, which indeed she either did not see, or seeing, reflect upon. Poor Celestina therefore, who never suspected the real source of Willoughby's affected coldness, nor could imagine why his mother, who always found pleasure and comfort in her company, should now fly from her, concluded she had offended them both, and passed the morning in tears. At dinner, however, Mrs. Willoughby, as if conscious of her injustice, behaved to her with even more than her accustomed tenderness. After they had dined, as Matilda was still out, their reading went on as usual. Mrs. Willoughby took no notice of the swollen eyes and half-stifled sobs which still agitated the gentle bosom of her young friend; but without naming the cause, she seemed solicitous to remove every remaining uneasiness; and by her easy and affectionate manner Celestina became convinced that concern for her son's departure, and not anger towards her, had occasioned the coldness which had so much alarmed her; and her soft heart was thus restored to tranquillity.

---

1 Kissing.

Chapter II

Though Mrs. Willoughby took infinite pains to appear cheerful, and to hide the progress of the illness which was undermining her constitution, her efforts to appear better than she was, could not deceive her physicians; who now proposed that she should go either to Lisbon or the south of France.[1] This prescription however she endeavoured to evade, by assuring them that travelling so late in the year would infallibly injure rather than be useful to her; but she promised to follow their advice early in the ensuing spring, and to pass the winter at Bath. Thither she repaired in November, with her daughter and Celestina, to remain some months. Willoughby declined joining them at the end of term, contrary to his usual custom: he informed his mother, by letter, that he had made a party with some of his friends to pass the Christmas vacation at Alvestone, and that on their way back to Cambridge they would stay two or three days at Bath.

Matilda in the mean time, who frequented every public amusement, was become a Bath beauty, followed and admired by that description of men whose opinion is considered as decisive in the world of fashion. Miss Willoughby was always most elegantly dressed; for to be so was the principal study of her life. She was always with people of rank, was of an honourable family, had a good fortune,[2] great connections, a pretty person, and was, to use the common phrase, 'extremely accomplished;' that is, she knew something of every thing, and talked as if she knew a great deal more. Among the men of *ton*[3] who contributed to feed her vanity and raise her fashion,[4] was Mr. Molyneux, the only son of an Irish Baronet, of whom the bounty of a grandfather had made him independent. With a handsome figure, a good fortune, and a title in reversion, Mr. Molyneux was every where courted and admired; and by lounging about from one public place to another during the summer, and passing his winters, whether in England or Ireland, in the very first world,[5] he had acquired so high a polish, that his manners and his

---

1 Lisbon in Portugal and the French Alps were both medically recommended over English spa towns such as Bath, especially in the treatment of tuberculosis.
2 Dowry.
3 Style.
4 Her popularity.
5 In the most important or best-connected circles.

dress, his expressions, and even his air, were copied by all the rising beaux.[1] His understanding was just of that level which rendered him capable of being pleased with this species of fame; and having no great warmth of heart, he had no other motive of choice in marrying than that which arose from his solicitude to maintain his importance as a man of taste in the fashionable world. He had indeed no great inclination to marry at all; but his father, now far advanced in life, pressed him so earnestly to take a wife, and he was so besieged by the kind entreaties of two maiden aunts who had a great deal to give him, that tired by their importunity, and willing enough to oblige them in a matter which was indifferent to himself, he at length, in the thirty-fifth year of his age, fixed on Miss Willoughby, as a pretty woman, well born, and above all—very much "the rage." Proposals from such a man were of course accepted by the mother and the daughter; Willoughby was pleased to hear his sister was likely to be so well established; and in a few weeks it was settled that the wedding was to take place in February, when Mrs. Willoughby and her family proposed returning to London.

When Willoughby came with his Cambridge friends to Bath, to fulfil the promise given to his mother, he was introduced to his future brother-in-law. But a very short observation convinced him that they were not designed for friends; and that however closely they might be allied, Mr. Molyneux would still be to him a mere acquaintance. Willoughby was ever in the pursuit of knowledge; his mind, already highly cultivated, his heart warm and open, and his manners, with all the ingenuous simplicity of youth, had the natural good breeding which only good understanding can give. Whatever was the real character of Molyneux, it was no longer distinguishable under the polish of fashion; to obtain which, alone, seemed to be his study; all his ideas of good and evil, of right or wrong, centered there. If books had been the object, in the circle where he moved, he would have qualified himself to talk upon them; but as they were not, his reading never extended beyond a short novel, a pamphlet, or a newspaper. To strike out something new in a cape or a carriage, something which the great would imitate and the little wonder at, was half the purpose of his life: to have any affections was reckoned extremely vulgar; and as he really had as few as well possible, it cost him but little trouble to divest himself of them entirely, and to obtain

---

1 Fashionable young men.

that *sang froid*[1] which is the true criterion of a man of fashion. It is absolutely necessary to be in the House of Commons. A seat he had for a Cornish borough; where he gave a silent vote to the Minister for the time being; and neither cared nor enquired whether it would benefit or injure his country, about which he was perfectly indifferent. Yet with a mind occupied almost entirely by trifles, his handsome figure, and his affluent fortune and fashionable manners, gave him that consequence which is often denied to virtues and talents. His air was that of a man of rank; and the calm coldness of his manner gave an idea of latent powers, which he was supposed to be too indolent to exert.

Matilda, in many respects, seemed to be his very counterpart. Since they had been so much together, she had adopted his thoughts and caught his phrases; and her brother, though he did not think her by any means improved by the imitation, allowed, that if similarity of character gives happiness in marriage, his sister had a prospect of being completely happy. But when he looked at Celestina, which he avoided doing as much as possible, he saw in her improvements so different from those of Matilda, that all his resolutions to wean his mind from dwelling on her perfections faded before her. She was now in her seventeenth year, with a face and form which instantly attracted the eye, even before the beauties of her understanding had time to display themselves. These latter she never obtruded on observation; but was as silent in company as Matilda was talkative and gay. The loveliness of her form therefore it was that immediately struck the young companions of Willoughby; who both, the instant they quitted the room where they had been introduced to Mrs. Willoughby, her daughter, and Celestina, asked of Willoughby farther particulars of his adopted sister, declaring they had never seen so charming a girl, and expressing their wonder at the calmness with which he had frequently spoken of her. This conversation was so uneasy to him, that he could with difficulty conceal his vexation; and as his college friends from time to time renewed it, that circumstance, added to the pain he felt in forcing himself to behave to Celestina with cold and distant civility, shortened his visit to three days; at the end of which time he took leave of his mother, who again mentioned to him her views in regard to Miss Fitz-Hayman; to which Willoughby, who was less than ever inclined to listen to her on that point, returned vague but gentle answers; escaping from it as

---

1   Cold blood, detachment.

well as he could without giving any thing like a promise, he hastened back to his books, among which he hoped to lose the idea of Celestina, which he could not cherish but at the hazard of rendering either his mother or himself unhappy.

He promised to attend in London his sister's wedding, which was now to take place in a month, and for which preparations were making:[1] but about a week before the day fixed for Mrs. Willoughby's departure for London, an inflammation on her already injured lungs seized her so suddenly, that there was only time to send an express[2] to Cambridge for her son, who, notwithstanding his utmost expedition, arrived hardly an hour before his excellent parent expired.

As she had before taken leave of her daughter and Celestina, the greater part of that melancholy hour was given to her son, ever the object of her tenderest affections. What passed was known only to Willoughby, who, the moment his mother was no more, gave way to such an excess of sorrow, as deprived him for some hours of his senses; and when they were restored, the sight of Matilda's calmness, who did not seem to him to feel half the concern she ought to do, and the perfect composure of Molyneux, who evidently felt nothing, seemed to him so insupportable, that he shut himself up in his own lodgings and refused every offer of consolation. Though Celestina had long apprehended that the life of her beloved benefactress was in a much more precarious situation than she could herself allow, or than Matilda was willing to see, yet this cruel and yet unexpected blow quite overwhelmed her: but Willoughby, as unable to bear the sight of her grief as displeased at the stoical composure of his sister, fled with equal solicitude from both of them; and having given directions for removing the remains of his mother to the family seat at Alvestone, he hastened thither himself to receive and pay them the last offices;[3] which being done, he wrote to his sister, recommending it to her to return to London with Celestina, and to send for an elderly maiden relation to remain with them till her marriage, which the death of her mother had of necessity postponed: he promised to see her in town in the course of a fortnight, there to execute, as far

---

1 Even among fashionable people, weddings were smaller and less elaborate than they were to become later. When there was no reason for a long engagement they quickly followed the betrothal.
2 A letter sent by special mounted messenger rather than by the post coach like ordinary mail.
3 Women, young or old, were not expected to attend an interment and seldom did so.

as he could, those parts of his mother's will which demanded immediate attention.

In pursuance of these directions the two young ladies set out for London, Mr. Molyneux following them in his own carriage. The sight of the house which had now lost its mistress, threw Celestina into all those agonies which the recollection of past happiness and past kindness, from a lamented friend, gives to a heart so tender and so sensible as her's; while Matilda, who shed a tear or two from feeling something of the same sensation, presently recovered herself, and received her lover, who waited upon her[1] immediately after his arrival, without betraying any symptoms of emotion which could give him cause to apprehend that the repose of his future life might suffer any interruption from the too exquisite sensibility of his wife.

At the time he had appointed, Willoughby rejoined them. Though he now saw them with less emotion, his melancholy seemed to be deeper than at first. With his sister he avoided all conversation that was not absolutely necessary; with Celestina he was even more reserved, and never, as in their happier days, brought his book and sat with her, or sought her conversation as his greatest pleasure. He contrived indeed, under pretence of having affairs to settle abroad,[2] to see her only at dinner or supper; and frequently, under pretence of illness, absented himself from both.

After having been with them a few days, during which this reserved and altered behaviour almost broke the heart of Celestina, who seemed to have lost, by the death of the mother, the friendship of the son, he sent up one of the female servants to her room, when she retired thither after breakfast, to beg to speak to her in his sister's dressing room. This formal message, so unlike the brotherly familiarity with which he used to treat her, cut her to the heart, but she immediately attended the summons.

Willoughby bowed on her entrance. They both sat down: Celestina trying to check the tears she found rising to her eyes, and the sighs which swelled her bosom. His looks, so pale, so changed from what they were, his attitude, his silence, all contributed to distress her; while he seemed collecting fortitude to go through the talk he was to execute. After a short pause, he took from his pocket book a paper, opened it, and counted out three Bank notes, of six hundred

---

1 Called at her house.
2 Out of the house.

pounds each,[1] on the table; then advancing towards her with them in his hand, he presented them to her, saying in a voice which he did not intend should faulter—"There, Madam, is the sum which Mrs. Willoughby—which my mother, by her will, bequeaths you, and which as her executor, I most willing pay you. Allow me to wish you every happiness—and ..." He would have gone on: but Celestina, who had arisen on his approaching her, turned pale and sat down. "You are not well," said he: "the recollection of my mother..."

"Does indeed overcome me," answered Celestina. "*I* have lost a mother—and a brother too—Yes! I have lost all!"

"Pardon me, Miss de Mornay," replied Willoughby, "I meant not to distress you ... and...."

"Miss de Mornay!" repeated Celestina, again interrupting him— "*Miss* de Mornay and *Madam*. Ah! Mr. Willoughby! those appella- tions of distant civility convince me that I have no longer a friend— a brother...."

"Nay, but my dear Madam, be not, I beseech you, guilty of so much injustice. Let me execute the directions given me by my dear deceased mother, whose orders you know were, that within two months after her decease these should be put in your possession." He then again offered the notes to her.

Celestina put forth her trembling hand; but instantly withdrew it.—"I cannot take these notes indeed, Mr. Willoughby," said she. "What can I do with them? I, who am a minor, a stranger, an orphan; who have no relation, no guardian—no friend! I did indeed hope," continued she, her eyes filling with tears from the recollection of her forlorn situation—"I did indeed hope that you, Sir, would have the goodness to have kept it for me till...."

She stopped from inability to proceed. "Till when, my dear Miss de Mornay?" cried Willoughby with eagerness he seemed endeav- ouring to check.—"Certainly I would if it had been in my power; but it was my solemn promise to my mother to pay it into your hands, or into those of any person whom you should appoint."

"And cannot I name *you* as being that person?"

"Pardon me, dear Celestina," answered Willoughby, speaking hastily, as if fearful of relapsing into the fondness he once felt, and desirous of quitting a painful subject—"pardon me, it is not possible

---

1   In leaving Celestina £1,800, Mrs. Willoughby enables her to live inde-
    pendently on the annual interest of her capital, though not in the com-
    fort or with the status she has enjoyed in the Willoughby household.

for me to be of that service to you which most assuredly I should rejoice to be if...."

"Dear Celestina!" replied she. "Ah! Willoughby! I have seen for many, many months, that I am no longer your once dear sister Celestina. Call me Madam and Miss de Mornay, as you did just now, rather than flatter me with the sound, when the sincerity of your regard is gone! Well Sir! since, for reasons which perhaps I ought not to penetrate, it is no longer in *your* power to act by me as a brother and a friend, I will no farther intrude on your kindness than to beg you will tell me how I ought to place the provision thus made for me by my benefactress."

Willoughby half stifled a deep sigh; and after a moment's pause said—"I would advise you to place it immediately on government security, in the names of two persons on whom you can rely, till you become of age. Dawson, who was, you know, always employed by my mother, is more conversant than I am in these matters. If you will give me leave I will send him to you; and I am convinced you may safely trust to his honor and probity."

He then again offered the notes he had in his hand. Celestina took them in silence, being in truth unable to speak; and turning hastily away, he reached the door, where he stopped as if irresolute; then in a low and faltering voice he said—"As I shall probably see you no more, unless in mixed company, before I return to Cambridge, I cannot take this my last leave without assuring you, that however circumstances may, alas! *must* prevent my showing it, my heart can never be indifferent to the welfare—to the happiness of my sister Celestina."

There was no time for the trembling auditor to answer this address, to reflect on the peculiar way in which the whole was delivered, nor on the strong emphasis laid on the words *may* and *must*; for he was in a moment at the bottom of the stairs, and Celestina, who remained in breathless agitation, with the door of the apartment still open, heard him a moment afterwards call to his servant for his hat, and the door of the house presently shut after him. She then sat down and burst into tears, for which she was, on a little reflection, ashamed to assign a reason even to herself. "For what do I weep," said she—"or why am I disappointed? What did I expect? that Willoughby was attached to me? Surely no! for he never gave me any reason to imagine it, and of late has sedulously avoided me, as if he supposed me weak and vain enough to misinterpret the friendship and regard he used to show me. Let me, while he does stay, convince him that he may, without prejudice to his views in regard to Miss Fitz-Hayman, still treat me and consider me as his sister, and that I never thought of being looked upon otherwise, which surely he must have fancied, or he would not behave to me as he does!" Another flood of tears relieved the swelling heart of Celestina after this soliloquy. She then dried her eyes, dressed, and acquired so much command over herself as to meet Willoughby at dinner without betraying any symptoms of the uneasiness and mortification she still suffered; and when the next day he took leave of her and Matilda, she bade him adieu with the same apparent calmness.

Three months passed, and the time fixed for Matilda's marriage arrived. Willoughby then wrote to desire his sister would excuse his devoting only a single day to her on that occasion: he would attend he said to give her away,[1] but was obliged by indispensable business to return immediately afterwards to Cambridge. Matilda remarked how strange it was that her brother, who had now been some time of age, was so bigoted to his books that he could not leave them for longer than a day even on such an occasion; but his pleasures and hers differed so greatly, and their tempers and pursuits were so opposite, that no sympathy had for some years existed between them; though on the part of Willoughby there was always great affection for her; and on hers, as much regard for her brother as it was her nature to feel for any body. This difference of sentiment and inclination however had insensibly so far estranged them from each other, that the company of Willoughby was oftener a restraint than a pleasure to his sister, and therefore as he felt little regret in losing it, she thought not much about his motives for depriving her of it.

The evening before that on which Matilda was by special licence[2] to be married to Mr. Molyneux, her brother arrived: but instead of the gaiety the occasion required, or even that which had formerly been usual with him, his melancholy and regret seemed to have become habitual by indulgence. He hardly spoke: and when he did, it was with such languor that Matilda might with reason have been

---

1   The original form of the Church of England marriage service required someone to "give" the bride to her husband, usually her father or another male relative, though the sex is not specified and in the absence of either this role was occasionally taken by a woman, as at Charlotte Brontë's wedding.

2   Matilda and Molyneux need a special licence from the Bishop of London because she is marrying in London, probably in a private house, not in her own parish church, and has not had the "banns" or proclamation of the intended marriage called in her parish church on three Sundays before the marriage, as the law generally required.

alarmed for his health, if she had been capable of attending seriously to any thing but herself. Celestina, to whom he behaved with
more distant reserve than ever, could not be insensible or silent
about a health and life which she thought to be so precious to his
sister and his friends, and therefore she spoke to Matilda, when they
retired after supper, of the change so evident in her brother. Matilda
answered coldly that it was owing to nothing but his burying himself as he did among his books, and losing all relish for other company. "I wish," added she, "that these Fitz-Haymans were come over,
that he might live in the world again, and be like other people,
which he must be when he is married." Celestina could not heartily join in with this wish, and even doubted whether Willoughby ever
would be quite like those who were called "other people" by his sister. She dropped the conversation however, and retired to her pillow
with more solicitude for the happiness of Matilda, which was to be
determined the next day, than Matilda was capable of feeling for herself. The image of Willoughby, such as he was a few years before, was
strongly painted by her imagination: she ran over all their former
early pleasures; their walks, their reading, their gardening together at
Alvestone while yet children; then Willoughby, such as he now was,
so amiable yet so changed, obtruded himself on her mind; and being
unable to look forward with any degree of pleasure, she felt with
redoubled sorrow that those days of innocent confidence and ingenuous tenderness, could never—never return!

Chapter III

When the party met the next day, every body had left off their
mourning, and every face appeared cheerful but those of Willoughby and Celestina: the latter, when gaily rallied by the friends of Mr.
Molyneux, endeavoured to recover her tranquillity; and as to Matilda herself, she gave away her hand with as much ease as if it was a
matter of course. Molyneux received it with equal composure; and
as soon as they were married, they sat[1] out, accompanied only by
Celestina and Mr. Hamilton,[2] a near relation of the bridegroom, for

---

1   A common past tense for "set."
2   In earlier times a couple often remained at the bride's home following
    the marriage. By the latter part of the eighteenth century, one or more
    of the bridesmaids or relatives often accompanied a newly-married cou-
    ple on a wedding journey; the modern concept of the honeymoon
    developed later.

an house which Mr. Molyneux rented in Hampshire. Willoughby saluted his sister; and as he handed her into the coach[1] he again wished her happiness. It was impossible to avoid doing the same as Celestina passed him, but he faltered, and could hardly articulate his compliment, which while he yet tremulously attempted to express, holding one of her hands between his, Mr. Hamilton, who had been detained by giving some orders to his servant, came up, and taking her other hand said—"Come, come! as you don't go with us, Willoughby, the care of this lady devolves upon me and I shall not allow these sorrowful partings to make her as melancholy as you are yourself all her journey." Celestina was then unresistingly led away; while Willoughby, who followed her to the coach door, found at that moment his heart assailed by pangs it had never felt before, but which he knew too well to be jealousy in its most corrosive form. As the coach drove away, he stood looking after it; now repenting that he had not accompanied his sister and her husband into Hampshire, then determining to order his horse and follow them; now detesting Hamilton, of whom he had never thought before, and then resolving to conquer a passion which a thousand circumstances made it the height of folly to indulge. The coach which contained the object of it was already out of sight; but Willoughby still stood on the spot from whence it had been driven, so lost in the indulgence of these sensations, that he forgot where he was, and was roused from his reverie only by the arrival of a friend with whom he had made an appointment to go in his chaise[2] part of the way to Cambridge.

This friend he was ashamed to disappoint, nor could he form any excuse to account for his suddenly changing his mind and following his sister, whom he had steadily declined to accompany under pretence of urgent engagements. While he yet debated, the chaise was ready, and with an heart torn with contending passions, and a mind intent only on Celestina and the advantage Hamilton enjoyed of being so long with her, as during the stay of Molyneux in Hampshire and in the tour they were afterwards to make, he proceeded, absent, silent, and miserable, to the end of his journey.

Celestina with equal oppression of spirits was yet more unfortunate, because she was afraid of enquiring too narrowly into the source of her concern, nor did she dare to indulge it, but was com-

---

1   As a wealthy man Mr. Molyneux owns at least one coach, which is capable of containing a party of six, though four more comfortably.
2   French for "chair," a light one-horse carriage for one or two travellers.

pelled to assume cheerfulness very foreign to her feelings. Mr. Hamilton, who had never taken much notice of her before, now seemed disposed to amuse himself by coquetting with her; but she had so little inclination to encourage him, that, as he was too perfectly a man of the world to give himself much trouble about any woman, he soon left her to her own amusements. In a few days after the bride and bridegroom arrived at their house, it was filled with company; and Matilda, wholly occupied with parties all the morning, and play[1] in the evening, had never time to think of Celestina, who soon found herself neglected by the only person whom she could now call her friend; and the disappointment which still sat so heavy on her heart—the failure, as she believed, of Willoughby's regard—was now embittered by the coldness or rather carelessness which she experienced from his sister.

In a few weeks a party was made to visit Plymouth and the Western bathing places.[2] Celestina went with them as a matter of course, but she felt herself dwindling fast into the humiliating character of a dependent companion, and sometimes fancied that her place in the coach might have been occupied by another more to the satisfaction of her friend: yet Mrs. Molyneux was never rude to her; and sometimes related (with apparent kindness) how her mother had adopted her from a convent, and that therefore she ever should consider her as her sister. Celestina always felt herself more mortified than gratified by these relations; and by degrees they became so irksome to her, and the whole style of conversation among Matilda's friends so little to her taste, that she insensibly acquired an habit of absenting herself, and of living very much alone either in her own room or in the walks which wherever the party fixed she contrived to find, and whither the image of Willoughby, such as it had been at a very early period of her life impressed on her young heart, incessantly accompanied her. This was more particularly the case when in the course of their tour Mr. and Mrs. Molyneux undertook to shew their friends Alvestone, where Willoughby had ordered every thing to be prepared for their reception as if he had been himself there. Matilda re-visited this beautiful place with no other emotions than those of gratified pride; but on Celestina it had a very different effect: this was

---

1 Gambling.
2 Sea-bathing was recommended by doctors from the 1760s on, and steadily increased in popularity, accommodated by the growth of seaside resorts and eventually by the holiday industry. Women bathers entered the sea from wheeled wooden "bathing machines" drawn by donkeys.

the scene where the happiest hours of her life had passed. The dressing room where they all used to assemble when the only parent she had known was its mistress, brought her forcibly to the recollection of Celestina. The chair on which she used to sit, the furniture which she had worked[1] herself, and the pictures she had collected, were so many memorials on which Celestina could not look without recollecting a thousand instances of her general goodness or her particular tenderness, and feeling with bitter regret the irreparable loss she had sustained. The park and the gardens too furnished her with many sources of painful contemplation, mingled however with a degree of melancholy so soothing, that nothing would have been to her so great a punishment as being obliged to exchange it for the desultory and uninteresting conversation, which, in the little time spared from the card table, engaged the party within the house.

The party however troubled themselves very little with her: and she was left at liberty to retrace the walks which she had so often traversed with Willoughby while Matilda leaned on one arm and she on the other, and to gaze on the prospects which he, while yet a boy, had pointed out to them with so much pleasure. She remembered all the proposed improvements of which he delighted to talk. A rapid stream bursting from the hollow of a rocky common that bounded the park, and made its way through it, had been by the former Mr. Willoughby widened at a great expense, and now fell several feet into a vale which he had at a still greater cost, floated with water. On the sides of this fall, which had been formerly part of the common, grew some old oaks and beech, and among these the mountain ash and weeping birch had been planted and now spread their various foliage and half concealed the water that dashed from rock to rock between them. These steep banks had ever been the various seats of Willoughby; who there sitting between his two sisters, and holding each of their hands, had very frequently amused himself with projects to encrease the roar of the water or deepen the shade of the wood that fringed its side. This place was the daily resort of Celestina during the week she remained at Alvestone, and thither she usually carried some of those books from the library that she remembered Willoughby had read to her. These were principally poetry: and the re-perusal of them, the place, the season, a thousand tender remembrances enforced by each, served at once to soften and depress an heart naturally tender and affectionate, which, deprived of almost

---

1 Embroidered or worked in tapestry.

every other object of its regard, cherished with painful pleasure the idea of Willoughby, such as he once was, and when they passed here so many innocent enchanting hours. But when she imagined that in a few months he would probably re-visit these scenes with another, with Miss Fitz-Hayman, who would then be his wife, and that she herself should never again be admitted to wander among them with their beloved master, sick despondence took possession of her soul, and it was with difficulty after these reflections that she could reassume courage enough to mix with the friends whom Mr. and Mrs. Molyneux had assembled to listen to insipid pleasantry and attend to uninteresting conversation.

But whatever regret Celestina felt in recollecting past hours of felicity which she knew could never return, she left Alvestone with extreme reluctance, and had it been proper, or possible, would most willingly have remained there alone. In quitting it never to return, she felt almost as much concern as she had done when in taking leave of Willoughby she fancied that she should see him no more till he was married to Miss Fitz-Hayman.

Of that match Mrs. Molyneux now very frequently spoke as a matter entirely settled, and Celestina no longer doubted of its speedy completion. This circumstance, (which gave her uneasiness that she was unable either to repress or entirely to disguise), the encreasing indifference of Matilda towards her, and the constant succession of company in which Mr. and Mrs. Molyneux lived, united to raise in her a wish to quit them; and finding that the hints she gave of such a disposition were received with perfect carelessness, and that such a removal would probably not be objected to, she every day grew fonder of her project, and during their stay at Sidmouth fixed on a cottage about four miles from it, where she thought she might reside, if not happily at least in that quiet obscurity which her circumstances rendered prudent, and her distaste to the world in which she now lived, pleasant. She found that she could there be accommodated with board and lodging, and there she would now have remained if Mrs. Molyneux had not, when she understood her project, insisted on her returning to London with her after finishing their tour.—"Go with me however," said she, "the rest of our journey, and till we meet the Castlenorths, who are to be in town in October; and then if you have this rural passion still so strong upon you, you shall take your own way." Though there was little appearance of affection in this invitation, Celestina thought she ought not to decline it, and therefore, though meeting the Castlenorths was what she most solicitously wished to avoid, she determined to go with her friend to town, that she might not give her any pretence for forgetting her entirely, or incur the censure of the world for leaving abruptly the only protection she could claim.

Chapter IV

The return of Mr. and Mrs. Molyneux to London was postponed from time to time till November. Lord Castlenorth had been too ill to set out on his journey to England at the time he proposed and the family meeting which was to settle all that related to the marriage was now delayed till after Christmas. Willoughby however testified no impatience: he had promised to meet his sister and her husband in town on their arrival; but instead of doing so, he sent such an insufficient excuse as must have appeared very strange to Matilda had she thought much about it; but immersed in pleasures and pursuits of her own, she gave herself very little time to reflect on her brother's conduct, and was far from supposing that he absented himself because he could not see Celestina without encreasing and confirming a passion which he had many reasons against indulging, and of which he was determined to cure himself by absence and reflection. The negociation with his uncle, which had been carried so far by his mother, he neither declined nor forwarded; but suffered it to remain nearly on the footing she had left it, flattering himself that by the time Miss Fitz-Hayman arrived in London, he should have so far conquered his early attachment as to have an heart as well as the hand, which he had promised to his mother's entreaties, to offer her.

Though his endeavours to forget Celestina had hitherto been quite unsuccessful, he had however acquired so much resolution as to determine not to see her, till the arrival of his destined wife, and the final settlement of every thing that related to his marriage, should put it out of his power to break the engagement he had made to Mrs. Willoughby in her last hours, and to sacrifice every thing to his passion. The struggle he underwent however was dreadful, and by continually repeating to himself the necessity there was for his forgetting Celestina, he so accustomed himself to think of her, that he in reality soon ceased to think with interest of any body else; and though he endeavoured to persuade himself that he should have courage to acquit himself of what he tried to think his duty to his family, to his mother's memory, and himself, there was no intelligence he so much dreaded as that of the arrival of his uncle's family in England.

Celestina on her part, passed her time in a way very unpleasant to her. Mrs. Molyneux, now mistress of herself, plunged into unceasing dissipation;[1] and as Celestina was frequently desired to accompany her, and always to make one of the parties she collected at her own house, she found that the expenses of dress alone would greatly exceed the income of her little fortune, and that she should soon exhaust it to live among people whose society gave her no pleasure, and who for the most part considered her only as she was capable of filling up a table[2] or the corner of a coach when it was vacant. Her quickness of apprehension and extreme sensibility made her too frequently remark, that the table or the coach might in the apprehension of Matilda always be as well, and sometimes better filled; and these observations, together with her growing dislike to Mr. Molyneux, and the people with whom he associated, who not unfrequently treated her with the impertinent familiarity which they thought themselves at liberty to use towards Mrs. Molyneux's *companion*,[3] renewed, before she had been six weeks in town, her wish to quit them for ever, and to enjoy in her own way the small independence given her by her lamented benefactress.

The certainty that Miss Fitz-Hayman was so soon to become the wife of the only man for whom she ever had felt the least degree of partiality, hastened the execution of her project. She now heard every day of the great beauty, the extraordinary accomplishments, and the immense fortune of the future bride, while Mrs. Molyneux was exercising her fancy on the equipages, and other preparations which were so soon to be on foot for the wedding of her brother; a subject that Celestina always listened to with impatience, which, though she with difficulty concealed it from others, she was painfully conscious of herself. The eternal harangues of Mrs. Molyneux on taste and elegance had always been fatiguing to her, but she was more than usually disgusted when the purpose of these lectures was to decide upon or to describe the bridal fineries intended for Willoughby and Miss Fitz-Hayman.

A letter now arrived from Lady Castlenorth announcing her intentions of being in London with her Lord and her daughter the following week; and at this intelligence Celestina, no longer hesitating, wrote to the person near Sidmouth, to whom she had spoken

---

1 The term suggests late hours, gambling and frequent socialising.
2 For cards.
3 A salaried dependent, of much the same status as a governess.

the preceding summer; and finding she could be immediately received at the lodging she had then looked at, she packed up and sent by the waggon the small collection of books given her by Mrs. Willoughby, which with her cloaths and the legacy vested in the funds, were all her worldly possessions; and that evening after supper, when by a chance very unusual with them Mr. and Mrs. Molyneux were without company, she declared her intentions of going into the country the next day.

Mr. Molyneux, twirling about a wine glass and humming a tune, seemed to attend very little to the information; his wife, after hearing it with almost equal indifference, said—"I cannot imagine, my dear, why you think of going into the country now, or what you propose by it."

"Nothing more," replied Celestina, piqued at the coldness of her manner, "than to accustom myself at once to a mode of life which my narrow fortune renders, if not absolutely necessary, at least highly prudent."

"Prudence," cried Molyneux with a smile which Celestina thought a contemptuous one, "is an acquisition very unusual at eighteen: but a girl of spirit, with so pretty a person as your's is, should be rather ambitious than prudent, and should try to make her fortune by marriage instead of hiding herself in the country. Numberless young women about town have done extremely well, who, without any compliment, have not had your share of beauty."

"Very possibly, Sir," replied Celestina; "but unless my mind was disposed as their minds probably were, which I believe it never will be, the personal advantages you so flatteringly allow me, will never obtain the affluence you think so desirable."

"What do you mean to say?" answered he. "What! do you pretend that you would not marry as other women do for money or title?"

"For neither, upon my honor."

"Pooh! I thought you had more sense; but since it is so, my dear Celestina, I wish you all possible felicity in your new plan of pastoral amusement, and doubt not but that some tender and amiable Philander,[1] in the shape of a young west country curate, will enable you to realize to your heart's content all your ideas of disinterested love and rural happiness."

---

1   From its Greek root, a lover. The name is used in a number of poems and plays, e.g., Ludovico Ariosto's *Orlando Furioso* and Francis Beaumont and John Fletcher's *The Laws of Candy*.

Molyneux then sauntered away, and his lady looking in a pocket mirror, and picking her teeth with the nicest[1] care, took up the argument.

"You know Celestina that I have the greatest regard for you, and that I have argued with you for ever about this nonsensical resolution, which I cannot imagine what put into your head. You will be tired to death, child, in the country at this time of the year. However if you will go, do stay here at least till after my brother is married. We shall have half the world with us then, and I shall want you for twenty things."

At the mention of Willoughby's marriage, Celestina, though so much accustomed to hear of it, changed colour, and her voice as well as her look might have betrayed the uneasy sensations she felt, if Mrs. Molyneux had not been always too much occupied by herself to attend very narrowly to another.

"Pardon me, dear Madam," said Celestina, "I certainly cannot be wanted on that occasion. You will have so many other friends about you that I shall not be missed; and I have no right, indeed I never had any, to be upon an equality with the persons who will then be assembled about you. Let me therefore find my own place in society, and learn at once to submit to it."

After some other conversation, Celestina, still unwilling to appear in the slightest degree ungrateful for past kindness or too impatient of her present situation, agreed to stay another week in town; and retired to her own room relieved by having thus declared her intentions and fixed the time when her present uneasy state of dependence would be at an end.

But of this delay she repented, when the next day notice was received by Mrs. Molyneux of the arrival of Lord and Lady Castlenorth at their house in Grosvenor-street. Mr. and Mrs. Molyneux instantly waited on[2] them; the next evening they were to return the visit in form; and thus Celestina was compelled to be present at a meeting she had been studiously endeavouring to avoid.

Lord Castlenorth was one of those unfortunate beings, who have been brought up never to have a wish unprevented[3] or a want ungratified. He was born when his father was far advanced in life,

---

1 Most delicate.
2 Paid a brief formal visit leaving an address card, which invited a return visit.
3 Unanticipated.

the sole heir to one of the most ancient[1] families and opulent fortunes in England; and was of so much consequence, that till he was near eighteen he was hardly ever suffered out of the sight of his father. He was then released by death from the officious affection which had long been very troublesome to him; and with every thing on his side but a good constitution, he set out on a wild career of pleasure, in which, before he had materially hurt his fortune, he was stopped by the apprehension of declining health. His figure was one of those which look as if

"The blasts of January would blow them thro' and thro'"[2]

and the irregularities[3] of his life had so much impaired a habit[4] naturally weak, that at thirty he was a mere shadow, and then was told by his physicians that he must resolve on a residence of some time in the south of Europe if he would avoid going to that country "from whose bourn no traveller returns:"[5] to which having an invincible aversion, he lost not a moment in complying with their advice. But as he soon recovered some degree of health, he grew every day less attentive to injunctions they had given as to his manner of life; and relapsing into his former indiscretions, he was again reduced to extremities, and when very little hope of his life remained, was recommended by one of his medical friends in London to put himself under the care of Dr. Maclaurin, a Scottish physician, who had been settled for two or three years at Naples with his wife and family.

There he was treated with the most assiduous attention, not only by the Doctor himself but by Mrs. Maclaurin and her daughter, then near thirty, who was so reasonable as to allow herself to be five and twenty. She was tall, and had a tolerable face, with which her ambi-

---

1   A Norman, Robert Fitz-Hamon, was granted lands in Gloucestershire
    and seized much of Glamorganshire in Wales after the Norman invasion
    in 1066. The family had died out by Smith's time. Smith's note: Fitz-
    Hayman, Earl of Glocester, came in with the Conqueror [William I], the
    heiress of which family married a natural son of Henry I, by Nesta,
    daughter of Rhees Prince of Wales.
2   *The Winter's Tale*, 4.4.111–12.
3   Smith suggests that Castlenorth is debilitated by venereal disease and
    heavy drinking.
4   Constitution, physical makeup.
5   If he wants to avoid dying. *Hamlet*, 3.1.81–82.

tion to be admired, suffered her not to be content in its natural state. She had been brought up to attend most sedulously to her own interest, and to pursue the establishment of her fortune by marriage: she had therefore learned early to fawn and flatter; and to the cunning of her mother united some portion of the abilities of her father. Mrs. Maclaurin was one of that species of being who are by courtesy denominated good sort of women. All her virtues were negative; and of the few vices she had it in her power to practice, she contented herself with malice and defamation, and even in those she never indulged herself unless very certain that the objects were incapable of retort and totally defenceless. She had now however but little opportunity of gratification; for though she had lived three years in Italy, she understood not a word of the language, and her attempts to mend the world being therefore made, in one not understood by those in whose favor they were exerted, were very little comprehended, and of course failed of affording her much satisfaction. Her talents being thus perforce confined to her own household, had taken another turn, and had been applied to the acquisition of money, and of securing a good match for her daughter.

The Doctor, though really a man of some abilities, had not hitherto been successful enough in his profession to be enabled to give her a fortune: the project of marrying her well was equally interesting to him; and among the various patients he had received into his house since he resided at Naples, the elder son of a very opulent merchant in London, and an old Baronet, who had several daughters older than Miss Maclaurin, very narrowly escaped her multiform attractions by the impertinent remonstrances of their families. Lord Castlenorth had no relations but Mrs. Willoughby, who was very unlikely to interfere in any matrimonial project; he had besides a much larger fortune, and was of a much higher rank, than any of those for whom the family of Maclaurin had intended the honor of their alliance; but the very circumstances which rendered the prospect of such a marriage most alluring, seemed to preclude the probability of success.

Among the few things Lord Castlenorth had learned of his father, the principal was to value himself on his descent; and, as far as related to his own family, he was a genealogist[1] almost as soon as he could speak. As he advanced in life, he found himself of so little con-

---

1 One who studies genealogy, the family trees and inter-marriages of (usually titled) individuals and families.

sequence for individual merit, that he was compelled to avail himself of the names of his ancestors, from whom only he derived any importance at all; and the 'puny insect shivering at a breeze,'[1] swelled with conscious pride when he recited the names of heroes from whom he had so woefully degenerated.

This pride of ancestry was now the most distinguishing feature in a character where it appeared with the greatest prominence, from the faintness and insipidity of the other traits, for being no longer able to pursue the dissolute manner of life which he had adopted rather from fashion than inclination, he had now in other respects no character at all.

Miss Maclaurin, who began to study him as soon as he was received by her father, soon saw it, and saw it with dismay; for she supposed that it would be an insuperable bar to those hopes, which she thought she might otherwise very reasonably entertain.

The Doctor however had too many resources to be so easily discouraged. He fabricated with admirable ingenuity a story, of which he justly supposed the ignorance and indolence of his patient would prevent his ever detecting the falsehood. He said that he was really a Hamilton,[2] and had taken his present name in compliance with the whim of a distant relation who had on that condition given him his property. The only objection being thus removed, Miss Maclaurin had a fair field for her attractive talents; and they were so effectually exerted, that in about five months after Lord Castlenorth's reception into the family of Maclaurin, he became himself a member of it, and Miss Maclaurin returned to England as his wife.

That her father might still retain, without too scrupulous an enquiry, his relationship to the house of Hamilton, and that her mother's coarse figure and coarser manners might be no disgrace to Lady Castlenorth in the sphere where she now prepared to blaze, she prevailed upon them to retire to their native country on a pension which there gave them consequence: while her Ladyship, who while she was Miss Maclaurin had nothing doubted of her own eminent

---

1 Alexander Pope, *Epistle IV (On Riches). To Richard Boyle, Earl of Burlington*, 108.

2 The main branch of the Hamilton family held the Earldoms of Arran and Orkney from the twelfth century on, and was granted a Dukedom after the unification of England and Scotland under James I. In a clan multiply-related to the Stuarts and other powerful Scottish families, many cadet members have been distinguished in the army and navy and in the arts and sciences.

perfections, was now so convinced of their irresistible power by their having thus established her in a situation so much above her hopes, that she thought herself born for the government and amendment of the world, and from that period had been advancing in arrogance and ostentation till the present hour; when at the age of fifty, with an unwieldy person and a broad face, where high cheek bones appeared emulous of giving some protection to two grey prominent eyes, whose lids seemed inadequate to shade them, Lady Castlenorth was as well by her rank as her talents and her travels, qualified in her own opinion for universal dominion. Not content therefore with governing her Lord with despotic sway,[1] (which indeed saved him the trouble and probably the disgrace of governing himself) she affirmed towards the rest of the world a style equally dictatorial. Her opinion was strongly enforced on every topic that came before her; in private anecdote, in public debates, in literature, in politics, in fashions, she was equally omniscient; and whether the conversation ran on taxes or on taste, in laying out grounds or on setting out a dinner, in making peace or a poem, she understood all, descanted on all, and could decide on all, in a way from which few of her auditors had at the moment courage to appeal.

By the side of this majestic figure, her Lord, the descendant of the old Earls of Gloucester, of Welsh Princes and English Kings, sunk into insignificance. His diminutive figure, now shrunk by age and sickness, his sallow and withered countenance, and his feeble step, formed a decided contrast to his robust and Juno-like lady,[2] by whom he suffered himself to be led about, without ever pretending to differ from her opinion, unless in matters of heraldry or genealogy, where he still ventured to take the lead, in which she was for the most part willing to indulge him. His Lordship's ill health had made him also conversant in physic;[3] a science in which, notwithstanding her hereditary claim to it, Lady Castlenorth had not shown much disposition to contend with him: but as there was more trouble and disgust than honour to be obtained by a constant attention to it, as applied to his real or imaginary complaints, she had very frequently delegated her authority, and at length quite relinquished her knowledge, to a relation, who being a widow (and said to possess a pretty

---

1   Cf. John Milton, *Samson Agonistes*, 1054. There the Chorus, however, considers that "despotic power" should be the husband's prerogative.

2   Juno, Queen of the Roman gods, is usually represented in literature and painting as dark and powerful.

3   Medicine.

fortune though nobody ever knew where it lay) now about six and forty, had with infinite philanthropy dedicated her days to relieve the infirmities of her fellow creatures without any other advantage than that of being received in turn at their houses. She knew every receipt,[1] whether of diet or medicine, that could be named as preventative or cure; understood the preparation of every quack remedy, and the qualities of all the drugs of which they are compounded: nor was she less acquainted with the human frame; and would in all companies give the history of any complaint to which it is subject in technical terms, to the wonder of some and the terror of many hearers. Such were the manners of Mrs. Calder; and her person was one of those, which but for their singularity, nobody would ever recollect as having seen at all. She now resided almost constantly with Lord and Lady Castlenorth, to both of whom she had contrived to render herself necessary. With them she had been abroad, (where she had greatly improved her stock of knowledge, and had actually written a treatise on the goitres[2] of the Alpine peasants, which Lady Castlenorth was polishing for publication,) and she was now of the party who were assembled at Mrs. Molyneux's; where the last but not the least in consequence appeared also—the destined bride of Willoughby.

The claim of this young lady to eminent beauty, or to any thing more than a barely tolerable person, would certainly not have been allowed, had she not been heiress to the illustrious house of Fitz-Hayman; but the escutcheon of pretence,[3] which she had a right to, seemed to give her a pretence also, to much of what nature had very scantily allowed her. She was as tall and almost as large as her mother, whom she greatly resembled. Her complexion was brown, and as her hair was not dark, the want of contrast produced a muddy and heavy effect, which nothing could have relieved but two dark eyes, whose powers were assisted by a greater quantity of rouge than unmarried ladies are even by the French customs usually allowed. What expression they naturally had however was not pleasing, and

---

1   The word also meant "prescription."
2   Lumps caused by a swelling of the thyroid gland in the throat, prevalent in some Alpine areas.
3   An escutcheon is the representation in wood, plaster or stone of a shield on which a coat of arms is depicted, in a great hall or over a gateway, for instance. She has true claims to high rank, like the Pretender to a throne—though "pretence" here seems closer to "pretentiousness,"—but none to beauty.

what they borrowed from this addition added more to their fierceness than their lustre. They were eyes of "high claims and expectations,"[1] which demanded rather than solicited admiration, and signified pretty plainly the real disposition of a character, inflated with ideas of its own consequence, and considering more than half the world as beings of another species, whose evils she could not feel for, because she was placed where it was impossible she could ever share them.

To the personal arrogance of her mother, she added the hereditary pride of her father: the first had taught her that hardly any man could deserve so perfect and accomplished a creature; the second, that it was more desirable to unite herself with Willoughby, and thus continue her own illustrious race, than lose or share her consequence by marrying a nobleman of superior rank. Some degree of personal partiality too, contributed to render this resolution more pleasing to her; for though she had not seen her cousin for between three and four years, his graceful and beautiful form when he left Eton, with his dark auburn hair flowing over his shoulders, had made a very lasting impression in his favor.

Chapter V

Such was the group, which, at a very late hour in the evening, entered the dining-room of Mrs. Molyneux, who, with her husband and Celestina, received them in the usual forms. Lady Castlenorth, as usual, took the lead in conversation, having first satisfied herself that Mrs. Molyneux had sent for Willoughby, and heard her assurances that he would certainly be in town the first moment he possibly could after hearing of the arrival of his noble relations.

"What sort of taste, my dear," cried her Ladyship to Mrs. Molyneux, "is this apartment fitted up in?—Is this the present style in England?—I think it extremely ugly."

This was trenching[2] on Matilda in a very tender point. Taste was her reigning foible; and the house had, on her recent marriage, been fitted up under her directions at an immense expence. To have her elegance called so abruptly in question, therefore, was very far from

---

1   Smith is probably thinking of a woman's eyes with "high claims and terrifying exactions," in Lawrence Sterne's *Tristram Shandy*, Vol. 8, Chapter XXV.
2   Cutting into, attacking.

being pleasant, and she answered coldly—"I am sorry you dislike it: it is, I believe, the newest style of doing rooms. To what does your Ladyship object?"

"Oh, to the whole. These sort of papers are unclassical[1] and glaring: I don't like the colour of your furniture either."

"Nor I," interrupted Mrs. Calder; "'tis terrible for the eyes; does not your Ladyship[2] find it dazzling and inconvenient even by candle-light?" She then began to explain the effect of glaring and strong colours on the visual orb, when Lady Castlenorth, who had no intention to throw the conversation into her hands, turned abruptly towards Celestina, of whom she had hitherto taken no notice, and said, looking steadily at her while she addressed Mrs. Molyneux, "That, I think, is the young woman whom your late mother said she took out of a convent somewhere in France, is it not?" Mrs. Molyneux answering in the affirmative, Lady Castlenorth, her eyes still fixed on the object of her enquiry, said, "Aye, I thought I recollected her:—Umph!—and so Mrs. Willoughby provided for her, did she?—Well! and is she to live on with you, as she did in your mother's time?"

"Only a few days longer, Madam," said Celestina, who had borne very impatiently this rude and unfeeling scrutiny; "I am then going to reside entirely in the country."

"I am glad of it, child," replied the lady; "for I always consider it as a misfortune when girls are educated above their fortune, and introduced into a style of life they have no pretensions to. Indeed, I gave Mrs. Willoughby my opinion about you repeatedly in your infancy. I did not then know that her circumstances allowed her, in justice to *her husband's* children, to provide so amply for another. However, though it was a great deal for her to do, it is not by any means a fortune to authorise you with prudence to continue to live about town. You took, I think, your Christian name from the order of Nuns among whom you were reared; and your surname—I mean the name they gave you—it has escaped me?"

---

1   The Adam brothers, especially Robert (1728-92), introduced a spare and delicate "classical" style of furnishing in the latter half of the eighteenth century, with papers and plasterwork in white, cream or pale blues and greens. Matilda favours a fashion for the new and exotic: there was a growing taste for "Gothic," Middle-Eastern or Indian styles and artefacts, with darker colours and heavier furnishings.
2   "Lordship" in the original.

"My name, Madam," said Celestina, whose tears were restrained only by indignation, "is de Mornay."

"True; I recollect it now. I remember I enquired of Mrs. Willoughby, whether when they gave you that name they had any reason to fancy you any way related to the family of the famous du Plessis Mornay;[1] but I think she told me no, and that you received that appellation because the Superior to whose care you were entrusted had some fanciful partiality to the name."

To this no answer being given the conversation took another turn, but was still engrossed by Lady Castlenorth; while Mrs. Molyneux, wearied to death, proposed cards, and making a table with the noble pair, Mrs. Calder, and her husband, she sat down herself by Miss Fitz-Hayman, and endeavoured to enter into conversation with her.

Miss Fitz-Hayman however, who never loved her cousin because she had heard her reckoned handsome, and who was out of humour to find that Willoughby was not yet arrived, though there was barely time for him to have come express,[2] received all her advances with more than her usual haughty indifference; and while she answered in short sentences or mere monosyllables, she now examined with looks of dislike the studied but becoming dress of Mrs. Molyneux, now, with yet more unpleasant expression, glanced with averted head, from the corners of her eyes, on Celestina, who without any study at all was infinitely more beautiful.

These scowling looks of mingled malignity and contempt, added to the behaviour of Lady Castlenorth towards her, had by this time rendered the room so disagreeable to her, that she left it as soon as she could. A loud rap at the door however soon after announced the arrival of other visitors; and some ladies coming in who had finished their circle of visits for that evening, Mrs. Molyneux, as tired of the daughter's silence as she had before been of the mother's loquacity, proposed a table at vingt un,[3] which Celestina was immediately desired to join.

---

1 Philippe du Plessis Mornay (1549-1623) served King Henry IV of Navarre with equal distinction as First Minister, diplomat and general. Sympathetic to the French Protestants, the Huguenots, at a time of religious bigotry and civil war, he was also a devout lay theologian who risked the condemnation of Catholic clerics to attempt conciliation between the Huguenots and the Catholic majority. He was related to the French royal house, the Bourbons, and to a network of aristocratic families.
2 At great speed.
3 A round game of cards where the winner reaches without exceeding 21 points.

The party were hardly placed at it, before Mr. Molyneux was informed by his gentleman[1] that Mr. Willoughby was below and asked to speak to him. "Desire him to come up," replied he, without any seeming consciousness of the formidable nature of the interview he was to go through.

"He is in boots, Sir," replied the servant, "and desired me to say that he is going immediately to his lodgings."

"Oh but we shall not let him go," said Molyneux. "Do Mrs. Molyneux," continued he, addressing himself to his wife, "do go down and bring up this brother of yours."

Mrs. Molyneux rose and left the room. Lady Castlenorth, still appearing to attend to her game, turned her fiercely-questioning eyes, first on her daughter, who might have blushed if her complexion had been calculated to shew the suffusion of blood, and then unluckily they were attracted by the more unequivocal and deep rose colour, which for a moment took possession of the face of Celestina, who sat next to her.

There was no time to comment on this appearance before it was heightened by the entrance of Willoughby, who was immediately led by his sister to Lord Castlenorth, then to her Ladyship, and at length to Miss Fitz-Hayman. He paid his compliments to all with his usual graceful manners, but not without an expression of pain and embarrassment in his countenance, which he seemed vainly trying to shake off. He had yet distinguished nobody in the room but those to whom he had been speaking; but on recovering from the low bow he had made to Miss Fitz-Hayman, he saw Celestina; and starting, he said in a hurrying way—"Miss de Mornay! I thought you had left my sister! I hope I see you well!" Celestina answered only by a curtsey; and Willoughby, turning away towards Mrs. Molyneux, told her that he was a good deal fatigued, and must beg her to excuse him for the rest of the evening, but that he would be with her the following morning to breakfast. "Your Lordship," added he turning to his uncle, "will perhaps allow me to pay my respects to you and Lady Castlenorth in the course of the morning": then without waiting for the reply which his Lordship was in great form waiting to give him, he hurried out of the room, and the card tables very soon afterwards broke up.

Though Willoughby was very much altered since Miss Fitz-Hayman has last seen him, the change appeared greatly in his favour. His undress,[2] and the agitation he was apparently in, which she imputed

---

1 His personal servant or valet, usually "man."
2 Informal clothing.

to the effect of her charms, combined to make him appear more interesting both to the mother and daughter; and as they went home, Lord Castlenorth, who grew every day fonder of the proposed marriage, spoke much in praise of his nephew's figure and manner. "He has a great deal," said he, "of the family countenance. He strikes me, indeed he always did from a boy, as resembling greatly the picture painted on board[1] of William, son of Robert Fitz-Hayman, Seneschal[2] to Henry II, who obtained the grants of the estate in Gloucestershire. His arms[3] were azure, a lion rampant, gardant or,[4] the original bearing of the family; you see it so in the great window of the hall at Castlenorth; the next is that of his wife, party per pale,[5] two griffins counter sailant, sable, langued gules.[6] This is my first quarter[7] for the name of Bigot, a daughter of which house, this William, son of Robert, married." Lord Castlenorth was now got on his favourite topic, and in the numberless quarterings of his present bearing,[8] he quite forgot the merits of his nephew, and was busied among wyverns[9] and boars, pearls,[10] saltiers,[11] fesses[12] and bend dexters,[13] till they arrived at their own house. The imaginations however of the rest of the company finding nothing to arrest them in a detail so often repeated, had all left him to settle his chevrons and chevronels[14] his own way; even the attentive

---

1 On wood.

2 Controller of the household (steward) to Henry II (1133-89), who inherited his throne as a child, now mainly remembered as the monarch who ordered Thomas à Becket's murder.

3 Coat of arms, blazon or armorial bearings.

4 On a blue background, a gold lion standing on its hind legs and facing the viewer (gardant).

5 In contrasted pictures or colours.

6 Two griffins (legendary beasts with eagle heads and wings and lions' hindquarters), facing opposite ways, in black, with crimson tongues.

7 In heraldry a shield is divided into at least four "quarters" or areas; the first, the dexter chief, is the top right-hand quarter; Castlenorth describes his own.

8 Armorial bearings, the marks or emblems signifying rank and descent.

9 Winged dragons with eagle feet and barbed tails.

10 The small white or silver balls set on a coronet and reproduced on armorial bearings.

11 Diagonal crosses, better known as saltires.

12 Two horizontal lines dividing a shield in three.

13 A bend dexter means two parallel lines from the top right to the left base of a shield. The opposite, a bend sinister, signifies illegitimacy.

14 A chevron is a device on a shield like an upside down V; a chevronel is half its size.

and complaisant Mrs. Calder was considering whether a lady in the company they had left, who had related her complaints to her, was in a right course of medicine; Lady Castlenorth was laying up a little magazine[1] of literature, which she intended to open on Willoughby the next day; and her daughter was contemplating in her mind's eye, the handsome person of Willoughby, the figure they should make at Court and the triumph there would be when without degrading herself, by an unequal alliance in point of family, she should notwithstanding carry to her husband so splendid a fortune, and titles so ancient and illustrious.

Chapter VI

The party the noble visitors had left were very differently employed. Mrs. Molyneux, almost always accustomed to be heard with attention and submitted to with deference as a beauty and a woman of exquisite taste, was piqued and offended by the air of superior intelligence assumed by Lady Castlenorth, who treated her like a child that knew nothing. Miss Fitz-Hayman too had not expressed any admiration at her dress and figure, but had viewed her with supercilious silence; while Mrs. Calder, from knowing her to be a young married woman, had with more curiosity than elegance enquired whether she was likely to give the Molyneux family the heir so much desired by the older part of it; a question which extremely disgusted her. Lord Castlenorth, (who had complimented her upon her person, particularly on her long Chinese eyes, and the form of her face, which he said was extremely like that of Gertrude Fitz-Hayman, some time Maid of Honor to Catharine of Arragon[2] and afterwards Countess of Powis,) was, she declared to Mr. Molyneux, the only tolerable creature of the party. "My uncle," said she, as soon as they were alone, "my uncle is a reasonable being; but for the rest! did you ever see a plainer woman than Miss Fitz-Hayman? her cloaths might be French, but I am sure she looks absolutely Dutch in them. It's really a misfortune at her time of life to be so large."

---

1 A store or repository, often military.
2 Henry VIII's first wife, whom he divorced to marry Anne Boleyn when he broke with the Catholic church and declared himself head of the church in England. Smith authenticates her characters by relating them to historical persons and events.

Molyneux carelessly answered—"You see she is sensible of the misfortune by her endeavours to conceal it: but 'tis more witty than wise, I think, to find fault with her. Willoughby *can see* I suppose as well as you can, and I don't think it very politic in you to give him your authority for disliking her. Let him marry her, and then hate and abuse her as much as you will."

"Oh!" replied the lady, "I shall always detest her, and...."

"So I dare say will he," interrupted Molyneux; "but let them be once married, and all that is very immaterial to you: it is by no means so, that your brother cannot, till he does marry, pay the second five thousand pounds of your fortune, unless he sell the Withcombe estate, which indeed the mortgagee is, as far as I can learn, very impatient to take possession of with this charge upon it, which he will immediately pay off. You see that Willoughby has no choice—matrimony or the dismembering his estates; and pray never put it into his head to hesitate." This affectionate brother in law then went to his own dressing-room, and Mrs. Molyneux taking a candle, surveying herself in the great glass, and wondering how it was possible such a figure and face could fail to attract universal admiration from all ages and sexes, retired to her bed.

The contemplations of poor Celestina, who had left them the moment the company dispersed, were much more painful. The sight of Willoughby, his surprize, and, as she thought, his displeasure at finding her still there, were as poisoned arrows in her breast. But the pride of conscious worth, aided by her disinterested affection for him, enabled her, though not to heal, yet to endure without weak complainings, the exquisite pain they inflicted, and to give her courage immediately to execute the design she had long formed of withdrawing herself from his sight for ever. It was now impossible for her to set out the next day, but that immediately following it, she fixed for her departure; and after a night in which she enjoyed very little repose, she rose early in order to make the immediate preparations for her journey, which she determined, in order to save expence, to make in the Exeter stage.[1]

---

1 The stage coach companies offered a service for journeys between towns to people who had no carriage or conveyance of their own. Coaches travelled fast, though allowing through passengers time to eat and stretch their legs while the horses were changed at the inns which were the "stages." They were cheap and reliable, starting before and continuing after daylight hours in all but the worst weather. But because of the mixed and sometimes drunken customers, genteel people and especially unaccompanied young women avoided them where possible.

As she was desirous of giving as little trouble as possible to Mr. Molyneux's servants, who were all people of great consequence and would any of them have thought such a commission degrading, she determined to go herself into the City,[1] where places were to be taken. It was yet so early when she went down to execute this intention, that only the housemaid was stirring, and the windows of the parlour only were opened: there Celestina sat while the maid went into the kitchen to get her a glass of milk and water, which she had asked for: and while she yet trifled with it, being indeed afraid to venture into the streets till she saw more people in them, she heard the servant, who was at the door dusting the hall and steps, speak to somebody who entered, and the instant afterwards Willoughby came into the room where she was.

She arose trembling and amazed from her seat. "Miss de Mornay," said he, "so early prepared to go out?" Celestina answered—"yes," and sat down again. He laid down his hat on the side board; and as if he knew not what to say, went to the window.

Celestina sat motionless; and Willoughby, after standing there a moment, seemed ashamed of his silence yet afraid to speak. He traversed the room, mended the fire, and complaining of the cold, at length ventured to enquire of Celestina what induced her to venture out at so early an hour of so unpleasant a morning? She replied calmly, for she had by this time regained her composure, that she had business in the City.

"Business in the City!" cried Willoughby; "and at this time of the day! Ah! Celestina there was a time when you would not thus have answered my enquiry." He was going on, when Celestina interrupted him:

"There was indeed," said she with a deep sigh, "a time when you would not have made it."

"Not have made it!" answered he; "was I not then ever interested in all that concerned you, and was any action of yours indifferent to me?"

He faultered and stopped. "I was once simple enough to think so indeed," said Celestina, "and in those days of fortunate illusion you certainly would have made no such enquiry as the present, because I should then have done nothing of which you would not have known the motive, nor have taken any measure without the con-

---

1 The East End or commercial part of London where many of the coaches started and where tickets were sold.

currence of my brother and my friend; but as you told me yourself—would I could forget it!—that it was no longer in your power to retain those characters towards me, I am learning to forget that I ever was so happy as to fancy that no change in my situation, especially a change for the worse, could rob me of that regard so valuable always, so particularly valuable now!"

"Gracious heaven!" cried Willoughby, entirely thrown off his guard by her words and manner—"How have I acted, what have I said, to deserve this reproach from you Celestina? When we parted last...."

She again interrupted him—"Did we part like friends? like brother and sister?"

"No," replied he hastily; "but I tore myself from you like a man who sacrifices, to the performance of a fatal promise, his own happiness, and who is the victim of family pride and family necessity." This sentence was decisive. His resolution forsook him at once, and his long stifled affection burst through all the restraints he determined to lay on it. "Oh! Celestina!" continued he, "you whom I loved before I knew what it was to love! you whom I now adore with a passion too strong for my reason! do not, I beseech you, aggravate my sufferings. I promised to my mother—and you know how well she deserved to be obeyed—I promised to unite myself with her niece; I promised to extirpate from my heart an inclination that even then I could not conceal. Rash and ridiculous promise! No, Celestina, it is impossible for me to cease loving you! All my behaviour, which you have thought cold and unfriendly, was a part I was acting in opposition to my real affections! I can sustain it no longer: I cannot bear that you should think of me with indifference and yet—Oh! my mother, what a cruel task have you imposed on me! Celestina, pity me; I am more wretched than you can imagine!"

His agitation now became too violent: he seized the hand of Celestina, and fervently kissed it, while her own sensations were such as no language can describe. That Willoughby loved her, that what she had considered as indifference was owing to the struggle between his duty and his tenderness, was transport such as obliterated every other sentiment. But this delirium lasted but a moment: her reason, her genuine affection for him, told her, that to indulge this tenderness was injurious to him, and she determined to show that she could sacrifice herself to his advantage, and that contented with his brotherly attachment, she could resign him to the fortunate Miss Fitz-Hayman. The terms however in which she declared this, the softness of her voice, and her eyes filled with tears, were little calculated to reconcile Willoughby to the resolution, which, after a long dialogue, she urged him to adopt; she assured him that whatever might be her own fate, she should never forgive herself were she to be the means of his breaking a promise so solemnly given, and given at such a time, to her dear deceased benefactress.

"No! my brother," said she, "she is dead, but my obligations to her can never be annihilated; and what would become of me, were I ever to feel myself reproached for ingratitude to her memory, were I to destroy the fabric she had raised for the happiness of her beloved son, and to fancy that the spirit of my more than mother, which I now often invocate with conscious pleasure, should, instead of beholding her Celestina with complacency not unsuited to her present state of happiness, see her degraded into a selfish and unworthy being, who repays her benefits with the blackest ingratitude."

Willoughby, whose love, once suffered to obtain the advantage, now acquired more power every moment, combated these objections with very dangerous eloquence; telling Celestina that he had determined the evening before, on a sight of Miss Fitz-Hayman, who was insupportable to him, to put an end to the negociation, and say plainly to his uncle that it was impossible for him to fulfil an engagement in which his heart never had any share. Celestina represented to him the situation of his fortune; the absolute necessity there was for his marrying one who could repair its deficiency, and restore him to the splendid affluence of his ancestors; but for this he talked of economy and simplicity, by which when they lived entirely at Alvestone he should be able to repair every thing; then for a moment indulging his vivid imagination in painting the happiness they should enjoy there together, (images of felicity which reflected in stronger colours those which Celestina had a thousand times formed, though knowing they could never be realized,) he thought suddenly of the fatal promise he had given to his mother, and his heart seemed to shrink from the idea of breaking it to obtain even the highest human happiness, which under such circumstances he felt would be dashed with gall. He obtained however from Celestina, but not without difficulty, a promise that she would lay aside her intentions of going into the City that morning to prepare for her journey, of which he would not hear; and she prevailed upon him to wait on Lord Castlenorth, as he had assured the family he would do: "Though wherefore should I do it," said he, "unless to put an end at once and for ever to all thoughts of this odious marriage?"

"You ought surely," replied Celestina, "to wait on the brother of your mother tho' no such connection had been thought of: and no dislike which you may have conceived to Miss Fitz-Hayman as your wife, should induce you to forget what you owe to your uncle."

By arguments thus reasonable, Celestina, while she prevailed on Willoughby to do what was, he was forced to own, proper, would have riveted his chains, if indeed they had not already been immoveable. The noble candour and disinterested generosity of her soul, gave tenfold force to the charms of her person, which since he had last seen her, Willoughby thought greatly improved: and the tenderness of her manner, the certainty of her affection for him, which she tried to conceal with more kindness than success, had altogether such an effect on him, that nothing but the fatal promise which lay so heavy on her heart, could have prevented his marrying her immediately, in despite of every consideration of prudence or family engagement.

Chapter VII

While Celestina remained with Willoughby, the very tumult and agitation of her heart had sustained her courage, and like a fever that lends momentary strength to the patient it is destroying, this disorder of her spirits had supported her against the flood of tenderness that overwhelmed her as soon as she was alone. A conflict then began between her affection for him and her duty and gratitude towards the memory of his mother, which was almost too severe to be endured; but however soft her heart, her reason was equal to the task of checking a dangerous or guilty indulgence of that sensibility; and after long arguing with herself, she found she loved Willoughby better than every thing but his honor and his repose.

The first, and too probably the second, she saw too plainly that he must forget, by yielding to an affection, which, circumstanced as he was, would perhaps be as fatal to both as it certainly was to his pecuniary interest. She had heard Mr. Molyneux say, who had his reasons for repeating it before her, that nothing but his marrying a woman as opulent as Miss Fitz-Hayman could prevent his selling the greater part of his estates; "and in that case," added he, "I don't see how he can avoid disposing of Alvestone too; for with the income he will then have, to think of keeping up such a place as that, would be quite insanity." Celestina knew that no blow could fall so heavy on the heart of Willoughby, as the cruel necessity of selling this his paternal seat; and though she was flattered and delighted when he had just before declared to her, that to obtain her every deprivation would be easy, she knew, while she now more coolly reflected on it, his local attachment to be so strong, that it was very probably his love would soon yield to the regret which would arise from their sacrifice. "What would become of me," said she as she meditated on this matter, "were I to be the wife of Willoughby, and to see him unhappy that I was so? He would have broken his faith to his mother; he who has always been taught to hold the slightest promise sacred; he would see his estate dismembered; even Alvestone, the place he so loves, would pass into the hands of strangers, and it would be to me he would owe his indigence and his unhappiness! How dare I suppose that my affection, warm and sincere as it is, could make him any amends for all those mortifications. Oh! let me not suppose it, nor ever think of risking it. I can bear to quit him now—I believe I can—but how should I endure to find myself the source of repentance to him! how should I ever survive seeing him decidedly unhappy, with the consciousness that he owed his being so to his partiality for me?"

These reflections, and above all the obligation by which he had bound himself to obey the last injunctions of his mother, determined Celestina as to the conduct she ought to adopt; and having once seen it by the light lent by integrity and disinterested love to her strong and excellent understanding, she hastened to execute it, and certain that he was engaged for the rest of the morning, she had no sooner breakfasted than she told Mrs. Molyneux she was going to make some purchases for which she had occasion before she left London; and getting into an hackney[1] coach, was driven into the City, where she secured a place in the Exeter stage, which was to leave London at a very early hour the next day. She returned to the house of Mrs. Molyneux about twelve o'clock, and then learned, that she and her husband were engaged to dine at Lord Castlenorth's, where a very large party were to assemble. In the card which Lady Castlenorth had sent to invite them no mention was made of Celestina nor was any separate card sent to her. "It is mere forgetfulness I fancy," said Mrs. Molyneux as she mentioned it to her: "you will go however, as the ceremony of an invitation is not very material."

"Pardon me," replied Celestina, "it appears to me of so much consequence in the present case, that I certainly shall not go without it. I am indeed very glad to be excused, and I am sure you will not urge

---

1 Hired from a rank, a hackney coach was used, like a taxi now, for short town journeys.

me to violate etiquette in a matter where to forebear doing it is so particularly desirable."

Mrs. Molyneux, very solicitous about the contents of certain band boxes with which her woman entered at that moment, forebore to press her farther, and Celestina desiring her to let her know when she was dressed, that she might see her before she went, retired to her own room, leaving her friend to the pleasing and important occupation of the toilet,[1] in which half what is now called morning,[2] was usually passed by Matilda.

Celestina had promised Willoughby to give up for that day her intention of fixing her journey; but this promise she thought herself well justified in breaking. The entertainment at Lord Castlenorth's was given on his account: of course he would be engaged the whole day; and since she must go, she desired nothing so much as to be spared the fruitless pain of a farther discussion of the subject, and the misery, which she was not sure her resolution would support, of bidding him a last farewell.

At a little after five however, after she had undergone the form of sitting down alone to table, where she ate nothing, and had then retired to her own room, Mrs. Willoughby's woman came to say that her mistress was dressed. Celestina had once determined to tell Mrs. Molyneux how soon she meant to quit her, and to have taken leave of her, but on reflection she thought her doing so might betray her resolution to Willoughby, from whom it was necessary to conceal it till it was actually executed. She now therefore intended to leave a letter of thanks and to take leave of Mrs. Molyneux as if it were only till the next day.

But when the moment approached in which she was in reality to bid adieu—perhaps for ever—to the friend and companion of her infancy—to the daughter of her beloved friend—to the sister of Willoughby—her heart sunk within her; and hardly had she strength to go to the door of Mrs. Molyneux's dressing room, on opening which she saw her friend standing before the glass putting the last finish to her very elegant dress, while with her eyes fixed on her own figure, she was arguing with more than her usual warmth with some person who sat beside her, and who Celestina presently discovered to be Willoughby himself, in boots, and his hair out of

---

1 Dressing table; also dressing, hairdressing and cosmetic preparations to receive company.
2 "Morning" meant any time before the main meal of the day, which was in high society usually about five o'clock.

powder.[1] His countenance was pale and dejected; and while his sister talked to him he leaned with one arm on another chair, and seemed rather musing than attending.

"I am glad you are come," said Mrs. Molyneux to Celestina as she entered, "for here is George behaving quite absurdly: he will not go he says to Lord Castlenorth's, though the dinner is made on purpose for him. Do Celestina—he minds your opinion always more than mine—do try to make him understand how very absurd and oddly he acts."

"I have no talents," Celestina would have said but the words died away on her lips: and before she could collect courage to finish the sentence, Molyneux, who was now ready, came in, and seeing Willoughby unprepared to go, expressed his surprize in terms which were warmer than Willoughby could hear with perfect command of temper. "Surely Sir," said he, "I am my own master. I am not disposed to go, and I will not go!"

"And what am I to say," cried Mrs. Molyneux, "to Lady Castlenorth, to my uncle, and to my cousin?"

"Just what you please," replied he.

Molyneux, finding by the tone in which his brother in law spoke, that he would not be dictated to, now called his wife out of the room, and Willoughby and Celestina were left alone.

It was now that all her fortitude and strength of mind were necessary. Her duty evidently was to persuade Willoughby to accompany his sister and to complete a marriage which his mother had when dying enjoined: a marriage so necessary to the acquisition of all that the world calls happiness in life, and on which depended the continuance of his family estate in his possession. But her heart refused to assent to what her reason pointed out as the conduct she ought to pursue, and the affection he now so evidently had for her, adding to the strength of her long attachment to him, she found it impossible to urge his quitting her for ever, though she thought she had yet courage enough to tear herself from him if she heard not his complaints nor witnessed his agonies while she combated her own.

"I cannot—I will not go to these people," said Willoughby after a short silence: "why should I? since to marry Miss Fitz-Hayman

---

1   Willoughby is not dressed for an evening party. Men and women with claims to gentility used hair powder, usually silver-white, but sometimes yellow, red or blue, not necessarily every day but on formal or social occasions.

would be the height of cruelty to her—since I am incapable of dis-simulation—since—In short, Celestina, I feel it to be impossible for me to live with her—to live without you: and I have determined to declare myself in writing to that effect."

Celestina, whom this speech was not calculated to calm, answered, trembling—"Indeed I think you wrong, Mr. Willoughby. As your uncle, as your mother's brother, Lord Castlenorth has undoubtedly a claim to this mark of respect. It is not probably expected to be any thing more than a visit of form, and surely you ought not rudely and without reason to decline it."

"If it *were indeed* meant only as a visit of ceremony," said he—

"It is in your power however," interrupted Celestina, "to appear to consider it so: your not going must seem very extraordinary; your going certainly leads to no consequence."

"If you think so," replied Willoughby; "if you think I ought to go.—But why did they not ask you?"

"Why should they ask me?" answered she. "I am almost unknown to Lady Castlenorth; and in the little time I ever did see her, I appeared to be no favourite. Believe me, so far from being displeased I am rejoiced at the omission."

"Insolent, odious woman!" cried Willoughby. "If any thing could add to my dislike of her and her daughter, it would be the supercil-ious airs they gave themselves towards you even in the short moment I saw them there. But my Celestina shall never be exposed to their insulting scorn; and if I myself this time undergo the punishment of keeping up the hateful farce which I have so unhappily been engaged in, it shall be with a determination to put an end to it."

At this moment Mr. and Mrs. Molyneux entered the room; and Celestina wishing them all an agreeable day, left it; having sustained with some difficulty the various emotions which were contending in her bosom. Willoughby soon after left the house, to dress at his own lodgings, which were in the neighbourhood, and having promised to join his brother and sister at dinner, they soon after departed themselves, much better satisfied with him than they were before his short conversation with Celestina.

Chapter VIII

Celestina, though more unwilling than ever to go, had prescribed to herself in her cooler moments a line of conduct, from which, feeling it her duty to adhere to it, she now determined not to depart. In arguing with herself on its propriety, and strengthening her faltering resolution, she passed the night. At four o'clock the servant who was commissioned to awaken her, came to her door: she arose and dressed herself by candle-light: the morning was cold and dark: every object appeared dreary and forlorn: she hurried on her cloaths however, and endeavoured to drive away every recollection that might enfeeble her spirits too much; but, as she passed the door of the drawing room, she remembered that it was there she had seen Willoughby perhaps for the last time, and almost involuntarily she went in, and by the light of her solitary candle, contemplated a whole length picture of him which had just been finished for his sister: the likeness was so strong, that by the wavering and uncertain light that fell upon it, she almost fancied he was about to speak to her: she started at the idea, and feeling a sort of chilly terror at the silence and obscurity of every thing around her, she turned away and hastened to the servant who had prepared her tea in the parlour: she had however hardly time to drink it, before the hackney coach which had been ordered the night before was at the door; and having seen what little baggage she had not before sent put into it, she stepped in herself, and was soon at a distance from the residence of Mrs. Molyneux, from the friend of her early years, and was launched alone and unprotected into a world of which she had yet seen nothing but through the favourable medium lent by affluence and prosperity to those who from thence contemplate difficulties they are never likely to encounter and calamities they probably never can participate.

That a young woman, who might still have enjoyed those indulgences, should renounce them at an age when they have so many charms; that Celestina, who had been educated with so much delicacy, and accustomed since her first recollection to every indulgency, should thus voluntarily enter on a life of comparative hardship and deprivation, may appear improbable, but when it is added that she quitted the man to whom she had so long been fondly attached, and leaving him to her fortunate rival, devoted herself to a life of solitude and regret, such an effort of heroism in a woman not yet quite nineteen, might be classed among impossibilities, were it related to any other than Celestina: but her character was an uncommon one: though she had always been told by Mrs. Willoughby that her birth was very uncertain, and that nothing was known of it but that it was disgraceful to her parents, since they had taken such pains to conceal it, she felt within herself a consciousness of hereditary worth, an innate pride, which would never suffer her to believe herself descended from mean or unworthy persons: her open and commanding countenance, where sat dignity mingled with sweetness; her nymph-like and graceful form, which might have rivalled the models of Grecian art; were advantages of which, though she was not vain of them, she could not be insensible, and if she had any foible, (a perfect character it has been said must not be represented because it cannot exist) if she had any foible, it was carrying a little too far, though she carefully concealed it, that sort of pride which seemed born with her, and which, after all that has been said against it, is often, especially in a young and beautiful woman, a fortunate defect.

The circumstances of her birth had seldom been touched upon in the family, for it was a topic which could not but be painful to her: but if ever any thing relating to it had been accidentally introduced, when Mrs. Willoughby was conversing with her three children, (as she often termed Willoughby, Matilda, and Celestina) Willoughby would say laughingly that it was impossible she could be born of French parents: his mother had been sometimes half angry at this assertion, in which however he usually persisted, asserting, with prejudice that she declared to be entirely English, that no native of the South of France ever had a complexion or a form like hers. After she grew up, though these perfections became more eminent, Willoughby never appeared to notice them; with the improvement of her form, her mind kept pace; and as it acquired every day more strength, she gradually became more sensible of her obligation to her benefactress; but while she indulged her gratitude towards the friend on whom she depended, she felt that she was not born to be dependent.

This elevation of spirit now supported her; and the consciousness she was acting right, blunted for a while the poignancy of that pain which she too sensibly felt in tearing herself from Willoughby. Obliged to act for herself, having no breast on which she could with propriety lean, her naturally exalted soul acquired new firmness, before which trifling inconveniences disappeared; and with an heart occupied by the beloved image of Willoughby, and the sacrifice she was making for him, she hardly remembered that she had never in her life been in a stage coach before till she found herself seated in one under the dark gateway of an inn in the city at five o'clock in a dreary winter morning.

Two female passengers had already taken their places; one of whom expressed great anxiety for a number of hat boxes and caravan[1] trunks which the people belonging to the inn were placing

---

1   Large traveller's trunk suitable for an extended journey.

in different parts of the coach, while the lady particularly recommended to their care one box, which she assured them contained her new *laylock*[1] bonnet, an article for the safety of which she was so solicitous that she would have taken the great machine in which it was contained into the coach, had it not been opposed by the coachman, and presently after by a man who had been drinking with him, and who now preparing to enter the coach, protested vehemently against this whim of his sister Mary.—"Who d'ye think will be scroughed[2] and crammed up," cried he, "with your confounded trumpery? No, no such thing. Here Daniel, prythee[3] take and stow it somewhere or another: it shall not enter the coach, I'll be sworn."

The man then placed himself by the side of the other female passenger, opposite to Celestina, and appeared to be as anxious for his own ease as his sister was for the safety of her wardrobe. The coach moved on, but it was still quite dark, and silence prevailed for the first four or five miles, interrupted only by some fretful expressions from the lady of the bandboxes, at the inconveniences to which people were subjected by going in stage coaches, and some exclamations against the unfortunate dampness of the morning, which she declared would certainly penetrate the covering and entirely spoil her *laylock* bonnet, which she said cost her three guineas.[4]

"The more fool you," cried her brother, who was of a character Celestina had never had an opportunity of seeing before, that of a country tradesman affecting to be a wit and a buck—"the more fool you, sister Mary. What! D'ye think a three guinea bonnet will make you look three years younger? No, no take my word for it, your flounces, and fringes, and furbelows serve for no purpose at all but to shew your wrinkles."

"Wrinkles!" repeated the lady disdainfully, "what do you mean, John Jedwyn? I declare you are so rude and disagreeable I always repent travelling with you. I wish you would find out another subject."

"Egad," answered Jedwyn, "I cannot have a worse one than your wrinkles, that's true enough; and upon my soul," added he, looking confidently in the face of Celestina and then in that of the other female passenger, who though pale and thin, was very young and very pretty, "here is two better subjects, one aside of me and t'other opposite: no, no, sister of mine, now day breaks a little, and lets a

---

1 Dialect form of lilac.
2 Scrunched.
3 Pray thee; please.
4 A guinea is one pound and one shilling.

body see how the land lays, you'll hear no more about your wrinkles; for as Hamlet says—let me see—aye—'here's that metal that's more attractive;'[1] hey, Miss?"

Celestina, to whom this "hey Miss" was addressed, who had till now been very little aware of the species of rudeness and impertinence to which her mode of travelling might subject her, was shocked and alarmed at this address from a person, who, had he seen her a few days before, would have approached her with awe and spoken to her with diffidence. She remained silent however, casting a look on the man sufficiently expressive of the contempt she felt for him: but he was not of a humour to be easily daunted or repulsed, and without seeming to understand her, began, with purse-proud pertness to relate as if it was a narrative which all the world should be informed of, that he was a grocer and chandler at Exeter, in a very flourishing trade, and in partnership with a gentleman who had married one of his sisters: "and this *laylock* bonnet lady," continued he, "is my elder sister, who has been a *wisiting*[2] this half year and better an old aunt of ours at Camberwell.[3] She is an old maid herself, but devilish rich, and from a sort of fellow feeling you know she intends to make our Mary here her heir. The old girl must hop the perch soon, or all her money won't get her dear niece a husband it's my opinion, unless may be an Irishman or a strolling player."

This second attack on herself, and his visible admiration of Celestina's beauty, compleated the ill humour of his sister, who with a look where anger and scorn contended for preeminence, remained silently swelling, while the facetious trader again addressed himself to Celestina.

"What, do you never make talking? Come, since now you have a history of me, let's hear a little who you are, and where you are bound to?"

"Sir," replied Celestina, "it is impossible that either can be of any consequence to you."

"How are you sure of that?" cried Mr. Jedwyn with a loud laugh: "now I think nothing is more likely than that we may be better acquainted. Tis nothing now I believe for a young man of spirit, as well in the world as I am, to take a fancy to a pretty woman."

---

1 Cf. *Hamlet*, 3.2.99.
2 Though Jedwyn lives in Exeter, Smith gives him a Cockney (London) accent, which pronounced v as w in the eighteenth and nineteenth centuries.
3 In East London.

"A fancy!" exclaimed Miss Mary Jedwyn, with great acrimony—"a fancy! Jack Jedwyn I am amazed at you!"

"And why amazed, my ancient spinster?" retorted he. "What the devil! I am my own master I hope. To be sure you are some fifteen or twenty years older than me. But what of that?—So much the worse for you. I hope I a'nt to be governed by a duenna.[1] What a plague, mayn't I talk to a handsome girl I wonder without your putting in your squinnygut[2] opinion?"

"If you intend to insult me," answered the lady, trying to hide under the appearance of calm contempt her great disposition to cry:—"if you intend to insult me, I am sure I heartily wish I had got the better of my fears and travelled alone in a post *chai*;[3] for no rudeness as I might have met on the road could be worse than yours."

"That's your gratitude now," cried Jedwyn, "for my coming up clear from Exeter to fetch you at a time when I had no business in London nor should a had for these six weeks: that's your thanks for my kindness, and for listening to your nonsensical fears and frights. Rude to you! oh Lord! as if any mortal man who has eyes would ever look at you twice. No Mary! make yourself easy; that weazen, winterly visage of yours is safeguard enough if you were to travel from here to Jericho."

He then began to mimic his sister, and enlarge on the terrors to which she was, he said, perpetually subject, lest some sad daring rake[4] of a man should carry her away: and had he been less gross and disgusting, Celestina would hardly have forborne a smile at some part of the ludicrous representation he gave of this apprehensive delicacy and trembling nicety, for which she could not, in the personal attractions of Miss Jedwyn, find any reasonable grounds; for she was very tall, very thin, and very yellow: her long, scraggy neck, appeared hardly adequate to the support of a head, where art had so redundantly been called in aid of nature, that it seemed to abound in shining black hair, nicely curled, without powder, which was suffered to wanton over her forehead and flow down her back, while a little white beaver hat, perched on one side, was meant to give to her countenance that bewitching archness which she had observed that mode of head dress to bestow on the young and lovely.

---

1 Spanish: a governess or chaperone, but here used for an older woman.
2 Dialect for a skinny, meagre person.
3 Miss Jedwyn perhaps believes the word "chaise" is plural and gives what she thinks is the singular form.
4 Seducer.

Mr. Jedwyn having exhausted all his immediate stock of wit on his sister, now left her to digest the indignation he had raised, and applied himself again to Celestina. Having no idea that any thing but money bestowed consequence, and having lived the greater part of his time among those who had less of it than himself, he had never been accustomed to allow of any superiority, nor could comprehend how a young woman so humbly situated in life, as to travel in a stage coach, could help being charmed into liking by his wit, and awed into complaisance by his importance.

On such a man the native dignity of Celestina failed totally of its usual effect. He became more and more troublesome; so he was piqued but not repressed by the coldness and even contempt of her manner. He told her, among much other impertinence, that all her shyness should not hinder him from finding out who she was; and then with yet more offensive familiarity addressed himself to the other young woman, who he thought belonged to her, and who heard his conversation with terror and dislike as great as that of Celestina.

His behaviour at length becoming insupportably uneasy to her, Celestina, when the coach reached the village where they were to breakfast, determined not to subject herself to it any longer; she therefore ordered her tea to be carried into another room, and a post chaise[1] to be ready as soon as she had drank it.

As she sat at her breakfast, she saw the young woman, whose countenance had greatly interested her, walk by the window slowly and dejectedly, one hand held to her forehead, and an handkerchief in the other. Ever ready to assist the unhappy, the generous heart of Celestina was touched with compassion towards this forlorn stranger.

"She is as young as I am," said she, "and perhaps even more unfortunate. Why should I not take her with *me*, if she is, as I suppose, travelling the same road? why should I leave her exposed to the insults of that odious man, which, humble as her fortune seems to be, she ill knows how to bear. I may at least, though I cannot otherwise assist her, save her from passing the remainder of the journey improperly and unpleasantly." Celestina then rang the bell, and directing her fellow traveller to be called, desired her not only to partake of her breakfast, but to accompany her the rest of the way in a post chaise which she had ordered, to escape from Mr. Jedwyn.

---

1 A hired carriage generally used for the mail and seating one or two passengers.

The young person, notwithstanding the kindness of Celestina's address, still continued standing, and with a faint blush said,

"You are very good Madam:—but—though we happen to be in the same coach I am sure I ought not to put myself on a footing with you: I am only a servant, travelling into the country to my friends to recover my health, and it would be very wrong in me to intrude on a lady like you."

Celestina, won by this humble simplicity, soon reassured her new acquaintance, and soon after Jessy Woodburn, (which was her name,) followed Celestina to the chaise; where having paid the coach in London, she now had directed her box to be placed.

Mr. Jedwyn left the hot rolls and chocolate with which he was regaling himself, to remonstrate at the chaise door against this secession. Celestina, without giving him any answer, drew up the glasses the moment she was seated, which gave Jedwyn an opportunity to say to the postillion,[1] who was not yet on horseback, that if he would in the course of a fortnight find out who the lady was, and whither she went, he would make up the half crown he then gave him to half a guinea.[2] The boy readily promised to execute to the best of his power so lucrative a commission; and Celestina and her companion were soon at a distance, and proceeded on their journey much pleased with the exchange they had made of a conveyance.

Chapter IX

Celestina having by her easy and gentle manners conquered part of the extreme diffidence of her companion, began to question her about her situation in life; and as she had one of those faces and one of those voices which win every heart where any spark of feeling is found, Jessy soon found herself enough at ease and even flattered by the interest she seemed to take in her fate, as to acquire courage to relate the following narrative.

"I must go back a great way, Madam, since you command me to tell you all I know of myself; even as far as my grandfather, who is still living, and who is one of the richest farmers in our part of Devonshire using his own land, as all his family I have heard have

---

1 A postillion rode the left hand one of a pair of horses harnessed to a coach or carriage.
2 Half a crown was two shillings and sixpence, half a guinea ten shillings and sixpence.

done before him for a great many years. He married a clergyman's daughter who had been educated very well, greatly indeed above the sort of life she was to lead as a farmer's wife. But she was very pretty. Her father left her unprovided for, and so she married perhaps more for money than love. My mother was the only child they ever had, and my grandmother, though her own education had only served to make her unhappy, would fain[1] have had her daughter brought up as she had been herself; but her husband, of a very hard and obstinate temper and repenting perhaps of having married a wife too fine for him, was so far from allowing her to have any education, that he went to the other extreme; insisting that his girl should do as his mother did thirty or forty years before, and not only be taught to understand all the business of the farm, but to live as he did himself, and as he obliged his wife to do, the same as the farming men.

"The consequence of this difference of opinion was fatal to my poor mother: one of her parents took every opportunity of giving her notions above herself, which very naturally, she easily took; and the other seemed to delight in humbling and degrading her: when she was about eighteen she lost her mother, and then was forced to submit to the harsh and unnecessary confinement imposed upon her by her father, from whom she endeavoured to conceal her passion for reading, which only gained strength by this unreasonable restraint. Home was very uneasy to her, but she could hardly ever leave it but by stealth. As she was likely to have a very good fortune, she had numberless suitors; but my grandfather would suffer none of them to see her; designing to marry her to a relation of his own almost as old as himself, to whom she had an invincible aversion, which through the timidity of her nature she dared not declare.

"A neighbouring farmer, with whom my grandfather had for many years been at variance, and with whom he had had two or three lawsuits, had two sons, both brought up to his own business; the eldest was married and had a family, but the other had been spoiled by his mother, and the notice taken of him by the neighbouring gentlemen on account of his skill in field sports; he had indeed always been rather fonder of being with them at cricket matches, and races, than minding his farm. He found means to introduce himself to my mother, though he had been positively refused by my grandfather: he won her affections, and after several private

---

1 Would have wanted to.

meetings she agreed to go off with him: the consequence of which was her having the door of her paternal house shut against her for ever.

"For a little time after this marriage my mother was received at the house of her father in law, but on his death it became the right of the eldest son, who had a number of children; and as my father's family were all irritated and disappointed by the obstinate resentment of my grandfather towards his daughter, they soon behaved with such unkindness towards her, that she prevailed on my father to quit them and take a little farm of his own, which he with difficulty borrowed money enough to stock, for he had long since paid away in discharge of old debts, all the money left him by his father. He had been so long used to an idle, or rather a gay life, that he could not now accustom himself to the labour requisite on so small a farm. My mother however by incessant attention remedied for some years this deficiency on his part; and though nothing was laid by, they contrived to live; my mother making from time to time attempts to obtain her father's pardon, though she received nothing but cruel and positive refusals, either to see her or her children, or ever to give them the least assistance.

"This hardness of heart, which should have excited pity, only made my father treat my poor mother with harshness too. A young man of fortune in the neighbourhood just then coming of age, was often at this seat near our little farm, and took such a fancy to my father that he was always at his house, living as he lived, and associating with gentlemen from London, and women they brought down with them. He never came home but in such a terrible humour, that I and my sister, who were then about ten and nine years old, used to be terrified to death; yet when he was gone, as he sometimes was for weeks together, my mother lamented his absence and the loss of his affection, much more than the fatigue, poverty, and sorrow, to which his conduct exposed us all.

"Present anxiety and the fear of leaving me and my sister to a fate as deplorable as her own, together with the incessant toil attending the care of a farm wholly neglected by her husband, gradually destroyed her constitution, till at last, Madam, her heart was quite broken. When she found she had only a few hours to live, she entreated the clergyman of the parish to go to her father, and beg, if he would not see her, that he would only send her his forgiveness, for she could not die in peace without it.

"Even that he had the cruelty to refuse! I lost my dear mother, Madam; and my sister, who was always of a weak constitution, followed her soon afterwards to the grave. Ah! how often have I wished that I had died too. Troubles now multiplied around us: my father's great friend had by this time so compleately ruined himself, that every thing was seized and he left the country. My father having no longer a house to be at, was forced to live at home; but it was only for a little while; for during my mother's illness every thing had been neglected, and we could not pay our rent; so the landlord seized,[1] our cattle were sold, and we were turned out of the farm and went to a miserable cottage in the next village; where, as my father was so unused to work, we subsisted for a while on the reluctant charity of my uncle, whose daughters were always reproaching me with taking their bread from them. Believe me, Madam, I did all I could do to earn it for my father and myself: but what could hands so feeble as mine do towards supporting us both? I made an attempt to see my grandfather, and to implore his pity and protection towards one who had never offended him; but he ordered me to be driven from his door, and never again suffered to appear there: orders which those he had about him were ready enough to execute. I returned home quite disheartened indeed, but still endeavouring to the utmost of my power to procure a support by my labour for my father and myself; I even went out to work in the fields; but all I could earn was so insufficient that we often wanted necessary food, at least I have often wanted it. But my father had made an acquaintance with a widow woman in the next village, who was said to be worth forty or fifty pounds. She was young too and not ugly, and in less than a year after my dear mother's death, he married her, and we removed to her house.

"The extremes of poverty I had before known, bitter as I thought them, were comparatively happiness to what I now endured. I became the servant of my mother in law,[2] only without wages. She soon brought my father an increase of family: to them then I was nurse, and very soon had neither sleep by night or respite by day. I thought it my duty to bear every thing for my father, without murmuring, but as my fatigue and suffering encreased, my dejection encreased too, and I was sometimes through mere despondence unable to fulfil my heavy tasks, in which if I failed in the slightest degree, I was insulted with opprobrious language and told to go to my rich grandfather.

---

1 Repossessed everything (an intransitive verb in this legal sense).
2 Stepmother.

"Alas! my rich grandfather continued inexorable; but home was so dreadful that I determined to go to service, being near twenty, and able I thought to undertake any place that could be offered me; for a harder than that I now filled, it was impossible to meet with.

"I applied to a relation I had at Exeter, who after some enquiries procured me a place in the family of an attorney in London, who was willing to dispense with my want of experience in favour of my being a country servant. Thither therefore I went, and entered as cheerfully as I could on a new mode of life; endeavouring to forget that I ever had any expectations of a better. The dark, damp places where the servants of persons in the middling ranks of life, live in the city, appeared very dreadful to me; and it was my business, after a day of fatiguing work, to sit up for my master or the clerks, who were often out very late. My mistress too was a very fine lady,[1] and kept a great deal of company, and it was part of my employment to wait on her own maid, who was also a sort of housekeeper, and much more difficult to be pleased than the lady herself: she took care indeed that I should never want business; but determined as I was never again to be a burthen to my father, I went through the duties of my place, heavy as they were, with courage and steadiness; so that even this second mistress, however unwilling to be pleased, could not find fault with me.

"Among a great number of clerks that my master kept, there was one who was employed merely to copy, and was not admitted among the rest, though he looks I am sure more like a gentleman than any of them. He did not lodge in the house, but came every morning early to his work, and sat at it, poor young man! till five or six o'clock at night, when he dined with us servants, after the family and other clerks had done. Often indeed, instead of eating, he would sigh all dinner time as if his heart would break; and I could not help fancying that he had been used to live quite in other company; though he never seemed above ours, but was always very obliging, though he was melancholy.

"It happened once, that my master had some extraordinary business to do that required great haste; it was some papers that were to be sent to India; and Mr. Cathcart, the young man I have been speaking of, hearing my master say how afraid he was he should not get ready, offered to work all day on Sunday, when none of the rest

---

1 Jessy is ironic here. Her mistress, though an attorney's wife, imitates the habits of aristocratic women.

of the clerks would have staid from their pleasure on any account. My master was pleased with his willingness to oblige, and he sat down to his task. Nobody was in the house but him and me; for it was the custom of my master and mistress to dine in the country on a Sunday with my mistress's mother at Edmonton;[1] and all the gentlemen in the office went different ways. The footman attended my mistress; and Mrs. Gillam, her maid, always went to see her acquaintance, who lived at the other end of the town,[2] and very often came home sadly out of temper because her place was not so fine and so fashionable as their's; and then I was sure to suffer for it, as indeed I did for all her ill temper when she had nobody else to vent it upon.

"Ah! Madam! often of a Sunday in the summer I have gone up into our dining room, because the street was so close and narrow that below we hardly saw day light from one end of the year to the other; and I have opened the sash,[3] and looked against the black walls and shut windows of the houses opposite, and have thought how dismal it was! Ah! I remembered too well the beautiful green hills, the meadows and woods, where I so often used to ramble with my sister when we were children, in our own country, before we were old enough to know that my poor mother was unhappy, and had learned to weep with her! How often have I wished those days would come again, and how often have I shut my eyes and tried to fancy I saw once more all the dear objects that then were so charming. Alas! the dream would not last long! or if it did it served only to make me feel more unhappy, when, instead of being able to indulge it, I was obliged to go back to hard, and what was yet worse, to dirty work in our dismal kitchen. In Devonshire I had been used to work hard enough; but I had always fresh air to breathe, and could now and then of an evening sit at our cottage window, and look at the moon, and fancy that my mother might be there with my sister, and that they saw and pitied their poor unfortunate Jessy. Tears then relieved me; and I gathered courage to bear the next day the ill humour of my mother in law, which now that it was over I fancied was not worse than the ill humour of Mrs. Gillam. My father's harshness indeed was worse than either, because I loved him, and every time he used to speak cruelly to me, and seem to wish me away, it was like a dagger in my heart!"

---

1 Then still a village a little east of London.
2 The West End or fashionable side of London.
3 Wide-paned window that pulls up and down.

The tears of the unfortunate Jessy here interrupted her narrative a moment, and Celestina took occasion to say—"But what were you going to tell me about Mr. Cathcart? You seem to have forgotten him?"

"Ah! Madam!" replied she with a deep sigh, "I thought after I began to talk of him, that I was doing wrong, and that it was better not to say any more about him: besides, Madam, though you are so good and so condescending, it is not perhaps proper for me to trouble you with all the reasons I have to be sorrowful."

"Indeed I wish extremely to know them," replied Celestina; "and particularly I desire to know all that relates to Mr. Cathcart. The little you have said, has interested me greatly."

"It was on the Sunday, Madam, that I was speaking of, when every body was gone out, that poor Mr. Cathcart first spoke to me alone. Often before that to be sure I thought he pitied me, when he saw me doing work too heavy for my strength; and often he has offered to help me, and did not disdain to assist me though the footmen did; and yet I am sure his look and his manners were a great deal more those of a nobleman than any thing else. Mrs. Gillam however was always so angry if she saw him speak to, or help me, and used to put herself into such passions, that he was afraid almost of looking at me before her least it should be the occasion of my being used ill.

"On the Sunday, Madam, that I was speaking of, he had finished all my master left for him to do, between six and seven o'clock: for he wrote such a beautiful hand so quick that his writing seemed done by enchantment. That day he had eat no dinner: but a little after six o'clock he came down into the kitchen, where I was sitting: 'Jessy,' said he, 'will you make me some tea: I am fatigued and I think it will refresh me.' Ah! Madam! how pleased I was to do any thing for him. As he sat on the other side of the table drinking his tea, I looked at him, and thought his eyes seemed inflamed as if he had been crying, and he seemed more melancholy than usual. 'What is the matter, Mr. Cathcart?' said I, 'you have tired yourself too much?'

"'Yes,' answered he, 'I have been writing a long time; but I have finished my business, so I never mind my headache.' He seemed desirous of turning the discourse, and reaching across to the side of the table where I sat, he took up a torn book, which, while I was sweeping the clerk's office the day before, my master had thrown to me, bidding me burn it, for that he would not have such trumpery lay about there. I never had time to read, though my poor mother had taught me to love it: and I had thrown this book into a drawer, from whence I had taken it but a moment before Mr. Cathcart came down.

"He enquired how I came by it, and when I told him, asked if I had read it? I answered that I had no time. 'It is my book,' said he, sighing from the bottom of his heart as he spoke; 'and it is the story of a poor young man, who was as unfortunate as I am: but he had the resolution to end his calamities; he indeed was not enchained to life as I must be.[1] Heaven and earth!' exclaimed he, as if at that moment oppressed by some idea altogether insupportable, 'how long shall I remain the wretch I am?'

"He started from his chair, and walked about the room with looks so wild that I was terrified to death: I went to him trembling, and besought him to be calm, to tell me if I could do any thing for him: he looked eagerly at me a moment and burst into tears—'Ah! Jessy,' cried he, 'you pity me, and all the return I make is to terrify and distress you!' For a moment Madam, after this gust of passion, he became calmer, and sat down; then as I stood still trembling by him, he took my hands within his and put them to his burning forehead and eyes; but after a moment seeming to recollect himself, he sighed, let them go and said—'I hardly know, Jessy, what ailed me just now; but I was so tired, my spirits were so exhausted by having been so long at the desk employed in such tedious kind of writing, that when I looked at you—when you seemed concerned for me—I am so little used to meet any friendly looks here, that your pity affected me strangely; I felt just then how terrible, how very terrible my fate was; and this proud rebellious heart, unsubdued yet to my cruel destiny, deprived me for a moment of my reason.'

"'Thank God,' replied I, 'you are now easier: indeed you did sadly frighten me. Tell me, dear Mr. Cathcart, why did you talk so, and why are you so unhappy?'

"'I will tell you, Jessy,' answered he, 'though you are the only person in the house who ever shall guess at my real situation. I am unhappy:—not because I was born and educated a gentleman, and am now reduced to a condition worse than absolute servitude, but because those I love and feel for more than for myself are fallen with me; because my labour—and yet I am sacrificing my life to follow

---

1   Probably Cathcart refers to Johann Wolfgang von Goethe's *The Sorrows of Young Werther* (1774), which was quickly translated into English and became a cult book. The hero kills himself rather than adapt to his unhappy circumstances, a story that evidently appealed to many contemporary readers.

it—my labour is insufficient to support a woman, delicately brought up, and her four infant children!'

"Ah! Madam! all the sorrow I had ever known was nothing to the cold death-like feeling which seemed to wither up my heart, when for the moment I thought Mr. Cathcart was married and had a family! I did not know at that time why it hurt me so: but I was not able to speak, while he, after remaining silent a minute, said—'By my work today I have earned a guinea more than my weekly stipend: surely therefore instead of murmuring thus, I ought rather to be thankful that I have had power to do this, for tomorrow I shall receive it, and tomorrow I shall be able to carry to my Sophy and her children some necessaries which they have long wanted, but which I could not before spare money enough to procure for them, out of what I earned weekly as the only support of us all.'

"Poor as I am, Madam, I could not help unlocking my tea chest where I kept my little savings; and though I trembled like a leaf as I did it, I put a guinea and some silver, all I had, into a paper, and carried it to him. 'Mr. Cathcart', said I, 'pray be not offended, but take this trifle, and make use of it for your family; they want it more than I do, and you cannot think how much happier it will make me if you have it, than if I lay it out on myself.'

"'Gracious God!' cried he, 'this is too much. No, my dear, generous girl, do not imagine I will take what you have so hardly acquired. Believe me, Jessy, this instance of sensibility and kindness, charming as they are, only render me more wretched. In the meanest servitude, in the lowest degradation, amid the hardest labour, I have found a soul so much superior to those I have met with in polished society: but your form, your manners, your sentiments, are not those of your station: surely you were not born what I now see you?'

"'Indeed,' replied I, 'I was: my father is now a labourer; I have no mother; nor any friend willing, if they are able, to do any thing for me: but while I am able to work I must not, I will not be discontented, whatever hardships I may undergo, if you, Mr. Cathcart, will but let me be your friend. Let me see your children; indeed I shall love them; and if your lady will give me leave I will work for them: I can bring any thing she will give me to do home, and work in my own room instead of going to bed.'

"I do not know Madam, how I was able to say so much, for I felt my heart to throb as if it would break all the time I was speaking. Oh! Madam! I was suddenly transported as it were to heaven when Mr. Cathcart, thanking me a thousand times for my offer, told me that the children he supported were not his own but his sister's, whose husband had been undone by the villainy of some people with whom he had been connected in trade, and by the wickedness of an attorney; it is impossible to describe how I was relieved to find he was not married! For though I am sure I should have loved his children dearly because they were his, yet methought[1] I loved them much better now."

Sensations she had herself felt in regard to Willoughby, now forcibly occurred to Celestina: she remained silent however, and Jessy went on.

"After this time, Madam, Mr. Cathcart took every opportunity of speaking to me; and I got leave to go out one evening, and he took me to see this beloved and unfortunate sister. It was in one of those little new houses which are run up in a road leading from Islington[2] to London, that Mr. Cathcart's family lodged: his sister, Madam, was so like him that the moment I saw her I could have died for her; and I forgot all the reluctance with which I agreed at his earnest request to go to see her: she seemed to be four or five years older than he is, and was very pale and thin, but she had such beautiful eyes, and hands so white!—her form was so graceful, so commanding, that her very plain dress, and a close cap, such as widows wear, could not disfigure her, or make her look otherwise than like a gentlewoman. When her brother led me in, she held out her hand to me, and begged I would sit down: though in such a poor little lodging, I felt that she was so much my superior that I could not obey her without hesitation; but she presently by her gracious manners dissipated my fears, and I sat down by her close to a frame[3] on which she had been working. A cradle, with a sleeping baby in it, stood at her feet, by which a little girl of three years old sat, as if watching the infant, and on hassocks near the window were placed two little boys, the elder not above six years old, who were learning their tasks. As soon as my reception was over, she smiled on her brother with more cheerfulness than it seemed possible a moment before for her countenance to assume; and desired he would assist her in getting some tea for me. Cathcart went down stairs, and then she entered into conversation with me: 'My brother,' said she, 'has often told me how unfit you are for the condition in which he found you, and if I may judge by your appearance, you certainly were not born to it. Had my

---

1   It seemed to me.
2   Then a village just north of London, though the intervening space was already being filled in.
3   A wooden device to hold sewing or embroidery taut.

dear Frank been any other than he is, I should have supposed him influenced by beauty; but I know that mere personal loveliness in any rank never affected him, and many reasons induced me, Jessy, to consent to see you—reasons which relate to him as well as yourself.

"'He has told you, Jessy, that he was born to prospects very different from those now before him—prospects which are I fear vanished for ever. My misfortunes, which are such as I dare not attempt to relate to you, have extended to him: yet does he with unexampled generosity, give himself up to servitude, to assist me and my poor children. Judge whether such a brother is not dear to me—judge whether I ought not to love all that he loves, and to comply as far as possible with all his wishes.

"'I have of late seen with infinite pain, that in addition to all the calamities of indigence, a passion has seized him, which must encrease, and may perpetuate, his misfortunes, and I consented, and even wished to see you, that I might fairly state to you the situation he is in, as to circumstances; in the hope—a hope in which I trust I shall not be deceived, that your good sense, and even your regard for him, will lead you to avoid an error so seducing as that of becoming his wife.'

"I do not know Madam, how I looked at that moment, but I believe Mrs. Elphinstone thought I should faint, for she gave me immediate assistance by opening the window, fetched me a glass of water, and very earnestly entreated me to try to recover myself before her brother returned. I should be too tedious, Madam, were I to relate all that passed even in the few minutes we were together afterwards. I found that Cathcart's regard for me was such, that he was willing to forget what he had once been, and what he might still be, and to unite himself for ever with the poor and humble Jessy. Ah! Madam, had it not been for Mrs. Elphinstone's sake, who with her children had no other dependence, I should have feared no poverty, no distress with him; but should have been too happy to have begged round the world with him: as it was, I saw that I ought not to think a moment of a marriage, which would at best only encrease his difficulties. Oh! how I then wished that my grandfather were less cruel, my poor father less imprudent!

"After this first interview with Mrs. Elphinstone, I saw her whenever I could get leave to go out, which was not indeed very often: but my master, who did not want humanity, seeing me look dreadfully ill, ordered Mrs. Gillam to let me go out whenever she could spare me, for air. Mrs. Elphinstone, who watched every alteration of my countenance, guessed at all I suffered; and at length she became so fond of me, that she rather desired than opposed the completion of her brother's wishes. The struggle I underwent nearly cost me my life: but at length, Madam, I have left them both. I could not bear to see my dear Cathcart every day more and more unhappy: I could not bear to become a burden to him: for some time I redoubled my diligence, and exerted myself greatly beyond my strength, from a hope, that by becoming necessary to my mistress, I should obtain an encrease of wages, out of which I thought it possible that I might be able to save something: but the upper servant took pains to render all my endeavours ineffectual; and my health declined so rapidly under the labour and anxiety I endured, that Cathcart, whose uneasiness compleated the measure of my sufferings, at length proposed that I should quit my service, as the only means of saving my life, and try what my native air would do to restore me.

"I hope my father will receive me without unkindness, and suffer me to stay till I am able to take another service; and sometimes I am willing to flatter myself that my grandfather may relent, though it is more possible than probable."

"And where," enquired Celestina, "have you left your lover?"

"Ah! Madam," replied the weeping Jessy, "he still remains writing for the existence of his sister and her children: at his pen from early morning, to eleven or twelve at night. By such assiduous application he is enabled indeed to earn double the money he would otherwise do; but his dear health is fast declining, and God only knows," continued she, clasping her hands together, "whether I shall ever see him more: but if not, one comfort, one great comfort is, that we shall not be separated long:—in heaven nothing can part us!"

"Let us however hope," said Celestina, "that your tenderness, your fortitude, and generosity, will be rewarded on earth. Your father then knows nothing of our arrival?"

"Ah! no, Madam: I dared not write to him for fear he should have been angry with me for having quitted my service, and have refused to receive me. Now I hope, when he sees me so sadly altered, for I am not at all like what I was when I left him, he will have some pity upon me, and suffer me at least to stay in his house till I have strength enough to undertake another service."

"You shall go with me, however, tonight," said Celestina, "and you shall stay with me till you are fitter than you now appear to be to undergo an interview with this cruel father."

The poor Jessy, oppressed by this goodness, could not speak, but she kissed the hand of her benefactress with a respectful gratitude, and a mournful but not unpleasing sadness kept the generous and soft hearted Celestina silent till their arrival at the inn where they were to remain that night.

Chapter X

Early in the evening of the following day, Celestina and her humble friend arrived at the lodging she had taken: it was a small new built brick house, on the edge of an extensive common: enclosures[1] at a distance relieved a little the dreary uniformity of the view from its windows, and a village church, with a few straggling houses scattered round the edge of the heath at the distance of about half a mile, gave some relief to the eye, and some intimation of an inhabited country: winter had alike divested the common of its furze and heath blossoms, and the few elms on its borders, of their foliage. All was alike dull, and unpleasant: but Celestina remembered that she had now escaped from the Castlenorths, from the sight of preparations for Willoughby's marriage, and that if she was not to live to see him happy, she should not now witness his struggles and his distress: she tried to believe that she could receive intelligence of his marriage with composure, and be glad in the reflection that he had obeyed his mother; but her heart revolted, and all she could promise herself was, to exert her resolution to obtain such a state of mind, as might enable her to hear, without very acute anguish, of an event, which notwithstanding all that had passed at her last interview with Willoughby, she still considered as inevitable.

The next day after her arrival was passed in settling herself in her new habitation by the aid of Jessy, who helped her to arrange her books and her wardrobe. The pensive simplicity of her new friend's character won upon her every hour; and now, deprived as she was of all her former connections, and of every prospect of happiness for herself, she was sensible of no other pleasure than what arose from the power of soothing the sorrows of her unfortunate companion, and forming schemes for restoring her to the favour of her grandfather; and to her unhappy lover, in whose fate she became as much interested from the artless description Jessy had given, as if she had herself known him. It was necessary however to part with her: but

---

1 Ground formerly "common," for grazing by the villagers' animals, but now enclosed or fenced by the local landowner for his own use, and forested for the encouragement of game.

as she appeared in too weak a state of health to encounter the rude reception she might meet with from her father and her mother in law, if she appeared before them without notice, Celestina thought it best to keep her till an answer could be obtained from them, and she therefore hired a messenger, by whom the letter the trembling Jessy indited was dispatched to the cottage of Woodburn, which was about seven miles distant. Towards evening he returned, and brought a reluctant and surly consent from her father to receive her for a little time till she recovered her health. The terms in which this answer was written, though Celestina endeavoured to give them the best interpretation she could, were cruelly painful to poor Jessy, who wept over the letter, while Celestina, with the most generous pity, assured her, that if her father's behaviour to her was unkind, and her stay at his house uncomfortable, she would again receive her, and that she should be welcome to remain with her till her health was re-established, and till means could be found to procure for her the favour of her grandfather, who, on enquiry of her hostess, Celestina found to be as Jessy had represented him—a very rich farmer, now quite superannuated, and almost childish; who having once determined to resent his daughter's marriage, had persisted in it from the hard obstinacy of his nature, and had been supported in it by the arts of an old female relation who lived with him, and who, while she made a purse every year out of what was entrusted to her, looked forward with avidity to his death, when she hoped to possess the whole. Celestina procured an horse and a man to lead it, the expense of which she paid herself, and on the third day after their arrival at Thorpe Heath, Jessy took leave of her lovely and generous benefactress, who was now left to reflect, without interruption, on her own destiny.

Till lately she had not been conscious of the force of her attachment to Willoughby; for it began so early in life, that she had never been alarmed by the uneasiness which seizes the heart on its first reception of a new passion: she now however found that her existence had been delightful to her, only as his idea had mingled itself with every hour of it, and that now, when she believed she ought no longer to indulge herself in thinking of him, she could think of nothing else with either interest or pleasure: the benevolence and tenderness of her heart still afforded her some satisfaction, while she could exert it in favour of the unfortunate, and the power of befriending the desolate and unhappy Jessy had called off her attention a little from her own uneasy feelings; but now, having done all she could at present do for her, her heart was again sensible of the cruel deprivation to which she was condemned, and her mind occupied in reflecting on what Willoughby would think, what he would say, when he learned she was gone; in conjectures on his behaviour to the Castlenorths, and in trembling solicitude whether he would write to her, or without any farther indulgence of an attachment, which he knew he ought not to cherish, drive her from his recollection, at least till he had obeyed the injunctions of his mother, and by compleating the marriage she had insisted upon, put it out of his power to think of Celestina otherwise than as his sister.

Two or three days passed thus, before Celestina could acquire in any degree her usual serenity, and sit down to her books, her drawing, or her work.[1] By music, which she now fancied would sooth and calm her spirits, she could not amuse herself; for though she had a piano forte[2] which used to be called her's, yet, as it had never been formally given to her, and as Mrs. Molyneux had not mentioned it, Celestina would not take it on her quitting London. At length the first uneasy sensations on her change of situation a little subsided. And she began to consider of a letter which she thought it indispensably necessary to write to Mrs. Molyneux.

In the mean time the ardent and eager temper of Willoughby exhibited in London a scene, which, could Celestina have known, it would have redoubled all her anxiety. The dinner of which he had been with difficulty induced to partake at Lord Castlenorth's, had served only to fill him with new and invincible disgust towards the whole family, and hardly could he command himself so as not to betray it. The restraint, however, which, in consideration of their relationship to his mother, he determined, whatever it cost him, to put upon his sentiments, gave to two of the persons concerned a favourable impression of him: Lord Castlenorth, fond of form, and of that reserve which he fancied supported dignity, liked his nephew the better he said for not assuming the familiar and too easy manners, so disagreeable to him in the behaviour of most of the young men he saw; and Miss Fitz-Hayman, who liked his person better on every interview, and who never could for a moment suppose that any man could behold hers with indifference, imputed to respect and admiration that distant politeness which was intended to conceal aversion. Lady Castlenorth, however, who had seen more of the

---

1   Needlework.
2   Invented in Padua around 1710, the piano rapidly became popular, superseding the spinet and harpsichord.

world than her daughter, and had not the same prejudices as her husband, was by no means pleased with the observations she made in the course of the day, nor with the pleasure she saw for the first time in the eyes of Willoughby when the moment of their departure arrived. This was not till four in the morning. The late hour of dinner, and the parties which were made for cards, brought on a supper at near two, of which Lady Castlenorth seemed to expect her guests would partake: they staid therefore; Lord Castlenorth retiring early, by the advice of Mrs. Calder; and the universality of Lady Castlenorth's knowledge being displayed the whole time to the extreme fatigue of Willoughby, and by no means to the satisfaction of his sister, who found in her aunt a desire to monopolize not only all the conversation, but the attention of every man present, to whom she contrived to address herself by turns, and with whom she appeared immediately offended, if Mrs. Molyneaux, whom she considered and treated as a pretty automaton,[1] attracted even for a moment any of that admiration that she was generally, at her own parties and among her own friends, accustomed to engross.

Willoughby was set down by his sister at his own lodgings, and Mrs. Molyneux herself knew nothing of Celestina's departure till breakfast the next day; when busied with preparations for a ball subscribed for by some noblemen of her acquaintance, she received it, and testified no other concern than by saying coldly—"I wish she had staid till to-morrow, for she has really something of a taste, and I should have liked to have had her here when I dress." This important dress, however, was too momentous to suffer her to think long of any human being; and when her brother called upon her about three o'clock, she was adjusting the ornaments on a tiara of her own invention, and had forgotten for the moment not only the sudden journey of Celestina but Celestina herself.

Willoughby sat down by her; and in hopes of Celestina's coming in, entered into conversation on frivolous subjects, to which he in fact gave so little attention that he hardly heard the answers his sister gave him. He desired, however, to prolong the time of his stay as much as possible, that without asking for Celestina, he might see her; and he knew, that busied as Mrs. Molyneux was, he should have an opportunity of speaking to her without observation.

---

1   A clockwork toy; the word was also applied to clocks and watches in the seventeenth and eighteenth centuries, perhaps here suggesting a figure that strikes the hours on a large public clock.

The tiara was at length ornamented, and no Celestina appeared: Willoughby then enquired why she did not assist at an operation so important, and heard with pain and amazement that she had left the house at five o'clock that morning.

"And whither is she gone?" said he in a voice hardly audible: "and how could you suffer her to go?"

"Oh! as to that," answered Mrs. Molyneux, quite regardless of his distress, "she has taken those lodgings you know in Devonshire that you have so often heard her speak of; and for her going, you know she has long determined on it, and indeed I did not oppose it, thinking as things are, it was the very best resolution she could take."

"As things are!" repeated Willoughby, trying vainly to stifle the painful sensation his sister's coldness and insensibility gave him: "I know not, Mrs. Molyneux, what you mean exactly, but ..."

He was proceeding, when the hair dresser,[1] who on these great occasions was employed in preference to her own maid, was announced; and Mrs. Molyneux, ordering him into her powdering room,[2] walked immediately away, and left Willoughby sitting like a statue by the dressing table she had left.

He remained there near a quarter of an hour, in a state of mind difficult to be described: the danger to which Celestina must be exposed, alone and unprotected; the probability of his losing her for ever; nay of her sacrificing herself to one of those pretenders whom he doubted not her beauty would attract, in the same spirit of disinterested heroism, as that which had determined her to quit London; the excessive tenderness he was conscious of towards her, against which he found every hour the impossibility of contending, and the encreasing disgust that he felt in contemplating the chains he had promised to put on, all contributed to overwhelm his mind with anguish, from which he saw not how it was easy or even possible to escape.

His first idea was to obtain a direction to Celestina, and follow her immediately; but he knew the delicacy of her mind, and he felt perfectly what was due to her situation:—reflections which checked those intentions almost as soon as they were formed; and before he could decide on what he ought to do, he received from Molyneux,

---

1 Fashionable hairdressers came to their customers' houses rather than keeping a salon.
2 Wealthy people set aside a small room adjacent to the bedroom, partitioned in such a way that the hair could be powdered without spoiling their clothes.

who had just come in and gone out again, an unsealed note, containing these lines:

"Dear George,

"I am just returned from Lincoln's Inn, where I have been to meet Atkins and some other cursed bores about money: I cannot get what I want of them: do contrive to let me have five hundred this evening for my pocket, and I wish you would arrange things so as to have the remainder of the unpaid five thousand and interest ready by this day sennight[1] or it will much inconvenience me. Castlenorth is your man; and it is but speaking for the money to have it. Let us see you to-morrow to dinner.

Yours ever,

P.H. Molyneux."

This note, so peremptorily requiring what the writer knew Willoughby could not obtain but by hastily confirming those measures which were so displeasing to him; this unfeeling precipitation, which appeared only a *finesse*[2] to compel him to plunge into them, roused Willoughby from the state of undetermined anxiety he had been in, into anger and indignation: his first solicitude however was to raise instantly the five hundred pounds for that evening's play, which was clearly the meaning of his brother in law; and snatching up his hat, he left the house, determining, in the first emotions of his resentment, to enter it no more. He took his way towards the City, and applying to a banker in Lombard-street, in whose hands his father had kept his money, and who had had considerable advantages by his own affairs during his minority, he obtained, not without solicitation the most painful to his pride and on terms as hard as would have been demanded by a common money lender,[3] the sum he wanted; which he enclosed in a cover,[4] and sent by one of the clerks, with these words:

---

1   Week (seven nights).
2   Manipulation, strategy.
3   Charging interest on a loan was by now legal and recognised as essential if commerce was to thrive: 5 per cent was reckoned to be the highest acceptable rate of interest for a private loan, while "usury" was the term given to charges of 8-10 per cent or more. The banker is charging a usurious rate.
4   Envelope.

"Mr. Willoughby encloses to Mr. Molyneux the sum for which he has so pressing an occasion, and assures him he will lose no time in procuring the rest, that all pecuniary transactions may be at an end between them."

It was with great difficulty he bridled the natural vehemence of his temper, and forbore to express with bitterness the displeasure Molyneux's proceeding had given him. More resolute than ever not to be dictated to by his brother in law, and detesting more than before the marriage which was thus intended to be forced upon him, dissatisfied with every idea that occurred to him, and having no friend in London to whom he could open his oppressed heart, he determined at length to procure a direction to Celestina, and returning immediately to Cambridge himself, consult a friend he had there, on whose judgment and attachment he had an equal reliance, how he should avoid an alliance with the woman he detested and the hazard he now incurred of losing the woman he adored.

He sent therefore a servant, as soon as he returned to his lodgings, to procure from the servants of Molyneux a copy of the direction that had been put on the trunks sent to Celestina. This being obtained, he ordered a post chaise, and late as it was, and without giving any account of himself either to his sister or the Castlenorths, he set out for Cambridge, and arrived at his college about four in the morning of the next day.

Chapter XI

Celestina in the mean time became better reconciled to the plan of life she had adopted; and after being near a week at her new abode, during which time she heard nothing either of Willoughby or his sister, she wrote to the house as follows:

"My dear Mrs. Molyneux will be glad to hear that her wandering friend is settled contentedly, if not happily, in her new abode, and has already subdued her mind to her fortune so much as to regret only the society of those she has been so long accustomed to love, and by no means the scenes in which she has left them. My habitation is in the house of a man who was formerly master of a coasting vessel, in which occupation having made money enough to support himself and his wife in their old age, and all his children being married and provided for, he built this house a few miles from the port where he used to trade: their only servant is a mere West country paisanne,[1] who does the business which the good old woman herself is unequal to: whose not frequent, but somewhat loud and shrill remonstrances to Jenny, when she is careless or neglectful, are the only sounds I ever hear to remind me that there are such things as anger or contention in the world. The scene around me is now dreary enough; but in a few weeks spring will produce new pleasures for me; and I shall hail the first primrose with as much delight as I can feel from any thing, but from that most welcome sight, the face of an old friend. My dear Matilda, you pity, I know, the merely negative life I have chosen: enliven it then sometimes by your kind recollection, and find time now and then to write to me, if it be only to say you are well. Your brother's marriage may at this period occupy you; yet I hope you will not even now forget me, nor fail to recollect the tender interest which must ever exist for your happiness, and that of all you love, in the grateful heart of your affectionate

      Celestina de Mornay."

Feb 7, 17—[2]

    This letter arrived a day after Willoughby's abrupt departure. Between the continual and unceasing hurry in which she lived, and her vexation at that event, she hardly read it, but threw it carelessly by on her toilet, where it remained forgotten like the writer of it.

    On the day Willoughby had dined and supped in Grosvenor-street, the whole family had been much dissatisfied with his conduct except his uncle; who retaining much of form and ceremony in his own manners, was willing to impute his coldness to respect, and his distant civility to veneration: but the mother and daughter were by no means content with his deportment; and though they concealed their feelings as it were by mutual consent, their pride was equally alarmed, and both resolved to have an early explanation. Lady Castlenorth, however, whose policy only had power to restrain awhile the ebullitions of her wounded pride, waited one day in hopes that Willoughby would in a family conference testify more ardour for the match than he had done in mixed company; but Willoughby never appeared; and her indignation now knowing no bounds, she ordered her coach, and on the next, stalked with more

---

1   Peasant, farm worker.
2   Later we learn that the date is 1788.

than usual majesty into the dressing room of Mrs. Molyneux just as she had finished her breakfast, which was, owing to the hour on which she went to bed the preceding morning, even later than usual.

Lady Castlenorth hardly spoke to Mrs. Molyneux when she entered, but demanded in an imperious tone what was become of Mr. Willoughby.

The lady to whom she thus abruptly addressed herself was as haughty and of as high consequence in her estimation as Lady Castlenorth herself; and feeling and resenting her rude and peremptory stile, she answered, with almost as little complaisance in her manner, that she knew not.

"You don't know, Madam!" exclaimed the imperious Viscountess; "you don't know! Very extraordinary surely. What am I to understand from all this?"

"Of that also I am ignorant," replied Mrs. Molyneux. "Mr. Willoughby, Madam, is his own master; and I really can no more account for than direct his actions."

"Astonishing!" re-assumed Lady Castlenorth: "that a man situated as he is, who is not an absolute ideot, should behave in this manner in an affair on which his very existence as a man of fashion depends: but don't imagine, Mistress Molyneux, that *my* daughter ..."

"Dear Madam," interrupted Matilda, irritated by the supercilious and insolent tone in which her Ladyship spoke, and particularly the emphasis she put on the word Mistress,[1] "I beg and entreat that you will spare your anger. I at least cannot deserve it, for I have no influence over my brother. I dare say he has some reasons for having left London so abruptly, though I assure you I do not know them."

"You don't!—I do: he is gone after that creature, whom your mother, to her utter disgrace, brought up in the family, and with whom she suffered her son to live in habits of intimacy which shock me every time I think of it."

At this moment Mr. Molyneux entered with a letter in his hand, and hardly in his haste noticing Lady Castlenorth, he told his wife that the letter was that instant delivered to him by an express, that his father was dying, and that they must immediately set out for Ireland at his earnest entreaty.

"Hasten therefore," said he, "to prepare yourself, for the chaise I

---

1 Because Lady Castlenorth is emphasizing that Matilda has no title.

have sent for will be at the door in a moment. Your Ladyship will excuse us I am sure on such an occasion," added he, addressing himself to Lady Castlenorth. "Matilda, we have not a moment to lose: direct your maid to prepare what you want to take with you, and to follow herself with the baggage that may not be so immediately necessary."

"And where is Willoughby?" cried Lady Castlenorth, raising her voice: "I insist upon seeing him."

"I believe he has left London," answered Molyneux; "but I assure you I know not whither he is gone. I dare say your Ladyship will soon hear of him. In the mean time pray pardon me; it is impossible for me now to have the honour of attending you."

He then left the room, as his wife had done already; and Lady Castlenorth, bursting with anger and indignation which she had nobody to listen to, returned in all the fury of mortified pride to her own house.

While she was there meditating how to revenge the neglect shewn to her daughter, of which she now no longer doubted, Willoughby was pouring out all the distresses of his heart to a friend whom heaven seemed to have sent him for their alleviation.

Mr. Vavasour, his most intimate friend, had been absent when he left Cambridge on his hasty and reluctant journey to London, but was now returned, and to him Willoughby immediately disclosed the cause of that uneasiness which his friend perceived he suffered under even before he spoke.

"What shall I do?" said he, as he leaned on the table, "how extricate myself from the most insupportable of engagements? how satisfy this narrow and unfeeling Molyneux: my soul revolts from the odious necessity of being obliged to him for forbearance: yet to sell my estates—is more painful to me than any measure but marrying Miss Fitz-Hayman. Yet my promise, my assurances to my mother—I see not how I can escape from the difficulties that encompass me."

"You make more of them surely, my dear George," replied Vavasour, "than is necessary. What! should either a promise or an exigence compel you to be miserable for life; then indeed there would be no escape: but now, surely, my friend, your escape is not difficult."

"Were you situated as I am then, how would you act?"

"Why, I would without hesitation declare off with the woman I did not like, and marry the woman I did: that is, if I were disposed to marry at all."

"And would you do this, Vavasour, contrary to a solemn promise given to her who cannot now release me from it? and then how can

I act in regard to Molyneux? be the consequence what it will he shall never again dun[1] me for money, and ..."

"Never!" interrupted Vavasour warmly, "if you will listen to me. I am not quite of age it is true, but my fortune is such, that nothing is easier than for me to raise this paltry five thousand pounds, or twice the sum, on no very exorbitant terms. I have already taken up money for my own pleasures, and shall I hesitate when my friend has real occasion for it? In a week's time the money shall be ready for you. Pray then let us hear no more of any difficulties of that sort, and as for your promise—the good lady, when she extorted it, could never think it binding."

"Speak not lightly of her, my dear friend," said Willoughby, "that I may feel all the kindness of the former part of your speech without alloy: she was a woman whom, had you known, you would have reverenced and loved, and it was in kindness only that she made me give her an engagement[2]...."

"To make yourself miserable. I am, you know, George, an Epicurean;[3] you are somewhat of a Stoic[4] I suppose; and if that is the case, fulfil your promise, take your heiress, and philosophize at your leisure. I have never seen your Celestina, you know; but from your description of her, and your long attachment, I should pity you—I am afraid I should despise you—I am sure I should not love you— were you to sacrifice such a creature to any pecuniary consideration. Come, my dear fellow, assure yourself that if five thousand pounds or more will relieve you from what weighs on your spirits about Molyneux's matter, it is yours; the other affair you must settle with your own heart, and I leave you to argue it together."

Vavasour then quitted the room; and Willoughby, released from his anxiety about his debt by the generosity of his friend, gave himself up to all those pleasant images which presented themselves to his mind. To be united immediately with Celestina, to carry her down to Alvestone, and there to enter on a plan of economy which should in a very few years retrieve his circumstances, was a vision which he

---

1 Demand money from. "Duns" were men hired to harass debtors into paying their creditors.
2 Promise.
3 Epicurus established the "Garden" school of philosophy in Athens about 307 BC. Since he taught that goodness is identical with happiness, his philosophy was easily vulgarised and equated with self-indulgence.
4 From the Stoic school of philosophy founded by Zeno around 300 BC at Athens: rational, self-controlled.

found so much delight in cherishing, that he drove from his mind as much as possible the painful objections that still cruelly intruded themselves to destroy it: the conversation of Vavasour helped to put them entirely to flight; and Willoughby, persuaded that by the process of economy he had formed he should soon be enabled to pay his friend the money so generously offered him, agreed without much hesitation to accept it. The young men then settled that they would go the next day but one to London, stay there long enough to negotiate this business, and then go down together to Alvestone, from whence Willoughby, who had no inclination to encounter Lady Castlenorth personally, determined to write to his uncle, resigning all pretensions to the honor intended him, and immediately to complete his marriage with her who had so long been mistress of his heart. This arrangement, once made, became every moment more seducing to his imagination; still the words of his mother, the solemn charge given him with her last breath, returned now and then to disturb his visionary felicity: but Celestina, always so lovely in his eyes, leaning on his arm amid the shades of Alvestone, the delight of his friends, the patroness of his tenants, the protectress of the poor, was an image so deliciously soothing to his fancy, that by indulging it he at length persuaded himself that his mother, who had so very tenderly loved her, would, could she be sensible of all the happiness they should share together, applaud his violation of his promise and sanction his choice.

Vavasour, gay, generous, open hearted, and volatile, always eagerly following himself his own inclinations, and as warmly solicitous for his friend's gratification as his own, encouraged as much as possible all tendency in Willoughby to throw off any adherence to what he deemed tyranny beyond the grave; and by the time the negociation for the loan was completed, which took them up near a week, Willoughby had no longer any scruples remaining. His only business in town then was to pay Molyneux, whose conduct had offended him so much that he had not been to the house: as soon however as the money was ready, he wrote a note to his brother in law, signifying that he would on the next day meet him at his attorney's chambers to settle all accounts between them. The servant who was sent brought the note back; and Willoughby then first learning that his sister and her husband were embarked for Ireland, deposited the money at a banker's, and wrote a cold letter to Molyneux, signifying that it waited his orders. He then gave directions to his own solicitor to take proper receipts on the payment of it, and with Vavasour hastened down to Alvestone, in the neighbourhood of which place he knew Celestina was, but he had determined not to see her till he had obviated every objection she could make to his plan of happiness, by breaking at once and for ever with the Castlenorths; a task on which, resolved as he was to execute it, he could not think without a mixture of concern and apprehension that he was ashamed of feeling, and dared by no means betray to his friend Vavasour; who, without knowing any thing of the Castlenorths himself, had made up his mind that they were an odious and disagreeable set, and from such, whatever might be their rank, he always flew away himself, and encouraged his friends to do it at whatever risk. If he was careless and even rude towards those whom he did not wish to please, he was altogether as amiable and attentive to those to whom he sought to be acceptable. His dislikes and his attachments were equally warm, and the latter had hitherto been rather warm than permanent.

Chapter XII

While these things were passing at Cambridge and in London, Celestina underwent the cruellest anxiety at not hearing from Mrs. Molyneux; but all her conjectures ended in the painful conclusion that the preparations and celebration of Willoughby's marriage entirely engaged her, and prevented her writing. All her reason was now summoned to support her against the shock which the certainty of this event would give her. With a beating heart, and in breathless agitation, she ran over the paper which once a week a travelling newsman brought from Exeter, and where she knew the marriage of a man of so much consequence in the neighbourhood would not fail to be inserted.

No such intelligence however appeared; and Celestina, imagining that the marriage had notwithstanding certainly taken place, endeavoured, since she could not conquer her regret, to divert it, by trying what she could do towards softening the sorrows and relieving the distress of the unfortunate Jessy, whose patient endurance of evils, evidently severer than her own, whose fortitude in tearing herself perhaps for ever from the man she loved, and sacrificing the indulgence of her affection to his interest, made Celestina sometimes ashamed of the murmurs she found excited in her heart by less inconveniences, and blush at the reluctance with which she had submitted to the loss of a man, whose regard for her seemed already to have yielded to the influence of pecuniary advantage, and family convenience.

But in despite of every argument she could bring to subdue the pain arising from the recollection of lost happiness, and totally silence the Syren[1] voice of hope which now and then presented the possibility of more favourable days, the uncertainty whether the event to which she laboured to become reconciled had really happened, disturbed and rendered her restless and uneasy. Jessy, to whom she now sent to desire her company for a little time, joyfully accepted the summons; and in her company Celestina felt great satisfaction, though she had never disclosed to her any part of the sorrow that oppressed her, or given the remotest hint of her attachment to Willoughby. All the indulgence she allowed herself was, that of sometimes chusing to walk towards a knoll at the extremity of the common, which afforded an extensive view towards the west; from thence, by the help of a telescope lent her by her landlord, Celestina had discovered a clump of firs in Alvestone Park; and though they were near ten miles distance, and without a glass appeared only a dark spot above the rest of the landscape, she found a melancholy pleasure in distinguishing them, and would frequently, as she leant on Jessy's arm in their pensive rambles, fix her eyes on that distant object, gaze on it steadily for two or three minutes, and then with a deep sigh turn away, and walk silently home.

She encouraged however the artless Jessy to talk to her of Cathcart; and the poor girl, pleased with every opportunity of repeating his name, and flattered by the tender interest Celestina took in their story, was never weary of speaking of him. She at length acquired confidence enough to produce some of the letters he wrote to her; and Celestina, who had very naturally imputed much of the praise Jessy had bestowed on his writing and on his style to the fond partiality of her affection for him, was surprised to find in these letters the most manly, clear, and sensible style she had almost ever met with. The generous emulation which appeared between these lovers, their disinterested tenderness, and the steadiness of their mutual attachment, raised in Celestina admiration and even respect, and every hour encreased her inclination to contribute to their happiness.

But these intentions she had no way of executing but by means of Willoughby, who was, as she knew from long experience, ever ready to befriend the unfortunate; and on such an occasion she

---

1 In Greek myth, the sirens were sea-creatures like mermaids who had the power to lure mariners to their deaths through the beauty of their singing.

thought, that as soon as he was married she might, without any impropriety, address herself to him; and as the farm which old Winnington, the grandfather of Jessy, possessed, adjoined to his estate at Alvestone, Celestina imagined he could hardly fail of being some influence, which she knew he would be ready to exert for her unfortunate friend.

In meditating how to administer to the afflictions of others, her own sorrows were at least mitigated: but the calm she outwardly assumed was the mere effort of resolution, while her anxiety to hear of Willoughby and of his sister encreased every hour; and as the delay grew more unaccountable, it became almost insupportably painful.

It was now the beginning of March: the weather was uncommonly cold and dreary; and a deep snow, which had fallen some days before, had confined Celestina and her companion almost entirely to the house. It was very unusual to see any person pass by the house, near which there was no public road, and the inclemency of the season rendered it still less frequent: Jessy, therefore, who went to the window by accident to fetch some work that lay there, mentioned to Celestina, as a matter of some surprise, that two foot passengers, who had the appearance of gentlemen, were crossing the common towards the house.

Celestina, who was at that moment meditating, with her eyes fixed on the fire, on the long, long space of time that had elapsed since she had heard of Willoughby, and on all the events that might have taken place in that period, gave very little attention to this intelligence, and on Jessy's repeating it, answered that probably it was some persons who had lost their way in the snow and were coming to the house for directions to regain the road.

To Jessy, however, the idea of Cathcart was ever present: one of the strangers was not unlike him in figure as she fancied, though both were wrapped in great coats; and the possibility of his having come in search of her, had no sooner struck her, than with eager eyes and a beating heart she watched every step they took: at length they entered the little gate that divided the garden of the house from the common; Jessy was then convinced that neither of them was Cathcart; but her curiosity was strongly excited, and listening to the questions they put to the servant who went to the door, she distinctly heard one of them enquire for Miss de Mornay.

Celestina was now in her turn alarmed; and trembling, though she knew not why, she desired Jessy to go down and ask who it was, but before she could be obeyed the door opened, and she saw, with emotion to which language cannot do justice—Willoughby himself!

The first idea that struck her was, that he was come to announce his marriage; and the air of triumph and satisfaction his countenance wore, seemed to tell her he was the happy husband of Miss Fitz-Hayman. Long as she had been accustomed to dwell on this idea, she shrunk with terror from its supposed reality, and pale and trembling drew back, as he eagerly advanced towards her:—"My heavenly girl! my own Celestina!" cried he as he took her hand. This address, from the married Willoughby, seemed an insult: she withdrew her hand with an air of resentment, would have spoken but could not, and unable to support herself sat down.

Willoughby, whose own anxious emotions had too much prevented his considering how she might be affected by his abrupt appearance, now saw that he had been too precipitate. He placed himself by her, and again taking the hand she had withdrawn, he enquired, with more tenderness and less impetuosity, if she was sorry to see him. Again Celestina would have spoken, but her native pride again refused to assist her; and while she was vainly endeavouring to acquire resolution enough to congratulate him on his supposed marriage, she learned that he had not only broken for ever with Miss Fitz-Hayman, but was come to offer himself to her, who had from his childhood been the sole possessor of his affections.

This sudden and unexpected happiness was too much. Her reason, which in the severest calamity had never quite deserted her, now seemed unequal to tidings so overwhelming, and for a moment or two she sat like a statue; till Willoughby, in that well known voice, and with that graceful and manly tenderness which had rendered him ever[1] so dear to her, related all that had passed from the hour of their last parting, and the resolution he had adopted of sacrificing that wealth, which could not bestow happiness, to the long and incurable passion he had conceived for an object so deserving, and without whom no advantages of fortune of situation could give his life the smallest value.

Tears of gratitude and affection now fell from the eyes of Celestina; and as he found the tumult of her spirits subside, he went on to relate to her, with the most generous delicacy, the plans he had formed for their future life, and the means by which he hoped to retrieve his affairs, without sacrificing his happiness. Tenderly however as he touched on these subjects, his violated promise to his mother returned with all its force to the recollection of Celestina.

---

1   Always.

Willoughby, whose eyes were fixed on hers, saw the painful idea by their expression as soon as it arose, and in a voice that trembled from emotions he could not express, he endeavoured to obviate the objections he feared she was about to make, even before she could utter them.

All his eloquence, however, could not silence that monitor in the breast of Celestina, which told her that there was more of sophistry[1] than of sound reason in his arguments; but fondly attached to him as she was, it was sophistry too enchanting for her to have courage to attempt detecting it. She wished to be convinced Willoughby was right; to see him happy had almost from her earliest recollection been the second wish of her heart; for perhaps to have the power of making him so had always, even unknown to herself, been the first; that happiness seemed not to depend upon her; and she determined (after one of those short struggles, in which, when inclination and duty contend, the former has too often the advantage,) to stifle within her own bosom every painful remembrance, to think as he thought, and in rendering happy the son of her benefactress, to acquit herself through her future life of the debt of gratitude she owed her.

Celestina, therefore, made no objection to the proposals Willoughby laid before her, which were, that they should be married privately in about ten days, and take up their abode at Alvestone in the same stile they meant always to reside in. These preliminaries being arranged, Willoughby besought her to permit him to introduce Vavasour to her, who had been waiting below; he went down himself to bring up his friend; and Celestina, in that moment of his absence, endeavoured to recall her presence of mind, and habituate herself to think with less agitation in the happiness of being the wife of her beloved Willoughby.

Vavasour, from the ardour with which his friend had spoken of her personal perfections, was prepared to find her very lovely; and Willoughby on their first interview watched his looks, trying to discover if his expectations had been answered: they were completely so: the agitation she had suffered had raised the glow of her cheeks, and given more softness to her eyes, in which the tears yet trembled; while the natural dignity of her manner received in his opinion new

---

1   The original proponents of spin, the Sophists, flourishing in Greece in the fifth century BC, were travelling teachers who held that political persuasiveness is a skill that can be acquired rather than the result of representing a just cause; thus: speciousness, manipulation of the facts.

charms from the remains of embarrassment which she endeavoured to shake off, and in which, after a few moments, she succeeded so well, that they all became as much at their ease as if they had all been as long acquainted as Willoughby and Celestina.

Jessy, who had left the room on Willoughby's first entrance, was now desired by Celestina to return. During her short absence, while she prepared a repast of cold meat for the hungry travellers who had walked from Alvestone, Celestina related to them as much of her history as interested both of them in her favour; and Willoughby, who found in every sentiment and every action of Celestina something to encrease his tenderness and admiration, was charmed with the generous pity she had shewn to her humble friend, and promised her all his influence to obtain for her the provision she had a right to expect from her grandfather, and unite her to her deserving lover.

Willoughby hung with fondness approaching to adoration on every word Celestina uttered, and forgot, that for this time the delight of seeing her must be short; Vavasour, gay, volatile, and enjoying with extreme good humour the happiness of his friend, was little accustomed to think at all; and Jessy was in too humble a situation to offer her opinion: on Celestina only, therefore, the prudence of the whole party depended; and as the snow was very deep, and they had between eight and nine miles to Alvestone, she at last ventured to hint that it was time they should go.

To Willoughby, the necessity of quitting her had never occurred, and he now heard of it as a sentence of banishment; but Celestina repeating that she should be very uneasy if in such weather they delayed so long a walk to a late hour in the evening, he saw that he should make her really uncomfortable by his stay; and having obtained leave to see her the next day, and every day till they were to part no more, he at last consented to go, that he and his companion might reach Alvestone before the night fell.

When he released the hand of Celestina, which he kissed a thousand times as he bade her adieu, she turned towards the window, and her eyes followed him across the heath till the furze and thorns at a distance concealed him from her sight. The very traces of his footsteps in the snow were dear to her; and in that frame of mind which renders it hardly conscious of its own sensations, she still gazed on *them* when she could distinguish *him* no longer. Jessy, though she could easily account for her silence, became after some time uneasy, and speaking to her, roused her from her reverie: she then sat down in her usual place, and attempted to quiet the perturbation of her mind by re-assuming her usual occupations; but the sudden transition within the last three hours, from lifeless despondence to a prospect of the utmost felicity she had ever imagined, was too violent to suffer her spirits to return to their usual calm. The recollection of her deceased benefactress, and of the fatal promise Willoughby had given her, recurred in despite of her endeavours to escape from it: and though, resolute as he appeared to be, to reconcile himself to its violation, there was nobody who had power by their interference to prevent the execution of the determination he had made; though nothing was likely to prevent the marriage on which he had resolved;[1] yet the mind of Celestina remained impressed with a confused sensation rather than any distinct prospect of the happiness she had been offered; and the transactions of the day appeared like a dream, from which she feared, by examining its reality, to be awakened.

Chapter XIII

Neither the person or the mind of Celestina were of that sort which make the strongest impression on the first view; and interesting as her figure and face were, it was the grace as well as the symmetry of the former, and the expression rather than the beauty of the latter that made her altogether so enchanting. Willoughby and Vavasour were now with her every day; and while her lover found in every hour of those days more reason to congratulate himself on the choice he had made, his friend grew insensibly so interested for Celestina, that volatile and unsteady as he had been till then, he found, that though, considering her already as Willoughby's wife, he could form neither hopes or designs for himself, yet that her happiness was the first wish of his heart; and that without violating his warm friendship towards his friend, he, for the first time in his life, envied a man who was going to be married.

The present happiness of Willoughby could be exceeded in his idea only by that which he imagined he had secured to himself by having determined to live only for the happiness of Celestina; and in continually contemplating her perfections, he endeavoured to justify to himself the measures he had taken, and to dismiss from his mind the unpleasing circumstances which might have robbed him of her for ever. He had written, after many attempts, to Lord

---

1 The original has "resolved upon."

Castlenorth, declining to carry any farther a negociation in which his inclinations had never any share; and though he softened this mortifying information as well as he could, he was sensible of the bitterness and resentment it must create, and indeed was so little satisfied himself with his performance, that after the fifth or sixth, he would still have delayed or wholly have evaded sending the letter, if Vavasour had not with many arguments and much difficulty persuaded him, that, resolved as he was to break with the family, any letter he could write in explanation, would be less offensive than total silence.

Celestina was very solicitous to know how he had acquitted himself towards his uncle; yet, as he seemed sedulously to avoid the subject, she feared to give him pain by recurring to it, and yielded perhaps too easily to the artifices she saw he used to draw her thoughts from it: while he, studying every turn of her speaking face, often saw, by the pensive cast it assumed, uneasy thoughts arise in her mind; and on those occasions, exerting himself to dispel them, he delighted to recall their sparkling vivacity to her eyes:

"E'l lampeggiar dell' angelico riso"[1]

which never bestowed greater charms on any countenance than on that of Celestina.

It was now decided that as soon as the settlements[2] were finished, which Willoughby had directed rather according to his love than to his fortune, and which were likely to take up about three weeks, Celestina was to become mistress of Alvestone. He had promised her to forbear making about that delightful place any of the alterations he meditated, till his income was so far retrieved as to allow him to do it with prudence, but he had a thousand reasons ready why Celestina should go there every day; for to reside there entirely, till she was married, she had refused with such firmness as left Willoughby nothing to urge with any chance of success. Partial as

---

1 Francis Petrarch, *Rime Sparse*, Poem 292, line 6. Smith's note: Petrarch. The lightning of the angelic smile.

2 Settlements were pre-marital agreements drawn up by a lawyer and signed by the couple and witnesses which would stipulate such matters as the wife's annual allowance and her jointure, the sum she would receive if she survived her husband. Without a pre-marital contract, whatever belonged to the bride before she married, and all money acquired during the marriage, became the property of the husband.

himself to this spot, where she had passed the happiest hours of her life, she yet, in her present situation, felt distressed and uneasy at the thoughts of visiting it; but Willoughby pressed it with so much earnestness, that, as the weather was now fine, and she had defended herself as long as she could, she at length, on condition of having Jessy with her, agreed to go there for a whole day, and that Willoughby should fetch them both in his phaeton.[1] *C'est le premier pas qui coute*,[2] says a French proverb; and he longed to have this day over, knowing that the memorials of his mother, which Celestina would there meet with, and which he feared would give her some uneasy sensations, would, after she was accustomed to see them lose their effect on her mind, and that she would insensibly learn to behold them rather with agreeable than uneasy sentiments.

He persuaded himself that such a revolution had been effected in his own mind, and that notwithstanding his clear recollection of certain forcible words his mother had used in their last melancholy interview, he was, in making himself happy, doing that, which, if she had yet any knowledge of human events, she would most warmly approve.

Intoxicated with his passion, which reason and taste seemed so entirely to justify, and an extorted promise only to oppose, Willoughby no longer suffered any uneasy recollections to cast a shade over the bright prospect opening before him. He now saw Celestina, the woman he had from his infancy adored, in that spot where his local affections were so fondly settled. Nothing seemed likely to impede his passing with her there a life of uninterrupted felicity; and till their union could take place, his greatest anxiety was to detach her imagination from all those objections which might yet linger in her mind, and to confirm her in the persuasion that to constitute through her future life the happiness of the son of her benefactress, would be her best acquittal of those obligations she owned to her in the early part of it.

Instead, therefore, of suffering her to visit immediately the particular parts of the house which he knew would most forcibly recall ideas which might distress her, he desired Vavasour to attend on Jessy, and follow them into the garden, where, when they were at a little

---

1 Open carriage, named after the Greek sun god.
2 It is the first step that is so difficult. The aphorism is attributed to the French aristocrat and distinguished letter-writer, Mme du Deffand, in a letter of 7 July 1763, and given currency by Voltaire, but it probably predates both, and was used by many later writers.

distance, he related to Celestina the measures he had already taken to restore or rather to introduce her amiable and injured friend to the favour of her grandfather. Celestina warmly approved his proceedings, and gratefully acknowledged his kindness, while the hope of seeing Jessy rescued from the severe hardships to which she must otherwise be exposed, and rewarding the disinterested attachment of her deserving lover, was most grateful to her generous heart. Willoughby himself never seemed so perfect as when thus employing his time and his power in the service of the unhappy. The fine scenery around her never appeared to such advantage as now, when she leaned on one arm while with the other he pointed out to her its various beauties; and at this moment the very season seemed to add something to her felicity. Within a few days the whole face of nature was changed: the snow, which had covered every object with cold uniformity, had now given place to the bright verdure of infant spring; the earliest trees and those in the most sheltered situations had put forth their tender buds; the copses were strewn with primroses and March violets, and the garden glowing with the first flowers of the year; while instead of the usually rude winds of the season, those gales only blew which

"Call forth the long expecting flowers
And wake the purple year!"[1]

Myriads of birds, who found food and shelter amid the shrubberies, and wood-walks, seemed to hail with songs their future lovely protectress,

"Hopp'd her walks and gambol'd in her eyes:"[2]

and while every thing was thus gay and cheerful without, the house, when she entered it, shewed her only contented faces: the old servants, its ancient and faithful inhabitants, had known and loved her from her earliest childhood, and rejoiced in the hope of ending their days in her service; the tenants, who loved their young landlord, were glad to find, that instead of carrying his rents to London he was coming to settle amongst them; and the poor, who had now for

1 Thomas Gray, "Ode on the Spring," lines 3-4: "Disclose the long expecting flowers/ And wake the purple year."
2 Cf. *A Midsummer Night's Dream*, 3.1.147.

some time severely missed Mrs. Willoughby's annual residence among them, invoked blessings on her son, from whom they were assured of more constant consideration, from his own noble nature as well as from the influence of Celestina, who, as they well remembered, was formerly the successful mediatrix between them and their deceased mistress, when her own daughter had frequently heard their petitions with indifference, or avoided them with disgust.

In a few days after this first visit to Alvestone, a fortunate circumstance occurred to facilitate the good offices Willoughby had undertaken in favour of Jessy Woodburn. The old female relation who had acquired unbounded influence over her grandfather died suddenly; and the old man, thus restored to the little power of reflection his very advanced age left him, and alarmed by the death of a person younger than himself, no longer refused to listen to the remonstrances of a clergyman in the neighbourhood, who had by Willoughby been engaged to speak to him in favour of his daughter's child. He consented to see her, provided no attempt was made to introduce her father to him, towards whom neither time, age, or sickness,[1] had blunted the asperity of his hatred; but though these odious passions retained, from habitual indulgence, all their inveterate malignity, the softer feelings of natural affection were dead in him; rather yielding to importunity than prompted by inclination, he consented to receive his granddaughter to officiate about him as a servant, and stipulated that during his life she should be no expence to him; thus grasping to the last moment of his existence, that which he had never enjoyed, and could no longer want. As he had nobody he valued more, he consented however, after many persuasions, to make a will, by which he gave her every thing, on the express condition, to use his own phrase, that her father "might never be the better for it."

It was necessary, though this important point was carried, that Jessy should, by residing with him, preclude the possibility of being again superseded by some of those mercenary beings who are in all ranks of life ready to surround the couch of the dying miser: a necessity Celestina admitted with reluctance, and Jessy with tears and regret; but they were both consoled by the reflection that a very short time must in some degree re-unite them by the removal of Celestina to Alvestone, which was within a walk of the farm at which her friend was now to reside.

---

1   An echo of *A Midsummer Night's Dream* 1.1.142, "War, death or sickness did lay siege to it."

Willoughby, having thus far succeeded for the interesting *protegée*[1] of Celestina, determined to complete his generous work by attending to the situation of Cathcart. He knew nothing could more highly oblige *her*, to contribute to whose slightest satisfaction was the supreme pleasure of his life; and his own good heart prompted him to lose no time in relieving the unmerited distresses of a deserving young man: he wrote, therefore, (without communicating what he had done) to Cathcart, enclosed him a bank note for his expenses; and informing him of all that passed in regard to Jessy, desired that he would relinquish his place with the attorney, and come down to Alvestone, where Willoughby meant that the same day which gave him Celestina should unite Cathcart to her humble friend.

The joy this unexpected turn of fortune gave to Cathcart can better be imagined than described. That sickness of the soul,[2] which long despondence and anxiety had produced, vanished at once: his immediate care was to secure his sister's and her children's support during his absence; and reserving to himself no more of Willoughby's generous present than sufficed for the expences of his journey, he took a tender leave of Mrs. Elphinstone, assuring her that the first use he would make of his good fortune should be to assist her; he then set out on a hired horse for Alvestone, where he arrived ten days before that which was fixed upon for his patron's happiness and his own.

If Willoughby had been greatly interested for him before he saw him, he was much more so now that he found him very intelligent and well informed, with abilities that might have made his way to any situation of life, and a heart that would have done honour to the most exalted: his knowledge, which was very extensive, was without pedantry, and his gratitude without servility. The meeting between him and Jessy, at which Willoughby contrived that Celestina should be present, was very affecting; and after the first transports of happiness so unexpected had a little subsided, Willoughby explained to them his views for the future. "You, my dear Jessy," said he, "must not think of leaving your grandfather, who must know nothing of your marriage while he lives, which can, according to the course of nature, be only a very little time; and as you may see each other every day, this partial separation may for that little time be easily

---

1 A person under the protection of another in a superior position.
2 Cf. Proverbs 13.12: "[...] hope deferred maketh the heart sick," a frequent allusion in Smith's work.

borne. As for you, Cathcart, you will stay with me: I have, in consequence of my new plan of life, many regulations to make, and many accounts to settle, in which you can be of great use to me. Poor Beechcroft, my old steward, is in his eightieth year, and the palsy has lately made such ravages in his intellects, that he is unequal to the common business of his office; while he lives however, and thinks himself capable of executing his trust, I am very unwilling to mortify him by taking the affairs out of his hands: at his death I shall not replace him, but become my own steward; and you, my good friend, can be of the most effectual service to me in preparing every thing for this arrangement: while your neighbourhood to the estate of which you will probably soon become master, will give you an opportunity of inspecting it, and settling those plans for the future which will I hope and believe make you a very fortunate man."

While the considerate kindness of Willoughby endeared him every hour to Celestina, and while the hearts of Cathcart and Jessy overflowed with gratitude, it would have been hardly possible for a happier party to have been any where found than that which now occasionally inhabited Alvestone, if the painful recollection of Willoughby's violated promise could have been entirely expelled from the conscious recollection of Celestina, and if Vavasour had not sometimes felt towards Celestina something bordering on serious love, which was a sentiment so new to him, who had never thought with respectful affection of any woman before, and had passed too much of his time in scenes of fashionable debauchery, that he hardly knew himself what it meant. He formed however no designs, for his temper was generous, candid, and artless; so artless indeed that he took no pains to conceal what he felt almost without understanding his feelings; and frequently fixed his eyes on Celestina with so impassioned a look, or spoke to her, or of her, with such unreserved marks of fondness and admiration, that Jessy and Cathcart both saw it with some alarm; but Willoughby, too liberal for jealousy, and knowing his friend more inclined to general libertinism among the looser part of the sex than capable of a particular attachment to any woman of character; sure of Celestina's affection, and imputing Vavasour's attentions to his admiration of beauty wherever found, either noticed not his manners, or held them to be wholly without consequence; while Celestina, perfectly unconscious of the power of her own charms, treated him with that affectionate familiarity which his own open and lively manners encouraged, and which his friendship for Willoughby, and the obligations they both owed to him, justified.

Only three days were now to intervene before that fixed for the double wedding which was to be celebrated in the parish church at Alvestone, in the presence only of two trusty servants, and Vavasour, who was to act as father to both the brides.

Very different prospects of life from those which now were before Willoughby and Celestina, had opened to Mr. and Mrs. Molyneux, who, on their arrival in Ireland, had found Sir Oswald Molyneux just alive: he lingered unexpectedly a few weeks after their arrival, and then died, leaving to his son an immense fortune, of which Sir Philip[1] hastened to take possession, and to display, as soon as decency permitted, his wealth and his interest; while Matilda, now Lady Molyneux, lost no opportunity of availing herself of the *eclat*[2] which almost boundless fortune gave to novelty. Nobody was so much followed and admired; no taste was so universally adopted, no parties so splendidly attended, as hers; and having thus attained the summit of what she fancied happiness, she was in no haste to return to England till she had exhausted the felicity Ireland offered her, and cheerfully acquiesced in her husband's proposal of staying one summer at their magnificent seat about twenty miles from Dublin. In the mean time she had heard from her brother, whose resentment towards her husband did not extend to her, of his having broke with the Castlenorths, and his intentions in regard to Celestina. She disliked both Lady Castlenorth and her daughter, and therefore was pleased with their mortification and disappointment: she had now no pecuniary claims on her brother, and heard therefore with indifference his resolution to marry a woman without fortune; and as to Celestina, though she was incapable of any affection for her, yet she thought she would make a good quiet wife for her brother, and be well adapted to that insipid domestic life, his turn for which she had always pitied and despised. As Willoughby's just resentment against Sir Philip had never given her any concern, she gave herself no trouble to remove it; and Sir Philip himself, above all attention for the feelings of others, and too much of a man of the very first fashion to understand the claims of relationship, or to feel those of friendship, was as unconcerned as if no such resentment had ever been deserved; and while they both enjoyed their newly acquired consequence in Ireland, Willoughby was suffered to

---

1 As the son of a baronet, Matilda's husband now inherits his father's title and estates and becomes Sir Philip Molyneux.
2 Fame, celebrity.

proceed his own way at Alvestone without remonstrance and almost without notice.

But neither the neglect of his sister, or the sullen resentment of his uncle and Lady Castlenorth, from whom he heard nothing, now gave Willoughby any concern: his happiness it was out of their power to disturb or prevent, since one day only intervened before he was to be the husband of Celestina.

Chapter XIV

Vavasour, born to a splendid fortune, and left by the early death of his parents to the care of guardians, who, while they took sufficient care of his property, had very little influence over his mind and his morals, had never yet formed a wish which it was not immediately in his power to gratify: the growing inclination, therefore, that he found toward Celestina, was painful and uneasy to him, for he had too much honour, and too true a regard for Willoughby, to suffer a thought injurious to him to dwell on his mind; and had he been capable of entertaining wishes or forming schemes against his happiness, he knew that Celestina's attachment to him was not to be shaken, and that he should excite her contempt and abhorrence instead of continuing to enjoy that confidence and regard with which she now favoured him.

But the more hopeless his partiality for her was, the more restless he of course became in its encrease: for several days he endeavoured to conquer or at least to conceal it by redoubling his gaiety: he romped, laughed, and rattled, till his violent spirits became very distressing to Celestina: all however would not do; and as he had no notion of enduring any kind of uneasiness while there was a chance of relieving himself, he at length resolved to quit Willoughby, and not to return to him till after he was actually married; and his resolution he prepared to execute the following morning, which was the preceding one to that which was fixed for the marriage.

"I shall leave you this morning, George," said he to Willoughby, as they were at breakfast together.

"Leave me!" cried Willoughby in much surprise: "for what reason?"

"Because I hate all formal ceremonies, and have besides business elsewhere."

"Ridiculous! surely you are not in earnest?"

"Perfectly so, believe me: never more in earnest in my life. I'll come back to you in a week or ten days, but I positively go this very day."

"Thou art a strange fellow, and there is never any telling where to have thee.[1] Did you not promise to be father to the brides?[2] What will Celestina say?"

"Why probably as you do—that I am a strange fellow."

"You make me uneasy, Harry," said Willoughby very gravely. "Whimsical and unsettled as you are, it must be surely something more than mere whim which urges you to leave me at such a time."

"Not at all," answered he gaily: "it is the time in the world you can best spare me; and upon my soul I have business to do which I have foolishly neglected, and which I must either go after now or a fortnight hence, when I intend to be with you; and so, my dear George, we'll talk no more about it: my servants are getting ready, and will be at the door in a minute: oh they are driving round. Well, George, God bless you, my dear fellow. Give my love to the girls, and tell Celestina to save me a great piece of bride cake."

Willoughby would again have remonstrated, but Vavasour, in his wild way, ran on rallying him about his marriage, and refusing to listen to him, till the curricle[3] was ready; into which he stepped, after again promising to return in a fortnight, and immediately drove away.

Willoughby, though long accustomed to these starts of caprice from his thoughtless friend, was equally surprised and disconcerted at a resolution for which he could not account: he was far from the remotest idea of the real cause; and, occupied as his thoughts were by Celestina, he investigated not so deeply the motives of his friend's actions as at another time he might have done.

On the preceding day, moved by his tender reproaches that she had no confidence in his honour, and affected needless precaution, Celestina had acceded to his wishes that she would allow him, as the day was fixed for Thursday, to fetch her to Alvestone in the morning of Wednesday, where Jessy was to meet her, and that she would then take her last leave of her humble abode on Thorpe Common.

As soon, therefore, as Vavasour, was gone, he despatched Cathcart for Jessy, and hastened himself to Celestina, who was ready for him.

---

1 Cf. *1 Henry IV*, 3.3.115.
2 To formally "give" the brides to their husbands as required in the marriage service.
3 Light, fast carriage pulled by two horses abreast, popular with young men.

As they journeyed towards the house that was henceforth to be their home, Willoughby, with more than usual tenderness in his voice and manner, entered into a more minute detail than he had ever yet done of the plans he had formed for their future life: with the sanguine hand of youthful hope, he drew a picture of uninterrupted felicity, which Celestina, involuntarily sighing, thought too perfect to be realized; and with timid apprehension, for which she could not account and was unwilling to betray, she internally asked herself wherefore she could expect to deserve or enjoy blessings so much superior to the common lot of humanity.

All, however, that might have been to another an alloy to happiness, was none to her, so far as it related only to herself. In marrying her, Willoughby had resigned all prospect of ever restoring his family to the splendid fortune and high consequence possessed by his ancestors, nor could he even retrieve the estate he had left, or keep up the place he was so fond of, but by relinquishing all superfluous expences, and confining himself to that mode of life, which was some years since adopted, but would now be thought below the pretensions of a man possessed only of a thousand a year: in fact Willoughby found, on a close inspection of his affairs, that by living within that income, he might in about ten years clear, without dismembering, his estate. "It is enough for happiness, my Celestina," he would say; "it is enough to afford us all the decencies, and all the comforts of life, and to assist those who may not have either. Oh how little reason we shall have to envy those who have more." Celestina assented with her whole heart; and if ever an uneasy reflection arose there for a moment, representing that for her he resigned the splendour and luxury in which he might have lived, she recollected her opinion of the greater part of those who moved amid a succession of those luxuries, and asked herself whether there was one among them who was so much respected by others, or so well content with himself, as Willoughby probably would be, living as he proposed. She remembered how often, when she was accustomed to see nearly[1] many of those, who, by adventitious advantages, dazzle at a distance, she had been compelled to assent to the truth of that severe expression of the satirist's, which says, that it may be seen—

---

1 Close up.

"Of how small estimation is exorbitant wealth in the sight of God by his bestowing it on the most unworthy of all mortals."[1]

The departure of Vavasour, of which Willoughby had, with some marks of regret and surprise, on his first meeting Celestina informed her, had given her concern, as it seemed to have been a disappointment to him; but for herself, she felt rather relieved by the absence of a too lively guest. There was at times an unguarded vivacity about him, of which she was not always able to check the excess; and though she had never any idea of his partiality to her, nor thought him capable of a serious attachment to any woman, there had of late been a warmth and earnestness in his manner which she was afraid of being called prudish if she attempted to repress, and yet she could not but feel that it was improper to allow it in her present situation, and would be more so when she became the wife of Willoughby. On their arrival at Alvestone, the lawyer was ready with the settlements: they were immediately executed[2] in the presence of Cathcart and Jessy; and when that unpleasant ceremony[3] was over, a walk filled up the time till dinner. Nothing was ever so gay and happy as Willoughby: Celestina was now mistress of his house: his happiness was secured almost beyond the reach of fate: and since only a few hours were to intervene before their marriage, he tenderly chid Celestina for her pensive gravity, and endeavoured to engage her thoughts by necessary arrangements that he proposed in the house, and by enlarging on those topics which she had listened to with so much complacency in the morning.

---

1 "D.A," (Dr. John Arbuthnot), quoted in Alexander Pope's *Thoughts on Various Subjects*, no. LXXII: "We may see the small value God has for Riches by the People he gives them to."
2 Signed, and witnessed by Cathcart and Jessy.
3 Pre-marital legal contracts or settlements, as noted earlier, secured rights to the wife, who without them would be wholly dependent on her husband's favour for an annual allowance or financial support after his death. Thinking about the settlements is unpleasant because it must take into account such matters as the jointure, the sum Celestina will receive if Willoughby dies first, and how her daughters' or younger sons' rights will be secured if she dies first and he remarries. The bride's family would usually initiate any legal settlement, as the woman had everything to lose if she married without one. Here Willoughby arranges it, providing generously for Celestina, though the agreement would not come into force until after the marriage.

After dinner another walk was proposed: but just as they were rising from table, a servant entered with a letter for Willoughby, which he said had been brought express from Exeter.

He broke the seal, which, like the hand of the direction, was unknown to him: he ran over the contents hastily, changing countenance as he read; and then enquiring if the messenger waited, hastily left the room.

Celestina, who watched his looks, was alarmed both by them, and his manner of leaving the room. A moment's reflection subdued her apprehensions; but they were presently renewed and heightened by his sending to speak with Cathcart; who, after being with him almost a quarter of an hour, returned by his directions to inform her, that he was gone on horseback to Exeter to meet some people who had sent to him about business which would admit of no delay; he begged Cathcart to tell her that it would be soon dispatched, and that he should certainly return in a few hours.

Celestina knew, from his own account, every circumstance of his fortune; she knew that except the mortgages on his estate, the interest of which had been punctually paid, he had no pecuniary claims to answer but his debt to Vavasour: she was equally certain that he had no dispute with any body, and that therefore it could not be an affair of honour,[1] and she thought it certain that if Lady Molyneux or any of his relations had been in the neighbourhood, he would have made no mystery of their arrival: his abrupt departure, therefore, without seeing her, surprised and troubled her; and neither her own reason, which urged how unlikely it was that any disagreeable business should detain him, or the arguments of Cathcart and Jessy, could quiet or mitigate the anxiety which every moment of his absence encreased.

Four, five, six hours, had now been passed by Celestina, while it was light, in traversing the avenue and the road that led towards Exeter; and after it became dark, in listening at the door to every noise. It was ten o'clock: a still, star-light night: a low wind conveyed now the distant murmur of the water-fall in the park, now the voices of men from the village, where every thing soon sunk into repose. Neither Cathcart nor Jessy could longer disguise their fears, though neither knew what to dread: but while they affected to believe Celestina's apprehensions in great measure groundless, their anxious

---

1 A quarrel that could only be settled by a duel with swords or (more usually) pistols.

returns to the door to listen, their restless inquietude, and various conjectures, convinced her too evidently that they participated the fears they pretended to condemn.

At length about eleven o'clock, a horse, or as they were willing to believe, horses, were heard to come fast along the road: the park gate opened and shut with violence. It was Willoughby they all fondly hoped: all ran out eagerly, impatient to meet him: as the horseman approached, however, they distinguished him to be not Willoughby, but the servant who had attended him.

"Where is your Master, Hugh?" said Celestina; "is he coming? is he well?"

The man took a letter from his pocket, and answered in a dejected tone—"No, Madam, not coming: he sent me with this letter to Mr. Cathcart."

Celestina followed trembling, while Cathcart ran into the hall, and by the light which hung there, read these words:

"Dear Cathcart, come to me immediately. I shall not return to-night. I know not if—But assure Celestina of my safety. Lose not a moment in coming to

yours ever, G. W."

Swan, Exeter,
Wednesday night.

The painful suspense Celestina had before endured, was happiness and ease in comparison of the vague but terrible apprehensions that now seized her. What could detain him against his wishes? what meant the unfinished sentence—"I know not if—?" what could he want with Cathcart? and why not disclose the cause of his stay, and his business with Cathcart, if it was only an affair of little consequence, since he could not but know how much his sudden departure must alarm her. The note too seemed to have been written with a trembling hand; the lines were crooked, and the letters hardly formed, and the paper blotted: all denoted hurry and confusion, very unlike Willoughby's manner in matters of mere business; and the indications of some impending evil, alarming enough in themselves, were exaggerated by the terrors which had now taken entire possession of the mind of Celestina. Unable to restrain her emotions, she ran, hardly knowing whither she went, to the stable, where the servant who had brought the note was getting ready the horse on which Cathcart was to go. She eagerly questioned the man who was with his master? He answered that he did not know: that he saw nobody with him, but he had heard at the inn that two ladies had come hither that morning, who had sent the messenger to Alvestone; that he believed they had been with his master, but he did not know, and when his master spoke to him, and gave him the letter for Mr. Cathcart, he was alone, and seemed very uneasy, saying however little more to him than to desire he would make what haste he could.

This account served only to encrease the terrible obscurity which tormented Celestina. A thousand other questions occurred. Were these ladies yet at the inn? Did they travel in their own chaise? Had they servants with them? Hugh could not answer the first question; but the other two being such as lay more within the reach of his observation, he answered that there were certainly neither servants nor horses at the inn belonging to any stranger when he came away.

Cathcart was by this time ready; and seeing the extreme inquietude of Celestina, he assumed the appearance of tranquillity he was far from feeling, said that it was probably some business relative to Mr. Willoughby's estates, which had been overlooked and neglected; that at all events he would be back in a few hours, when it was almost certain that if Mr. Willoughby did not return himself, he should be commissioned fully to acquaint her of the reasons of his detention, and convince her that her fears for his safety were groundless: in the mean time he besought her to endeavour to quiet her spirits and to take some repose. Cathcart then departed; and Celestina, leaning on the arm of Jessy, returned to the house; but to follow the advice he had given her, was not in her power; the little she had gathered from the servant served to awaken new alarms, not less painful, though very different from those which had at first assailed her: then she had a confused idea that the abrupt departure of Vavasour had been occasioned by some misunderstanding between them, which had produced a challenge;[1] it was unlikely, but it was not impossible: now she gave up that conjecture for another, and supposed that Willoughby might have formed some connection or engagement with some woman, who, hearing of his intended marriage, had thus prevented it by using her prior claim to his hand: this supposition was, however, more improbable than the other, from his known integrity and unblemished honour, from his long and tender attachment to her, and from the whole tenor of his morals and his conduct; but however unlikely, it was not quite impossible;

---

1 To a duel.

and the anxious and alarmed spirit of Celestina ran over the remotest possibilities, but found in all only exchange of anguish.

As Cathcart had promised to return in a few hours, Celestina, certain of not being able to sleep, would not go to bed; and Jessy, who shared all her solicitude, sat up with her. As the time approached that Cathcart had named for the probable period of his return, they were again both at the window, and again eagerly listening to every noise. The sun arose, but discovered not the object of their solicitude; and Celestina, now unable to rest within the house, besought Jessy to go down with her to the end of the long avenue of elms and into the road, as if the attempt to meet those they expected rendered the suspense less distracting.

Weary of conjecture, and fatigued both in mind and body, they moved slowly and melancholy along: neither of them spoke, for neither had any comfort to offer the other. Of the labourers, who were come by this time to their work, they enquired if they had heard of their master, or seen Mr. Cathcart on the road. But no intelligence could be gained of either. The peasants, however, alarmed by the questions and by the looks of those who asked them, all eagerly offered to go any where, to do any thing their master's service might require, and begged Celestina to employ them: but though she had several times, during the long and anxious night, thought of sending a messenger with a letter to Willoughby, or even of going herself, she now remembered that all the intelligence she could gain from the first expedient, she would probably receive from Cathcart before any messenger could get to Exeter; and for the second, that it might be displeasing to Willoughby, were she to appear thus prying into his action and mistrustful of his honour.

Nothing, therefore, remained but to bear, with what firmess she could, suspense which every moment rendered more insupportably cruel. Hardly conscious of what she was doing, and insensible of personal fatigue, she had advanced near a mile beyond the park, and had partly crossed a sandy heath, over which the high road lay, when Jessy hastily cried out that Cathcart was coming; he saw them at the same moment; and hastening on, leaped from his horse as soon as he came near them.

His countenance was little likely to quiet their fears: he was as pale as death, and his lips trembled as he spoke to Celestina, and assured her, in a voice that seemed to contradict the words it hardly articulated, that Mr. Willoughby was well, perfectly well, and had authorised him to say everything to her that might make her easy.

The hurried manner in which he spoke this, the impression of

uneasiness on his countenance, and the improbability that Willoughby should be well and not return himself, all struck forcibly on the
mind of Celestina, and convinced her that something very fatal had
happened. "You deceive me, Cathcart," cried she in the wild and
tremulous voice of despair, "I know you deceive me. Something very
dreadful has befallen him: he is dead, or dying: I will go to him, however—I will know the worst."

Cathcart now took her hands, and with the utmost earnestness
began again to repeat his assurances that Willoughby was not only
alive but well.

Celestina, interrupting him, asked—"Why then do I not see him?
why is he detained? and what business of fatal import could keep
him so long? Cathcart, I will not, I cannot be deceived: tell me at
once what I have to suffer, and I will endeavour to bear it; but this
incertitude, these apprehensions, I cannot endure another hour, nor
another moment."

While this dialogue passed, he had taken one of her arms within
his, and having made a sign to Jessy to take the other, they led her
gently towards Alvestone park gate. Cathcart was silent for a
moment, as if considering how he could soften the shock which it
was necessary for him to give her; while Celestina continued impatiently urging him to tell her the worst, whatever it might be. "Let
me repeat to you, dearest Madam," said he, "let me repeat to you, that
you have nothing to fear for the life of our dear friend; and surely
whatever other intelligence I have to impart ..."

"Other intelligence!" cried Celestina: "you have then something
to impart which all my fortitude is required to sustain. Willoughby—
but no! it is impossible: he cannot be unworthy—he cannot have
cruelly deceived me—it is impossible...."

"It is indeed," replied Cathcart, "in my opinion impossible for Mr.
Willoughby to be guilty of any unworthy action. You, Miss de
Mornay, have, I am convinced, a strength of understanding very
uncommon...."

"Cathcart," cried Celestina with energy, "this is no time for flattery: prove your opinion of my understanding, by daring to entrust
me with this fearful secret: the knowledge of it cannot give me so
much pain as your hesitation."

"I would very fain obey you!" replied he. "What then will you say
if I tell you, that, though I am wholly ignorant of the cause of a resolution so extraordinary, so unexpected, I am afraid it will be very
long before you see Willoughby again, and that he is now many
miles distant from us; though upon my soul, by all my hopes here

and hereafter, I swear that I neither know the motives of his departure nor whither he is gone."

Celestina, prepared as she was for some heavy blow, found this hideous uncertainty more than she could sustain: that Willoughby should have quitted her, probably for ever, without assigning any cause, at the very moment they were to be united; that he should not himself have seen her to have softened the pain this cruel and unaccountable event must inflict; that he should not even have written to her, but should, in this abrupt and unfeeling way, abandon her to all the misery of endless conjecture, regret, and disappointment; were circumstances so unexpected, so insupportable, that her reason, which would have sustained her in almost any other exigence, seemed for a moment to yield to this: she became extremely faint, her knees trembled, a cold dew hung on her forehead, and all the effort she could make was, to signify by a motion of her hand that she could go no farther.

They were then more than half a mile from the park gate: but the road along which they were passing was worn, and a bank on either side offered her a seat. Cathcart and Jessy sat down by her, both silent, and almost as much affected as she was. She learned her head on Jessy, and after a moment a deep sigh a little relieved her. She turned her eyes mournfully on Cathcart, with an expression he perfectly understood, as seeming to say, "tell me all—and I will try to endure it."

"Do not think, I conjure you, my dear Madam," continued he, "that the ardent and tender affection of Mr. Willoughby for you is diminished. Were it possible for me to do justice to the agonies I saw him in, when he told me that a strange necessity—a necessity he could not explain—compelled him to quit you:—if language could describe the wretchedness in which he seemed to be involved...."

"Do not describe it, dear Cathcart," said Celestina, speaking with difficulty. "I can bear my own misery, terrible as it is, better than the thoughts of his."

"Mitigate his sufferings then, amiable Miss de Mornay," interrupted Cathcart, "by collecting all your fortitude, and remembering how much reliance you ought to have on his honour and his affection; and let me be able to say, when I write to him, that this sad separation has not injured your health, nor your opinion of him: believe me, such is the only intelligence that can administer any consolation to the torn heart of my noble friend."

"I will try then, Cathcart, that he shall have it. You know where to write to him? He expects to hear from you, and from me he wishes not to hear?"

"He told me," reassumed Cathcart, "that as soon as he was able he would write to you himself: that he was going immediately to London: whither he should go afterwards he knew not; but that hateful mystery—Then he stopped; seemed to repent having said so much; charged me to assure you of his everlasting affection; started from his seat; walked about the room wildly; then again repeated his charge to me that I would not leave you, or suffer Jessy to leave you, but that you would remain at Alvestone till you heard from him; again he hesitated, doubted, and wringing my hand, asked me, with disturbed looks and in a tremulous voice, if ever wretchedness equalled his. I would have besought him to tell me from whence it arose; but as if foreseeing whither my enquiry would tend, he stopped me: 'Cathcart,' cried he, 'you know I have great confidence in you, and that I would entrust you with this fatal mystery, which I go now to clear up; but I have sworn never to divulge the cause of my—what can I say?—Oh! Celestina! best and loveliest of human beings! what must be those sufferings which Willoughby dares not communicate to you!—which your pity and tenderness....' Again he broke off, and hurried out of the room. He returned, however, in a few moments, somewhat more calm; and alarmed as I had been by his agitation, by the wild eagerness of his manner, and the incoherence of his words, I thought it better to soothe him than to attempt to obtain an explanation which it cost him so much even to speak of: I contented myself therefore with assuring him of my implicit obedience to all his commands, and of my conviction that whatever might be your distress and anxiety, you would acquiesce in all his wishes, and that your reliance on him, your affection for him, would not be shaken by this involuntary separation, 'which, dear Sir,' continued I, 'will surely be temporary only': I was going on, but he checked me—'I know not,' said he, with quickness—'I know not—involuntary, God knows it is, but when it will end!—Oh Celestina! is this the day which I have with so much delight anticipated!' He now struck his open hand on his forehead, again started away from me, and again relapsed into all the agonies of sorrow."

Celestina had not hitherto shed a tear. Stunned by the greatness and singularity of her misfortune, terrified by the evil, which its obscurity rendered doubly fearful, her senses were for some moments suspended; but Willoughby weeping, and in despair—Willoughby torn from her by an invisible and resistless hand—awakened all her tenderness, and tears filled her eyes, as, with a deep sigh, she cast them towards heaven, and with clasped hands and in a faint voice cried—"Wherever he goes—whatsoever he does—may God protect and bless him; and if the remembrance of poor Celestina causes him any unhappiness, may he forget her. Indeed, Cathcart," added she, "indeed his happiness, and not my own, has been always the first wish of my heart." She would have gone on, but her voice failed her. After a moment's silence, however, she seemed to have found some degree of fortitude and strength—"Let us return to the house, my dear Jessy," said she, "while I am able, and let us there consider what it will be right to do."

Cathcart, glad to see her more composed than he had dared to hope, now again led her forward with the assistance of Jessy. But their help seemed no longer requisite: she hurried on with as much quickness as if she expected her suspense to be terminated on her reaching the house; where she arrived, out of breath, trembling and agitated. She spoke not, but hurried through the hall into the library, where they usually sat; and there the first object that struck her was Mr. Thorold, the clergyman who had been engaged to marry them, the same who had, at the request of Willoughby, so effectually exerted his zeal and friendship in introducing Jessy Woodburn to her grandfather, and of whose society Willoughby was very fond. He laid down his book on the entrance of Celestina, and prepared to salute her with cheerful congratulations, for it was not now more than eight o'clock; he had put his horse into the stable himself as was his custom, and walked into the library, where he had been some time expecting Willoughby, and began to wonder, as he was a very early riser, at his delay.

All his ideas of bridal festivity however were driven from his mind the moment he beheld the countenance of Celestina. "My dear Miss de Mornay," cried he, approaching her, "are you ill?—has any thing happened?" Celestina, struck by the sight of him, could not answer, but sat down in the first chair she found, and Cathcart, seeing how greatly she was affected, took Mr. Thorold by the arm and led him into the garden.

Celestina in the mean time leaning against Jessy, who hung weeping over her, attempted again to recover her resolution and composure. She sighed deeply. "Jessy, my love," said she, when she could command her voice, "I wish to return to Thorpe Heath. Methinks I am now an intruder here: send, therefore, for some conveyance for me; and think for me, my dear friend, for I fear I am incapable of judging for myself."

The timid and soft tempered Jessy was but little likely to direct or support her. "Let us, dearest Madam," said she, "speak to Cathcart again before you take any resolution: let us hear Mr. Thorold's opinion."

"Do you then attend them for that purpose," replied Celestina, "for myself, I cannot hear them. I should I think be better were I left alone for a few moments: I will go, therefore, to my own room—my own room? alas! I have none in this house! Let me go, however, Jessy, to that which I used to call mine. I would recall my dissipated and distracted spirits, I would acquire some degree of reason and resignation; and since wretchedness is now irrevocably mine, I would teach this rebellious heart to submit to it."

Jessy answered not; and Celestina rising, walked slowly through the hall, leaning on her friend's arm, towards the stair case. As she passed, she saw Willoughby's hat and gloves on the table where he generally placed them; a book he had been reading to her, as they sauntered in the garden the preceding day, lay by them: Celestina started as if a spectre had met her: the painful contrast between her present situation and that of a few hours before struck her forcibly: she shuddered, and snatching up the book, hastened away with it, as if she apprehended somebody would take it from her.

When they reached the door of the apartment which she had chosen for her dressing room, she turned to Jessy, and with a melancholy and forced composure bade her adieu for an hour. "You will go, my dear," said she, "to Mr. Thorold and Mr. Cathcart, and say to the former, with my compliments, that I will endeavour to see him if he will be kind enough to stay till ten o'clock and breakfast here, and tell him too that I depend much on his friendly advice, and that it cannot be given to any being who wants it more or will be more sensible of its value."

END OF THE FIRST VOLUME.

VOLUME II

Chapter I

The reflections of Celestina when she was alone were full of bitterness and anguish. It was in vain that she wearied herself with conjectures on the cause of her misfortune: she could find no probability in any that presented themselves. It could not be caprice, nor that cruel delight which men have sometimes taken in wantonly inflicting pain, and torturing by disappointment the hearts they have taught to love them, for of such conduct she knew Willoughby to be incapable; it could not be a dispute with Vavasour or any other young man, for such, however alarming, must soon have been decided; nor could it be any pecuniary difficulty that had thus divided them, since Willoughby, in talking over their future prospects, had related to her the situation of his fortune with the utmost clearness and precision; it could hardly be a prior matrimonial engagement, for from his infancy he had loved her, he had repeatedly told her that he never had the least partiality for any other woman, and he was truth and candour itself; it could not be any impediment raised by the Castlenorths, for however great might be their displeasure and disappointment, they had no power over Willoughby's actions, and he did not love them well enough to make it probable that their persuasions or remonstrances could induce him to give up the favourite project of his life, and abandon her whom he so passionately loved to disgrace and misery.

Whatever was the cause, however, of the sudden resolution he had taken, misery was certain: she observed that in the dialogue which Cathcart repeated as having passed between him and Willoughby, no mention was made of a probability of his return—no hope thrown out, that their union was rather suspended than put an end to. All was dark and comfortless;[1] and in the mystery which surrounded the whole affair, there was something of terror and apprehension which seemed more insupportable than the certainty of any evil except Willoughby's death.

Cathcart, however, had given her a motive to support her courage, in telling her that nothing but the knowledge of her bearing his loss without injury to her health or her affection for him,

---

1 Cf. *The Tragedy of King Lear* 3.7.83.

could soothe or diminish the anguish with which Willoughby was himself oppressed. "Let me endeavour then," said she, "to give him this satisfaction, as the last proof I shall perhaps ever be able to give him of my tender, my unalterable love. Condemned as I am to everlasting regret, dashed from the summit of happiness to long and hopeless sorrow for the rest of my life, let my resolution in suffering with calmness shew that I should have deserved the happiness which heaven once seemed to have settled as my lot. Heaven only knows wherefore I am condemned to lose and lament it."

The solemn promise which Willoughby had owned his mother had asked and received of him in her last moments now occurred to her. "Perhaps it is for the intended breach of that promise," cried she, "that we are punished: yet from whence? the ear that heard it, the anxious maternal heart that obtained it, are dust! My benefactress comes not from the grave to claim it: it was known only to her, to her son, and to me. Who is there who could enforce it now, and to whom would Willoughby listen, after obviating all the objections I urged against its violation?"

This fatal promise, however, had always hung heavy on the heart of Celestina, even in her happiest moments, and she seemed now to be paying the price of having ever consented to break it. Still, still the inexplicable mystery remained; and the hand from which the blow came that had divided her and Willoughby was equally hid in obscurity.

When a misfortune, however heavy, is certain, the mind sinks resistless beneath it; and feeling all remedy ineffectual, it ceases all attempt to apply any: but this was not the case with Celestina: while the cause of her being torn from Willoughby was unknown, there appeared a possibility that it might be removed; and though he had held out no such hope in his conversation with Cathcart, her reason now seized this idea as her only resource. He had besought her to bear their separation with patience; he had hopes then surely that it would end: he had entreated her not to forget her affection for him; surely he had expectations then that he might again claim it. Her sanguine temper encouraged these faint rays of comfort, which a few moments before seemed to be extinguished for ever. The first shock was passed; the tears she had shed had relieved her overburthened heart, and she prepared with some degree of serenity to go down to Mr. Thorold, Cathcart, and Jessy, and to consult with them on what she ought to do.

When she again entered the room, the little group which were assembled in it, their melancholy and anxious looks, and the different expectations with which their meeting had been appointed, combined to affect her, and to shake the little resolution she had with so much difficulty acquired: she sat down, however, and Mr. Thorold, with a degree of fatherly tenderness, approached her and took her hand.

"My dear young friend," said the excellent man, "this dignified composure is worthy of your excellent understanding. Do you think me deserving the honour of being your adviser, if, in the present state of circumstances, you feel that you want one?"

"I do indeed severely feel," replied Celestina faultering, "the necessity of a friend who is able to advise me; and where, dear Sir, can I find one so equal to it, if you will but undertake the trouble?"

"Well then," replied Mr. Thorold, "we will not go over the occurrences that have happened, nor attempt to account for them: some unforeseen events have divided you and my friend Willoughby, and I am very sure, that whatever they are, they must, if irretrievable, embitter the rest of his life: he wishes you, as I understand from Mr. Cathcart, to remain here at least till you have letters from him. Do you intend to do so?"

"I hardly know," answered Celestina faintly, "what I ought to do."

"It seems to me," said Mr. Thorold, "that whatever reason has had so much influence on him as to compel him to quit you, should render your abode in his house improper."

"I will return then, sir, since that is your opinion, to the lodging I left at Thorpe Heath."

"That will be very melancholy and unpleasant to you I fear."

"It certainly will: but what have I to do now but to learn to suffer? Local circumstances will have little power to add to the sorrow I must endure, while uncertain of what is become of Mr. Willoughby: doubting whether I may not have been the cause that some evil has befallen him, and sure of nothing—but that I must be wretched if I never see him again."

"I would very fain[1] comfort without deceiving you if I could. I hope you will see him again: yet nothing surely but some very extraordinary event could have taken him from you; but you hear that he was well—that he promised to write to you: it is possible that letter may explain what all our conjectures can do little in clearing up: let us leave them, therefore; and do you, my dear Miss de Mornay, resolve to fulfil his parting injunctions as far as prudence

---

1 I would very much wish to.

will permit. I cannot say I approve of your staying here, or of your going back to indulge your uneasiness in the mournful seclusion of your cottage; let me propose therefore a middle way, by which you will receive this expected letter without quitting the neighbourhood, and be ready to obey any wish of our dear Willoughby, without receiving it at Thorpe Heath, where you would have nobody to assist you in its execution. Will you go home with me?"

Celestina, who already felt the value of such a friend as she seemed to have acquired in Mr. Thorold, and who foresaw that she must lose Jessy, who could not stay long from her grandfather, would willingly have embraced this offer. She knew that Willoughby had the warmest friendship for Mr. Thorold, and that he would probably approve of such a proposal; but she was unacquainted with his wife, and dreaded to intrude herself into a family where she might find only the master of it disposed to receive her: she objected therefore to the trouble she should give, and to the impropriety of introducing herself, thus unasked, to the acquaintance of his lady; but Mr. Thorold obviated all her objections, assured her she should have an apartment to herself, and that his wife would consider her as his daughter, his daughter as her sister; and Celestina, who could not think without pain of going alone to Thorpe Heath, which she had left with prospects so very different, and from whence her books and cloaths had been removed, consented to go with Mr. Thorold, and to remain with him at least till she heard from Willoughby.

It was then settled that at least part of the original errand which had brought Mr. Thorold to Alvestone should be completed, and that Cathcart and Jessy should be married, since her father was already waiting to give her away, and since Cathcart was to remain at Alvestone by the particular directions of Willoughby on their parting. Celestina could not be present at the ceremony, but while it was performing prepared herself with as much resolution as she could for her little journey. When they returned from the altar, she kissed in silence the weeping Jessy, who clung round her unable to bid her adieu: she recommended to Cathcart the closest adherence to every injunction laid on him by Willoughby, and besought him to come himself over to her with the expected letter as soon as it arrived; and then with faultering steps went to the chaise which was in waiting for her by Mr. Thorold's orders. He placed himself by her; and she was thus removed, probably as she thought for ever, from the house, of which, only a few hours before, she considered herself as the fortunate mistress.

As she passed along the avenue, the bench under one of the great elms, where she had so often sat with Willoughby in their childhood, and where only a few days before he had been recalling those delightful times to her recollection, struck her most: it looked like a monument to the memory of lost happiness! As the great gate of the park shut after the carriage, she felt exiled for ever from the only spot in the world that contained any object interesting her; and though little disposed to think of poetry, almost involuntarily repeated—

"O unexpected stroke, worse than of death!
Must I thus leave thee paradise? thus leave
Thee native soil, these happy walks and shades...?"[1]

Mr. Thorold, to whom sorrow was sacred, attempted not to call off her thoughts from their present mournful employment; but glad to see that her sorrow broke not out in those violent and convulsive expressions which many women would have given way to, he contented himself with administering to her in silence all the offices of friendship; and when they arrived at his house, which was about five miles from Alvestone, he got out and went in first to prepare his family for the reception of their unexpected visitor. After a few moments he returned, and assured her that both Mrs. Thorold and his daughter would be happy to see her, and think themselves honoured by her abode with them; "but," added he, "perhaps you had rather go to your own chamber than be introduced immediately to strangers." Celestina had already repented of having accepted Mr. Thorold's offer, however friendly it was, and felt that in her present state of mind the most forlorn solitude would have been better for her than the restraint she must unavoidably submit to, and the enquiries that, if not by words, the looks of all who saw her would make into the cause of the strange revolution that had happened in her circumstances: but it was now too late to retreat, and she determined to go through at once a ceremony, the delay of which would not render it less distressing.

She answered, therefore, with more steadiness of voice than could be expected, that she could not too soon avail herself of Mrs. Thorold's kindness, and was immediately introduced to her and her only unmarried daughter.

Mrs. Thorold was what the world agrees to call a very good sort of woman, but one of those who are best described by negatives; she had no positive failings, but a sort of feminine pride, which made her

---

1   John Milton, *Paradise Lost*, Book XI, 268-70.

very anxious that none of her neighbours, at least none of the rank of private gentlewomen, should have handsomer cloaths, or better furniture, or a nicer house; and while she carefully guarded her own dignity, she indulged somewhat too much curiosity in enquiring into the minutest particular by which the consequence of others could be diminished or encreased.

Mr. Thorold, whose strong understanding taught him to see and bear her foibles, had taken the utmost pains to check in his daughters a propensity to imitate them. The three elder had been married some years, and were settled in the neighbourhood of London. Arabella, the youngest, was now about two and twenty, rather pretty in her person, and pleasing in her manners: with much of her father's sense, she had a little of the vanity of her mother; but it had taken another turn: though she dressed fashionably, and her sisters always took care, by sending her the newest modes from London, to enable her to give the *ton*[1] in that remote country,[2] she piqued herself less on that advantage than on being reckoned extremely accomplished. In consequence of this rage, she played on several kinds of instruments mechanically, for she had no ear, and sung in a feigned voice, for nature had denied her a natural one. In languages she was more successful: under the instructions of her father she had early been taught Latin, and that knowledge facilitated her acquiring the French and Italian, which she wrote and understood better than she spoke them: she took likenesses in crayons; painted landscapes in oil; and the apartments were furnished with her worsted works and embroidery.

Celestina had hardly gone through the first ceremonies of her reception than she found a relief from the inquisitive looks of the mother and daughter, in admiring these performances. "You do my trifling productions a great deal of honour," said Miss Thorold, "and your praise cannot fail of being very gratifying to me, as I understand you are yourself so extremely accomplished."

"Indeed," answered Celestina, "you have been misinformed. I can boast of no such advantage: but I am extremely fond of music and of drawing, and used to please a very partial friend by attempting them: since her death, my time has passed in a very unsettled way, and I have now no motive to tempt me to recover what in that desultory life I have lost of the little I knew."

---

1 Set the fashion.
2 County (Devonshire).

Miss Thorold, who had heard Celestina represented as excelling, was not sorry to find she possessed no such very great advantages over her; and Celestina, to whom any thing was preferable to conversation, pressing her to sit down to the harpsichord, she complied with that air of confidence which the certainty of excelling gives; and till dinner she continued to play sonatas and lessons, all of which Celestina failed not to applaud, though she had so little idea of what she heard, that she could not have assigned one to its proper composer: her thoughts were fled after Willoughby; and from the strange reverse she had experienced, nothing had power to detach them. Dinner, tea, and supper, at length were over; the presence of Mr. Thorold prevented his wife from asking questions which were every moment rising to her lips; and Celestina was permitted to retire to her own room at an early hour. The extreme fatigue she had suffered the night before, and the solicitude of spirit she had endured for so many hours, had so exhausted nature that she sunk into slumber; but it was disturbed and broken by hideous dreams. In the morning, however, she found herself better: her mind had not yet recovered from its consternation, but she could now think of all that had happened with more steadiness. In the letter she expected from Willoughby, she had something to look forward to, which might alleviate but could not encrease her anxiety, as whatever cleared up the mystery would, she thought, be a relief to her, and certainty, however painful, she was sure she could endure better than wild conjectures and terrifying suspense.

Chapter II

All the following day passed without any tidings of Cathcart, in search of whom the anxious eyes of Celestina were continually turned towards the window. Mr. Thorold went out to his farm and among his parishioners in his usual way, and had charged his wife to let Celestina be mistress of her time, and not to importune her with questions or even with conversation: to Arabella also he had given the same injunctions: but the native politeness of Celestina had made both the ladies believe she was pleased by their conversation and interested in their concerns, and to avoid the appearance of rudeness or singularity, Celestina now forced herself into some degree of attention to their endeavours to entertain her, listened to the details Mrs. Thorold gave of the affairs of the neighbourhood, and gave her daughter her opinion of the most elegant mixture of colours in a workbag she was composing for one of her sisters, heard with patient politeness a long poem, written by young Thorold, who was now at Oxford, and assented to the justice of Arabella's complaints that there was very little rational society in the country, that every body now forsook their distant seats to pass their summers at some watering place, and that unless one could enter into the amusements of an inferior circle, there was to be found in the country no amusement at all.

So passed the long long day, and another and another in the same manner, relieved by nothing but the silent though tender sympathy with which Mr. Thorold himself seemed to enter into the feelings of his fair, unhappy guest. He looked at her with eyes that told her all the concern her situation gave him; and appeared hurt that both his wife and daughter, though they behaved to her with all the attention and kindness possible, seemed not to understand, that on a mind like hers, in its present situation, the common occurrences of life could not be obtruded but to pain and fatigue. He however spoke not to them, of what, he feared, they had not delicacy of feeling enough to comprehend; but knowing of the expected letter from Willoughby, he became towards the noon of the fourth day almost as anxious for its arrival, and almost as uneasy at its long delay, as Celestina herself.

Her solicitude was by that time become insupportable. She could no longer conceal it under the appearance of attending to her hosts; but took the opportunity of Mrs. Thorold's being engaged in domestic business, and Arabella at her music, to steal into the garden; where she hid herself in a sort of alcove cut in an hedge of holly and other evergreens that bounded the garden towards the road, and there gave way to the tormenting apprehensions that corroded her heart. It was now Tuesday: Willoughby had been gone since the preceding Wednesday evening; and had he gone to London immediately, and written from thence as he promised, the letter must long since have reached Cathcart by the return of the post: but she knew that unless he was greatly changed it was not to the post[1] he would entrust the conveyance of a letter on which her existence perhaps depended; the delay therefore aggravated all the terrors she felt; but another day past, and she was still obliged to endure them. To disguise her distress however was impracticable; and without hoping to impose upon her friends by so common an artifice, she was at length compelled to say, that she had an headache which was very severe unless when she was

---

1 But send it by express, though this was more expensive.

in the open air; and that she was rendered by it quite incapable of conversation.

Having thus obtained the liberty of wandering alone in the garden, she passed there the whole morning of Wednesday: sometimes reflecting with the bitterest regret on the different prospects which were before her on the Wednesday of the preceding week, and sometimes bewildering herself in conjectures, on the cause of their having thus vanished from her.

Spring had within that period made a rapid progress; but Celestina no longer heeded the beauties that surrounded her: hers was now that state of mind when—

"'Tis nought but gloom around; the darken'd Sun
Loses his light; the rosy-bosom'd Spring
To weeping Fancy pines, and yon bright arch,
Contracted, bends into a dusky vault: —
All Nature fades extinct...."[1]

Even flowers, of which she was passionately fond, had lost the influence they once had over her fancy. She saw them not; or seeing them, only recollected that Willoughby had shewn her at Alvestone a bed of such hyacinths, whose bloom and fragrance he had fondly anticipated, knowing how much she delighted in them: she remembered with a sigh each particular leaf and blossom that composed the last nosegay he gathered for her, on the morning of that day, when they were divided, never, as she now feared—to meet again!

Such were her sad recollections, as, hardly knowing what she did, she traversed the grass walk which was divided by a hedge of evergreens from the road. Her mournful reverie was interrupted by the sound of a horse's feet. She flew to the gate: it was Cathcart! who on perceiving her threw himself from his horse and gave her the long expected letter, which she received with such marks of extreme agitation, that Cathcart, afraid she would fall, left his horse to find its way to the stable, and came to support her.

She leaned on his arm, attempting to speak, and after a moment's pause said, "Cathcart, you have had a letter also?"

"I have."

"Before I have courage to open my own, tell me—is Willoughby well? and are there hopes of our seeing him again?"

---

1   James Thomson, *The Seasons*, "Spring," 1009-13.

"He is well," answered Cathcart; "but of seeing him again he gives me no hopes: to you, perhaps, he may be, and I hope is, more explicit."

Celestina staid not to reply; but hurrying as well as she was able to her own room, tore open her letter, which was in these words:

London, April 3, 1788.[1]

"What must be the misery the man endures, who only a few days since had the immediate prospect of calling Celestina his, and who is now compelled not only to leave her, but to leave her uncertain whether he may ever again dare to entertain that hope—whether he shall ever see her more! How I have loved you, Celestina—how I still love you—I surely need not repeat. This passion you well know—

"Grew with my growth, and strengthen'd with my strength:"[2]

you will not therefore believe that any circumstance can diminish—any time efface it. Yet such are the barriers that may be between us, that perhaps I may never dare again to see you; or only when I have submitted to the dreadful sacrifice required of me, and given my hand to one to whom my heart must ever be a stranger: and yet, Celestina, if to this I ever do submit, it will only be to enable me to place you in the situation you deserve as to fortune, and because it matters not, if I cannot pass my life with you, with whom it may be my destiny to pass it; for then, it must in every event be equally unhappy. Celestina! I am aware of the appearance my conduct must have in your eyes; aware of it without having the power to explain it. I have sworn that I will not unveil this fatal mystery till I either can see you, with all those delicious hopes *unempoisoned* that were so late mine, or till I have learned to regard you—not with less affection, for that is impossible, but with—I bewilder myself—I know not what I would say—only let this be understood as my meaning, that

---

1 This is the first complete date given. Celestina is born in 1770, and the main part of her narrative covers the years 1787-90, with the fictional action ending a year before the date of publication. But the inset narratives of Sophy Elphinstone in this volume and of Celestina's parents in volume four extend the time-span back to the Seven Years' War (1756-63) and the American War of Independence (1775-82).

2 Alexander Pope, *An Essay on Man*, Epistle II, 135-6: "The young disease, that must subdue at length,/ Grows with his growth, and strengthens with his strength."

wherever I may be, or whatever I may become, my fondest affection, my love, my esteem, must be yours. It is more probable that I shall go abroad; and you, Celestina, whither will you go? Suffer me to name my wishes, though I hardly dare hope you will comply with them—Why should you not stay at Alvestone? If *ever I return to it*, you will be its mistress; if I never return, you might find a melancholy pleasure—But again I am wandering from my point: I will not dictate to you, my lovely friend, I, who am incapable of judging what I ought to do for myself; for in the midst of my reflections a thousand bitter possibilities distract me: Celestina may renounce me as unworthy of her; may learn to despise me, or what is yet more dreadful, she may learn to love another. Oh! Celestina! should this ever happen—should you ever give that heart, which it was the glory of my life to possess, to another!—and yet, situated as I may find myself, it may perhaps be—But I must conclude while I am able, and call off my thoughts from myself, to promote Celestina's future comfort, if I can yet contribute to it, who have perhaps been its destroyer.

"Do not write to me. Expressions of your anxiety and regret I cannot bear. It is as much as I can now do to keep my senses. Gracious heaven! that ever I should say to Celestina, do not write to me!

"Cathcart has my directions how to act in all pecuniary matters at Alvestone, and to stay in the house till he takes possession of his own, which I suppose will be as soon as old Winnington dies: then he will continue to superintend the farm, and to receive the rents, out of which I have directed him to pay you fifty guineas every quarter, and to answer any farther demands that you may make upon him: and you must not, Celestina, refuse this; for remember that the master of the whole fortune should now have been yours, and that you have a right to this trifle—perhaps to much more. But if these reasons are insufficient to conquer your reluctance, remember, Celestina, that Willoughby, the unhappy Willoughby asks it of you, as the greatest alleviation his wretchedness now admits of.

"Wherever you are, let Cathcart give me constant information; and whenever I can tell you that the weight which now presses on my heart is removed, I will write—write! no I will then fly to my Celestina from the extremity of the earth. Perhaps I may now be in a few days on the sea; but I go no farther but to the South of Europe. Celestina, it would be a very great comfort to me to hear from Cathcart, before I go, what you intend to do: it would be a still greater to know that you determine to remain at least this summer at Alvestone: but you are now with a most excellent man, who is capable of advising you: in him, Celestina, you will have a friend and protector.

"Oh! why is it my lot to refer you to another for protection, when to be your friend, your lover, your husband, was so lately the first hope, as it has ever been the first wish of my existence. But I am running again into useless repetition. Celestina, if I ever seemed worthy of your regard, give not away hastily those affections which were mine! If ever I can claim them again—we may be happy; if not—but I cannot finish the sentence—I know not what I would write, nor am I able to read over what I have written. May God bless and protect you! Adieu, dearest Celestina!

George Willoughby."

Celestina read over this letter the first time in such perturbation, that except a general notion that notwithstanding Willoughby had *involuntarily* left her they should meet no more, she had very little idea of its contents.

Hers were sensations of anguish which no appeal to friendship, no participation of her sentiments with another, could mitigate or appease. Cathcart knew no more of the motives of Willoughby's conduct than she did herself; Mr. Thorold was equally ignorant; and to neither of them could she look for consolation. She tried to recover her composure; she a second time read the letter: it grew more and more inexplicable; and after having anxiously waited for it so many days, its arrival seemed now only either to embarrass her with new conjectures, or to torment her with apprehensions of his marrying Miss Fitz-Hayman, for to that the close of the first sentence evidently alluded. Nothing but the natural strength of her understanding could have supported her under the first tumultuous sensations of redoubled consternation and wild conjecture, which now assailed her. The longer she studied the letter, the more impossible she found any explanation of Willoughby's conduct: still the assurances of his unshaken attachment sweetened the bitterness of her destiny; he was living; he still loved her; her situation, therefore, however uneasy, was not desperate; and, as the first astonishment at the incomprehensible contents of a letter, which was expected to clear up every doubt, subsided, she saw less cause of despondence, and again she examined every separate paragraph, trying to extract from all that would bear it, something to cherish that hope, without which her existence would have been insupportable.

Every request of Willoughby had with her the force of a command; but that he made in regard to her continuing at Alvestone was so worded, as if he hardly himself thought she ought to comply with it. The impropriety of it appeared evident; but in every other instance she determined to be governed by his wishes, and as far as was now in her power to contribute to his satisfaction by affording him all the consolation that depended upon her. Of the pleasure of living for a beloved object, though perhaps personally disunited for ever, of believing that wherever he was, her ease and happiness were ever in his thoughts, she was fully sensible; and she now found in it a consolation so soothing to her mind, that she was soon enabled to return to Cathcart, who awaited for her in the parlour, with more composure than on her leaving him it was likely she would soon obtain. She found herself unequal to entering on a discussion of the letter, which she gave Cathcart to read; and on his returning it in silence, but with a look sufficiently expressive of his astonishment, she told him, that nothing remained but for them to fulfil as nearly as possible all the injunctions of Willoughby. "He desires me not to write to him," said she. "Even in that I shall, with whatever reluctance, obey him at present, and so I certainly shall in what relates to following the advice of Mr. Thorold. A little time will be necessary before I can fix on any plan of life: but as my dear Willoughby expects to hear of me from you, tell him that I bear our separation, cruel as it is, with fortitude and calmness, convinced as I am that our connection is not broken by any cause that ought to make me blush that it had ever been intended." She stopped a moment to recover her voice, which faultered and almost failed, and then added— "No, Cathcart, whatever has divided us, I have the firmest reliance on Willoughby's honour."

"And on his love," said Cathcart, "you may, dear Madam, with equal firmness rely: and though these perfect convictions render this strange separation more wonderful, they will I trust sustain your courage through it—I say through it, because I am almost certain it will be of no long duration."

"Ah! Cathcart!" cried Celestina mournfully, "I would I could think so! But it is indeed very fruitless and very painful to enter again on these bewildering conjectures, in which, as there is no end, there is little use: and I have need of all my spirits to enable me to support an evil, for which I cannot account; I will not therefore waste them in guessing or lamenting but employ them to obey him to whom my heart must, in every change of circumstance, and though I were certain never more to see him, be fondly and faithfully devoted. Tell him so, my good friend: tell him how well I bear this severe blow, more severe as coming from an unknown hand; and assure him that if he will allow me to write to him, I will not distress him by useless complaints, or aggravate his sorrow by representing my own."

Again she stopped, while Cathcart expressed his admiration of her just and noble resolutions; and after a moment, finding the exertion too much for her, she added hastily— "tell him thus much, Cathcart, in the letter you will of course write to him this afternoon; and tell me that your next letter shall inform him, if it is still uneasy to him to receive a letter from me, of the arrangements I will make under the guidance of Mr. Thorold for my future life: but say, that they will be such as will render his generous intentions as to pecuniary matters needless. I would fain explain my thoughts in that respect; but in truth I am not able just now. Some hours of reflection will be necessary to me. Farewel, therefore, dear Cathcart, for this morning; I shall of course see you again in a few days."

Cathcart assured her he would be with her again the following Friday; or the intervening day, if he received any new intelligence from Willoughby. She then charged him with many kind wishes and remembrances to Jessy, who was now, he told her, so confined by her grandfather that she could not get to her, and then took his leave to return to Alvestone, and execute the wishes of Willoughby by giving him a minute detail of all that had passed with Celestina.

Chapter III

Mr. Thorold, who was informed that Celestina had received letters from Willoughby, felt a true friendly impatience to know their contents: but feeling also how much his lovely guest must in any event be agitated, he not only forebore to intrude upon her with any enquiries himself, but in order that she might not suffer even from the looks of his family, which he knew could not fail to express solicitude arising from less generous motives, he sent her up a note to her own apartment, in which he begged she would not come down to dinner, to put herself, through form,[1] into any situation that might be in any degree painful. This exemption was particularly gratifying to her, as the younger Thorold was this day expected at dinner, and was to remain at home for some weeks; and his elder

---

1 Etiquette.

brother, a Captain in the army, who had been some time in Ireland, was to meet him in the evening. Celestina was unfit for company, and above all, the company of strangers; and again she regretted that in the first unsettled tumult of her spirits she had agreed to Mr. Thorold's proposal, instead of going back to the lodgings she had formerly inhabited: she was now, however, compelled to remain where she was, till she could determine, with the advice of Mr. Thorold, whither to go. She thought it probable that he might wish her to remain with him; but to this, except his friendly regard for her, and the advantage of being near Cathcart and Jessy, she had no inducement; and wherever she was, she determined it should not be as a mere visitor for any length of time, but that she would pay for her board. Again the quiet and liberty of her cottage on the heath recurred to her; but when she enjoyed that quiet, her heart had not undergone those vicissitudes of happiness and misery, which had now, she greatly feared, excluded tranquillity from her bosom for ever; what had then afforded her a species of melancholy pleasure, the distant view of a spot in Alvestone Park, would now serve only to render her more unhappy, and to encourage that tendency to repine, which her reason told her she should, both on Willoughby's account and her own, rather resolve to conquer than endeavour to indulge: she believed, however, that if once some resolution was formed as to her future residence, she should be easier herself, and be better able to satisfy Willoughby. To this subject, therefore, she turned her thoughts, and examined with a heavy heart several different plans that offered themselves to her mind.

Nothing could be more comfortless than her reflections: she was not only an orphan, and a stranger in England, but knew not whether there was in the world any being whose protection she had the remotest right to claim. Lady Molyneux had never written to her since their separation, and even if Willoughby should approve of her again seeking the protection of his sister, which she had great reason to doubt, she knew not whether Matilda and her husband would receive her; and from that want of heart she had too often discovered in them both, she could not think of making the experiment. She had no intimacy with any other person; for though many of the families she had been accustomed to visit while Mrs. Willoughby lived, had daughters, who had cultivated an acquaintance with her, she had already seen enough of the general conduct of the world to know that she should now be no longer an acceptable guest, and that an individual to whom court is made assiduously, while shining as an equal among fashionable circles, is soon forgotten; or if remembered, despised, when those adventitious advantages surround her no longer. She had heard from Vavasour, for Willoughby himself had always carefully avoided the subject, that the sudden desertion of Miss Fitz-Hayman, to whom Willoughby was supposed to be so firmly engaged, and his resolution of marrying his mother's adopted daughter, had been very much talked of in the extensive circle who were connected or acquainted with the family: she could not doubt but that their sudden separation on the very eve of their marriage was as generally known: and had she found any temptation to return to the society she had quitted, this painful certainty, the prying curiosity that would be excited, and the malicious conjecture that would be made, would effectually have counteracted it.

Towards evening she found sufficient courage to entreat Mr. Thorold's attention for half an hour. He came to her immediately, and she put into his hands the letter she had received from Willoughby.

He read it with great attention, and as it should seem with great concern, and then, in the expressive manner that was usual with him, gave it back to her without speaking.

Benevolence and pity were now visible in his features, which were masculine, strong, and frequently stern; but Celestina was hardly enough accustomed to him to understand his silence completely. "You see, dear Sir," said she timidly—"you see that Willoughby refers me to you, and I would very fain avail myself of the benefit of your advice."

"It is always at your service," replied Mr. Thorold; "but on what occasion do you now ask it?"

"I wish to know," replied she with still greater hesitation, "what you think it advisable for me to do? where you think I ought to settle myself?"

"I am sorry," answered he, "you think it so soon necessary to turn your thoughts that way. I hoped that you would stay here at least for some weeks; and really I can give you no other advice than to do so. The mystery which I cannot develop,[1] may by that time be removed, and we shall have time not only to hear more of Willoughby, but if nothing occurs on his part to re-establish you at Alvestone, to cast about for a proper and permanent situation for you: think no more, therefore, my dear ward, for such I consider you, of leaving us

---

1 Uncover.

at present, and rather exert your admirable understanding in quieting your spirits, and in acquiring fortitude to bear adversity and evil, if they should be finally your portion; or equality of temper to enjoy, what it is more difficult to enjoy well—happiness and prosperity."

Celestina would now have spoken of the inconvenience to which so long a visit might put his family, and the little claim she had to such unusual kindness from him and Mrs. Thorold; but he suffered her not to continue these apologies, seemed little pleased that she attempted to make them; and then re-assuming his good humour, he left her, bidding her try to recover her looks, and to dismiss as much as she could from her mind the distressing events of the last ten days.

Celestina now found that she could not immediately remove without offending the friend to whom Willoughby had recommended her, and prepared, since she could not be indulged with solitude, to mix with his family, and be as little as possible a weight on those, who, whatever might be their good humour, could not be expected to enter into her sorrows; the next morning therefore at breakfast she joined Mrs. Thorold, her daughter, and her two sons, to both of whom she was immediately introduced, and from whose scrutinizing looks she sought refuge in talking with forced cheerfulness to Arabella.

Captain Thorold was the eldest of the family, and Montague the youngest. The former of these young men had been adopted by his uncle, who, after a life passed in the army, had died a general officer at a very advanced age, and had left his nephew his whole fortune, which was near fifteen hundred a year, after the death of his wife, who surviving him only a twelvemonth, Captain Thorold had now been some time in possession of his estate, and of a considerable sum of money.

But accustomed from his infancy to the unsettled life of a soldier, he still continued it from habit and choice; and though his father and his family were very solicitous to have him marry and settled near them, he seemed to have no inclination to resign his freedom for the pleasures of domestic society. Novelty and amusement were his pursuits, and his fortune gave him the power to indulge himself. He had what is generally called a very handsome person; but without his military air, his figure would have been rather esteemed clumsy than graceful. He had lived much among the circles who give the *ton*, dressed well, and had that sort of understanding which recommended him to general society, and particularly to that of the ladies, with whom he was an almost universal favourite, and who had agreed to call him the handsome Thorold, even before he became possessed of a fortune, which in the opinion of most of the belles at country quarters,[1] and still more in the opinion of their mothers, more than redoubled his attractions. Thus spoiled from his first entrance into life, he had learned to consider himself as irresistible, and supposed every woman he saw his own, if he chose to take the trouble of securing her.

His air and manner were tinctured with the consequence he derived from this persuasion; and from having indulged himself in the cruel vanity of extensive conquest, he was incapable of any lasting or serious attachment. At the first public meeting at any town he happened to be quartered at, he elected some goddess of the day; with her he danced, he walked, he rode, he coquetted; and by studied looks, and tender speeches, soon persuaded the inexperienced girl that she had secured in her chains the handsome Thorold. The delusion of the young woman herself, and the envy of the cotemporary belles,[2] sometimes lasted till the removal of the corps to another station: when he took a cold farewel, and left her to suffer all the pain of disappointed love and mortified vanity: but he not unfrequently indulged himself in witnessing the distress this wanton folly inflicted; and after some days of attention so marked and unequivocal as to give the lady reason to suppose an absolute declaration of his passion was certainly to be expected, he suddenly broke off the acquaintance, pretended to forget their intimacy, bowed to her when they met with the air of a stranger, and beginning the same career with some other pretty girl of the place, he affected to treat with disdain and wonder the reports he had himself raised of his permanent attachment to the first lady, and laughed with her rival at the melancholy moping looks, or glances of angry disappointment, of the deserted beauty, declaring himself amazed at her having the vanity to suppose him serious, because he had shewn her a few trifling attentions which meant nothing.

This conduct of his son had given Mr. Thorold great uneasiness a few years before, but lately, as he had been in Ireland, and in very different quarters, his father had heard no more of it, and flattered himself that now, at near thirty, this unsettled temper and unjustifiable levity would end in his marrying and quitting the army. But though a very fond father to all his children, Mr. Thorold loved the Captain less than the others; partly perhaps because he was so early removed from

---

1   In provincial towns where the army was quartered.
2   Beauties of her own age.

him, and rendered independent of his care, and partly because his temper and disposition resembled not his own; while Mrs. Thorold doated on her eldest son, whose figure and fortune gratified her vanity, and whom she thought no young woman could possibly deserve, unless she possessed at once fortune, beauty, and fashion.

Montague Thorold, who was but just turned one and twenty, and was designed by his father for the church, was as modest and unassuming as his brother was arrogant and pretending. He was a very good scholar, with a passion for poetry, and was just of the age to be in love with every handsome woman he saw; and without having the courage to speak to any of them in prose, he celebrated his divinities in verse, and sighed forth his tender sentiments in sonnets and elegies, which enriched the magazines, and now and then the public prints, under the fictitious names of Alphonso or Lysimachus.

Such were the two young men who were now added to the tea table of Mr. Thorold, where all the family were assembled except Mr. Thorold himself, who always breakfasted early and then went out to his farm or among his parishioners.

Mrs. Thorold had told her sons that a young lady was visiting at the house, whose history she had given them in short hand, describing her as a dependant on the late Mrs. Willoughby, whom her son had very simply[1] intended to marry at Alvestone; but the evening before the appointed wedding day had broken off the match, from prudential motives as she supposed, and by the advice of some of his friends who had come down from London.

This was the idea Mrs. Thorold had herself conceived of the affair, and she had no means of being undeceived; for Mr. Thorold, who knew that with her a command was better than an argument, and whose authority was pretty firmly established, had ordered her positively to ask no questions of his guest, and had peremptorily refused to answer those she put to himself. She obeyed, but not without many murmurs; but knowing that Mr. Thorold would be much disobliged by her refusal to entertain Celestina with kindness, had put a restraint upon herself, and shewed her hitherto much civility, though not without many complaints to Arabella, when they were alone, of her father's absurdity in forcing people into the family, and refusing even to satisfy her who and what they were, or what claim they had to the kindness he exacted for them.

---

1 Foolishly.

From his mother's sketch of their visitor the evening before, Captain Thorold had very little curiosity to see her; and Montague, whose heart was in one of its most violent paroxysms of love for the fair daughter of an attorney at Henly, with whom he became acquainted about a fortnight before, was occupied in composing an elegy on absence, and thought he could with indifference have beheld at that period Helen[1] herself: he had enquired of his mother and sister if their guest was handsome: Mrs. Thorold answered—"No, not at all handsome in my opinion;" and Arabella said—"Yes, surely, Mamma, she is rather pretty-ish."

On her entering the room, however, both the gentlemen were instantly of an opinion very different from that of their mother and their sister: yet Celestina had not now that dazzling complexion, or that animated countenance, which were once so dangerous to behold; she was pale and languid; her eyes had all their softness, but the lustre was diminished; and the enchanting sweetness which used to play about her mouth was now supplied by a melancholy smile, the effect of a faint effort to conceal the anguish of the heart.

Such as she now appeared, however, the Captain thought her very lovely; and Montague almost instantly forgot the nymph[2] for whom he had been dying in song all the morning, and saw in the interesting languor of Celestina—in her faded cheek, and downcast eyes, a sentimental effect, which none of the fair creatures whom he had celebrated had ever so eminently possessed: but if such were his sentiments before she spoke, his admiration arose to extravagance, when, after breakfast, his sister engaged her in a walk in which the two gentlemen attended them, and when he found that her mind corresponded with the elegance of her form; that she was very well read, had a taste for poetry, and understood Italian, of which he was enthusiastically fond. Captain Thorold, on whom these advantages made less impression, was not quite pleased during this walk with the unusual talkativeness of his brother, who generally suffered him to take the lead in conversation. He now attempted to put him by two or three times, and to relate anecdotes of people in high life: of what General Wallace said to him at Dublin Castle upon his intro-

---

1   Helen of Troy, whose abduction by Paris, as told in Homer's *Iliad*, is the cause of the war between the Greeks and the Trojans, was supposed to be the most beautiful woman in the world.

2   Term for a young woman in the pastoral literary mode still popular then.

duction to the Duchess of —,[1] and of a *bon mot*[2] of Lady Mary Marsden's at supper one evening: but Celestina, who cared nothing about the General, the Duchess, or Lady Mary, let the conversation drop without expressing any pleasure in it, and again lent her attention to Montague, who desired her to correct his accent while he repeated—

"O primavera, gioventu dell' anno...."[3]

Celestina modestly assured him she was incapable of correcting him; but he besought her so earnestly to recite the lines to him that she inconsiderately attempted it, and in the most enchanting accents began—

"O primavera, gioventu dell' anno,
Bella madre di fiori
D'erbe novelle e di novelli amori:
Tu torni ben—ma teco
Non tornano i sereni
E fortunati dì delle mie gioje:"

The cruel remembrance that now pressed upon her heart made her voice tremble, and gave it additional tenderness. She tried to recover it; and going into a lower tone, went on with—

"Tu torni ben—tu torni
Ma teco altro no torna
Che del perduto mio caro tesoro
La rimembranza misera e dolente."

She could go no farther: the tears were in her eyes; but she tried to smile, and to stifle the deep sigh that was rising as she said—"I cannot go on, for really I remember no more."

---

1 A common strategy in the eighteenth-century novel is to substitute a dash for a name, implying that a real person is meant.
2 Witticism.
3 Giovanni Battista Guarini, *Il Pastor Fido* 3.1.1-10: "O Spring, firstborn of the year, beautiful mother of flowers, of new grass and new loves, you happily return—but the calm and fortunate days of my happiness don't return with you. You happily return, you return, but with you nothing else returns except the bitter and painful memory of my lost, dear treasure." The first six lines were set as a madrigal by Claudio Monteverdi.

The young man, fascinated by her manner and her voice, now recollected—with reluctance recollected, that these seducing tones were drawn forth by the reality of those sufferings the poet described. He looked at her in silence; and as he marked the sad and pensive expression that remained on her countenance, that astonishment, which he had hardly time to feel before, arose: he thought it impossible that Mr. Willoughby, having the power to marry such a woman, and having once formed the resolution to do so, should by any persuasions be diverted from his purpose; and he found that in the single hour he had been with her, he admired her enough to sacrifice every thing to her, were it possible that her regard could be transferred to him.

The improbability that it ever could, struck him forcibly, and rendered him as silent as Celestina herself; while the Captain, who had now an opportunity of engrossing her attention, rallied her on being so much affected.

"I have no notion now," said he, "of giving way to those sort of things. I love gay and cheerful poetry. One is tired of weeping at the fictitious misery of fictitious persons. I remember being some time ago at a conversation in Dublin, where we talked of the fashionable indifference which every body has now for tragedy; and my friend Hargrave, who has written, you know, several things himself, was condemning it as the certain marks of the vitiated taste and imbecility of the age: I took up the argument on the other side; and Lady Mary Marsden thought as I did. Indeed every body present allowed that it was quite absurd to go to a play, which is intended to amuse and entertain, only to be made uneasy. She agreed with me that people have concern enough in real life, and need not go seek it in way of diversion."

"And did her Ladyship," enquired Montague Thorold, "give no other reasons?"

"I think those are very good reasons," replied the Captain.

"They might be so," answered his brother, "for a woman of fashion; but I am persuaded literary people and people of taste think quite otherwise; and the ancients,[1] whose superior intellectual advantages are not to be disputed—"

"Oh prithee[2] Montague," interrupted the Captain, "don't run us down with college cant. I am talking of the world we live in; and the

---

1 The Greeks and Romans. Montague Thorold is on the side of the Ancients against the Moderns in the eighteenth-century dispute over the superiority of classical knowledge.
2 Pray thee; please.

opinions of people who lived two thousand years ago are no more in question now than their dresses." He then went on to retail other opinions of Lady Mary Marsden, who was, as it seemed, the oracle of the hour in the society he had just left. Celestina heard him with apparent attention, but in truth without knowing what he said; his brother, rendered impatient by being interrupted in his conversation with her, walked away; and Arabella, who loved to hear descriptions of fine people, and to attend to fashionable conversation, kept up the dialogue till the end of their walk; when Celestina went to her own room, Arabella to her dressing table, and the Captain, finding his mother at work in the parlour, thought he had a right to ask her a few questions about Celestina, in return for the perpetual tone of interrogation she had kept up towards him ever since his arrival.

To Mrs. Thorold, the next gratification to that of asking questions was the pleasure of answering them: she told her son, therefore, not only all she knew, but invented answers on some points which she only guessed at; and he understood, from her information, that Celestina had been very partial to Willoughby; and so strong was this partiality described, that he began to doubt whether the proposed marriage had not been a mere finesse[1] to throw her off her guard, and get her wholly into his power; and whether his abrupt departure had not been in consequence of the success of this disingenuous but not unprecedented method of proceeding.

Captain Thorold had seen Willoughby frequently in his last visit at home, and knew that he had every advantage which a fine person and engaging manner could give him; he was well acquainted with the society among which he lived, and had heard some of them, but particularly Vavasour, described as being very gay[2] and unprincipled; he had therefore little difficulty in supposing that Willoughby resembled those with whom he associated, and that Celestina had been the victim of these arts which he supposed no man ever scrupled to practise where the object was so well worth the trouble; especially one so unprotected as she was, where no rigid father was in the way to obstruct their designs, or Chamont-like brother[3] to avenge the wrong they might commit. Willoughby now, however, seemed quite out of the question; and he doubted not, but that after a short interval given to sentimental regret on the loss of a first lover, she would

1 Trick.
2 Libertine, sexually immoral, without homoerotic implication.
3 The fierce brother of the heroine Monimia in Thomas Otway's *The Orphan*.

listen to other vows, and encourage the passion, which he thought it might be very amusing to entertain her with, without meaning however to offer himself to fill such engagements as Willoughby had broken. While he meditated on this project, he could not help smiling at the cullibility[1] of his father, who had thus, he thought, taken into his protection, and made the companion of his wife and daughter, the deserted mistress of Willoughby.

Chapter IV

The following morning Cathcart was early at the house of Mr. Thorold; and Celestina, who rose now earlier than usual, (to enjoy, if it could be called enjoyment, a few hours, before she was compelled to hide her sorrows under the appearance of attention to the family she was with) met him as he came from the stable; and instead of going into the house, she desired he would walk with her towards the village. "You have news for me," said she; "but if I may guess by your countenance none that will relieve the weight I feel on my heart."

"I am afraid not," replied he: "yet indeed I have nothing to say that should encrease it. Mr. Willoughby is well; he writes to me with more cheerfulness than I expected, and assures me that he has a long letter for you, which he shall send from Dover, where he shall finish it."

"From Dover! He is then set out on this expedition. Ah! Cathcart! and ought not such intelligence to add to my concern?"

"Not at all," replied Cathcart. "You knew before that it was his intention; and he tells me that on the event of this journey depends his ever seeing Alvestone again. There is certainly a chance of its terminating favourably; at all events, if this absence is to end your suspense, you should not only submit to it, but endeavour, my dear Miss de Mornay, to keep up both your health and spirits."

"Alas! Cathcart," answered Celestina, "there is nothing so easy to the happy as to give such advice, nothing so difficult to the wretched as to take it."

She then enquired into the other particulars contained in Willoughby's letter; and after informing herself of the day when he

---

1 Gullibility.

expected to be at Dover, and how long it might probably be before she should receive the letter he promised her, she turned the conversation on Jessy, whom she expressed an eager wish to see: and soon after Montague Thorold, who impatiently watched her wherever she went, came to tell her that his mother waited breakfast for her.

Cathcart, however, declined the invitation to breakfast with them, and wishing Celestina a good morning, and promising to be with her again in a day or two, he went in search of Mr. Thorold, with whom he said he had some business.

Many succeeding days passed without any interesting event. The Captain took every occasion to impress on Celestina an idea of his consequence, and the fashionable style he lived in, to which she gave very little attention; while his brother, whenever he left him an opportunity, talked to her of books, or read to her passages in favourite authors of which he heard her express approbation: she was prevailed upon to sing duets with Arabella; and he was enchanted with her voice and manner; she sat down to draw the flowers he gathered for her, while he hung over her in raptures, or held her pallet, or read a botanical description of the plants she was painting. Captain Thorold rode out occasionally to visit such of the neighbouring families as he considered worth his attention; Arabella was often of his party, and Mrs. Thorold engaged in domestic concerns; and then if Celestina could not escape to her own room before Montague, who was always upon the watch for her, could interrupt her, he entreated her so earnestly to walk with him, was so obligingly solicitous to please her, and seemed so mortified when she attempted to excuse herself, that she could seldom resolve to refuse him her conversation, even when she was most willing to be alone; and in the similarity of her tastes and studies, and in the brotherly though silent sympathy he appeared to feel for her sorrows, there was something soothing to her sick heart, which rejected every idea of love but for Willoughby: conscious of which, and supposing that no man could consider her otherwise than as destined to be his wife, or to die unmarried, she dreamed not that she was granting to young Thorold indulgence fatal to his repose.

He was himself soon aware of the danger, but he courted it; and though he understood that the heart of Celestina was engaged, he fancied, that without any pretensions to her love, he should be happier in being admitted to her friendship, than the unrivalled affections of any other woman could make him. He was too artless, and too proud of his judgment, to attempt to conceal this attachment from his father, who, had Celestina been disengaged, would have preferred her, with her small fortune and uncertain birth, to the richest heiress in the country: but knowing how she was circumstanced, he saw his younger son's encreasing partiality with some concern, and took an opportunity, when they were alone, to tell him the real circumstances of Celestina in regard to Willoughby. "I can consider her," said he, "no otherwise than his affianced wife. They are parted by some cause of which I am ignorant, but which will probably be removed: in the mean time her youth and beauty render her situation very dangerous; as from her being a foreigner, an orphan, and probably the natural daughter of some person of high fashion in France, who has taken care to destroy all evidence of her real family, she is without relations and without protection. Willoughby's father was my old friend. When I was an indigent curate he gave me a living, which, though I have now, from being possessed of greater preferment, resigned, I consider as my first step toward affluence. I am therefore, bound to the family by gratitude, and to young Willoughby I am bound by personal friendship and esteem. Except something too much bordering on rashness in his temper, I hardly know any man so faultless and so worthy of regard. He adores Miss de Mornay, and I am convinced the happiness of his life depends on their union. Finding him torn from her for the present, at the very moment this union was to take place, I entered at once into all the uneasiness that must have assailed him, and I voluntarily offered my protection to her, which he has since acknowledged in a letter to me to be the greatest kindness he could receive. Don't fancy yourself in love with a young woman who is in fact married. Any other kind of attention or regard you shew her will oblige me; but let us have no making love, unless you would drive her away and greatly disoblige me."

The young man readily promised what at the moment he was sincere in, that he would not make love to Celestina; but he did not promise not to feel the passion, against which it was too late already to guard him. Mr. Thorold however supposed, that after this explanation there was nothing to fear from the extreme susceptibility of his younger son; and for the eldest, he was too certain that he had not a heart on which the charms and virtues of Celestina, or of any other beautiful and interesting woman, could make any permanent impression. He was easy therefore in a situation which would have made many narrow minded and selfish parents very much otherwise; and did not think the presence of his two sons at home a sufficient reason for withdrawing his generous kindness from Celestina, to whom he was indeed affectionately attached for her own sake, and to whom he loved to consider himself as a guardian and protector.

Mrs. Thorold, always busied about the intrigues and schemes of the rest of the world, saw not very minutely into those of her own family. As to her eldest son, she contemplated him as a superior being, who had a right to marry the greatest heiress of the kingdom. She heard him speak so often of Lady Marys and Lady Carolines, that she concluded he might have any of them whenever he pleased; and had set her imagination so high as to his merits and his fortune, that she never supposed he could think of bringing her any other than a titled daughter in law. Celestina, whom she looked upon as a creature whose title to respect was very questionable, a dependant from her birth, and now little better than a dependant on herself, was not a person likely to make any impression on Captain Thorold; and the prejudice operated on her person and her manners. Mrs. Thorold could not see that she was handsome, or feel that she was interesting; and when the attention of young Thorold was very strongly marked towards her, his mother only ridiculed him, telling him that he was never easy but when playing the Philander, and that he cared not with whom.

Nothing, therefore, interrupted the progress of that serious passion, which Montague Thorold determined to indulge, and of which Celestina was perfectly unconscious. The more unreserved flattery and free address of the Captain she knew how to repress; and received all his advances with so much coldness, that his pride was piqued; and unused to the slightest repulse, he determined not to brook it from one, who had, in his private opinion, very little right to assume dignity or affect disdain.

The manner he took up towards her in consequence of these opinions, was so very disagreeable to her, that it forced her more than ever into the society of his brother; before whom, though the Captain held him very cheap as a boy and a pedant, he could not well address to her such speeches as he had ventured to utter several times when he seized an opportunity of speaking to her alone, or unheard by the rest of the family. Whenever, therefore, she was compelled to be below, she contrived to have Montague Thorold sit next to her, to accept his arm as they walked, and to address her discourse to him: and flattered by this evident preference, he let no occasion pass of proving how happy it made him.

So passed heavily for Celestina, the days that intervened between that when she last saw Cathcart, and that on which she expected Willoughby's letter from Dover. The day arrived at length; and Celestina, who happened to be sitting with Arabella and her brothers when the letters were brought, could hardly support herself while the Captain took them from the servant, and reading the direction of each, threw them across the table, now one to his sister, now one to his brother, and bade Montague carry a third to his father. There was none for Celestina, though Cathcart had told her it would be directed to her at the house of Mr. Thorold. Of this bitter disappointment, however, she spoke not, but tried to conceal the change it occasioned in her countenance, and hastened, as soon as she could, to weep alone, over the sad idea that Willoughby's diminished, perhaps annihilated love, had allowed him to torture her with suspense which he might so easily have avoided by punctuality.

Another almost sleepless night was the consequence of this delay: but though without rest in the night, Celestina rose as soon as day appeared. At no other time but early in the morning she had now any chance of being alone either in the garden or the neighbouring fields, and the air seemed necessary to her overburthened spirits. In the fields, she seemed to breathe more freely, and her heart, which often felt as if it would burst, was relieved while she was allowed to weep unmarked and uninterrupted.

A narrow road, shaded by thick rows of branching elms, led towards the village, which was that way almost a mile from the house of Mr. Thorold, who did not inhabit the parsonage but an house he had built on a farm of his own. Celestina, to avoid being seen from the windows of the house, which commanded the garden and the meadows near it, took her way down this lane. Her thoughts ran over the strange events of the preceding years, in which she had experienced so much anguish, anguish embittered by the transient promise of supreme happiness. As she reviewed her whole life, it seemed to have been productive only of regret. "Why," cried she, "was I ever born? Alas! my existence was the occasion of misery to those who gave it me! Why did dearest Mrs. Willoughby take me from a confinement where I was dead to the world, and where perhaps neglect and hardship might long since have released me? What will now become of me? If Willoughby forgets me, how shall I find courage to drag about a wretched being? useful to nobody, for whom nobody is interested, and which seems marked by heaven for calamity!"

These melancholy reflections led her on, till a turn out of the road brought her to the style[1] of the church yard. She leant pensive-

---

1 Stiles, by which walkers could gain access to another field or area by mounting a step, rather than by a gate which might be left open allowing livestock through, were once very common in England and are still in use.

ly over it, and read the rustic inscriptions on the tomb stones. One was that of a young woman of nineteen: it was her age; and Celestina felt an emotion of envy towards the village girl, whose early death the rural poet lamented in the inscription.

"Merciful heaven!" cried she, "is early death ever really to be lamented? and should I not be happier to die now than to live; as perhaps I shall not be forgotten?" Insensibly this idea took possession of her fancy; and with her pencil she wrote the following lines in her pocket book, not without some recollection of Edwards'[1] thirty seventh and forty fourth sonnets:

SONNET

Oh thou! who sleep'st where hazle bands entwine
The vernal grass, with paler violets drest;
I would, sweet maid! thy humble bed were mine,
And mine, thy calm and enviable rest.
For never more, by human ills opprest
Shall thy soft spirit fruitlessly repine:
Thou cans't not now thy fondest hopes resign
Even in the hour that should have made thee blest.
Light lies the turf upon thy virgin breast;
And lingering here, to love and sorrow true,
The youth, who once thy simple heart possess'd,

---

1   Smith probably refers to poems by Bryan Edwards (1743-1800), who inherited plantations in Jamaica, and wrote mainly historical works on the colonial history of the West Indies. He was in England again between 1782 and 1787 as a neighbour in Sussex, and advised her in the publication of her *Elegiac Sonnets* (1784). But the only volume of poetry I can trace to him is his *Poems Written Chiefly in the West Indies* (1792), which contains nothing to which the narrator could allude here. It is possible Smith saw sonnets in manuscript which were intended for publication but never published. She might refer to *Miscellanies in Prose and Verse*, by "Miss Edwards" published Edinburgh, 1776. Two poems in this volume, "Elegy on the Death of a Sister, who died in the sixteenth year of her age" and "To the Memory of Miss Jeany Scott," though not sonnets in the usual sense, are elegies for the death of a young woman which thematically resemble Smith's sonnet. They are not numbered 37 and 44 in the 1776 volume, however.

Shall mingle tears with April's early dew;
While still for him, shall faithful Memory save,
Thy form and virtues from the silent grave![1]

Celestina, who had a natural turn to poetry, had very rarely indulged it; but since she had passed so many hours with Willoughby, his passionate fondness for it, and his desire that she should not neglect the talent she had received from nature, had turned her thoughts to its cultivation; and now almost the first use she made of it was to lament that she lived, since none of her acquirements were to please him, for whom alone she wished to possess either life or talents.

She had finished her sonnet, and read it over aloud: she changed a word or two, again read it, and was putting it into her pocket book, when she was startled by the sight of Montague Thorold, who appeared behind her, though she had not heard him approach. "Do not," he cried, "be offended, dearest Miss de Mornay, if I thus break in upon your solitude; and do not," continued he, taking her hand, in which she still held the pocket book—"do not punish me by putting away what I have so earnest a desire to hear."

Celestina, half angry replied—"I have nothing, sir, worth your hearing."

"I have offended you," said he, in the most respectful tone—"I see you are offended. If you knew my heart, you would know how much better I could bear any misfortune than your contempt and anger."

Celestina, whose slight displeasure was already at an end, answered with a smile, that he certainly deserved neither: "but come," continued she, "you were sent I dare say to call me to breakfast and we are loitering here."

"I was not sent," answered he. "I believe it is yet earlier than you imagine it to be. You are not then offended at my interrupting you?"

"Oh no! think of it no more," said Celestina, wishing to change the discourse. "Is it not a delicious morning?"

He answered not her question; but fixing his eyes on hers said— "See how soon a second trespass is attempted when the first is so graciously forgiven. May I ask, as the most inestimable favour, to hear once more the lines you were reciting?"

---

1 Reprinted as no. XLIX in Smith's *Elegiac Sonnets* and in Stuart Curran's edition.

"Once more!" repeated Celestina. "Have you heard them once already then?"

"I will say I have not, if my acknowledging that I have will displease you."

"I do not think," said Celestina carelessly, "that will mend your case much: but however the lines were not worth your hearing, and...."

"Every thing you even repeat from another," cried he, eagerly interrupting her, "is worth hearing: how much more worth hearing, when that fascinating voice is employed in expressing the sentiments of that elegant and lovely mind. Oh! Celestina!—But forgive me, Madam; it is presumption indeed in me to address you so freely; yet Celestina is the only name in the world that seems to me fit for you. The common terms of formal civility are unworthy of you. Let me then call you Celestina, not in familiarity, but in veneration, in adoration; and entreat you, implore you to oblige me."

Disconcerted at his vehemence of manner and extravagance of expression, Celestina now thought it better to put an end to such very warm applications, by shewing him the little value in her eyes of the favour he solicited. She gave him the paper, therefore, saying coldly—"You are anxious for a very trifling matter; and as you have already heard the lines, it is hardly worth the time you must give, hastily written as they are, and with interlineations and erasures, to make them out."

"Give me then time to do it," cried he, as he kissed the paper and put it in his bosom. Celestina, more disconcerted by his manner than before, said yet more gravely, "I beg I may have them again immediately."

"You shall indeed," replied Thorold; "but I must first read them."

"Read them then now," replied she.

"It is impossible," cried he, "for here is Arabella and my brother coming to meet us; and it is the first time that being with you, I have felt their interruption as a favour."

During this dialogue Celestina had walked rather quickly towards the house, so that they were by this time within sight of the garden gate, from whence Captain and Miss Thorold advanced slowly towards them. Montague, as if conscious of the impropriety of what had passed, now affected to be talking of indifferent matters; and Celestina, ruffled by his wild enthusiasm, and eagerly anticipating the letter which she hoped that day would bring her from Willoughby, felt herself made uneasy by the steady and enquiring eyes of the Captain, who had acquired a very rude habit of staring people out of countenance. She was compelled however to endure it, not only while breakfast lasted, but afterwards when Arabella engaged her assistance in painting a trimming which was to compose the ornament of a gala dress for the balls at Tunbridge, whither she was going in June with the eldest of her married sisters, who was in an ill state of health.

Chapter V

Arabella Thorold, desirous of availing herself of the superior taste and skill that Celestina possessed in such ornamental matter as she was now busy about, the merit of which she knew she might, where she was going, take entirely to herself, now invited her guest to the work table at which she was employed; Montague took up a book to read to them aloud, while his brother sauntered idly about the room, now praising Celestina's performance, now correcting that of his sister; then humming a tune, looking at his watch, or throwing about the colours or the pencils, he seemed determined to interrupt his brother's reading, and particularly when by Montague's voice and gesture he saw that he hoped particularly to interest and attract the attention of his auditors. This scene, of which the painful anxiety of Celestina for her letter made her unusually impatient, was at length put an end to by the entrance of the servant from the post; and Celestina receiving, in trembling agitation, a letter with the Dover post mark, she flew with it to her own room, and read as follows:

"Dover, April 11, 17—[1]
"The vessel which is to carry me from England and Celestina is now waiting for me; and I have delayed writing to her till this last moment; not because I have ever ceased to think of her with the warmest solicitude, but because I have not till now been able to collect courage to bid her a long adieu! I am going, Celestina, to the South of Europe. Perhaps my stay may be very short: perhaps I may, for the rest of my life, be doomed to be a solitary wanderer. But however destiny may dispose of me, let me entreat you, by all that regard which once made the happiness of my life, to take care of your health; try to regain your cheerfulness; and believe me, Celesti-

---

1   1788.

na, strangely against me as appearances are, I have not deserved to lose your confidence, nor have I any wish so fervent as for your happiness. I cannot write to you on pecuniary affairs. Cathcart has, in regard to every thing of that sort, my full directions. Whenever he and Jessy become house-keepers for themselves, you will be their welcome guest, and my heavy heart will be relieved of much of its anguish: till then, I entrust you to the care and direction of the excellent friend you are now with: may it not long be necessary for me to—But I dare not trust myself on this subject. Write to me; for now the measure I have been driven to is adopted, I can hear from you without fearing that my resolution may be shaken. Heaven bless and protect you, dearest Celestina! This is the first wish I form, when, after my uneasy slumber, recollection returns in the morning, and the last before I attempt to sleep at night. Alas! it is often only an attempt! But there is no end of this—Farewell! most beloved Celestina, farewel!

G. W."

This letter was if possible more unsatisfactory than the last. No reason was yet given for his having left her, no certainty held out of his return; but all, if not hopeless, was so comfortless, so obscure, that her resolution to investigate the cause of all that had happened, again failed. She feared even to attempt putting aside the fearful veil that was drawn between them. He was now in another country, from whence his return seemed uncertain; and she seemed the most desolate and forlorn being that existed on that which he had left. Her heart sunk within her in remembering that she might never see him more—that he hardly seemed to wish she should. Again she read his letter over. He was sleepless, restless, unhappy; and for his suffering she wept more than for her own.

The plan he mentioned of her residing with the Cathcarts, was the only one to which, since their separation, she had looked forward with any degree of satisfaction. But that there was yet little probability of executing: for old Winnington was in even better health than he had been for some years; and though the tender assiduity of Jessy had won much even on his insensible heart, he suffered her to have no authority; and often being seized with fits of jealousy and suspicion that she went to meet and assist her father, he would insist upon her not quitting him a moment; so that she had sometimes for many days together no opportunity of seeing her husband, and had never once, since her separation from Celestina, been able to reach her present abode. Celestina had not been an hour alone, before Montague Thorold tapped at her door. She dried her eyes, and pulling her hat over them, opened it to him.

"Will you not walk?" said he, apologizing however for his intrusion. "I am afraid I disturb you: but the morning is so beautiful; and we are all going to see a pond fished, with two friends of my brother's from Exeter, who are just come in."

"I cannot indeed," answered Celestina. "Pray excuse me."

"I would not press you for the world," said he, "to do any thing that is disagreeable to you. But the air will be surely useful to you. You—have been weeping, Miss de Mornay! And...."

"If I have," replied she, interrupting him, "you may be assured, Sir, that I have reason enough for my tears, and would wish to enjoy them alone."

"Precious tears!" cried he with a deep sigh. "The letter was from the fortunate Willoughby!"

"Fortunate do you call him?" But Celestina, as if offended that any tongue but hers should name him, stopped, and turning from the door, went into her own room.

At this moment Arabella ran up stairs to fetch her cloak and gloves, and seeing her brother Montague at the door of Celestina's room, cried, as she passed him—"Hey day! are you in waiting as Page or Gentleman Usher?"

"As neither," answered he in some confusion. "I was merely asking if Miss de Mornay would walk with us."

"Oh! I dare say not," replied his sister, smiling maliciously as she looked over her shoulder at him—"I dare say not. Montague, what are you in now? Are you Romeo—'Oh! that I were a glove upon that hand, that I might touch that cheek!'[1] or are you Castalio?— 'Sweets planted by the hand of heaven grow here.'[2] You always make love I know by book. What! shall I call Edmund to take the part of Polydore? I think you will make it out[3] among you."

Celestina, who had heard this speech, though it was not meant

---

1   *Romeo and Juliet* 2.1.66-7 (Romeo is a Montague).

2   Thomas Otway's *The Orphan* 2.402. In this Restoration tragedy, the heroine Monimia marries Castalio unknown to his twin brother Polydore. Overhearing Castalio make an appointment to go to her room at night, Polydore, thinking her a mistress rather than a wife, takes his brother's place and so in effect rapes her. When the truth is discovered, Polydore incites Castalio to kill him, Monimia takes poison and Castalio stabs himself. Arabella makes an offensive joke here.

3   Fill the parts.

that she should, was equally amazed and hurt at it. It had however a very different effect from what the speaker intended; who having no wish that Celestina should join them, because she desired to monopolize the conversation of the two strangers, thought, by rallying her brother, to break off his entreaty. Montague, mild as he was, was piqued extremely, and would resentingly have answered, if his sister had not immediately disappeared, and if Celestina had not at the same moment opened her door and said—"You compel me, Mr. Montague, to walk whether I will or no."

"Pray forgive me," said he, interrupting her. "I would purchase no pleasure at your expense."

Arabella now returning down stairs, was surprised to see her preparing to go. "I thought you declined walking Ma'am," said she formally. Celestina made an effort to conquer the resentment she justly felt, and replied coldly that the morning was so pleasant she thought it would be a pity to lose it.

Her apprehensions indeed were, that had she remained at home, Montague, who had persecuted her the whole day, would have remained also; and the hint his sister had given of the rivalry of the brothers had at once shocked and amazed her. After a moment, however, she began to fancy that her speech had more malice than meaning in it: but the uneasiness of her situation, and the necessity of soon removing from it, recurred to her more forcibly than ever. She endeavoured, as she went down stairs, to regain her composure, apprehensive that the strangers, if not the family, might remark her emotion. But she soon found that there was little to be apprehended from either the one or the other: Captain Thorold was walking arm in arm before the house with Captain Musgrave, the elder of the two gentlemen, and Miss Thorold wholly monopolized the attention of Mr. Bettenson, a very young man, heir to a considerable fortune, who had a few months before, on his leaving Eton, purchased a Cornet-cy[1] of horse, very much against the inclinations of his father, whose only son he was. He could indeed give no other reason for his preference to a military life, but that he supposed it to be a very idle life, and that he should look uncommonly well in the uniform of the corps. This however did not succeed to his wishes, though he was very far from being aware how entirely they had failed. He had a very round back, very narrow shoulders, a long forlorn face, to which the

---

1   A cornet was the fifth-ranking commissioned officer in a troop of cavalry, and carried the colours.

feathered helmet gave neither grace nor spirit; and the defects of his mean and ill formed figure were rendered more apparent by that dress, which is an advantage to a well made and graceful man. He had twice danced with Belle Thorold at the provincial assemblies[1] towards the end of winter, and now, after having been in town for a few weeks, prevailed on Captain Musgrave to introduce him to a family, where he supposed he might find a monstrous good lounge for the rest of the time he was to be quartered in the neighbourhood. Celestina no sooner saw Miss Thorold's behaviour to this young man than she accounted at once for the dissatisfaction she had shewn at her joining the party; for she endeavoured by more than her usual vivacity to monopolize all his attention; she watched with uneasy curiosity every glance of his eye towards Celestina; and seeing that he hardly noticed her being among them, and was not struck with that beauty which the Captain and Montague had so admired, she presently reassumed her usual confidence in her own attractions, and thought only of securing the advantage she had gained.

Celestina, not having the remotest wish to interfere with her conquests, and being displeased and offended at the curious looks and whispers of the two other military men, who continued to saunter on before, was again under the necessity of listening to Montague, who never failed seizing every opportunity obliquely to hint to her the encreasing admiration with which she had inspired him, though he at the same time gave her to understand that he knew he had nothing to expect but her pity and her friendship.

This was however repeated till it became very uneasy to her; and the more so, because so respectful was his address that she seldom knew how to shew resentment, and so sincere appeared his repentance, when she expressed any, that she could not long retain it.

As they now followed the rest of the party, Celestina took occasion to ask Montague for the paper she had been teazed out of in the morning. "I know not," said she, on his evasive answer "whether my folly in giving it, or your absurdity in keeping it, be the greater. Pray restore it, and let us think no more of such trifling."

"I will give you," answered he, "a copy of it, which I have already began to write; but for the original—" He stopped, and suddenly seizing her hand, pressed it to his breast; where, under his waistcoat, the paper was enfolded. "There," said he—"there is your paper. I

---

1   Large dances held in public rooms and open to payment by subscription, as distinct from those held in a private house.

have put it next my heart, and never shall it be displaced unless you give me some yet dearer memorial to remain there."

Celestina withdrew her hand in confusion; and feeling more than ever the necessity of putting an end of such sort of conduct, she said, with evident displeasure and concern—"You behave, Mr. Montague, not only improperly in this foolish matter, but cruelly and insultingly toward me, who have, you know, at this time no proper home to receive me; but since you thus persecute me with conversation, from which though I cannot escape, I can only hear with concern and resentment, I must as soon as possible find another temporary abode, and acknowledging all your father's kindness, quit his house."

The young man, who amidst his wild enthusiasm, wanted neither sense nor generosity, was now shocked at her supposing he meant to insult her; and terrified at the idea of her being driven to inconvenience by leaving his father's house—"I am always offending," said he, in a voice expressive of the concern he felt, "and I am afraid often wrong; but pardon me once more, Miss de Mornay, pardon and pity me, and I will not again trespass on your patience with discourse which perhaps you ought not to hear; though surely the happy Willoughby himself would not be alarmed at the hopeless admiration of a man—who knows, that he can never pretend to any other than distant and humble adoration:

'It were all one
That I should love a bright particular star ...'"[1]

He was going on, when Captain Thorold, who had imperceptibly slackened his pace, caught these words, which were spoken in a theatrical tone, and stopping with his friend, Celestina and Montague were immediately close to them. "So, Montague," said he, "at the old game. Miss de Mornay, I bar all quotations. 'Tis not fair for Montague to avail himself at once of his own talents and those of all the poets and sonneteers he is acquainted with."

"He will avail himself of neither, Sir," answered Celestina, "and I assure you I wish our conversation to become more general."

"There, Montague," cried the Captain, "you see you have tired Miss de Mornay in your *tete a tete*;[2] let us see if Musgrave and I cannot successfully entertain her."

---

1   *All's Well That Ends Well* 1.1.80-2. Helena: "'Twere all one/ That I should love a bright particular star/ And think to wed it, he is so above me."
2   Confidential talk.

Celestina, who did not promise herself much advantage from the change, since Captain Thorold's address to her was often as warm as his brother's but never so respectful, now hastened forward to join Miss Thorold; but she received no notice either from her or her little military beau: they were by this time however near the end of their walk, and were met by the family of Mr. Cranfield, to whom the pond belonged which they were to see fished. The children, several fine boys, now at home for their Easter holydays, were assembled round it eager and delighted. Montague, who was a great favourite in the neighbourhood, was engaged in talking with their mother and with them; while their father, having civilly noticed the whole party, entered into conversation with the gentlemen; and Miss Thorold and Mr. Bettenson still continuing to entertain each other, regardless of every body else, Celestina, who was fatigued by her walk, and still more by the uneasiness of her reflections, sat down under one of the trees which over-shadowed the pond; and her thoughts, which had long been distracted by interruptions, were immediately with Willoughby. So intirely indeed was she for some moments absorbed in reflection, that though she saw objects moving before her, and heard the shouts of the boys, the mixed voices of the party who surrounded the water, and the servants who were drawing the nets, she totally forgot where she was, and was insensible even of that want of common politeness which the whole party evinced in so entirely neglecting her. Montague, however, could not long be guilty of it; but disengaging himself from Mrs. Cranfield, who was one of those incessant talkers from whom it is difficult to escape, he came towards her; and fearful of renewing the displeasure she had so forcibly expressed a quarter of an hour before, he only named his fears that she might receive injury by sitting on the grass; to which, as she gave a cold and reluctant answer, he added a deep sigh, and then leaning against the tree under which she sat, he fell into a reverie as deep as her own. From this mournful silence she was roused by the sudden appearance of an horseman, who rode very fast near her, and who, on lifting up her eyes, she immediately discovered to be Vavasour.

A thousand painful sensations arose on the sight of him; though the first idea that occurred was, that he came from Willoughby. He passed her, however, without seeing her, and reaching the party who were beyond her, he gave his horse to his servant and joined them.

By the manner in which Vavasour addressed Mr. Cranfield, and the manner in which he was received by him, Celestina immediately understood that he was an expected guest. "He comes not to me," said she. "Willoughby sends no friend to me! He is far, far off! and perhaps his most intimate acquaintance may now shun as assiduously as he once sought me."

Then the fears she had once entertained that some difference of opinion had occasioned a quarrel between him and Willoughby recurred to her; and remembering how different her situation had been when he abruptly left Alvestone, and how very cruel was the change, she grew distressed at the thought of meeting Vavasour, and meeting him before so many strangers: she again repented having walked out, and her soul sickened at the many uncomfortable occurrences to which she was continually exposed.

In a few moments, Vavasour, who seemed to have lost none of his vivacity, had been introduced to the Captain and Miss Thorold, but he hardly made his bow to them before he said to the latter—"Miss de Mornay is with you still, Madam; is she not?"

"With us?" replied Arabella. "Oh! yes—Miss de Mornay is with us."

"She is well I hope?" enquired Vavasour eagerly.

"You may satisfy yourself by personal enquiry," said Mrs. Cranfield, "for there is the young lady. She and Mr. Montague really form a very picturesque appearance."

Vavasour, now turning his eyes on the opposite side, saw Celestina, and instantly advanced towards her with an eagerness of manner which he took no pains to check. She arose on his approach; and hardly knowing how to receive him, so various and painful were her sensations, she held out her hand to him, then withdrew it; and when he spoke to her with all that good humour with which he used to approach her in her happier days, it brought those days back to her mind so forcibly, that she could not conquer her emotion, and burst into tears. Vavasour was immediately checked; and said, with evident concern—"My dear Miss de Mornay, the pleasure I felt in again seeing you conquered for a moment the recollection of what has happened since we parted last."

"It is a subject," said Celestina, trying to recover herself, "on which I cannot now talk: yet—" and she moved a few steps forward to escape the earnest looks of Montague Thorold, which were fixed on her face—"yet I cannot help asking if you have seen your friend since—"

Vavasour, walking on with her to avoid the observation of the company, said—"Seen him? to be sure I have: I was continually with him in London all the while he remained there."

Celestina now proceeded in silence, struck with the idea that

Willoughby had certainly acquainted his friend during that time with the reason of their abrupt separation. She had not, however, courage to ask him; but having wiped away the tears which a moment before filled her eyes, she turned them upon him with a look so expressive of what passed in her heart, that Vavasour, who could not misunderstand her, answered, as if she had spoke to him— "I do not *certainly* know the cause of George's very sudden and extraordinary change of measures; but I have reason to believe the Castlenorths, though how I cannot tell, were the occasion of it. Though I was with him every day, I had very little conversation with him, for he always affected to be, or really was hurried if I saw him in the course of the day; or, if towards night, complaining of fatigue, and taking laudanum,[1] without which he said he could not sleep. When he informed me of his having left you at Alvestone without accounting for his absence, he saw my astonishment, and put an end at once to my enquiries by saying—'Vavasour, you know my unbounded confidence in you, and that any thing that related merely to myself would be known to you as the first friend of my heart; but do not ask me any questions now: I cannot answer them truly, and therefore I will not be liable to them: even your friendship and zeal can here do me no good.' This," continued Vavasour, "precluded all enquiry; nor could I obtain any farther satisfaction, when a few days afterwards, the very day indeed before he left London, he desired I would meet him at the chambers of Edwards, our mutual attorney, where in spite of my resistance, he paid me the money which you know I lent him, with the interest, with as much regularity as if I had fixed that time for payment; and when I very warmly remonstrated on the unfriendly appearance this had, besought him to oblige me by keeping the money, and expressed something like resentment at his conduct, he said, with a sort of affected calmness, and almost sternly—'Vavasour, I am going abroad. I may die, and I will not leave any thing between us to be settled by Lady Molyneux, who would be my heir at law; and do not you,' added he, 'my good friend, get a habit of throwing your four or five thousands about you, but learn to value money a little more....' 'And friends a little less,' said I, interrupting him in my quick way; 'for that, Willoughby, is the next lesson I expect to hear from you. This money, however, Edwards shall keep till you are quite sure you do not want it.' 'I am already sure of it,' said he, 'and do beg, my dear Vavasour, that you will

---

1 A mixture of opium and alcohol taken as a painkiller or soporific.

immediately pay it into the hands of the person from whom you borrowed it for my use, as the only way in which it can now contribute to my satisfaction.' Willoughby then left me with the attorney, of whom I enquired if he could guess where he got the money; Edwards assured me he could not, as he knew nothing more of the affair than that he was that day to pay it at his chambers to me."

This circumstance seemed, in the mind of Celestina, to confirm the notion Vavasour had started, that the Castlenorths were somehow or other the cause of Willoughby's having left her; yet, as they could have no power over him from affection or friendship, their influence, if indeed they possessed any, must arise from their riches; and what was such a supposition but to suppose him a sudden convert to mercenary politics,[1] from being generous and disinterested even to excess, if such noble qualities could ever lean towards error. The mind of Celestina no sooner harboured such an idea than her heart rejected it; but all she heard from Vavasour tended only to augment her perplexity and her sorrow, which, as he perfectly understood, she saw that he would if he could have removed.

Almost afraid of asking any question, where it was easy to see he could not answer without wounding her, she acquired, after a few moments, resolution to say—"Where, Sir, did you at last part from him? What did he then say to you?"

"I took leave of him at the hotel where he lodged, and where I had been with him for about an hour before the chaise came to the door. He was sometimes very grave, and even dejected for a few moments, then tried by hurry and bustle to drive away his dejection. I asked him why he went to the south of France, where he had been before, rather than to Spain and Sicily, which he had often expressed an inclination to see: he answered, that he had business in France; 'but it is more than probable,' continued he, 'that I may see Spain and Sicily, or Turkey for aught I know, before I return to England.'"

"And did he," enquired Celestina mournfully—"did he say nothing of me? Did he not even mention me?"

"Very often," replied Vavasour, "for indeed I forced him into the conversation."

"Did there *need force* then?" said Celestina in a plaintive tone, and ready to melt into tears.

"Yes," answered Vavasour; "for though I believe he thought of nothing so much, he seemed frequently unwilling to trust his voice

---

1   Used in its original meaning of scheming or trickery.

with your name; and sometimes, after we had been speaking of you, he sunk into a gloomy reverie, and reluctantly spoke at all. One great object of his solicitude was your future residence. He seemed however very easy while you were under Mr. Thorold's protection. Tell me, are you yourself happy in his family?"

"Happy!" said Celestina, "*can* I be *happy* any where?"

"Perhaps not just now: but you know what I mean when I use the common term *happy*. Are you satisfied with your residence? do you mean to continue there?"

"I hardly know," sighed Celestina, "what I mean. So heavy, so unexpected was the blow that fell upon me, that my stunned senses have not yet recovered it; and for happiness—I am afraid it never can be mine."

"Well, my sweet friend, though I hope and believe otherwise, we will not talk now either of our hopes or fears: but are the family you are with pleasant people? of whom do they consist?"

"Of Mr. Thorold, to whose worth you have heard Willoughby do justice, of his wife, his daughter, and, at present, of two sons."

"Yes, I see the Captain is among you."

"You know him then?"

"A little. Some friends of mine are acquainted with him. He is a man of great gallantry I have heard, and affects the very first world;[1] does he not?"

"Really I hardly know. Yes, I believe he may be that sort of man."

"Celebrated, I think, for having sent more young women broken hearted to Bristol[2] than either Charles Cavendish or Ned Hervey.[3] That is the sort of praise that attracts your hearts, while we rattle-headed fellows, who are very honest though not very refined, who say no more than we mean, and address you—not as goddesses, only to laugh at you for believing us, but as mere mortal women, are called rakes and libertines and I know not what; as

---

1 Pretends to be in the highest society.

2 Literally, broken-hearted to try to recover their health at the spa, Bristol Hotwells. But the flippant expression could be used of any woman disappointed in love.

3 These are not allusions to real people; rather, Smith substantiates the social prestige of Vavasour and Willoughby by showing Vavasour on familiar terms with young men with the family names of the Dukes of Devonshire and Bristol.

if twenty such careless, I had almost said harmless, lads as we are, do half as much mischief as one of those plausible, sentimental, sighing sycophants, who mean nothing but the gratification of their own paltry vanity."

"Bless me, Mr. Vavasour," cried Celestina, won a moment from her own anguish by this odd remark, "you seem as much discomposed as if the redoubtable Captain had sent some favourite of your own to Bristol."

"No, upon my soul—my favourites—I speak pretty plainly you know: my acquaintance have in every instance but one lain among people not easily sent to Bristol. Come now, don't affect prudery. I tell you though, Celestina, that had such a fellow sent a sister of mine to recover health, ruined by the disappointment of expectations he had raised, I believe I should try if I could not stop his career."

"It is fortunate then, perhaps, for the Captain, that you have no sister."

"I may, however, have friends," added be, earnestly fixing his eyes on the face of Celestina—"I may have friends, for whom I may be as much interested as I could be for the nearest relation; and whom I would put upon their guard."

"I would very fain misunderstand you," said Celestina, "because I think you ought to know that, situated as I am, I need no such precaution: or you must have a mean opinion of me indeed, if, knowing Mr. Willoughby, you can suppose that she who has once been attached to him, can throw away a thought upon Captain Thorold."

"Aye that's true—all very true and very fine: but look ye, my dear Celestina, I've no way of judging of others but from myself, and (though to be sure I don't speak from experience in these honourable sentimental sort of treaties) I am confoundedly afraid that had I been engaged to Helen, and found that by some cursed counter stroke of fortune her divinityship was not to be had, that after a little raving and swearing and scampering about the world to get her out of my head, I should have fallen in love with—"

"With Andromache,"[1] said Celestina, helping him to a comparison, and smiling.

"Oh no!" answered he, "she was too wise and too melancholy for me: your weeping and tragical beauties would make me cry, but

---

1   Wife of the Trojan prince, Hector, and mother of his son, thus with
    more dutiful, less glamorous associations than Helen.

never could make me love. Faith I think Briseis or Chryseis[1] would have been more to my taste."

"Or Cressida[2] perhaps?"

"Oh! she would have suited me exactly."

"Well Sir!" said Celestina, re-assuming her gravity, "you undoubtedly follow the golden rule in judging of others; but give me leave to assure you that in the present instance it would mislead you, and that you are the only man in the world from whom I could listen to such a supposition without resentment. You, however, do not, I know, mean to hurt me."

"No that I don't by heaven," cried he, kissing her hand, "and so do now tell me how and when I can see you again."

"I cannot tell; since it probably depends on your stay in this country."[3]

"That depends then upon you."

"Upon me!"

"Yes, upon you: for I came down with no other intention in the world than to enquire after and see you; and for that purpose only have consented to undergo the company of Cranfield and his wife; very good sort of people indeed, but confounded bores; who have invited me down these two years, and whose invitation nothing but their being within four miles of Thorold's would have made me accept."

Celestina was at a loss what answer to make to this, because she did not know whether he meant to impute his solicitude to the care he took of Willoughby's interest, or simply to his friendship for her, for of any warmer interest than friendship she had not the remotest idea. She had, however, no time to answer, for Montague Thorold, who had followed them with his eyes ever since they parted from

---

1   In Homer's *Iliad*, Chryseis, daughter of a priest, is awarded to King Agamemnon of Greece as his slave when the Greeks invade her native island. Her father's spells enforce her return, but Agamemnon takes Achilles' slave Briseis in compensation, causing the wrath of Achilles, one of the main themes of *The Iliad*. By the comparison with slaves Vavasour implies he prefers a mistress or a prostitute to a wife or to courting an unattainable woman.

2   Cressida does not figure in Homer's *Iliad* but appears in medieval versions of the Troy story, and is the heroine of Chaucer's *Troilus and Criseyde* and Shakespeare's *Troilus and Cressida*. In both, she is unfaithful to her lover when her circumstances change.

3   County.

the rest of the company, now came hastily on towards them to say his sister was returning home.

Celestina rejoined them immediately; and after Mr. and Mrs. Cranfield and their guest had been invited and consented to dine with the Thorold family the next day, they separated, Vavasour betraying a violent inclination to attend Celestina home, and seeming to repress it with great difficulty from the habit he was in of doing whatever pleased himself without considering whether what he did was, according to the established forms of the world, rude or polite. He felt, however, that to quit his hospitable friends on the moment of his arrival would be carrying his carelessness a little too far; and therefore after lingering as long as he could, he reluctantly left her to Montague Thorold, who had walked silently by her for some moments, and wished her a good day.

Chapter VI

Celestina, in whose mind a thousand painful thoughts had been revived by this interview, was too much lost in them to attend to Montague Thorold, who still in silent dejection walked by her, while his brother was engaged with Arabella and his military friends. Montague had narrowly watched her the whole time she had been conversing with Vavasour; and, though hopeless himself, could not see her receive another with such an appearance of interest as he had remarked towards Vavasour, without mortification. "Mr. Vavasour," said he at last, "for that I think is the gentleman's name—Mr. Vavasour is an old acquaintance of yours?"

"A very particular friend of Mr. Willoughby's," replied she; "and of course a friend of mine."

"A single man I suppose?"

"I believe so," said Celestina; "at least I never heard he was married; and you see he has not a very sober, married look."

"No really, very much otherwise. But he does not seem to have communicated any portion of his gaiety to you."

"I am not indeed greatly disposed to be gay," said Celestina; "and since I am not merry, would it not be as well to be wise? Do, Mr. Montague, give me that silly paper: its detention is useless to you and disagreeable to me."

"Pardon me then if for once I am guilty of what offends you. I cannot part with it. But it is my first and shall be my last offence."

"I hope so," said Celestina very gravely. "The thing is in itself of no consequence, and I wonder you should be so childishly anxious to keep it."

"Your hands have touched it; your letters are upon it; you composed the lines."

"Well, Sir," cried she impatiently, and willing to put an end to a speech to which she feared the Captain might listen; "since you will not give it me or destroy it, the only favour I have to ask is, that you will never speak of it again, either to me or any other person."

"A needless precaution!" exclaimed he, "a very needless precaution is the latter; and, alas! in the former I cannot trespass long, for in a few days, a very few days, I return to Oxford, and I shall then be no more liable to excite your displeasure: you will cease to recollect that such a being exists."

"No indeed," said Celestina; "whoever is dear to Mr. Thorold, to your father, to whom I am so much obliged, must have a claim to my recollection and my good wishes."

"Oh! how cold does that sound from those lips," said he, "and how little those expressive eyes are calculated to talk of mere good wishes. They are so enchanting when they say more, when they look as they did just now on Mr. Vavasour. How I envied him the simple 'God bless you!' and—'Adieu, Mr. Vavasour,' and the look that accompanied them."

"Ridiculous!" cried Celestina. "Really, Mr. Montague, the style to which you have accustomed yourself destroys all conversation. If however that adieu was so enviable, I will bid you farewel with quite as much sincerity. God bless you, and adieu, Mr. Montague." They were now very near home, and Celestina, hastening forward, crossed the garden by a nearer way and reached her own room.

She there began once more to meditate on her situation. Every day that she had passed at Mr. Thorold's house had encreased her desire to leave it, and she now more than ever regretted that she knew not whither to go. Her concern was encreased by a note brought to her from the neighbouring village, from whence she had early that morning sent to her former abode at Thorpe Heath to enquire whether, if she had occasion for them, she could again have her former lodgings: the answer imported that the old man and his wife had died within a few days of each other, the week before, and that the house now belonged to one of the sons, who had a large family of his own, and intended to remove into it himself, as being more convenient than his former habitation.

This forlorn hope being entirely over, her reflections on her situation became more painful, since she now knew not one place in the world where she could with propriety go. She had once or twice consulted Cathcart on the subject; who not being aware of the circumstances which rendered her present abode uneasy to her, and knowing how much Willoughby desired her to continue there, rather discouraged than promoted any scheme for her removal; flattering himself, that the time was not far distant when her presence would give, in the opinion of Jessy and his own, a charm to the house they hoped to call their own.

Celestina was well aware of his reasons for wishing her to remain where she was, and did not love to explain hers for desiring to remove, least she should appear at once fastidious and vain. She could not relate to Cathcart, what after all might be fancy, that Mrs. Thorold did not love her though she was civil to her; that Miss Thorold beheld her sometimes with dislike and never with friendship; and that of the two brothers, the elder often affected to entertain her with conversation, such as, though she could not directly complain of it, she could not hear without being offended and mortified; while the younger never ceased pursuing her with declarations of romantic attachment, less disgusting, but equally if not more improper for her to listen to.

In Mr. Thorold she had always a steady friend and a disinterested adviser; but to him she could not state the reasons that made his house uncomfortable and his kindness useless, nor complain that his wife and daughter slighted, or his sons made love to her; and though he possessed a very uncommon share of discernment, he seemed determined not to perceive either himself. On no plan of removal, however, could she at present determine, and had fixed on nothing but to find an opportunity to hint her discontent to Vavasour, when she was called down to dinner.

The two military strangers were gone; but Celestina found they were engaged to dine there the next day with the Cranfield family and Mr. Vavasour; and Mrs. Thorold, who piqued herself above all other things on giving as good entertainments as some of her neighbours who kept men cooks, was so impatient to prepare for the dinner of the next day, that she could hardly give herself time to eat that of the present, but hurried way to her store room the instance the cloth was removed. Arabella had yet a more important concern to attend to: Mr. Bettenson had been so lavish of his compliments, which were indeed the only sort of conversation *he* was at all perfect in, that she had no doubt of having made, if not an absolute conquest, at least such an impression on his heart as another interview would make indelible; and though his extravagant praises, and the heavy language of two rolling black eyes, (which in lustre and shape Montague compared to two pickled walnuts,) had not so far blinded the judgment of Arabella but that she saw he was extremely weak, she considered his great fortune, and that if he could not lead, he would probably submit to be driven, for which she thought she had all possible talents and was sure she had all possible inclination. He had not a title indeed, but was the third or fourth cousin of a man that had; of course he was a man of family himself; and had he not been so, had his birth been mean and his person less tolerable, his fortune would not have suffered her a moment to consider either as of any consequence. But though she entertained a very great inclination, and a very well grounded hope to secure Bettenson, she had not the least objection to make an experiment at the same time on Vavasour, who had a still better fortune with a very handsome figure; and who she had heard described, as one of those agreeable rakes, who are blamed and loved by all their acquaintance. She had heard too that he declared himself not to be a marrying man; the greater therefore would be her glory, should she happen to charm him into other sentiments; and when she looked in the glass she thought nothing more probable. As to Celestina, besides her engagements with Willoughby, she considered her as quite out of the question. Neither Captain Musgrave or Bettenson had taken any notice of her, and the latter had declared he thought her far from handsome. Arabella therefore saw nothing to impede her success; and even fancied, that as she intended to be infinitely lively and entertaining, the melancholy air and pensive face of Celestina would produce a contrast extremely to her advantage; while her mother therefore was busy with her jelly and custards, Arabella was preparing her artillery against the hearts of her expected guests; and Celestina, who dared not venture out least she should meet Montague Thorold, who had placed himself where she could not escape him, remained the whole evening alone in her own room, where she formed a sketch of the letter she intended to write to Willoughby.

This employment, by fixing her thoughts entirely on the object which broke in upon every other that at any time of necessity engaged them, quieted and soothed her spirits; she forgot every thing but her wish to convince him of her unfailing attachment, and to pour out before him a heart that was entirely his own. She determined, however, not to finish her letter till after she had talked to Vavasour; and then recollected that she could not tell Willoughby the result of that conference, without assigning her reasons for desiring to quit a protection, where he had himself directed her to remain.

This was an irksome task to her; for if he should happen to think her objections frivolous, he would be displeased that for those she removed, and if he thought them just, the idea of rivalry would add to the uneasiness which she knew her unsettled situation would occasion to him. Thus undetermined, she could rest on nothing but the hope that Vavasour might, from his dislike to one or other of the Thorolds, (for he was too frequently extremely fastidious and disliked with all his heart) agree with her in the necessity there was for her change of abode, without enquiring into all the reasons that made her desire it.

By the bustle she heard below in the housekeeper's room, which was under part of hers, and by the frequent running up and down of Arabella's maid, and the universal hurry of the household, except Mr. Thorold, who on these occasions retired to his study for the evening, Celestina found she should rather accommodate than offend if she declined supping below. She sent down a note therefore, saying she was much fatigued with her morning's walk, and begged to be excused for the evening, and received a verbal answer that Mrs. Thorold desired she would do as was most agreeable to her. Montague, however, who despairing of her coming out to walk, had at last sauntered away alone, no sooner found on his return that he was not to see her at supper, than he went up himself, and tapping softly at the door, enquired if she was not well?

"Oh! perfectly well," said she, "but tired by my walk of this morning, and not disposed to eat any supper."

"Surely," cried he, "if you are tired you will need something. You did not drink tea, and yet will have no supper; let me get something for you?"

Celestina declined this however as politely as she could; but Montague was not to be repulsed so easily. He went down therefore, and returning in a few minutes, besought her to open the door and take some of the wine and water he had brought her. Distressed by civility, which it seemed so rude to refuse and so painful to accept, she hesitated a moment, and then opened the door, when taking one of the glasses she thanked him and would have wished him good night; but he looked earnestly in her face—"Ah!" said he, "tears! you have been weeping again! always in tears! You have been writing to—writing to the fortunate Willoughby?"

"Pray don't teaze me so," cried Celestina: "if I have cause for tears, you should remember that the greatest kindness you can do me is permitting me to indulge them: and it signifies not who I write to."

"It signifies no more indeed," said Montague, with a deep drawn sigh, "than as it excites my envy and my regret."

"Well, well, good night to you," interrupted Celestina. "Pray don't let me keep you from supper."

"Oh!" said he, putting his foot within the door so as to prevent her shutting it, "I have had my supper. One look suffices me:

> 'Loose now and then
> A scatter'd smile, and that I'll live upon.'[1]

Ah! you remember those delicious lines of that most elegant of our English poetesses:

> 'It is to be all bathed in tears;
> To live upon a smile for years;
> To lie whole ages at a beauty's feet;
> To kneel, to languish, to implore,
> And still, tho' she disdain, adore.
> It is to do all this, and think thy sufferings sweet.'[2]

Shall I go on? for the whole of that beautiful song is exactly descriptive of my feelings:

> 'It is to hope, tho' hope were lost,
> Tho' heaven and earth they passion crost'[3]

But are you angry?"

"I am at least tired," said Celestina, "and must beg you would no longer detain me."

"Give me your hand then in token that we part in peace.

> 'Ma poi di pace in pegno
> La bella man mi die'[4]

---

1 *As You Like It* 4.1.104-05.
2 Anna Laetitia Barbauld, "Song I," 7-12. Smith's note: Mrs Barbauld.
3 Barbauld, "Song I," 19-20.
4 Pietro Metastasio, *Canzonetti*, "IV: La Partenza," 35-36: "But then as a pledge of peace/ She gave me her beautiful hand." Smith's note: Y Metastasio.

"There, Sir," said Celestina coldly, "there is my hand, and now good night."

"Oh that I dared seal my forgiveness upon it," cried he, eagerly pressing it. "But I dare not."

Celestina withdrew her hand, and again repeating a cold good night, he at length permitted her to shut the door.

These frequent declarations, which she could not affect to misunderstand, greatly disturbed her; and so well aware was she of the impropriety of suffering them, that she was determined no consideration should induce her to remain another week, if Mr. Montague was not really returning within that time to Oxford. She had heard him repeatedly laughed at by his father, his brother, and his sister, for his paroxysms of love: if his present attention to her was only a return of the fit, she felt herself degraded by being made the object of it; and if it was more serious, she thought herself to blame to suffer his assiduities, on account of his father, though she knew not very well how to put an end to them. Much less appearance of passion would have made many young women believe him ready to take the lover's leap, or to apply laudanum or gunpowder as a remedy; but Celestina, though not unconscious of her personal advantages, had none of that overweening vanity which make so many of inferior attractions fancy themselves irresistible, nor any of that unfeeling coquetry, which would be gratified by the despair of a man capable of real attachment: she wished to put an end to Montague's persecuting admiration both for his sake and her own; and after some reflections, concluded, that it would be better to take an opportunity of speaking to him the next day, and declaring to him that his extravagant behaviour would compel her to quit the house and lose the acquaintance of his family; for she thought, notwithstanding all his romantic flights, he had so much good sense, that he would see the impropriety, and indeed the cruelty of his conduct, if it were once fairly represented to him. She now almost repented that she had not listened with more patience to the boasting egotism of the Captain, and had taken shelter from his equivocal compliments in the more agreeable because more literary conversation of Montague; and again she reflected, with bitterness of heart, that whether Montague went or stayed, his brother's character, and indeed his manners towards her, made her remaining where she was extremely improper; yet that no eligible situation offered: and for the first time, since she had left Lady Molyneux, she formed a half wish to be again with her, though she knew she had there little kindness and no real friendship to expect.

Chapter VII

The preparations for a splendid dinner succeeded admirably, and Mrs. Thorold was in high good humour when her guests arrived. Arabella was still better pleased: for Bettenson, immediately on his entrance, had protested that she never looked so well in her life, and Musgrave whispered to her, that "if she minded her hits[1] she would be sure of the pretty boy," for so he, the Cornet, was termed by his Captain. Intelligence so conveyed would have disgusted and offended a young woman of delicacy, but Belle Thorold was too eager for conquest, and too resolutely bent on securing a man of fortune, to feel or to resent the freedom of this address from Musgrave, to whose praises of her she knew much of the attention of Bettenson was owing. Mr. and Mrs. Cranfield and Vavasour soon after arrived; and Celestina saw with surprise the pains Miss Thorold took at once to attract the notice of Vavasour, and encrease the admiration of Bettenson. She had never before seen her in the company of young unmarried men of fortune, and now observed with concern how totally she defeated her own purpose. She threw herself into numberless attitudes which she fancied becoming; applied her hand incessantly to rectify a curl, or adjust her necklace, by which she thought to display its beauty as well as that of her hair, and her throat, which she had been taught to fancy eminently handsome. She whispered about nothing, laughed at some joke which nobody understood but herself and Musgrave, then affected to be angry at something he said to her, then talked to him by signs across the table, and by way of being charming was rude and childish. But this sort of behaviour she had seen practised by some very fashionable young women; it was perfectly adapted to the level of Bettenson's capacity; and she had not judgment enough to see that it must offend any man who had either good sense or good breeding. Vavasour, who in the presence of Celestina would have seen perfect beauty or extraordinary merit with indifference, took no other notice of Arabella than just served him to remark to Celestina that she was one of the most conceited and pert girls he had ever seen. This served, as they walked after tea in the garden, to introduce the discourse she wished to hold with him: but it was extremely difficult to escape a moment from the vigilant assiduity of Montague Thorold. "Pray," said she to Vavasour, "pray be more guarded: her brother will hear you."

---

1 A hit in fencing, used as a metaphor for success in attracting a husband.

"And that brother," said he, somewhat abruptly, "you seem very much afraid of offending, though he seems to me to be a puppy;[1] how can you let him prate to you as he does?"

"Indeed," replied Celestina, "you would not dislike him if you knew him; and it is amazing to me that you, who are really so good humoured, should take such dislikes to people before you can possibly know them."

"And when I do know them I often dislike them more. Why now, in this family, who is there but the father that has any understanding, and he has too much of the priest about him. But here comes your highflying Oxonian.[2] Surely it's hard not to have a moment with you, though I want to talk to you about Willoughby."

"I will speak to Mr. Montague," said she, "and tell him so." She then stepped back a few paces, and meeting Montague Thorold, who was approaching to join them, she told him that Mr. Vavasour had something to communicate to her on behalf of their mutual friend Willoughby, and that she should esteem herself obliged to him if he would prevent their being interrupted for a few moments.

Montague, with a melancholy and submissive look, laid his hand on his heart and said—"One word from you is enough to him who lives but to obey you." He then went back to the rest of the party, casting a wistful look after Celestina, who, turning into another walk with Vavasour, said eagerly—"Well, and now what you have to say to me from Willoughby? have you heard from him?"

"No," replied Vavasour; "I could not well do that since yesterday, nor do I indeed expect it for some time to come: but do you know, Miss de Mornay, that I consider myself as Willoughby's representative, as a sort of guardian to you, and am going in that character to talk to you very seriously."

"Well," cried Celestina, conscious that her own conduct was irreproachable, "my sage guardian and revered monitor, begin then with your remonstrance or exhortation, whichever it is to be."

"You must give me leave to be serious on this occasion," answered he.

"Most willingly," replied Celestina, interrupting him; "and the more so because I never remember in all our former conversations to have had one serious discourse with you, and I long to see how you acquit yourself."

---

1 An impertinent youth.
2 Oxford man.

"I don't like the people you are with," said he, "and wish you were any where else."

"I wish I were any where else myself; yet I like the family, and believe them to be very good sort of people."

"Come, come, Celestina, you cannot be ignorant of what I mean: Captain Thorold, as I told you yesterday, is that dangerous and hateful character, a male coquet."

"He never coquets with me I assure you," said she, "for I never give him an opportunity."

"No, because at present his brother has the advantage of him. If you do not coquet with the military man, at least you listen to the scholar, and it may be he is the most dangerous of the two. It is the general idea of the country[1] that he is in love with you; that—"

"The general idea of the country!" cried Celestina, "how can the country possibly know any thing about him or about me?"

"My dear friend," interrupted Vavasour, "you cannot be ignorant that in these places the people could not exist if their curiosity did not keep their idleness from total stagnation. They will talk, and let them about one another, but I won't have them talk of you, who are of another order of beings: in short, I am jealous of you *for my friend*, and don't like to hear that Lord Castlenorth has paid off all Willoughby's incumbrances,[2] and that he has procured him the reversion of his titles,[3] to engage him to break off his connection with you, which it is said he formed before he came of age, and therefore thought himself obliged to fulfil."

Celestina cried with great emotion—"Dear Sir! but how false and foolish is all this."

"It is so," resumed Vavasour; "and what follows is equally or more so, yet it is I find generally believed."

"And what is it?"

"Why that Willoughby, having scruples about suddenly leaving you, and leaving you in comparative indigence, Lord Castlenorth has given you five thousand pounds; which, with what was before left you by Mrs. Willoughby, and the promise of a very considerable living in the gift of the Castlenorths to a clergyman if you marry one, have rendered you a desirable object in Mr. Thorold's eyes as a wife for his youngest son, whom finally you have accepted of, and are to

---

1 County.
2 Debts.
3 Has ensured through influence at court that Willoughby will inherit his titles on his death, if he marries Miss Fitz-Hayman.

be married to very soon; as Miss Fitz-Hayman has insisted upon this before she gives her hand to her cousin, which is also to happen very soon in Italy."

"Miss Fitz-Hayman!" said Celestina, turning pale; "and pray, my good Vavasour, where have you learned this legend?"

"In London," replied he, "I collected enough to make me uneasy about your situation. I picked up more since I came down to the Cranfields, for his wife is a gossip of the first pretensions; and as to the Fitz-Hayman part of the story, their going abroad so soon after Willoughby has, I take it for granted, confirmed it in the opinion of every body."

"Are they gone abroad then?" said Celestina.

"So say the newspapers; and I fancy rightly." He then took one from his pocket and read this paragraph:

"Dover, April 26, 17—[1]
"Yesterday Lord and Lady Castlenorth, and their daughter, the Hon. Miss Fitz-Hayman, with a great retinue, sailed from hence on their way to the South of Europe."

Celestina was silent a moment; for not all her faith on the unchangeable affections of her lover could guard her from a momentary shock: recovering herself however, she said—"They may be, and I suppose are gone; but—certainly—certainly Mr. Willoughby had no share in their going. You surely do not think he had? As we know some part—great part of what you have heard, to be utterly false and unfounded, why may it not all be so? Certainly you do not believe any of it."

"Pardon me," answered Vavasour, "I believe that this young man, this Montague Thorold, is what they call in love with you; for the rest, I know some of it is false, and I believe the greatest part of it is so."

"Gracious heaven! you have doubts then, Vavasour: doubts whether Willoughby—But it is impossible you *can* doubt it. You know he is all honour, generosity, integrity, and goodness."

"I know I always thought so, or I should not have loved him better than any man breathing. But don't let me alarm you; I cannot doubt when I recollect all I ever knew of my friend: yet I very honestly tell you, that the mystery he made to me of his reasons for

---

1 1788.

going abroad, the gloomy reveries in which I so often saw him, his evident struggles with himself, and a thousand odd circumstances which struck me when we were last together—upon my soul, Celestina, I know not what to think, and should deceive you were I to tell you that I have no doubts: yet they arise rather from my mistrust of human nature in general than my opinion of George as an individual: but when I look at you, and remember that he was within one day of calling you his, I cannot upon any common principles account for his conduct, and am sure that no common motives can justify it." Celestina, whose heart sunk within her while it could not deny the justice of this remark, sighed deeply, but remained silent; and Vavasour went on—"Be *his* motives, however, what they may, it is certainly your determination to await the event of this mysterious journey?"

"It is certainly," said she faintly.

"Well then, is there not any more eligible situation for you than one where you are the subject of such reports as I have just repeated to you? Suppose, if it be only for supposition sake, they were to reach Willoughby: if he still loves you...."

"If!" repeated Celestina; "good heaven! you believe then that it admits of a question?"

"I did not mean to hurt you. But my dear Celestina, there is nothing so insecure as our affections I am afraid; and you must recollect too many instances of their change to suppose it *quite* impossible that...."

"Well, I will interrupt you no more. If then—if Willoughby still loves me...."

"He will suffer extremely from such a report; and should—though I allow it to be very improbable—*should* any change have happened, your apparent approbation of Montague Thorold will justify that caprice which nothing else *can* justify."

"Ah! Vavasour," said Celestina, in faultering accents, "I see, I too evidently see, that you believe your friend is lost to me for ever, and that all you have now said is merely to prepare me for a blow, which, if it fell on me suddenly, would, you think, destroy me: but believe me, Vavasour, believe me, suspense such as I have long endured—such as I at this moment endure—is, I *think*, more insupportable than any certainty could be, unless it were the certainty that Willoughby is more miserable than I am: that I think I could not bear: but for the rest, however I might suffer in my pride or in my love, I trust that my mind would in time be reconciled to whatever is inevitable; and perhaps," continued she, struggling with the violent emotion she felt—"perhaps that very pride might assist me to cure the anguish of disappointed and improperly indulged affection. But yet it is surely impossible Willoughby *can* have acted as these suspicions in regard to Miss Fitz-Hayman would make me imagine, and still write as he writes to me! However, Vavasour, I again entreat you, if you know more than I do, to conceal nothing from me through misplaced and needless tenderness."

"You know me very little," answered Vavasour, "or you would know how little concealment and dissimulation are in my nature. My dear Miss de Mornay, I have faithfully related to you all I know of our friend, and even my half formed doubts I have not attempted to conceal from you: be now equally ingenuous with me, and tell me, whether you think your present situation is either the most pleasant or the most eligible you could possibly chuse."

"It is not pleasant," answered Celestina, "because I am not mistress of my time; but it is eligible surely, because Willoughby himself in some measure placed me in it, and it is to his wishes I am to attend while he is yet interested about me, and not to the vague and unfounded reports of people who care nothing whether I am happy or miserable, so long as they have something to talk of."

"But reflect a moment whether Willoughby, when he mentioned his desire of your continuing here, was aware that Captain Thorold would *therefore* remain at home all the summer, or that Montague Thorold would chuse to make you the object of his poetical panegyric: you cannot but know that he does both; and were you wilfully blind to it, his behaviour to-day would have sufficiently convinced *me*."

Celestina could not deny his extreme particularity in company, and his private declarations were less equivocal: without however acknowledging either to Vavasour, she said in general, that for many reasons she should not be displeased to change her residence if she knew whither to go.

Vavasour then began to lament that he had no mother, no sister, of whose friendly reception of her he could be assured; "but," added he, "my dear Miss de Mornay, give me a day or two, and some proper place will perhaps occur to me, or rather to an excellent female friend whom I will apply to. In the mean time I will see Carthcart, as I propose to ride over to Alvestone to-morrow, and we will talk the business over together." He then took her hand, and in a manner more tender and less lively than was usual with him, asked her if she would pardon him for any thing he might have said to give her pain. Celestina assured him she could not forgive because she had never been offended, but that she must ever be greatly obliged to him for the friendly part he had taken; and then, fearing that some invidious remarks might be made by the company they had left if they were any longer absent, she desired Vavasour to rejoin them, while she went for a few moments to her own room to recover from the still apparent emotion which she had been thrown into from what had passed.

She had hardly, however, time to breathe, before she saw Montague Thorold walking anxiously on the lawn before her windows, looking towards them as if he knew she was returned to her apartment, and almost immediately afterwards Mr. Cranfield's carriage drove up to the door to take them home. Celestina, now, therefore, composing herself as well as she was able, hastened down to the company, who, except Montague and Vavasour, were hardly conscious of her rejoining them: Mr. Cranfield being busied in giving to the elder Mr. Thorold a long detail of a cause that had been lately decided at the sessions in which he had a principal share; Mrs. Thorold and Mrs. Cranfield engaged in settling the affairs of the neighbourhood, and comparing notes on the frequency of Mr. Langly, the curate's visits to Mrs. Poole, the widow of a rich farmer, a matter in which these good ladies were mightily interested; while Miss Thorold was violently flirting with Bettenson; and the other two military men walking together, were talking over their former adventures, and Musgrave laughing at Captain Thorold for being thrown out, as he termed it, by his brother with Celestina. "What the devil," said he, "d'ye bury yourself alive in this manner for, if Montague is to supplant you? Faith, my dear Edmund, 'tis so much against the honour of us all, that if you don't make more progress I shall try what I can do myself. Don't you see that her attachment to Willoughby is all stuff, and that she throws out her lure[1] for this Vavasour? If you like her, what a cursed fool you must be to let her slip through your fingers."

"As to liking," replied Captain Thorold, "you don't suppose I intend to commit matrimony. The girl is handsome, and has more sense than most of them...."

"And therefore 'tis more worth a man's while to make a fool of her. There I perfectly agree with you; for though, if I were condemned by any devilish mischance to marry, I should dread nothing

---

1   A device used by a falconer to recall a falcon, used metaphorically: she tries to attract you.

so much as one of your sensible women, yet it is glorious to see how a little foolish flattery can set the sense of the shrewdest of them at nought. But by the way, Edmund, how did you get off with that business in Ireland?"

"Which? for I had so much business upon my hands that I don't know what you mean."

"Why between you and Miss O'Brien: was there not an impertinent brother or—"

"Oh! aye poor Fanny O'Brien. 'Twas the old story: Fanny was very pretty, and faith I was very fond of being with them all, for there were three others, all sweet little dears. Their mother, a good sort of a widow, was a little upon the *qui vive*[1] when she heard I had a fortune and so forth, and somehow or other I lived a good deal at the house, and talked nonsense to the girls in my way you know, till this Miss Fanny took it into her head to fancy herself in love with me, and to suppose I had told her that I was so with her, though if I did upon my soul 'twas only by implication. I dangled to be sure, and dined and danced with her; but I meant nothing, and was obliged at last to tell her mother so, who very plainly signified to me, one evening after I had passed the day with them, that it was time to understand me. Well, I gave her to understand then, as civilly as I could though, for faith they were a good sort of a family, that I had no thoughts of marrying, and the good gentlewoman waxed wroth about it, and told me I had done a very unhandsome thing in winning her daughter's affections. I could only lament they were so easily won, and return them undamaged by me. Something I said, however, gave Mrs. O'Brien offence, and she desired to see me no more; a prohibition which I of course did not attempt to disobey; and some other pretty girl falling in my way, faith I thought no more of my poor Fanny, till being one night at an assembly at Dublin, I saw a great bustle soon after my entrance, and was told that Miss O'Brien had fainted away upon seeing me, and was gone home extremely ill. 'Twas no fault of mine you know that the girl was so simply[2] susceptible: but her brother, a fierce young sailor, who came a day or two afterwards from his ship, thought otherwise, and talking to me rather cavalierly, we agreed that the matter must be settled in the Phoenix

---

1 On the lookout, from a French sentinel's challenge, "Qui vive?" (Who goes there?)
2 Foolishly.

Park by a brace of pistols. *Un beau jour* [1] we accordingly met there, and exchanged each a couple of shots with all possible politeness, in which it was my fortune to lodge a bullet in the flesh of his left arm, which was immediately extracted. I heard there was no danger; and as he was of course satisfied, I came off to England the next day, having taken my passage some time before."

"Your folks here at home never heard of the hazard you ran?"

"No, I believe not. My father is a little too apt to lecture and preach on such occasions, and so 'tis as well sunk I believe; and since I've been in England faith I've had no inclination to amuse myself in the same way, nor indeed any opportunity, except with this Celestial beauty, and she don't seem to take to me."

"The greater will be the glory," replied Musgrave. "I own I should like of all things, were I thee, to drive out a solemn, settled, sentimental affection from such a heart as hers, and jockey thy brother Montague."

Here the gentlemen were interrupted by the departure of Mr. and Mrs. Cranfield and Vavasour; after which Musgrave and Bettenson took leave themselves, having first received a general invitation from Mrs. Thorold and her daughter; who, though by no means pleased to observe that Vavasour, entirely occupied by Celestina, had beheld and heard her with frigid indifference, was yet much consoled by being almost certain that she had secured the heart of the little Cornet. She judged very right. Musgrave, to whose care the father of Bettenson had recommended him, had purposely introduced him to Arabella Thorold, under the idea of detaching him from two milliners, to both of whom he had been making very serious love ever since his residence at Exeter; and the elder Mr. Bettenson was so desirous of saving him from a connection of that kind, which he was thus likely to form, that he no sooner heard of his growing partiality to Miss Thorold, than he besought Captain Musgrave by every possible means to encourage it, declaring that fortune alone was no object to him, and that he should consider himself happy if his son was fixed in his choice of the daughter of so worthy and respectable a man as Mr. Thorold.

1 One fine day.

Chapter VIII

The short remainder of the evening past very unpleasantly to Celestina while she continued in company, for Montague, to whom she could not prevail upon herself to be rude, was yet so dissatisfied, either from the constraint he observed she wore towards him, or from her long conference with Vavasour, that he could not conceal his concern, and sighed so loud and so long, as to attract notice and some very acrimonious speeches from his mother. Mr. Thorold too, she thought, looked uneasy, and Arabella evidently disliked her more than before; while the Captain's rude examination of her countenance, from which she always shrunk, was now more painful to her than ever. She got away as soon as possible; but was far, very far from finding repose in solitude. All that Vavasour had said now returned to torture her; and instead of finding sleep when she retired to her pillow, the same uneasy thoughts and harrassing conjectures which had long rendered it of difficult acquirement, had now received such a reinforcement as made it impossible for her to sleep at all.

She rose with the dawn of day, hoping she might in the course of it see Cathcart; and yet from him she had little to expect as to her removal, unless he could find for her some farm house in the neighbourhood of Jessy, where she might have board and lodging. But even to this scheme there were objections: it would be too near the Thorolds: the young men might still visit her, and the reports still obtain which Vavasour had repeated to her; because, though Montague was really, she found, returning to Oxford in a few days, there would be other occasions of his being at home. It was also too near Alvestone, which, since she almost despaired now of seeing again with pleasure, she wished to escape seeing even at the distance from which she frequently beheld it; when the clump of firs and some of the high grounds in the park, conspicuous from almost every part of the country within ten or fifteen miles, often drew from her heart many a bitter sigh.

About eight o'clock, she saw Cathcart enter the little lawn before the house and immediately went down to him. He approached her with more than ordinary cheerfulness; but in answering her questions told her he had not heard from Mr. Willoughby.

"I flattered myself you had," said Celestina, sinking again into dejection, "for I thought, Cathcart, you seemed unusually cheerful."

"If any thing could make me long so," replied he, "when you, my dear Madam, and my noble friend are divided and uneasy, it would be the intelligence I have received about my sister, whose situation, you know, and my solicitude for her and her children, was indeed the only one Mr. Willoughby's goodness would have left me, if he had himself been as happy as he deserved to be."

"And what then have you heard," enquired Celestina, "of Mrs. Elphinstone?"

"That her husband, who has been long wandering about the world, is at length settled, in a very remote situation indeed, but one which he happens to like and which is likely to become profitable. He is appointed to superintend the fisheries established by a society of gentlemen in the western islands of Scotland, and is already put in possession of a good house in the Isle of Skye. Thither my sister is about to follow him; but I have prevailed upon her to send to me her two youngest children, whom I shall put to nurse in some farm house where Jessy or I can visit them every day: the other two are as many as it will be possible for her to take care of, and when she is settled, I have engaged to conduct the little ones to her. She has already received money from Elphinstone to enable her to set out well equipped, and waits only to see me before she takes leave of London, and, she says, she hopes for ever."

"And when do you go?"

"I propose setting out for London on Thursday, unless you or Mr. Willoughby have any commands for me that may detain me longer."

"Alas! Cathcart," said Celestina, "I am afraid you will receive no intelligence of Willoughby by that time: but I can find, I believe, something for you to do for me which will rather expedite than detain you."

Cathcart then assuring her how happy every opportunity of shewing his gratitude would make him, Celestina said—"Well then, my commands are simply these, that instead of going on horseback you come hither in a post-chaise on Thursday morning, and take me with you to see my dear Jessy, as I cannot go without having that satisfaction, and afterwards, Cathcart, you shall take me to London with you."

Cathcart expressing some surprise at her resolution, she told him that she would account for it as they went; that Devonshire was at present very unpleasant to her, and that she fancied change of place would relieve her spirits more than all her reason and her philosophy, "which, to tell you the truth, Cathcart," said she, "may be accused of acting a little like Horatio; and I sometimes am tempted to say to them—

'Is then the boasted purpose of your friendship

To tell Calista what a wretch she is?
Alas! what needed that?'[1]

But however, I find really, Cathcart, that I cannot here obey our dear friend in the points he most insists upon, those of keeping my cheerfulness and preserving my health, and I have a mind to try his remedy and ramble a little. Perhaps I may go to Scotland with your sister. Do you think she would admit me as a travelling companion?"

"Admit you, dear Madam," said Cathcart. "Surely she would be but too much honoured. But you can never be serious?"

"It is, however, very likely that I may become so. At present, my resolution is to take leave of this family and go with you to London. You will see Vavasour to day, and you may tell him so."

They then settled the house at which the post-chaise was to be ready for her the next morning save one. Cathcart returned to Alvestone; and Celestina to the house, where she proposed taking the earliest opportunity of acquainting Mr. Thorold with her determination.

She considered herself rather as Mr. Thorold's visitor than as the guest of any other of the family; and wished to have his approbation for the step she was about to take, without however assigning the reasons that actuated her to take it. She had frequently fancied of late that he saw more than he chose to notice, and that, though he was too generous to repent the friendly invitation he had given her, he was too prudent not to foresee ill consequences from her long continuing to accept it. In the midst of a large family, to which he was greatly attached, Mr. Thorold lived much of his time alone. His study and his parishioners divided the day, and, except at dinner and for about an hour afterwards, his wife and children saw very little of him. Celestina was uneasy till she had spoken to him; and therefore when he rose to go for his walk after dinner, she enquired whether he would allow her to go part of the way with him, as she wished to speak a few words to him alone.

Montague blushed deeply as she thus addressed herself to his father; who led her however out of the room, and taking her arm within his in his usual friendly way, took the way towards the village street, where he had, he said, some patients to visit that evening; for

---

1   Nicholas Rowe, *The Fair Penitent* 3. 2. 37-9. Calista: "Then all the boasted Office of thy Friendship,/ Was but to tell Calista what a wretch she is;/ Alas! What needed that?" Horatio is the hero's friend, and advisor to Calista.

he was the physician as well as the pastor of his people. After a few minutes of embarrassing silence on the part of Celestina, she collected courage enough to tell him, that in consequence of some intelligence she had learned from Mr. Vavasour, she had determined to go to London.

"Not under *his* convoy I hope?" cried Mr. Thorold, eagerly interrupting her.

"No," answered Celestina, a little startled by the manner in which he spoke: "Not by any means with him, or under his care, but with Mr. Cathcart, who is going on business of his own."

"You know, my dear Miss de Mornay," said Mr. Thorold very gravely, "that my house and my best advice are equally and always at your service: you may have reasons for quitting the one and rejecting the other, into which were I to enquire it would produce for me nothing but mortification. I will not then enquire; I will only entreat you to consider well, whither and with whom you go. Mr. Vavasour has, I apprehend, no mother or sister, and you cannot be ignorant that he has the character of indulging himself in liberties, which even in this age of freedom make him rather a marked man."

"My dear sir," replied Celestina, "I have not the most distant idea of quitting your protection for one so little proper as Mr. Vavasour's must be, though he is the most intimate friend of Mr. Willoughby. But my meaning merely is...."

"Come," cried Mr. Thorold, interrupting her, "I will explain your meaning, or rather the meaning of Vavasour. He has been talking to you about my son Montague. He has represented the impropriety of your listening to such sort of conversation as I know Montague has more than once entertained you with. It is not so?"

"I own it is," said Celestina in some confusion.

"I do not blame him," rejoined Mr. Thorold, "and if his vigilance is the effect of *friendship*, I commend him. Nor do I, my dear ward, disapprove of your wishing to shun the boyish importunity of Montague. I only entreat you to reflect well on your removal, and to remember, that notwithstanding Mr. Vavasour's intimate connection with Willoughby, I consider myself as having some claim to your confidence and as in some degree answerable for your disposal of yourself."

"You are very good, dear Sir, and deserve I am sure my gratitude as well as my confidence. You deserve too that I should speak to you with the utmost sincerity." She then related to him, all that Vavasour had said to her of the reports that had obtained relative to her and Mr. Montague; and concluded by saying, that though she highly esteemed his son, and had the most grateful regard for the whole family, she could not listen to these reports without concern, because they might be displeasing to him and injurious to views he might have for his son, even putting herself out of the question. "I think therefore, dear sir," added she, "that it will be better for me to put an end to my visit for this time, and to travel into the North with a sister of Mr. Cathcart's, who is going thither: change of scene will relieve my spirits, and wandering give me perhaps a new relish for the beauties of Devonshire; where, believe me, I shall be most happy to return, whenever I can do it without subjecting my best friends as well as myself to uneasiness."

"I am vexed," said Mr. Thorold, "that the romantic temper of Montague has made this removal necessary in your idea. He goes very soon to Oxford: indeed in a few days: and afterwards, perhaps, you would find my house less objectionable. As to the gossip of the country, you are I hope too wise to mind it, and I have long since learned to despise it. *That*, therefore should not weigh with me at all. But in return for your charming sincerity, I will speak very plainly to you. Montague is a young man of good abilities, and of an excellent heart; but the violence of his passions keeps me in perpetual concern least they should deprive me of all the happiness that I may hope to derive from such a son: and already I have twice, with great difficulty, delivered him from engagements he had made with young women quite unworthy of him: engagements which, though he soon saw the folly and impropriety of them, he fancied his honour obliged him to keep. Another—I know not who; one perhaps not much superior to these, (as I learned by a friend who keeps a steady eye upon him,) had succeeded to the imaginary possession of his affections when he last came home. I was uneasy at it; but perhaps considered my own feelings too much and yours too little, when I saw with pleasure his instant admiration of you. I encouraged it, because I hoped, that in learning what true merit was, he would hereafter be less liable to be misled by the poor semblance of it, when aided by a pretty face, or a slender shape: at the same time I thought I had sufficiently guarded him against any excess of attachment, by representing to him your situation and convincing him it would not be only presumptuous but hopeless. I believe, however, from some late observations I have made, that I have judged ill; and to save him from maladies that might be trifling or curable, have exposed him to the severer misfortune of feeling a real passion where he can meet with no return."

Celestina could not with sincerity disclaim what she had so much reason to fear was true. Affecting, however, to believe that Mr. Montague would soon lose the impression when she was no longer present, and would find many infinitely more worthy of his affection, who might be proud to receive and at liberty to return it, she renewed the subject of her going to London, besought Mr. Thorold still to honour her with his friendship, and promised to return to him again in the winter if no objection should arise to his receiving her. She heard with gratitude the advice he gave her about Vavasour.—"Do not," said he, "put yourself too much in his power under the idea of his being the chosen friend of Willoughby. He is called, and I believe is, a man of honour, in the common acceptation of the term; but I am afraid there is little real honour among those who are in any respect so very licentious as Vavasour is said to be in regard to your sex; the stile in which he lives among a certain description of women, is not only the means of degrading all in his opinion, but hardens the heart while it corrupts the morals: and with all Vavasour's boasted honour, I dare say he is a man, who, if he happened to take a fancy to the mistress of his friend, would steal her affections and her person without hesitation, and suppose, that by an appeal to the sword or pistol to vindicate the wrong he had done, the action, however unprincipled, would derogate nothing from his honour."

"Sure, sir," said Celestina, "Willoughby would not have so much friendship for Mr. Vavasour were he such a man?"

"I don't know, my dear," answered Mr. Thorold, "that Vavasour is such a man; but you will allow at least that it is very probable; and as to Willoughby's friendship, I am afraid that is no criterion of merit. The college friendships of young men—But let me not make you too much out of humour with the world, while I mean only to put you upon your guard against the evil with which it too often teems towards unprotected youth and loveliness. It grieves my heart to let you go. But—upon the whole, if you promise to write to me often—to remain with this sister of Cathcart's, who is, I conclude, a woman of character, and to take no new course without informing me; above all, to keep yourself quite out of the power of Vavasour, and not to be introduced to any of his acquaintance by way of staying with them, unless you are very certain who they are; I say, on all these conditions I will not oppose your going, though it hurts me to consent to it."

Celestina, having thus relieved her mind by explaining herself to her generous friend, became better satisfied than she had been for some time, and found at least an alleviation of the concern that preyed on her heart, in the idea of change of place. She parted soon after from Mr. Thorold, whose business she was fearful of interrupting, and walked back towards the house, intending to open her intentions of leaving them, to the rest of the family, when they were assembled to their tea.

Montague, however, who had never left sight of her, but had followed her and his father at a distance during their walk, now hastened across the field she was in to meet her. His eagerly enquiring eyes were fixed on her face when he came up to her; but not daring to ask the subject of her conference with his father, nor able to turn his thoughts from it, he only said—"Well, Miss de Mornay, you have left my father?"

"You see I have," said Celestina, smiling, "and I have left him well satisfied with the reasons I have given for quitting his hospitable roof on Thursday."

"Quitting it!" exclaimed Montague, turning pale—"quitting it! What are you going to leave us then? and before I go to Oxford?"

"My good friend," replied she, "you did not surely suppose that I was to be a perennial visitor at your father's. I have now been here almost a month, and you must certainly allow that to be a very long visit from a person, who, till within five weeks, had not the good fortune to be known to your family at all."

"I know not," said Montague, sighing, "what I thought, or what I supposed; but I would to heaven I could forget having ever seen you, as easily as I am convinced you will lose the remembrance of me."

Celestina, with one of those fascinating smiles which lent such peculiar charms to her countenance, now assured him that he was mistaken: "indeed," said she, "I shall always remember you all, with pleasure and with gratitude."

"Well," answered he, "I thank you; and I thank you for not excepting me, and by putting us all together, shewing that you have no particular favourite in the family, but that one is as indifferent as another. But however, I wish you would not smile, for I cannot bear it."

"Ridiculous!" cried Celestina. "I am amazed, Mr. Montague, that with your understanding, you give way so frequently to such absurd fits of—I hardly know what to call it—a romantic stile of behaviour, which you seem to think women like, whereas I assure you that to me at least it is the most unpleasant in the world."

"When did you ever see me in this romantic stile, as you are pleased to term it, with any woman but yourself?"

"I never did, because I happen not to have seen you with any other women than those of your own family: but you know that your mother, your sister and your brother, nay, even your father, all have repeatedly said it was your way with every body."

"They are mistaken however; and I own *I* have often mistaken a transient degree of liking for love, which I never felt—no never—till I saw you!

> 'For several virtues
> Have I liked several women; never any
> With so full soul, but some defect in her
> Did quarrel with the noblest grace she owed[1]
> And put it to the foil.[2] but you! oh you!
> So perfect and so peerless, were created
> Of every creature's best.'"[3]

"There now," said Celestina, "that is exactly what I complain of: there is no rational conversation with you, capable as you are of adorning it; but, as Arabella very truly says, you do nothing but make speeches out of Otway or Shakespeare."

"Arabella did not say I made speeches, but that I made love; and I make love because I feel it—feel it to an excess which is dreadful, because I know, and have known from the beginning, that it is hopeless! But as this hurts nobody but myself, I don't see why it should displease you, or why you should affect to misunderstand, or attempt to laugh off a passion, which, whatever may be its effect on me, can never disturb your tranquillity or that of your fortunate lover."

Celestina finding him thus serious, though it would be better, and indeed more generous, not to pretend ignorance of his meaning, and to reason with rather than rally him; she therefore dropped the gayer tone with which she began the conversation, and said gravely—"Mr. Montague, I will not affect then to misunderstanding you. I am undoubtedly honoured by your partiality, and very much concerned if it is the source of present pain to you. Let it become rather a source of pleasure to us both, by reducing it to that generous and disinterested friendship which I may return with satisfaction, and for those warmer sentiments, which you now suppose are entirely diverted from any other object, seek one who can deserve and return

---

1   Owned.
2   Counteracted it.
3   *The Tempest* 3.1.42-8.

them, and spare me, I beseech you, the pain of believing, even for a moment, that I have brought solicitude and suffering into any part of a family to which I am so much obliged. I need not tell you my situation: you know it is a very comfortless and a very uncertain one: perhaps I may never see Mr. Willoughby again; or if I do, perhaps I may see him the husband of another. But in either case my attachment to him is unalterable; and were I sure to-morrow that we are divided never again to meet, I should only think of submitting in such a way as would least wound him, to a blow, which I am sure he will not voluntarily give me, but never of running the hazard of making unhappy some equally worthy man, by giving to importunity what I can never give to love—for my heart has been Willoughby's ever since I knew I had one, and it will be his, till I remember it no longer."

Montague gave no other answer to this than a deep sigh; and Celestina pausing a moment to recover herself from the emotion her words had occasioned, went on—"You love quotations, and undoubtedly recollect, though perhaps from an author I ought not to quote, these words: '*Il n'y a point d'homme pour celle qui aime; son amant est plus, tous les autres sont moins.*'"[1]

Montague now impatiently interrupted her—"You need not," said he, "thus refine on the cruelty with which you tell me that you can never throw away a thought on me. I knew it before; and in the wildest paroxysms of that passion which I glory in feeling and in cherishing, I never dared flatter myself that you would. Yet—perhaps even this fortunate Willoughby himself—this happy man, who may neglect you, leave you for another, and yet still be beloved—is not more capable of an ardent, a sincere affection, than I am. If he leaves you for ever—good God!—Even if he entirely deserts you, you will still love him—Even then no other would have any hope."

"None," said Celestina, "for then I will never marry. But, my good friend, this is an uneasy subject to us both; let us then never resume it. Allow me to offer you my friendship and my esteem, and to assure you that this sudden partiality, which believe me you will soon and easily conquer, is the only subject on which I cannot listen to you with pleasure."

They were now so immediately before the parlour windows, that

---

1 Jean-Jacques Rousseau, *Julie, ou la Nouvelle Heloise*, Part 1, Julie's Letter L: "For a woman in love there is no such thing as a man; her lover is more, the rest are less."

Montague, who saw the family assembled there at tea, dared not give way to what he felt; but asked her, in a lower voice, when she went. She told him the day after the morrow. Again he sighed; and when they got into the hall, turned towards his own little study, which was on the same floor, while Celestina went to join the party in the parlour; where she found Mr. Bettenson, who she understood was now the professed lover of Miss Thorold; and so entirely did he now occupy the attention both of her and her mother, that they hardly noticed the entrance of Celestina. She took, however, the earliest opportunity of a pause in their conversation, to signify her design of going on the following Thursday.

Miss Thorold contented herself with coldly saying she was sorry to lose her so soon; and her mother, even less civil, as her husband was not by, said—"And pray, Miss de Mornay, where are you going?"

"To London, Madam."

"To London. Bless me! and pray who are you going to there?"

"To a Mrs. Elphinstone, I believe, Ma'am."

"And alone?"

"No, Madam."

"Not alone? then who do you go with?"

"With Mr. Cathcart, Madam."

"Oh! with Mr. Cathcart; and pray, how do you go? In the stage?"

"No, Madam," replied Celestina, blushing at the indelicacy with which all these questions were asked before a stranger.

"How then pray?"

"In post chaises, Madam."

"Humph! Post chaises are expensive." Here she stopped; being unable to find any other questions, or rather not daring to ask any more, as her husband and eldest son that moment came in with Captain Musgrave. Celestina however interpreted the look she put on, as saying, "no matter how you go, so long as you do go," and again she congratulated herself on the resolution she had taken.

Chapter IX

Celestina, finding that Montague Thorold did not join the party, constrained herself to stay with them, least it should be imagined they were together. Captain Thorold, as if he took advantage of his brother's absence, sat down by her, and began in a half whisper to make her some of those speeches, between a sneer and a compliment, which always confused and distressed her. Soon after tea, however, Montague came in, and then, the evening being rainy, cards were proposed, to which his mother desired him to sit down; while Celestina, saying she had a few preparations to make for her journey which she might as well begin in time, went away, nobody asking her to take a seat at the card table.

She was no sooner gone, than Mrs. Thorold, addressing her eldest son, said—"So, Edmund, we are to lose our father's visitor at last, my dear."

"Are we?" said he carelessly. "What, is her *intended* come back?"

"Oh no," replied his mother, "the young lady is going to London it seems."

"Lord, Ma'am," cried Bettenson, "I'll tell you what Musgrave and I heard t'other day; didn't we Muzzy?"

"Faith I don't know whether we did or no, Jacky Boy, till you tell me what it was we heard."

"Why we heard—Lord why 'twas that night we drank tea and supped, you know, with that there family of the Killigrews—we heard that Mr. Montague Thorold was a-going to be married to this Miss de Morning, and that Mr. What d'ye call him—he that was to have had her, had given Mr. Montague a living to take her off his hands."

Either the purport of this speech, or the manner in which it was delivered, threw Captain Thorold and his friend Musgrave into bursts of laughter, which they very freely indulged; but poor Montague turned pale, and trembled with vexation: while Mrs. Thorold, pursing her mouth and drawing herself up, said—"Pray, Mr Bettenson, *where* did you say you heard this story? Edmund, what do you laugh at? I say—Mr. Bettenson, pray was it at Mr. Killigrew's you heard this absurd story?"

"Lord yes, Ma'am, and upon my soul I've heard it elsewhere. Why, Musgrave, don't you remember?—why half the people at Exeter I'm sure have talked to me about it."

"I'm very sorry for it," rejoined the old lady. "People give their tongues strange liberties methinks. My son I can assure them will never, at least with mine and his father's consent, form any such connection. What! with a foreigner! an alien as one may say! brought up upon charity, and I dare say not very honourably born, or how did Mrs. Willoughby get her so easily from her own country. People of fashion don't part with their children to strangers. For my part, I would be very civil to a young woman in distress, as 'twas Mr. Thorold's whim to have her here for a little time, but I am very sorry it has given rise to any such report, which I beg the favour of you gentlemen to contradict. A living indeed! it is very likely that Montague Thorold should accept of a living with such an incumbrance, or on any such conditions."

"But Madam," cried Captain Thorold as he dealt his cards, "what think you if poor Montague avows his penchant for the lady, and talks of dying without her instead of getting a living with her?"

"Think," replied his mother, reddening with anger—"why, think that he is a fool, and that you are very little better for encouraging a silly boy in such nonsense."

"Nay, Madam," cried the Captain, "I am sure I don't encourage him. I was only pitying him, as one naturally does all gentle youths who are crost in love."

Arabella, who knew that her mother sometimes suddenly threw off her every day character to appear in one far less amiable, when unchecked by Mr. Thorold, now feared that she might give way to one of these fits of ill humour and exhibit a scene before Mr. Musgrave and Mr. Bettenson which might give them no very favourable idea of the family temper; she therefore gave her brother Edmund a hint to forbear pushing the conversation any farther. He desisted; the game went in favour of Mrs. Thorold; and in the pleasure of winning five shillings, she forgot for that time the displeasure she had conceived against her youngest son.

Celestina was in the mean time preparing for her journey. She had nothing now but her cloaths to pack up; for her books and her drawing cases were at Alvestone, where Cathcart besought her to let them remain a little longer, promising that if events were finally determined otherwise than he was still willing to hope, he would take them all from thence and send them to her whithersoever she might desire. She wished most earnestly the next day over: for she had now learned to dread more than before some extravagance on the part of Montague Thorold, for whom, notwithstanding the trouble she had received from his continual persecutions, she could not altogether withhold her pity and her esteem. In his figure he resembled his father, whom she had so much reason to regard with grateful affection; and his faults were merely those of youth and a vivid imagination. Whether his partiality to her was of a permanent or transitory nature, it was pretty certain that it now gave him pain, of which Celestina could not consider herself as the cause without desiring to alleviate or rather to end it. At supper, however, she learned, with great satisfaction, that Mr. Thorold and his two sons were engaged out for the whole of the next day, and were to leave home early in the morning. She fancied, from several remarks[1] she made in the course of the evening, that this was purposely contrived: and the eyes of Montague, though he dared not otherwise speak, told her how cruelly he suffered from an arrangement which would deprive him of almost all the opportunities of speaking to her which her short stay might yet afford him. Though he saw that his mother remarked all his looks, and was restrained only by the fear of offending his father from openly avowing the anger she had conceived, he could not forbear watching every turn of Celestina's countenance; and, when he bade her good night at the door, sighing deeply and saying in a low whisper—"At what time do you go on Thursday?"

"Early I hope," replied she; and to avoid all farther questions hastened away.

The next day passed quietly enough: for Mrs. Thorold, sure of being delivered from a visitor who had never been agreeable and was now uneasy to her, thought it as well to be tolerably civil to her; and Arabella, who thought very little about any thing at present but securing her conquest over the heart of Mr. Bettenson, was hardly conscious that she was with them.

Late in the evening the gentlemen returned; but Celestina had left the parlour before their arrival, on pretence of going early to bed that she might be ready the next day for Mr. Cathcart, whom she had appointed to meet her in a post chaise at six o'clock. She took leave of Mrs. Thorold and her daughter therefore this evening, who received her thanks and adieus with great formality and no kindness. Very willingly would she have escaped bidding farewel to Montague Thorold the next morning, but she feared it would be impossible: Mr. Thorold had told her he should himself put her into the chaise; and he always rose so early, that this, she knew, would not put him out of his way.

As soon as her window was opened in the morning, which was almost as soon as it was light, she saw Montague Thorold standing under it. He kissed his hand to her when he perceived her, and looked so dejected that she could not see him without concern. She was very soon dressed, and went down into the parlour, where he no sooner saw her than he came to her.—"You are ready even before the time, so impatient are you to leave us," said he in a mournful voice. "Ah! Miss de Mornay! this house then will never again be blest with your presence!"

---

1 Observations.

"Indeed, Sir, I hope to see it very frequently again, and shall always be happy to hear of the health and welfare of its inhabitants. But is your father in his study? I must see him before I go."

"Do not, Celestina," said Montague very gravely—"do not so industriously try to deprive me of this last poor moment. Yet a little—and my unfortunate, my despised attachment will trouble you no more."

"You are mistaken, Mr. Montague," replied Celestina. "Any circumstance that you have occasion to deem unfortunate will trouble me long, wherever and whatever I may be: pray therefore, for my sake as well as for your own, exert your excellent understanding, and conquer this unlucky partiality towards a person, who, whatever may be her sense of your worth, or her gratitude for your good opinion, can never return it otherwise than by esteem and good wishes."

"I had rather you would hate, detest, and drive me from you," cried he, starting up and going to the window: "'twould be less cruel than this gentle reason, which I know to be just, but which I cannot obey: and yet indeed, Celestina, I have no hope: I am not quite frantic enough to suppose there can be any for me. All I ask is to be permitted to be miserable, and that, after all, you cannot prevent. Yes, there is yet another favour I would solicit, though I know—I know you will not grant it."

"Any thing I can do without impropriety," replied Celestina, "I certainly will do."

"I do not know," said he, in a depressed and solemn voice, "what *you* may call propriety or impropriety; but the favour I would solicit is to be allowed to write to you.—Nay don't interrupt me with a refusal before you hear me—to be allowed to write to you, so long as I confine my letters to literary subjects only, and that once or twice a year you would acknowledge the receipt of my letters."

"My dear Sir," cried she, smiling, "you would be weary of this project long before the first half year had elapsed. Had you never talked to me of I know not what particular regard, there might have been no impropriety in this, and I am sure the pleasure and advantage would have been wholly mine; but after the extravagantly gallant things you have said, how can I—"

"If I infringe the articles of our agreement," said he, "then send my letters back."

"But tell me," cried Celestina, interrupting him in her turn, "tell me what good can this possibly do you?"

"Good!" replied he: "you are not yourself insensible of a tender attachment to Willoughby, and yet ask what good it can do to be admitted to write to a beloved object. Good! Why, it will be the soft-ener, the sweetener of my existence! While I am writing to you, I shall forget that I am never to see you—I shall forget every thing but the pleasure of knowing that you will read what I am writing, that your hands will unfold my letter, your eyes pass over the traces of my pen; that sometimes I may amuse or interest you, and at others per-haps, raise in your bosom a compassionate sigh for my silent, my unhappy love! Besides, I shall by that means always know where you are.

> 'Soffri che in traccia almeno
> Di mia perduta pace
> Venga il pensier seguace
> Su l'orme del tuo piè.
> Sempre, nel tuo cammino
> Sempre m'avrai vicino.
> E tu!—che sai se mai
> Ti sovverai di me!'"[1]

Celestina had no time to answer this otherwise than by saying, that if he had sagacity enough to find out where she was he pos-sessed more than she did, who could not even guess where she might be. He answered that he could always know of Cathcart; and before she could urge the many objections she saw to his request, the chaise, with Cathcart in it, drove up to the door, and at the same moment Mr. Thorold came to them. He appeared sincerely con-cerned that she was going from him; desired her again to write to him; and while he was hastening breakfast, which he insisted upon her taking before she went, Vavasour rode into the court yard, and giving his horse to his servant, came into the room also.

Celestina, who knew that Cathcart had informed him of her res-olution to go, had felt some surprise that he had not called upon her the day before to express his approbation, and enquire how she intended to dispose of herself: but he was so volatile and inconsider-ate, that she thought it not impossible but that he might have for-gotten on Wednesday what he so vehemently urged on Monday; and she now rather wished he had, as she saw Mr. Thorold was very

---

1 Pietro Metastasio, *Canzonetti*, "IV: La Partenza," 9-16: "Allow at least my thoughts to follow in the footprints of my lost happiness, always on the road you take, always near you. And you!—who knows if you will even remember me!"

little pleased either with his present visit, or the manner in which he addressed her, without taking either of him or his son quite so much notice as the laws of civility required.

Celestina had frequently remarked the extreme inattention and disregard, which, as Vavasour felt, he never chose to take the trouble of concealing, for the opinions of those to whom he was indifferent; and he was indifferent to three fifths of the world, and not very solicitous about the rest, unless for a few, a very few friends, whom he loved. He disliked the Thorolds, without knowing or enquiring of himself why he disliked them; and eager and solicitous only about Celestina, he hardly gave her time to address herself to them, or returned their invitation to partake of their breakfast by the usual speech. A party who seemed so little pleased with each other, Celestina thought could not too soon separate; she therefore hastily drank her tea, and telling Cathcart she was ready, she gave the elder Mr. Thorold her hand, and thanked him, not without emotion, for all the kindness he had shewn her; she then wished Montague Thorold health and happiness, desired him to offer her compliments and acknowledgments to his mother, sister, and brother, and then Mr. Thorold leading her, and Montague walking silently on her left hand, she went out and stepped into the chaise.

Cathcart followed her, and Vavasour went round to speak to her at the opposite side. "You did not wish me good morning," said he, "and therefore I suppose you foresee that I intend going with you part of the way."

Celestina had no time to answer; for Mr. Thorold offering his hand once more to bid her adieu, she gave it him, saying—"Adieu! dear Sir; a thousand and a thousand thanks and good wishes." Montague, who stood by his father, at that moment caught her eye, and there was on his countenance an expression of sorrow which affected her so much, that under the sudden impulse of concern and pity she held out to him the hand his father let go. —"Farewel, Mr. Montague," said she. He seized it eagerly, and held it as if he would never part from it more: but Cathcart at that moment bowing to the gentlemen and bidding the postillion drive on, he was compelled to release it, though it was with a sigh as if his heart was half broken; and when the chaise drove off, instead of following it with his eyes, he turned away and went into his own room, unable either to see Celestina go or Vavasour following her.

The concern she felt for him kept her silent the greatest part of the way to the cottage near old Winnington's, where Jessy was to meet them. Cathcart, who was unhappy at the necessity of parting

from his wife, was not disposed to interrupt her; and though Vavasour now and then rode up to the door of the chaise and talked, she
was not in spirits to answer the gay nothings with which he
addressed her. The meeting with Jessy was more in unison with her
feelings. Jessy threw herself into the arms of her benefactress, from
whom she had been so long divided, and who she now saw only for
a moment before they were to be separated for a yet longer time.
Neither of them could say much, for their hearts were full: but had
they been disposed for conversation, Vavasour, who felt only pleasure
in having got Celestina away from the Thorolds, was very little
inclined to give them an opportunity: but in his rattling way rallied
Jessy, and then Celestina, whom he teazed about Montague Thorold
and his father, one of whom he called her pedant and the other her
priest, till she was half angry. Cathcart at length, however, prevailed
upon him to leave the friends alone; and as they walked together
before the door of the cottage, he enquired whether he had any
commands in London. "Oh none, I thank you," replied Vavasour, "for
I shall be there myself almost as soon as you. Pray where does Miss
de Mornay intend to lodge?"

Cathcart declared himself entirely ignorant; and then, for the first
time, from some expression or look of Vavasour's, he suddenly entertained a notion that there was something more than friendly solicitude for Willoughby's betrothed wife in the eager and assiduous
attentions of Vavasour; and he determined from that time to remark
more narrowly his behaviour to her.

"You do not intend to set out for London to-day, Sir?" enquired
Cathcart.

"Yes I do," answered Vavasour: "that is, I just ride back and make
my bow to those honest humdrum Cranfields, and then I am off for
Oakhampton, where I've told them I have business, and from thence
I shall take four horses, and so come up with you, my good fellow,
and our fair *compagnon du voyage*,[1] before you reach Honiton."

"And does Miss de Mornay know of your intentions, sir?"

"No; for I know what scalping savages all the people about here
are; and though there can be nothing you know in my attending
her on behalf of Willoughby, yet on her account one would not see
the clacks of the old cats within twenty miles round at work about
it, and so I have made up a story of having a lawyer to meet about
the affairs of my deceased aunt, who, luckily for the honour of my

---

1   Travelling companion.

veracity, had a farm or two near Oakhampton, which are now mine; and I intend the Cranfields, good matter of fact souls, shall fancy me carefully looking after my property and settling repairs and renewals with Mr. Palmer the attorney."

"You intend, no doubt, to tell Miss de Mornay of it, however, Sir?"

"Oh! yes, now I see her safely out of the hands of her confessor, or else perhaps he would have put it into her head that I am not a fit escort for her; though I think, Cathcart, thou art so grave and sage that thou'lt make as proper a third to our party as his reverence himself. Come never look so calamitous, but go and take leave of thy weeping wife, and let me and Celestina have a little conversation."

Cathcart then went into the house, and Celestina presently afterwards came to Vavasour, who continued walking before it. "Has Cathcart told you my plan?" said he, before she could speak. "I intend to go to London with you from Honiton, where I shall be almost as soon as you."

Celestina now recollected all Mr. Thorold had said to her; but the great friendship which had for so many years subsisted between Vavasour and Willoughby, and the undesigning openness of Vavasour's character, put all the suspicions he had raised to flight, even when this scheme seemed most strongly to corroborate those suspicions. "I had much rather you would not join us," said Celestina, "because, though I should certainly be glad of your company as well as Mr. Cathcart, yet perhaps a thousand ill natured things may be said about it."

She was proceeding, when Vavasour interrupted her. "Yes, that's just the politics you have learned at the Thorolds. What does it signify to you what any body says or thinks but Willoughby, and you know that he would put you himself into my protection on every occasion where he could not protect you himself. Come, come, Celestina, acknowledge that your old Mentor[1] has been warning you against having any acquaintance with such sad young rakes as Vavasour."

"If you think so," replied Celestina, "you undoubtedly know that he has reason for his precaution; and as for his calling you what I always fancied you rather piqued yourself upon being, I don't see why my Mentor, as you term him, should give you offence by that."

---

1   In Homer's *Odyssey*, Mentor is the tutor to Odysseus' son Telemachus: hence, an adviser or guardian.

"Rake as I am, however," answered he, "curse me if I would do a dishonourable thing towards George. No, by heaven, not if I were dying for love of you."

"I believe you indeed," said Celestina; "and such perfect confidence I have in your honour, that I should trust myself with you as with a brother."

"And never, you dear candid angel," interrupted he, "never shall you repent that confidence. But I tell you very plainly, that though I am upon honour with Willoughby I am not so with those Thorolds, and can allow nobody else to usurp that favour, which perhaps I might have taken it into my head to dispute even with my friend George himself if he had not made out a very early and almost an hereditary claim to you: as it is, however, I have no pretensions for myself, but I am confoundedly jealous for him; and now I have got you out of the way of that prating, piping, poetical pedant—that Montague Thorold, I shall be quite easy when I see you situated where you are not very likely to meet with him again: so you won't oppose my meeting you on the road; and, till then, my sweet friend, adieu!" He then, without waiting for an answer, ran to his horse, which his servant was leading about, and mounting it, was out of sight in an instant. Cathcart and Jessy then came towards Celestina; and the latter hanging on her neck, could hardly prevail on herself to bid her farewell; while Celestina, melting into tears, kissed her, and willing to shorten a scene so uselessly painful, stepped into the chaise, where Cathcart, having taken again a tender leave of his wife, immediately followed her, and they took the road that led across the common to the turnpike.[1]

Chapter X

The road they were travelling led along the side of Alvestone Park for near a mile and a half. Celestina had never passed it before but on the day when Mr. Thorold had taken her to his house; and then she had been so lost in mournful contemplations as hardly to notice whither she went. Now, however, the profound silence she had fallen into on parting from Jessy, was suddenly broken by an exclamation; for on looking up, she saw one of the park gates, and cried—

---

1 A highway with barriers at intervals where travellers had to pay a toll towards the road's upkeep.

"Alvestone! is it not?—oh! yes, I see it is: there is the house!" Cathcart answered that it was; and after another short silence, Celestina said—"To any body but you, Cathcart, I should be afraid of betraying my weakness; but you are now in place of a brother to me, and knowing my situation, will indulge my regret: I have a strange fancy to get out and go up to that tuft of beech trees on the brow of the hill. It is not far. I shall not be gone long. Will you wait for me?"

"My time is yours," replied he. "But will you allow me to observe that it is perhaps wiser to endeavour to conquer this useless regret than to indulge it?"

"I know it would be wiser," answered Celestina: "but alas! we are not always able to be wise. I think I shall be easier when I have once more taken, of that spot where I have often been so happy—a last adieu!"

"Heaven forbid it should be the last," cried Cathcart, as he assisted her to leave the chaise. "I foresee many, many happy days for you yet, when you will be mistress of that house."

"Ah! dear Cathcart," returned Celestina, half smiling through the tears that filled her eyes, "how happy a convert shall I be to the doctrine of second sight if your prophecy should ever be fulfilled. But no; I feel too certainly that this is the last time I shall ever behold this dear place."

She then went into the park over the stepping stile, and walking about half a quarter of a mile, reached the group of beech trees which shaded a high knoll in the park; from whence the house, half concealed by intervening wood, appeared to great advantage. It was now the beginning of May, and the trees under which she stood were just coming into leaf, while others scattered over the park were many of them of the most vivid green, contrasted by the darker shade of fir and cypress mingled among them. One of the trees of this clump was marked by Willoughby with her name, his own, and his sister's, and the date. It was five years since; and the bark had grown rough and knotted round the scars, but the letters still remained. It was to revisit this well known memorial that Celestina had been anxious; and now she could hardly bear the thoughts of leaving it. She recollected every trifling circumstance that happened when Willoughby cut those letters: the cloaths he wore, and his very look, were again present to her; while in the breeze that sighed among the trees she fancied she heard the sound of his voice, and that he pronounced the name of Celestina. In this state of mind she had almost forgotten that Cathcart waited for her; till a herd of deer ran bounding by her, and looking up, she saw following them in mimic race, several horses which grazed in the park. There was among them a favourite little mare, which Willoughby had been fond of from a boy: it had always carried him to Eton, and been the companion of all his boyish sports; and when it became old, had been turned into the park in summer and carefully sheltered in winter. While Mrs. Willoughby lived, it had been accustomed to be fed with bread once or twice a day from her hand, from her daughter's, or Celestina's; and since her death the old servants in the house, with whom it was a sort of contemporary, had accustomed it to the same indulgence; to which it had become so habituated, that on sight of any of the family it went towards them to be fed. This creature therefore no sooner saw Celestina's cloaths fluttering among the trees, than it left its companions, and came neighing towards her.

Celestina fancied the animal remembered her. She caressed it fondly, and with tears in her eyes, and a deep sigh, cried—"Ah! Fanchette, you recollect then your old friend, when perhaps your still beloved master is trying to forget her, and may already have succeeded but too well." She found herself too much affected with this idea, and turning her swimming eyes towards the house, the contrast between what she now was, and what, hardly a month since, she expected to be—the fearful apprehension that Willoughby had suddenly become a convert to avarice and ambition, and that Miss Fitz-Hayman, who had the power to gratify both those passions, would soon possess the place where she had fondly hoped to constitute the happiness of *his* life whose happiness was dearer to her than her own—all crouded with cruel force on her mind; and feeling her sensations become more and more painful, she tore herself from the spot which had so forcibly presented them, Fanchette still following, and importuning her to be fed. She walked slowly towards the park gate, and saw Cathcart, who began to be uneasy at her stay, coming to meet her. He understood the nature of her sensations too well to make any enquiries; but offering her his arm, in silence led her towards the chaise. Before she ascended the steps of the stile, she turned once more to look at the horse; kissed the sensible[1] animal as it licked her hands; and pronouncing a half stifled and tremulous "adieu Fanchette!" she got as hastily as she could into the chaise, and desired Cathcart to order the postillion on quickly. "Since I must go," said she, "I would be soon out of sight of this place, for I find I cannot bear it."

---

1   "Sensible" meant almost the opposite of what the word means now: affectionate, emotional.

"I feared indeed," replied Cathcart, "it would too much affect you."

Both then returned to their former silence; while Celestina, as her thoughts went back to past pleasures, and as her heart felt all the bitterness of disappointed hope, indulged herself without restraint in the sad luxury of sorrow. She no longer saw the objects she passed, or thought of whither she was going: but Alvestone was still present to her eyes, and she saw Willoughby wandering among its shades as if looking for lost happiness, and returning discontented to his house; whence the sullen magnificence and arrogant superiority of his haughty heiress had driven all domestic comfort. She heard him sigh forth too late his regret, and lament that for advantages he could not enjoy, he had relinquished the competence he might have possessed, with the tender attachment and grateful affection of his Celestina. Tears fell slowly down her cheeks as these distressing images presented themselves, and insensibly the tender adieu she had taken of the place, the tender wishes she had formed for the lamented friend and lover to whom it belonged, arranged themselves into verse, and produced the following

SONNET

Farewel ye lawns! by fond remembrance blest,
As witnesses of gay unclouded hours,
Where, to maternal friendship's bosom prest,
My happy childhood past amid your bowers.
Ye Wood-walks wild! where leaves and fairy flowers
By Spring's luxuriant hand, are strewn anew:
Rocks, whence with shadowy grace rude Nature lours
O'er glens and haunted streams!—a long adieu!
—And you!—oh! promis'd *Happiness!* whose voice
Deluded fancy heard in every grove,
Biding this tender, trusting heart rejoice
In the bright prospect of unfailing love:
Tho' lost to me—still may *thy* smile serene
Bless the dear Lord of this regretted scene.[1]

This disposition of mind, mournful as it was, afforded Celestina so much melancholy indulgence, that it was very reluctantly she was

---

1 Reprinted as no. L in Smith's *Elegiac Sonnets* and in Stuart Curran's edition of her collected poems.

roused from it by their reaching Honiton; where she was glad to find Vavasour not yet arrived: for though she was sensible of the friendly interest he took in whatever related to her, and imputed it to no other motive than regard for Willoughby, and pity for her own situation, there was an impetuosity in his manner, and a freedom in his discourse, which, though it did not offend her because she knew it was his usual way with every body, was yet often oppressive to her, and since Mr. Thorold's caution, had become more so than before. She observed too, that Cathcart was not pleased at his purpose of accompanying them to London, and had expressed more than once, in the little conversation they had together during their journey, his hope, that she would find his sister, Mrs. Elphinstone, such a companion as might engage her to continue with her.—Celestina, who was, perhaps, a little too fastidious in the choice of her company, from having in her early years had her taste set very high by Mrs. Willoughby, was become generally indifferent now, from the little expectation she formed of being gratified, and though her overcharged heart languished for the soothing pleasure of unburthening itself to such a friend as the simple and sensible Jessy, she knew it was very improbable that any one whom she might meet should replace her. She answered Cathcart, however, that she doubted not Mrs. Elphinstone's merit, since she was his sister, and was greatly prejudiced in her favour by Jessy's account of her. "But, my dear Sir," said she, "it is I who have the greatest reason to doubt of my reception, and I have thought since, the plan we hastily formed a very wild one. Mrs. Elphinstone, occupied by her family, may have as little occasion for a companion as taste for an intruder into her domestic circle; and she may perhaps, on your recommendation, accept, what her own inclination may be averse to receive. Besides she has a husband, of whom I know nothing, and to whom the presence of a stranger, when he expects only his wife and family, may be disagreeable. I own I have thought of a journey into the North with more pleasure than any thing else can now give me, for it is the only part of this island I have not seen something of, in those summer excursions which my dear Mrs. Willoughby was fond of making. But with whatever satisfaction my fancy has dwelt upon it, I ought not to think of it farther, at least till I have seen your sister."

Cathcart repeated again and again his assurances of the happiness her company would bestow on his sister, and continued to lay plans for the accommodation of their journey: while Celestina could not but think with internal anguish on her very forlorn situation, compelled to solicit the friendship and protection of strangers, or remain alone, unfriended and unprotected. She blest, however, again the fortunate chance that had brought her acquainted with Jessy and Cathcart, without whom her condition would be yet more desolate; and for once saw evidently the lasting good that had been produced by a transient evil, the troublesome impertinence of Mr. Jedwyn.

As they arrived at Honiton sooner than they expected, Celestina proposed going on as far as Axminster, nine miles farther, before they dined. To this Cathcart consented; hesitating however a moment whether they ought not to wait for Vavasour. Celestina seemed averse to it, and said if there was any rudeness in their going on without him, she would herself be answerable for it.

They proceeded therefore to Axminster, and were just set down to their dinner, when Vavasour, at the expence of almost killing the four horses which drew him, arrived.

His volatile humour never forsook him, and he seemed now unusually disposed to indulge it. He gave the most ludicrous account of the manner in which he had misled the curiosity of Mrs. Cranfield, by setting out very gravely for Oakhampton; and then cried—"Oh! and I tell you who I met as I rode back to Cranfield's; your languishing lover, Montague Thorold, looking, poor dog! so distanced and so dismal: he was composing, I fancy, an elegy on your departure, for I rode almost against him in the cross lane that leads from old Thorold's grounds towards Cranfield Hall, and he had a paper in his hand, on which he was so intent that he did not see me, till I awakened him with a ho hoop! ho hoop! as if I had been in at the death.[1] He started, and I was afraid, as I might have spoiled a thought, that he would feel some poetical indignation; but instead of that, he popped the paper into his bosom, as if he feared I should have seized it; and then, with as much humility as if I had been the head of his college, he pulled off his hat, and professing himself glad to see me, enquired where I had left you. I told him on your way to London, and that I was going back to Cranfield's; and we parted with the utmost politeness."

Celestina, who had really a friendship for Montague Thorold, could not hear of his anxious solicitude for her, without a mingled sentiment of regard and concern, which, as her face expressed every emotion of her heart, was immediately perceived by the quick and penetrating eyes of Vavasour. He did not spare her; but rallied her with more success than politeness on the influence this college lad,

---

1 A term from hunting: present when the hounds catch the fox.

for so he chose to term him, had obtained over her. "Upon my word," said he, "I shall think it necessary to put Willoughby upon his guard a little."

"And how do you know, Sir," answered Celestina, "that Mr. Willoughby will thank you for it? or, that admitting Mr. Montague Thorold was really more to me than a common acquaintance, which you do not seriously believe, how are you sure that your friend would not be rather pleased, that the affections he may wish to be troubled with no more, are transferred to another?"

"Transferred!" exclaimed Vavasour. "You admit then that such a transfer is probable?"

"Not probable at all: but certainly it would with most people be possible."

"And if it were with you, I am convinced that Montague Thorold is not the man to whom Willoughby would wish them to be transferred."

"He could, however, have very little pretence, after having resigned them himself, to dictate to whom they should be given. But of what use, Mr. Vavasour, is all this argument? Whether I shall ever see Willoughby again or no is very uncertain: But it is very certain that if I do not, I shall never marry at all."

Vavasour saw he had gone too far; and Cathcart at that moment returning to them to say the chaises were ready, the conversation dropped for that time; Celestina peremptorily resisting the efforts Vavasour made to induce her to go at least the next stage, in the chaise with him.

They reached Dorchester that evening; and Celestina, after a slight supper, complained of being a good deal fatigued with her journey, and going as soon as she could to her chamber, left the two gentlemen together.

Vavasour, naturally unreserved, even to indiscretion, and seldom taking the trouble to conceal his sentiments, was totally off his guard when he had drank five or six glasses of wine; and since Willoughby, who alone had the power to restrain any of his excesses, had been less with him, he had accustomed himself to take more than double that quantity when he either dined or supped. Celestina was no sooner gone therefore, than he ordered in another bottle of claret, and before it was finished, he had told Cathcart without reserve all that he thought. Taking occasion to toast Celestina, he said—"Tell me, Frank! what do you think of her? Is she not a charming girl?"

"Most undoubtedly," replied Cathcart, "she appears so to me, who know that her very lovely person is the least of her merit; to me, who owe her more than life, and who throughout mine shall have reason to bless the hour that first threw my Jessy in her way."

"Yes, by heaven," cried Vavasour, "she is an angel, and I cannot for my soul guess at this strange mysterious business of George's leaving her: for though it is a desperate undertaking for a man to marry at all, yet he had got over that, and doated upon her to a degree that I never imagined possible till I saw them together. I cannot understand it; and the more I think about it, the more incomprehensible it becomes. Tell me, Cathcart, do you think he will now ever marry her?"

"My dear sir," replied Cathcart, "I can only say with you, that the more I think, the less I comprehend of the affair."

"I'll tell you, Frank: I am pretty well persuaded that he never will marry her; nay, that he has made up his mind to tie himself to the fifteen thousand a year, and the Viscount's title, which are the appendages of his cousin: yet why, unless he had fully determined against all the temptations that match offered him—why carry matters so far with Celestina? and who the devil could those two women be who it seems put the matter by and sent him off in such a hurry?"

"I never could find out," replied Cathcart. "He was himself the only person who knew, and of him, as he avoided all explanation, I could not enquire."

"What! did you never ask whether they were young or old?"

"I asked; but the people hardly saw their faces. They came in the evening, and went away in the middle of the night; but from the little information I could make out, neither of them appeared young."

"I should have thought, (for you fellows that affect principle are not always to be depended upon,) that George had got into some silly scrape or other with some wench that he might have promised to marry: but any such entanglement might have been easily got rid of, without his flying away from Celestina or even from his country. Well! there is no making it out: but I believe it is clear enough that Celestina will now never be *his* wife, and that being once ascertained, Cathcart, do you know she is the only woman upon earth whom I shall ever think of making mine."

"Your's Sir!" exclaimed Cathcart.

"Aye, mine, Sir. I own 'tis rather extraordinary that even my divine Celestina should make *me* meditate on matrimony; but such a wonder was worthy of her only, and she has effected it. I never was uneasy half an hour in my life about any woman till I saw her at Alvestone, or rather till I became acquainted with her; for I have seen perhaps handsomer women, or at least those that were at first view more striking. Faith I found myself growing so cursed foolish about her, that supposing her then to be on the eve of marriage with my friend George, I thought it best to fly for it, and by going back to my old haunts—you know my way—I got her out of my head a little, and could have seen her Willoughby's wife coolly enough; but the moment I heard he had left her, this confounded love, I suppose you call it, began to play the devil with me again, and I could not be easy, knowing the folks she was with, without coming down to see after her. However Captain Thorold, (it was that puffing[1] fellow I was most afraid of,) had not, I believe, the least interest."

"Nor will any man have it, I fancy," replied Cathcart: "at least I am sure that nothing less than the certainty of Mr. Willoughby's marriage with another, would for a moment detach her from the invariable affection she has for him. I even question if that would make any alteration in her heart, though it might in her prospects."

"Pooh, pooh," cried Vavasour, "you have not studied women I find. Celestina has too much spirit and too much sense to mope away her youth and beauty, and dwindle into the neglected ugliness of ancient maidenhood, because Willoughby did not know his own mind. Her pride, and she is not without it, will help her to get the better of an attachment which will only be a source of mortification to her. No, no, let me be once sure that Willoughby gives her up, and I don't think it very presumptuous to say, that in a fortnight afterwards I carry her, to Ortney-bury, Mrs. Vavasour."

"'Till then, however, sir," said Cathcart—"till you are quite sure that all is at an end between Mr. Willoughby and Miss de Mornay, you will of course hold it a point of honour not to declare your intentions. It will distress her extremely if you do. For thinking of you as I know she thinks, she will conclude you are very certain that all ties are dissolved between them, or you would not address her in a way, which while those ties are undissolved, she will call a breach of honour towards your friend."

"Aye, that's very true," replied Vavasour. "But let her take care then how she shews a disposition to favour that sucking[2] parson—that Montague Thorold. Though I'm willing to allow Willoughby the preference, I am by no means disposed to give the *pas* to[3] such a

---

1 Bragging.
2 Baby.
3 Defer to, give way to.

green horn as that: and to tell you the truth, Frank, if I were sure she preferred him I might commit some d—d folly or other."

"Well, sir," cried Cathcart, rising to wish him good night, "she is not likely to be in his way; and if she were I am very certain Mr. Willoughby has nothing to fear from him; and as to yourself you know, you agree, that while he is in question you are entirely out of it."

Cathcart then left him to finish another bottle alone, and carried with him no very agreeable reflections. Notwithstanding all that had passed he could not divest himself of the hope of seeing Celestina united to Willoughby, whom alone he thought worthy of her. His own competence and happiness, which they only had given him, would, he felt, be incomplete if both or either of them were unhappy; and unhappy he thought they must be if they lived not for each other. Whatever scheme therefore interfered with a union he so much desired, he felt as a sort of injury to himself; and though the extreme good humour, generous spirit, and gay temper of Vavasour, made it impossible to dislike him, Cathcart was convinced, from the little he knew of his manner of life and very free principles, that were Willoughby wholly set aside, he was a man with whom the sensibility and purity of mind of Celestina would never allow her to be happy: he foresaw, therefore, nothing but uneasiness for her in his intended pursuit of her, and thought with redoubled anxiety of her situation.

As early the following morning as Vavasour could be prevailed upon to move, they renewed their journey; and about six o'clock that evening, having taken leave of Vavasour in Piccadilly, (who took Cathcart's direction,[1] in order to be with them the next morning,) Celestina was set down at the lodgings Mrs. Elphinstone had removed to in Suffolk-street, Charing Cross.

Chapter XI

Cathcart had given his sister notice of the arrival of Celestina, and therefore the joy with which Mrs. Elphinstone received her brother and the lovely person to whom he had been so much obliged, was unallayed by the surprise she might have felt at the unexpected entrance of a stranger.

---

1 Address.

Celestina was extremely pleased with her new acquaintance, and very soon forgot that she saw her for the first time. Her figure was very tall and thin, and would have had as much dignity as symmetry but that an habitual though slight stoop seemed to bespeak oppression of spirit and the weight of many sorrows. Her face very much resembled that of Cathcart; but the bloom of youth and glow of health were gone: still it was interesting, though languid and faded. Her eyes were eminently beautiful; and there was an air of mild resignation over her whole countenance particularly touching, which, even in her most cheerful moments, bespoke her rather studying how to bear the evils she seemed to foresee, than capable of enjoying the passing pleasure. Sorrow had left on her expressive features marks of its cruel power, and had anticipated the hand of time: for though she was not yet thirty, she appeared four or five years older; and her dress offered nothing to undeceive the imagination, for it was so plain that nothing but its extreme neatness and finer linen distinguished her from women in the humblest rank of life. Her manners, however, would, in any dress or any situation of life, have marked her for a well educated woman; and her voice was particularly pleasing to Celestina, who had been wearied by the harsh monotony of Mrs. Thorold or the affected lisp of her daughter.

Celestina had not been an hour in company with Mrs. Elphinstone, before she not only determined on going to Scotland with her if it were practicable, but felt so uneasy in the fear of a disappointment that she wished to have it immediately discussed. Cathcart, who easily understood her, then began to talk the matter over with his sister, and found, that from the hint of it which he had before given her, she had been assiduously removing every objection that could arise. She answered for Mr. Elphinstone, whom Cathcart had before described to Celestina as good natured even to a fault, and so fond of society as to have owed great part of his misfortunes to a passion for it; and Celestina, willing to be convinced of what she wished to believe, no longer hesitated. Nothing then remained but to prepare for their departure, which was fixed to be at the distance of two days. Cathcart undertook every preparation; and having settled every thing as far as it could be that evening, he took leave of Celestina, for whom Mrs. Elphinstone had procured an apartment in the same house, and went to a coffee house, where he had bespoke a bed, promising to be with them the next morning.

Celestina early on that morning arose to write the letter she had long meditated to Willoughby. She was not able to give such reasons for her quitting Mr. Thorold as he could not disapprove; and though he might perhaps think her present plan a strange one, he would be easy, she thought, in the reflection that it was attended with no personal danger and that she was with Cathcart's sister. One only objection now struck her, and that was the length of time which must elapse before she could receive his letters; but on the other hand, if the strange obstacles to their meeting remained, it was uncertain whether he would write to her; and if they were removed, she hoped that he would fly to her with equal eagerness whether she was in Devonshire or in the extreme parts of Scotland. She collected, therefore, every thing her tenderness suggested to make Willoughby easy about her if he still loved her, and was shedding involuntary tears over that painful doubt, when, as she had just concluded her letter, Vavasour very abruptly entered the dining room, where Mrs. Elphinstone had not yet taken her seat, being detained by the care of her four children, whom she attended to entirely herself.

Vavasour entered with the gay confidence of a welcome visitor; but was a little disconcerted by the languid coldness with which Celestina received him, and by the air of melancholy she assumed, and the traces of recent tears which he observed on her cheeks. He enquired if she was not writing to Willoughby; and on her answering "yes," asked her what she had said to him of her future intentions as to residence.

"I have told him," replied she, "that I am going to Scotland."

"To Scotland! impossible! you are laughing at me."

"Indeed I am going to Scotland," said she; "and I thought you had known it."

"To Scotland! No, I imagined you would take lodgings either in London or its neighbourhood, and wait for letters from George, which must soon be here and be certainly decisive."

"That is by no means certain," answered Celestina; "and whatever the purport of those letters may be, I may bear it there as well as here."

Vavasour now enquired more minutely into her plan; against which he first levelled his whole powers of ridicule, as being wild, romantic, unpleasant, and productive of nothing by disappointment and fatigue; but finding Celestina proof against all the ludicrous lights in which he could represent it, he became serious, and vehemently inveighed against the folly and hazard of a journey to the most desolate and dreary country of Britain, to reside with people whom she did not know, and who were themselves only adventurers on a wild and speculative scheme that would probably be abortive. He represented very forcibly the discomforts she must meet with, and the little pleasure or knowledge which the view of such a country could offer to counterbalance them: but she was as indifferent to local circumstances as to the ridicule of those who would, he said, laugh at her pilgrimage to the shrine of St. Columba;[1] and he had exhausted almost all his arguments without making any alteration in her resolution, when the entrance of Mrs. Elphinstone and Cathcart obliged him to desist.

From their conversation he had the mortification of hearing that every thing would be ready for their journey the next day but one, and of finding that Cathcart never supposed he meant to object to any plan of Celestina's, who was entirely mistress of her actions. Unused to any opposition, Vavasour could hardly brook it, even from those who were his equals; and though he had hitherto behaved to Cathcart as if he had considered him as such, his spirit now revolted at what he thought the opposition of an inferior and a dependant. He became silent during breakfast, and was very evidently displeased; and as soon as he could he desired Cathcart to walk with him for half an hour in the Park.[2] He there remonstrated very warmly against Celestina's going, and urged, among many other reasons, the objections Willoughby would make to it. Cathcart, convinced from this conversation that it was necessary for her to be removed as far as possible from Vavasour, kept his temper, and referred his impetuous opponent to Celestina herself. He went back, therefore, to Mrs. Elphinstone's lodgings to make another effort, but had the additional mortification of finding the ladies gone out to make purchases, and all his subsequent attempts that day to see them were abortive. The next, he attended very early at their door, and saw a chaise there, into which he found them almost instantly stepping, to dine at Richmond with an old relation of Mrs. Elphinstone's and Cathcart's, of whom it was necessary for the former to take leave; and all Vavasour's disregard for forms could not authorise his intruding himself upon them there. He called in the evening in Suffolk-street, but they were not returned; and was there again at ten o'clock, and told they had gone to bed. At day break the next morning he proposed to beset the door, though almost hopeless now of detaining Celestina. The habits of life, however, he was accustomed to, and some additional wine drank the evening before to conquer

---

1   On Iona, which like Skye is one of the Western Islands of Scotland. St. Columba (521-597) is credited with the conversion of Scotland to Christianity.
2   St. James's Park, just south of Suffolk Street across Pall Mall.

his vexation, contributed to keep him long after day break from being on the watch; and on his arrival about seven o'clock, he learned from Cathcart, who was just setting out for Devonshire with the two little girls and a servant he had hired to take care of them, that Celestina and his sister had been gone above two hours, and were probably many miles on the North road. Vavasour received this intelligence with indignation and resentment, which Cathcart pretended not to observe; and busying himself in placing the[1] little girls in the chaise and settling their baggage, he in a few moments wished Vavasour a good morning, and left him to curse his destiny at his leisure, which he did very liberally for some moments; and then determining to think no more of Celestina, he plunged, in order to forget her, into those scenes where he was certainly not apprehensive of meeting any body like her; and with a party he formed there, he went in a few days to Ortney-bury, his seat in Staffordshire, where he tried to persuade himself that he hated and despised all modest women, and never would give himself a moment's concern about one of that description again.

Very differently did Montague Thorold sustain the loss of Celestina's company, and the cruel probability, amounting almost he believed to a certainty, that he should never see her again. While he remained at his father's house, which was hardly a week after her quitting it, he fed his unhappy love by collecting many little memorials of her, which he preserved as sacred relics with all the fond idolatry of romantic passion. A cambrick handkerchief which she had dropped, marked by her own hands and her own hair, was one of the principal of these, and in it he constantly kept folded up the sonnet, written with a pencil, which he steeped in milk to preserve the letters from being creased; a card on which she had sketched a landscape, and a profile which he attempted to make of her one evening by a shade,[2] though his trembling hand and want of skill had deprived it of much resemblance, were added to the packet which he thus wore in his bosom, and which he so delighted in contemplating, that he forgot all other claims upon his time; and regardless of what his family said or thought, passed whole days alone in the fields, or when he was with them, was reserved, silent, and restless.

---

1 The original has "his."
2 Silhouette portraits were fashionable. They were made by reproducing and blacking-in the outline of the sitter's head as cast by lamplight against a "shade" or thin screen of fabric.

Mr. Thorold saw all this with great concern, but still flattered himself that absence, and returning again to his studies and his college friends, would insensibly wean him from the indulgence of a fruitless passion; and sometimes he entertained a vague and distant hope that if Willoughby resigned all pretension to the hand of Celestina, the merit and attachment of Montague might have a claim to her gratitude and her affection. But of this he gave not the most distant hint to his son, and parted with him without naming Celestina, or seeming to notice the state of his mind in regard to her.

Celestina in the mean time was journeying towards Scotland with Mrs. Elphinstone and her two little boys. As Cathcart had hired a chaise to carry them to Edinburgh, where Elphinstone was to meet them, they travelled slowly; but as the weather was delightful, and her companion became every day more agreeable to her, Celestina was in no haste to reach the end of her journey. Every thing in this part of England was new to her; and since the fatal hour of her separation from Willoughby she had never been so calm as she now felt herself, though far enough from being happy. The oftener she read over the letters she had received from Willoughby, which were her constant companions, the more steadily she reflected on his principles and his character, the more firmly she became persuaded that whatever was the cause of their separation, it was not owing to his preference of another, to idle caprice, or to any motive which should make her blush for his morals or his heart.

In this reliance on the honour of the man to whom her heart was fondly devoted, she found so much consolation, that she drove from her as resolutely as she could all those suspicions which had embittered her mind on the information Vavasour had given her. She thought it very possible that the Castlenorths *were* gone abroad, because Lord Castlenorth was never well in England; and his lady, of more consequence among the English in Italy than she could be in London or even at Castlenorth, was much fonder of being looked up to there, than in being lost in the crowd of those who were of equal or superior rank at home. Their daughter too affected foreign manners and foreign sentiments; and with the figure and countenance of a coarse English female peasant, assumed sometimes the animated vivacity of the Neapolitan beauty, and sometimes the insinuating languor of the Venetian; and when in England, had very frequently declared her dislike of the people and the country, and expressed her wonder that those who could converse in any other, should use the harsh and vulgar language of the English.

That a family thus disposed should not remain in their native country, and above all, after the mortification they must have met with from Willoughby's rejection of their alliance, was not extraordinary; but Celestina endeavoured to persuade herself, that though they were on the Continent it was with no intention of renewing their negociation with him, to which their pride would never suffer them to stoop; and that, though he should meet them there, it would be on his part involuntary, and only as the nephew of Lord Castlenorth, by no means as the lover of his daughter.

Notwithstanding all her arguments, however, and all her dependance on Willoughby's love and constancy, she was sometimes conscious of returns of suspicion and fear; and unable wholly to stifle the pangs she then felt, she endeavoured to think less of herself and more of others; and above all, to interest herself for Mrs. Elphinstone, who seemed every hour more worthy of her regard.

In the course of their conversation she found, that Mr. and Mrs. Elphinstone, reduced as they had lately been in circumstances, had once been in a very different situation of life; and she could not resist the inclination she felt to learn what reverse of fortune had thrown them into the distressed condition which Jessy had described to her, and which had made a deep and painful impression on the generous sensibility of Celestina: but however her anxiety was excited, she had so much delicacy as to avoid wounding her new friend by shewing it: unlike that very common description of people, who love to enquire into the sorrows and misfortunes of others, not with any view to relieve or even to soothe them, but merely to gratify an impertinent curiosity, and to rise higher in their own idea by the comparison, while they cry like the Pharisee—"Lord I thank thee that I am not as other men are, even as this publican."[1]

To an heart such as heaven had bestowed on Celestina, there was something in misfortune not only respectable but sacred; and she behaved towards Mrs. Elphinstone with infinitely more attention than she could ever prevail upon herself to shew to Mrs. Thorold, amid all her bustle of affluence and her claims upon the veneration of the world from good dinners and rich connections.

Mrs. Elphinstone, however, who was aware that Celestina knew part of her history, was very solicitous to relate to her the whole of it; conscious that in her opinion she should lose nothing, and that Celestina had in some measure a right to enquire into the life of a person to whom she had given her confidence, and who was a can-

---

1 Cf. Luke 18.10-14.

didate for her friendship and her esteem. She waited therefore a fit opportunity the second day of their journey to drop something of her family; and seeing that Celestina wished to know more, she said, smiling—"It is something like the personages with whom we are presented in old romances, and who meet in forests and among rocks and recount their adventures; but do know, my dear Miss de Mornay, that I feel very much disposed to enact such a personage, and though it is but a painful subject, to relate to you my past life?"

"And do you know, dear Madam," replied Celestina, "that no wandering lady in romance had ever more inclination to lose her own reflections in listening to the history of some friend who has by chance met her, lost in the thorny labyrinth of uneasy thoughts, than I have to listen to you."

"Well then," rejoined Mrs. Elphinstone, "you shall hear all that has befallen me, 'even from my girlish days.'[1] Mine has been a life, not marked, I think, with any thing very extraordinary but invariable ill fortune, which, though I could not escape it, I trust I have sustained with fortitude. But here," continued she, pointing to her children, "here are my little supporters: without them, without feeling that they were a trust committed to me by heaven, from my sacred attention to which, no personal sufferings, no care for myself, could exempt me even for a moment, I am afraid that I should have tired long ago in the rude and various path I have trod. But my exordium will be longer than my history.

"My family are of Scottish origin. My father, one of its younger branches, was settled as a merchant in London, and was engaged in the American trade,[2] by which he was making a respectable provision for his family, of three daughters and three sons, of whom my dear Frank was the youngest, when the course of his business brought him acquainted with the family of Mr. Elphinstone, who had possessions in the West India islands.

"The father of Mr. Elphinstone inherited some of these from his family, but, of a great part, became possessed by purchases made of lands in the islands ceded to England at the peace of 1762.[3] They at first promised to answer his most sanguine expectations; and on the strength of those promises he quitted the West Indies, where he had lived many years on his own estate, and came to London, establish-

---

1 *Othello* 1.3.131: "I ran it through even from my boyish days."
2 Importing cotton and sugar among other goods, therefore dependent on the slave trade and possibly actively engaged in it.
3 The end, in the West Indies, of the Seven Years' War.

ing his household in a stile of expence more suitable to his imaginary than his real fortune. His family consisted of a wife, who had never been in England before, and who brought with her all the pride she had boundlessly indulged in Antigua, five children, and as many negroes.

"A few years convinced Mr. Elphinstone that he had reckoned somewhat too fast on his annual income; but he was not disposed to diminish the shewy and expensive style in which he first set out; and had he himself thought of it, the opposition he was sure to meet with from his wife and children would have deterred him from any attempt to put a scheme of oeconomy in practice.

"His daughters were most expensively educated, and still more expensively dressed, their mother wisely making a point of their being always the best dressed girls in the school to which they were sent, though among their schoolfellows there were many children of the nobility. The two boys were placed at Westminster School,[1] where the elder was soon distinguished for having more money and less understanding than any boy of his age, and where the tyrannical disposition which he had been suffered to exercise over the unfortunate black people among whom he had passed his childhood, broke out in so many instances, that he was as much hated for his overbearing temper as despised and laughed at for his ignorance and his vanity.

"The youngest, who is now my husband, was in every thing the reverse of his brother: open, good humoured, and undesigning; too gay and careless to think, too quick to learn, which, however paradoxical it may sound, is in many instances true—the boy who knows he can learn in half an hour a task which another cannot conquer in a day, is very apt to let alone learning it till application becomes too late. Alexander Elphinstone however was so much a favourite, that when he neglected to do his business somebody or other was always willing to do it for him; and when his father took him from school to place him at an academy where he was to be qualified for a merchant, he was as much regretted as his brother detested, who had now acquired in the school the name of Squire Squashy, which he never afterwards lost.

"It was about the year 1770, that Mr. Elphinstone, the father, in seeking for a counting house to place his youngest son, was intro-

---

1　Westminster School, a public (that is, fee-charging) school situated in central London, probably began as a monastic school for the Abbey but was reorganised on secular lines under the Tudors.

duced to my father. The pomp with which the old gentleman was surrounded, the high style in which he accustomed himself to talk, the detail of his estates, (though some of them brought him every year in debt,) his negroes, and his sugar works, dazzled my father's eyes, who had been accustomed only to a plainer stile of life, and less flattering views of profit. He was pleased with the thoughts of taking into his counting house the son of a man so opulent; and when he saw the young gentleman himself, was immediately prejudiced in his favour. Elphinstone was then a tall boy of sixteen: his dark complexion was enlivened by black eyes full of spirit and vivacity; and his countenance, if not handsome, was expressive of an open and ingenuous mind. The premium which my father asked was agreed to, and young Elphinstone became one of our family, which consisted of my father, his second wife, by whom he had no children, my two sisters, and myself; for of my three brothers, one was placed at the Temple,[1] another was gone to the East Indies, and the youngest, my dear Frank, was then at school.

"My mother-in-law[2] was one of those common characters which are so difficult to describe unless it be by negatives. She was not ill natured; she was not a woman of understanding; she was not handsome; she was not young; she was not well born or well educated: but my father, who had married her to take care of his family, and to put the three thousand pounds she possessed into his business, was well enough contented to see that she did not behave ill to his children, that she brought him no more, and that she had always a plain dinner ready for him when he came from 'Change;[3] was satisfied with going on a Saturday to a country house at Clapton, near Hackney, and receiving the visits of the wives and daughters of traders like himself; and had been brought up with no higher ideas of elegance than what were answered by their society, or fancied any superior entertainment was to be found than what she enjoyed in the front boxes at a play twice a year, or in a Christmas attendance at Hackney Assembly.

"It is true that on these occasions she loved to be fine, to wear rich silks and good lace, to clean and exhibit her mother's rose-diamond ear rings, and to wear my father's picture by way of bracelet, fastened by garnets on her comfortable round arm. But

---

1 At the Inns of Court, in training as a lawyer.
2 Stepmother.
3 The Stock Exchange.

these were indulgences about which he never contended: and was rather pleased that Mrs. and the Miss Cathcarts began to be considered as people of some consequence in the circle in which they moved, while he gradually obtained in the city the name of a warm[1] man.

"I was not more than eleven years old when Mr. Elphinstone became a member of our family. One of my sisters was four years older, and the other a year younger; but my eldest sister, at about the age of seventeen, was married to a young West Indian[2] of whom my father had the care, and went with him to settle in Barbadoes. My sister Emily and I grew up to consider Elphinstone as our brother; but I soon learned to think of him with particular partiality, and to grieve at the frequent occasion which my father had to complain of him. He was wild, eccentric, and ungovernable: sometimes rode away to races when he ought to have been settling with the grocers, (for my father was now deeply engaged in the West India trade,) and sometimes got into scrapes with his old schoolfellows, and was found at the watch-house[3] instead of the counting house; or if he attended those solemn meetings at which the price of freight or the quality of Osnaburghs[4] was discussed, he turned the venerable persons of the old merchants and grocers into ridicule; and while they thought he was making calculations, was frequently drawing caricatures of them in all their majesty of wig, upon the leaves of his memorandum books. But with all this, he was so capable of business, so ready with his pen, and so perfectly master of accounts, that my father often said he could do more business in an hour than he himself could do in three; and that if once he became steady, he would make a great figure of a merchant.

"His father, the elder Mr. Elphinstone, found it convenient, after his son had been with us a year or two, to cultivate very assiduously an acquaintance with our family. Mrs. Elphinstone, who had reluctantly consented that her youngest son should be brought up a merchant, now condescended to visit us, and in her drawling ways to attempt civility. The Miss Elphinstones were directed to forget the distance between Cavendish-square and Mincing lane,[5] and to visit

---

1　Prosperous, well-to-do.
2　Then a European living or owning property in the West Indies rather than someone of African or Caribbean descent.
3　The eighteenth-century equivalent of a police station.
4　Lengths of coarse linen made in Osnabruck, Germany.
5　Between the fashionable West End and the City, the commercial district.

us often; while we were of course mightily delighted to receive invitations to their routs,[1] and to be admitted to add to the crowd which four or five times in a winter filled their rooms in Cavendish-square.

"Insensibly my good mother in law acquired a taste for what was then called the other end of town; and no longer contented with the gratifications of Haberdasher's Hall, or the Crown and Anchor,[2] which had once been the utmost limits of her ambition, she learned to sigh for the Soho Assembly, for five and twenty tables, and the company of 'titled Dowagers and Yellow Admirals.'[3]

"If this unfortunate mania seized her, it was not wonderful that it extended itself to us. Emily had a very fine voice, and the Miss Elphinstones had concerts to which she was invited. We both had learned among ourselves to act parts of plays; the Miss Elphinstones had at their house at Ealing[4] a private theatre, and we were promoted to parts in their drama. Looking upon us as inferior to them in our persons, in our education, in our family and in our fortunes, no idea of rivalry ever disturbed this intercourse, and insensibly we passed more time with them than we did at home; whither I should always have returned with murmurs and regret, if it had not been the only place where I could meet young Elphinstone without witnesses, the only place where some folly at the moment did not seem to make him forget the preference he professed to give me.

"Such was the situation of the two families, when the eldest son of the Elphinstones, the gentleman who had been distinguished at Westminster by the appellation of Squire Squashy, arrived from a twelve months tour in France and Italy, and with him a sort of tutor who had been sent with him at a very exorbitant salary. To all the

---

1 Large parties.
2 Popular sites for City Assemblies, for balls and social events attended mainly by people in trade.
3 In an otherwise undated letter of 1782 to her sister from Hampton, Hannah More described a rout as: "one hundred and fifty or two hundred people met together, dressed in the extremity of fashion; painted as red as bacchanals; poisoning the air with perfumes; treading on each other's gowns; making the crowd they blame; not one in ten able to get a chair; protesting they are engaged to ten other places; and lamenting the fatigue they are not obliged to endure; ten or a dozen card-tables, crammed with dowagers [widows with grown-up sons] of quality [high rank], grave ecclesiastics and yellow [naval captains allowed to retire as Rear-] Admirals." *Memoirs*, 242-43.
4 Then a village west of London.

native arrogance and invincible stupidity of his original character, this elder brother had added the pertness of fancied knowledge and the consciousness of travelled superiority; a more disgusting character could hardly be imagined. He was now not only above all the rest of the world, but infinitely above his own family: his mother was silenced by—'Good Madam! how is it possible *you* should know?' his father, by a silent shrug of contempt and a disdain of argument; while his sisters, who piqued themselves upon their elegance and fashion, were ridiculed for being *si bourgoise*,[1] that they were hardly within the possibility of being made *comme il faut*.[2] As to my sister and myself, who were with them when he arrived, he looked at us once through his opera glass, enquired who we were, and hearing we were the daughters of his father's merchant and lived in the City,[3] he never, on any occasion that I can recollect, deigned to notice us again. Unhappily, the gentleman who had travelled and who still continued with him, saw with different eyes my poor little Emily, then not quite fifteen: he affected to be highly pleased with her singing, and undertook to give her instructions. He would teach us both French, and corrected our acting. We were invited to pass two months at Ealing, at a house which Mr. Elphinstone rented, and to which his daughters had given the name of Cypress Grove, though not a cypress higher than a gooseberry-bush was near it; and there we were to act plays: in which, though the elder hope of the family declined taking a part and absented himself from the set entirely, his travelling friend, whose name was Beresford, was of great consequence; and Alexander Elphinstone was permitted by my father to quit, on those occasions, the high counting stool and sharp desk[4] for the throne of King Pyrrus,[5] or the triumphal car of his namesake Alexander.[6]

---

1 So citified (middle or lower-middle class; from trading families).
2 Presentable.
3 In the East End or commercial area of London.
4 With a tight or demanding workload.
5 Perhaps in Ambrose Philips' play, *The Distressed Mother*, or in a play extemporised from the Roman historian Plutarch's *Lives of the Noble Grecians and Romans*.
6 Alexander the Great (356-323 BC), King of Macedonia, conquered much of the then known world including Persia and India. Pyrrhus (319-272 BC), King of Epirus, was doubly related to the family of Alexander and said to resemble him in character. But his military successes against Macedonia and Rome were so costly of his soldiers' lives

"I will own, that young as I then was, being not quite sixteen, my childish heart was enchanted with these amusements, especially when he bore a part in them to whom that heart was already so fondly attached. Unsuspecting and artless, I dreamed not of the mischief which lurked under all this festive pleasure; and incapable of thinking for myself, I was a very insufficient guard to my sister, who was still younger and more thoughtless; yet to me was she entrusted; unless, which did not very often happen, my mother left the card table to be a spectator of the amusements of the younger part of the company.

Emily, however, was always with me; but it is true that young Elphinstone was always with me too, and in listening to him, I heard not or attended not to the more dangerous conversation with which Mr. Beresford entertained my sister. He contrived most artfully to put her upon her guard against all confidence, which he knew must ruin his scheme; and the first idea I had of my poor Emily's misfortune, was, when on awaking one morning I found she was already risen, contrary to her usual custom. I was not, however, alarmed, till, on beginning to dress myself, I found the drawers where we kept our cloaths were emptied of every thing of hers; even then I had only a confused idea of what had happened, till, in looking wildly round the room, I saw a note upon the table, which I opened in trembling astonishment, and read thus:

'MY DEAR SISTER,
'To avoid any arguments in regard to a step I was determined to take, I have said nothing to you that I meant to leave you. I hope you will forgive it: and assure yourself I am safe, and in the care of a man of strict honour, who will himself write to my father; and I do not know that I am accountable to any body else but to him for my actions. You shall hear of me soon; when I shall have

---

as to give rise to the expression "Pyrrhic victory," one hardly worth winning. In his *Lives*, Plutarch tells how Pyrrhus, in a military emergency, dreamed of Alexander, long dead, lying in bed sick and offering to help him. When Pyrrhus asked how he could help in such a state, Alexander replied in the dream, "With my name only." He then showed Pyrrhus the right course to follow. Schoolchildren were encouraged to act out scenes from classical (Greek and Roman) texts to engage their interest in their studies. We can assume that the Miss Cathcarts and Miss Elphinstones, like Smith, knew Plutarch's *Lives* well in translation.

exchanged the name of Emily Cathcart for that of your still affectionate sister,

Emily Beresford.'

"My ideas were at once so painful and so confused, that I lost all recollection for a moment, and running down stairs half dressed as I was, I asked in breathless agitation for my sister—my sister Emily! The servants who were up, (for it was yet early morning,) stared at me without comprehending my distress; and I found nobody disposed to attend to me till the younger Elphinstone met me and eagerly enquired what was the matter. I put the note I held into his hand, sat down in the seat of a window, and burst into tears. He saw in a moment what my ignorance of the world had in some measure concealed from me; and knowing that Beresford was the last man in the world likely to marry, he knew that Emily was lost. Neither my father or his wife were then at Ealing; and he paused a moment on what could be done.

"He then endeavoured to console and reassure me, and went to his father and his mother to inform them of what had happened. The old gentleman came to me in a few moments, advised me to go immediately home and acquaint my parents, and sent a servant for a post chaise, in which he said his younger son should attend me. I hardly know how I left the house; but I remember Mrs. Elphinstone did not appear, and that the young ladies expressed none of that concern which I thought I should have felt for the rest, had any one of them disappeared under circumstances so prejudicial to their fame."

The travellers now arrived at Stilton, where they were to rest that night. It was late, and Mrs. Elphinstone appearing a good deal fatigued, Celestina besought her to delay any farther gratification of her curiosity till the next day. She then assisted her friend in giving her children their supper and putting them to bed; and after a short repast together, they retired to rest in two beds in the same room, where the children were already asleep.

Chapter XII

The following day they proceeded early on their journey, and Mrs. Elphinstone thus reassumed her narrative.—"In our way from Ealing to London, Alexander Elphinstone endeavoured by every argument in his power to strengthen my resolution, and calm those fears I expressed at meeting with my father and mother; who would, I apprehended, be enraged against me for a misfortune they had themselves taken no pains to prevent. This dreadful meeting must however be hazarded: I tottered as well as I was able into the dining-room, and sending for my father out of his counting-house, I put into his hands the fatal note, and informed him as well as I could of what had happened. He was too reasonable to blame me for an error he had as little foreseen himself; but hastening out of the room with Elphinstone, enquired, as I afterwards learned, whether he thought Beresford meant to marry my sister? Elphinstone, with some hesitation, answered that he feared not. 'Let us then,' said he, 'endeavour to find her, and if it be possible, hush up this unhappy affair before it becomes more known.'

"Elphinstone most willingly agreed to assist him in the search, and my elder brother was sent for from the Temple for the same purpose. *His* anger and indignation were much more turbulent than my father's. He vowed vengeance against Beresford, and sat out in pursuit of him in such a temper of mind as made me dread the consequence should he find him.

"To find him, however, every effort proved abortive. Among other places, my Mr. Elphinstone went to enquire for him at the lodgings his elder brother had taken in Piccadilly. The Squire received him with that contemptuous coldness which he thought was all he owed to a merchant's clerk; and upon his eager enquiry after Beresford, and learning the reason of it, he said—'What a fuss is here, indeed, about a little grisette:[1] why, one would think Beresford had carried off an heiress. Let him alone, and I dare say he will bring her back again.' His brother, enraged at this insult, spoke to him very freely, which he returned no otherwise than by calling him quill-driver, and maccaroni[2] of Mincing-lane. The brothers parted in wrath; and the younger returned home lamenting his fruitless search, and devising new measures for the next day. These, however, were equally successless. Poor Emily was lost to us for ever; and the feeble hope that Beresford might have married her every day became fainter.

"This unhappy affair put an end to our intercourse with the Elphinstone family, and was indeed the first signal of a long series of

---

1 Lower-class young woman.
2 There was a Maccaroni Club in London at this date, founded by rich, well-travelled young men with a taste for foreign food and fashions. Hence a dandy or person with uncommon tastes and opinions might be ridiculed as a maccaroni.

calamities. I observed that my father grew extremely uneasy at something that related to the situation of his affairs: he began to complain that Mr. Elphinstone's remittances fell very short of what he expected; that he was paid no interest for the large sums he had advanced for him; and while he was deliberating how to get out of the difficulties these circumstances threw him into, he received information, that Mr. Elphinstone, deeply involved before, had been overwhelmed by the expences of his eldest son, and the failure of his remittances, had gone off in the night from his house at Ealing to Falmouth, whence he had embarked in the packet for Antigua; while his lady and family had shut up their houses at Ealing and in Cavendish-square, and were gone to Bath.

"These terrible tidings fell on my father like a stroke of thunder, and for some time he was unable to attempt applying any remedy to the evils he saw gathering around him. But from the torpor of immediate anguish, he was roused by the pressing demands of those, of whom he had on his own security borrowed money for the supply of Mr. Elphinstone. It was at a season when many months were to intervene before he could receive any remittances from his correspondent,[1] even if his correspondent should have honour enough to send them, and bankruptcy and ruin seemed inevitable. He had however, as he thought, a friend in a very eminent banker, who a few months before, on his engaging so largely with Mr. Elphinstone, had heard some report that that gentleman, had influenced him in favour of the banker with whom *he* was connected; on which my father's friend, a man of immense property, had then written to him thus—

'MY DEAR SIR,
'The intimation I have this day received of your connection about to be formed with Mr. Elphinstone, is the occasion of this address. It would be injurious to that friendship you so constantly professed towards me, to doubt a moment, that, to have an occasion of serving me, would be a real pleasure to your good self. From a conversation between Mr. Elphinstone and my brother Peter, (who were acquainted by meeting at the house[2] of Sibley and Co.) I am very apprehensive we run the risk of losing a connection so pleasing to me, by *his* influence and inclination to another house. Upon your friendship, dear Sir, I rely to save me from so great a mortification

---

1   His partner in the West Indies.
2   Business.

and concern: as I flattered myself the connection between your house and ours, was formed for many many years. Let your goodness towards me, therefore, prevent your other connections from breaking it; and I hope your friendship for me admits of no diminution, as mine towards you never will assuredly. My very best and sincerest wishes *waits* in the mean time on worthy Mrs. Cathcart, your good self, and every member of your amiable family, who am,

      my dear Sir

          your most sincere

             and faithful friend,

          and obliged humble servant,

               TIMOTHY HEAVYLAND.'

London, Jan. 30, 17—.

"To this *affectionate* and *sincere* gentleman (whom my father had instantly obliged in dropping all thoughts of complying with Elphinstone's request,) he now wrote; and describing with great simplicity his present embarrassment, which he hoped would be only temporary, besought him to advance him five hundred pounds for the present demands of tradesmen, till remittances came in, and till he could obtain assistance from his other friends: to which he received the following answer—

'SIR,

'Your's is come to hand. Our house, on making up your book, find they have already advanced you £26l.18s.2¼d. above your credit. We hoped you would have made this up by payments forthwith, instead of asking a loan; are sorry it is not in our power to comply therewith. I cannot take upon myself to advise them thereto, as I find myself blamed for being the occasion of the present advance, and, that our house are uneasy at the non-payment thereof. Hope you will think immediately of repaying it; and will oblige thereby,

          Sir,

          your humble servant,

             TIMOTHY HEAVYLAND.'

"The eyes of my poor father were now compleatly opened, and all the horrors of his fate were before him. Young Elphinstone, still sanguine as to his father's property and his father's honour, was on this occasion his great resource. He was indefatigable in stemming the torrent of ill-fortune thus brought upon us; and succeeded so well by various expedients, as to support for a while the sinking credit of the house; but seeing my father become every day more and more anxious, and doubtful about the elder Mr. Elphinstone, he proposed to go over to Antigua himself; and to this proposal added, that of marrying me and taking me with him. My father, who found his health giving way under the accumulated calamities that had lately befallen him now thought it better to accept this proposal, and by a union of families make it Mr. Elphinstone's interest to be just. We were married then, after a reluctant consent wrung from the haughty mother of my lover, and three weeks afterwards embarked for the West Indies.

"I was not yet old enough to consider the situation of our fortune with any great concern: but I parted from my own father with a sad presentiment that we were to meet no more, and I dreaded my introduction to the father of my husband. But I loved *him*; he was the most cheerful and sanguine creature in the world; and painted to me only scenes of prosperity and happiness, which I was well pleased to contemplate as true representations. Gracious heaven! could I then have foreseen all the misery that was in store for me, how should I have shrunk from a destiny so insupportable! how should I have wished that in a violent storm we met in the Bay of Biscay, we might perish.

"We arrived, however, after a tedious passage, at Antigua; and I was relieved from the discomforts of a long voyage, to encounter, as I believed, what I dreaded more—the disdain and rudeness of my father in law. I landed, trembling with this apprehension, disgusted with every thing I saw, and overcome with heat and sickness: but the first intelligence we heard was, that Mr. Elphinstone had been dead about a week of an epidemical distemper, and that his houses and plantations were in the possession of the agents of his eldest son.

"It was in vain that my husband desired to be admitted to reside on one of them till he could see into his father's affairs: the people who had been placed there refused him any satisfaction; and it was only by applying to the governor that he at length obtained a sight of the will, by which he found that his father had left every thing to his elder brother, and an annuity to his mother of eight hundred a year; with five thousand pounds, to each of his daughters and to his youngest son: but as the estates were not charged with these last legacies, nor able to pay them if it had, his nominal fortune gave him but little comfort, nor alleviated the concern with which he saw too evidently that all the sums of money lent by *my* father to *his*, were entirely lost.

"The pain this gave him, the incessant fatigue to which he exposed himself in going to Granada and St. Vincent's, where his father had made purchases, at length overcame the natural strength of his constitution. After we had been about four months in the West Indies, living with his friends, he was seized at Granada with one of those fevers so common in that climate. An old French lady, who lived on her own estate near the lonely habitation where he was taken ill, had pity upon him, took him to her house, and by her extraordinary care carried him through the disorder: but he was very long in a state of infantine weakness, and could articulate nothing but a request that he might see his wife. It was some time before I received intelligence of his situation, and some time longer before I could get to him. The kindness of our foreign friend did not stop there: I was now in a state which excited her generous compassion towards me, and she insisted, that instead of returning to Europe in a situation so unfit for a voyage, I should stay with her, till the birth of my child.

"Poor Elphinstone's weak condition of health indeed, rendered such a voyage as impracticable for him as for me. We accepted therefore the generous hospitality of Madame du Moulinet, and at her house in Granada my eldest child was born.

"During the five months we remained there, we heard that the elder brother was come over himself to Antigua and had taken possession of every thing. We had therefore no business to go back, where we had no authority nor indeed any provision; but as soon as our hostess would give us leave, embarked again, to return to England more destitute than we had left it, and with a little unfortunate baby to share our distress.

"We arrived there, after an absence of thirteen months; and hastened to London as cheaply as we could, for we had very little money. My poor Elphinstone left me at the inn where we stopped, and went to my father's house. Never shall I forget the look with which he returned to me: his bloodless cheeks, his wild eyes, his trembling lips, spoke before he could utter a syllable. He sat down; looked earnestly on me a moment, then on his child, which was sleeping in my arms, started up, ran from us, staggered towards the wainscot, and fell.

"My screams brought the people of the inn into our miserable room. They took up the unhappy young man, and gave him what assistance they could, supposing that he had fallen into a fit. After a moment, he recovered his speech, and entreating to be left alone with me, told me that my father was dead insolvent, all his effects sold, and my mother in law[1] gone to reside with her relations in the North: 'and 'tis I have undone thee, my Sophy,' cried he—''tis I and my family who have reduced thee to beggary, and now I have not a place wherein to shelter thee and this dear helpless innocent.'

"Agony now choked his utterance; and all my resolution was necessary to prevent his relapsing into the state he had just recovered from. Stifling therefore my own anguish, I besought him to take courage; declared that I feared nothing while he was with me and well, and urged him to think of some place where we might pass the night and recover courage to encounter what was before us.

"He seemed comforted by my calmness, and recollected an old servant of his father's who kept a lodging house in Northumberland-street. Thither we determined to go; the man was gone from thence, but some other people who let lodgings now inhabited the house: they had a bed chamber on the second floor to let; and knowing something of us, took us in.

"Fatigue of body overcame for a short time the agony of mind my poor husband had felt. He was asleep by me; my infant was at my breast; but *I* could not sleep; all the horrors of poverty were before me, and my agitated spirit ran over every hope which yet remained for us, but rested securely on none.

"The morning at last came; and I now desired Elphinstone to enquire out my eldest brother, who when we went away had chambers in the Temple; and to discover what was become of my dear Frank, whom we had left at school, and to whom I was always fondly attached. Poor Emily too recurred to me, but for her, alas! I dared not enquire.

"He went out, therefore, after breakfast, and returned in about an hour with looks that gave me no favourable impression of his success. My eldest brother, he told me, had left his chambers, and had been married some months to a young woman of some fortune, at least in expectancy, being the only child of her parents, with whom they lived; and that her father, an attorney of practice in Warwick-court, Holborn, had taken my brother into his business. 'I saw him however,' said Elphinstone; 'but he received me so coldly that I shall hardly repeat the visit.'

"My heart sank cold within me, and I had hardly courage to ask what was become of Frank.

"'He is at I know not what academy,' replied Elphinstone. 'Your

---

1   Stepmother.

brother John told me, very coolly, that though he was so lucky as to have a provision by marriage himself, it was out of his power to provide for all his father's family; and thought it quite enough, that he had been at so much expence for Frank, 'who must now,' said he, 'do something for himself, for I cannot undertake to pay his schooling another year: and you, Sir, as it is owing to your family that my father was ruined, I hope you will now take this burthen off my hands; for my wife's family are very much discontented at my bearing it.'"

"'Gracious God!' cried I, 'what will become of us! Oh, my poor baby! why wert thou ever born!'

"'To embitter our calamities,' cried Elphinstone. 'Rather ask, my Sophy, why I was ever born, who brought them upon thee, and on that dear little victim.'

"We had so little money left, that it was necessary to think of something directly: Elphinstone therefore went out again to enquire after his mother and his sisters, from some of those families who had, during their splendour, been the fondest of their society and the most frequently at their house. Among these was one lady who had always professed the greatest affection in the world for them all; never spoke to Mrs. Elphinstone but as her dear friend, nor to her children under any other appellation than her sweet creatures, or her amiable young friends. Elphinstone gave me, as nearly as he could, the words in which she answered his enquiry.

"'Why, my dear, dear Sir, you must think how shocked and amazed I was—for your poor good mother!—to be sure I had a most sincere regard for her—and your sisters too; good sweet young women—so amiable, so accomplished!—I'm amazed they never married.—Well, poor things—God knows, to be sure, what is best for us:—Whatever is, is right,[1] as Pope observes.'

"'But, dear Madam, I must beg to learn where my mother and my sisters are?—I am but just come from the ship that brought me back to England.'

"'Is it possible!—Poor young gentleman!—I am sure I wish I could inform you of any thing agreeable. You don't know, then, perhaps, that every thing in Cavendish-square, and at Ealing, was sold under executions,[2] as I heard; but I heartily hope it was not so. Such

---

1 Alexander Pope, *An Essay on Man*, Epistle I, final line: "One truth is clear, 'Whatever is, is right.'"
2 Seizures and sales of a debtor's houses and goods following his bankruptcy.

a respectable family! and so many fine young people! and your poor good mother!—I saw her at Bath last winter, after those disagreeable affairs, and was sorry to see that she had lost a great deal of her cheerfulness. To be sure that was not to be wondered at. I told her how sincerely I wished her a pleasant voyage, poor worthy woman!' After being compelled to listen to a great deal more of this fulsome cant, he at length learned that one of his sisters boarded with an apothecary's family at Bath, being in an ill state of health; and that his mother, and the other two sisters, finding Mr. Elphinstone, who was distinguished as Squire Squashy, little disposed to do them justice, had, by advice of their friends, embarked for Antigua; so that we probably passed them at sea.

"This was terrible! Every resource seemed to fail us, and in a few days famine was likely to stare us in the face. My beloved brother Frank, however, was, among all my own distresses, ever near my heart; and I determined for his sake, and because I would leave nothing unattempted for Elphinstone and my child, to go myself to my eldest brother, to implore the kindness of one, and obtain a sight of the other. I said nothing, however, to Elphinstone of this intention, fearing he might oppose it. I set forth alone, with my baby in my arms, for I could not leave it, nor could I afford to hire a coach. I rapped at the door; and enquiring for Mr. Cathcart, was told by the footman who opened it, that I might wait in the passage, and he would see. In the passage I waited some minutes, and was then told that Mr. Cathcart was busy with some gentlemen, and that I must send in my business and call again.

"Ah! Miss de Mornay, you have no relations, I think; nor can ever, nor will ever, I hope, feel how sharper than a serpent's tooth it is[1] to meet cruelty and scorn from those to whom the sick heart looks for pity and protection.

"I was unwilling to send in my name and a verbal message, as there were people with him; I therefore sat down on a bench where porters and servants sit in those passages, and wrote with a pencil—'It is your sister Sophy, who cannot call again.' This brought out the great man, for great he suddenly was become. His likeness to my father, the tender recollection that he was my brother, made me forget all his unkindness the moment I saw him, and I was throwing myself and my child into his arms, when a cold—'how d'ye do Mrs. Elphinstone?' fixed me to the place. I suppose he thought by my

---

1 Cf. *The Tragedy of King Lear* 1.4.250-52.

looks that I should faint, and was afraid of being exposed to his servants and new relations, for he took my hand, faintly kissed my cheek, and leading me into a little dark parlour where there was no fire, desired me to sit down.

"Some remains of natural affection, which, in a young man, is very rarely totally extinguished, seemed to be contending with pride, avarice, and mean policy, and for a while kept him silent: he then enquired coldly into our situation, and as I related it, (for he had no idea it was so bad,) I saw those affections gradually shrink from the detail: his heart seemed to become harder as its tenderness became more necessary; and he declared to me at last, that I had formed erroneous ideas of his situation if I thought it was in his power to be of any service to me. I rose to go; but desired a direction to Frank, which he gave me very unwillingly; for since I could contribute nothing to his support, he thought it useless for me to see him. I do not know very well how I got out of the house of this cruel brother, who never introduced me to his family, or seemed to wish to see me again: but I recollect that when I came into Holborn I became so very faint and sick, that I was obliged to get into a coach to return home, which I paid for by changing the last guinea I had in the world.

"Ah! my dear Miss de Mornay! veteran in sorrow as I have since been, I look back with wonder on the scene I afterwards passed through; I wonder how I supported it. We lingered on for three months at these lodgings; my beloved Frank often, and always happy to be with us. He was now near sixteen; very tall and very manly, and repeatedly declared to Elphinstone that he was well able to get his bread, or to assist him in any way of business he could enter into. Business however was not to be obtained without money; but my father's creditors knowing how well Elphinstone was acquainted with his affairs, engaged him to assist them in recovering debts due to him, and allowed him from time to time some very trifling compensation, which was our only support.

"As long, however, as he was well—as long as my little boy blest me by its innocent smiles, I murmured at nothing; and the little time I could spare from nursing him, and after he was in his cradle of a night, I found exquisite pleasure in applying those little arts I had learned as matters of amusement, to the purpose of profit. They produced not much; but in our situation every thing was an help; and our simple meal, partly the produce of my industry, and shared with my brother Frank, after Elphinstone came home of a night, was infinitely a sweeter banquet than the insipid though splendid tables of the affluent had formerly afforded me. At length, however, the persecution of ill fortune, which seemed to have relaxed a little, began anew, and misery fell upon me where I could least bear it. Elphinstone was seized again with an infectious fever, differing only from that he had at Grenada, in the symptoms occasioned by difference of climate. On his attendance on the creditors, our daily and scanty subsistence depended: with his confinement, every aid of that sort ceased; and I saw him languishing in a sick bed, in all the depression of a malignant fever, without the means of giving him the necessary assistance.

"A neighbouring apothecary, however, attended him, who told me that wine was absolutely necessary to be given him in large quantities. Where was I to get it?—For the first time, I had recourse to a pawnbroker, and my dear, dear Frank was my agent: for now, attached entirely to us, he quitted his school, where, indeed, he knew more than the master, and gave himself up wholly to our service: while my brother John, not sorry to be relieved from the expence of supporting him, remonstrated, or rather quarrelled with him once, and, obtaining an excuse for shaking him off, saw him no more.

"I had a watch, and a few trinkets; these were first disposed of, and then such clothes as I could spare; for I could not endure the thoughts of taking any thing that belonged to Elphinstone, though my trembling heart too often whispered that he would want them no more. Youth, and the strength of his constitution, carried him on many days through a rapid and generally fatal distemper; and, at length, my fainting courage was sustained by the hope of his recovery, when my lovely infant was seized with the same terrible disorder; and I was told, that as it was almost always fatal to children, I must not hope.

"I know not, then, what became of me; but I think, that for some hours I was not in my senses. I recollect being seized with an earnest wish to have my child attended by a physician I had heard named, as eminent for his humanity as for his peculiar skill in this disorder; and, as Frank was not at that moment with us, I wrapped myself in an old cloak, and leaving my poor infant to the care of his father, who was just able to sit by the cradle and look at him with eyes of hopeless agony, I went away myself to implore this physician to come to us; and had just sense enough to remember the direction I had received to his house, but none to notice the objects around me, or to care what people might think, who saw me, with wild looks and uncertain steps, hurrying through the crowd of the busy and the happy.

"I had proceeded as far as the corner of Cecil-street, when a croud of carriages and passengers impeded the crossing; I was making my way through them, heedless of the danger, and hardly hearing the noise, when a footman, in a livery glittering with lace, stopped me, and told me he was ordered by his lady to beg I would step to the door of her carriage and speak to her.

"'Oh! I cannot; I cannot, indeed,' replied I, without enquiring who his lady was: 'my child—my child is ill—I am going for advice for him.' I would have passed the man; but he followed me, and pointed to an elegant vis-a-vis[1] that was drawn up close to the broad pavement. 'Here is my lady, Ma'am,' said the man.

"I looked up:—it was my Emily, my long lost, lamented Emily! I gave a faint shriek, and hardly heard her in a low and tremulous voice articulate—'My sister! my sister Sophy!'

"Not quite in my senses when I left my lodgings, this interview quite robbed me of them. I caught hold of the door of the carriage, or I should have fallen in the street. Every object swam before me; and I retained only recollection enough to cry, 'My child! my child! save my child!' and to hear Emily repeat—'What child? what can I do for you? Good Heaven! what can I do for you?' But I was unable to answer. I found myself, however, in a few moments, placed in the carriage, and Emily holding her salts[2] to my nose, and chafing my temples. When my senses returned, my child was their first object; and again I exclaimed—'Oh! do not, do not detain me; I must go to save my child—my poor little boy!'

"'My dear, dear sister,' cried Emily, 'pray summon[3] your recollection, and tell me whither you would go; we will drive to the place directly.' In my anxiety for the life of my infant, I forgot the culpable conduct of my sister; and, telling her where the physician lived, she gave orders to her coachman to hasten thither instantly. A strange stupor overwhelmed me; I could not speak till we came to the door of the house: I then looked out; I would have flown out of the carriage. He was not at home: but just as we were leaving the door, he drew up to it.

"Then my voice and recollection returned to me. I besought him most earnestly to go with me. He was that moment come from his first round of visits to change his horses, and begged we would wait

---

1   Carriage holding two people seated face to face.
2   Of ammonia.
3   The original has "summons."

a few moments: but Emily urged him so earnestly to get into her carriage, saying she would take him to my lodgings and bring him back, that he could not resist her importunity. He went with us then; and so totally was my mind absorbed in the danger of my child, that I heeded not the strange contrast between my appearance and the gay splendour of my sister; I forgot what she was, and almost who she was; and only enquired, when the physician had seen my child, whether he would live.

"I saw by his looks his opinion to the contrary; nor, indeed, did he attempt to conceal it: but he besought me to attend to my own health, and to that of my husband; gave directions about us all, and departed with my sister, refusing the fee I offered him, and telling me he would come again early the next day.

"Elphinstone, amazed as he was at the scene that had passed, had no power to enquire the meaning of it, and I had none to explain it: all my resolution was roused to attend my dying infant; but all could not save him—he died: and I now tell it with dry eyes, though, when it befel me, I thought no blow could be so severe, and that I could not survive it:

'For since the birth of Cain, the first male child,
To him that did but yesterday suspire
Never was such a gracious creature born!'[1]

"Yet I have lived now above ten years longer, my dear Miss de Mornay; and have learned that there are such evils in life as make an early death a blessing.

"I was delirious, I know not how long, between the excess of my affliction and the opiates that were given me to deliver me awhile from the sense of my misery. In the mean time my sister sent a careful person to attend me, and saw me every day herself, though I no longer knew her, or any body but Elphinstone, whose hand I held for hours, imploring him not to let them take my child from me. Emily did yet more: she supplied us with every thing we wanted, attended herself to the funeral of my poor baby, and then took lodgings for us at Kensington, that we might be removed from the place where we had suffered so much calamity. In her frequent visits she spoke not either to Elphinstone or Frank, unless they first spoke to her; and never but on the subjects of my health and ease. I was not

---

1 Cf. *King John* 3.4.79-81.

yet quite restored to my senses when we removed. She sent us, by a porter, the next day, a forty pound note, with these words:

'MY EVER DEAR SOPHY,

'Having been lucky enough to be of some use to you, I rejoice that we have met: but now, if our future meetings should be unpleasant to you, it depends entirely on you whether they shall be repeated. Whatever may be my failings, or my errors, I trust that among them will never be reckoned, want of love to my relations, whether they will acknowledge or no,

Your still affectionate
EMILY.'

"As soon as I was capable of reading and understanding this, all that had passed came back to my recollection. I had been supported, then, for many days, by the wages of shame; and now had nothing but a gift from the same hand, to save my husband, my brother, and myself, from actual hunger. 'Oh! my dear father,' cried I, 'can you forgive your unfortunate child; or rather, your unfortunate children! and ought I to refuse taking from this lovely lost one, whose heart, so generous, so full of sensibility, cannot surely be quite hardened in a course of evil!'—I shall tire you, my dear Madam, if I am so minute: suffice it to say, that I saw my sister; that she owned all her guilt, and all her folly; without having the power, or, at that time, perhaps, the wish, to quit a manner of life, where she possessed boundless splendour and luxury, for such a precarious subsistence as women can earn in business. My remonstrances she heard with gentleness, and mingled her tears with mine: but she pleaded gratitude to the friend who supported her, and the impossibility of her abandoning him, or existing if she did. I was afraid of enquiring who this was; but I found that it was some man of high rank who had taken her from the worthless Beresford, and with whom she had lived ever since.

"Her purpose seemed to be to detach my thoughts as much as possible from her situation, and to fix them on my own: and indeed it was very necessary; for we had now, in consequence of Elphinstone's long illness, no support whatever but what her tenderness afforded us.

"As Elphinstone recovered his health, his sanguine temper returned, and again he formed various projects of entering into business. It was now the midst of the American troubles;[1] and some part

---

1   The American War of Independence, 1775-82.

of my father's property, which was thought recoverable, was there. Elphinstone, who now from long habit and from his natural disposition, was become unsettled and fond of speculative schemes, proposed to the creditors to go over there in search of these sums. I was still too ill and too much depressed by past sufferings to give very minute attention to this plan: I only resolved not to be left behind, but to share his destiny whatever it might be. In a fortnight or three weeks he was every day in town, and the latter part of that time returned in remarkably gay spirits, and told me of I know not what prospects that were opening to him; to which, indifferent to every thing beyond a mere subsistence, now that I had lost my boy, and long accustomed to hear of visionary fortune, I gave very little applause, till he came home one day elated beyond what I had ever seen before, and told me that an offer had that day been made to become a sort of under secretary to a man high in administration,[1] into whose house he was to be taken; that he was to enter on his place the following week, had taken a lodging for me in the neighbourhood, and hired two female servants and a footman to attend.

"I wondered at, and rather blamed his precipitancy; but he assured me he was right. Frank went with us, as he was to be a sort of secretary, in his turn, to Elphinstone, who was now domesticated with his patron, while my brother and I were in very handsome lodgings in Westminster. I do not know by what means the money came, but from this time it was as plenty with Elphinstone as it had before been scarce. In a few months his views were so much enlarged that he took a house for me, increased the number of his servants, and from one thing to another our establishment was at length on a footing of splendour, against which I remonstrated in vain. He assured me that his future success depended on his keeping up such an appearance; that the emoluments of his place fully entitled him to it; and that I should soon see him permanently fixed in a situation, such as would put us out of the power of fortune.[2]

"In the mean time, as I never loved London, and as my health was very much hurt by a long continuance in it, I prevailed on him to let me have a small house at Shene, near Richmond, where it would not be necessary, for me at least, to be always in company, which began to be unavoidable in London. To this proposal he consented at first with reluctance; but afterwards, I thought he was not sorry to

---

1 The government.
2 Chance.

have his house in town at liberty to receive the parties he now made there, by which it became distinguished for good cheer and high living. I had by this time two boys; one of them I have since lost, and the other is the eldest of these: and with many a silent and stifled sigh I wished their father would think, while in this prosperous train of fortune, of making some provision for his increasing family.

"He heard me always with his usual good temper, and as constantly assured me that he was laying by money every year; though I never could guess how or from whence it came.

"Frank, however, was not only supported like a gentleman, but had really more money than, had he been less prudent and steady, would have been proper for so young a man.

"Of this, notwithstanding the infectious example of the people among whom he lived, and even of Elphinstone himself, he always brought a part to me to put by for him. On these occasions I sometimes questioned him of their manner of life in London, whence I now entirely absented myself; and though he gave me such answers as would, he thought, prevent my inquietude, he was too ingenuous to be able to conceal the whole truth. Thus my prosperity was embittered by the fear of falling again into adversity, from which we had been delivered by miracle; and I lived in perpetual dread of evils I had no power to prevent. Alas! the greatest evil was already arrived—the estrangement of Elphinstone's heart!—I saw it in a thousand instances; but I knew that reproaches and importunity would not recal it; and I endeavoured, whenever he came down to Shene, to appear cheerful, lest he should be quite won from me by those whom he now frequented.

"Though he has an excellent understanding, he became insensibly intoxicated with his good fortune, and never gave himself time to think how soon it might be at an end, till this fatal period actually arrived. His patron was dismissed from his employment, and the golden dream vanished at once.

"I then knew, that out of immense sums of money he had made, by means, of which I understand nothing, he had not reserved five hundred pounds; and I knew that a mistress whom he had supported in great splendour, had pillaged him of twenty times that sum. But he was now humbled and unhappy! I forgave all his failings; and should have blessed the chance that had restored him to me, had we but had a competence to live upon.

"After all our plate and fine furniture in London was sold, and our debts called in, we found ourselves about two hundred pounds worse than nothing. But Elphinstone still told me he had friends; and now commenced a course of solicitation and attendance, to which the humblest and severest labour is in my mind infinitely preferable: and in the mean time our subsistence was derived from his writing for the papers, and now and then by an eighteen-penny political pamphlet.

"I did not notice, that in the height of our prosperity my brother John assiduously courted our regard; and Elphinstone had procured him many advantages: among others, that of being steward to a nobleman, by whom he made a great deal of money; so that he was, on our decline, more prosperous than ever. With our failure, however, his love failed also; and all we could now obtain of him was, to take Frank as a sort of assistant into his business.

"My poor Emily, who from gratitude and pity I could never wholly forsake, was at this time abroad with her friend; and I had nothing to support me against the heavy tide of adversity but the consciousness of having done my duty, and the firm reliance on heaven which that consciousness gave me. Four years we lingered on, sometimes flattered by hope of some trifling place, and sometimes supported by small remittances from Elphinstone's mother; while she complained heavily of the conduct of her eldest son, who had deprived her and his sisters of every thing he could take from them.

"Oh! never may those who have it in their power to secure an independence, foolishly throw it away, and trust to the fallacious assurances of that friendship which flourishes only in the sunshine of affluence!

"Day after day did poor Elphinstone now attend those men, who but a few months ago were his assiduous friends: many, into whose pockets he had been the means of putting thousands, now shut their doors against him; while, of those who could not so easily escape from his importunity, some blamed him for the expence at which he had lived, talked of the advantages of oeconomy, and of the demands of their own family—others very gravely harangued on the caprice of fortune, the ups and downs of the world, thanked God they had but a little, but that little was, they hoped, secure; yet most truly lamented that it was too little to enable them to follow the warm dictates of their hearts, in aiding a friend they so much respected and esteemed; and with this sort of language bowed him out, whose favour and recommendation they had only a few months before solicited with meanness equal to their present ingratitude.

"Wearied at length by this sad experience of a world to which he was still too much attached, and where, from the vivacity of his sanguine temper, he was long unwilling to relinquish the hope of rising again into consideration, he took up once more his old projects of recovering the money due to his father in America: and though that country was no longer under the government of Britain, and his expectations of success greatly diminished, he contrived to persuade those persons who were interested, to furnish him with a small supply of money; and we went, a wandering and unhappy family, to America.

"I could give you, my dear Miss de Mornay, a long detail of our pilgrimage—of our being once fixed on a farm in the back settlements, and exposed to terrors from the Indians, which, with all my courage, it was utterly out of my power to support; but I have already been too prolix, and tired you with a long history of sorrow, from which your sensible heart requires some relief.

"Alas! I cannot give it you while I dwell on my own sad story; I will therefore, as briefly as I can, conclude it, by telling you that we were four years in America, and two in Antigua; where my husband joined his own family, and tried to establish himself as a merchant. But he was, by this time, considered as a schemer[1]—as an unlucky man—as one not born to be prosperous; and this design ended, like the rest, in disappointment.

"I have obtained, however, some advantages by my itinerant life; I have learned resignation, and have seen, that almost every condition of humanity has evils equal to mine, though I have sometimes thought them insupportable. But in acquiring patience, hope, I own, has escaped me: nor have I now any other wish, than to see my children well, and to be able to find them bread.

"The distinctions of rank have long since too been lost to me, who have passed from competence to extreme poverty, from extreme poverty to high affluence, and have again fallen to all the miseries of dependence and indigence. When Frank, therefore, first declared to me his attachment to Jessy Woodburn, I opposed his marriage, not from pride, but from the apprehension of redoubling his difficulties. I then, it is true, depended almost entirely on the generous assistance of that excellent brother; but, believe me, that would never have induced me to oppose what was requisite to his happiness. I had not known Jessy long before I lost every idea of opposition to it, and I wished to see them married long before I knew what favourable prospects might one day open to the object of his affection. To foresee to whom she would owe the realizing those prospects, to whom she would afterwards be the means of my being known, was, you know, impossible."

1   Projector, speculator.

"And where, my dear Madam," enquired Celestina, "where was Mr. Elphinstone at the time you speak of?"

"He was gone again to Antigua, on account of his mother's death. I was left with four children, and so little money, that heaven only knows what would have become of them and of me, had it not been for Frank."

"And your sister Emily!—I cannot help being interested for her with all her failings."

"Ah! would to heaven I knew what was now her lot! I lost all traces of her after my going to America; nor could mine or Frank's most assiduous enquiries ever since, gain any intelligence. She has changed her name, or taken some other means to avoid us; circumstances that make me fear she is sunk below her former brilliant but discreditable and destructive condition. When I think of her and of my children, my stoicism forsakes me—and of her, unless I could snatch her from a manner of life so terrible, I endeavour not to think; for the thoughts of what she is, and of what she may be, I am very frequently unable to bear. You will allow, my dear Miss de Mornay, that my own situation requires all my courage. A new and perhaps an abortive project now carries me to the remotest part of Scotland—with a heart, I hope not callous, but exhausted by long suffering. My husband is amiable, good tempered, and, I believe, truly attached to me; but he is so volatile! so unsteady! misfortune has made him restless, and his desultory life encreased the original blemish of his temper—a want of firmness; from which have arisen some of the evils that have pursued us.

"One of his some-time friends procured him the little appointment he now holds, rather to get rid of his importunity, I think, than to do him real service. It may, however, afford us a residence and a support, and I need not say that its distance from the scene of our former prosperity and former adversity is to me its greatest recommendation. If my husband can learn to be content among the cold and dreary Hebrides, if my children have there health, food, and shelter, never shall I be heard to repine; and indeed my journey, in having you for my companion, begins under auspices so favourable, that my heart, dead to hope as it has long been, is yet not insensible of something that nearly resembles it."

This conversation brought the travellers to the end of their third day's stage; and Celestina, more than ever interested for Mrs. Elphinstone, forgot for a moment every thing but the series of undeserved calamities to which she had been listening.

END OF THE SECOND VOLUME.

VOLUME III

Chapter I

At the end of a week, Celestina, with Mrs. Elphinstone and her children, were arrived at the small village of Kirby Thorn, where, as the youngest of the little boys had appeared the preceding day to droop, his mother determined to pass the night. Celestina, who saw her friend greatly alarmed by the indisposition of the child, endeavoured to appease her fears by imputing it to the fatigue and heat of their journey. But the terrified mother saw every moment new grounds for her apprehensions, and the next day the child was evidently much worse. Four and twenty hours more passed in painful solicitude, and then Mrs. Elphinstone knew that it was the measles; and became much easier, though the eldest boy had every symptom of having taken the same disorder.

Mrs. Elphinstone never left her children a moment; and Celestina, with the tenderest solicitude, assisted her. The elder boy was of a sanguine[1] and irritable[2] constitution, and the eruptive fever ran high; while the situation they were in, at a little inn, where the servants and children of the house had not had the distemper,[3] was rendered extremely uncomfortable by the fears of its other inhabitants, the murmurs of the landlady and the reluctance of the servants.

Celestina, with that cheerful benignity which was on all occasions ready for the service of the distressed, now acted for her friend almost the part of a servant; and in her frequent visits to the kitchen for what was wanted in the sick room, she saw three servants, a postillion and two footmen, and observed that they seemed fixed here, and were not at present travelling. The men were remarkably well behaved, and observing the discontent of the people of the inn, had more than once offered to go out for her on any messages she might have occasion to send.

The mind of Celestina was, however, too much occupied by the little invalids to suffer her curiosity to be awakened by this circumstance; and she never enquired to whom these servants, nor a very plain but fashionable post chaise, about which she saw them some-

---

1 Susceptible to fever.
2 Sensitive.
3 Disorder, illness.

times busied, belonged. The children were in the height of the distemper, and the anxious mother and Celestina entirely occupied about them, when a very decent person, about fifty, who had the look of a housekeeper to some person of fashion, came to the door of their room, which was left open for the sake of air, and asking permission to come in, told them, that her lady, Lady Horatia Howard, had ordered her to wait on them to enquire if her servants or any thing in her power could contribute to the ease of the children, or the ladies to whom they belonged.

Mrs. Elphinstone returned a proper answer to this very polite and humane message; and after the person who had delivered it was withdrawn, Celestina pausing a moment, said that she recollected the name of Lady Horatia Howard, and that she was one of the friends most esteemed among the numerous acquaintance cultivated by Mrs. Willoughby.

It was now debated between them whether, after so obliging a message, Celestina should not make herself known to Lady Horatia: Mrs. Elphinstone was inclined to think she ought; but Celestina seemed rather disposed to avoid it.—"It is true," said she, "that I recollect my dear Mrs. Willoughby to have been very partial to her, but it is probable that she has long since forgotten me, and that I shall be exposed to the disagreeable necessity of announcing myself, and recalling to her mind circumstances which I cannot remember but with pain. Perhaps, too, she may know the strange occurrences which have since happened; and though I remember her conversation to have been very refined and elegant, perhaps she may expect, if she honours me with her notice, that I should prove myself worthy of it, by relating all that has happened; for who knows in what light the Castlenorths may have represented my conduct. I am unequal to all this, I fear; and unless to avail myself of our former acquaintance will be of any use to you, my dear Mrs. Elphinstone, I shall not, for my own sake only, endeavour to renew it."

In the few hours afterwards, however, Lady Horatia, who had heard from her servant of the fine form and amiable manners of the young person who was so attentive to the sick children, contrived to have a door left open by which she must pass; and seeing her, immediately knew her. On her return into the room therefore, Lady Horatia sent her woman again, with her compliments, begging to know if the name of one of the ladies was not de Mornay, and if it was, requesting the favour of speaking to her.

Celestina could not now decline going; and following the messenger, was shewn into a room where Lady Horatia sat alone.

"Pardon me, dear Miss de Mornay," cried she, the moment she entered, "if instead of waiting on you, I request to see you here. The truth is, I am foolishly affected by the sight of illness. That which has attacked your little friends is not however, I hope, dangerous?"

Celestina, who by the freedom and kindness of this address was immediately relieved from some little uneasiness which she had felt from this unexpected interview, answered with all her usual ease and grace, and Lady Horatia, who seemed extremely pleased with having met her, enquired after Lady Molyneux, and such other of their former friends, as she thought would renew no unpleasing recollections: for though she did not know all that had happened, she was well aware how cruel a blow the death of Mrs. Willoughby had been to Celestina, and had heard some confused reports that the marriage of Willoughby and Miss Fitz-Hayman was interrupted by his prior attachment to his mother's ward; but she knew not how far Celestina had been preferred to the haughty heiress; and though she had always a partial kindness to her when she used to meet her at Mrs. Willoughby's, she had lost sight of her entirely afterwards, and, after some enquiries, concluded she was gone back to France.

The sight of her now, at a remote inn in the North, was as agreeable as it was unexpected; and though the difference of their ages seemed to preclude any great degree of intimacy before, for Lady Horatia was passed the middle of life, yet now she felt herself strongly disposed to cultivate a pleasure thus thrown her way. Celestina could not be insensible of the honour she derived from the notice of a person more eminent for her goodness and her talents than her birth or her fortune, and always pleasing, she grew infinitely more so where she desired to please. In a few hours, therefore, they became so happy with each other, that Lady Horatia could not part with her but with regret; and Celestina would have left her with reluctance on any other occasion than to attend the children of her friend, (which, during her absence, Mrs. Hemmings, Lady Horatia's woman, had done, with an attention that prevented Mrs. Elphinstone's suffering from the engagement of Celestina with her lady.)

The children became better and their mother easier. Lady Horatia saw and liked her, and invited both her and Celestina to give her as much of their time as they could spare from their little convalescents. In consequence of this invitation they were now a good deal with her, and Mrs. Elphinstone on some occasion expressing how fortunate she thought herself that in so remote a place she had the honour of becoming known to her, Lady Horatia said, smiling,— "And I dare say you think it very extraordinary too, my dear

Madam; for unless you had known me before it would be difficult to account for my being here. Did you never remark that unhappiness makes people restless?"

"Oh, yes! very often," replied Mrs. Elphinstone with a sigh.

"It has had that effect on me," said Lady Horatia; "and satiated with every thing in what is called the world, where I have passed the greater part of my life, I often leave it and ramble about, careless of every thing but change of place; my old faithful servants and a few books being the sole companions of my travels. I have for these last four or five years given up my house in the country, and passed all the summer in wandering about Switzerland, France, and England. This year I am going into Scotland, for no other reason than because I have not been there before: at this village one of my horses fell lame: and as it was indifferent to me where I was, I agreed to my servant's request of staying here a day or two. While I waited, you arrived here, and I own very sincerely that I became interested for the children and for the ladies, such as Hemmings described them to me. I hope we shall none of us be sorry for the accidents that detained us here, when the little boys are quite well, as I am persuaded they will be now in a few days. They will have passed happily through a very troublesome distemper, and I think you will each of you have added a friend to your stock: the advantage, however, will be still more evidently mine, for I hope to have added two."

A few days confirmed the good opinion which Lady Horatia entertained of her new acquaintance and her acquaintance of her. If she was particularly attached to Celestina, it was because she was young enough to be her daughter, and because she told her that she could not look at her, especially when she was reading or employed in any thing that gave a serious cast to her features, without remarking her likeness to a person she had once fondly loved.

Celestina, whose thoughts were perpetually fixed on the strange mystery which hung over her birth, and who caught at every thing likely to clear it up, blushed deeply the first time she made this remark, and asked whether this person was a foreigner?

Lady Horatia sighed in her turn, and said, no! it was a brother of hers, who had not been long dead. "He was a soldier," said she, "and lost his life in America, in that war which tore it from the British empire.[1] Judge yourself of the likeness, though I well know it must be accidental."

---

1 American War of Independence, 1775-82.

She then took out of a travelling trunk a little filligreed[1] casket, in which were several valuable trinkets and several pictures. Three were the portraits of gentlemen.—"Come," said Lady Horatia, "to prove whether this resemblance is merely a chimera[2] of mine, let us ask Mrs. Elphinstone if among these pictures she sees one which is like any body she knows; for my dear Miss de Mornay, do you know this similitude of countenance struck me when you were a child with Mrs. Willoughby; and now that your features are more formed, it is, in my mind, wonderfully strong. But, my sweet friend, why do you appear so uneasy?"

"I cannot very well tell," replied Celestina, trying to force a smile: "I am sure to bear a resemblance to any body dear to your Ladyship must be ever pleasing to me, though I will know that it must be, as you observe, quite accidental."

Mrs. Elphinstone then coming in, Lady Horatia shewed her the three portraits:—"Come tell us, Mrs. Elphinstone, if you know any living friend whom either of these portraits resembles?"

Mrs. Elphinstone took them, and looked steadily a moment on each; then fixing on one, she looked more intently, first on that and then on Celestina. "Indeed I think I do," cried she: "I surely see a resemblance—a very strong resemblance, between this picture and Miss de Mornay. Bless me, how very like! the shape of the face, the mouth, the dark-brown eyebrow, the colour of the eyes, the setting on of the hair round the forehead and temples; except that it is less fair, that the features are proportionably larger, and that you wear a cap, in truth, my dear friend, it might have been drawn for you."

"And yet," said Lady Horatia, smiling mournfully, "this was drawn for a brother of mine, who could, I fear, be no relation to our lovely friend here: so strangely it happens that features coincide."

"It is fortunate, very fortunate for me, Madam," said Celestina gravely, "if this resemblance has had the effect of prejudicing your Ladyship in my favour."

"You have merit enough to justify it, though I had conceived an affection for you without any introduction. But we will talk no more of resemblances, if such discourse makes us melancholy."

Lady Horatia then turned the conversation; and the next day, as the two little boys were by this time well enough to continue their

---

1 Ornamented with jewels and gold or silver thread.
2 In Greek myth, the Chimaera was a monster part lion, part goat and part serpent; hence, an illusion, a phantasm.

journey, they moved on about twenty miles together; Lady Horatia begging for that day to have Celestina with her, while her woman went with Mrs. Elphinstone, to assist in the care of her children.

Celestina, who knew only in general that Lady Horatia was a widow of very affluent fortune, who gave up much of her time to literary pursuits and literary connections, and much of her fortune to the assistance of the unhappy, now learned that domestic misfortunes had contributed, with her natural turn of mind, to estrange her entirely from those scenes where Celestina had sometimes formerly seen her; and that having lost an only daughter, (the last of her children,) of a deep decline,[1] she now tried to call off her mind from the subjects of her mournful contemplations by change of place, and had never, since that period, resided long at any of her own houses, but had passed almost the whole year in travelling; stopping wherever she found a pleasant spot, and often remaining several days, or even weeks, at some remote house. She had once or twice, she said, engaged friends to go with her on these expeditions, but had always found the difficulties they made so much counterbalance the pleasure they were capable of affording her, that she now travelled alone. "Some," said she, "were tired, and some were tasteless; some were talkative and some were insipid. You will certainly think me fastidious; and perhaps I am so; but indeed it is more difficult to find such a companion as suits me in every respect, than appears at first view.

"Women of my own age, who are established in the world, cannot of course leave their families and connections; those who are not, are for the most part unhappy from pecuniary or family distresses, and the mind, depressed at that period of life, has lost its power of resistance, and sinks in that hopeless languor from which I often want to be myself relieved by cheerful conversation. The young do not travel for prospects, or enjoy cataracts and mountains: they are looking out for lovers; and are wearied when there are neither men to talk to or adventures to be hoped for. I have tried two or three young ladies; and found, that as we had no ideas in common, our conversation was soon exhausted; and when I was near any place of summer resort, or passed through a town at the time of a race or a music meeting, their hearts were beating to enter into scenes which I was only solicitous to fly from. Do you know, however, that if I had not met you absolutely engaged on this Scottish journey, I should

---

1 Usually tuberculosis, the biggest killer of young people in the eighteenth century; but the term could cover a number of debilitating illnesses.

have been strongly tempted to enquire whether you would allow me to make the experiment once more, where I am strongly impressed with an idea that I should meet with better success."

Celestina answered, that her good opinion did her the utmost honour: and by degrees the tender and maternal solicitude Lady Horatia expressed for her, drew from her the little narrative of her life. Lady Horatia expressed the greatest aversion to Lady Castlenorth. "It is true," said she, "I do now know her much from my own observation; for she is a woman whose conversation I have always disliked and avoided; but from some anecdotes of her that have been related to me by those who know her well, I believe it may with truth be said of her, as was said of a celebrated political character, that she has 'a heart to imagine, a head to contrive, and a hand to execute any mischief.'[1] Willoughby is young, open-hearted, and artless: by no means likely to suspect, or likely to detect artifice so deep as what she is capable of; and I am well convinced that there are no contrivances at which she would hesitate, either to carry a favourite point or avenge its failure."

Celestina was extremely comforted by this opinion given by so good a judge. Every other sorrow was comparatively light to that which she felt from the idea, whenever it forced itself upon her mind, that Willoughby had, through ambition, or caprice, or avarice, voluntarily deserted her; and every opinion that strengthened her own hopes of his unaltered affection, and imputed his leaving her to the evil machinations of the Castlenorths, was soothing and consolatory.

Lady Horatia Howard was now travelling towards Edinburgh, and made the time of Mrs. Elphinstone her own, for the pleasure she derived from her company, and still more from that of Celestina, to whom, during this journey, she became so much attached, that she made her promise to come to her whenever the abode she was now going to should be inconvenient, or whenever she was under the necessity of changing it. An invitation so flattering was gratefully accepted; and Lady Horatia having shewn both her travelling friends every polite and generous attention, took leave of them with regret

---

1 Smith is recalling a sentence by Edward Hyde, Earl of Clarendon, in *The History of the Rebellion*, Vol. 7, 84. Writing of John Hampden, politician and officer in the Parliamentarian army in the rebellion against Charles I, and judging from a Royalist point of view, Clarendon says that he had "a heart to contrive, and a tongue to persuade, and a hand to execute, any mischief."

on their leaving Edinburgh with Elphinstone, who was there waiting for them. She gave Celestina directions whither to write to her for the remainder of the summer, and again made her promise to come to her in the winter, if she left her Scottish friends; and at all events to contrive to pass with her two or three months of the next summer. After taking leave of her, a very tedious and very dreary journey of many days brought the Elphinstones and Celestina to the sea side, where they were to embark for the Isle of Skye.

Mrs. Elphinstone, accustomed to see so many different countries, was yet struck with dismay at the sight of the black and dreary heaths over which they travelled; and in spite of all her attempts to sustain her courage, she looked at her children with eyes where maternal anguish was too visibly expressed. Elphinstone, however, to whom novelty had always charms, was not yet weary of his situation, and he was as gay and unconcerned as if he had been leading his wife to the most beautiful estate in England. Celestina, though very little delighted with the country they had passed through, was determined to testify no dislike to it that might add to the painful dejection of her friend, and by making light of the inconveniencies of the journey, and putting their hopes and prospects in the fairest light, she supported her drooping spirits, which the thoughtless and somewhat unfeeling vivacity of Elphinstone himself, served rather to depress than to support.

Chapter II

Arrived at this insular[1] abode after great fatigue, Mrs. Elphinstone, recalling all her fortitude, busied herself in making it as comfortable as she could; and assumed, at least, the appearance of cheerfulness, though Celestina saw with concern that it was often but appearance. Celestina herself, however, whose mind had too long been unpleasingly called off from that object on which she best loved to fix it, was far from being displeased by the perfect seclusion of the place. She could now wander whole days alone, amid the wild solitude in which she found herself, listening only to the rush of the cataract, which, dashing through broken stones, sparkled amid the dark heath on either side of it; or the sullen waves of the ocean itself, which on all sides surrounded her. The ptarmigan,[2] bursting from its heathy

---

1 Island.
2 Smith's note: a bird of the grous kind, common in the highlands of Scotland.

covert, or the sea fowl screaming from the rocks, were the only sounds that broke these murmurs; but she found her spirits soothed by the wildness of the places she visited; and far from regretting the more cultivated scenes she had left, she rejoiced that since she no longer could hope to see Willoughby, she was released from the necessity of attending to any other person.

The immense distance that was now between them, she sometimes considered with dismay; but at others she remembered—

"That distance only, cannot change the heart."[1]

She trusted on the long tried, the long assured tenderness of her lover, and was willing to indulge the soothing hope that they should meet again to be separated no more, and that he was labouring to remove the fatal obstacle, whatever it was, that now divided them.

After having been above five weeks on the island, a large pacquet arrived from Cathcart. It enclosed, among many to his sister, one to Celestina from Willoughby; and this, more than any she had yet received from him since his absence, seemed to assure her of his unfailing attachment. It was less confused than those he had formerly written, and seemed the production of a mind more master of itself: and, though it did not speak in positive terms of his immediate return, Celestina fancied that many of the expressions alluded to that hour; and her heart found this idea so deliciously soothing, that she would not suffer her reason to deprive her of any part of the pleasure she found in indulging it.

A few of the residents of this and the neighbouring islands were by this time acquainted at the house of Mr. Elphinstone. The young, (and of young people their visitors principally consisted,) were all charmed with Celestina, who, whatever was her inclination for solitude, never refused to make one in the ramble of the morning, or to join the cheerful dance of an evening. Elphinstone, naturally good humoured, and particularly desirous of pleasing her, soon became anxious to promote these parties, which Celestina, whose heart was open to new sensations of pleasure since the receipt of Willoughby's last letter, did not decline; not only because she found much in these remote regions to gratify her curiosity, but because she foresaw that, from the shortness of the summer so far North, the days when these

---

1   William Cowper, "An Epistle to Joseph Hall, Esq." 10–11: "... and friends may part/ But distance only cannot change the heart."

amusements were practicable were drawing to their conclusion, and that she soon should be left unmolested, to listen to the roaring of the waters, and the sighings of the wind round the naked rocks, against which it incessantly beat.

It was now the end of July, and Celestina had already visited Iona and several other islands. Sometimes these excursions had been made with Mrs. Elphinstone, but oftener without her. Elphinstone kept a boat, which was always ready for the service of Celestina, and when his wife could not go with her, a Miss Macqueen, a very agreeable young highland lady,[1] always made the third.

Several little isles, which afford no habitations for winter, are scattered among the larger islands, which are called the Hebrides. One of these lay within sight of Elphinstone's house, (which was close to the shore,) at the distance of about a mile and a half. It was remarkable for the grotesque form of the cliffs which arose round it, and for a stream of the purest water, that bubbled up at the highest ground, and fell into the sea through a chasm of the rock. Celestina, to whom Elphinstone had shewn it, laughingly called it her island; and he, in return, had said that were she established on it, it would become more dangerous than the island of Calypso.[2] Among other little plans of amusement, which the decline of summer insensibly rendered more infrequent,[3] it was agreed that on the first fine day some cold provisions should be taken, and that they would all dine together on one of the natural stone tables in Celestina's island.

A fine day was found; the party, which were Mr. and Mrs. Elphinstone, Miss Macqueen, and two gentlemen, were ready, when one of the boatmen who usually accompanied them was no where to be found. Elphinstone, equally impatient and eager, whatever was the importance or insignificance of the matter he was engaged in, was going himself in search of the missing man, when one of those who remained in the boat followed and told him that there was a young man a few yards farther on the shore, who would take the place of him that was absent, and that it was better not to wait: Elphinstone, satisfied so long as his party was not interrupted, accepted the offer,

---

1   The Highlands (Northern Scotland) are not distinctly divided from the Lowlands in the south, though very different national characteristics are often attributed to their inhabitants.
2   In Greek myth, Calypso, the daughter of Atlas, lived on the island of Ogygia. When Odysseus was shipwrecked there, she kept him captive for seven years.
3   The original has "frequent."

and the boatman beckoning to a highlander who stood at some distance, he ran towards them and was admitted into the boat.

The party now put off from shore. The water was beautifully smooth, the sky clear, and the wind in their favour; very little exertion therefore on the part of the men who were entrusted with the navigation, landed them safely on the ilk.[1] It did not contain more than three acres of land, and the sole inhabitant of it was a solitary herdsman, whose temporary dwelling, composed of loose stones, turf, and heath, he had raised under the protection of a large cliff of grey slate, that seemed to have started away, in some strange concussion of nature, from some other island, and to have fixed itself as a sea mark[2] amidst the perpendicular and abrupt rocks that fenced this on every side. The spring burst out near its base, and here the party sat down to make their gay repast.

When it was over, the gentlemen went away; and while the boatmen were at dinner, pushed out the boat themselves and began to fish near the shore, while Celestina, leaving the ladies together, walked away alone to the western coast of the island.

The sun was already declining in an almost cloudless sky, and gave the warmest splendour to the broad expanse of ocean, broken by several islands, whose rocky points and angular cliffs caught the strong lights, in brilliant contrast to the lucid hue of the heath with which their summits were cloathed, and which on the northern and eastern sides threw a dark shadow on the clear and tranquil bosom of the sea. The sea birds, in swarming myriads, were returning to their nests among the ragged precipices beneath her; and Celestina, recalling to her mind the "green delights"[3] of Alvestone,

"Its deepening woods, gay lawns, and airy summits,"[4]

compared it, in pensive contemplation, with the scene before her; yet different as they were, she thought that with Willoughby any place would be to her a paradize; and that even in such a remote spot as this she should be happy if it gave only a subsistence with him.

---

1 Island (dialect).
2 Any feature, geographical or otherwise, used as a guide to navigators.
3 James Thomson, *The Seasons*, "Summer," 956.
4 Smith may be thinking of lines from Robert Colvill's "Sir Ambrose and Fair Portia," Canto 2, 74–76: "The pathless wilds and muirs.... gay lawns and stately towers."

This train of thought a little indulged, made her have recourse to her pencil, and produced an address to him in the following

SONNET

On this lone island, whose unfruitful breast
Feeds but the summer-shepherd's little flock,
With scanty herbage from the half cloath'd rock,
Where osprays,[1] cormorants, and sea mews rest;
Even in a scene so desolate and rude
I could with *thee* for months and years be blest;
And, of thy tenderness and love possest,
Find all *my* world in this lone solitude!
When the bright sun these northern seas illume,
With thee admire the light's reflected charms;
And when drear Winter spreads his cheerless gloom,
Still find Elysium in thy sheltering arms;
For thou to me canst sovereign bliss impart,
Thy mind my empire, and my throne thy heart.[2]

The broad orb of the sun was now only half seen above the horizon; and Celestina, who had little marked the progress of time, rose, and hastened to join her companions; as she turned for this purpose towards that part of the island where she had left them, she saw the highlander, who had been taken by chance into the boat in consequence of the absence of another, start up from the ground at about two hundred paces from her, where he seemed to have been concealed behind a cairn or pile of rude stones, and hurry away towards the part of the shore where the boat had been left. The incident however made no great impression on her mind, but from the singular appearance of the man who was in a complete highland dress, which is now not often seen,[3] and which made him, as he walked

---

1 Smith's note: the sea eagle.
2 Reprinted as no. LI in Smith's *Elegiac Sonnets*, and in her *Collected Poems*, ed. Stuart Curran.
3 The defeat of Prince Charles Edward Stuart and his army at Culloden in 1746 marked the end of military attempts by the Stuarts to regain the British monarchy. William, Duke of Cumberland (known as The Butcher), pacified the Highlands. Among other measures to break the power of the clans, wearing the clan tartan (plaid) had been forbidden, but it was now gradually returning.

very quickly on before her, seem exactly the figure a painter would have chosen to have placed in a landscape, representing the heathy summits and romantic rocks of the Hebrides.

She soon rejoined Mrs. Elphinstone and Miss Macqueen. The three gentlemen almost as soon approached to tell them it was time to return; and they arrived again at their home after a little excursion with which all seemed pleased, though Celestina had suffered some raillery for having so long deserted them.

Every day now passed nearly alike, diversified only now and then by the company of a stranger from some of the other islands, and sometimes a party in the boat. Elphinstone was not yet tired by the project which brought him hither, for to use an expression of his wife's, which she uttered with a melancholy smile to Celestina, "the new was not yet off." He was therefore gay and alert; persuaded himself, by calculations, which he made after his own sanguine[1] manner, that he was not only a benefactor to the public, but should in a few years realize a great fortune by facilitating the capture of herrings among the western islands of Scotland.

The season[2] for the proof of his exploits in this way was now rapidly approaching, and he became every day more busy: but his wife looked forward to it with less pleasure: she languished for her little girls, who were at the other extremity of England, and thought with dismay of the tempests of winter, which would shut her out from the little communication she yet had with that country. But whatever was her regret, she suffered it not to disturb the transient happiness her husband seemed to enjoy, nor to communicate any gloom to the milder cheerfulness of Celestina, whose company was her greatest resource against that cold despondence, which, in despite of all her fortitude, sometimes seized on her heart.

Celestina had now been almost three months an inhabitant of the Isle of Skye, and felt nothing unpleasant in her insular situation but the length of time that must always elapse before she could hear from Willoughby or even from Cathcart. A second packet was however brought to Mrs. Elphinstone from the latter before the expiration of the eleventh week of their abode. With eager impatience it was opened. Celestina received her part of it with a beating heart; but on unsealing it found no letter from Willoughby. A letter, in a hand which she did not at the moment recollect ever to have seen

---

1 Confident, hopeful.
2 Autumn.

before, attracted her attention and mingled it with something of terror. She looked eagerly at the name, and saw it signed with that of the elder Mr. Thorold. Her spirits sunk! was it some ill news of Willoughby, which he communicated that he might soften the blow? She hurried it over in such breathless agitation as hardly gave her leave to understand what she read, which was to this effect:

"Your old friend, amiable Celestina, though he has only had one letter from you since you left him, reminds you of himself once more, and is sorry that, like every thing in this world, his letter will convey to you a mixture of pleasure and pain.

"My daughter Arabella is married, to her own wishes and those of her mother. In point of fortune she has done well. We cannot here obtain every thing. I hope she will be happy, and am sure she will be rich, which, in the opinion of most fathers, you know, puts the former point out of doubt. You will guess that Mr. Bettenson is the gentleman who is now numbered with my family. My wife has been gone with the new married couple some weeks to the seat of Mr. Bettenson's father in Norfolk.

"You know I love home; and I love that those who are less delighted with it should not be needlessly disturbed when they are out; for which reason I have never communicated to his mother, that Montague, after attending his sister's wedding here, did not return to Oxford as he talked of doing; that I know not whither he is gone, and have only had one letter from him since, in which he assured me he is well, and desires I would not be uneasy about him.

"It is very difficult to be otherwise. This eccentric young man makes me tremble for him perpetually. Having no clue to direct my guesses, I have no conjecture where or with whom he is; and think it better to say as little as I can about an absence on which a thousand unfavourable constructions may be put. Ah! my lovely ward, how fortunate it would have been, if, when his judgment directed his heart, it could have been accepted where—but this is wrong, or at best useless. Farewel! May heaven protect you! and I pray you not to forget

your most faithful friend,

E. THOROLD."

Relieved from her first apprehensions, Celestina felt extremely concerned at the absence of Montague Thorold; so painful to his father, perhaps so discreditable to himself. She read over the letter again, and fancied it very evident that Mr. Thorold imputed it to some new attachment; and giving a sigh to the recollection of all it must cost such a father to see such an unfortunate turn of mind blast all the acquirement of learning, and all the advantages of genius, she turned her thoughts to Willoughby, and felt with renewed poignancy the disappointment of not having heard from him.

Another and another week passed without any intelligence, and all the soothing hopes Celestina had so fondly encouraged gradually gave way to fear and apprehension. At length a second packet arrived: it contained a letter indeed from Willoughby; but so far was it from confirming the favourable presages of the former, that she saw in it only a prelude to the event which other information made her believe would soon happen—the marriage of Willoughby and Miss Fitz-Hayman. Lady Horatia Howard, whose attachment to Celestina had taken very deep root, had written to her from London, whither she was now gone, and had told her, with as much tenderness as she could, that such was the general report among the relations of the family, and what was generally believed in the world. From the same channel she also learned that Sir Philip and Lady Molyneux were expected in England early in the ensuing winter, and that a large house in Portman-square was fitting up in the most splendid stile for their reception.

Lady Horatia concluded a most friendly letter to Celestina thus:

"But my dear Miss de Mornay, however all these things may be, let me hope that you will not hide yourself in the Hebrides all the winter: why should you? Talents and virtues like your's were never intended for obscurity. Come then to me, and assure yourself of the truest welcome. You need not apprehend meeting Mr. Willoughby and his bride, for it is understood that they are to remain some time abroad; and before they return to England, you will have learned to conquer those painful emotions which the sight of them now perhaps might give you. Your understanding sets you above the puerile indulgence which inferior minds claim by prescription towards a first love. The man whom any common consideration could induce, after having won your affections, to desert you, never could deserve you; and if some insurmountable barrier is between you, you will learn to consider him as a friend, and consult his peace in regaining that cheerfulness which he meant not to destroy; but which to see destroyed, must overcloud his days, however prosperous they may otherwise be."

There was in this letter more meant than was expressed; and on considering it, the wonder and uneasiness of Celestina were redoubled. But however obliged she thought herself by the friendly interest Lady Horatia took in her happiness, and however just her arguments might be, she felt no inclination to quit her present solitude; and since she had now less hope than ever of meeting Willoughby, she had less than ever a desire to return into the world, but gave herself up to that melancholy despondence, against which hope, and her own sanguine and cheerful temper, had till now supported her.

To indulge this encreasing sadness, it was now her custom to walk out alone after dinner, and to make for herself a species of gloomy enjoyment from the dreary and wild scenes around her. A little time before, she had been imagining how pleasant the most desolate of these barren islands might be rendered to her by the presence of her beloved Willoughby. She now rather sought images of horror. The sun, far distant from this northern region, was as faint and languid as the sick thoughts of Celestina: his feeble rays no longer gave any warm colouring to the rugged cliffs that rose above her head, or lent the undulating sea that sparkling brilliance which a few weeks before had given gaiety and cheerfulness even to these scattered masses of almost naked stone, against which the water incessantly broke. Grey, sullen, and cold, the waves now slowly rolled towards the shore, where Celestina frequently sat whole hours, as if to count them, when she had in reality no idea present to her but Willoughby lost to her for ever—Willoughby forgetting her, and married to Miss Fitz-Hayman!

She had more than once remarked, in returning from her walks, that a man, who kept always at such a distance that she could merely discover to be a highlander, seemed to be observing her; yet as he never came near her, and always disappeared before she got near the house, she could not imagine him to be one of the people belonging to Elphinstone: but puzzled rather than alarmed by his appearance, for which she could not account, she insensibly ceased to notice him. Mrs. Elphinstone, occupied as she was by her own domestic uneasiness, was still most tenderly attentive to Celestina, and endeavoured to communicate to her some of that still and mournful acquiescence which served her in place of philosophy. Celestina had not yet suffered enough to learn it; but she forbore to add to the melancholy of her friend by indulging her own while they were together; and this restraint threw her more than ever into entire solitude, though the autumn was so far advanced that the weather frequently drove her from the open hill, or the vale under it, to the casual shelter of some natural cave, by the side of which, the torrent, encreased by the storm, hoarsely rushed, and was answered by the roar of other streams, whose hollow murmurs swelled in the gusts of wind that whistled through the mountainous tracks, and compelled even the fowls of the desart to seek shelter, where only it was afforded, within the caverns of the cliffs, or among the matted heath that cloathed their summits.

The delicate, the elegant, the lovely Celestina, she whose talents would have adorned the most informed society, and whose beauty might have given new lustre to the fairest assembly, was thus a self-banished recluse in the remotest and most uncultivated part of the British dominions. Her wish now was, to pass her whole life here, in that sullen[1] calm which she at length hoped to obtain; and the rudest scene of these islands now appeared to her infinitely preferable to any of the pleasures Lady Horatia Howard offered her, since they could only serve to remind her of Willoughby; perhaps to shew her how happy he could learn to be, united with another.

The frequency of storms now prevented many of those visits which had, during summer, a little broken, for Elphinstone, the uniformity of solitude; but it was the height of the season for catching herrings, and he was busy, and for the present happy; while his unfortunate wife, who, desolate as her present situation was, yet dreaded the hour when this bustle should sink into discontent and give place to other projects, received him on his return from those expeditions to other islands, in which he was now frequently engaged, always with cheerfulness, which he did not, or would not see, was forced; and sometimes with smiles, which to every body but him very evidently were the smiles of stifled anguish.

Celestina answered Lady Horatia's letter as it deserved, but to Willoughby she determined not to write. That trembling solicitude

1 Quiet.

with which she had been accustomed to expect letters from him, it was now, she thought, time to subdue, for she persuaded herself that never again they would bring to her any thing but anguish and regret: and yet by those contradicting sensations to which violent attachments subject the human heart, she incessantly indulged herself in thinking of all those happy hours which she had passed with him, whom she fancied deserved little or no regret, of whom she ought not to think at all, and yet was so fond of recollecting, that every conversation was irksome to her, and every employment a task, which took off her attention a moment from him.

"Ti perdo! ti lascio, non ti vedro piu—"[1]

she repeated incessantly to herself, sometimes with tears of tenderness, and sometimes with those painful emotions of mingled anger and regret which press on the heart when pride and resentment are struggling with affection. In other moods she reproached herself for thus cherishing this unhappy passion, tried to recal those days of resignation when, without hope of ever being his, she yet preferred Willoughby to all mankind; and to dismiss from her mind for ever the recollection of the few weeks when he had awakened that hope, and called forth all her sensibility only as it should seem to render her wretched; then she exclaimed in her native language—

"Felicité passée
Qui ne peut revenir;
Tourment de ma pensée!
Que n'ai je en te perdant, perdu le souvenir."[2]

In these gloomy moods, she was quite unable to remain a moment in company, especially in the company of Elphinstone, who, with the true projector's infatuation, fancied every body else as much interested about the fishery as he was; and persecuted her with details of how many *busses*[3] he had out and how many *lasts*[4] they had

---

1 Unidentified: I lose you, I leave you, I will never see you again (Italian).
2 Jean Bertaut, "Chanson XXVIII," 45–48: "Past happiness/ That cannot return;/ Tormentor of my thoughts!/ That in losing you, I haven't lost the memory of you." The passage was often quoted, by Voltaire and J.B. Rousseau among others, and was set to music by P. Cerveau and K.F. Zelter.
3 Two-or three-masted boats used in herring fishery.
4 Boatloads.

taken; what was the best method of curing them, and of the superiority which a few years would give the fishery in which he was engaged, over the Dutch.

Celestina began to dread the conversation; and had it not been for Mrs. Elphinstone, of whose suffering merit she was every hour more sensible, she would not have forborne to express her weariness and disgust. A hearer was necessary to Elphinstone; and when he had nobody else to talk to, this unenviable place was filled by the inwardly-impatient Celestina. It happened, however, that she was released from this for some days. Towards the end of November, Elphinstone went to the Isle of Harris, on his business, as he fancied, and the wind being against his return, she no longer listened to the method of curing herrings, but returned to her shortened but less interrupted walks. In one of these, towards the close of a very lowering and cheerless day, when her way was along the rugged cliffs that, on the western side of the island, hung over the sea, she composed the following sonnet:

THE PILGRIM.

Faltering and sad, the unhappy pilgrim roves,
Who, on the eve of bleak December's night,
Divided far from all he fondly loves,
Journeys alone, along the giddy height
Of these steep cliffs, and as the sun's last ray
Fades in the West, sees, from the rocky verge,
Dark tempest scowling o'er the shorten'd day,
And hears, with ear appall'd, the impetuous surge
Beneath him thunder!—So, with heart opprest,
Alone, reluctant, desolate, and slow,
By friendship's cheering radiance *now* unblest,
Along life's rudest path I seem to go;
Nor see where yet the anxious heart may rest,
That trembling at the past—recoils from future woe![1]

---

1 This sonnet is no. LII in Smith's *Elegiac Sonnets* and in Stuart Curran's *Collected Poems*.

Chapter III

Elphinstone had now been absent some days, and the wind, which was contrary and violent, prevented his return to the place of his abode. Mrs. Elphinstone became uneasy at the storms which detained him, and Celestina participated in her anxiety. At length the wind sunk, and, towards the evening of the fifth day of his absence, was fair to bring him from Harris. Mrs. Elphinstone, who had been a good deal alarmed by the hurricanes of several preceding days, and had wearied her spirits by watching the weather and keeping an anxious eye towards the impracticable[1] sea, found herself indisposed and shivering; and telling Celestina that she believed she had caught cold, she went early to bed, remarking, as she bade her good night, that Elphinstone would probably be at home in the morning.

Celestina, left alone, went out as was her custom, even although the evening was already closed in; and standing on the edge of the rocks, near the house, remarked the singular appearance of the moon, which was now rising. It was large, and of a dull red, surrounded by clouds of a deep purple, whose skirts seemed touched with flame. Large volumes of heavy vapour were gathering in the sky, and the heaving surges swelled towards the shore, and broke upon it with that sullen regularity that foretels a storm. From the North, arose distinctly the pointed rays of the Aurora Borealis:[2] fiery and portentous, they seemed to flash like faint lightning a little while, till the moon becoming clearer, rendered them less visible.

Not a sound was heard but the dull murmurs of the sea on one side and the rapid waterfalls on the other, whose encreased noise foretold with equal certainty an approaching tempest. Celestina, who was in that disposition of mind to which horrors are congenial, walked slowly on notwithstanding; but quitting the cliffs, on account of the gales of wind which now blew from the sea, she went along a narrow pass, where there was a cairn or heap of stones loosely piled together, the work of the first wild natives of the country; and as that was as far as she thought it proper to venture from the house, though it was not more than eight o'clock, she leaned pensively against it, and watched with some surprise the fluctuations of the clouds that were wildly driven by the wind across the disk of the moon, and lis-

---

1 Impossible to cross.
2 Aurora Borealis or Northern Lights: a striking display of coloured lights in the night sky, sometimes visible in Scotland and further north. A similar phenomenon occurs in high southern latitudes.

tened with a kind of chill awe, to the loud yet hollow echo of the wind among the hills; which sometimes sobbed with stormy violence for a moment, and then suddenly sinking, was succeeded by a pause more terrible.

It was in one of these moments of alarming silence, that Celestina thought she saw the shadow of a human form for a moment on the ground, as if the person was behind her who occasioned it. She was very little subject to fear; but the loneliness of the place, and her own desponding spirits together, made her start with terror and turn round. Something immediately glided away; and convinced that the first impression had not been the work of fancy, she hastened with quick steps from the place, and hardly at the distance of above a hundred yards, ventured to look behind her. She fancied that she saw a man standing in the place she had left; and the strange superstitions of the islands, of which she had heard much since her residing on them, crowding at that moment on her mind, she became extremely terrified, and hurried on with such unguarded speed, that a little before she reached the house she trod on a loose stone, that turned under her foot, and she fell with some violence and with considerable pain; which, together with the fear she had before felt, produced a momentary stupor, from which she was awakened by finding herself eagerly raised from the ground by some person, who wildly expressed his fears for her safety, and in whose voice she recognized, with astonishment that deprived her of utterance, Montague Thorold. Surprize at that moment conquered the pain she felt: "Oh! Mr. Montague!" cried she, "is it possible? for heaven's sake what brought you hither?"

"No matter what," replied he eagerly: "think not—ask not about me!—when you are yourself hurt—in pain—bruised, I fear, by your fall!"

"I have no hurt so great," said Celestina, rising and attempting to walk: "I feel no bodily pain so acute, as that which your extraordinary conduct gives me."

"Let me assist you into the house," interrupted he. "Do you not see that the tempest, which has been gathering the whole evening in the south-west, is now driving hither with uncommon fury?"

"And let it come," answered she languidly: "I am just now so very unhappy myself—I feel so much for the unhappiness of my friends, particularly of your father, that it is indifferent to me what comes."

"It is not for *me*, at least that you feel," answered he: "that I know but too well: but undoubtedly you will be greatly concerned for poor Elphinstone, whose boat has been beating about ever since night-fall, within a mile of the shore, at the imminent hazard of being dashed to pieces."

At this information Celestina forgot herself, forgot the uneasy astonishment into which the unexpected presence of Montague Thorold had thrown her, and the danger of Elphinstone occupied all her thoughts. "Oh! where!" cried she, "where is he? shew me the bark which is in so much hazard, and for heaven's sake call the people, who are not, perhaps, aware of its danger."

"Alas!" answered he, "several men have been upon the shore above half an hour, alarmed, as I was, at the danger the vessel was in of striking on the rocks, which she has got among from the unexpected shifting of the wind; but in their present state no human assistance can do them any service."

He had, during this dialogue, taken her arm, and led her towards a point of the rock, where she saw, by the pale and uncertain light of a moon, wrapped continually in volumes of clouds, the boat struggling among the dark heavy waves which often totally concealed it, and continually driven by the sudden gusts of violent wind from the point it was attempting to reach.

She now saw and shuddered at the peril of those who were in it: but still fancying it was possible to afford them assistance, she felt impatient and almost angry that Montague Thorold, holding her arm within his, stood gazing when she fancied he might be helping. "Why stand here," cried she, "when we might be of use in summoning people to the assistance of those poor creatures?" While she yet spoke, and while Montague, though not less alive to their distress, was less sanguine in the hope to assist them, and therefore still hesitated, she disengaged herself hastily from his arm, and flew towards the house, no longer conscious of any thing but their danger: before she could reach it, though the distance was not a quarter of a mile, the wind suddenly blew with treble fury, and a hail storm accompanied it, against which she found it difficult to stand. She found the door open, and Mrs. Elphinstone, whom the wind and the talking of the servants had awakened, already below. Trembling with apprehensions, which the sudden appearance of Celestina encreased—"Good God, my dear friend, what is the matter?" cried she, "and why are you out in so dreadful a night?"

"Ah! dear Madam!" replied Celestina: "Mr. Elphinstone—his boat—"

"What of him?" interrupted her terrified friend: "is he drowned? is he lost?"

"No, no! I hope, I believe not," cried Celestina; "but a boat, which they say is his, is beating off the island, and the people are afraid it will go to pieces."

This was enough for the unhappy Mrs. Elphinstone, who seeing, in its most dreadful light, the evil which threatened her, now ran herself wildly towards the beach; while Celestina, overtaking her with difficulty, persuaded her to accept her assistance—assistance which she was very little able to give.

The sad event had happened before the trembling friends had reached the headland. The boat striking on the sunken rocks, to save it from which the united efforts of the little crew had been exerted in vain, was staved to pieces, and the unhappy men, already exhausted with fatigue, were unable to resist by swimming, the violence of the sea. Mrs. Elphinstone and Celestina looked out in vain for the place where a few moments before the boat had been seen: no vestige of it remained, and they saw only, by the waning moon, which but served to lend new horrors to the view, the wild waves dashing over these rocks in sheets of white foam; while the fury of the winds and the beating of the rain hardly allowed them to stand on the precipice that overlooked the scene of stormy desolation.

Celestina doubted but little of the calamity, and therefore endeavoured to persuade her unfortunate friend to return to the house; but this was impossible: she continued to wander backwards and forwards for some moments, till terror quite overcame her; and she threw herself on the ground, saying, in a low and solemn voice to Celestina—"Elphinstone is drowned; I know he is; and here I will wait to see his corpse, which will be driven on shore in the morning." Then starting up, she would have gone down to the shore, from an idea which suddenly occurred to her that he might yet be saved by swimming. Celestina, not knowing whether it was best to prevent or to indulge her, unable to dissimulate and affect hope she did not feel, was in a situation hardly better than that of her distracted friend whom she supported, when Montague Thorold joined them. Mrs. Elphinstone, occupied only by the terror of the moment, took no notice of the extraordinary circumstance of a stranger, whom she had never seen before, thus suddenly appearing; but unconscious of every thing, and heedless of who he was, requested in accents of piercing anguish his assistance to help her down the winding path which led to the beach. He lent it, though very certain that the catastrophe had already taken place which by her eager and wild enquiries he saw she yet thought doubtful; and giving her one arm, while with the other he clasped the trembling hand of Celestina, they reached the place, where seven or eight men were already assembled.

The moon was by this time down, and the darkness was only broken by livid flashes of faint lightning, which, with the thunder muttering at a distance, encreased the horrors of the storm. Amid the black and swelling waves, however, objects were seen floating, and many of these heavy seas had not broken on the shore, before these objects were discerned to be the bodies of those who had perished, and that of the ill fated Elphinstone was one of the first which was thrown on the beach, and too well known by his unhappy wife. She now no longer remembered all the causes of uneasiness that her husband had given her; but saw only Elphinstone, once so fondly beloved, the possessor of her first affections, and father of her children, a disfigured corpse before her. Her native strength of understanding, and the calmness acquired by habitual suffering, forsook her at once, and grief produced a momentary phrenzy, during which fearful paroxysm, Celestina, whose presence of mind was now summoned to the assistance of her poor unhappy friend, had her conveyed with great difficulty to the house; where Montague Thorold attending them both with the most assiduous tenderness, she watched for many days over the disordered intellects of the ill fated Mrs. Elphinstone before she saw them restored.

At length the violence of her affliction, which Celestina found means to soften by presenting her children continually to her, and talking to her of those that were absent, sunk into the calm torpor of despair. She heard nothing, she saw nothing but the children, whom she would not suffer to be a moment absent from her; and the agitation of her mind preying on her slender frame, she was reduced to a state of languor which made Celestina tremble for her life.

Celestina had, immediately after the fatal event, written to Cathcart, desiring his directions, and even entreating him to come himself to fetch them all from a place where there was now no reason for their stay. But she knew that it must be five or six weeks before she could have an answer; and hardly dared trust herself to meditate on the scenes of distress she must in that time encounter.

Amid all the horrors however which had surrounded her, she had not forgotten the fears and alarms to which she knew the absence of Montague Thorold exposed his father, her benefactor; she seized the first interval, after the death of Elphinstone, to urge to him the cruelty of his conduct, and to entreat him to return home; but he replied, that nothing on earth should induce him to leave the place where she was, while there was a probability of his being of use to her; and that whether she admitted him to see her, or drove her from him, the island should be his residence while she remained in it. All that then remained for her was, to write to Mr. Thorold, which she did under cover to Cathcart, acquainting him as briefly as she could of the unexpected appearance of his son, and all that had happened since.

Having thus far acquitted herself, she found herself in a situation in which it was almost impossible for her to help receiving the assistance of one to whom she trembled to be obliged, while she knew it encouraged and augmented a passion that empoisoned his life. On him, however, she was compelled to entrust the regulation of the last melancholy offices that were to be performed for poor Elphinstone, who was interred in a little ruined chapel about two miles from his late residence; his wife consenting reluctantly to this disposition, and taking opiates[1] incessantly to procure that torpor which alone prevented the more violent ebullitions of grief from seizing her again, when the remains of her husband were removed.

Recourse to opiates became gradually a habit with Mrs. Elphinstone; and though Celestina trembled for the consequences, she thought it almost inhuman to oppose the application of any remedy, which, under such circumstances, won her friend from sorrow even for an hour. Yet the frequent absence it occasioned, compelled her to be very long and very often alone with Montague Thorold, to whose manly tenderness on the late sad occasion she could not be insensible, and to whose unceasing attention she was every hour more obliged. In the first conference they had held when the melancholy event to which they had been witnesses allowed them to talk of themselves, Celestina, after urging him to return to his father by every motive with which reason and truth supplied her, repeated to him with great firmness her resolution never to marry if Willoughby was not her husband, and represented very forcibly the cruelty as well as absurdity of his pursuing her; to which he replied, that he knew all she represented before he came thither, that his only wish was to be allowed to see her, though at a distance, and his only gratification, that of being suffered to breathe the same air; that it was the natural privilege of every human being to pursue their happiness when it injured nobody; and that finding his consisted in being near her, though without even the hope of her admitting him into her

---

1 As tincture of opium was a common soporific and painkiller, it is not surprising that Mrs. Elphinstone should take some with her to Skye. It was, of course, addictive, and so was generally used sparingly.

presence, he had followed that axiom, and had for some weeks been the distant and unseen companion of all her walks. "I was the highlander," said he, "who supplied the vacancy I had before taken care to make when you went your excursion on the water. I am the person of whom you had sometimes caught a glimpse at a distance, and who would never have approached you nearer, had not my fears for you the evening of the storm thrown me off my guard, and induced me to conceal myself within a few yards of you, behind those piled up stones against which you leaned. Ah! I heard you sigh—I heard the name of Willoughby repeated with tenderness! but I bore it all! and nothing, believe me, nothing but your fall, your apparent danger, could have compelled me to break the vow I had made never to intrude upon you—never to offend you with my unhappy passion!"

Celestina could not help being affected with the melancholy solemnity with which he uttered those words; but making an effort to prevent his perceiving it, she said—"It is absolutely necessary now that you again take up as much of so proper a resolution as relates to not speaking to me on a topic which to you must be useless, and to me painful; and while you persist in remaining here, let me at least owe it to your complaisance not to be distressed by declarations to which I cannot, ought not, will not listen."

Montague Thorold, then laying his hand on his heart, assured her that if she would allow him only to see her, indulge him only with being useful to her in her present remote and comfortless residence, he never would again name to her the passion which he knew, he said, he must carry to the grave; and from that moment he kept his word; though Celestina saw, with more emotion perhaps than the warmest declarations could have given her, his painful struggles and continual contention with himself; but while her pity for him encreased, she studied more carefully to conceal from him that she felt any, and behaved with as much calm politeness as she could have done towards the most indifferent man in the world.

To beguile the tedious moments during which they were compelled to wait the hoped for arrival of Cathcart, and while the sea that surrounded them was agitated continually by the wintry tempest, Celestina had recourse to the books with which poor Elphinstone, who, among all his faults and errors, was not without taste, had furnished a closet in the house. Mrs. Elphinstone, moved by the representations of Celestina to attend to her health for the sake of her children, whose sole dependance was now on her, consented by degrees to listen while Celestina read. Montague Thorold, whose residence was at the cottage of a highlander that boasted of having two rooms and a chimney, about a mile farther on the island, was sometimes admitted to these parties; and as Celestina was soon fatigued, and as he read remarkably well, Mrs. Elphinstone appeared pleased with his taking occasionally the office of their reader, and gradually he became accustomed to attend them every afternoon, and to read aloud to them till the hour of their simple supper.

Among the books in this little collection, there were several that Celestina recollected as the peculiar favourites of Willoughby; and the remembrance of those days when he read them to her, though never a moment absent from her thoughts, were now most forcibly recalled by hearing them again repeated. Some pieces of poetry particularly affected her, from their simple pathos, and the manner in which Montague Thorold read them; while they often drew tears from the unhappy Mrs. Elphinstone, an effect at which Celestina rejoiced, as her grief was now settled into the still and sullen melancholy unsolicitous of consolation and incapable of receiving it; which, while it produces a degree of apparent calmness, preys with fatal power on the heart.

Thus passed the heavy hours; till at length, after a fortnight longer delay than they had reckoned upon, letters were received from Cathcart: they contained intelligence that old Winnington was dead, and Jessy in such a state of health as made it almost impossible for Cathcart to leave her.[1] He therefore besought Celestina to accept the protection of Montague Thorold for herself, for Mrs. Elphinstone, and her children, and to hasten to his house, where he was now as able as happy to receive them, as soon as was possible and safe. Mr. Thorold wrote also to Celestina, and expressed his hope that the wild eccentricity of his son, which had occasioned to him so much pain, might at least be of service to her, and entreated her to allow him to attend her and her unfortunate friend into Devonshire, where he assured her he would prevent her receiving any trouble from the importunities of Montague, should he be weak enough to presume too much on her favour. He wrote also to his son; but after the contents of that letter Celestina did not enquire, and Montague carefully concealed them.

It was now determined that the plan laid down by Cathcart and Mr. Thorold should be pursued. Montague undertook the arrangement of every thing, and within ten days they were ready to depart.

---

1   The usual euphemism for having a baby—but Smith forgets this development later.

The weather alone seemed now likely to prevent their crossing the water; Mrs. Elphinstone, who had till now feared nothing, being so apprehensive for her children, that every gust of wind, every swell of the sea, made her shrink back with dismay, and postpone from day to day a little voyage which she yet earnestly wished over. It was the end of November, and very good weather could hardly be expected. Dark and gloomy days, with storms of wind and rain, succeeded each other; and Celestina, whose thoughts had been of late called frequently from her own mournful contemplations to the acute distresses of others, now relapsed again into the desponding state of mind which her long absence from Willoughby and his apparent neglect of her unavoidably threw her into. She had confined herself a good deal to the house since Montague Thorold had been so much with them, because there either Mrs. Elphinstone or the children were usually in the room, and she by that means avoided being alone with him; but now, as he was more engaged by the preparations of their departure, which he had undertaken to superintend, and in settling poor Elphinstone's accounts with his employers, Celestina again ventured out of an evening whenever she could escape unseen.

In one of these walks, along the edge of very steep rocks, where the scene presented only desolation: the dark and turbulent sea on one side, and on the other a succession of mountains, which seemed to have been thrown upon each other in some tremendous convulsion of nature, she turned towards the yet more dreary North, and reflected on the condition of those whom the poet describes as "the last of men,"[1] the inhabitants of Siberia, of Lapland, and those extreme regions where "Life at last goes out."[2]

"Alas!" cried she, "if they have not our enjoyments, they suffer not from those sensibilities which embitter our days. Their short summer passes in laying up necessaries for their long winter; and with what their desolate region affords them they are content, because they know not that there are comforts and conveniences beyond what it affords them. Void of the wish and the power to observe other modes of life, they are content with their own, and though little superior in point of intellect to the animal from which they derive their support,[3] yet they are happy, if not from the possession of good, at least

---

1 James Thomson, *The Seasons*, "Winter," 936-37: "Hard by these Shores, where scarce his freezing stream/ Rolls the wild Oby, live the last of men."
2 *The Seasons*, "Winter," 889-90: "[...]farthest Greenland, to the pole itself/ Where, failing gradual, life at length goes out."
3 The reindeer.

from the absence of evil; from that sickness of the soul which we taste from deprivation and disappointment."

A deep sigh closed this short soliloquy; and after indulging a little longer this train of thought, it produced the following sonnet:

THE LAPLANDER.

The shivering native, who by Tenglio'[1] side
Beholds with fond regret the parting light
Sink far away, beneath the darkening tide,
And leave him to long months of dreary night,
Yet knows, that springing from the eastern wave,
The sun's glad beams shall re-illume his way,
And, from the snows secur'd within his cave,
He waits in patient hope—returning day.
Not so the sufferer feels, who, o'er the waste
Of joyless life, is destin'd to deplore
Fond love forgotten, tender friendship past,
Which, once extinquish'd, can revive no more:
O'er the blank void he looks with hopeless pain;
For him those beams of heaven shall never shine again.[2]

A few days after this, an interval of calm weather gave to Mrs. Elphinstone courage to determine on embarking: but the evening before that on which it was finally fixed that they should go, she told Celestina, with a solemnity of voice and manner that convinced her she was not to be diverted from her purpose, that she could not be satisfied to leave the island without visiting the spot where lay the remains of her husband. Celestina, without much hope of success, represented to her how wrong it was to yield, or rather to encourage sorrow, unavailing to its object, and injurious to those who were his living representatives, by depriving her of her calmness of mind when exertion was most necessary, and injuring her own health, now so particularly precious to them. To these arguments her poor friend replied, with melancholy composure, that she should suffer

---

1   Stuart Curran's note in Smith's *Collected Poems*: perhaps the Arctic river called in Norwegian the Tana and in Finnish the Tera, that forms the boundary between the two countries, or the Tana Fjord into which it empties.

2   Printed as Sonnet LIII in Smith's *Elegiac Sonnets* and in her *Collected Poems*, ed. Stuart Curran.

more in reflecting on her omission than she could do in fulfilling what she had persuaded herself was a duty. Celestina therefore agreed to accompany her that evening. Montague Thorold had already shewn her the place, and Mrs. Elphinstone desired to have no other witness to her sorrows, than the soft hearted and pitying friend, without whose generous sympathy she would probably long before have sunk under them.

It was near two months since the death of Elphinstone, when this melancholy farewel visit was to be paid by his widow. A calm but sullen day, with an overclouded sky, threatening snow, was succeeded by a dark but mild evening. The distant sun had left a few lines of red light in the western horizon; and the moon, within a day or two of being at the full, edged with fainter rays the opposite clouds, through which it appeared not but at intervals. The unhappy widow, leaning on the arm of her tender friend, walked slowly and with languid steps, as she was guided towards the ruined chapel, and a universal pause of nature seemed to respect her sorrows! Not a breath of air wandered among the channels of the hills, and the waterfalls murmured low and hollow at a distance; the sea was calm, and being low on the sands, was hardly heard; while the birds, and few animals who inhabited the land, were retired to their repose.

Around this little chapel, now more than half in ruins, a few rude stones were raised to the memory of the dead of former times. The grass and weeds concealed many, and on the rest no figures but those of crosses rudely cut were now visible. Elphinstone had been interred within the walls of the edifice itself; his widow desired her friend to enter it with her, to shew her the place, and to leave her.

As they approached the spot, the ground sounded hollow beneath their feet, and a mournful echo ran round the damp walls. The moon, darting for a moment through the ruined stone work of the dismantled window, shewed them a broken table that had once been the altar, on which some pieces of the gothic[1] ornaments of the chapel, and several human bones, were scattered, and near it, the newly turned up earth, on which a few stones were loosely piled, discovered the grave of poor Elphinstone. Celestina could not trust her voice to point it out; but leading her friend to it, she immediately comprehended that there lay the remains of her husband, and fetching a deep sigh, she stopped at it.

---

1 Medieval.

"I had better not leave you surely," cried Celestina mournfully. "I cannot bear to leave you in this dreadful place."

"Pray oblige me," replied her friend; "it is the last indulgence I will ask, and I promise not to stay long."

"I will wait for you without then," replied Celestina; "and pray, dear Sophy, consider your children, and let it not be long that you indulge this sad propensity."

She then went out of the chapel; and seating herself on one of the ruined monuments near its entrance, yielded to all the gloomy thoughts which the place, the hour, and the occasion inspired. "Ah! who knows," cried she, "whether I too may not have reason to lament even as this poor mourner, whose groans tear my heart to pieces while I listen to them! I hear her! she implores forgiveness of the shade[1] of her departed husband for all the involuntary offences she committed against him: she, whose whole life has been one course of suffering, solicits forgiveness of him to whom those sufferings were owing: she forgets his faults towards her, and recollects only that he once loved her, that he was the husband of her youth, and that he is gone for ever; while she trembles for the future fate of him, whose errors she only remembers to recommend them to mercy! Dreadful then is the final separation even from those, of whom, though we have reason to complain, we have once loved: ah! what must it be when an eternal barrier is put between us and those whom we unreservedly and passionately love. Willoughby! if I have regretted so deeply our separation, what would become of me should I ever hang over the grave where thy adored form moulders in the dust. Oh! God! grant that I never sustain a trial like that!"

Overwhelmed by these sad thoughts, and terrified at the encreasing darkness and fearful silence, which was broken only by the deep sighs of her unhappy friend prostrate on the grave of her husband, she started up to recall her from her mournful employment, when Montague Thorold, breathless with haste and anxiety, approached her; she was glad to recognize him, and took the hand he offered her; while he cried impatiently—"Wherefore is all this, my dear Madam, and where is your friend?"

Celestina led him to the place, shuddering as she approached, while Mrs. Elphinstone, recovering herself by an effort of resolution, and having perhaps disburthened her oppressed heart and satisfied her mournful propensity, agreed immediately to go with them, and

---

1 Spirit.

having turned once more her streaming eyes on the spot as she quitted the chapel, she suffered each of her friends to take an arm, and lead her home in silence; where Montague Thorold advised her and Celestina to take immediately a few hours rest, as the tide would serve very early in the morning for their embarkation in the vessel which now lay ready to receive them.

They followed his advice; and before day break on the twentieth of December, near seven months after their arrival in the Isle of Skye, they quitted it; and landing safely on the coast of Scotland, they proceeded with very great fatigue, though fortunately without being intercepted by such heavy snows as they had at such a season reason to apprehend, to Edinburgh, where it was necessary for them to rest some days before they proceeded on their long journey to the other extremity of Great Britain.

Chapter IV

As Mrs. Elphinstone was too much dejected to allow her to go out, Celestina, who had great pleasure in visiting antiquities, and whose active mind was perpetually in search of new ideas, was compelled either to relinquish these gratifications, or to permit Montague Thorold only to accompany her. He was generally so guarded in his conversation, that, though it was easy to see how much he suffered in suppressing his passion, Celestina had no reasonable ground of complaint. He found, however, at Edinburgh, that it was particularly uneasy to her to visit the places she wished to see without some other companion, and recollecting that one of the professors was well known to his father, he made use of the claim that acquaintance gave him, and by that means Celestina received all the attention and hospitality for which the Scottish nation are so justly praised. The gentleman to whom she thus became known, had several daughters, amiable and elegant young women: with them she saw all that the capital of Scotland afforded worthy of observation; with them she visited the ruinous chapel and magnificently mournful parts of Holyrood House,[1] and gave a sigh to the fate of the lovely, luckless Mary,[2] who was almost its last resident sovereign.

---

1 Seat of the Scottish royal court in Edinburgh.
2 Mary Stuart (Mary, Queen of Scots), daughter of James V of Scotland, married the heir to Francis I of France. Widowed young, she returned to Scotland and married Henry, Lord Darnley, who had her court musician

Then parting with her newly acquired friends with mutual regret, she proceeded on her road to England, nothing particular occurring on the way for some time except the slow but evident amendment of Mrs. Elphinstone's spirits, and the symptoms of encreased attachment in Montague Thorold; who, if he loved her before with an attachment fatal to his peace and subversive of his prospects, now seemed to idolize her with an ardour bordering on phrenzy. In despite of the resolution she had avowed to him, in despite of those he had himself formed, this ardent and invincible passion was visible in every thing he said and did. He seemed to have forgotten that he had any other business in the world than to serve her, to listen to the enchantment of her voice, to watch every change of her countenance. His whole being was absorbed in that one sentiment; and though he had promised not to consider the advantages, which his own wild Quixotism,[1] aided by accident, had thus obtained for him, as making the least alteration in the decided preference of Celestina for another, he insensibly[2] forgot, at least at times, her unalterable affection for Willoughby; and seeing, notwithstanding all her attempts to conceal it, that she pitied him, that she was not insensible of his attempts to please her nor blind to his powers of pleasing, he cherished, in defiance of reason and conviction (from which he fled as much as possible) the extravagant hope that the barrier, whatever it was, between her and Willoughby would be found invincible, and that the time, though it might yet be remote, would at length arrive when he should himself be allowed to aspire to her favour.

The human mind, however strong, yields too easily to these illusions, whence at least it enjoys the soft consolations of hope, and sees rays of light, which, though imaginary, perhaps are all we often have to carry us on with courage over the rugged way, too thickly sown with real, or, missing them, with imaginary and self-created evils.

It is therefore little to be wondered at, if Montague Thorold, so sanguine in temperament, of so little experience in life (for he was

---

David Rizzio killed, and was soon after killed himself in circumstances that threw suspicion on Mary and on the man she then hastily married, James Bothwell. She was forced into exile in England, where she was imprisoned for nineteen years and eventually beheaded for conspiring to kill her second cousin Elizabeth I.

1   Gallant but foolish behaviour, from the deluded chivalry of Miguel de Cervantes' hero, Don Quixote.

2   Little by little.

yet hardly twenty two) and so much in love, should thus eagerly feed himself with hopes of its ultimate success, and be wilfully deaf to every argument which reason would have brought against the reality of the gay visions he cherished.

Celestina, pitying and esteeming him, was very anxious to reduce this unhappy and fruitless prepossession to the bounds of friendship and esteem, and though she at this time thought of Willoughby with so much internal anguish that she never on other occasions willingly named him, yet she now took occasion sometimes to speak of him, and purposely laid her train of conversation in such a way with Mrs. Elphinstone, as gave Montague Thorold to understand that her sentiments in regard to him who had first possessed and still was master of her heart, could never suffer any material change, or be transferred to another, even though she was sure that she was personally divided from him for ever.

After some days travelling, which the languor of Mrs. Elphinstone, and her extreme anxiety about her children, rendered tedious, the party arrived at York, and there it was determined to remain two days. Celestina, who had nobody to receive her at the end of her pilgrimage with peculiar delight, was not very eager to finish it; Mrs. Elphinstone, seeing nothing but poverty and dependence before her, of which her mind, being enfeebled by grief, was little able to bear a nearer prospect, was yet less anxious; and Montague Thorold cared not how long a journey lasted which gave him what he must at its termination lose, the happiness of being with, and of being useful to the mistress of his heart.

When they arrived at York, there was an appearance of snow; it fell with violence during the night, and by ten o'clock the next morning the north road was rendered impassable.

The travellers were well assured that in a day or two it would be sufficiently beat[1] for them to proceed with safety, and as their original intention was to remain at least two days, the farther immaterial delay with which this circumstance threatened them, gave to none of them any concern.

The snow, however, continued to fall very heavily, and the cold became almost insupportably severe. The party were drawn round a good fire at the inn, and Mrs. Elphinstone had just put her children to bed, when an unusual clamour and bustle below attracted their attention. Horses were called for, and a loud voice was heard to say—

---

1 Beaten down.

"If four are not sufficient, my master will have fourteen rather than be stopped a moment."

"This is some matrimonial expedition,"[1] cried Montague Thorold, "or why all this haste?" The idea, which the ladies allowed to be probable, excited some degree of curiosity, and when the waiter soon after came in to lay the cloth for supper, Montague could not forbear enquiring if the horses which were a short time before so eagerly called for were not for the accommodation of a young couple hastening into Scotland. The man replied that the gentleman was going into Scotland, and had been stopped by the snow about seven miles off, the horses he had to his chaise being unable to draw him; but that he understood he was quite alone, that horses and men had been sent to his assistance, and that he was expected there presently.

The man, who probably loved to hear himself talk, went on to inform them, though they now no longer felt any great degree of curiosity, that the gentleman's valet de chambre[2] and one of the postillions, who had come forward, (who were warming themselves at the fire below before they returned back as they were ordered,) had declared that they were almost dead with cold; "but as for that, Sir," continued the waiter, "he says, that is, Sir, the *walet de sham*[3] says, says he, 'my master if once he've got a scheme in his head, 'tis not cold, no nor water, nor fire neither, as will find it an easy matter to stop him, and then,' says he, 'as for fatigue to his own self,' says he, 'or danger, or any thing of the like nature, or expence, though it cost him a hundred, aye or a thousand pounds, why my master,' says he, 'minds it no more than nothing; 'tis all one to him; yet to be sure,' says he, 'he is a good master in the main, and no sneaker,[4] neither in money, nor liquor, nor no other accommodation to servants.'"

"And pray," said Montague Thorold, "who is this courageous, bountiful, and accommodating gentleman?"

---

1 An elopement. Parental consent for children under 21 and the calling in church, for three Sundays, of the banns or proclamations of an intended marriage were not requirements for marriage in Scotland as they were in England. English couples whose families refused consent would sometimes marry across the border, often taking the Great North Road from London, which passed through York, and occasionally pursued by a father or brother attempting to stop the marriage.
2 His "man" or body-servant.
3 A Cockney accent pronounced v as w in the eighteenth and nineteenth centuries.
4 Miser.

"I did not think to ask his name, Sir," replied the waiter, "but I can know in a minute." He then, without waiting for an answer, ran down stairs, and returning almost instantly, said that the gentleman was Squire Vavasour of Staffordshire.

"Vavasour!" cried Celestina in a faint voice, and turning as pale as death. "Good Heaven! to what purpose can Vavasour be travelling in such haste towards Scotland?"

"Vavasour!" cried Montague Thorold, his countenance betraying all that passed in his heart: "Vavasour! Ah! Miss de Mornay, it was to you he was undoubtedly going. Willoughby is returned, and sends his friend to reclaim his betrothed wife."

"Sends his friend! oh! no, no," answered Celestina with quickness, "that cannot be: were Willoughby returned, he would not send; rather it is some sad news he has to impart, and I must prepare myself for it—I must bear it be it what it may."

The cruellest anxiety now took possession of both Celestina and Montague Thorold; they both dreaded an explanation, though unable to bear the suspense. Thorold went down to see what he could gather from the men; but Mr. Vavasour's servant was gone back to meet his master, and the postillion had only come with him from the last post town. Celestina in the mean time now traversed the room, now went to the window, and now appeared to attend to the conjectures Mrs. Elphinstone offered, that perhaps this journey might in no respect relate to her, but might be owing to one of those sudden starts of caprice in which Vavasour was known to indulge himself.

This state of suspense and conjecture, which is of all others least easy to be borne, did not last long, for in about a quarter of an hour the carriage, in which Vavasour himself was, arrived.

Celestina now debated within herself whether she ought to send to him, to inform him of her being on her way to England, or suffer him to proceed, whither she doubted not he was going, even to the Hebrides in search of her. This internal debate was however short: her extreme solicitude to have news of Willoughby superseded every other thought; and whether Vavasour was going to Scotland to announce her fate to her by the direction of Willoughby, or merely in consequence of some whim of his own, she knew that he in all probability could give her some intelligence of him of whom she most wished to hear. Montague Thorold, who trembled least in consequence of this interview all the day dreams in which he had been indulging himself should be at once destroyed, would have represented to her some imaginary improprieties which his wish to find them raised in his mind.

Celestina, however, had, with all her candour and humility, a decisive spirit, the effect of her great good sense, which, when she had once examined and determined on any subject, did not leave her open to the trifling perplexities of feeble and unimportant debate. She considered, that even if Vavasour *was* going on some eccentric idea of his own to follow her into Scotland, it would be cruel and unjust to suffer him to pursue such a journey at such a season, and therefore steadily resisting all the representations of Montague Thorold against it, she addressed to him the following note:

"Miss de Mornay presents her compliments to Mr. Vavasour, and having learned by accident that he is at this place, requests the favour of seeing him to-morrow morning to breakfast with Mrs. Elphinstone and with her at half past nine."

Montague Thorold, being unable wholly to prevent, thought he could at least impede the delivery of this note till the next day; but Celestina was too impatient to hear of Willoughby to be blind to the artifice which Montague was too much in love to manage very dexterously, and therefore quitting the room herself, she found one of the waiters, who she enjoined to give the note to the gentleman who was just arrived, as soon as he had done supper.

This was not perhaps very discreet: but Celestina thought much at the moment of Willoughby, and very little of Vavasour, and in her anxiety to hear news of the one, she reflected not on the way in which it might be conveyed by the other, who, after a long and cold journey, having finished his supper, was not likely at least to be a clear and calm messenger, and a moment's reflection would have convinced her that he was not a man who from motives of delicate forbearance and polite deference would put off the interview to the time she had named.

No sooner was the note from Celestina delivered to Vavasour, then he ran up stairs with an impatience amounting almost to phrenzy, his eyes flashing fire, and his countenance expressive of the violent emotions with which he was agitated; he hardly noticed Mrs. Elphinstone, but casting a look of angry surprise at Montague Thorold, whom he immediately knew, he approached Celestina, took her hand, and eagerly kissing it, told her in a hurried manner that he was hastening to Scotland to give her intelligence of a very great consequence, and to deliver her a packet from Willoughby.

"From Willoughby!" cried Celestina, so extremely affected by his abrupt entrance that she was ready to faint. "Is he well? is he returned to England?"

"No," replied he, without seeming sensible of the nature of her sufferings, "not returned to England, or likely to return, but—"

"Is he married then?" said Celestina, interrupting him in a still more trembling voice.

"Not yet, but I have a letter for you which—"

"Give it me," cried she, hardly able to breathe. He had it not about him, but ringing for his servant, gave him the key of his portmanteau, and bidding him bring a large sealed packet, which he said he would find there, the man immediately returned with it; and Celestina, without speaking to Vavasour, hurried away with it in breathless agitation, Mrs. Elphinstone, alarmed at her looks, following her in silence.

All this time Montague Thorold had remained leaning against one of the piers:[1] with contracted brows and clasped hands watching the countenance of Celestina, while his own changed from pale to red, from red again to pale. He had always returned the dislike which Vavasour had shewn towards him as much as his nature could return dislike; and this was encreased by the abrupt and unfeeling manner in which Vavasour had executed a commission, that, whether it brought to her welcome or unwelcome tidings, demanded, he thought, more delicacy and more preparation. When Celestina and Mrs. Elphinstone were gone, he felt no inclination therefore to stay with Vavasour, who walked up and down the room as if expecting their return; but was preparing to leave it, when, as he crossed to the door, Vavasour, turning short towards him, asked how he came to be at York with Miss de Mornay.

"How I came, Sir!" replied Montague Thorold with equal abruptness. "Have you any right, Sir, to enquire?"

"Yes," replied Vavasour contemptuously, "I have a right."

"To enquire into my actions, sir?" interrupted Thorold; "surely not!"

"To enquire into those of Miss de Mornay, Sir, *I have* a right."

"Well, Sir, if she allows of that right, to her you may then apply; but you will be so good as to leave me at liberty to be at York, or wherever else it is convenient to me to be."

"Not with her, Sir, you must not; not with Miss de Mornay, be assured. As for the rest, pray understand, that were it not for the

---

1 The supports of the mantelpiece.

circumstance of your being seen in company with her, *I* should never recollect that such a person was in the world as Mr. Montague Thorold."

Thorold, though naturally of a gentle disposition, was little disposed to hear the contemptuous arrogance of any man: he therefore answered with more quickness, that it was an honour he could well dispense with, to be thought of at all by *such* a man as Mr. Vavasour. The tone in which he spoke this, and the emphasis he laid on the words *such* a man, provoked the haughty and impetuous spirit of Vavasour; and words rose so high between them, that Mrs. Elphinstone, who was only in the next room, came in, and extremely terrified at their violence, besought them to separate. Vavasour, whose passions were at all times too strong to suffer him to listen either to reason from others or to his own, gave very little attention to the remonstrances; but Montague Thorold, on seeing her extreme uneasiness, and on hearing the name of Celestina, became in a moment apparently calm; and assuring Mrs. Elphinstone that she had no reason to be alarmed, he addressed himself coolly to Vavasour, and said, that if he had any business with him he would be at his service in the morning: he then besought Mrs. Elphinstone to return to Celestina; and taking her hand, led her out of the room, assuring her in a whisper that he would not return that evening to Vavasour, nor have any farther contention with him. "Make yourself easy, therefore, my dear Madam," said he, "and tell me—how is our lovely friend? what are the contents of a letter which required so extraordinary a messenger?"

Mrs. Elphinstone answered, that Celestina had appeared in great emotion while she read the beginning of the letter, and then telling her that she should finish it in her own room, had left her, in encreased agitation she thought, but without tears.

"And shall you see her no more tonight?" enquired Montague Thorold.

"I rather believe not," replied Mrs. Elphinstone.

"And do you think," said Thorold, "do you think, my dear Madam, that the agitation, the emotion you remarked, was the effect of joy, or grief—"

"Of grief, of disappointment, of regret, I think," answered she. "I believe Celestina is now convinced that every probability of her becoming the wife of Mr. Willoughby is at an end for ever."

"Then," cried Montague Thorold, unable to repress the violence of his feelings; "oh! then there will be hope for me!"

There was something like the transports of phrenzy in the man-

ner in which he uttered this, and Mrs. Elphinstone was shocked at
it. "Be not too sanguine, Mr. Montague," said she, "I do not believe
that the affections of Miss de Mornay are to be easily or lightly transferred, but if they were, think of the powerful claims upon them that
are rising[1] against your's." "Claims! what claims?" cried he: "who
shall dare to dispute with me an heart to which—"

"Nay, nay," answered Mrs. Elphinstone, "this is all phrenzy and
wildness. Do you not know that you have no claim, though I am
willing to allow all your merit; and do you not see that Willoughby,
in being compelled to resign her, recommends his friend Vavasour to
her favour, and therefore sends him hither."

"Vavasour!" cried he: "recommend Vavasour to her! And would
Celestina, who, with all that dignified gentleness, has a great deal of
spirit, with a proper consciousness of her own value; would she bear
to be consigned, like a bale of merchandise, to a friend, and to such
a man as Vavasour? Impossible! he dare not think of it: but I wish he
may, for her insulted pride will mitigate the pain of her disappointed love, and she will be mine—the charmer will be mine."

The look, the manner, in which this was uttered, encreased the
concern of Mrs. Elphinstone, who, from her own recent and severe
sufferings, had learned to dread any thing like romantic eccentricity.
She laid her soft cold hand on the burning hands of Montague
Thorold, as they were wildly clasped together—"My dear Sir," said
she, in the gentlest accents, "I owe you a thousand obligations for all
the attention you showed me in my late calamitous situation, and ill,
very ill, should I repay those obligations, if I did not try as a friend
to mitigate these violent transports. Believe me, the heart of Celestina, fixed in her early life to one object, is attached to that object with
more than common firmness: Vavasour's frantic fondness, and your
real merit, will, in my opinion, be equally indifferent to her; and I
verily believe, that if Willoughby marries another, as I conclude he
will, Miss de Mornay will never marry at all."

Montague Thorold could not bear this. The idea of rivalry had
been painful; but the pain was mitigated by his knowledge of her
character and of the character of Vavasour, which, with all its avowed
libertinism, he knew Celestina could not even tolerate, and certainly not approve: but the idea of her living only for Willoughby, even
when Willoughby lived for another, was insupportable, and since he
was unwilling to own it was possible, he would therefore have been

---

1 The original has "using."

ready to quarrel with any body but Mrs. Elphinstone for supposing it probable: but to every being who was unfortunate, and especially if that unfortunate being was a woman, the kind heart of Montague Thorold overflowed with good will and sympathy: he therefore checked himself; and saying he should be impatient to hear of Miss de Mornay in the morning, he wished Mrs. Elphinstone a good night, and left her.

Chapter V

It was not till after two or three readings, with a palpitating heart— a heart so much agitated as hardly to leave her the use of her reason, that Celestina perfectly understood the meaning of Willoughby's letter, which ran thus:

"The only apology, dear Celestina, that the unhappy Willoughby has to offer for his conduct is, to relate to you all that has befallen him since that fatal night when he parted from you at Alvestone. The emotions which I must feel while I write, I will endeavour to suppress, both for your sake and my own; it shall be, if I can command myself, a history of events rather than of the sufferings to which those events have condemned me.

"You know, that after the abrupt and unaccountable note that I received, I hastened to the inn at Exeter, where I was informed some persons, who had business of the utmost importance which admitted not of a moment's delay, waited to see me. The terms in which the note was written were such as gave me a strange alarm, though I knew not what to dread. This uneasy astonishment was not lessened, when, after much appearance of mystery, I was introduced to—Lady Castlenorth.

"You know the woman, and can imagine how ill her harshness, when irritated by the malignity of disappointed pride, was calculated to soften the blow which it was her pleasure to give me herself. She told me, that having heard I was on the following morning to become your husband, she felt it to be her duty to save me from the horrors of such a union, by informing me that she knew you to be the daughter of my mother, the daughter of that Mr. Everard who was my tutor, and that the woman she had with her, who had been a servant in the house at the time, could give the most indisputable account of your birth.

"Stunned as by a stroke of thunder, I turned towards the woman, of whose face as a servant of my mother's I had not the least recollection. I know not what I said to her; I only remember that she gave, in a confused and vulgar way, an account of what she pretended to have been witness to. I suffered her to talk on, for my very soul was sinking with anguish. My mother's honour destroyed! my Celestina torn from me! My soul recoiled from the idea as from an execrable falsehood. Yet when I remembered the solemn injunction that beloved mother gave me in her last moments to marry Miss Fitz-Hayman, the promise she drew from me never otherwise to unite myself—when my agonized mind ran back to the displeasure she sometimes expressed at my fondness and admiration for you—I dared not, with all the pain and all the horror I felt, I dared not throw from me with indignation this odious intelligence; I dared not load the hateful communicators of it with the odium which would have been dictated by my swelling heart, had it not been checked by these sad recollections which pressed upon me in despite of myself, and gave me something like internal evidence of the facts I would very fain have denied.

"There was, in the countenance of Lady Castlenorth, something of insolent triumph, which I could not bear. She made a merit of her disinterested conduct, and talked of virtue, and honour, and integrity, till I was blind and deaf: she then threw out some reflections on my mother's memory, which roused me from the torpor of amazement and sorrow to resentment; she uttered some malignant sarcasms against you, and I flew from her.

"She had, however, completely executed her purpose, if it was that of rendering me the most wretched of human beings; and in quitting the house, which she did soon afterwards, had the barbarous pleasure of knowing that she had destroyed my peace for some time—if not for ever.

"To return to you, Celestina, under the doubts which distracted me was impossible. To become your husband—so lately the fondest, the first wish of a heart that doated upon you, was not to be thought of, while ideas of so much horror obtruded themselves on my mind: yet to leave you without accounting for my absence, to leave you to all the torturing suspense of vague conjectures, to leave you to suppose I had deceived and forsaken you, was cruel, was unpardonable: it was, however, what, after a long and dreadful struggle, I determined to do. I might, indeed, have put an end to your conjectures by delivering you over to others more tormenting—by communicating the doubts Lady Castlenorth had raised; but this I found I could less bear to do than even to leave you wholly in suspense.

Believing her capable of any thing which revenge or malice could dictate, there was reason, notwithstanding all my trembling apprehensions, to suppose it more than possible that she might have invented the story, and have bribed the woman with her to give evidence of its truth.

"To this possibility my mind clung with the eagerness of a drowning wretch; and I could not resolve to sully before you the memory of my angel mother, which I knew you hold in such tender veneration; I could not determine to raise in your delicate and sensible mind doubts and terrors which might make such fatal impressions as might impede our union, even if the fallacy of this invention to divide us was detected. In a state of mind then which I will not attempt to describe, I at length determined to send for Cathcart, and without explaining even to him the motives of my sudden journey, to secure, if I could, your continuance at Alvestone, and to set out myself to discover the real circumstances of your birth; and never to return till I had the most thorough conviction that you were not the daughter of my mother, or till I could learn to consider you, if it were so—only as a beloved sister.

"Ah! Celestina! I little knew the task I undertook; yet with anguish and depression, to which no words can do justice, I set about it. My first step was, to find out Watson, my mother's old servant, who had never, I knew, left her for many years. I knew that after her death, and on receiving the legacy of fifty pounds that her mistress left her, she had retired to the house of her son, who was married and settled at Whitehaven. I might have written to have enquired after her; but then I must have waited some days in suspense I could not bear; and while I was in motion I felt my misery less, from an idea that I was doing something to end it. I sat out therefore on horseback for Whitehaven, and on my arrival there learned that she had been dead about six weeks. This first hope of certainty thus frustrated, it occurred to me that perhaps among her papers there might be some memorandums that would be useful; and as she always hired and discharged the inferior servants, and kept an account of the time and terms of their service in a book, I flattered myself that I might find some date of the time when Hannah Biscoe, who pretended to have been in her confidence and to have been entrusted with a secret of such importance, really lived in the family.

"I told her son, that to see all the papers his mother had left, was of importance to me. He readily brought all he had. There were some books of accounts, and some memorandums about servants, but none that gave me any light, or were of any importance to my enquiry, for none went back above ten years. The man told me there were more; but that not knowing they were of any consequence, or even supposing them likely to be called for, he had given them to his children, who had cut them to pieces. 'I believe, however, Sir,' said he, 'that there are some letters in a drawer of a bureau, which I remember to have seen during my mother's illness: I will fetch them if you think they will be of any service.'

"I desired him to do so, and he brought me about twenty letters: some of them were from my mother, while she was in London in the years 1779 and 1780, and Watson was at Alvestone with you and my sister, of which she had, as you well remember, the care on all occasions where it was necessary for my mother to be absent. You were then about nine, and Matilda about eleven years old. The only sentences of any kind of consequence were these: 'I have no notion of any real danger from the landing of troops from the fleets of France and Spain. No landing can take place; and 'tis all nonsense and bravado. I thought you had more sense, Watson, than to catch the panic of the vulgar and the ignorant, which they rather like to communicate. However, since you write so pressingly to know what should be done if any thing should happen, I give you an answer, first, that nothing will happen; and secondly, if you have any alarm, which a reasonable being would consider such, take my two girls and bring them up hither instantly. But I shall be down at Alvestone in about ten days, and nothing can happen within that time believe me.'

"*My two girls*, was the only sentence in this letter on which I could lay any stress. *My* two girls! Well, and what then? have I not heard my mother a thousand times say, *my* two girls? *My Matilda, my Celestina*, were names indiscriminately used: my *children*, even my *daughters*, were terms not unfrequent with her. Ah! little, little did her generous and benevolent heart suppose that *such* advantage might be taken of that generosity—of that benevolence; for her—even now—no—I do not, I cannot, I will not believe that Celestina has any other claim to her friendship, to her protection, than what arose from that generosity and benevolence. Now, do I say?—can I say it? Oh heaven! how dreadfully contradictory are the sentiments that agitate and tear my heart!

"Let me, however, recall my scattered thoughts: and remember, that it is a simple history of facts only, and not of feelings, that I promised to relate.

"Another letter was written to Watson, when Mr. Everard, after a very tedious illness, which had long confined him in town, went down to Alvestone in the year eighty, for change of air, rather than to his own parsonage, where some repairs were then going on. This letter was expressive of great solicitude and anxiety: but from thence what could be inferred? nothing but that the dear and benevolent writer was solicitous for the health of a friend to whom she had long been attached. There was not in this a word on which the most invidious observer could dwell; nor was there in any other letter a syllable to give me any confirmation of what I dreaded to find. Still I procured from the person who had succeeded to Watson's effects, every paper and every book that remained; but I found nothing; and returned to London as miserable, as dissatisfied as I left it.

"Nothing made me more wretched than the questions with which I was now persecuted. I fled from society; stopped at a small village in the neighbourhood of London, where I avoided every body who was likely to know me, and thought only how I might satisfy my own torturing doubts, and escape those of others.

"The most obvious method seemed to be, to find out the woman who had accompanied Lady Castlenorth, and question her when she was no longer under the influence of her employer: but this I could not do without getting, at my uncle's house, information which I knew not how to set about. To go there, was hateful to me. I could not now bear the sight of people whom I had never loved, and to whom I imputed all the misery I laboured under.

"My servant Farnham had been little used to those sort of nego-tiations, and knew not much better than I did, how to ingratiate him-self into the favour of the persons, through whose means only he could procure the intelligence so necessary to us. He went, however, about it as well as he could; but all I learned was, that Lady Castlenorth had, soon after her journey into Devonshire, sent the woman who accompanied her away into her native country, which was either Norfolk or Suffolk, and with so much secrecy that nobody knew whither she was gone, or how she was provided for: but Farn-ham with some difficulty drew from the rest of the servants, with whom he found means of conversing, that she had boasted, in some moments of vulgar exultation, that her fortune was made for ever.

"No clue, however, could I obtain by which I could find out this woman; and after much fruitless enquiry, where the art of the adver-sary with whom I had to engage baffled all my assiduity, I deter-mined to go to Lord Castlenorth, to state to him the stigma that his wife had thrown on the honour of my mother, his sister, and to demand that I might have proofs of the facts she alledged, such as she could now give, or that she might acknowledge the wickedness and injustice of her aspersions.

"I was not aware, till I conversed with Lord Castlenorth, to how debilitated a state indolence, ignorance, pride, and prejudice, can reduce the human mind. His, however, was of so singular a cast, that instead of being shocked at the injury done to his sister's honour, he affected to resent, in spite of his family pride, my doubts of his wife's veracity, flew from the point to which I attempted to bring him, and we parted in mutual disgust: at least I was disgusted, and more wretched and more hopeless than before I had made this attempt.

"Every effort to discover the retreat of the woman failing, my next measure was to go to the convent at Hières. It was owing to these cruel circumstances, Celestina, that I left you in doubt while I remained in England; it was owing to these, that I left England in the hope—though it became every day more mingled with apprehension—that I left England without accounting to you for my conduct.[1] Were these surmises groundless, why should I empoison your delicate mind? why should I sully for a moment the sacred fame of my mother by divulging them? were they found to be at length too well substantiated, it would be then time enough to inform you of them.

"On my arrival at Hières, I went directly to the present Confessor of the community out of whose care my mother took you. I found him to be intelligent, obliging, and officious. From him I learned, that the present Superior was a young woman of good family, who had been compelled to take the veil, and who would probably have very few real scruples as to giving me all the information she could.

"I succeeded easily in my research, as far as it depended on these two persons. I found that the memorandum of my mother's having taken you out of the convent, by the name of Celestina de Mornay, remained; and I found, with emotions on which I must not dwell, that there was another memorandum of expenses, 'for the little *English* child, received at the request of Madame de P—.' Such is the literal sense of the French words. Who then was this Madame de P—? An old nun, who had lived in the house above five and twenty years, and who was the only person who recollected any circumstances of your reception, told me that she well remembered that this Madame de P— came from Bayonne, or some part of the country in the neighbourhood of that town; and that she was an intimate friend of the then Abbess, and her name, of which only the

---

1 Thus. There is probably a printer's error here.

initials were expressed in the memorandum, was la[1] Marquise de Pellatier.

"I enquired of the old nun, if she knew on what ground it was you were represented as an English child? she replied, that she knew no more than that when first you were received under the care of the Superior, you were said to be the child of English parents, or at least that one of your parents was of that nation: but that soon afterwards this was, by the Abbess's authority, contradicted; it was forbidden to be mentioned in the community: and it was ordered that you should from that time be spoken of as Mademoiselle de Mornay; while intimations were given that you were a relation of her own; born of a concealed marriage; and that your father being dead, and your mother married to another person, you were to be considered as belonging only to the community in which you were destined to pass your life.

"Ah! Celestina! what food was here for those corrosive conjectures which preyed on my heart. Having exhausted however, every kind of information which it was here possible to procure, I set out for Bayonne; where some of the family at least of Madame de Pellatier were, I understood, to be found.

"She had herself been dead some years. I met, however, with her son, a gay young man of four or five and twenty, from whom I could obtain nothing but a general confession that his mother probably had, from the general tenor of her life, occasion in more than one instance to exercise the secrecy and kind offices of her friends, and very probably obliged them in her turn: and when I explained to him my reasons for the anxious enquiries I made, which I thought the only means likely to interest him for me, he said that he was '*vraiment au desespoir*' at the little *embarras*[2] into which I had fallen: that la belle demoiselle[3] might be my sister or might be his; that he had not the least hope of being of service to me in unravelling the mystery, for he had destroyed all his mother's papers in pursuance of her dying directions some years before, and did not believe the slightest trace remained of any connection with an English lady, or an English family. I enquired where his mother lived in the years 1770[4] and

---

1 The original has "le."
2 "Really in despair" at the little "difficulty."
3 The lovely young lady.
4 Celestina's age is given as nineteen when she composes her sonnet to the dead village girl in the parish churchyard. Smith presumably means "in her nineteenth year."

1771, which was about the time of your birth, and where in the year 1772, the time of your reception in the convent; he replied that she was then sometimes at Paris, where she was believed to have an arrangement with Count W—, a German nobleman, sometimes at Pezenas and sometimes at Hières. From all this I could gather nothing to my purpose; and Monsieur de Pellatier soon quitting his house in the neighbourhood of Bayonne to go to Paris, I returned thither also, infinitely more unhappy than before my research.

"All I have related, Celestina, is so little convincing when it is put together, that perhaps I ought not to lay any stress upon it, when to such slight and unsatisfactory ground of conjecture, is opposed the character and the principles of my mother: yet shall I tell you truly, that the energy with which she pressed me with her last words to marry Miss Fitz-Hayman; the displeasure she always shewed at my expressing any partiality towards you; her grief at the death of Mr. Everard, which it was easy to see she never recovered; some words which, though I could not clearly understand them, escaped her lips almost with her last sigh, and in which the name of Celestina seemed united with some ardent prayer, or some earnest injunction, while, in her cold convulsed hand, she pressed mine to her trembling lips; oh! Celestina! those sounds I have since interpreted into a confession of this fatal secret. Still, still inarticulate as they were, they vibrate on my heart: and now, united with the story of Lady Castlenorth, and the circumstances I have gathered of your being born of English parents—all, all unite to render me wretched.

"Yet there is not the least likeness between you and my mother; there is not the remotest resemblance between you and Mr. Everard, who had remarkably strong features and very red hair: oh! Celestina! what am I to conjecture? what am I to do? can I, ought I, on such grounds, to resign you? Can I ever learn to consider you only as my sister? Where shall I go next? how satisfy my doubts? how ever possess again a moment's happiness?

"Every other evil is light to this. Even the disorder of my affairs, the necessity I shall soon be in to sell Alvestone, is hardly felt. On my leaving England, I raised money at an enormous premium in order to pay Vavasour what I could not bear to owe him, uncertain as I was what would become of me. This, together with my absence, has alarmed some of my mortgagees, who talk of foreclosing their mortgages; while my own neglect of my affairs has, in despite of Cathcart's assiduity, contributed to my embarrassments. But what are these inferior distresses, compared to the wretchedness of a heart, adoring Celestina yet afraid of indulging his passion lest it lead him into guilt? Ah! every evil fortune could inflict but this, I could bear.

"But again it is necessary to recall my pen from the description of feelings to the narrative of fact.

"Lord and Lady Castlenorth and their daughter arrived in the early part of the summer in France. I was then absent on the research I have related to you, but heard they had been very earnest in their enquiries after me at Paris; and on my return thither, some months afterwards, I received a letter from Lord Castlenorth, earnestly desiring me to join them at Florence or Naples. The letter imported that the alliance he once wished was no longer in question; but that finding his health every day declining, he wished to see the only male relation he had, on the settlement of some family concerns.

"This invitation I ought not perhaps on other accounts to have refused; but the hope of being able to gain some farther intelligence of the circumstances which occupied my mind incessantly, determined me at once to accept it. I went then, and met them at Florence, where my uncle received me with as much overacted civility, as when we parted last he had treated me with supercilious scorn.

"I found him, however, not more reasonable than before: the prejudices that had taken possession of his mind were so strong that he was angry and amazed that what made the whole business of his life could be to any other person matters of mere indifference. He talked to me incessantly of remedies for the gout, of the medicines he was taking, and of their effects; told me how he slept and how he eat; and read dissertations without end of chronic disorders in general; and from this discourse he glided by some link which escaped me, into his other favourite science, heraldry. Oh! the quarterings and bearings which I was compelled to affect hearing; the genealogies I was distracted with; and the marriages and intermarriages to which I appeared to listen, while in fact I knew nothing of what he said, and only endured this sort of martyrdom in the hope of seeing Lady Castlenorth, who on my first visits did not deign to appear.

"All these latter harangues were, I found, intended to impress on my mind the pride and prudence which would attend a union with my cousin, his daughter and the advantage it would give me above any other alliance I could form. My patient acquiescence was imputed to returning inclination for this boasted connection: and when I was thought to be sufficiently impressed with the ideas thus meant to be conveyed to me, and to be weaned from the weakness I had betrayed, I was admitted, without any solicitation however on my part, to the honour of seeing Lady Castlenorth and her daughter.

"The elder lady was the only one of them with whom I wished to have any conversation, and her love of hearing herself talk obtained me this favour, in spite of all the displeasure she had conceived against me: but it was very difficult to bring her to converse on that subject which alone interested me: she would talk politics, or give me a dissertation on the nature of the soul, or on the eruptions of Vesuvius,[1] descant on the age of the world, or on her *own* age, (if her auditors would allow her to be not quite five and forty:) but of Celestina she would *not* talk; and if ever I, in spite of her evasions, introduced the conversation, she affected to hear me with horror, and to consider every mention I made of a person whom she called so connected with me, as the most indelicate and improper conversation with which I could entertain her. She was for the most part surrounded, when I was admitted to her, with abbati,[2] and the oracle of a circle she had herself formed, in which it was generally impracticable to entertain her with any other conversation than that she chose to lead to.

"Her daughter, who had formerly received me with so much haughtiness, and who had since been offended in the tenderest point, a point too in which her extreme vanity had rendered her particularly susceptible, affected no longer the overweening pride which in our first interviews had been so repulsive, but a soft melancholy, which sits well enough on some people, but was in her more likely to move mirth than pity: she seldom spoke to me; but when she did, it was with the air of one whose just indignation was conquered by softer sentiments. I knew I never could deserve those sentiments from her, and therefore was very sorry to see them, even though certain they were feigned.

"But it was here only I could hope to gain any information of the woman, Hannah Biscoe, who pretended to have lived with my mother near twenty years since. Lady Castlenorth evaded, with wonderful art, ever giving me any trace of this circumstance, and of her daughter I knew it was in vain to enquire; but there was a little smart

---

1 Vesuvius was of interest to antiquarians and geologists of The Royal Society, art collectors at home and British expatriates and tourists to Naples. Pompeii and Herculaneum were now being excavated, and there had been a major eruption of the volcano in 1787. Examination of the layers of lava was revealing that the world might be older than the Genesis account allowed.
2 Literally, Italian priests, but used here ironically to mean would-be-learned men.

Italian girl, called Justina, who had attended on Miss Fitz-Hayman for some time, and who had been in England with her, and I took occasion, as often as I could see her, to say some obliging thing to her, and sometimes to make her a trifling present. Justina, in consequence of my taking so much notice of her, began officiously to put herself in my way; and I believe her vanity prompted her for some time to suppose I had very different motives for my attention than those with which I was really actuated.

"But in a foreign woman of that rank even vanity usually yields to avarice. When I had obtained an opportunity of clearly explaining myself, Justina undertook to procure me a direction to the woman whom I was so solicitous to find. She produced it in about a week, but artfully evaded my question as to how she came by it. I sent off my own servant instantly with it, determined to follow him myself if the information as to her place of abode proved to be true. I received an account from him that a few days before his arrival at the house in Suffolk, where she was said to live, she had removed from thence and the people either did not know or would not tell whither she was gone.

"This seemed so like an artifice of Lady Castlenorth's to prevent my making the enquiry which she knew I had so long and so earnestly desired, that I could now no longer doubt but that Justina had betrayed me: but during this disquieting suspense time wore away, and you Celestina—what did you, what could you think of me?

"I entertained the strongest hopes, that since Lady Castlenorth so industriously kept me from the person she had herself produced as likely to give me authentic and indisputable testimony, that she knew her evidence would not bear investigation, and to this hope I eagerly adhered. My mind, however, was too much irritated by the idea of such complicated treachery to allow me to keep terms with her as I had hitherto done: I was wandering about Italy all the time of Farnham's absence: on his rejoining me, I went back to the residence of Lord Castlenorth, and very peremptorily taxed his wife with fraud. I denied that Hannah Biscoe lived with my mother at the period she pretended to have done so; and that least I should discover the deception, that she had been sent away from the place where I had with difficulty discovered her.

"Lady Castlenorth affected the calm indifference of injured innocence, the proud consciousness of ill treated integrity; she affected to declare that she was desirous of my seeing this Hannah Biscoe, that she knew not of her departure from the place whither she went, which was the house of a brother in law, nor was in any way concerned about her; 'but,' added she, rising and going to a cabinet where she kept papers; 'you shall presently be convinced that she did live with your mother in the year 1770.'

"She took out a letter, which I saw immediately to be my mother's hand. It was directed to Hannah Biscoe at Mrs. Willoughby's, South Audley-street, where my mother's town house then was. These were the words:

'HANNAH,

'I desire you will immediately on receipt of this go to Kensington, and deliver the enclosed to the person for whom it is directed, and let me know by the return of the post whether the orders I gave in a former letter were executed, and how every thing goes on there.

M. WILLOUGHBY.'

Alvestone,
April 26, 1770.

"I returned the letter to Lady Castlenorth, and expressed myself very warmly; insisting upon it that from such evidence nothing could be derived or even guessed at: but she bade me, with a contemptuous smile, remember, that when I questioned this woman at Exeter she had told me, that you were for the first months of your life nursed at Kensington, whither she went almost every day to see you, and that at five or six months old you were sent abroad; and when my mother went to the South of France, on pretence of recovering her health, eighteen or twenty months after the death of my father, you were conveyed thither, and there put under the care of a friend, who placed you soon after with the Superior of the convent of St. Celestine, at Hières, as a relation of her own.

"The coincidence of this story, with what I had heard before relative to Madame Pellatier, struck me with more force than any thing I had yet learned. I left the house of Lord Castlenorth more miserable than I had ever been before, and again set out for Provence, hardly knowing why, and not caring at all what became of me.

"Ever since that period, Celestina, I have been wandering from place to place in search of information which I cannot obtain, and, which obtained, would certainly render me wretched, if indeed any wretchedness can be greater than that which in my present state of miserable uncertainty it is my lot to suffer.

"Are we then, Celestina, are we related by blood? and is there an invincible bar between us? Was my mother, that admirable, that excellent, and almost faultless woman, capable of living in a state of continual dissimulation as to you, and of hiding one fault by another, which might have been followed by consequences so hideous to my imagination? Oh! Celestina, it seems sacrilege to her memory to think it: yet her aversion to my expressions of tenderness towards you, her conduct in a hundred instances I can recollect, her strong injunctions, the promise she extorted from me to marry Miss Fitz-Hayman—a promise urged with such vehemence, even in her last moments!

"Could the poor consideration of pecuniary advantage influence her then? did it ever influence her? And the repetition of your name with her last breath, mingled with words that might be a prayer for you, but which I have since thought was possibly the fatal secret which she determined to divulge only in death. The sad recollection of that scene, her countenance, which I continually behold, her voice, which murmurs still in my ears, all, all contribute to empoison every moment of my life, and to make that tender affection, that ardent love, which was once the joy of my existence and the pride of my heart, the severest curse with which heaven can pursue me.

"Yes, Celestina, unless I dared indulge that fondness with which my heart overflows, I would I could forget you for ever, and determine never to see you more, for I despair of ever seeing you as I— Pardon me, I am lost in the confusion of sensations I cannot describe; and at this moment I hope so miserable a being does not exist on this earth. Write to me, Celestina: you have more strength of mind than I have; you are not, like me, the sport of agonizing passions. Write to me; tell me what you would have me do farther to unveil this sad mystery, or to throw it from us for ever, if that may be. I have told Vavasour what it appeared impossible longer to conceal from him: he is warmly my friend, and you may employ him in any way in which you think he can be useful. Celestina, I commit you to his protection! till—till when, heaven only knows; and I dare not trust my pen with another word: only I entreat you to write to me; and may every happiness that virtue and innocence, and excellence like your's deserve, ever be the portion of my Celestina, whatever becomes of the unhappy

G. WILLOUGHBY."

Thus ended this long letter, and thus was explained the strange circumstances that had cost Celestina so many tears. But she wept not now: she read the letter over twice: her first tremulous emotion subsided; but her stunned senses had not recovered their tone. It was late; it was cold; her candle had burnt nearly out. She put the letter on her pillow; and unable to undress herself, threw herself on the bed in her cloaths, and lay pondering on what she had read, on Willoughby's situation and her own, till the tedious night was at an end.

Chapter VI

Vavasour, who had passed great part of *his* night over a bottle, was not, however, at all more disposed to sleep towards morning than if he had been in bed, but at half after seven o'clock he sent the house-maid to know if Miss de Mornay was up, and, if she was, directed the servant to give his compliments to her, and let her know that he should take it as a favour if she would allow him to speak to her for a few moments before her other friends were assembled.

Celestina had but just fallen into an unquiet slumber, when she was awakened by the maid who tapped at the door, from an uneasy dream indeed, but from a change of uneasiness. With her returning memory, all the purport of Willoughby's letter returned; and Vava-sour's message added most painfully, the recollection that she must discuss it all with him.

She ordered him to be told, that she was not very well, and could not immediately attend him: then shaking off the heavy lassitude which uneasiness and want of rest had occasioned, she called to her aid all that strength of mind and rectitude of heart with which she was eminently endowed by nature; and having again read over Willoughby's letter, began to consider what she ought to do.

With a doubt of such a nature on his mind, she resolved, what-ever it cost her, never to meet him but as his sister; unless, which was very improbable, the strong and bewildering circumstances which had given rise to such an idea could all be removed. With so much purity did she love him, that she felt, that were he happy with anoth-er, and his esteem and tenderness for her undiminished, she could be content through life to find her felicity in witnessing his. She resolved, therefore, after much debate with herself and some pangs of unavoidable regret, that since this dark and unpassable barrier was raised, either by nature or by artifice, between her and the only man she had ever thought of with fond partiality, she would never marry, but would leave him at full liberty to compleat that union with Miss Fitz-Hayman, which might at once fulfil his engagement to his mother, wean him from that lingering fondness for her which it was folly if not guilt to indulge, and retrieve his pecuniary concerns from those embarrassments which were now hastening to overwhelm him.

Having formed this heroic and proper determination, she endeavoured to compose her countenance, to quiet the agitation of her mind, and to meet Vavasour with that degree of calm spirit which she imagined, from past experience of his behaviour, such a meeting would require.

This, however, was easier to imagine than to execute. She wished indeed to meet him without witness, because she knew he possessed too little of that delicacy which would teach him to repress any part of his knowledge before strangers, as Mrs. Elphinstone and Montague Thorold were to him: but when she opened the door of the room where she knew he waited for her, the blood forsook her cheeks, her trembling hands refused the little exertion necessary to turn the lock, her feet refused to carry her forward, and she would have returned without speaking to him for that time, if he, who was eagerly waiting her approach, had not heard her light foot steps in the passage, and opened the door while she yet stood hesitating at it.

He was struck by the sight of her swollen and heavy eyes, the languor of her air, and the paleness of her countenance; and his usual address, which had more of warmth and vivacity than elegance, was softened by the real concern of which he was at that moment sensible. He took her hand, which trembled within his as he led her to a seat—"I am sorry," said he, "to see that you are not well."

Celestina tried to speak, but could not. Vavasour had but an indifferent notion of administering consolation, nor could he contrive to condole with her for what he secretly rejoiced at himself; so that between his dissembled concern and his undissembled satisfaction, he sat a moment or two silent; and then remarked, that the letter he had brought gave a very good account of George's health.

Celestina, without having any very precise idea of what she said, answered faintly yes; and by this time Vavasour added, that it contained also, he supposed, like what he had at the same time received, the history of a devilish awkward, mysterious business.

Celestina, who found herself unequal to the conversation, thought it better to put an end to it at once and for ever. She therefore, by an effort of resolution, commanded voice enough to say— "Mr. Vavasour, you understand undoubtedly that every idea of the alliance between your friend and me, is at an end for ever. As for the reasons that exist against it, a thousand motives make me wish they may remain secret; from this moment, therefore, you will very much oblige me, by forbearing to speak of Mr. Willoughby otherwise than as my best friend, and by concealing from the world a secret, in which it can have no interest, but which will give pain to many to have divulged."

"Divulged!" cried he, laughing: "what then, do you suppose it is any secret?"

"To be sure I do," she replied.

"Oh! yes," answered he, "that is mighty likely, when Lady Castlenorth has taken such pains to talk of it every where already."

"Lady Castlenorth!" cried Celestina; a faint blush rising in her pale cheek.

"Aye, to be sure," said Vavasour carelessly, "that she did months ago. Why don't you know, that beside the interest she had in dividing you and Willoughby, because her daughter is in love with him it seems, she always hated his mother; and that death itself is no barrier against malice like her's."

"Do you think it probable or possible that this story may be entirely the effect of that malice."

"Why faith no. I own I do not. You know—at least people tell me so who do know, that it was whispered about a great many years ago, and even said, that Everard was privately married to Mrs. Willoughby. But what signifies talking about it," added he, seeing her again change colour—"You have just been desiring me to say nothing about it. George seems to me to have made up his mind about it: he will marry his cousin, and retrieve his estates, as was his first plan; and my fair Celestina" (and he took her hand) "will look out for somebody else to transfer those affections to that he resigns."

"No, Sir," said Celestina, withdrawing her hand hastily from him, "they are not, I assure you, so easily transferred."

"I am glad to hear it," replied Vavasour, without being at all discomposed by her manner; "for then I hope this pedantic young fellow, whom I find here travelling with you, will not have the presumption to suppose he has any chance of obtaining them? Pray tell me—how comes he here with you? is he any relation of the people you are with?"

This was a question it was impossible for Celestina to answer ingenuously. The piercing and enquiring eyes of Vavasour, inflamed and fierce from the late hours and free use of wine the preceding night, were fixed on her face. She changed countenance; felt that she did, and again her complexion altered. The various emotions with which she was agitated, consciousness that she must no longer think of Willoughby as a lover, yet could never admit another to that distinction, consciousness too that Montague Thorold must appear in the eyes of the world to have succeeded to that place, and anger that Vavasour should thus presume on the confidence of Willoughby to question her with a freedom he had otherwise no pretensions to, all combined to affect, to distress, and to deprive her for a few moments of that presence of mind, which, from the strength and clearness of her understanding, was usually at her command.

Vavasour, who, from the time he found Willoughby must in all probability resign her, made no doubt of succeeding to her affections; who had no idea of the sensations which pressed on her heart, from his total inability to feel them himself; became irritated and impatient at the silence his own impetuosity had occasioned. He sat eagerly reading on her countenance the emotions of her heart, and interpreting them his own way: again he repeated his question— "How came young Thorold with you? Is he related to these Elphin-stones?"

"You must enquire of him," Celestina was on the point of saying; but the fear least a quarrel between them should be the consequence of her so answering, checked her. She tried, therefore, to evade the question. "Of what concern is it," said she, "how he came hither. We were talking of Mr. Willoughby. Pray tell me—is he aware that our supposed relationship is talked of? Does he know the pains Lady Castlenorth has been at to circulate the story?"

"'Tis impossible for me to know that," said Vavasour, (as it really was;) "it is much more in your way to tell me, how this college boy came hither with you."

"I know no right you have to enquire about it," answered Celestina faintly, "because I cannot see that it is a concern in which you are at all interested."

"You will give me leave then to make my own conclusions; or rather," added he, in a louder voice, on seeing Montague Thorold enter the room, "rather to interrogate the gentleman himself."

This was exactly what Celestina had been most solicitous to avoid; the impetuosity of Vavasour, the surprize and answer she saw flashing from the eyes of Thorold, her sleepless night and long agitated spirits, the fear of she knew not what consequences from these two inflammable spirits, and her inability to check or repress those over whom she had no pretence to assume any authority, were together a combination of cruel circumstances which might have overcome a stronger mind than her's. Mrs. Elphinstone was dejected from situation, and languid from recent sorrow of her own: to her, therefore, Celestina would in any case reluctantly have applied; and now she could not leave the room to seek her without leaving together two men who seemed so highly irritated against each other that the first moment of her absence would probably bring them to extremities. To speak to Vavasour, was to address the winds of the sea: she saw that he was hardly sober, that he was incapable of feeling for her distress, or of listening to any thing but his passionate impetuosity: it was on Thorold alone she had any hopes of prevailing; but in the moment of her deliberation this hope seemed escaping her.

Before she could determine on what to do, Vavasour had, in a manner at once contemptuous and hasty, addressed himself to Montague Thorold, and enquired how it happened that he was at York attending on Mrs. Elphinstone and Miss de Mornay?

"How it happens, Sir?" said Thorold. "Is there then any thing so very extraordinary in it? May I not be at York or at Canterbury?"

"Yes," replied Vavasour, "when you are Archbishop of either; and then you will be, for ought I know, in your right place; but at present I think you in the wrong one."

"What you think, sir," replied Thorold, "is the last thing that ever can be of any consequence to me; and if my actions are, as I apprehend, of as little to you, I imagine we can find some pleasanter topic than either the one or the other on which to entertain this lady."

He then approached Celestina, who was, he saw, ready to sink from her chair; and softening his voice, said—"You are ill I am afraid."

"No," replied she; "but I am alarmed and uneasy; and I beg of you," continued she, lowering her voice, "I beg of you to keep your temper, let Mr. Vavasour say what he will."

"I cannot promise that," said he in the same tone; "but I can promise never voluntarily to do or say any thing that shall give you a moment's pain. Do not be so distressed, I beseech you; let me find Mrs. Elphinstone. You tremble: you seem ready to faint."

"I am indeed," replied she, "affected from numberless causes. If you will be so good as to call Mrs. Elphinstone, I will be much obliged to you."

Thorold went immediately to obey her; and Vavasour approaching her, cried—"I see how it is; that young fellow is to console you for the loss of Willoughby. Your partiality to him I always suspected, and am now too well convinced of it."

"Well, Sir," cried Celestina, assuming in some degree her usual spirit; "and admitting it to be so, I do not really understand by what pretence you call me to an account for it."

"By my own long and ardent affection for you," cried he; "of which, however you may now chuse to affect ignorance, you cannot have been ignorant. I sacrificed it to Willoughby's prior claim, and to your visible attachment to him; but I am not humble enough to withdraw my pretensions in favour of such a new boy as Montague Thorold."

"I am obliged to you, Sir," answered Celestina, "for the predilection you avow in my favour; though it cannot command my affection, it demands my sincerity; and I therefore assure you, that though I am now perhaps at liberty, I have no intention of engaging myself again. I shall hope to be allowed to consider both you and Mr. Thorold as my friends, while I absolutely decline any preference to either."

The pride of Vavasour was hurt extremely by this speech. Though he was not personally vain, yet he had from his infancy been so accustomed to have his own way, that opposition from any quarter was new and insupportable to him. Mrs. Elphinstone and Thorold at this moment entering the room, he for once checked himself; and breakfast being ready, he was invited to partake of it, which however he declined, but told Celestina, on retiring, that he must desire to see her again alone in an hour.

Celestina now attempted to repress the various emotions with which she was agitated, and to quiet the throbbing of her heart. She sat down to the table, and tried to eat, but could not; while Montague Thorold, watching with eager fondness every turn of her countenance, officiously tried to engage her to partake of the breakfast that was before her.

As soon as she could, however, she withdrew; and after a moment's pause alone, her scattered and oppressed senses were collected enough to bring before her all that had happened, and tears, which she had not hitherto been able to shed, came to her relief.

Her reason too, came to her assistance, and strengthened the resolution she had formed after her first perusal of Willoughby's letter. But though she was able to decide on what she ought to do herself, she saw many painful circumstances likely to be created by the violence of Vavasour, and the impossibility of prevailing either on him or on Montague Thorold to leave her and Mrs. Elphinstone to pursue their journey with the other; or, what she would still have preferred, of continuing it without the attendance of either.

When the mind is oppressed with any heavy affliction, the less serious evils which at other times it can repel or submit to, are felt with painful impatience. Mrs. Elphinstone, drooping and depressed from her past sufferings and future apprehensions, could no longer interpose to check the impetuosity of two young men, each of whom thought himself at liberty to attend on Celestina: while Celestina herself, who never meant to encourage either, and whose heart was so recently wounded by the dread of having lost that protection on which she was wont with fondness to rely, was yet more unequal to the exertion which was necessary to part these men, who were determined to look upon each other as rivals, or to keep them within the bounds of civility if they persisted in remaining together.

Anxious to proceed towards the house of Cathcart, and to put her children under the care of her brother, while she herself tried to enter on some mode of life by which to procure them a subsistence, Mrs. Elphinstone became impatient of any farther delay; while Celestina, though equally anxious to get forward, trembled at the thought of a journey, which she foresaw would produce a quarrel, and perhaps a duel, before they had proceeded three stages.

Sometimes she thought of leaving the whole party abruptly, and going on as speedily as possible alone: but besides her unwillingness to leave Mrs. Elphinstone, she foresaw that if she did this Vavasour would follow and overtake her; and Thorold would hardly content himself with attending her friend, while certain that Vavasour was with her. After much consideration, therefore, nothing seemed to remain, but to endeavour to prevail on Thorold to go forward without them; than which, nothing seemed much more unlikely to succeed, unless it was the same attempt on Vavasour. She felt, too, a reluctance in asking a favour of Thorold, which he might interpret as encouragement she never meant to give him; and was afraid that the assurances she must make him in regard to her total indifference towards Vavasour, might afford him reason to hope, that towards him she would be less inexorable.

It was necessary, however, immediately to make the essay; and therefore sending for Mr. Thorold, she with trembling hesitation told him, that the letters brought by Mr. Vavasour had been decisive in regard to ending the intended alliance between her and Mr. Willoughby. But she had hardly uttered the word Willoughby, before the countenance of Montague Thorold was animated with all the warm hopes to which this intelligence gave birth. She saw it with concern; and with as much resolution as she could, besought him to attend to her, while with a faultering voice, and her tears with difficulty repressed, she went on—"That I shall now never be the wife of Willoughby is certain: but do not misunderstand me; I have determined never to be the wife of any other person. I shall go, for the rest of the winter, to Lady Horatia Howard, and afterwards retire to some village as remote as possible from that part of England where I once expected to pass my life. This resolution is unalterable. But though I never can return to you the favourable sentiments with which you have honoured me, my friendship, my gratitude, my esteem, it is in your power to secure and—"

"Friendship! gratitude! esteem!" cried Montague Thorold. "Can I be content with such cold words: I, who can never for an instant disengage my thoughts from you: I, who worship your very shadow, and who cannot bear the thought of quitting you even for a moment! Oh! Celestina! Celestina! if ever the most pure and violent love deserved a return—"

"Forgive me," cried Celestina, "if in my turn I interrupt you. Do you not mistake your sentiments, or, by an abuse of terms, call a transient liking by that name which ought to belong only to that refined affection of the heart which leads us to prefer the happiness of another to our own, and to sacrifice every inferior consideration to the sublime pleasure of promoting that happiness."

"Heaven and earth!" cried Thorold impetuously, "and do I not feel that sentiment in all its purity for you? Would I not lay down my life to procure you any real—almost any imaginary good."

"Prove it," interrupted Celestina, "prove it by obliging me in the request I am going to make: a request in which I must not be refused, and which, before I make it, you must absolutely promise to grant."

"I promise," returned Thorold, who had at that moment no idea whither her request tended, "I promise to obey you, even though you desired my death. If the sacrifice I make has any merit in your eyes, how cheaply would your approbation be purchased even by the loss of existence."

"All that is very absurd and very wild," replied Celestina. "What I ask you can easily do, and ought to do without reluctance."

"Name it," cried he, "and see how well I can obey you."

Celestina then told him, that Vavasour, fancying his friendship with Mr. Willoughby gave him a right to attend her, meant, she feared, to go on with her and Mrs. Elphinstone to London; "and from the dialogues which have twice passed between you and him," added she, "there is reason to apprehend that your continuing together may be attended with very unpleasant consequences: neither Mrs. Elphinstone or I have courage to encounter the sort of contention which may arise between you: and to avoid the hazard of it, allow us to thank you for all the trouble you have taken for us, and now to bid you adieu till we meet again in Devonshire."

Montague Thorold, who from the moment he understood her had listened with impatience, now protested that the promise he had just given could not be binding in an instance that must be as injurious to his honour as cruel to his feelings. "Why should you suffer this Mr. Vavasour," said he, "to force himself upon you, while you drive me from you? what is this chimerical[1] claim that he derives from Willoughby, who has resigned his own: and how poor and spiritless must I appear, who having been permitted that of seeing you thus far on your journey, consent to resign to another the honour of attending you to the end of it: to another, who assumes a right no better founded than my own; and to whom I am to give place for no other reason but because he rudely demands it. You would despise me, Madam, and I should deserve to be despised, were I capable of so mean a desertion."

This was exactly what Celestina feared; but persisting in her resolution to escape the alarm to which she must be subject from Vavasour and Montague Thorold's being together during the journey, she told the latter very calmly, that unless he consented to oblige her, and to go forward under pretence of being obliged to return home, that their acquaintance must here end for ever.

Even against this fear, his reluctance to yield, or to appear to yield the right of attending her to Vavasour, awhile supported him. The dread, too, least Vavasour should now succeed for himself, and that he should see those hopes destroyed for ever which he so fondly cherished since Willoughby was out of the question, made him resist still more forcibly the injunctions Celestina desired to lay upon him. At length, his fear of offending her, his real love for her, and the sight of her uneasiness; her assurances that Vavasour never would have any particular interest in her favour, (though at the same time she bade him understand that he had himself no better claim,) and his wish to shew her how much he preferred her satisfaction to his own, prevailed upon him to sacrifice his pride and his fears to her entreaties; and making himself acquainted with the place where she was to be with Mrs. Elphinstone in London, where he obtained permission to attend her as soon as she arrived, Montague Thorold, though still reluctantly and with great compulsion on himself, departed alone, and on post horses pursued his way to London.

Having thus prevailed on Thorold to depart, Celestina again sat down to recollect her fatigued spirits. She had some hours before

---

1 Imaginary.

determined to write to Lady Horatia Howard, and accept of the invitation so repeatedly offered her, as soon as she saw Mrs. Elphinstone safe in the protection and assistance of Cathcart, who was to meet them in London.

This letter, therefore, she wrote and forwarded; and as neither the weather or any other circumstance was now likely to render their progress hazardous, Mrs. Elphinstone agreed that they would set out at a very early hour the next morning.

The day, however, was of necessity to be ended where they were; and it was very certain that Vavasour would pass it with them. He had ordered for them every thing they were likely to have occasion for, in a stile infinitely superior to what they would themselves have thought of; and when they met at dinner, he received them as his guests, and when his natural vivacity was heightened by that sort of triumph that he felt on finding that Thorold was gone, his exulting spirits were such as to be cruelly oppressive both to Mrs. Elphinstone and Celestina.

Incapable of entering into *their* feelings, he had no idea of repressing his own. He fancied there no longer existed any obstacle to his project in regard to Celestina; and as that project had long been the first of his heart, and had become doubly important from the opposition it had met with, he concealed no part of the pleasure he felt at what he fancied the absolute certainty of its immediate accomplishment.

This was conduct that was insupportably distressing to Celestina. He spoke without scruple of the resignation Willoughby had made of her hand, and seemed to have as little delicacy as to the occasion of it. Of an attachment to him, abstracted from every idea of becoming his wife, Vavasour had no idea; and Celestina had no courage to urge it, so entirely did his want of feeling, and the proud certainty he shewed of his own success, overwhelm her. All she could do was, to entreat Mrs. Elphinstone not to leave her with him, and to assist her as much as possible in attempting at least to check that assuming manner, for which neither her former friendship for Vavasour, nor the regard Willoughby had for him, could, in her opinion, offer any apology.

Fortunately, however, for both her and her friend, two young men of fortune, much acquainted with Vavasour, arrived at the inn early in the evening, and seeing his servants, enquired for him, and were shewn into the room almost as soon as dinner was over. Celestina and her friend took the earliest opportunity to withdraw; and Vavasour's attention to his guests over their wine, delivered them for the rest of the evening from his company.

He had taken care, however, to inform himself of all that related to their journey the next day. But eager as he was to have Celestina in the chaise with him, he was compelled to desist from the request he at first ventured to make, on her representing the impossibility of her leaving Mrs. Elphinstone; to whom, though Vavasour heartily wished her once more in the Hebrides, he had at length the complaisance to offer his place in his own chaise, as being more commodious than the hired ones to be found on the road; and agreed, on her acquiescence in that arrangement, to follow himself in a hack[1] chaise with his servant.

The gentlemen who had passed the evening with him at the inn, were not less fond of the pleasures of the table than he was himself; and their orgies had been prolonged till it was no longer worth while for him to go to bed. With a very little alteration of his dress therefore, and with a great deal of wine still in his head, he was ready in the morning to set out: but such was his appearance, and such his manners in consequence of his debauch the preceding evening, that Celestina was more than ever solicitous to avoid him; and had it been possible for her to have thought of him before with the slightest degree of partiality, his looks and his conversation of this morning would have filled her with terror and disgust.

As she travelled on, however, by the side of her dejected friend, who had no spirits for conversation, she could not, amid all the reflection on her own circumstances, which filled her mind, avoid considering, with melancholy regret, the situation of this young man, who, with some talents and many virtues, was thus yielding to the wild current of passion and vice, and destroying his constitution and his fortune before he knew the value of either. She then with mournful recollection contrasted his character with that of Willoughby, who had at once all his vivacity, tempered with so much sweetness, so much attention to the feelings of others; who had all his generosity of spirit and openness of heart, without any of his careless dissipation; and whose brighter talents were not obscured by vice, nor degraded by folly; and as all his virtues, all his amiable qualities were enumerated, her heart felt all the acuteness of sorrow, in remembering too that under their influence she had lost the hope of passing her life: yet the cruel pain of the reflection that these hopes were now at an end, was immediately mitigated, when she considered, that this she might perhaps still do, as his sister and his friend;

---

1 Hired.

but her reason, however it began to recover its tone, could never say any thing to her that for a moment taught her to reflect with pleasure, or even with tranquillity, on the thoughts of his being united to Miss Fitz-Hayman.

On reperusing Willoughby's letter, which she had now acquired courage to study more minutely, she saw with new uneasiness, what in the first tumult of her spirits had escaped her, or at least made but a slight impression—that he recommended her particularly to the care and protection of Vavasour; and that, as he had probably intimated the same trust to Vavasour himself, she should find it very difficult to disengage herself from his attendance. The longer she dwelt on Willoughby's expressions, the more she apprehended he was but too well convinced that the whole story of their relationship did not originate with Lady Castlenorth. She foresaw, that while even the shadow of a doubt remained, their union never ought to be thought of: but having nobody with whom she could properly discuss the various and contradictory ideas on this bewildering subject that passed through her mind, she looked forward with earnest impatience to the hour when she should receive the maternal counsel and soothing consolation which Lady Horatia Howard alone was likely to afford her.

The journey, however, was to be performed; and though she carefully avoided, during the two days that it lasted, being alone with Vavasour, yet she suffered extreme pain from the encreasing conviction that he presumed on Willoughby's total resignation of her, and openly declared that he thought himself a candidate for her favour, whose fortune and pretensions of every kind rendered him secure of success.

At length the party reached London, and Cathcart received his sister and her friend at the lodgings he had prepared for them on being informed of the time of their arrival.

The meeting between him and Mrs. Elphinstone was too affecting to the already depressed spirits of Celestina. She retired early to her own room, having with difficulty prevailed on Vavasour to quit her, and there endeavoured to acquire steadiness to talk over with Cathcart, the next morning, the purport of Willoughby's letter; and then to take leave of him and her poor dejected friend, as Lady Horatia Howard had received with avidity the information of her intended visit to her, and was to send her coach for her at one o'clock on the following day.

Chapter VII

The morning at length arrived, and the friends who had so long found all the consolation their circumstances admitted of in being together, were now to part; uncertain when, or if ever, they were to meet again. Mrs. Elphinstone, sinking as she was under oppression of many present sorrows and future apprehensions, yet found them all deepened by the loss of Celestina, who had so generously assisted her in supporting them: and Celestina felt, that when to soothe the spirits and strengthen the resolution of her friend was no longer her immediate task, she should dwell with more painful and more steady solicitude on her own singular and unfortunate situation.

Cathcart, warmly attached as he was to both, from gratitude and from affection, had no power to speak comfort to either. Early in the morning he had met Celestina, and gone through Willoughby's letter: but though his mind sometimes strongly resisted the idea of that relationship of which it spoke, he had nothing to offer against it; and could only sigh over the incurable unhappiness with which he saw the future days of friends he so much loved would be clouded.

Silently they all assembled round the breakfast table; but nobody could eat. Cathcart tried to talk of Jessy, of his house, of his farm, of his fortunate prospects, and of his sister's two little girls, whom he had taken home; but there was not one topic on which he could speak that did not remind him of the obligations he owed to Celestina and Willoughby, nor one idea which arose unembittered with the reflection, that they, to whom he was indebted for all *his* happiness, were themselves miserable.

About twelve o'clock Vavasour came into the room in his usual way; enquired eagerly of Celestina when she went to Lady Horatia Howard's, and when he could see her there; and without waiting for an answer to his enquiry, told her that he had that morning met Sir Philip Molyneux, and that Lady Molyneux had been in town about a week. Every body who were related to Willoughby was interesting to Celestina; and from Lady Molyneux she had always supposed more might be collected than from any other person: but now her mind was too much oppressed and too much confused to allow her to distinguish her sensations, or to arrange any settled plan for her future conduct towards Lady Molyneux. She received Vavasour's information, therefore, with coldness; and indeed her manners towards him were very constrained and distant, which he either did not or would not notice; rattling on his usual wild way, though he saw the dejection and concern of the party; a circumstance that more than ever disgusted Celestina, who began some time before to doubt whether the credit which Vavasour had for good nature was not given him on very slender foundations: for to be so entirely occupied by his own pleasure and pursuits as to be incapable of the least sympathy towards others, to be unable or unwilling to check for one moment his vivacity in compliment to their despondence, seemed to Celestina such a want of sensibility, as gave her a very indifferent opinion of his heart.

Mrs. Elphinstone quitted the room to make the last preparations for her departure: but Cathcart, who had settled every thing before, remained with Celestina and Vavasour. He would have given the world to have passed these moments in conversation with her; but the presence of a third person, and especially of Vavasour, put an end to all hope he had of an opportunity of explaining to her, with that tenderness and caution which the subject required, some circumstances relative to Willoughby's fortune, which had lately come to his knowledge. New embarrassments seemed threatening him; and a law suit, involving part of the property which belonged to Alvestone estate, seemed likely to encrease these embarrassments; while the mortgagees were gradually undermining the estate itself; and the absence of the master encreased the impatience and mistrust of those who had claims upon it.

All this, Cathcart thought Celestina ought to know; yet in their first interview that morning he had not courage to tell her of it, and now Vavasour left him no chance of doing it; for while he yet deliberated, the coach sent by Lady Horatia Howard stopped at the door, and the moment was come in which he was to take his leave of her.

He took her hand, and kissed it with an air of grateful respect; but he could only say—"I shall write to you in a few days, and, I hope, give you a good account of my sister and of Jessy."

"I hope you will," returned Celestina faintly.

"And," added he, "you will of course like to hear of all that passes material in our neighbourhood?"

"Certainly I shall," replied she. "Adieu, dear Sir. I cannot *say* much, but you know what I feel for you all."

Vavasour had taken her hand to lead her down stairs; but she disengaged it from him, and said to Cathcart, as she gave it to him— "Let us go to your sister." He led her to the door of the room; where at that moment Mrs. Elphinstone entered, pale and breathless: her eyes were heavy, and fixed on Celestina, but she did not weep. Celestina's tears, however, were more ready, and, as she embraced her friend, they choked the trembling adieu she would have uttered, and fell in showers on her bosom. The emotion was too painful; and Cathcart, desiring to end it for both their sakes, disengaged his sister gently from the arms of the trembling Celestina, while Vavasour, again seizing her hand, hurried her down stairs, and as he put her into the coach, told her he should call upon her the next day. She would have besought him not to do it, as a liberty he ought not to take in the house whither she was going; but before she could sufficiently recover herself to find words, the coach was driven away, and in a few moments she found herself at the door of Lady Horatia Howard, in Park-street, Grosvenor-square, and it became necessary for her to collect her spirits, to acquit herself as so much kind attention deserved.

Lady Horatia received her with unfeigned pleasure, and with a degree of maternal kindness that set her almost immediately at ease with herself. She was put into possession of her apartment, and bade to remember that it was her's as long as she would occupy it, and that her time was always to be her own. "I am going out," said Lady Horatia, "to dinner to-day. I have a great notion you had rather dine at home?" Celestina owned she had. "Be it so then," replied she: "and whenever you prefer being at home to going with me, I shall be pleased at your using that freedom, without which such a situation as I am able to offer you would be not only of no value but a species of slavery." While she said this in the kindest manner, Celestina observed that she looked very earnestly at her eyes, which were red with weeping; and examined, with a kind of mournful enquiry, her features, which bore traces of the concern she had felt in parting from her friends; and having thus examined her countenance some time, her own, which was remarkably expressive, assumed a look of surprise tempered with concern; and then, as if she checked herself, she rang for her woman to receive orders about Celestina's dinner, and while they remained together, she gave the conversation a more general turn.

When Celestina was alone, she ran over in her thoughts the transactions of the last month, and wondered what Fate would do with her next. But not of herself alone she thought: Willoughby, unhappy and unsettled; his mind thrown from its balance by disappointment; his talents lost in the bewildering uneasiness of uncertainty, and his temper injured by the corrosive anxieties of pecuniary inconvenience; he, who had such a mind, such a heart, such talents, such a temper; who deserved every happiness, and yet had hitherto known none; Willoughby, wandering about the world to obtain confirmation of a fact, which, when known, would only complete his misery;

was an object from which the thoughts of Celestina could never a moment escape: and a thousand times she wished she had never been born, since to her, to whomsoever she owed her birth, Willoughby certainly owed his unhappiness.

It was time to consider of obeying the injunction he gave her, towards the close of his letter, to write to him; but on this subject she determined to consult Lady Horatia Howard, as well as to ask her advice in what way she should act in regard to Vavasour, whose importunities she dreaded, yet from whose visits she knew not how to disengage herself.

Under such protection, however, she knew that much of the inconvenience she must in other circumstances feel from Vavasour's behaviour would be obviated; and that the sense as well as the situation of Lady Horatia would prevent that improper familiarity which, when she was only with Cathcart or Mrs. Elphinstone, whom he looked upon as inferior and as dependent, it was too much his nature to assume.

With more complacency, she thought of Montague Thorold, and always of his father with a degree of affectionate reverence. As to the young man, though her heart never admitted, in regard to him, the slightest tendency towards that sort of partiality which could ever grow into love, yet she had received so many marks of real and ardent attachment from him, she thought so well of his talents, and so much better of his heart, that she could never divest herself of solicitude for his welfare. Perhaps—for in what heart, however pure, does not some such weakness lurk—perhaps, the stories she had heard of his former universal propensity to form attachments, and which were intended to prejudice her against him, had an influence on her mind of which she was herself unconscious, and that her self-love, though no human being ever appeared to have less, was gratified by having thus fixed a man so volatile and unsteady, though she never could, nor ever had given him reason to suppose she could, return the passions she had thus inspired.

While there remained any hope of ever seeing Willoughby such as he had once been, she had felt an utter repugnance to suffer the assiduities of Montague Thorold; but Willoughby's apparent neglect of her for some time before she left the Isle of Skye, and the little probability there now was that they could ever meet in peace, since the receipt of his letter, had gradually and almost insensibly accustomed her to the attentions of Montague Thorold: and though she felt for him nothing like love, she could not help being sensible of a great difference in her sentiments towards him and towards Vavasour.

One seemed to live only to obey and oblige her; the other, presuming on the advantages of fortune, or on those which Willoughby's friendship gave him, appeared rather to demand than to solicit her regard—rather to resent her neglect of his suit, than court as a favour her acceptance of it: and if Celestina had any fault, it was a sort of latent pride, the child of conscious worth and elevated understanding; which, though she was certainly obscurely, and possibly dishonourably born, she never could subdue, and, perhaps, never seriously tried to subdue it. She felt, that in point of intellect she was superior to almost every body she conversed with; she could not look in the glass without seeing the reflection of a form, worthy of so fair an inhabitant as an enlightened human soul; and could she have been blind to these advantages, the preference Willoughby had given her so early in life would have taught her all their value.

It is not the consciousness of worth that is offensive and disgusting, but the tribute of respect that is demanded of others who have perhaps no such conviction, and of whom it is therefore unreasonable and arrogant to expect that they will acknowledge what they cannot perceive. Nobody was ever yet eminently handsome in person, or eminently brilliant in intellect, who did not feel from self evidence that they possessed those advantages; though many, from the infirmity and weakness of their tempers, fancy they exist where none but themselves can find any shadow of them.

Good sense, one prominent feature of which is a due attention to the opinion and to the self love of the rest of the world, will rarely suffer those who possess it to obtrude even real advantages on the notice of others; and without good sense, little distinction appears between the real bloom of youth and beauty and the factitious charms purchased at a perfumer's: both are, if not equally disgusting, equally devoid of all that can make them estimable or valuable. Of this good sense, Celestina possessed such a share, that conscious as she was of that superiority of which she was continually told, no village girl had ever more unaffected simplicity of manners; and while her mind was irradiated by more than common genius, and her knowledge very extensive for her time of life, she was in company as silent, and as attentive to the opinion of others, as if she had possessed only a plain and common understanding, with no other cultivation than what a common boarding school education afforded.

Her pride, therefore, so moderated, was rather a virtue than a blemish, and taught her to value herself, but never to despise the rest of the world.

There was about her, too, much of that disposition which the French call *Amenété*:[1] a disposition to please by seeming interested for others; by entering into their joys and sorrows, and by a thousand little nameless kindnesses, which though they consisted perhaps only in attending patiently to a tale of sorrow, told by a mourner of whom the world was tired or who was tired of the world, or listening with concern to the history of pain and confinement related by the valetudinarian, smiling at the fond enthusiasm of a mother when she described the wit or beauty of a darling child, or admiring the plans which an improver had laid down for the alteration of his grounds, were all so many testimonies of a good disposition, in the opinion of those towards whom these little civilities were exerted, that Celestina had formerly had almost as many friends as acquaintances wherever she appeared. In the circle where she was now to move, more splendid even than that where Mrs. Willoughby's kindness had placed her, it was probable that under such introduction as that of Lady Horatia Howard, all the charms of her person, talents, and temper, would be seen to the utmost advantage.

Unaccustomed as Vavasour was to look far into consequences, he had discerned this as soon as he heard of the invitation Celestina had received; and he foresaw so many impediments to the pursuit of his wishes, as well from the severity and prudery which he had heard imputed to Lady Horatia, as from the interference of rivals, that he would very gladly have persuaded her against accepting it, had he had any pretence to offer for his objections: but having none, and not daring to invent any, he had confined himself to mutterings against prudish old cats, and representing to Celestina that she was going to confine herself as an humble companion to bear all the caprices of a superannuated woman of quality. Celestina heard him at first with concern, from an idea that he had heard Lady Horatia misrepresented; but when, on his afterwards repeating this conversation, she found that he knew nothing of her character even from report, and only described her in so unpleasant a light from his wish to deter Celestina from finding an asylum in her house, anger conquered her concern, and even her complaisance, and she besought him in very strong terms never again to name Lady Horatia Howard to her, unless he could prevail upon himself to remember that she deserved, from her character rather than her rank, the respect of every man, and particularly of every *gentleman*.

---

1   Tact, empathy.

Vavasour had desisted then from talking of her in this style; but he was not at all more reconciled to the abode Celestina had chosen; where, if he was admitted to see her at all, it would probably be only in the presence of those who would be little affected with his professions of that love which every day became a greater torment to him, and little dazzled by that fortune which he had to offer as the price of its return.

Celestina, however, to whom he had repeatedly said that he would visit her, thought she could not too soon apprize Lady Horatia of her situation; and the first hour they were alone together, Lady Horatia expressed such a desire to know all that had passed in regard to Willoughby, since she saw her on her journey into Scotland, that Celestina, without hesitation, but not without great emotion, related it all, and put into her hands the letters received from Willoughby.

Lady Horatia read them, and attended with great interest to what Celestina related of the sudden appearance of Montague Thorold and the avowed pretensions of Vavasour; and after deliberating some time, she smiled, yet not with a smile of pleasure, and said—"It appears, my love, as if you were only come to tantalize me for a moment with your company; for beset as you are by these young men, I see I shall never be able to keep you long."

"Ah! Madam!" replied Celestina, "neither Mr. Vavasour nor Mr. Thorold can excite a wish in me to quit your protection while it is convenient to you to afford it to me; and for my first, my most beloved friend! my—what shall I call him?—he talks not of returning to England: and if he does—"

"And if he does return," interrupted Lady Horatia, "you must, and rightly formed as your heart is, you do I am sure understand, that while the faintest mist of doubt hangs over you, you ought never to meet him, unless indeed one of you were married."

"Allow me to ask, Madam," said Celestina, in a tremulous voice, "allow me to ask your Ladyship, who were so well acquainted with Mrs. Willoughby, whether from any recollection of remarks made in her life time, you have any persuasion as to the foundation of those doubts."

"You might have seen," replied Lady Horatia, "from the purport of a letter I wrote to you while you were in Scotland, that I had even then heard rumours of the cause of your separation from Willoughby, which Lady Castlenorth had very industriously set forth. I judged, from what I then heard, that if it was not true, her art would be so effectually exerted that you would never discover the deception; and that you must be rendered unhappy. It was therefore I advised you to detach yourself as much as you could from what is childishly called a first love. I thought, that what Mr. Willoughby was then said to be on the point of completing—his marriage with Miss Fitz-Hayman—was the very best thing he could do, both for his own sake and your's: for if it should be found you are related, the very idea is attended with too much horror to be dwelt upon; and even if it is a fabrication of Lady Castlenorth's, unless it can be clearly proved to be so, your whole life might be embittered by it; besides, my dear Celestina, how could Mr. Willoughby, circumstanced as I understand he is in regard to money matters, how could he afford to marry you?"

Celestina sighed deeply from the recollection of the arrangements as to all those affairs which Willoughby had so fondly made, and to which she had so fondly listened; then recovering herself, she repeated her question, which she thought Lady Horatia had evaded—"But has your Ladyship any recollection of circumstances in Mrs. Willoughby's conduct or life, that give you reason to believe this unhappy story may *not* be the fabrication of Lady Castlenorth?"

"Not from my own knowledge," replied she, "for I was in Italy with General Howard, who was then in an ill state of health, at the time Mr. Willoughby's father died and for two years afterwards. When I returned to England, I was absorbed in domestic uneasiness, and heard, without attending much to them, those gossiping stories which fly about for a week or a month till some newer scandal causes them to be forgotten. Yet I do recollect, I own, hearing some hints of Mrs. Willoughby's partiality for Mr. Everard, and that they were supposed to be privately married: but I accounted for it, when I attended to it at all, by recollecting that Mrs. Willoughby was, at the time of her husband's death, a young and beautiful woman, with a good fortune, and an admirable understanding; advantages, which, while they created envy and malignity in the minds of an hundred people who possessed nothing of all that, among her own sex; produced as many pretenders to her favour among the other; every one of whom, though some were men of rank and all of course eminent enough in their own eyes, were dismissed by her on their first application with a polite but positive refusal. These men were piqued, and these women were spiteful; and they together found out a reason for the unheard of refusal of a young and admired widow, by supposing her attached to her son's tutor; not one of them, from the information of their own hearts, being able to conceive it possible that she made this sacrifice to maternal tenderness, and refused her hand to a second husband, because she would suffer nothing to interrupt the attention she owed to the children of the first."

"You do not then believe," said Celestina eagerly—"you do not then believe, my dear Madam, that there is any truth in this odious story?"

"Pardon me," answered Lady Horatia; "I did not say so."

"Gracious heaven!" exclaimed Celestina, "is it possible you can believe it?"

"My dear young friend," said she calmly, "I have lived so long in the world, that though I do not hastily and on slight ground believe such a report, yet I should not *wonder* were it in the event to be verified."

Celestina, who had always in her own heart opposed the idea of her being the daughter of Mrs. Willoughby, though she felt and submitted to the necessity of seeing Willoughby no more while one doubt remained unsatisfied, now changed colour, affected as well by the manner of Lady Horatia as by what she said. She had not, however, courage to press her farther, but spoke of the visit intended her by Mr. Vavasour—"I wish it were possible," said she, "to convince him at once that I shall never listen to the proposal with which he is pleased to honour me. As Willoughby's friend," added she, and sighed, "I shall be always glad to see him; but, in any other light, never—"

"I think you wrong however," replied Lady Horatia, "in wishing so hastily to dismiss him. He is a man of family, of fortune, and, as you allow, not disagreeable in his person; and for his morals, they are not worse, I suppose, than those of other young men; he is allowed, I think, to be generous, good tempered, and not to want sense. If every idea of Willoughby is at an end, why not relieve yourself and him from a state of uneasy retrospection by receiving the address of one whom he cannot disapprove."

"Are you in earnest, Lady Horatia?" cried Celestina.

"Certainly I am," replied she: "at least, I venture very seriously to advise you not dismiss Vavasour so hastily, but receive him as an acquaintance till you are sure you disapprove of him as a lover."

"Dear Madam!" resumed Celestina, "were I capable of giving away my hand so lightly, is Mr. Vavasour a man who you would think could make me happy?"

"Nay," replied Lady Horatia, "if there is any body whom you prefer that is another point: I only say, that if you feel yourself perfectly disengaged, I cannot think Vavasour ought to be dismissed hastily. Perhaps half the young women in London would think a more desirable match could not offer."

This conversation was interrupted by the entrance of a servant, who announced the arrival of the person who was the subject of it; and Vavasour immediately entered the room.

He condescended to pay to Lady Horatia more respect than he generally showed to those who were indifferent to him. Hers was, however, that sort of company in which he by no means found himself at ease; and his eagerness to entertain Celestina alone, once or twice broke through the restraint which he imposed upon himself.

Lady Horatia, who was candid and liberal, saw in him only an unformed and unsteady young man, whose morals and manners required nothing but time and good company to render estimable. She saw the prejudice Celestina seemed to entertain towards him, as a mere prejudice; and on his rising to depart, gave him a general invitation to her house.

Celestina, who knew the refinement of her mind, and the delicacy of her taste, was amazed at her seeming to approve him; and when he was gone, ventured to say—"What does your Ladyship think of Mr. Vavasour?"

"Why really very well," replied she. "He is very young, and quite unformed; but with those giddy manners, and amid that unpolished conversation, there is no want of understanding."

Celestina again sighed. "No," answered she, "no want of understanding certainly; for Willoughby was not likely to select him for his friend had that been wanting: but yet they were so unlike—so very unlike—that I have often wondered at their long and intimate friendship. Vavasour is so head long, so impetuous, so self-willed, and sometimes so boisterous, while Willoughby, with more imagination, more genius, more strength of understanding, is so calm, so reasonable, so attentive to every body—"

She was too much affected to proceed in the catalogue of his virtues, a subject on which she had hardly ever touched before; but stopped, from the emotion she felt; and Lady Horatia, who saw and pitied the source of that emotion, changed the conversation.

Vavasour, flattered by the reception he had met with from the present protectress of Celestina, and more in love than ever in proportion as she was in his opinion infinitely handsomer now than ever, was now very frequent in his visits; while Celestina's whole mind was occupied by the necessity she was under of writing to Willoughby, and the difficulty she was under how to answer with propriety such a letter as that she had received from him. At length, with many efforts, and more tears, the letter was written and approved of by Lady Horatia; and Celestina endeavoured, in compliance with the wishes of her friend, and with more earnestness than success, to dismiss from her mind some of its corrosive sensations, and to enter, if not with avidity, at least with cheerfulness, into that style of fashionable life, which, though she could not always enjoy, she never failed to adorn.

Chapter VIII

Vavasour had been with her every day since her arrival in town, which was almost a week, and Montague Thorold had never appeared. While Celestina at once wondered at his absence and rejoiced at it, (though perhaps her sensations were mingled with a slight degree of mortification,) for she disdained every species of coquetry, she yet felt humiliated by the sudden cessation of that attachment which he had taken such pains to convince her, could not be destroyed even by despair.

Impatience, however, to hear of Willoughby, was still predominant in her mind: and for this purpose she wished to see Lady Molyneux. No acquaintance subsisted between her and Lady Horatia: and therefore she determined to write and beg leave to wait on her old friend. This she executed in a note to the following purport:

"Miss de Mornay being in town for a short time, solicits permission to wait on Lady Molyneux at any time when her Ladyship may be disengaged."

This note was delivered to Lady Molyneux in company. She read it, and as if she had forgotten totally the claim Celestina had upon her from their having been brought up together, and from her mother's fondness for her, she asked carelessly whether the messenger waited for an answer; the servant replied, that he did. Lady Molyneux had formed an idea that Celestina, of whom she had not thought for many months, was now wandering about the world in a dependent and inferior situation, and might perhaps expect an invitation to stay with her, which she had no inclination to give; she therefore in a cold and careless way bade the footman tell the person who brought the message, that being then engaged with company she could not write an answer, but would take an opportunity of letting Miss de Mornay know when she should be at home. She then entered again into conversation with her guests; and it was not till the next day that she remembered having heard from Celestina at all; when seeing the note on her table as she was going to dress for the opera,[1] she gave it to her maid, and bade her put her in mind to send an answer to it and fix the first morning she should be disengaged.

Celestina in the mean time received the verbal answer to her note with more concern than surprise. She had not expected much kindness from Matilda, who during so many months had never once written to, or enquired after her; but she could not without internal anguish reflect that it was the daughter of her more than mother, the friend of her orphan youth, and the sister of Willoughby, who was thus insensible of all those feelings which swelled her heart when the scenes of that orphan youth, and the pleasures of that infantine friendship, were remembered.

Amid these painful reflections, however, there was one that gave her some degree of consolation. She thought that Lady Molyneux could not, either from any knowledge of her own, or from the reports spread by Lady Castlenorth, believe that any relationship by blood subsisted between them; for she supposed it to be impossible for her in that case to treat with so much cold neglect a person whom she knew to be her sister. On this, therefore, she dwelt, as a circumstance favourable to the notion she most wished to entertain; and as two or three days passed on without her hearing from Lady Molyneux, her eagerness to enquire of her subsided into a strong belief that she knew nothing.

Vavasour assiduously attended every day at the house of Lady Horatia during this interval, and contrived to obtain for himself some degree of interest in her favour. The openness and candour of his temper, was with her an apology for half his faults; while his youth and natural vivacity obtained his pardon for the rest. His fortune was splendid and his family ancient and respectable; while his person was such as could hardly fail to please; and his manners, careless and wild as they were, appeared to advantage in the eyes of Lady Horatia; who had been disgusted by the coldness and apathy, either real or affected, of many of those young men of fashion who frequented her house.

On Celestina, however, the frequent opportunities she had of

---

1   The Opera House in the Haymarket, designed by Sir John Vanbrugh, opened in 1705. A box cost half a guinea (ten shillings and sixpence) a night, gallery seats five shillings. The building burned down in June 1789, a few months after the fictional time here, and was rebuilt.

observing Vavasour, had a very opposite effect. In *her* mind a standard of perfection had been early formed, and every man she now saw was pleasing or otherwise as they resembled or differed from Willoughby. She continued therefore to treat Vavasour with encreasing coldness; and saw with concern that Lady Horatia was every day more solicitous for his success.

Willoughby, in the mean time, continued to wander about Europe without any fixed plan, and merely flying from himself. Still anxious to gather information on the subject which had destroyed all the happiness of his life, and having little hopes of obtaining any but by means of Lady Castlenorth, he often conquered his reluctance, and visited his uncle at a villa he now inhabited near Naples; where he was always received with pleasure, and where, save only on the point which alone interested him, Lady Castlenorth seemed to descend from her natural character, to endeavour by every means in her power to gratify and oblige him: and her lord, who really loved his nephew as much as his imbecility of mind allowed him to love any body, and who saw in him and in his alliance with his daughter, the only chance of perpetuating a family which was the great object of his pride, became hourly more eager to see him, and more gratified by his company. It has been observed, that there are two reasons which equally operate in determining some people to marry—love and hatred; and something resembling both these sentiments agitated the heart of Miss Fitz-Hayman. Of an involuntary preference to her cousin, she had been sensible from the first moment she saw him; and his indifference, his preference of Celestina, and even his positively declining the honour of her hand, had mortified without curing her of her partiality; though resentment and disdain were mingled with the inclination she could not conquer, and which neither his absence nor his coldness had prevented from gaining on her heart. When she saw him again, new force was given to this passion; he was less handsome, less animated; but more interesting and more pleasing; while his melancholy and dejection, though created by another object, gave him so many charms in the opinion of Miss Fitz-Hayman, that her pride yielded to them; and as it was now very certain that he had no attachment but to Celestina, whom, since she fully believed their relationship, she knew he never could marry, she doubted not of being able to inspire him with an affection for her, and, in returning to England his wife, of fulfilling at once her parents' wishes and her own.

Lady Castlenorth, whose love of intrigue time had by no means diminished, and whose arrogance had been deeply wounded by the failure of her original plan, which she fancied Willoughby would with so much eagerness have embraced, was now doubly anxious to avail herself of the advantage she had gained by having prevented the intended union of Willoughby and Celestina. Pique and resentment operated upon her mind with even more force than attachment and regard would have on another. Besides, in the marriage of her daughter with any man of superior rank and independent fortune, she found great probability that her influence would be lessened and her government disclaimed; but in uniting her daughter with Willoughby, whose fortune was in disorder and whose temper was remarkably easy, she foresaw the continuation of her power, and that she should neither see her daughter take place of her,[1] or escape from her influence.

Whatever was the wish of her friends, the assiduous Mrs. Calder officiously adopted; and when she found how much Lord Castlenorth had set his heart on concluding the marriage between his daughter and her nephew, she applied all her rhetoric to prove its advantages, and all her art to secure its success.

Willoughby was unconscious of the plans that were thus forming in the family of his uncle, and did not think it possible that their pride would allow them to solicit again an alliance which he had once declined: he therefore went to them without any apprehension that he was encouraging expectations he never meant to fulfil, and had indeed no other design than to lay in wait for traces of that involved mystery, which he still thought had been created by the intrigues and machinations of Lady Castlenorth.

In art, however, she was so much his superior, that the very means he adopted to obtain satisfaction, was, in her hands, a means of bewildering more deeply. She now affected the most perfect candour; and whenever she saw him touching with a tender hand on the subject, she appeared to feel for his uneasiness, and ready to give him every satisfaction in her power.

Willing to avail himself of this apparent disposition in his favour, he one day, when he was sitting alone with Lady Castlenorth, asked her, whether she had now no traces of Hannah Biscoe, the servant who alone seemed possessed of the circumstances into which he most wished to enquire. Lady Castlenorth answered with great apparent ingenuousness, that she did not exactly know, as she had no connection at all with her, but that if he wished to make any enquiry her woman should write out the directions to[2] her relations, which she did not herself recollect.

---

1 Take a higher rank than hers.
2 Addresses of.

Willoughby eagerly seized on this offer, and begged that these directions might be immediately written out for him. Lady Castlenorth instantly called her woman, and questioned her as to her recollection of the abode of the relations of this Hannah Biscoe; the woman named what she knew; her lady directed her to put it down, and Willoughby left the house, flattering himself that he had at length obtained a clue which might lead him to escape from the labyrinth of error and mistake where he had so severely suffered.

It was, however, by no means Lady Castlenorth's plan to suffer Willoughby to return to England in search of this woman, whose direction she seemed so willing to give him; and as from the eagerness and agitation he expressed on receiving this paper, it appeared but too likely that he meditated going himself, in order to preclude the possibility of his views being again frustrated, she found that all her art would be necessary to prevent his escaping her.

Fortunately for her views, Lord Castlenorth was seized a few hours afterwards with one of those illnesses which had so often reduced him to the brink of the grave; and the presence of his nephew, which he so earnestly desired, the generous and feeling heart of Willoughby could not deny; while he endured the cruellest restraint in staying, and thought every hour an age till he could go himself to England, and renew his hitherto hopeless research after the real situation of Celestina.

Thus passed, however, a month after the arrival of Celestina in London; and then the arrival of an English gentleman at Naples brought him her letter, written in answer to that she received at York. Nothing could equal the impatience with which he had expected this letter, but the pain he felt at reading it. He learned by it that she was returning to London, where he fancied so many objects would combine to soften her concern for their separation; and he fancied the letter expressed too much calmness, and that she submitted to the separation which he had himself indicated as too likely to be inevitable without feeling half that regret and anguish which he expected she would have described. The reluctance she expressed to be left to the protection of Vavasour, made him believe his presence interfered with her preference to some other person— a preference, of which the very suspicion threw him into agonies at the very moment his reason told him that he ought not to think of her for himself. Jealousy now added to the pangs of disappointed love, and the letter which Celestina had endeavoured to word so as to calm and sooth him, and to teach him to submit to that necessity of which he allowed the force, seemed to him to breath only indifference, and to prove that she saw him, without regret, relinquish his claim to those affections, which were already in possession of another.

All his sufferings were confirmed and encreased, when a day or two afterwards he had an opportunity of conversing with Mr. Jarvis, the gentleman who brought the letter, and who was hastening to Rome. He had been often in company with Celestina at parties where she attended Lady Horatia Howard; and believing, as all the world now did, that Willoughby was certainly to be married to Miss Fitz-Hayman; and that the marriage of Celestina would be a subject of satisfaction to him, he related without hesitation the reports he had heard of her being soon to give her hand to Mr. Vavasour.

To the amazement Willoughby expressed at the first intimation of such a match, Jarvis, who entirely mistook its cause, said—"Yes, it is wonderful to be sure, considering all we know of Vavasour, that he should seriously intend to marry."

So acute was the pain which the intelligence Willoughby had just received gave him, that he could make no answer to this; and Jarvis fancying him out of spirits for some reason or other which he never thought of enquiring after, soon left him to meditate on what he had heard.

There was room for "meditation even to madness,"[1] when he recollected a thousand circumstances that had till now appeared of no moment; he was convinced that Vavasour had long admired Celestina; he had himself resigned her, or at least intimated that he dared not think of her; and the person, the fortune, the impetuous ardour of Vavasour, which his agitated mind represented as irresistible, now all crouded on his recollection, and he doubted not but that before he could reach England, Celestina would have given herself away.

Yet with the horrid mystery unremoved, on what pretence could he wish or even think of impeding a marriage with a man of whom his regard was evinced by his long friendship, and who had so affluent a fortune? As a lover, he could himself no longer interfere; as her relation, he could not bear to consider himself; and were he only such, an alliance with Vavasour could not be objected to on any reasonable grounds.

The longer he reflected, therefore, on what he had heard, the

---

1   Cf. *Othello* 2.1.297-98: "practising upon his peace and quiet/ Even to madness."

more unable he became to support his reflections; and they concluded in a resolution to set out immediately for England; a determination which he communicated to his uncle the same day, who was affected by it even to tears.

Lady Castlenorth had, in conversation with Mr. Jarvis, heard the report of Celestina's intended marriage, and knew immediately how to account for the extreme uneasiness Willoughby betrayed, and his sudden resolution to depart for England. When Jarvis, who proceeded immediately on his journey, was gone, she found an opportunity a few hours afterwards to speak to Willoughby on English news, and the change of his countenance confirmed her conjectures. This was an occasion not to be lost; she ventured, what she usually avoided, to name Celestina, and to express her satisfaction that she was likely to be so well married. "After all the conversation there has been about this young person," said she, affecting to have a great deal of feeling for her, "I am very glad that the poor girl will be so well established. A man of Vavasour's independent fortune can well afford to please himself; and I doubt not but that you and Lady Molyneux must on every account rejoice at her change of name, and that nothing more will be said of her origin." Though Lady Castlenorth affected to speak with sentiment, and to soften her voice, her piercing and enquiring eyes were demanding from the countenance of Willoughby that explanation which she knew it would give of his real sentiments; and she saw the blood forsake his cheeks, his lips turn white and tremble, and a mingled expression of doubt, fear, anger, and disdain, marked on his features. "If I were certain, Madam," said he, "that all the odious reports, on which you, who first promulgated them, have invariably refused to satisfy me as you might do—if I were sure they were all true—"

"If!" interrupted Lady Castlenorth: "can you then doubt their truth? Will you compel me to make, by adducing those proofs, a matter public which you ought on every account to wish might be buried in eternal oblivion?"

"Will I compel you, Madam! Yes surely I will if the means are in my power. 'Tis for this only I have been so much with you; not to compel you indeed, but in the hope of prevailing upon you, if you really possess the evidence you have often meditated, to give it me all without reserve."

"Well," cried Lady Castlenorth, "I have now given you a direction to the only person who is in possession of this evidence. You might have procured it as long since as when I interfered to save you from the horrors of a marriage which must have rendered you and the object of your unhappily placed affection miserable for ever: but then you flew from me, and resented my friendship as if it had been an injury. Since that time it is not my fault if you have been unable to find this person, whom I have never secreted, and of whom I know little or nothing. Satisfied in having saved you from an abyss of guilt and misery, I trusted to time and your own principles to convince you of the injustice your suspicions did me. You have searched for proofs in those places where your mother is said to have been with her young charge: tell me, have you ever found any reason to believe the facts I told you to be of my invention—to have been totally unfounded?"

Willoughby was conscious he had not; yet at the same moment he discovered that Lady Castlenorth had watched him, and knew of the journies he had made to Hières and to other places. Vexed and angry, not knowing what to think, or whether he was imposed on by her superior cunning, or was needlessly tormenting himself in pushing the enquiry farther, he could not command the various uneasy sensations with which he was agitated; and therefore abruptly leaving the room, he hastened to his lodgings, and gave directions for his immediate departure for England.

He was concerned, however, for his uncle, and returned in the evening to take leave of him: he found him sitting with Mrs. Calder, who was reading to him a sort of *catalogue raisonnée*[1] of the various ills to which the human body is subject; and as they passed in melancholy review before him, he stopped her to consult her on his own symptoms, and to enquire of her whether she did not think such and such complaints were about to add to his bodily infirmities. Mrs. Calder, who was always obliged to every body who fancied her skill enabled her to answer such questions, was delighted with the opportunity this afforded her of exhibiting her knowledge to Willoughby, from whom she could never procure the smallest voluntary attention; and the conversation became so irksome, that having waited near an hour, and seeing it not likely to end, Willoughby at length started up and approached to take his uncle's hand, when Miss Fitz-Hayman, in all the languor of unhappy love, swam into the room.

On her entrance, Willoughby sat down again, as being unwilling to have her suppose he rudely fled from her approach. She put on an air of affected humility, and looked as if she thanked him for even this slight mark of attention. She gave a loud and deep sigh, pro-

---

1 Annotated or detailed catalogue to an exhibition.

longed as much as possible; her eyes, robbed of their fire, were turned mournfully upon him—"You are going from us, Mr. Willoughby?" said she, in a subdued and faint voice.

He replied, that business, which could not longer be delayed, made his return to England necessary.

Another deep sigh was all the lady's answer to this information: but Lord Castlenorth cried—"I am sorry to hear you say so, George—very sorry. I did hope that we might have all returned together as soon as my complaints subside a little. As to business, you ought to remember that all your money matters might be easily settled if you pleased."

"I thank you, Sir," replied Willoughby, who saw whither the discourse would tend; "but those matters are the least of my concern."

"Stay, however, one day," said Lord Castlenorth, "that you may execute some business for me. Surely, nephew, you will oblige me so far."

Though every hour's delay was death to him, he at length agreed, on his uncle's repeated entreaties, to stay four and twenty hours longer at Naples; and then leaving the room, he was followed by the officious Mrs. Calder, who desiring leave to say half a dozen words to him alone, he suffered her to shew him into another room.

She put on a most rueful countenance, stroked her handkerchief, plaited her ruffles,[1] and uttering an "oh dear!" between a sigh and a groan, she continued thus—"My dear good Sir! I wish to have a little conversation relative to your situation in this dear worthy family, for every member of which my poor heart bleeds."

"And yet, Madam," interrupted Willoughby impatiently, "there is, perhaps, hardly a family among your acquaintance who are, in the opinion of the world, so little objects of compassion."

"The world!" exclaimed the lady. "Lord bless me, what signifies the opinions of the world? The world cannot see as I do into all their feelings. There's your most excellent uncle, as worthy a man as ever existed, sinking, poor good dear man! under five complaints, all incurable, and denied, alas! the only satisfaction this world has to give him—seeing his darling daughter settled to his wishes, which would smooth his path to heaven, and leave him nothing but bodily pain—which is severe enough—nothing but bodily pain, as I observed, to contend with. Oh! Sir, what heart felt satisfaction it must be to you!

---

1   The ruffled edgings to the neck of her gown extend into ties, which she twists.

what comfortable reflection for a good heart, such as inhabits your breast no doubt—I say, what delight it would be to you, to hold forth the amiable hand that should—

'Rock the cradle of reposing age,'[1]

and sooth the latter days of so excellent and worthy an uncle."

The whine, and the hypocritical grimace with which this speech was delivered, would have conquered the gravity of Willoughby at any other time: but he now felt his disgust irritated by impatience, amounting almost to rage; but he repressed his feelings with difficulty, unwilling by opposition to lengthen the conversation, which Mrs. Calder suffered not to languish, but thus went on—"Ah dear! what a melancholy reflection, as I observed, it is, to consider, that, poor good man, this is not likely to happen; and instead of it, this darling daughter, this fine young woman, heiress to such a noble fortune, so beautiful, so accomplished, so elegant—undeniably the first match in England—so lovely in person, so amiable in mind, so elevated in understanding—far, alas! from being happy, sees her youth pass away in a hopeless passion, which from her infancy she has been taught to cherish, and which now her reason, aided by her affronted pride, tries in vain to repress. Oh! Mr. Willoughby! Mr. Willoughby! the happiness that you refuse, by how many would be courted! the heart that you disdain to accept, by how many would be adored! Dear creature! when I see how thin she is grown, and know the cause of it so well!—when I hear her sigh, and know how injurious it is to her dear delicate constitution, I really Sir—you will forgive my zeal—have looked upon you with amazement, and have asked myself whether you have eyes—whether you have a heart—"

"To what, Madam," interrupted Willoughby, who could no longer endure her harangue patiently—"to what does all this tend?"

"Tend, dear Sir!" replied Mrs. Calder; "why certainly to open your eyes if possible to a sense of the happiness you are throwing away; to prevail on you to answer the expectations of all your friends, consult your own interest, and to become all you ought to be."

"You mean well, I conclude, Madam," answered Willoughby, "by all this; but you mistake greatly, when you suppose that the alliance to which you allude would contribute to the happiness of any of the

---

1 Alexander Pope, "Epistle to Dr. Arbuthnot," 408.

parties for whom you are interested. I have no heart to offer Miss Fitz-Hayman; and if the partiality which you represent exists any where but in your own imagination, it would be ungenerous to encourage and unworthy to avail myself of it, feeling as I do that I never can answer it as I am very willing to allow the young lady's merits deserve: excuse me, therefore, if I entreat of you never to consider me as being likely to be more closely united with the family of Lord Castlenorth than I at present am, and to declare to you, that by persisting in pressing it, my uncle will put it out of my power to testify for him that regard and affection which I really feel."

Willoughby then left the room; and Mrs. Calder, piqued and mortified at the little success of her rhetoric, went reluctantly to give an account to Lady Castlenorth, by whom she had been employed, of the ill success of her embassy.

Chapter IX

Willoughby, notwithstanding every effort and every art made use of to detain him, pursued his way to England: but at Paris, the fatigue he had undergone, and the anxiety which had so long weighed on his spirits, combined to throw him into one of those fevers, to which, from his infancy, he had been subject; and for three weeks he was in the most imminent danger. Amid the wild ravings of the delirium that perpetually occurred during the severest paroxysms of the complaint, he called incessantly on Celestina; and complaining that Lady Castlenorth had taken her from him, entreated of his servant, a man who had lived with him for some years, to send for her that he might see her before he died. This, in the simplicity of his heart, his faithful attendant would have done, having no idea that any thing could be of more consequence than the wishes of his dear master, for whose life he was so cruelly alarmed; but when he asked him whither he was to send, Willoughby put his hand on his heart, sighed deeply, and replied, either that he did not know or that it would be of no effect; and that, indifferent what became of him, she had already refused to come to him, and was gone to Scotland with Vavasour.

When the violence of the disease subsided, he ceased to name her; and his servant, afraid of renewing his recollection, carefully avoided any hint of what he had dwelt upon during his delirious ravings. Slowly, and with two relapses, he recovered strength enough to proceed to Calais; but nine weeks had elapsed since the information he had received from Vavasour; and it was near three months after that time before he arrived in London.

His first enquiry was after Vavasour, who was, he found, in Staffordshire; and his heart was relieved by the intelligence, for he dreaded least he should have met him in London, perhaps married to Celestina. His next was after his sister, whom he still loved, and in favour of whom he was willing to forget all the neglect he had experienced from her, as well as the causes of displeasure given him by her husband.

After Celestina he feared to ask by a direct message to herself, and he therefore sought somebody who could tell where she now was, of which he concluded he should have intelligence from Lady Molyneux.

Lady Molyneux attended his summons; and while he embraced her, with tears of fraternal fondness, from a thousand tender recollections that crouded on his heart, he saw her equally unmoved by their meeting and unconcerned at his illness, of which he still retained melancholy proofs in his altered countenance and reduced figure. He took an early opportunity of turning the discourse on Celestina; and saw, with encreased amazement, that far from being interested in the enquiry which had occupied his whole thoughts so long, Matilda was perfectly indifferent about it, or if he moved her a moment from the stillness of fashionable apathy, she shrunk from the subject with something like disgust; seemed afraid of the trouble of investigation, and careless how it might terminate; wishing rather to hear nothing about it, than to hazard—not the tarnishing her mother's honour, for to that she seemed insensible, but the probability of being obliged to own for a sister, one whom she had hitherto considered a dependent; and of seeing her brother, from a point of honour, undertake to provide for her as a relation. Avarice, the heterogeneous[1] child of selfish vanity, was become a leading feature in the character of Matilda: she found so many uses for money in adorning and in indulging herself that she loved nothing so well, except the adulation it procured for her; and so much power has this odious passion to pervert the heart, that instead of feeling concern in contemplating the sunken features and palid cheek of her brother, she could not, nor indeed did she attempt to check, a half formed idea of the pecuniary advantage she should receive from his death.

---

1 Incongruous, unexpected.

While such were her thoughts, Willoughby asked her when she had last seen Celestina?

"Oh!" replied she, "I have seen her only once in a room, and that was by accident. I was never at home when she called; and I hate that old Lady Horatia Howard that she lives with, and so took no great pains to meet them when I returned her visit.[1] I have seen her though in public five or six times lately, but the girl seemed to me so very much altered, and to give herself such intolerable airs, that I rather shunned than sought her."

"Airs!" cried Willoughby. "She must indeed be greatly changed if she deserves such censure: but tell me, Matilda—what kind of airs?"

"Oh! the airs of a beauty," answered she, "which you first taught her to assume, and which she has made a tolerable progress in, since this old cat of fashion has taken it into her head to make such a fuss about her, and since she has been surrounded with such a set of senseless boys. There's your friend Vavasour constantly one of her suit,[2] and there was a notion of his being fool enough to marry her, but I fancy that was given out merely by her exorbitant vanity, for I dare say Vavasour knows better."

The heart of Willoughby sunk within him; but he was unable to express what he felt: and Lady Molyneux went on—"However, I have heard since, I think, that the girl has been addressed by another young fellow—one of the Thorolds I think—whom I have lately seen with her, which would be more suitable and more likely to be a match."

"You have seen her then often?" said Willoughby, in a faint and faultering voice.

"Yes, in public," replied his sister; "but I have had no conversation with her." Lady Molyneux then changed the conversation, and soon afterwards left her brother more unhappy than she had found him.

He was by no means able to see Celestina in his present state of wretched uncertainty: yet to know that by traversing two or three streets he could once more behold her, once more gaze on that lovely countenance, and hear that voice so soothing, so enchanting to his ear; was to him a state of tantalizing misery, from which he knew nothing could relieve him but detecting the falshood of Lady Castlenorth's report; and this he could only hope to do by another journey into Yorkshire, in order to find that Hannah Biscoe to whom

---

1 When Lady Molyneux left her card at the house, a mere formality.
2 Crowd of attendants; admirers.

he now thought he had certainly obtained a direction, and this he proposed doing immediately.

Celestina, however, surrounded by crouds of admirers; Celestina, forgetting all the tenderness she once felt for him and rendering all his researches fruitless even if they proved to him that he might again plead for the renewal of that affection, was an idea that unceasingly tormented him; and so painfully did the intelligence affect him which Lady Molyneux had given, that the ferment of his spirits produced a return of his fever; in a slighter degree, but still so as to confine him to his room; where, in a few days, he received a visit from Vavasour.

Vavasour was totally unconscious of the species of distress which Willoughby suffered; and since he himself had resigned her, and agreed to complete his engagements with the family of Castlenorth, for so his conduct had been generally understood in England, had no notion that the addresses of another, and particularly of his friend, could be otherwise than pleasing to him. He began, therefore without remarking the concern and coldness of Willoughby, imputing it only to his visibly deranged health, to relate to him his own views in regard to Celestina, and to complain of her preference of Montague Thorold. "The devil take me," said he, "if there is in England or in Europe another woman for whom I would take a fifth part of the trouble which this bewitching girl has already given me. Curse me if I am not ashamed of myself when I think what a whining puppy she has made of me; ten times I have left her, and ten times have returned, to prove to her that she might use me like a dog."

"Miss de Mornay," said Willoughby, in a voice affected by the various sensations he felt—"Miss de Mornay must be greatly changed, Sir, if she is become capable of any improper levity towards any gentleman who professes regard for her: at the same time you will recollect, Mr. Vavasour, that she is mistress of herself, and at liberty to reject those whose offers may not be acceptable to her. From the experiments which you have been pleased to make, (though from our long friendship I should rather have expected you to have applied to me before you made them)—from the experiments you have been pleased to make, it seems clear that Miss de Mornay has no favourable intentions towards you, and I would advise you by all means to decline the pursuit."

"May I perish if I do!" replied Vavasour, with all his usual impetuosity. "No, George, unless it can be made to appear that young Thorold—that little curatizing fellow—without a shilling, and with nothing but his impudence and scraps of plays to recommend him, has better pretensions than I have, curse me if I will give it up!"

This second intimation of Celestina's encouraging the addresses of Montague Thorold, was a second dagger to the sick heart of Willoughby. He dreaded an explanation, which, while it might serve perhaps to subdue all his fears as to Vavasour, might create others equally insupportable. He could not, however, remain many minutes in the breathless agitation of such suspence, and therefore said—"I really don't know any thing about Thorold. I hardly recollect that there was such a man."

"What!" exclaimed Vavasour, "not know him? Not know that she went immediately from Alvestone to the house of that old priest his father?"

"Yes," answered Willoughby, "that I certainly knew; for it was by my request that the elder Mr. Thorold became her guardian."

"Well, nothing was so natural, I suppose, as for his reverence to delegate the trust to his son; and as his deputy, I suppose it was, that he went with his ward to Scotland, and was her guardian all the time she was among the highlands and the islands."

"Impossible!" cried Willoughby. "He did not—could not have been there."

"He was by heaven!" exclaimed Vavasour; "and when I met Celestina, with your letter, at York, I found that young fellow attending on her and Mrs. Elphinstone: but *I* was authorised by yourself to wait on her; and I obliged *him* there to resign a post, which, when I think of his having so long filled, and apparently with her approbation, by all that's diabolical I could tear his puritanical soul out!"

Nothing that Willoughby had ever felt was equal to the anguish which pressed on his heart at this moment. The coldness he fancied he had found in Celestina's last letter was now accounted for; and all the warmth of grateful praise, with which in her former letters she had spoken of Mr. Thorold, was imputed to her growing affection for his son. Lost as she might be, and probably was to him for ever before this intelligence, unless he could content himself with that share of sisterly affection which was all she ought to bestow, there was something so terrible to his imagination in her feeling a warm attachment to another, that he could not think of it without horror, nor conceal from Vavasour the effect it had upon him. His mildness of manners forsook him; and speaking less like himself than like Vavasour, whose vehemence he seemed to adopt, he cried, in a voice that trembled with passion—"How dared he pretend to Celestina!"

"He not only dared then," interrupted Vavasour, "but dares still;

and has contrived to get Lady Horatia Howard to be of his party. He has fascinated the old woman with his piety and his poetry, and I see very plainly that the young one will throw herself away upon him unless you prevent it."

"May I perish," cried he, "if I do *not!*" Yet at that moment the recollection too forcibly occurred to him that he had no right to prevent it, unless by urging a claim as her relation, from which his soul recoiled. So painfully acute were his present sensations, that he was unable to breathe, and without attending longer to the exhortations of Vavasour, who eagerly pressed him to interfere immediately, he abruptly left the room, and sent by his servant a message to Vavasour, saying he found himself so ill that he was gone to bed; but should be glad he would call again for an hour in the evening.

Instead, however, of attempting to procure that repose which his encreased fever required, he went to the trunk where Celestina's letters were deposited, and with trembling hands taking them out, he ran them over, even from the first she wrote to him after their separation, to the last which Mr. Jarvis had delivered to him at Naples.

His apprehensive jealousy so powerfully awakened, now taught him to fancy, that from the moment of Celestina's acquaintance with Montague Thorold, her letters had become gradually cooler, and that the last two plainly evinced her cheerful acquiescence to that reluctant and only conditional resignation, which *he* had with so much anguish of heart been compelled to send her, while he explained the cruel circumstances that had torn him from her and from happiness.

The longer he dwelt on her letters, the more this idea was strengthened, and the more insupportable it became. His illness, originally occasioned by anxiety, returned upon him; and though without delirium, his fever was nearly as high as when he was in so much danger at Paris.

He now determined to send to Lady Horatia Howard; and he attempted to write to her. But he could hardly command his pen, and found himself wholly unequal to the more difficult task of composing such a letter as could alone be proper. He threw away the paper in despair; and calling his servant, ordered him to find out immediately some means of becoming acquainted with the servants of Lady Horatia Howard, and procure intelligence of what visitors were most at the house, particularly if a Mr. Thorold of Devonshire was there often.

The man hastened to enter on a task by no means difficult to him. He contrived the same afternoon to introduce himself to one of the footmen of Lady Horatia at the porter house[1] he frequented, and learned that his mistress and her young friend, of whom he spoke as of an angel, were gone for a fortnight or three weeks on a visit into Oxfordshire; that Mr. Vavasour used to be a good deal at the house when first Lady Horatia came to town; that now he was much less frequently there; but that Mr. Thorold was there almost every day, and read to the ladies whole evenings; who, since these reading parties at home, went much less into public than they had done before.

This intelligence distracted Willoughby by redoubling every apprehension he had felt. The man, however, was sent back for further information, and made to ask if Mr. Thorold was of their party in the present journey, and if there was any talk among the servants of an intended marriage between him and Miss de Mornay.

In answer to these queries, he had the mortification of hearing that Montague Thorold was to meet the ladies at Oxford; and that it was, in the family, generally understood that he was the accepted lover of Celestina, and highly approved by Lady Horatia.

It was now that the corrosive jealousy that had long tormented him had a decided object, and fixed with the most envenomed power on the heart of Willoughby. The impossibility of his interfering to prevent Celestina giving herself to another while he himself remained in such a situation as the present, and dared not even see her; the little probability he saw of removing the doubts that distracted him; and the apprehensions least if they were for ever effectually withdrawn Celestina would not[2] rejoice that they were so; the cruel idea of Montague Thorold's possessing that heart which he once knew to be all his own, and the preference of that elegant mind of which he had with so much delight contemplated the improvement; were thoughts that incessantly pursued and tormented him: and he had no means of obtaining any information of the conduct of Celestina, or of her return to town, but by his servant, who was now employed whole days to gather from the domestics of Lady Horatia, intelligence, which, when obtained, served only to encrease his misery.

The anecdotes he gathered from his sister served too but to aggravate his distress: yet when he saw her, (as he generally did once every day,) from whatever point the conversation set out, it always

---

1 Ale house.
2 There is no "not" in the original.

ended in questions about Celestina: and Lady Molyneux, who had insensibly familiarised her mind to the idea of her brother's dying a bachelor in consequence of his early disappointment, now saw with concern that his attachment to Celestina, though it prevented his marrying any other, was yet so rooted in his heart, that should he find, as she believed he would, the imagined relationship a mere fiction, he would most undoubtedly return to her with more ardour than before they were parted: and notwithstanding the embarrassed state of his affairs, which every day became more serious, would marry her, and disappoint every view of fortune—encrease of fortune—which her avaricious ambition foresaw might otherwise accrue to her.

Actuated, therefore, by very different motives, she co-operated with Lady Castlenorth in endeavouring to divide him from Celestina; and while one was strengthening the barrier raised between them, the other was trying to convince Willoughby that he ought not to wish for its removal.

The means of doing this were, she thought, to keep him at a distance from Celestina, and to pique his pride by representing her as attached to another. The first point was for the present secured by his illness; and she took care so artfully to insinuate the second, that aided as she was by the report of Vavasour, and by the continual repetitions of what he had seen on the journey from Scotland, that every hour the fatal impression sunk deeper into his heart, and his reason, or his reliance on Celestina's affection, had not sufficient power to resist it.

Thus passed five or six days after his arrival in London. He endeavoured to shake off his illness; for by a journey into Yorkshire, which he could not till it was conquered undertake, he could alone hope to obtain any satisfaction as to the original cause of their separation. Yet even from thence he now no longer dared to look forward to happiness, which even while he was employed in attempting to regain it, seemed escaping from him for ever.

But that he might undertake something to relieve himself from the wretched state he was now in, he put himself into the care of a physician, and set about getting out of an illness he had hitherto neglected or rather indulged. Though very languid, and with a great deal of fever still about him, he went to Lady Molyneux's; and in a day or two afterwards, he found himself better from change of scene and of place, he accompanied her on some of her visits, and called in at a card party, where she told him she must shew herself for a quarter of an hour. The rooms were full; and Lady Molyneux being, notwithstanding her declaration that she should stay so short a time, set down to a card table, Willoughby sauntered into one of the apartments where the younger part of the company were seated at a commerce table; where the first person that met his eyes was Celestina, elegantly dressed and more beautiful than ever, with myriads of charms playing round her face, and cheerfulness and pleasure dancing in her eyes; while on one side sat a young man whom Willoughby immediately recollected to be Montague Thorold, and on the other another gentleman, who, though he seemed to be more a stranger to her, was evidently charmed with her, and unable to keep his eyes from her face.

Fixed to the place where he stood unheeded among some other idle people who were looking on, he remained gazing at her for several minutes. His legs trembled so that it was with difficulty he supported himself, and his heart beat as if it would break. He debated with himself whether he should speak to her, or retire unobserved; but while he yet argued the point, a smile and a whisper that passed between her and Montague Thorold determined him to fly from the torments he felt, and which he found it almost impossible to endure another moment: he stepped hastily away to find his sister and entreat her to go; but so deeply was he affected, that, weakened as he was by illness, he staggered, and might have fallen, had not the shame of betraying so much weakness lent him resolution to reach a chair, where he sat a moment to recover breath and recollection.

Mortified tenderness and disappointed love gave him for an instant a sensation resembling hatred. He fancied he could quit Celestina never again to feel any interest in her fate; but, leaving her to the man she preferred, strengthen himself against his fatal and till now invincible attachment, by contemplating the fatal barrier which he had so long been trying to destroy, and to believe that artifice rather than nature had placed between them. Of this cause of their separation, no part had in fact been removed; and he reproached himself for the absurdity, folly, and even vice of his present conduct. Having argued himself into what he thought a resolution to feel no longer for Celestina, he hurried to Lady Molyneux, and told her, that if her game was not nearly at an end, he must leave her and go home in a chair,[1] as he found himself unable to bear the heat of the room.

---

1   A sedan chair, a mode of hired transport for one person used in towns, was a covered seat in a wooden box, often gilded and painted, and carried by at least two porters.

His sister answered, that she was only settling her winnings, and would attend him in a moment if he would wait for her. He agreed to do so, and going to the door that led out of that into the next room, he leaned against the side of it, turning his eyes as much as possible from the apartment where Celestina was.

Lost in the painful sensations inflicted by distracting jealousy and bitter regret, which he yet struggled to stifle, he distinguished not the objects: all, to him, uninteresting that moved before him. A croud of young people, however, who had just risen from their table, were pressing into another room where refreshments were distributed. He moved a little to make way for them, when he saw, close to him, and even borne against him by her companions, Celestina herself. Her face was at first turned from him; for she was speaking to Montague Thorold, who was on the other side; but finding herself crouding against somebody, she turned to apologise for the rudeness she was guilty of, when the well known figure, the well known face of Willoughby, emaciated and pale as they were, instantly struck her. An involuntary and faint shriek testified the impression they made; and Willoughby, who caught the weak sound of her distressful voice, was at first, by an irresistible impulse, hurried to her assistance; but see-ing the arm of Montague Thorold supporting her, and his counte-nance expressing all the interest he took in her emotion, he imput-ed that emotion to her consciousness of her attachment to her new favourite; and darting at her a look of impatient reproach, he forced himself through the croud, and without looking back, sat down breathless and trembling by Lady Molyneux, who was that moment coming forward to meet him.

The agitation of poor Celestina could not be concealed, nor could she for a moment or two escape from the enquiring eyes of those who remarked it. As soon, however, as she could disengage herself from the throng, she sat down, hardly daring to enquire whether what she had seen was real or visionary. She had returned from Oxfordshire with Lady Horatia only the evening before, and knew nothing of Willoughby's being in England; while, in addition to the amazement the sight of him occasioned, his apparent ill health impressed her with concern, and the displeasure with which he sur-veyed her, with terror.

Montague Thorold, who had seen Willoughby, and whose eyes were never a moment away from Celestina, knew at once the cause of her distress. He followed her, little less affected than she was her-self, to a sopha where she had thrown herself, and asked her, in a faint and tremulous voice, if he should fetch her any thing? she answered "if you please," so low that he scarce distinguished what she said; but stepping a few paces from her, he took a glass of lemonade from a servant and brought it to her. She took it, and carried it to her lips, almost unconscious of what she did, while Montague Thorold leaned over the arm of the sopha on which she sat, and watched the emotions of her countenance, with all the solicitude he felt strongly painted on his own.

At the same moment Willoughby appeared, leading Lady Molyneux through the room. The first objects that he saw as he approached the door, were Celestina and Montague Thorold: but having once seen them, he turned hastily from them; and seeming to give all his attention to his sister, he disappeared.

Celestina's eyes followed him with a look of inexpressible amazement and concern. She seemed to be in a fearful dream; and when she no longer saw him, her eyes were fixed on the door through which he had gone out. She heeded no longer what Montague Thorold said to her; but sat, with a palpitating heart and oppressed breath, till Lady Horatia, after twice speaking to her, roused her from her half formed and confused reflections by reminding her it was time to go.

She followed, in silence, where Lady Horatia led, and at the coach door wished Montague Thorold good night; for the only distinct sensation she felt, was a wish for his absence: but Lady Horatia, who was immediately going home, desired him to return and sup with her; which, without knowing what he did, he consented to, though too conscious while he did it that Celestina had rather be without him, for as he handed her into the coach, he felt her tremble so that she could hardly support herself, and he heard the deep sigh burst from her heart as if it would break.

Lady Horatia had not seen Willoughby, and had no idea of Celestina's sufferings. She talked therefore in her usual way of the people they had seen, and of some books that had been recommended to her; till observing that Celestina, who usually bore her part in the conversation, did not answer, she enquired if she was not well?

"Pretty well, I thank your Ladyship," replied Celestina; "but I am uncommonly fatigued to-night, and have the head ache." This answer satisfied Lady Horatia, who continued to address herself to Montague Thorold, till they arrived in Park-street; where Celestina would immediately have gone to her own room, so unfit was she for conversation and so unable to sustain it; but Lady Horatia ordering her woman to bring a remedy for the head ache, of which Celestina had complained, and that had before been of service to her, she, rather than alarm her kind benefactress, sat down near the supper table to wait for it.

But so great an effect had the violent though short perturbation of her spirits had on her countenance, that Lady Horatia immediately perceived it. "The head ache!" cried she in surprise, and taking Celestina's hand: "my dear, you have surely something worse the matter with you than a common head ache."

"Pray, dearest Madam," replied Celestina, "pardon me if I am utterly unable to say what is the matter. To-morrow I shall be better, and I know you will forgive me till then."

The manner in which she uttered these few words, as, trembling and faint, she advanced towards the door, alarmed and surprised Lady Horatia. She saw, however, by the countenance of Montague Thorold, that he could explain the cause of Celestina's uneasiness; she therefore suffered her to depart, and immediately made the enquiry of him.

He instantly informed her of what he had seen; and with no favourable description of the looks and manner of Willoughby, which had indeed appeared to him to be extremely cruel and insulting toward Celestina. Lady Horatia, with whom Willoughby was no favourite, and who extremely disliked his sister Lady Molyneux, saw his conduct in the same point of view as Thorold represented it; and, after some conversation on the subject, said, that though she was much concerned for the shock Celestina had received, yet that upon the whole it might perhaps be better for her that this circumstance had happened. "For now," said she, "I think she will, possessing, as she does, so much proper pride, be convinced, that even if the story coming from Lady Castlenorth has no foundation, as I myself suppose it has, that still she ought not to indulge her early prejudice in favour of a man, who, whatever he may have pretended or she may have believed, never intended to act honourably by her, and now not only deserts but insults her."

Thorold heartily assented to this opinion, and sat down to supper with a heart somewhat relieved from the extreme uneasiness which the emotion of Celestina on the appearance of Willoughby had given him. Still, however, he could not eat, he could not converse; but as soon as he could disengage himself, he took leave of Lady Horatia, and full of anxiety, and trembling lest all the hopes he had of late so fondly cherished should be blasted, he returned to his lodgings.

Chapter X

Celestina, in retiring to her own room, had hoped to recall her scattered and oppressed spirits, and clearly recollect all that had befallen her: but the angry, the disdainful look which that countenance wore where she had been accustomed to see only the smiles of approbation or the tenderly anxious looks of love, was the image still most prevalent in her mind, joined to the painful idea of the ruined constitution of him whose life was ever dearer to her than her own.

The cruelty of his being in London, of his going into public without ever having seen or wrote[1] to her, sunk deeply into her heart. "Ah! Willoughby," exclaimed she, "is it thus we meet again after such a parting? Is this the end of all your assurance, that you would ever be my friend? that you would learn to consider me as your sister if we were indeed related? alas! is it thus then you throw me off entirely, and seem sorry to remember that you ever saw me?" A flood of tears followed this cruel reflection; but after weeping some time, her pride came to her relief: she remembered the haughty neglect with which Lady Molyneux had treated her, and doubted not but that her influence with Willoughby had prevailed on him to expel her for ever from that place in his regard which the very reasons on which he resigned her as his wife, ought to give her as a defenceless and unhappy orphan, dependent on his family. She recollected now but too well the reserve and disdain, the look of mingled anger and scorn, which Willoughby's features spoke as she saw him the second time leading out his sister; and her mind dwelt on the expression of his eyes as they first met her's, when, though he must have seen how much she was surprised and affected by the sight of him, he flew from her without one consoling word, though it was evident she could hardly support herself.

"All is over then," cried she: "that tender friendship which would have been the consolation of my life, is at an end. Every tie that from our infancy united us is broken, and I have now no reliance but on the kindness of those who are comparatively strangers. Ah! is it generous thus to discard me, without even trying to soften the blow: but go, cruel, capricious man, go, and enjoy, with your opulent heiress, all that affluence can give: go, and become callous and insensible to all those noble sentiments that once animated your bosom, which once rendered you so deservedly dear to me. They are gone.

---

1   Used as a past participle.

Willoughby, selfish, cruel, unfeeling, and insolent, is not the Willoughby to whom my heart was devoted. Why therefore should I be thus wretched about him? why let his proud malignant sister triumph in knowing that I am mortified and unhappy? Let me try to drive his too painful remembrance from me; or at least to remember him only as the son of my beloved benefactress."

At the mention of that revered name, however, all her newly acquired resolution forsook her. The memory of her tender, her first friend, was so intimately connected with that of Willoughby himself, that her tears flowed for both; and against the unkindness of the latter neither her pride nor her reason could sustain her.

A sleepless night succeeded to this conflicting evening; and it was not till towards morning that Celestina determined to write to Willoughby, entreating him still to allow her that place in his friendship, which no fault of her's had, she thought, forfeited, and assuring him that whatever might be her destiny her regard for him was unchangeable, though she would never intrude upon him with it. Her tenderness conquered her resentment, and the idea of what she owed to the son of her early friend, whatever might be his conduct towards her, came in aid of that long rooted tenderness, and produced the resolution which she meant to execute in the morning. Having thus determined, her mind gradually became more tranquil, and her spirits being quite exhausted, she sunk into slumber.

But the fainter though still painful ideas of the evening before pursued her; and after tormenting her with numberless wild terrors, she fancied that she saw Willoughby with the same menacing look he wore the preceding night, with a dagger in his hand, approaching and threatening her to plunge it into a heart, which was, he said, perfidious and ungrateful, and had been the means of driving him to guilt and despair.

From an image of such horror she wildly started; and awaking, found Lady Horatia Howard sitting by her bed side, holding one of her hands, and gazing on her with great concern.

With the most soothing voice she spoke to Celestina, and endeavoured to quiet the excessive agitation of her spirits. Her reasonable and gentle arguments had their desired effect; and Celestina, ashamed of appearing insensible to the solicitude of such a friend, summoned all her resolution to her aid, and was able in about an hour to attend the breakfast table with something like composure. Her cheeks, however, had still that crimson glow which the perturbed state of her mind had given them: her eyes were heavy with tears, which in despite of all her efforts continued to fill them when the image of Willoughby, pale and thin, with anger flashing from his eyes, and contempt trembling on his lips, again arose in her imagination. Lady Horatia looked at her with more than her usual tender complacency;[1] for it was when her fine open countenance expressed pensive sorrow, that she was, from her then particularly resembling the regretted brother of Lady Horatia, to her more than usually interesting.

Before breakfast was removed, Montague Thorold was introduced. He was extremely dejected; and hardly able to return the compliments of Lady Horatia, who was always glad to see him, and who had undoubtedly given him all her interest with Celestina, and more encouragement to pursue his suit than was perhaps strictly prudent; since Celestina, though she could not avoid him, though she never could prevail upon herself to behave to him with unkindness, and though his talents and conversation, and perhaps that sort of respectful idolatry by which few women can help being gratified however they may wish to repress it, were, in some degree, pleasing to her, had yet repeatedly declared to Lady Horatia and to Montague Thorold himself, that she felt not, and was persuaded she never should feel for him, that tender preference, without which she never would marry. This declaration they both imputed to that affection for Willoughby, which the uncertainty of her own situation continued to nourish. Persuaded as they both were, that Willoughby had promised to become the husband of Miss Fitz-Hayman, which every body but Celestina had long believed, Lady Horatia doubted not but that the merit and attachment of Montague Thorold, the similarity of their taste, Celestina's regard for his father, and the easy competence which with him she could possess and which she often declared was the condition of life she would prefer, would altogether induce her to reward his ardent affection with her hand, as soon as it became certain that Willoughby, either from interested motives or from conviction of their too near relationship, absolutely and for ever relinquished all pretensions to it. She was, therefore, glad that the accidental meeting which had so much affected Celestina was likely to hasten this period; and far from seeing it in the unfavourable light Thorold himself did, she told him, as soon as Celestina left the room, that for him no circumstance could be more favourable.

Lady Horatia had long since transferred entirely to Montague Thorold those good wishes which she had at first expressed towards

---

1 Kindness, affection.

Vavasour. His great fortune, his handsome figure, and his apparent affection for Celestina, had for some time interested her for him; and she imputed his extravagant vivacity, and even his violent irregularities, to his youth and unchecked habits of gratification. Before her, Vavasour had at first so far restrained the intemperate sallies of his ungovernable temper, that she was for some time disposed to think well of his heart and his understanding: but soon finding that this semblance of moderation availed him not, and that he gained nothing on the inflexible heart of Celestina, he became tired of it, and relapsed into such a wild way of talking, and of boasting of actions still wilder, that Lady Horatia was no longer able to excuse him: and though she still received him at her house with civility, she entirely approved of the resolution Celestina had made never to listen to him as a lover.

It was just at that period that Montague Thorold, who on Celestina's first arrival in town had not availed himself of the permission he had obtained to see her, came to solicit of Lady Horatia that indulgence, and accounted for his absence by relating a long illness his father had just escaped; in which, as Mrs. Thorold was absent with one of her daughters, he had himself been his only and constant attendant. "You know," said he to Celestina, "how much I love my father, and how well he deserves that I should love him; and you will easily imagine what must have been my anxiety, when, for so many nights and days, I saw him experience the most excruciating tortures, and knew his life to be in the most imminent danger. Even the reigning, the triumphant passion of my heart—my love, my adoration of Celestina, was suspended, in the pain and solicitude I suffered for my father."

His looks, which were greatly changed since Celestina saw him before, witnessed how severe this pain and solicitude had been; and Celestina not only forgave, but esteemed him the more for that neglect, which had at first given her a slight degree of mortification. From that time, he had constantly visited at the house of Lady Horatia, and from his power of amusing her by reading and conversation, he was become so great a favourite, that he had no rival in her good opinion but Celestina herself. It was at her request he had met them at Oxford, and gone with them to Bath and Bristol. Celestina, who saw but too plainly that all this was but feeding a passion already fatal to the repose of a young man whom she highly esteemed, had in vain remonstrated with Lady Horatia on the subject; who answered, that *her* presence was a sufficient protection, and that as to his love, he would not indulge it the less for being refused the opportunity of speaking of it.

To this doctrine Celestina could not assent; but, in her situation, to dissent was of little effect; and all she could do to counteract the effects of this indiscreet indulgence of Lady Horatia towards Montague Thorold, was, to declare to him very solemnly, whenever he introduced the subject of his love, which was whenever they were alone, that though her esteem and regard for him were very great, she never could think of him otherwise than as her friend: and when he answered, that content with that esteem and regard he should be the happiest of mankind to be permitted by time and tenderness to win her love, she very frankly assured him, that the sentiments which were once her's for Willoughby, though towards him they might be at an end, could never, she was well assured, be transferred to another.

Montague Thorold, however, young, sanguine, and violently in love, was not easily discouraged; while the favour of Lady Horatia, the wishes of his father, and the complacency and kindness with which, notwithstanding her repeated declarations, Celestina treated him, all contributed to cherish a passion which insensibly absorbed his whole soul. Every action, every sentiment, every look of Celestina, at once encreased and justified this excessive passion; and he lived now only to think of her when he was absent, or gaze on her with adoration when she was present. Whenever he knew she was to be at any public place, (information which he was very assiduous and very successful in obtaining,) thither he went also; and though, unless he was invited, he never introduced himself into the parties she was with, he contrived so to place himself as to be able to see her, and was content.

The extreme dejection with which he had on the last morning entered the house of Lady Horatia, all fled before her assurances that the meeting between Willoughby and Celestina, however she might for a little time be affected by it, would prove of advantage to him. Elated more than ever by hope, he left Lady Horatia, having obtained leave to meet them at the opera, whither they were going that evening.

But with poor Celestina it was very different: hope had now wholly forsaken her, yet still she clung even to despair, when it gave her an excuse for dwelling on the beloved and regretted name of Willoughby.

She took out of her dressing box a locket, in which his hair was interwoven with that of his mother and of his sister, and which she had been used when a child to wear round her neck. She looked at it a moment, and remembered a thousand circumstances that brought the tears again into her eyes. She kissed it; she put it to her heart; and that soft heart melting at the tender images this slight memorial presented to it, the resentment which her pride had made her feel the evening before was forgotten; while, unable to bear the thoughts of having seen the last of Willoughby, of his having taken an accidental but eternal leave of her with anger and scorn, she determined instantly to execute her purpose formed the evening before, and with a trembling and uncertain hand wrote as follows:

"Do not think, dear Willoughby, that the unfortunate Celestina means to intrude upon you with her complaints, or to trouble you, after the present moment, with even her name. But when those recollections which she cannot at all once subdue press upon her heart, she finds it impossible, quite impossible, to submit to take of you an eternal farewell, without entreating, that though we never meet again, we may part in peace with each other.

"I might indeed urge to you, Willoughby, that if the account you gave me of our supposed relationship be realized, it ought not to excite your anger, but to give me a claim to your protection. If my heart did not, I know not why, revolt from the idea of being so nearly your relation, I might on that score claim your protection and your pity; I might be permitted surely to love you as my brother, since, alas! whether you permit it or not, I must still love you—but with an affection so disinterested and pure, that, be my situation in regard to you what it may, I feel nothing for which I ought to blush.

"You look very ill, Willoughby. You look unhappy: and on me you looked unkindly. I do not ask to see you, since my accidentally meeting you was evidently painful to you; but I ask to have a few lines from you to tell me that you are not ill, that you are not unhappy, and that your once loved Celestina is not become hateful to you. Believe me, I shall rejoice in your happiness wherever found. Do not then refuse to assist me in obtaining—not happiness, for that is no where to be found for me—but in obtaining that degree of content and resignation which may enable me to go through life without regretting the hour that I ever received it. This, Willoughby, is in your power, and you must be greatly changed indeed if you refuse, when you can so easily grant the last request that ever will be preferred to you, by the unhappy, but ever grateful and affectionate

CELESTINA DE MORNAY."

Park-street, Grosvenor-square,
March 23, 17—[1]

---

1   1789.

Though by no means satisfied with her letter when she had finished it, she despaired of pleasing herself better. She therefore sealed and sent it away by one of the footmen to the house of Lady Molyneux, as she knew no other address to Willoughby. The servant returned in about half an hour, and told her that Mr. Willoughby was not there, but that he had sent in the letter and received a message that it should be taken care of and delivered to him. She had flattered herself that if not a kind, at least an immediate answer would put an end to that almost insupportable state of anxiety which she had been in ever since she saw him. If he wrote to her with kindness, it would, she thought, soothe and console her: if he treated her by letter with as much coldness and disdain as he did during their short interview, she hoped that resentment would support her; and that though her pride might be wounded, her affection would torment her less.

She was now, however, to wait—perhaps a whole day in anxiety; and, what was more dreadful, be compelled to sustain this anxiety under the appearance of calmness if not of cheerfulness; for Lady Horatia, who had made an engagement with some of her friends to go to the opera, whither she seldom went herself, on purpose to gratify Celestina by hearing a new and celebrated performer, did not seem at all disposed to relish the proposal she had ventured to hint at breakfast, of being left out of the party of the evening: and though she was generally very desirous that Celestina should in all such matters follow her own inclinations, yet there were times when she seemed to expect some sacrifices to be made to her.

Her grateful heart was extremely sensible of all the kindness of Lady Horatia; who, from having taken her into her protection quite a stranger, was now so attached to her that her happiness seemed her first object. Having no very strong affection for her only surviving brother, who was a man immersed in politics and without pretence to natural affection; and having been torn early in life from a man she loved, and married by her father to one towards whom she was indifferent; having since followed her three children, who alone had reconciled her to her lot, to their early graves; her heart had become insensible to what are commonly called friendships, and she had for some years rather sought to amuse than to connect herself. But the graces of Celestina's mind, the sweetness of her disposition, and the goodness of her heart, had so won upon her, that the apathy of wearied sensibility, which she had so long been in, gradually gave place to an affection almost as tender as she could have felt had she been her mother; and this affection, created by merit, was strengthened by the resemblance which continually struck her between Celestina and her young brother, who lost his life in America, the loss, which, among all her misfortunes, she most severely lamented.

Her encreasing tenderness for Celestina, made her often reflect with uneasiness on her situation, and very earnestly wish to see her married. She was very sensible that her own life was not a good one; for early calamity had shaken her constitution and brought on in the early autumn of her days the infirmities of old age; and she knew, that after having taken her as her daughter, and accustomed her to share all the indulgencies which her own rank and income procured, it would be a very painful reverse of fortune were she to leave her in the narrow circumstances in which she found her. To save much out of her jointure had never been her wish, and was hardly now in her power. Her own fortune, in default of children, returned to her brother; and all she had to dispose of was about two thousand pounds. This she gave, by a will made in the fourth month of their being together, to Celestina; and with this, and what she before had, she thought that Celestina might, if married to Montague Thorold, enjoy through life that easy competence which was the utmost of her ambition. The embarrassed circumstances of Willoughby, which the good natured world had always exaggerated, and which Lady Horatia had considered as irretrievable; his very expensive place at Alvestone, which she knew it required a large fortune to keep up; the doubtful birth of Celestina, whom she always fancied too nearly related to him; and some prejudice against him, merely because he was the brother of Lady Molyneux, whom she so very much disliked; all combined in the mind of Lady Horatia a desire to impede every step towards the re-union of Celestina and Willoughby, and to promote her alliance with Montague Thorold, near whose residence, wherever it was, she proposed to take a house in summer, and to have them frequently with her in winter at her house in town.

Though she had not disclosed all her intentions, Celestina yet knew enough to be deeply sensible of the uncommon generosity of her friend, and the whole study of her life was to shew that she was so. She made it a rule never to oppose the wishes of Lady Horatia whenever they were clearly expressed; and therefore it was that she had often, contrary to her own judgment and to her own inclinations, suffered the assiduities of Montague Thorold; and seemed to the world to give him that encouragement, the ill effects of which she endeavoured to counteract, by ingenuously declaring to him the impossibility of her ever making the return he expected to his affection.

Too certain that Lady Horatia would be disappointed if not displeased if she declined on this evening to go out, and not having courage to tell her the step she had taken in regard to writing to Willoughby, she was compelled to struggle with her uneasiness, and to attempt concealing if she could not conquer it: but every rap at the door which seemed to be that of a servant, made her tremble: and while sitting at work before dinner, she could not help going to the window several times, nor listening to every sound that she heard in the hall. Time wore away, and her impatience encreased, and at length grew so evident that Lady Horatia remarked it. "What is the matter, my dear?" enquired she: "do you expect any one?"

Celestina, conscious that she was betraying herself, and fearing least she should be blamed for what she had done, of which she began already to repent as too humiliating, blushed at this question so deeply, that had not Lady Horatia been intent at that moment on her work, her suspicions must have been heightened. Celestina, however, not immediately answering, she repeated her question— "do you expect any body?" Twenty reasons might have been given for her seeming anxiety, and twenty people might have been named as likely to call; but not one of all these occurred to Celestina, who was little practised in dissimulation: she therefore answered faintly, "no;" and in hopes of turning Lady Horatia's attention from her, and of hiding what she felt, she proposed finishing the perusal of a poem which Montague Thorold had began to read the preceding morning.

"Do so," said Lady Horatia.

Celestina took up the book and began; but had no idea of what she was about, and of course read so extremely ill, and so unlike her usual manner, that Lady Horatia, looking at her very earnestly, said "Surely, Celestina—surely something is the matter?"

"No, indeed, Madam," replied she, "nothing except perhaps some slight remains of nervous agitation, from the circumstances of last night."

"Try, my dear, to conquer that," replied Lady Horatia, "and think of regaining the composure you possessed before; which such a circumstance, fairly considered, ought not to destroy."

Celestina sighed; and to avoid the necessity of giving an answer, went on with the book before her. She had hardly, however, read ten lines, when a servant brought in a letter and gave it her. She turned paler than death as she took it, and the book fell from her hands.

Lady Horatia, whose attention was now fixed upon her, eagerly asked from whom was the letter. Celestina had by this time read it; for it was only a note from a young friend, for whose painting she had promised to give some pattern.[1] She put it down: "It is only from Miss Clayton, Madam," said she, "about the patterns I am drawing for her."

"Dear child," cried Lady Horatia, "and is all this trembling and anxiety, this faultering and solicitude, about Miss Clayton's patterns? Celestina, I am afraid you are not ingenuous with me. Surely I deserve that you should be so?"

Celestina felt that this accusation, of want of confidence, and the claim made to it, were equally just. The measure she had adopted, at the risque of displeasing her best friend, had produced nothing but some hours of anguish, and would end probably in the conviction that Willoughby despised and condemned her: for it was now five o'clock; and it was very improbable that he should not, in all the hours that had intervened since she wrote, have been at his lodgings, or have had time to acknowledge the receipt of her letter. This mortifying reflection and the consciousness that she ought to have consulted Lady Horatia, quite overwhelmed her. She was pale and silent a moment; and then recovering her voice, with difficulty said—"I believe I have acted so foolishly, so improperly, that I hardly dare hope you will forgive me."

Lady Horatia expressing her uneasiness and surprise, Celestina, in a tremulous voice, told her what she had done. Pity rather than anger was created by the recital. "Certainly, my dear child," said Lady Horatia, "had you consulted me, I should have advised you against writing to Mr. Willoughby. Situated as you both are, no advances should have come from you. If he is convinced that you are so related to him as to make every thought of you, beyond such as that relationship authorises, guilty and odious, he should surely, on his coming to England, have sent to you if he was unwilling to see you, and have behaved with humanity and brotherly tenderness, though love were for ever out of the question: if he is not convinced of it, how will you account for his conduct, but by supposing, that, influenced by pecuniary motives or by caprice, he is desirous of forgetting all his former affection for you, and yet has not that generous openness of character which would urge him to quit you handsomely."

To the truth of these remarks Celestina had nothing to object; but their justice cruelly depressed her, and her sick heart recoiled from the idea of being obliged to appear in public. Again she ventured

---

1   An outline sketch which the painter would fill in; drawing masters often did this sort of work for their pupils.

very gently to insinuate a wish to be left at home that evening. "If you are really ill you shall," said Lady Horatia; "but otherwise I hope you will go."

"I am not really ill," replied Celestina, "if your Ladyship means only bodily suffering: but my spirits, my mind—"

"For the maladies of those," interrupted Lady Horatia, "there is no remedy more sure than change of scene and variety of amusement; and believe me, dear Celestina—believe me, (and I have suffered much from the maladies of the mind,) they only grow by indulgence: if we would conquer, we must contend with and not encourage them.—You will suffer much less to-night, if you are in a circle of friends, who love and admire you, than in brooding at home over the defection of one, who, if he ever did, certainly does not now deserve you—I beg, therefore, that you will go."

Celestina, unaccustomed to dispute any wish of her friend, yielded, with as good a grace as she could, to her remonstrances; and with a heavy and aching heart, went to finish her dress.

The hour of going out arrived; and Celestina found Montague Thorold, and a Mr. Howard, a relation of Lady Horatia's, ready to attend them.—As there was no escape, she endeavoured to assume the semblance of tranquillity, and to talk with them on indifferent matters: but the idea that Willoughby had left London without seeing her, or, being still in it, disdained to answer her letter, and utterly refused to notice her; hung so heavy on her heart, that she could with difficulty support herself; while the protracted state, in which she had been since the preceding evening, occasioned such a ferment in her blood, that her cheeks were of a feverish crimson; and the languid lustre of her fine eyes never appeared to greater advantage.—Deep sighs, which she tried in vain to suppress, stole from her heart; and Mr. Howard rallied her upon them, with that sort of common-place wit, which is so usual, and so irksome, when there is real uneasiness to contend with: while Montague Thorold answered every sigh of hers, with one yet deeper of his own; and watched every turn of her countenance with trembling solicitude.—Lady Horatia was to join another party at the opera; and Celestina was in hopes, that by obtaining a seat in one of the last rows in the box, she should be excused from the task of seeming to give any attention, either to the performance, or the people around her.—This, therefore, she contrived to do, and Montague Thorold placed himself by her.

Her thoughts were engrossed wholly by Willoughby—and by the cruelty of his refusing to answer her letter. She saw not the objects about her; she attended not to the humble and plaintive voice of Thorold, who now and then spoke to her; when Lady Horatia Howard turning to her, bade her remark, that into the opposite box had just entered Lady Castlenorth and her daughter.

Celestina instantly saw them, and as instantly concluded, that Willoughby's conduct towards her was owing to his being on the point of marriage with Miss Fitz-Hayman.—She had hardly felt her heart sink under this cruel idea, before Willoughby himself appeared, and Lady Castlenorth making room for him, he sat down between her and her daughter.

A look from the penetrating eyes of Lady Horatia Howard made Celestina turn away her head; but she then met the anxious and enquiring eyes of Montague Thorold; and again sought refuge in looking towards the pit—hardly knowing where she was, and not daring again to trust herself with the sight of the group placed immediately opposite to her. Willoughby saw her not; and after a while, her eyes, in despite of the pain she felt, sought him again. His countenance did not wear expressions of bridal felicity—he was, she thought, paler and thinner than the night before, and on his brow some corrosive sorrow seemed to hang: but Miss Fitz-Hayman, gay and animated, talked to him incessantly; and both she and her mother endeavoured to engross his attention by a flow of conversation. He listened to them,—but Celestina fancied, with more politeness than pleasure. He smiled; but she thought his smiles were the smiles of complaisance, and not of content. Still, however, his appearance in public with them was enough to convince her that his marriage was not far off. Her heart sunk at this sad certainty; for though she had long since endeavoured to wean her mind from the hopes of ever being his, she had still too keen recollections of that time when it was the first wish of both their hearts; and she was prepossessed with an idea, she hardly knew why, that with Miss Fitz-Hayman, he would be miserable.

That they had been parted by the artifice of Lady Castlenorth, she now more than ever suspected. But how Willoughby could be cheated into such a belief; and if he was, why he should entirely throw off, as a relation, her whom, as the chosen mistress of his heart, he had so fondly cherished, she could not comprehend; or could she in any way reconcile his conduct with that manly and liberal spirit, which had so eminently marked his character. As she gazed on his face, as on that of a stranger—the husband of Miss Fitz-Hayman—that face which she had been accustomed to contemplate with so much tenderness; and when she considered that, lost to her for ever, she now dared no longer look up to *him* as a friend, whom she had once hoped to find, through life, her fond and generous protector, her reflections became too bitter; and had she not feared that her going out would have attracted his eyes towards her; and known that Montague Thorold would have attended her, which she desired to avoid; she would have returned home—for her sufferings were almost insupportable.

She hoped, however to escape without his seeing her; and shrunk back as much as she could, pretending that her head-ache made the light particularly uneasy to her. Montague Thorold, though knowing too well the real source of her uneasiness, was yet as anxious as she was that Willoughby might not see her; and favoured her concealment as much as he could.

Towards the end of the opera, however, Willoughby, who seemed very weary of his seat, left it to speak to somebody he saw in the pit—Celestina saw him very near the box where she sat; and became so faint that she was afraid she must have sunk from her seat.—But her suffering still encreased, when, a moment afterwards, Mr. Howard, who sat next to her, called to him; and got up to speak to him. In answering his question, Willoughby turned towards him—his eyes immediately fell on Celestina, and Montague Thorold close beside her. An expression of mingled anger and scorn rose instantly in his countenance; he abruptly broke off his conversation with Mr. Howard, and walked away. In a moment Celestina saw him rejoin Lady Castlenorth, and Miss Fitz-Hayman. She saw him affect to enter into conversation with them; but that it was all effort. His eyes once or twice were turned towards her, but immediately withdrawn as if they had met a basilisk:[1] and after a very few minutes, she saw, by his manner, that he complained of the heat of the house, pleaded indisposition, and left them.

Celestina, overwhelmed with sensations too much to be borne, began to think the opera never would end; and that Lady Horatia, who saw her distress, had never before had so little compassion. At length it was finished, and as Montague Thorold handed her to the coach, she besought him not to stay to supper, if Lady Horatia should ask him, "for I must in that case stay, you know, to entertain you, and really I am so unwell, that it is cruelty to expect it of me." Gratified by the power of obeying her, even when the wishes were contrary

---

1 A legendary creature, half cock, half serpent, whose breath or look was fatal; also known as a cockatrice.

to his own; and full of hope that this last struggle, between her lingering love for Willoughby, and the certainty of his having left her for another, would terminate in his own favour, Thorold promised to be wholly governed by her, and took his leave at the door.

"Well, Celestina," said Lady Horatia, as soon as they were alone, "you are now, I think, convinced that Willoughby is, like most other men, capricious, and unfeeling. What was his conduct to-night, but the most insulting that it was possible to assume; and after receiving a letter too from you, which you confess was couched in the tenderest and most submissive terms, which, as a gentlemen, he ought to have answered, had you never had any claim whatever upon him. I hope, and believe, however, that such conduct will have the happiest effect—that of weaning you for ever from that excessive partiality, which from early prejudice you always appeared to me to think it a merit to cherish. If he quitted you, as he pretended, on account of the doubts raised in his mind, by that sorceress, Lady Castlenorth, why does he not, those doubts being now certainties, own you as his sister, and become your protector as relation? Why, if they are not ascertained, does he poorly shrink from the enquiry, and evade, under such paltry pretences, the engagements which you would surely release him from, if told that he no longer wished to accomplish them?"

Celestina tried to speak, but could not articulate and Lady Horatia, whose indignation against Willoughby seemed to increase by indulgence, went on—"Let me conjure you, then, my dear Celestina, to exert that large share of reason, with which you are endowed; and, expelling from your mind all that has passed, try to look forward to happier prospects—to prospects unclouded by doubt, and undarkened by the gloomy apprehensions of being despised by the family of your husband, and of being reproached as having embarrassed his fortune. Time and reason, the assiduous tenderness of a man who really adores you, will conquer all remains of regret; and you will, by degrees, learn to think of Willoughby, and of all the events of your early life, with the most perfect indifference."

Celestina thought that was impossible—but altogether unable to enter into the argument, she could only sigh, and in tremulous voice intreat to be permitted to retire; saying that, in the morning, she should have, she hoped, more resolution, and have got the better of the agitation of her spirits. Sleep, however, refused to visit her—the image of Willoughby, cruel and capricious as he was, incessantly haunted her. Having been long used to study his countenance, she understood all its expression; and when she had courage to fix her eyes on him, during the opera, no turn of it escaped her: all the comfort she could derive to herself from those observations was, believing that his attention to Miss Fitz-Hayman was forced; and that the solicitude with which she herself was avoided, arose, rather from some remains of tenderness, than from total indifference. "Surely," said she, "if he felt nothing for me, he would not fly from me, but treat me with polite indifference; or, with that candour and openness of heart which used to be so natural to him, he would avow his designs, and give his reasons for them; for he knows, that be his intentions or his motives what they may, I shall never reproach him; but, whatever I may feel for myself, rejoice, if he can find happiness."

Thus, the real affection of her heart for Willoughby, counteracted the effect of that native pride and dignity of soul, which, under other circumstances, would have supported her; and even of his quitting her, without finding that unanswerable reason for it, which was once supposed to exist, she thought rather in sorrow, than in anger.[1]

The morning came, joyless and uninteresting to her—she expected nothing but a repetition of common, irksome occurrence, with the suspense and misery of not hearing from Willoughby.—Lady Horatia's remonstrance, Montague Thorold's silent, but assiduous attendance, company whom she wished not to see, or parties abroad that could afford her no pleasure.

The day, and another and another, wore away, and still no letter from Willoughby arrived—the forlorn hope, which she had till now fondly cherished, that he still retained a lingering preference for her in his heart, now faded away; and an almost certain conviction succeeded, that he not only quitted her for ever, but disclaimed her even as a friend; and gave her up in silent contempt, without either offering her the protection of a relation, or feeling for her the regret which the loss of a pleasant acquaintance would once, she thought, have given him.

She repented she had concealed the letter she had written from Lady Horatia Howard; and while she was conscious that she ought to have no reserves towards her, she felt, that in her present anxious state of suspense, it would be some consolation to talk it over with her friend. But far from soothing her with hope, and attempting to account for the silent neglect of Willoughby, by any means that might palliate its cruelty, Lady Horatia exhorted her, more earnestly than ever, to call off her thoughts from a man, who was considered

---

1   Cf. *Hamlet* 1.3.228-29.

in every light so unworthy to possess them: and, she urged, more earnestly than she had ever yet done, her wishes, that the tender and generous attachment of Montague Thorold might be immediately rewarded.

Though to the necessity of giving herself to another, Celestina could by no means agree, yet she felt, that she must either learn to think with more calmness of her eternal separation from Willoughby, or sink under it—for such pain as the undecided wretchedness of the last two or three days had given her, human nature could not long sustain. She promised Lady Horatia that she would endeavour to regain her tranquillity; but besought her, for a day or two, to excuse her from mixing with company; and that in the mean time nothing might be said to Montague Thorold, to give him more encouragement than he had already received. From the loss of Willoughby, when he had seen her with him; and from his present disdainful silence, she supposed that he believed her engaged to him, and either resented her having entered into such an engagement, without consulting him, or still felt some pain in believing she had given herself to another—of which, she could not help owning, there was every appearance, from their being so frequently together; and from the report which had gone forth, which her protectress had not only left uncontradicted, but had rather encouraged. Of Montague Thorold, therefore, she now thought with concern and disquiet, as being partly the cause of the uneasiness she suffered from the certainty which every hour in its flight confirmed, that Willoughby had taken leave of her for ever.

END OF THE THIRD VOLUME.

VOLUME IV

Chapter I

When first Willoughby arrived in London, he had endeavoured to bring himself to a resolution of seeing Celestina; but her absence at that time on a tour of pleasure, and the assurances he received that she was engaged to Montague Thorold, not only diverted him from that intention, but gave his sister both time and opportunity to represent her as neither wanting or wishing for that attention, which he thought he should, as a friend, shew her. These insinuations had gradually their effect: not however in curing that invincible tenderness he always felt for her, but in mingling with it so much bitterness that his life became more than ever wretched. The accidentally meeting Celestina at an assembly, gay, unconcerned, and, as he believed, forgetting her former attachment to him in her new preference to Montague Thorold; the second meeting, which happened at the opera; and every thing that he heard both from his sister and in general conversation where Celestina was mentioned, all served to confirm this idea; while the letter which would have undeceived him, never reached his hands. It was left with Lady Molyneux; who, determined as she was to impede every advance towards a reconciliation between her brother and Celestina, made no scruple, on hearing from whom it came, to open, read, and, after some consideration, to destroy it.

Of the apparent neglect, therefore, which Celestina imputed to Willoughby, he had accused *her*; and thought, that if she had not determined to connect herself with Montague Thorold without any attention to his wishes or reliance on his regard, she would have written to or sent to him: while his neglect of a letter by which she thought she should awaken all the tenderness of friendship which she hoped he still retained for her, and the angry and disdainful looks with which he had twice met her, wounded both her affection and her pride. Thus, by the treachery of Lady Molyneux, all commerce even of civility was at an end between them; and such was the situation of Willoughby, when the Castlenorths arrived in London from Italy.

Embarrassed more and more in his affairs, and on the point of being overwhelmed with pecuniary distress, it was more than time that he should determine what to do; and this determination, the return of the Castlenorths to England was intended to hasten.

Always believing that to the artifices of Lady Castlenorth he had owed his being compelled to quit Celestina, and still hoping to detect those artifices, he had, by frequent visits at his uncle's, and by a sort of tacit and reluctant acquiescence in many of his plans, given Miss Fitz-Hayman great reason to suppose that he intended fulfilling his original engagement with her: yet now that he saw he must either continue to act what he could not but feel was a dishonourable and disingenuous part, or break with his uncle entirely, his uneasiness became more insupportable. The tortures which he had felt in observing the favour Celestina had shewn to Montague Thorold, by whispering and laughing with him, gave him a cruel foretaste of what he should suffer were he to see her married to him; yet his reason, whenever he was calm enough to listen to it, told him how absurd, how improper it was, to indulge such sensations of anguish and regret; since, if the relationship which had been hinted at did really subsist between them, he could never take any other part in regard to her than a friendly and fraternal concern in her happiness; and since the age, family, and circumstances of Montague Thorold were all without objection, he ought, if she believed such an alliance would make her happy, not only to rejoice in it but promote it.

From this, however, his heart absolutely revolted; and all he could prevail upon himself to think of was, to make for Celestina some more ample provision if he was once convinced of their relationship, and to wish her happy: for to see her happy, when another was to be the object of her love, he found would be to him the cruellest punishment that Fate could inflict.

Sometimes he thought, that since every other woman on earth was indifferent to him, he ought to learn to approve of Miss Fitz-Hayman, of whose apparently encreasing affection towards him he could not be insensible. But love was never yet the effect of effort; and while he compared her, with all her laboured accomplishments, to Celestina, he found too certainly that he never could love her, and that with such sentiments to promise it, was an unworthy prostitution of his honour.

His coldness, however, and visible reluctance, discouraged none of the other parties who desired this marriage: and Miss Fitz-Hayman, with all that pride which her birth, her fortune, and the exalted idea of her own merit, gave her, seemed to be either from her affection to Willoughby or some other cause, content to receive his hand with the hope of afterwards winning his heart. Convinced that he had no attachment but to Celestina, and certain that the impediments between them must effectually prevent him ever again thinking of her with the fond partiality he had done, she seemed very easy as to his indifference towards herself; foreseeing, perhaps, that their lives would be such after they were married as would very soon produce it, if they did not set out with it: or, to judge more candidly, she might think with pride and pleasure of conquering, as his wife, that coldness to which, as his mistress, she could not be insensible.

Lord Castlenorth had so determined a predilection for the match, which the difficulties he had met with had by no means abated, that he would not see any thing that appeared inimical to this his darling scheme. His great object was—and he forgot his infirmities as he pursued it—to procure for Willoughby the reversion[1] of all his titles, and to change his name to Fitz-Hayman. This he found would be attended with no great difficulty; and now, whenever he saw his nephew, he enumerated all the species of satisfaction which in his opinion would attend these acquirements, dwelling with great delight on the circumstance of the family arms remaining unchanged; though he offered to quarter[2] those of Willoughby, if their owner found any reluctance in parting with them entirely.

From these harangues, which nothing could for a moment render interesting to Willoughby, *his* imagination was often quite absent, and fled after Celestina, whom it represented as making the felicity of Montague Thorold, and enjoying with him that life of elegant and literary retirement, which he had himself fondly hoped to share with her. Frequently, when his uncle was talking to him of his ancestor, Reginald Fitz-Hayman, who in the reign of Henry IV, was slain by the celebrated Hotspur,[3] then in rebellion, after having twice unhorsed him, describing the circumstances of the combat, and still more minutely the bearings thereupon granted in addition to their former coat, Willoughby, far from attending to him, was meditating on some walk he had taken with Celestina during their short happiness at Alvestone the preceding spring; on the remarks she had made, and the improvements she had suggested; and having no idea of what his uncle was talking about, only understanding by

---

1 Succession to his titles after his death.
2 Thus combining the arms of Willoughby's father with those of the Fitz-Hayman family.
3 Harry Percy, son of the first Earl of Northumberland, and called "Hotspur" for his eagerness in repelling Scottish invaders, led a rebellion against Henry IV and was killed at the Battle of Shrewsbury in 1403. The story is told in Shakespeare's *Henry IV, Part 1*.

his tone when he ended a period, he said—"To be sure"—"Oh certainly"—"Very great"—"Undoubtedly"—without knowing or caring whether these words were well placed: while Lord Castlenorth was too much delighted with the pleasure of hearing himself talk on his favourite topic, to remark, that Willoughby knew not a syllable of what he was saying; and the latter had really acquired such a habit of inattention to those subjects about which his uncle paraded, that he not unfrequently had, in appearance, assented to plans relative to his fortune, and his residence after his marriage, when in reality he had not, on the discourse to which he seemed to listen, formed any one idea.

A few days only passed in this manner after the return of the Castlenorths to England, before the extreme pain he felt, the second time of seeing Celestina in public, made him sensible of his inability to continue long in this undecided and wretched state. From mere acquiescence in misery, or rather from an hope to escape from it by detecting Lady Castlenorth's schemes, he had become insensibly more deeply entangled in them: and he now began to accuse himself of very unjustifiable conduct; since not all the distressing circumstances of his fortune, not the certainty of Celestina being lost to him, nor the pleasure of saving his paternal estate, and particularly Alvestone, which, after Celestina, had always been his first object, could, on strict examination of his own heart, lead him to form a serious wish of becoming the husband of Miss Fitz-Hayman: and he was conscious that every part of his behaviour that had raised contrary expectations, was owing rather to his despair of obtaining one woman than to his wish of being united to another.

His mind was now in such a state of continual debate and perplexity, that nothing had the power a moment to amuse or please him. His sister, without an heart herself, had no notion of the corrosive sensations that preyed on his; his health, though far from being restored, was such as no longer offered her any prospect of becoming the heiress to what family property was left; and since her brother did live, her wish was to have him live in splendour, graced with the happiness of nobility, and reflecting honour on her by his affluence and prosperity. Her dislike of Lady Castlenorth and her daughter was long since lost in the more inveterate dislike she had conceived against Celestina, since she had been so much seen in good company in London, and so much celebrated for her beauty: she always therefore affected to consider his marriage with Miss Fitz-Hayman as a settled thing; and from the moment of the Castlenorths return to England, she joined, with more zeal than selfish indolence usually permitted her to feel for any thing, in promoting it.

Thus beset by his family, and on the other hand harrassed by the encreasing clamours of his creditors, who offered him only the sad alternative of selling Alvestone, and whose impatience was fomented by the artful management of Lady Castlenorth, Willoughby, for some little time lingered and hesitated: now thought that he ought to marry, when such advantages were to be acquired by it, now recoiled from the dreadful idea of passing his life with a woman who was indifferent to him, and whom he doubted whether he could ever learn to love. Even in the symptoms of her regard for him, which were unequivocal enough, there was something which rather disgusted than flattered him; and when he thought how different were their minds, their tempers, and their pursuits, no earthly consideration seemed to have sufficient weight with him, to make him resolve on putting on a yoke so uneasy to his imagination.

The repeated sight of Celestina made all his wounds bleed afresh. He found, that neither the suspicions of their relationship, or what he thought the certainty of her alienation from him, were strong enough to counteract the effect of the long rooted affection he felt for her: but he believed that if those suspicions once amounted to a certainty—if once he was thoroughly convinced Celestina was his sister, he should learn to conquer every other sentiment in regard to her but what he might with honour indulge.

For this reason, and because he found some satisfaction in the delay this journey would give him a pretence for, and thought that mere change of place would afford him some relief, he determined to set out in search of that servant, Hannah Biscoe, to whom he had obtained a direction in Italy, and whom he had been detained from visiting partly by his ill state of health and partly by the artifices of Lady Molyneux.

After she and Lady Castlenorth had met, however, her opposition to this journey was withdrawn; and he set out on horseback, attended only by his old servant Farnham, intending to reach the village to which he was directed, and which was on the borders of Lancashire, by easy journies.

Miss Fitz-Hayman, to whom he had said that every consideration urged him to a complete developement[1] of the mystery now that it seemed to be in his power, saw him depart with an appearance of reluctance; but Willoughby had seen her, even since her arrival in

---

1 Disclosure.

England, making parties for public places without him, if he happened not to be able or disposed to go; and found, that during his absence she would proceed in the same course of amusement; and that she and her mother would find no inconvenience for want of an escort, as they had brought over with them an Irish officer, who had been in the service of France,[1] with whom Lady Castlenorth had contracted an intimacy a few years before in Italy, which in their last journey to the Continent had been renewed and encreased: in consequence of which, Captain Cavanaugh had accompanied them to London, where he had apartments in the house, and was become one of the family. At all places of public resort he attended on Lady Castlenorth; sat by her at the upper end of the table to carve for her; and acted as a sort of gentleman usher[2] to the mother, while he treated the daughter with the most profound reverence and respect.

This gentleman was three or four and thirty. His face was handsome, and his figure, though large, uncommonly fine. He had seen a great deal of service and of the world; spoke all European languages except English, well, and with all the animation of a Frenchman, had enough of the national character still about him, to mark him for an Irishman.

He was, indeed, sufficiently proud of his country, and piqued himself on being descended from the kings of Leinster;[3] and Lord Castlenorth, to whom he contrived to render himself agreeable by a patient attention to long stories, by his knowledge of genealogy, by picking up for him old books of heraldry, and understanding the difference between a pale lozengy, and pale engrailed;[4] and affixing some importance to the enquiry, whether one of the quarterings of the arms of Fitz-Hayman, should in strictness be on field argent, a boar's head, couped gules, or couped Or.[5] Lord Castlenorth, among other doubts on this and equally important subjects with which he amused himself, sometimes considered whether the genealogy of Captain Cavanaugh might not be traced back in Ireland a genera-

---

1   Who had been an officer in the French army.
2   A court official in charge of the reception and announcement of visitors.
3   One of the four ancient provinces of Ireland, Leinster covers the east and southeast, including Dublin, and was a kingdom until the incursion of the English in the twelfth and thirteenth centuries.
4   Understanding the difference if the vertical band down the middle of an escutcheon has diamond-shaped or curvilinear markings at the edge. Smith's note: Terms used in heraldry.
5   On a silver background, a boar's head, severed, in red or in gold.

tion or two beyond his own in Normandy, a circumstance which excited his respect, and gave, in his opinion, weight and value to those qualities by which the Captain contrived to render himself, through the family, so very acceptable. Willoughby had seen him with them once or twice abroad, but had not then particularly noticed him among that croud of all nations and descriptions which Lady Castlenorth contrived to collect around her there. He now saw him, not without a slight degree of surprise, domesticated in the family; but his whole attention seemed to be given to the older members of it; and he hardly ever spoke to Miss Fitz-Hayman, who, when Willoughby one day took occasion to remark that he was on a footing of greater intimacy than formerly, answered, with something like a careless sneer—"Oh you know that Cavanaugh has long been my mother's favourite."[1]

In the societies of London, however, this intimacy became the subject of some malicious comments; and Lady Molyneux, who seldom let any thing of that sort escape her, could not forbear indulging herself in some remarks on Lady Castlenorth's friendship, even before her brother, who gave, however, so little attention to what he heard, that before he reached the end of his first day's journey he had forgot that such a person as the Captain existed, as he could probably have forgotten Lady Castlenorth herself, had not the purpose of his present journey, and all the transactions of the last twelve months of his life, brought her and the consequences of those transactions too forcibly to his memory.

While Willoughby was thus on his journey, the disquiet and unhappiness of Celestina, though she was compelled to appear to conquer them, were but little abated.

Nothing, in the opinion of Lady Horatia, contributed so much to wean the mind from indulging sorrow or encouraging weakness, as variety of company and continual dissipation; and in these, notwithstanding her reluctance, Celestina was continually engaged. She now more than ever regretted that she had relinquished that plan of life which she had fixed upon when first left, by the death of Mrs. Willoughby, to seek a new one. The quiet farm house in Devonshire where Cathcart and Jessy lived, the tender attention she should be there sure to meet with, the not unpleasing melancholy of Mrs.

---

1   As well as meaning "favourite friend," "favourite" was a euphemism for the lover, heterosexual or homosexual, of a monarch. Miss Fitz-Hayman is hinting that that his relationship to her mother is of this kind.

Elphinstone, and the perfect seclusion she might there enjoy from a world where nothing gave her any real pleasure, were ideas which were now always returning to her mind with new power. There, she thought her sad heart might be laid open to the pitying sympathy of her first and most beloved friend, and find some satisfaction amidst its own disappointments in witnessing the happiness of that friend, to which she had been so greatly instrumental; and there she might wander whole days among the fields and copses, indulging herself in repeating the name of Willoughby, in thinking of him, in reading again those books they had read together, painting the plants he admired, and composing melancholy verses, which above every other occupation soothed her mind. But when she had represented to herself all the mournful pleasure she should in such a situation enjoy, and half determined to gratify herself, the ingratitude of which she should be guilty towards Lady Horatia destroyed her resolves; and alas! she recollected too, that at the farm of Jessy she saw from almost every field, and from some of the windows of the house, Alvestone Park, where Miss Fitz-Hayman would soon be mistress; the sight she thought she could not bear; and her mind turned with terror from the idea of it. There were also very strong objections against her going into the immediate neighbourhood of Montague Thorold, if she meant not to give him encouragement; and these considerations adding to the impracticability of her quitting, without better reasons than a mere wish of retirement, such a generous protectress as Lady Horatia, determined her to wean her mind from an inclination she could not properly indulge, and to move on as well as she could in the wearisome circle; till the time arrived when Lady Horatia set out on her summer tour, which was to begin by going to Matlock,[1] from whence she was to go into Wales, and then end the summer at Cheltenham.

Vavasour had been so long absent, that Celestina began to hope his pride and resentment had subdued every wish to pursue her. In this, however, she was mistaken; a few days after the departure of Willoughby he called, and was admitted. Lady Horatia and Celestina, though neither of them were pleased to see him, yet received him with civility, and entered on common topics, such as the occurrences of the day afford; to these he appeared very inattentive, and turning abruptly to Celestina, he said—"Miss de Mornay, cannot I speak to you alone?"

---

1   In an area of picturesque beauty in the Peak district of Derbyshire.

She hesitated a moment, and then said—"I believe, Mr. Vavasour, there is nothing you can have to communicate to me, that ought to be a secret to Lady Horatia Howard."

"There is, Madam," returned he with quickness, and appearing much displeased with her apparent disinclination to oblige him, "for what I have to say relates in some measure to others, whose confidence I have no right to betray whatever I may chuse to do in those circumstances that relate only to myself."

Lady Horatia now rose, and said—"My dear, oblige Mr. Vavasour if he wishes to speak to you without witnesses." She then left the room.

"Now, Madam," said Vavasour, as soon as she had shut the door— "now you have no longer an excuse to repulse or deny me: Willoughby assuredly quits you for ever: and nothing ought, nothing shall impede my pretensions. Emily—my poor Emily herself— on whose account I own to you I have hesitated more than once, wishes my success, and bids me say, that convinced my happiness depends upon you, she withdraws every claim which she had on my heart, and beseeches you to believe it is not unworthy your acceptance."

"Emily, Sir?" cried Celestina in some surprise: "of whom do you speak? and how can a person to whose very name I am a stranger, be likely in such a case to influence me?"

"Don't affect," said he, "the ridiculous prudery of disclaiming any knowledge of her, because she does not rank among those who are falsely called virtuous women: by heaven she has virtues that might redeem the vices of half her sex; not one in a thousand of whom possess a twentieth part of her worth."

"I mean not," answered Celestina, mildly, "to dispute her value, but only to ask on what pretension you urge to me either the resignation or opinions of a person with whom I have no acquaintance?"

"Why will you pretend not to know her," resumed he with redoubled impetuosity—"why affect not to know that Emily, who has lived with me almost twelve months,[1] is the sister of your Mrs. Elphinstone, and of that Cathcart whom Willoughby picked up and placed as his steward at Alvestone?"

"I have heard there is such a person," said Celestina, "but I did not know she lived with you."

"Yes, she has lived with me some time, though I did not till late-

---

1 Smith leaves many years of Emily's life unaccounted for.

ly know her family. Unworthy and disgraced as you may think her, she should at this moment have been mistress of my house and my fortune, by what you would call legal claims, if I had not, like a cursed fool as I am, taken up a passion for you which I cannot get rid of, and which my generous little girl not only knows, but with disinterested affection, instead of trying to dissuade me from it, wishes me to succeed in. I have sometimes fancied, that your knowledge of my attachment to her was in my way; and that circumstance, together with the eternal mystery that always hung over Willoughby's intentions—in short, my hopes of being cured of a damned folly, by reason and absence, instead of matrimony, have altogether made me refrain from visiting you lately. But now I think, since George is gone out of town and returns only to be married to Miss Fitz-Hayman, there is an end of that; and for my experiment—curse me if I believe it will do; and so here I am again, more in love and a greater blockhead than ever. Don't, however, mistake me, Celestina: I will not, I cannot bear to be trifled with; nor will I sacrifice one hour, either to your coquetry or to the absurd partiality which I sometimes used to believe you had, for that whining, snivelling Montague Thorold. If there are no other pretensions than his in the way, I shall soon know how to settle the matter."

"Really, Mr. Vavasour," said Celestina, as soon as he would give her an opportunity of speaking, "your conduct and manners are so eccentric, that it is difficult to know what to say to you, which you will not call either prudery or coquetry, or impute to a partiality for some other person. Permit me, however, to tell you, with that sincerity with which I have always spoken on this subject, that I am sensible of the honour you do me, but that I never can accept it, even though my situation were to be more humble than it is, and though such a man as Mr. Montague Thorold had never existed."

"Oh! very well, Madam," cried Vavasour, impatiently interrupting her—"You must, however, allow me to ask your objections: are they to my person? my family? my fortune?"

"I have already said, Sir, that they are all unexceptionable."

"Well, Madam, I must then infer from your refusal, that you are engaged."

"No, Sir, that inference by no means follows. Pardon me if I say, that notwithstanding all the advantages you possess, it is possible for a person to decline the honour of your address without being engaged."

"However, Madam, do you or do you not deny that such an engagement does exist? Of that, I think, I have a right to enquire."

"Forgive me, Sir, if I answer that it does not seem to me that you have any right in the world to ask that question of me."

"Well then, I shall ask it elsewhere."

"Where you have, if possible, still less right," said Celestina, alarmed at his vehemence.

"You are, however, very quick at understanding to whom I allude."

"Certainly, after what you have just said, I cannot mistake your meaning. You allude to Mr. Montague Thorold."

"Damn him," cried Vavasour, rising, and speaking with vehemence that made her shudder, "that puppy crosses me like my evil genius. By any man at all worthy of you, I might perhaps bear to be supplanted; but by such a silly fellow as that—no, damn it, there is no enduring it—curse me if it does not make me frantic."

"Hear me then, Mr. Vavasour—hear me for the last time—for I never will again willingly expose myself to this sort of treatment. *I am not* engaged to Mr. Thorold: nor is it likely I ever shall be engaged to him; and farther, I again protest to you, that did no such person exist it would make no difference in the resolution I have made never to listen to the offers with which you honour me."

This declaration, repeated so strongly, served but to inflame those passions which Celestina hoped it would repress, and piqued his pride, without destroying what he called love. He walked backwards and forwards in the room a moment or two, and seemed to be reasoning with that extravagant warmth of temper she had complained of: but his eyes and his manner expressed plainly what he forebore to utter. After a while, he appeared to have conquered the inclination he felt to give way to the rage that possessed him; and sitting down by her, he softened his voice as much as he could, though it trembled through the variety of emotions he felt, and endeavoured to speak calmly while he said—"Celestina, if this be really the case—if I may venture to believe you, you will not surely refuse to satisfy me a little farther. I am not a vain coxcomb: but I know that neither my figure or my understanding are contemptible; I have a very affluent fortune; and I have an heart that, as you well know, adores you. Willoughby cannot or will not marry you; of that I think you can no longer doubt. You say, that you are not engaged to the young Doctor[1] Thorold; tell me then, what there is, that overbalancing so many points in my favour, renders them all ineffectual."

---

1 Sarcasm: Montague Thorold is not yet a Doctor of Divinity.

"And I will tell you candidly, Mr. Vavasour. My objections then are, to your morals—to your principles: they may not be, and I dare say are not, worse than those of other young men of fortune who have equal opportunities of following their own inclinations: but however that may be, they are such as would inevitably make me unhappy; and knowing that, it would be extreme folly were any advantages which affluence can offer to induce me to risk it."

"My morals!" cried Vavasour—"again my morals!—and pray what part of what you are pleased to call my morals is it that gives you so much offence?"

"All," answered she. "Your manner of life—your attachments—your connections, which you have just acknowledged you could not, without hesitation and reluctance, quit."

"Still you will misunderstand me. What I said in regard to Emily surely went to a very different meaning. I told you, that you are the only woman upon earth for whom I would quit her; and the greater my regard has been for her, surely the greater it makes out my attachment to you, for whom I would relinquish her. By heaven! I cannot tell how far my affection for her might have carried me, if my passion for you had not taken so deep root in my heart; and curse me, if amidst it all I do not still love her dearly, and would give half my estate to make her happy and re-establish her health; but poor dear girl—she will never, I am afraid, recover."

"If her illness is occasioned by her fears of losing you, Sir," said Celestina, "remove at once the cause of it by thinking of me no more. If you love her as much as you express, surely this cannot be difficult; and why, feeling this attachment to a person whom you think so deserving of it, should you, contrary to the dictates of reason, pursue one who never can return the good opinion you entertain of her?"

"Because of my morals! Ridiculous cant and falsehood. Don't I know that women all like the very libertinism they are pleased outwardly to condemn? Don't I know that the proudest, the most prudish among ye,[1] are flattered by the attention of those men who are called the greatest rakes, and that if any queer fellow sets up to be a moral man, ye all laugh at and despise him. This sort of stuff about morals, you have learned, I suppose, either from old parson Thorold, or this good motherly gentlewoman you live with: but you, who

---

1   This form of "you" may be thought an old-fashioned usage now, but it probably indicates, on the contrary, a slangy manner of speech.

have so much sense, cannot seriously persist in such methodistical cant;[1] and as to any objections about Emily—"

"Don't mistake me, Mr. Vavasour. I made no mention of her in the way of objection."

"Well then," cried he, interrupting her, "as to my morals in every other respect they are really exemplary. I play,[2] comparatively, very little; I don't drink a fifth part so much as half the people I live with; and I reckon myself, upon the whole, a very orderly, sober fellow."

"By comparison only," said Celestina, half smiling at his way of making out the account.

"Aye, by comparison. Every thing in this world is, you know, good or bad only by comparison. Come, come, Celestina, I was willing enough to allow for your prepossession in favour of George Willoughby, but to any other I cannot, I will not submit; nor will I allow any thing to this damned prudery. I know myself worthy of you, highly as I think of you. Yes, I deserve you, if it be only for my persevering love; and by all that's good I will not be denied."

"You really will, Sir," replied Celestina; who, more and more distressed by his perseverance, desired to put an end to it for ever if possible—"you really will; for I protest to you that I never can give any other answer than I have already given, and I beg, I entreat that you will desist from a pursuit that can produce for you only mortification."

"May perdition seize me if I do!"[3] returned he with renewed vehemence. "No! if I perish in the attempt, I will persevere!" He was proceeding in this strain, when Lady Horatia sent to let Celestina know she waited for her to go out; and she took the opportunity of

---

1 "Methodist" or "methodistical" was originally a contemptuous designation for the self-discipline and regular religious observance of the followers of John and Charles Wesley, in contrast to the laxity of many Church of England clergy. From 1729, when the brothers convened a group of like-minded theological students at Oxford, their passionate Evangelism, often conducted outdoors and addressed to the labouring and destitute classes, had an immense impact on the Church of England, forcing it to reform or lose its congregations, and on the cultural life of the country in general. Though the brothers remained within the Church of England, after their deaths the Methodist movement became a separate religious denomination with a large and continuing membership and influence. By "cant" is meant any moral or religious language used insincerely.

2 Gamble.

3 Cf. *Othello* 3.3.91-92: "Perdition catch my soul/ But I do love thee."

hastening away, glad to be relieved from a conversation so distressing; while Vavasour, finding all attempts to detain her ineffectual, left the house in one of those paroxysms of passion, which disappointment, from his having never been used to submit to it, always produced.

Chapter II

It would be difficult to say, whether Willoughby, wandering and solitary among the remote villages of Yorkshire, or Celestina, surrounded in London by what the world calls pleasure and amusement, was the most internally wretched. Celestina's last dialogue with Vavasour, had convinced her that Willoughby no longer thought of her even with that degree of friendship and tenderness which he had so often assured her nothing should destroy: and he was gone out of town merely to prepare for his marriage; and gone without deigning either to see her or answer the letter she had written to him. There was, in such conduct, so much unkindness and inhumanity, that she began to hope her reflections on it would by degrees abate the anguish she now felt: and she listened to Lady Horatia, who continually spoke of it as an unequivocal proof of Willoughby's want of an heart capable of a generous and steady attachment. To Montague Thorold, however, (who now again returned to town after an absence on business of some little time), she could not listen with so much complacency as her friend wished; and she repeatedly told him, that the greatest obligation he could confer upon her would be to desist from talking to her of love. The certainty, however, there now seemed to be that Willoughby no longer considered himself as interested about her; her positive rejection of Mr. Vavasour, and the encouragement given him by Lady Horatia to persevere, brought him continually to the house; where their morning parties of reading re-commenced; and whenever they went out to an evening engagement, Montague Thorold was there attendant: thus drinking intoxicating draughts of love, and indulging hope that it would finally be successful.

Willoughby now found without difficulty the person he sought: and whether it was that she had her lesson more completely, or was permitted to speak plainer of what she knew, she answered all his enquiries in such a way as served to perplex but not entirely to affirm the question, whether Celestina was his mother's daughter. The woman was, in her mind and ideas, one of the lowest of the vulgar: yet her simplicity seemed to be affected; and all the proofs which had been talked of did not amount to her declaring that she was present at the birth of Celestina or could produce any positive evidence of it. She spoke principally to the time when she said the little girl was at nurse[1] at Kensington; of which she related a great many particulars that staggered Willoughby more than ever, without convincing him: yet all the woman said, though it was consistent, had the air of having learned by rote; and there was about her a sort of guarded cunning which seemed to have been acquired, or at least improved by long practice. Willoughby attempted to discover whether she had not received money from Lady Castlenorth, and to find what were her present means of subsistence: but for these enquiries also she seemed prepared; and gave at least a plausible account of a legacy left her by a great uncle, that enabled her to live without servitude in her native country, where she boarded with a relation, and affected great piety and sanctity. She blessed God, she said, that she scorned for the lucre of gain to belye any one, dead or alive, much more her good mistress who was gone: but truth was truth; and she hoped, by the help of God, always to speak it plain and direct, without fee or reward: "and as for Lady Castlenorth," added she, "whom your honour thinks has paid me for speaking of this thing, pray consider, your honour, wherein it could be useful to my lady to put me upon saying a falsity. If I was base enough to take money of my Lady for it, which to be certain I never did, for what would that be, as your honour well knows, but selling my immortal soul? and what good, as I may say, would all the gold and diamonds in the world do me, if my precious soul was to perish because of them?"

This cant, to which Willoughby listened with continued patience, made him hope that he should, in some instance or other, detect her of inconsistency. But though he saw her repeatedly, and set Farnham to watch her still more narrowly and to talk the matter over with her as if in confidence, she was always so guarded that no contradiction could be discovered; and after waiting near a week at the village, Willoughby was compelled to give up every idea of certainly coming at the truth, and to return towards London without being positively sure that Celestina was so nearly related to him; yet forced to

---

1 Middle and upper-class mothers often sent their babies to live with the family of a woman (wet-nurse) who was breast-feeding or had just lost a baby of her own, and who was paid to breast-feed them for the first two or three years of their lives.

allow that he could not, in contradiction to all he had heard of a child nursed in secret at Kensington, bring any sort of evidence on which he ought to rely that she was not so.

Sick at heart, and feeling too sensibly that all his future life must be unhappy, his mind sunk in total despondence. Too certain it was, that under such circumstances he could not think of marrying Celestina: yet he was unhappily conscious that he could not bear to think of her marrying another. It was in vain he accused himself of something worse than folly. The moment his mind dwelt on that subject, he found that folly irresistible: and while he determined that one of the first things he would do on his return should be to make a provision for Celestina out of his remaining fortune, he sickened in recollecting that such a provision would probably but facilitate her marriage with Montague Thorold—and of Montague Thorold he could not think with patience.

Of his own situation in regard to the family of Fitz-Hayman, he thought with equal bitterness. He was but too conscious, that to obtain the information he wanted from Hannah Biscoe, which he had flattered himself would turn out very differently, he had renewed his attendance at the house of his uncle, and acted disingenuously and unlike himself. However indifferent or averse he was to his cousin, his honour forbade him any longer to trifle with those sentiments which she evidently entertained in his favour. What then should he do? This question came continually before him; and was continually debated without his being able to form any resolution on which he could for a moment rest without pain.

He sometimes thought, that since in losing the only woman whom he could love, he had lost all that could render his life happy, it was immaterial what became of him; and that since he must be miserable, it might be as well in following as in flying from what he still thought was in some degree a duty—completing the engagement he had made to his mother on her death bed. In doing this, he should gratify all his surviving relations, and retrieve his estate, which he must otherwise sell, as the mortgages upon it were rapidly devouring it: and to do this was, as he sometimes tried to persuade himself, to pay a debt he owed his ancestors. He had been educated by his mother in high ideas of the consequence and respectability, not only of her family but of that of his father; but of these prejudices his natural good sense had suffered very little to remain; so that if he now endeavoured to recall them in support of those arguments which he ran over in favour of his marriage, his understanding immediately revolted against them.

"I shall not only retrieve," said he, "but augment my fortune: not only save Alvestone, but add to my present estates the family possessions of my mother, which will otherwise become the property of strangers: the honours too so long inherited by her ancestors will be mine."

He frequently made efforts to fix his mind on these advantages; but the moment he began seriously to investigate their value, he beheld them with contempt.

"Ridiculous!" cried he. "My ancestors! What is this foolish family pride, for which I am meditating to sell my freedom, in acquiescence with narrow prejudice? I shall have a large estate; but will it make me happier in myself, or more respected by those whose respect can afford me any pleasure? I shall be called 'my Lord'—a mighty satisfaction truly!—The vulgar—for with such empty sounds the vulgar only are delighted—will bow to my Lordship, and I shall take place at county meetings above the neighbouring Esquires who are now my equals. I shall have a bauble called a coronet painted on my coach doors and my hall chairs, and shall become one of the legislature,[1] qualified for it only by the possession of that bauble. Perhaps half a dozen or half a hundred men and women of poor ambition, may court the notice and boast of the acquaintance of Lord Castlenorth, who would have let Mr. Willoughby remain unmolested by their kindness, and by such friends my house will be infested and my leisure destroyed. But I shall go to Court,[2] and be named as having appeared at the drawing room;[3] that will be very delectable certainly: and my wife's fine cloaths will be described at full length, and the taste of my equipage be commended in all the newspapers. It will be there told of me, that I am gone to this or that of my country houses; and my six bays, or greys, or blacks, will be celebrated in Hyde Park, or be conspicuous in the roads within twenty miles of London; while a thousand insignificant insipid beings, whom I neither know or desire to know, shall say 'what a beautiful carriage, what a well appointed equipage is that of my Lord Castlenorth.' All this felicity in the aggregate, and I know of no more that belongs to the possession of a title, is certainly well worth the sacrifice I shall

---

1 Will have a seat in the House of Lords.
2 The court of King George III and Queen Charlotte at St. James's Palace.
3 Signifying an occasion rather than a place, the term means a formal reception by the King or Queen, or both.

make to obtain it; and my ancestors, 'from their airy clouds,'[1] will be infinitely delighted by the story of their descendant.

"But what will that descendant be in reality? a mercenary, a miserable wretch: condemned to pass his life with a woman, whom, if he does not loathe, he does not love; to feel himself a purchased husband; and to have sold, in sad exchange, a man's best birth right, freedom, for a mess of pottage."[2]

To such soliloquies as these, succeeded determinations to carry no farther any semblance of attention to Miss Fitz-Hayman; but to go even from his present journey and without passing through London, immediately abroad.

To a mind unable to resist misery, there frequently appears a possibility of flying from it; and while Willoughby dreaded the thoughts of returning to London, he fancied that if he could cross over from Hull to the north of Europe, he should leave some part of his present unhappiness behind him. Unsettled and unhappy as he was, these debates with himself, these vague plans of quitting everything and becoming a wanderer on earth, became more usual with him: but still he decided on nothing. The idea of being compelled to sell Alvestone was the only one, however, that had great weight with him. To think that the place to which he had been so fondly attached should become the property of some upstart man of sudden fortune, was accompanied by a sensation of acute uneasiness. He imagined, those beautiful woods, the growth of centuries, fallen in compliance with the improving taste of a broker or a warehouseman;[3] the park ploughed up to be converted into farms; and the elegant simplicity of his house and his grounds, destroyed by gothic windows or Chinese ornaments;[4] the

---

1 Richard Polwhele, "The Fair Isabel of Cotehele, a Cornish Romance," Canto 5, 296: "They were as spirits on airy clouds[...]"

2 In the Genesis story (Chapter 25), Isaac and Rebecca have twin sons, Esau and Jacob. Coming back from hunting one day, Esau is so hungry and exhausted he sells his birthright (rights of inheritance) as the first-born to his twin in return for food, a "mess of pottage." Hence, to exchange one's integrity or expectations for a slight but immediate material gain.

3 A banker dealing in stocks and shares or a businessman in the import/export trade.

4 English domestic architecture was enjoying a Gothic Revival, the construction of neo-medievalism, for example at Horace Walpole's house at Strawberry Hill. But the expansion of trade and consequent import of foreign art objects inaugurated new fashions in furnishings and in garden design of a Chinese or Indian style.

shrubberies where he had wandered with Celestina, that turf, where he had ran by her side when she was learning to ride, and where they used to walk arm in arm together; that house, where he had hoped she would preside, and grace so lovely a scene with a mistress yet more lovely; all, all were to become the property of another! and the very name of Willoughby, and what was yet more painful, the name of Celestina, should never more, in those scenes, be remembered. Yet in a moment the cruel truth occurred to him, that whether this place belonged to him or to another, Celestina would never again visit it; that he should never again hear her voice calling him among the beech woods, or trace her footsteps on the turf; never listen to her as she read in his mother's dressing room, or hold her hand within his as they sat together on the woody banks of the water-fall, and marked its sparkling current leap from rock to rock. And without her, what would Alvestone be but a place where every spot would be haunted by melancholy images of departed happiness? How little the indulgence of these painful contemplations would be interrupted, or put an end to, by any satisfaction he could derive from the conversation of Miss Fitz-Hayman, his sick and reluctant heart too plainly told him; and then he again believed himself determined to sell all his estates and quit England; if not for ever, at least till time, absence, and the impossibility of his changing it, had better reconciled him to that destiny which condemned him to give up Celestina, and see her in the arms of another.

A desultory and unsettled life, had within the last year become habitual to him; and while he was actually moving from one place to another, his spirits preyed less corrosively on themselves. Since to live as he wished to have lived in his own country was impossible, he thought he should regret it less while he was wandering over others: and since he could not now contemplate the face and character he so fondly loved, he hoped that variety of characters and variety of faces would divert his regret if they could not cure his attachment. There was too an idea of freedom and independence, which accompanied his thus shaking off at once every incumbrance, that was not without its charms; and in this disposition he thought contemptuously of mere local preference as unworthy a strong mind, and determined to become a citizen of the world; and when in his imagination he had settled his route, through Holland and France to Sicily, which he had long wished to see, and from thence to the Archipelago,[1] he breathed freer, and felt himself more reconciled to existence.

---

1 The Greek islands.

He journeyed, however, slowly towards London while these debates were carrying on: and at York, whither he had ordered his letters to be directed, he found one from Cathcart which related some circumstances in regard to his affairs, that convinced him he could not, unless to the material injury of some persons who were connected with him, quit England without some regulation of those pecuniary concerns which he had so long neglected and would now willingly have escaped from. This letter determined him to return to London; though another letter from his sister, in which she mentioned, as an article of news, that Celestina was either actually married to Montague Thorold or on the point of being so, threw him into a state of mind bordering on distraction: reason, which had long fruitlessly contended against this fatal, and perhaps guilty attachment, now seemed tired of a contention so hopeless, and his mind became a chaos of conflicting passions, all equally destructive to his mental and bodily health.

To return to London, however, was become necessary; and Farnham, his old faithful servant, persuaded him to take post chaises for the rest of his journey. He arrived, after an absence of above three weeks, at the house of Lady Molyneux; and there heard, that a few days before, Lady Horatia Howard had publicly spoken of Celestina's marriage with the young divine[1] as a settled thing; that his father had bought for him a considerable living in Gloucestershire, where they were to reside, and where a curate was settled till he was himself qualified to take it;[2] and thither, as there was a very good house upon it, they were going immediately after their marriage. Willoughby heard all this without being able to make any reply, and then hastened to his own lodgings, from whence he dispatched Farnham for intelligence from the servants of Lady Horatia. The coachman, with whom he had some time before made an acquaintance and who was a very talkative fellow, immediately informed him of all he knew, and much that he imagined. He said it was very true, that Mr. Thorold lived almost always at their house, "and my Lady," said the man— "my Lady loves him for all the world as if he was her own son. There they are all morning reading play books and such together, as my fellow servants tell me, that is, my Lady and Miss and this here young divine as is to be; and then they goes out in my coach, all's one as if

1 Clergyman.
2 Until he has been awarded his Doctorate of Divinity at Oxford and ordained as a clergyman by the Bishop of the diocese in which he has a living (parish).

they belonged to the same family; and I do understand as how my Lady is to give her a portion[1] and they to be married out of hand, that is in a little time, and I believe that's the very truth of the thing, for my Lady have bought another coach horse within these ten days, and told me—'Abraham,' says she, 'I shall go early next month into Gloucestershire, instead of going to Matlock as I talked of, and I shall go in the coach instead of the post chaise, because I will have some friends with me.'"

This account, which Farnham faithfully repeated to Willoughby, confirmed almost beyond a doubt all Lady Molyneux had related to him. Some more recent intelligence that he had received from Cathcart as to the embroiled state of his affairs in the country, combined to render him desperate: and he had been so long harrassed between his love and his interest, his honour and his reluctance, that he suddenly took the resolution of putting it out of his own power to undergo again such variety of torments: like a wretch who leaps from a ship on fire into the sea, though certain of meeting death in another shape, he formed the determination of making himself, since he must be wretched, as completely wretched as possible. He thought of Celestina as his relation in vain; it abated nothing of that anguish with which he considered her as the wife of Montague Thorold; and so hideous were the images that forced themselves upon him, that he found his reason had no power to subdue them, and thought that nothing could so decidedly oblige him to check them as his marriage; and without giving himself time to consider how desperate was the remedy, he went immediately to the house of Lord Castlenorth, declared to him that he was satisfied as to the object of his journey, and took the most immediate opportunity after his return of expressing his solicitude to avail himself of his cousin's generous predilection in his favour, and to fulfil the wishes of his deceased mother and his surviving family.

The eager and tremulous manner in which he uttered all this, and which was in reality the effect of despair and anguish, Lord Castlenorth mistook for the anxiety and impatience of love. His nephew had never spoke thus decisively before; and seeing thus what he had so long fondly wished for out of doubt, his first idea was, to proceed instantly in securing to Willoughby the reversion of those titles on which he set so high a value himself. While, therefore, he set

---

1   The dowry or "fortune" usually provided by a woman's family on her marriage.

out in his chariot, supported by Mrs. Calder, who always attended him, to solicit the completion of a business which had hither proceeded but slowly, and fancied the happiness of all parties would be wonderfully advanced by his success, Willoughby, with such sensations as a determined suicide alone could envy, was making to Lady Castlenorth the same declaration; and was immediately afterwards allowed, or rather desired, to present himself at the feet of her fair daughter.

Chapter III

To play the lover is not difficult to most men, even where their hearts are not really interested. A few fine speeches, a little common place declamation, are easily produced and generally accepted: but Willoughby, always a very poor dissembler, and who felt, in despite of every effort to express them, sentiments towards Miss Fitz-Hayman bordering on antipathy, was very conscious that he should ill answer her ideas of a passionate lover, and his consciousness deprived him of the little power he might otherwise have had to dissemble.

He now, with encreased confusion of thought, repented that he had gone so far; but to recede was impossible; and with a countenance expressive rather of perturbation and wretchedness than of the pleasurable sensations inspired by successful love, he entered the apartment where Miss Fitz-Hayman had been prepared by Lady Castlenorth to receive his tender professions.

He approached her, and took her hand; muttered something about the final *éclaircissement* [1] of his doubts as to another person, (for he dared not trust his voice with the name of Celestina), and something about being, in consequence of that *éclaircissement*, released from his former engagements: then in a still more tremulous and uncertain tone, he solicited her permission to dedicate his life to her service, and to hasten those preparations for his happiness, which his former uncertainties and embarrassments had put it out of his power to solicit with that ardour which he should under other circumstances have evinced.

The falsehood he was uttering died away almost inarticulately on his lips, and his revolting heart reproached him for it, faint and reluc-

---

1 Enlightenment, clarification.

tant as it was. As he finished his speech, Miss Fitz-Hayman turned her large black eyes, which had till then been modestly cast down, full upon him. She seemed to have been trying to make them speak tenderness; but to him they expressed nothing but an imperious enquiry into the truth of his professions, from which he shrunk. In a moment, however, those eyes, so little calculated for the soft parley of affection, contrived to overflow with tears. She gave him the hand he had just before let go, and inclining her head tenderly towards him, said, in terms as gentle as she could command—"Oh! Willoughby! you know too well, you have long known my unfortunate partiality towards you—a partiality, which, with reluctance and with regret I own, not all your too evident coldness has conquered. Alas! could I now believe you sincere!"

"Believe it I conjure you," cried he in a hurried voice, and hastening to put an end to a dialogue which he found he could ill support—"Believe it, dear Madam! and believe, (what is true also)—that I have now no other engagement—no other attachment—and cannot but be—be truly sensible of your extraordinary merit."

"I will believe it," answered she: "I will endeavour to believe it, for I find, that even if I am deceived, the deceit is dear to me."

Willoughby then kissed her hand with as much warmth as he could affect; and running over, in the breathless tremor which consciousness of his disingenuous conduct occasioned, a few common place sentences about eternal gratitude and unalterable love; speeches which have probably been repeated ten million of times with as little sincerity but seldom with so much self reproof, he led her to talk of preparations, and equipages, and jewels: subjects on which she entered with such ease as showed that her mind had been familiarized to consider them, and that they were not without importance in her opinion. Poor Willoughby, who now felt his fate irretrievable, had very different sensations. Oppressed and bewildered by a variety of sufferings, yet compelled, by the part he had thus rashly determined to act, to stifle them all, his prevailing idea was, that since the Rubicon was now passed,[1] the sooner this dreaded marriage was over the better for him; since his mind must then combat, with more

---

1   The River Rubicon marked the boundary between Italy and Gaul in the time of the Roman Empire, across which a general returning to Rome was forbidden to bring his army without permission from the Senate. By crossing the river from Gaul and advancing on Rome with his army in 49 BC, Julius Caesar effectively declared a state of civil war. Hence: to pass some point of no return.

force than it could now do, those wild eccentricities, the offspring of despair, which were crouding fast upon him. He therefore pressed for an early day; not with the vehemence of love, but with that of a wretch who knowing he must die, wishes to hear his physician fix the period when his torments are likely to end. Miss Fitz-Hayman, however, either could not or would not discover this; and though his inflamed eyes, his short sighs, unsettled manner, and broken sentences, gave him altogether the appearance rather of a man suffering under some recent calamity than of a favoured and fortunate lover on the point of obtaining his happiness, the lady, either from her confidence in her own charms, or from some other cause, was perfectly satisfied with his behaviour; and before he left her, promised that she would not oppose the arrangement which she understood to have been made by her father—that in three weeks he should receive her hand.

This then was determined without possibility of recall; and Willoughby, too sensible already of the weight of those chains which he had thus easily forged for himself, now disengaged himself as soon as possible, and ran out of the house, impatient to be alone, and to contemplate in the stillness of his own room the prospect of misery into which he had thus rashly bound himself to rush. He walked very fast, and as if he was flying from himself, towards his lodgings in Bond-street, where, as he passed along it, a croud of passengers near one of the crossings impeded his passage. He regarded them not; but made his way eagerly among them, till he was immediately between a footman who waited at the door of a coach, and a young lady who was coming out of a shop to step into it. On his pressing rather hastily before her, the servant put him back with his hand. Willoughby, out of humour at that moment with himself and with all the world, and fancying the action of the footman impertinent, spoke to him very harshly and was almost provoked to strike him, when the lady, who had her foot on the step, appeared a good deal alarmed, and no sooner heard the sound of his voice thus menacing, than she caught the servant's arm for support; and at the same moment Willoughby, who had not till then seen her face, beheld the lovely but pale and terrified countenance of Celestina!

Thrown entirely off his guard, and not knowing what he did, he took the hand with which she had supported herself against the servant. "Celestina!" cried he—"Oh God! is it you, Celestina?"

She looked at him with eyes where surprise was softened by tenderness, and tried to recover voice enough to utter more than—"Willoughby!" which the immediate emotion drew from her: but he gave her no time; for fixing his eyes on her's, all that she had been to him, all that he believed she was now to another, and all that he had just agreed to be himself, rushed upon his recollection at once, and in an agony of grief, remorse, and despair, he threw her hand from him, and turning away, he walked, or rather ran towards his lodgings as if he had been pursued by the furies,[1] where, without giving his servant time to open it, he rapped at the door with violence enough to break it down; so fearful he seemed of again seeing Celestina as she passed in the coach, which, by the horses being in that direction, would, he thought, come that way.

Farnham, his servant, who opened the door, was amazed at his impatience so unlike his usual manner, and with still more surprise saw him, instead of speaking and enquiring for letters, as he always did when he came in, and was particularly likely now to do after so long an absence, rush by him as if he had not seen him; and hurrying up stairs by two steps at a time, shut the door of the dining room with a violence that shook the whole house, and turned the key.

This faithful servant had lived with him from the time of his leaving school, and was more attached to his master than to any other person on earth. He had seen with deep concern the sad change that had happened in his health and in his temper, since that unfortunate night when he so suddenly left Alvestone the year before, and had, in all his journies and all his illness, watched over him with assiduous and attentive care. He had often known him dejected, and almost sinking under his uncertainties and his disappointments, but had never till now observed such fury in his eyes and marks of desperation in his manner; and alarmed at the circumstance of his having locked the door of his room, Farnham was immediately beset with numberless fearful conjectures.

He was aware that his master's affairs were far from being prosperous, and imagined it possible that he might be pursued for debt: and as he knew his pride would render such a thing almost insupportable, he feared least in the sudden agony to which it might subject him, he might commit some violence on himself. Willoughby's temper was naturally very mild, and not easily inflamed to anger; but when that did happen, his anger was dreadful; and though Farnham had only once or twice seen it excited during his long service, he knew how terrible it was when thoroughly roused.

---

1   In Greek myth, the Furies, Tisiphone, Megaera and Allecto, were avenging spirits who pursued and punished wrongdoers, especially those who committed crimes within the family.

The conjectures that Farnham entertained were not to be supported calmly; and though he had always received strict orders never to enter the room where his master was busy, till he rang or called for him, he was now strongly tempted, yet dared not determine to disobey his commands. He could not, however, forbear going to the door and listening. He heard his master utter deep and convulsive sighs: he heard him walking by starts in the room; but, by the key's being left in the lock, he could see nothing. He then went softly into the bed chamber; and from thence a defect in the door, which opened from it into the dining room, enabled him to distinguish that Willoughby now sat by a table on which his arms were thrown, and on them he rested his head; while his hair, all in disorder, concealed every part of his face: then in a moment starting up, he traversed the room with quick and uncertain steps, now clasping his hands together, now throwing them wildly abroad. At length he stopped, and striking his forehead, said, in a voice rather resembling groaning than speaking—"Oh accursed, accursed wretch!—what hast thou done!"

Still more alarmed by these words, and by beholding the frantic gestures with which his master now leaned against the side of the chimney, now flew to the other side of the room, and now threw himself on a sopha, Farnham again debated with himself whether he should not go in at any event. There was a *couteau de chasse*[1] and a sword hung up in the room, and two brace of pistols in the cases, which Farnham had just put there, loaded as they were when his master travelled; and the poor fellow fancied that on these, whenever he passed them, his master looked wildly eager. This might be for some time fancy: but at length, either from accident or from his feeling at that instant some horrible temptation to escape from the evils that just then appeared quite intolerable, Willoughby stopped with folded arms opposite to these instruments of destruction, and while his expressive countenance was marked with the severest anguish, he murmured inarticulately some words which Farnham interpreted as a determination to put an end to his sufferings. Bent at any hazard to prevent his executing this fearful threat, the affrighted servant now searched with trembling hands for the lock, which he forgot he could not open. His master demanded, in a voice which struck him with terror, who was there? when luckily for him a thundering rap at the street door gave him hopes that some visitors might be coming who might more properly and effectually interfere, and he flew

---

1 Hunting knife.

down to let them in, regardless of Willoughby, who, coming out to the top of the stairs, called to him, and peremptorily ordered him to admit nobody.

It was Sir Philip Molyneux; who having just met Lord Castlenorth at the Minister's levee,[1] had heard from him that Willoughby, immediately on his arrival in town, had agreed to the conclusion of his marriage; and that in consequence of it he had himself been attending the levee to hasten the affair of the reversionary titles, which affair was likely to be speedily concluded. Sir Philip, therefore, having, received this intelligence, called as he went home to congratulate his brother in law, and to take him to dinner in Portman-square.

Little accustomed as Sir Philip was to make remarks on any body's appearance, and particularly on that of his inferiors, he was notwithstanding struck with the countenance of Farnham, as, pale and aghast, he opened the door to him; and as he went before him up stairs, he enquired what ailed him. "I hardly know indeed Sir," replied Farnham: "but my master, who came from Barnet only early this morning as you know I suppose Sir, off his Yorkshire journey, has been out somewhere since, and is come home in such a humour as I am sure I have never seen him in in all the years I have lived with him: be so good, Sir, however, as not to take notice that I spoke about it."

Sir Philip had no time to promise he would not, before they were at the door of the dining room, where Willoughby stood and sternly said to his servant—"How dare you, Sir, disobey me in this manner? did I not tell you, stupid hound, that I would not be at home?"

"Lord, Sir," cried Farnham in great distress, for he was little accustomed and could hardly bear to be thus harshly reproved—"Lord, Sir—it is only Sir Philip—and I am sure I thought—"

"Curse on your thoughts!" cried Willoughby. "Blockhead—are you to think for me?"

---

1   The First Minister's (William Pitt the Younger's) reception. "Prime Minister" was not then a term in general use, though the necessity for one leading minister with overall responsibility for public affairs was emerging during Pitt's tenure of office, especially after George III began to suffer bouts of what appeared to be insanity. Pitt was appointed Chancellor of the Exchequer, and therefore First Minister, in 1783 at the age of 24, and continued in power through the war with France in the nineties. Though running a relatively uncorrupt administration, he was in general against political and social reform of the kind that Smith's fellow radicals wanted.

"Hey day!" said Sir Philip, "what's all this? Don't be angry with poor Farnham. I would come in, for I was impatient to wish you joy."

"Joy, Sir?—of what?"

"Why I have this moment seen Lord Castlenorth, who has told me that every thing is settled at last. Come, I'm very glad to hear it, for it must be owned that this business, George, has advanced but slowly. Well! so now 'tis to be done directly? The old peer was quite frisky upon it, and forgot his asthma and his gout to stand till I was tired of hearing him, telling me of the regulation he had made as to your name; he becomes Earl and Viscount Castlenorth; and you take, as your title, that of Baron Ravensburgh. I heard the history too of how that came into the family. Well, but George, you'll go dine with us. Lady Molyneux will be glad, perhaps, to hear about it, and to wish you joy."

"Joy—damnation rather!" muttered Willoughby, as, snatching away his hand, he fled to the other end of the room: then by an effort recovering himself a little, he returned towards Sir Philip, and said, with forced calmness—"Prythee don't teize me with these hateful common place congratulations. Surely it is bad enough for a fellow to be forced to hear them afterwards, and indeed bad enough to be married, without having them rung in his ears for a month before hand."

Sir Philip, who now saw very plainly that his reluctance was by no means subdued, had no inclination to argue the matter with him. He had no idea why he might not be happy with Miss Fitz-Hayman or any other woman of equal fortune: but whether he was so or no, his own solicitude went no further than that his brother in law might not be reduced either to a state of indigence such as might disgrace his alliance or compel him to borrow money of his relations; and as Willoughby's marriage with Miss Fitz-Hayman would preclude the possibility of any such aukward circumstances, he heartily wished it, and had of late forgot his usual apathy to join with his wife in promoting it.

There was, he thought, no occasion for argument in the present case, since the affair was now, whether Willoughby liked it or no, irrevocably fixed upon. He therefore spared himself the fatigue of remarks or remonstrance on Willoughby's behaviour, and only said—"But you'll dine with us, George, today—will you not?"

"No, I cannot," replied Willoughby.

"Tomorrow then. We shall have a large party, and dine exactly at seven o'clock."

"I will if I can. But I can engage for nothing. I hate to be fettered by engagements: but if I can come I will. Shall I ring for your servants?"

"They are at the door," said Sir Philip, who immediately went away, without having any great reason to be satisfied with the politeness of his brother in law. Of that, however, he thought not: and if the behaviour of Willoughby afterwards occurred to him at all, it only created a momentary surprise, mingled with some degree of pity, which his absurdity, and not his evident unhappiness, excited.

His visit, however, had the effect of rousing Willoughby from that dreadful condition of mind into which the step he had taken that morning in regard to Miss Fitz-Hayman, and the sudden sight of Celestina, had thrown him. He now became able to collect his thoughts; and was at once conscious of the general folly of his conduct, and of his cruel behaviour to Farnham, who was so hurt by having seen his master in such a state, and by the unkind and unusual way in which he had spoke to him, that when the poor fellow came up to enquire if he would please to dress, the tears were in his eyes, and he was hardly able to speak.

Willoughby was of too noble a nature not to apologise for his fault the moment he felt it. He answered mildly that he should dress directly, and then said—"Farnham, I spoke angrily to you just now, and I am sorry for it. I was vexed, and could not command my temper. You were wrong too in letting in Sir Philip Molyneux. Another time remember, that when I give orders to be denied I except nobody unless I particularly name them."

Poor Farnham dared not say why he then ventured to disobey him; but in the most humble terms begged his pardon and said he was very sorry. "Well, well," cried Willoughby, with a deep sigh, "and I am very sorry, Farnham, that I was so foolishly passionate. Let us think no more of it." He then bade him get his things to dress, and tried, by taking up a book, to divert his thoughts from himself, and obtain at least a respite from the corrosive reflections that pursued him; but it would not do: he threw the book away, and felt, notwithstanding all his efforts, his wretchedness and impatience returning: while Farnham, who as he dressed his hair watched every turn of his countenance, saw but too plainly that his master was half distracted by something into which he dared not enquire. This gave a sort of unquiet slowness to his manner, which Willoughby observing, was on the point of relapsing into that sort of behaviour for which he had but the moment before expressed his sorrow, and impetuously bade him mind what he was about and make haste:

then hardly suffering him to finish his hair, he started up, and putting on his cloaths in the haste that denoted the unquietness of his mind, he sent for a hackney coach, and ordered it to set him down at the hotel in Soho-square. Farnham still apprehending that some fatal event might follow all the agitation of mind which he had witnessed, now approached again, and asked if he should be at home in the evening, or sup at home? To which Willoughby, no longer able to check himself, answered—"no!" as he drew up the glass, in an accent that terrified poor Farnham; who, more and more confirmed in his notion that something was about to befall his master, now concluded that something was a duel. The pistols and the sword indeed were still hanging up in the dining room: but yet he could not be easy; and, after some consideration, he determined to go and enquire among the servants at Sir Philip Molyneux's and at Lord Castlenorth's if they could at all guess what was the matter; and with most of the latter he was particularly acquainted, by having been much with them at Florence and Naples when his master was last abroad.

Chapter IV

If Willoughby was so deeply affected by the sight of Celestina, the sudden shock she had received from their abrupt meeting, and from his strange behaviour, had on her an equally painful though a different effect. That the impulse of the moment had urged him to take her hand, made her hope that some remains of affection for her yet lingered in his bosom, and that his former regard was rather stifled by anger than annihilated by indifference. She knew that the first might be removed, and that she might be restored to his friendship; but that if his heart had once become quite cold towards her, nothing could ever renew even that share of tenderness with which she could learn, if not to be happy, at least to be content.

It was some time before she could recover from the agitation of spirits into which this unexpected interview had thrown her: but when she at length became calm enough to reflect on it, she determined to say nothing of having seen Willoughby to Lady Horatia, as she knew it would appear to her only a fresh instance of his unworthy treatment of her; on which, how severely soever she felt it, she did not love to hear any comments even from her best friends. With all the resolution she could collect, therefore, stifling her internal anguish, she prepared to go with a large party in the evening to Ranelagh.[1]

While she was dressing for this purpose, a servant brought up to her the following letter:

"MADAM,

"That a stranger, and a stranger in my situation of life, should address you, would possibly appear, to any less generous mind than your's, a liberty that should be repulsed with disdain and resented by contempt: but I am persuaded that from you I may expect that liberal candour with which true virtue and unaffected goodness considers even those whom the generality of the world agree to condemn and despise.

"You know, Madam, what I have been and what I am. From Mrs. Elphinstone you have probably learned what were the circumstances of my early life; and Mr. Vavasour, with that sincerity which deserves to be so highly valued, has told you how long I have been under his protection.

"He has since, Madam, expressed some fears that this information may have been prejudicial to his interest with you, and least it should be so, allow me to declare to you, that I know myself too well to believe for a moment that I ought to be in question where you are beloved—too well to hesitate in declaring, that attached as I am to Mr. Vavasour, I can never make him as happy as he deserves to be.

"No, Madam; that happiness depends entirely on you. Such a passion as he feels for you, I believe no other person can deserve; and I know him to have so good a heart, I desire his felicity so sincerely, that I hazard this step in the hope of promoting it.

"Mr. Vavasour's generosity has left me nothing to fear for the rest of my life, were it even to be a long one: but I feel that a very few months will bring it to an end; and I feel it without concern; for, thoughtless and unworthy as my conduct has been, I have never found in its most brilliant periods, that the glittering trappings bestowed by mercenary love, could quiet the throbbing heart that beat beneath them: and now my only wish is, to be forgiven and received by my family, and to pass the short remainder of my days

---

1   Ranelagh Gardens was a resort in Chelsea Fields and popular with all classes of society that could afford the entrance fee, which was two shillings and sixpence, or five shillings on fireworks nights. At its centre was the rococo Rotunda, with an orchestra, and booths for people to take tea or wine.

with them. You can intercede with them successfully, for they can refuse you nothing. Deign then, Madam, to interest yourself for me, and at the same time be assured that it is my purpose to withdraw myself for ever from Mr. Vavasour, whenever he will suffer me to go, which shall, he says, be whenever you will give him hopes of listening to him.

"If generosity, sincerity, good nature, and understanding, may be sufficient recommendations to your good opinion, Mr. Vavasour eminently deserves it; and whatever faults he may have, your virtue will correct. He knows nothing of my writing to you; but I am conscious that I owe *him* such an effort where the felicity of his future days is concerned, and I feel that in addressing *you*, my presumption if not successful will be forgiven. I have the honour to be,

   Madam
     your most obedient servant
      EMILY CATHCART."

Celestina could not peruse such a letter without a mixture of admiration and pity for the amiable unhappy writer. Though her resolution in regard to Vavasour could not be changed, she thought that she should no longer delay acquainting Mrs. Elphinstone and Cathcart with the information she had obtained relative to their sister; but it required some consideration, at least in regard to Cathcart. The circumstance of Emily's letter added to the flutter of spirits which the meeting in the morning had given her. Montague Thorold, who dined with Lady Horatia, and was to be one of their party at Ranelagh, contrived to be more than usually importunate with her for more pity and favour than she had lately shewn him: while the ladies, and Mr. Howard, who joined them in the evening, completed her anguish and confusion, by talking of the marriage which was in a few days to take place between Miss Fitz-Hayman and Mr. Willoughby. One of these was acquainted with Mrs. Calder, and had heard from her that morning that every thing was settled, the title arranged, the equipages and liveries bespoke, and the jewels and cloaths concluded upon, all of which she detailed at great length; while another said, that *she* understood that the marriage was to take place at Castlenorth, and that from thence all the family were to proceed together to Italy, where they were to pass a twelvemonth. All, however, agreed that it was certainly to be concluded immediately, and Celestina could not any longer entertain a doubt of it.

Though her heart had always revolted from the idea of Willoughby's union with Miss Fitz-Hayman, she had been now so long accustomed to think of it, that she felt less poignant concern on that account, but if possible more than ever from his continued coldness, and the cruel neglect he had been guilty of in not answering her letter. "That he marries another," cried she, as she reflected on it, "I might learn to submit to without murmuring, if it can contribute to his ease or happiness in any way; but that he should quite desert and forsake me after so many assurances of esteem and regard, even when love was no longer in question; that he should disdain to own that connection by blood, if he is sure that it is so, which made him, with so much apparent reluctance, relinquish every other, that he should without pity leave me to a destiny which owes its unhappiness to him, seems so strange, so unnatural, so unlike him!—If I could once see him, hear him talk to me with friendly calmness, and tell me that he felt for me fraternal affection, or even the regard of long acquaintance, even what his mother's ward might claim from him, I think I should be comparatively happy, and should have no farther wish than to hear sometimes from himself that he was happy too. But to be thrown from him in his unfeeling and unfriendly way, to be forgotten and abandoned as if I had been found unworthy, not only of his affection but of his remembrance—oh! it is too much."

These reflections, and the uninteresting conversation of the company she was with, to which she was compelled to attend in order to escape the more irksome importunity of Montague Thorold, served but little to raise her spirits. They did not reach Ranelagh till a late hour: but on their entrance, the first party they met was Lady Castlenorth, her daughter, and Lady Molyneux. Captain Cavanaugh was on one side between the two former; and in deep conference with the latter was Captain Thorold.

The ladies, who could not avoid seeing Celestina, passed her with averted and haughty looks. Cavanaugh fixed his eyes on her with a look of bold enquiry, and Captain Thorold, as he passed his brother, said—"Ho! Montague, are you there? I did not know you were in town my boy!" He then gave a significant nod, as much as to say—"Aye, aye, I see how you are engaged," and passed on, renewing with great seeming earnestness his conversation with Lady Molyneux.

Though there was not in the world another set of people whom Celestina could be so little pleased to meet, and though she heard throughout the room, and from every group that passed them, the report of Willoughby's marriage, with various comments and circumstances, such as every body thought themselves at liberty to adorn it with, she felt a sort of satisfaction in seeing that he was not with them; and while there was not any thing she really so ardently desired as his happiness, yet so contradictory is the human heart, that she wished to believe he married Miss Fitz-Hayman reluctantly, though a marriage under such circumstances must above all other things render him miserable.

Montague Thorold, elated more than ever by hope, and encouraged to persevere by Lady Horatia, having now too, in consequence of the purchase his father had made for him, more pretension to aspire to her than his unsettled fortune had before given him; and sanguinely interpreting her gentle refusals, her friendly admonitions to desist, as giving him all the encouragement she could do, while her fate in regard to Willoughby was not absolutely decided; was on this evening particularly pressing and earnest; while her languor and weariness, the encouragement which she was conscious she seemed to have given him, her pity and even her regard for him, with the certainty of his ardent love for her, gave her altogether the air of listening to him favourably; and while her mind was frequently fixed on Willoughby, and she hardly recollected that Montague Thorold was talking to her, she seemed to be hearing the latter with complacency, and approving of conversation which it was not necessary for her to answer.

At length the short time Lady Horatia meant to pass at Ranelagh was over. She was fatigued, and Celestina rejoiced to hear her say she should go home. As Montague Thorold and Mr. Howard were with them, the other gentleman remained with the ladies who intended to stay longer; and Lady Horatia taking the arm of her relation, left Celestina to the care of Montague Thorold; and they were in this order proceeding towards the entrance, when standing near one of the niches, his hat over his eyes, and his head leaning against the way, they saw themselves close to Willoughby, who was, in that attitude, listening to some very earnest conversation with Vavasour, who stood by him.

The croud about the entrance was considerable: and Celestina, holding by the arm of Montague Thorold, was so near them, that they both at the same moment saw her. Willoughby started as if he had been crossed by a spectre; and without waiting to look a second time, he pushed through the croud and disappeared; but Vavasour came up to Celestina, and said in his usual way, taking abruptly the hand that was at liberty—"You must give me leave, Miss de Mornay, to see you to your carriage."

Celestina, dreading to give occasion to any thing like altercation between him and Thorold, answered coldly but civilly, that she thanked him; but Thorold, who had not forgotten or forgiven the mortification he received from him at York and on other occasions, could not now help resenting what seemed to be a repetition of such insulting behaviour. He therefore, walking very hastily on with Celestina, said—"No, Sir, there is no occasion for you to give yourself that trouble; for Miss de Mornay is under my care."

"I did not mean, Sir," replied Vavasour fiercely, "to ask your leave to wait on this lady: and I beg you will not take the liberty to address yourself to me."

"Pray, Mr. Vavasour," said Celestina, trembling, "do not persecute and terrify me with this sort of behaviour." She then saw by his countenance, and by the eager way in which he grasped the hand he held, that he was very far from being sober, and her terror encreased.

"I did not mean to persecute or terrify you," cried he: "no, by heaven! But damme if I can with any temper see that fellow always at your ear, and affecting to be favoured. Come, come, leave the pedant to his meditations, and don't forsake your old friends. The petticoats[1] that he is to wear are his protection."

"And this lady's presence, Sir," said Thorold, "is your's, or be assured I should answer you in a very different way."

Celestina, now alarmed even to agony by the menacing look of Vavasour, who quitted her hand and stepped before Thorold, screamed out to Mr. Howard and Lady Horatia; but the croud had so far divided them from her, that neither heard her, and before she could effectually interfere to prevent it, such words had passed between Vavasour and Thorold, as nothing but blood is, by the laws of honour, supposed to atone for. Celestina, who heard them in affright not to be described, now disengaged herself from both of them, and not knowing what she did, only having one confused idea that she might meet Captain Thorold in the room, she ran back thither alone.

Her beauty and her terror, whether it was thought real or affected, gave her, in the opinion of the first groups she met, the appearance of some young creature desirous to attract attention. Three or four young men surrounded her, and enquired what service they could do her. Breathless and ready to faint, she answered that she was in search of Captain Thorold.

"Egad," cried one of them, "Captain Thorold is a devilish lucky fellow."

---

1   To conduct the service in church, an Anglican clergyman wore (and often still wears) a black cassock, a full-length robe rather than breeches or trousers.

"And a very tasteless one," said another, "to leave such a lovely creature to seek for him."

Celestina now understood how entirely they mistook her; and collecting some presence of mind, said—"For heaven's sake, gentlemen, assist me to find him. His brother is engaged in a quarrel: a quarrel, I fear, on my account—and—"

She would have gone on, but unhappily for her the party of men who surrounded her were all of that description which are called bucks,[1] who fancy they distinguish themselves by shewing how little they deserve the character of men. One or two of these hearing of a quarrel, found they had no disposition to engage where there might be trouble or danger, and therefore walked away; but three others had now time to consider the eminent beauty of Celestina, and to have settled in their own minds that she was a girl without character, which her being alone, and even what she had told them of a quarrel on her account, seemed to authorise: they were therefore all determined not to let her go; and far from thinking of relieving the terror in which they saw her, and which they indeed believed to be a mere piece of acting, two of them took her arms within theirs, and held with her such discourse as encreased her alarm almost to distraction. She now knew not what she said. Terror for herself had so mingled itself with her fears of what might happen between Vavasour and Thorold, that she sometimes angrily entreated her persecutors to release her, then humbly besought them to seek for Captain Thorold, till at length, as they led her again towards the door, her fears were become insupportable, and shrieking, she entreated them rather to kill her than expose her to such horrors as she felt. At this moment, however, by a sudden spring, she disengaged herself: Willoughby was returning alone along the passage: she saw him, and threw herself into his arms.

"Save me, save me, Willoughby!" was all she could utter, before quite overcome with variety of terrors, she became almost senseless; her head resting on his shoulder, and his arms supporting her.

He looked sternly on the young men, and demanded the occasion of the lady's alarm. They replied that they knew nothing more than that she had run into the room alone, enquiring for a Captain somebody, and that they had endeavoured to find the cause of her fright and to assist her. Willoughby, who did not believe this, but who was more solicitous to recover the fainting Celestina than to

---

1 Fashionable, loud young men.

punish these idle boys, waved with his hand for them to be gone, and they immediately obeyed; for it was the defenceless only they had courage to insult. Willoughby then, by the assistance of a gentleman whom he happened to know, led Celestina, who was just sensible, into the room where the ladies' cloaks are received; and while his friend ran to get her a glass of water, Willoughby placed himself by her, and with one hand round her waist, supported her with the other; nor could be forbear, as he gazed on her pale but still lovely countenance, pressing her to that heart which had been so long fondly devoted to her. In a very short time she drew a deep sigh; and recovering recollection, begged his pardon, in a voice hardly articulate, for the trouble she had given him. She remembered that to the husband, the lover of Miss Fitz-Hayman, it must be trouble, and she withdrew herself from his arms before he could ask her, (so absorbed was he in the mingled sensations of pain and pleasure,) what had occasioned the alarm in which he had seen her. With a sigh still deeper than her's, he now made this enquiry. She answered, but not very distinctly, that high words had arisen between Mr. Vavasour and Mr. Montague Thorold, and that not able to check their impetuosity, nor to overtake Lady Horatia and Mr. Howard, who were gone on before, she had foolishly run back into the room to find somebody who might part them, when those young men had surrounded and insulted her, till in her fear she knew not what she did.

"And all this terror—all this excessive apprehension, was for Mr. Montague Thorold?" said Willoughby, in a faultering but not a tender voice: then, as if he had discovered nothing but what he had before known enough of to be easy under, he seemed at once to repress all appearance of interest as far as it related to Celestina, and said, with forced coldness—"I dare say, Madam, you have nothing to apprehend for his precious life. However, I will seek my friend Vavasour, and take care at least for to-night that it goes no farther, if you will tell me where I can find him, and whither I shall have the honour of conducting you."

Celestina was heart struck by the manner in which this was uttered. She turned her expressive eyes on his, to enquire whether he could really behave thus cruelly towards her; his eyes met her's; but as if he could not bear her looks he turned them away towards the door, where his friend now entered with the water, and almost at the same moment Mr. Howard came in, and told her that Lady Horatia had been in great alarm at her not following her to the coach, where she now waited for her. She did not give him time to finish the sentence, before she eagerly asked if he had seen Mr. Montague Thorold.

"Seen him?" cried Mr. Howard; "no certainly. Is he not with you?"

Celestina would then have related what had happened; but her returning apprehensions that something fatal might have already been the consequence, and the look with which Willoughby surveyed her, entirely deprived her of the power of speech; and Willoughby himself in a few words related to Mr. Howard what she had told him. "I do not know," added he, "what ground Miss de Mornay has had for the alarm she has been in; but I know Vavasour was not sober, and possibly may have been wrong headed: it will therefore be necessary perhaps for me to enquire after him; and as you, Madam, seem to be now recovered, and are safe in the protection of Mr. Howard, I will wish you good night." Having hurried over these words, he bowed to Mr. Howard, then with equal coolness to Celestina, and disappeared.

A shower of tears, the first she had been able to shed, fell from the eyes of Celestina as she lost sight of him. These tears however, and the water she had drank, a little relieved her; and Mr. Howard again representing the uneasiness in which he had left Lady Horatia, she collected strength enough to avail herself of the assistance he offered her; and leaning on his arm, reached the coach, where she was compelled, however unequal to the recital, to relate to Lady Horatia what had happened within the twenty minutes, (for more had not elapsed,) that she had lost sight of her.

Lady Horatia expressed great apprehensions for Montague Thorold; and thought, with great appearance of truth, that unless he had gone immediately away with Vavasour to decide their difference that evening, he would have sought them again, and have relieved them from the extreme apprehensions which he must imagine they must be under on his account—These conjectures, which were but too well founded, and which they had no means of satisfying, kept Lady Horatia and Celestina awake the whole night; towards morning, the former, who was less deeply interested, and more accustomed to the painful events of life than Celestina, found some repose; but Celestina herself was up by break of day, listening to every noise in the street, and trembling every moment least she should hear of some fatal accident; and her reflections, which no longer offered her any thing to hope, were busy in representing and magnifying all the evils which she had to apprehend.

The cruel suspense as to the extraordinary disappearance of Montague Thorold with Vavasour the evening before, lasted till near ten o'clock; when, as Lady Horatia and Celestina were sitting at a breakfast table, where the uneasiness they were both under did not allow them to eat, a servant announced Captain Thorold. Celestina turned pale as death at the name; but there was no time to express any part of the fear she felt before he entered.

His air was assuming, confident, and what the French call *glorieux*.[1] But from that Celestina could judge nothing; for she knew he had too little regard for his brother to have been much affected at any thing that might have befallen him. He paid his compliments in the common form to Lady Horatia, who was too much concerned to be able to answer them; and then turning to the silent, trembling Celestina, he said, with an unfeeling smile, "Well, Madam, your young champion is living."

"Good God," cried Celestina, "has he ever then been in danger?"

"Yes," replied the Captain, "he has been in all the danger that a man can be who has a brace of pistols fired at him; and is now in as much as is usual to a man who has a ball lodged in his shoulder."

Celestina could not speak; she could with difficulty breathe: but Lady Horatia now eagerly enquired the particulars, and learned that in consequence of violent language that passed between Vavasour and Montague Thorold, after Celestina left them the preceding evening, a challenge had passed, and a meeting been appointed in Chelsea Fields[2] at seven o'clock in the morning;—that Thorold, after quitting Vavasour, had in vain endeavoured to find out Lady Horatia and Celestina, and meeting his brother, and relating to him what had happened, was by him dissuaded from attempting it, as he could not see them without informing them of what had passed, and was yet to happen; that he had therefore gone home with Captain Thorold, who had, at the appointed time, attended him to the field,[3] where Vava-

---

1   Triumphant.
2   The then rural borough of Kensington and Chelsea, just north of the
    Thames, in which Ranelagh was sited.
3   Of battle.

sour was with a friend,[1] and where, the preliminaries being soon settled, each fired without effect; but neither declaring themselves satisfied, they fired again, and Montague Thorold received a ball in his shoulder, which was not extracted when his brother left him at his lodgings, whither he was immediately conveyed, and where he was attended by an eminent surgeon.

"And is he in danger, Sir?" said Celestina, with all that tremulous tenderness in her voice that her extreme sensibility gave her—"Is he in danger? is he in pain?"

Captain Thorold gave her a look which seemed to say "Humph— it *is* true, then, that you are violently in love with this brother of mine": and then answered—"The surgeon, on whose skill I have great reason to rely, does not seem to think him in danger; but till the ball is extracted, which will be attended with pain enough, it is not, I fancy, easy to speak very positively.—However, Miss de Mornay, Montague won't complain of the pain, let it be as severe as it will, while he recollects that he suffers in your defence, and hears, what I shall not fail to relate, how dearly you are interested for him."

Celestina could not say that this unlucky affair did not originate about her; indeed, she had not at that moment strength to enter on any explanation; nor could she deny, that she was extremely concerned, or make Captain Thorold comprehend that for a stranger, under the same circumstances, she should have been greatly, if not equally sorry:—As to Lady Horatia, who hoped that this accident would operate decisively on behalf of Montague, she rather encouraged than contradicted the idea that his brother seemed to entertain of Celestina's partiality towards him. And now the Captain, with as much unconcern as if nothing had happened, seemed only desirous of displaying his own consequence and his own perfections: as if to convince them both, that for a woman, who had ever seen him and his brother together, to prefer the latter, was an instance of most terrible want of discernment. Several times was Celestina, who could hardly support herself, on the point of withdrawing; but she thought, that were she to quit the room, it would look still more as

---

1   Each combatant in a duel was attended by a friend or "second" whose duty it was to examine the pistols or check the equal length of the swords if those were the chosen weapons, to measure out the ground to the agreed number of paces' distance at which the combatants would stand for an exchange of fire, to engage the services of a surgeon, and to go through the motions of requesting a reconciliation.

if she was sinking under apprehensions; and she besides feared, that were she absent, the zeal of Lady Horatia would induce her to explain to Captain Thorold more of her wishes and projects in regard to her and his brother than, feeling as she did the impossibility of their ever taking place, ought in discretion or in justice to be talked of.

For these reasons, wretched and distressed as she was, she had yet resolution enough to remain in her place; till at length Captain Thorold, having paraded about himself for near half an hour, withdrew.

Then it was, that, from the conversation of her friend, Celestina understood how much such an event would be expected to affect her sentiments in favour of Montague Thorold; and how impossible Lady Horatia considered it for her, after all the sufferings he must sustain on her account, to delay rewarding those sufferings and his long and ardent attachment to her longer than till his recovery: of which, notwithstanding what Captain Thorold had said of the possibility of danger, she seemed not to doubt; though she expressed great concern for the pain he must endure, and great anxiety to be informed of his actual situation. To all that she said, Celestina hardly answered a word—her heart was too much oppressed; and she could say nothing that would not appear either like insensibility, ingratitude, or like the anxious solicitude of love. She wished to avoid either: she wished to be alone; and though the determination Lady Horatia almost immediately formed to visit Montague Thorold herself, was a measure which must strongly confirm all the reports that she wished to discourage, yet it released her to her own reflections, and she was glad at that moment to see her friend depart.

Her own reflections, to which she was now left, were most uneasy.—She knew that such an affair must unavoidably be much and immediately talked of: she knew how much it would be misrepresented, and what conclusions would be made upon it. The expression used by Willoughby the evening before still vibrated in her ears: "What! and is all this terror, all this apprehension, for Montague Thorold?" It was displeasing then to him that she should feel an interest for Montague Thorold—and the little tenderness he had appeared to shew her, was repressed the moment he understood who was the subject of her alarm. Conscious that hopeless as she had long been of his affection, and submitting to the necessity of their separation, she had yet never bestowed on another the heart he had resigned, she could not bear to think how much every circumstance had contributed to make him think, that she had lightly given it to the first candidate; nor could her mind dwell without extreme concern, on the pain this affair would give the elder Mr. Thorold, whose hopes, were, she well knew, centered in his youngest son, and who would not only be distressed by the sickness and danger to which he had thus exposed himself, but be hurt at his having acted so contrary to those principles he had always endeavoured to inculcate, as to giving or receiving a challenge. Nor were the sufferings of Montague Thorold himself the least part of her concern: she apprehended he might be long confined in great pain; he might perhaps lose his arm, or even his life: and while she regretted the rashness which had been the occasion of this hazard, she could not but acknowledge, that it was impossible a young man of spirit could otherwise have answered the unprovoked ferocity of Vavasour.

Of him she thought with terror; and knowing that he was capable of any impropriety in the humour he was now in, she gave immediate orders, that if he came he should be denied.

All the circumstances of the preceding evening, which the fear that had beset her during the latter part of it had for a while driven from her recollection, now returned to it; and the repeated intelligence she had received through the day of Willoughby's marriage, all the particulars with which it had been related, the happy looks of Miss Fitz-Hayman, the proud triumph that sat on the features of her mother, and the forced friendship with which Lady Molyneux seemed to have connected herself with persons who were so lately the objects of her aversion, all confirmed the reports that were in circulation, so as to put their truth beyond a doubt.

In a few days she was to hear of their actually being married: to listen again to the detail of their nuptial splendors, perhaps to witness them: she was to be surrounded by a thousand impertinent people who would enquire and talk to her about the duel; and, with an heart so oppressed, must attend to them with patience, and answer them with civility. The whole prospect before her was too unpleasant; she fancied it impossible to be endured; and resolved to attempt, though at the hazard of appearing ungrateful, perhaps of disobliging her best and almost her only friend, to solicit leave to go down to Jessy, at least till the public conversation should have been turned to some other topic, and the public curiosity no longer excited by the marriage of Miss Fitz-Hayman, or the *rencontre*[1] of Vavasour and Thorold.

---

1 Meeting, usually hostile.

The natural softness of her heart made her, among all these sources of peculiar uneasiness, really and tenderly interested for Montague Thorold: and she awaited the return of Lady Horatia with as much solicitude as she could have felt if a beloved brother had been in such a situation: perhaps she would have felt more for nobody but Willoughby himself. It was, therefore, a great relief to her harassed spirits, when she heard, that while Captain Thorold had been in Park-street, the bullet had been extracted; that no bone had been injured by it, and that he was in as good a way as could be expected; his surgeon declaring, that from the nature of the wound, and the good constitution of his patient, he thought him in no danger, and should probably, at the end of a fortnight, dismiss him with his arm in a sling.

The satisfaction Celestina expressed on his account, was not however increased, when Lady Horatia added, that far from complaining of his sufferings, he exulted and rejoiced in them; flattering himself that she for whom he could willing have risked an hundred lives if he had possessed them, would feel some pity for him; and knowing how much power, in such a heart as hers, that sentiment had to produce others still more favourable.

Lady Horatia then went on to say very seriously to Celestina, that she ought no longer to trifle with such a man, but resolve immediately to give him her hand: not only as the reward of his merit, but to preclude the dangerous pretensions of Vavasour: "to whose perseverance," said she, "no refusal, no repulse seems to put an end."

"Dearest Madam," said Celestina, "*did* I ever trifle with Mr. Thorold—surely I never meant it—so far from it, I have an hundred times regretted that your Ladyship's partiality towards him, and the influence you have and ought to have over me, have combined to keep him in an error, which all my candid dealing with him has not had the power to refute. I have told him, whenever he has urged the subject, that he is in possession of my esteem and of my friendship, but that for my love I have it not to bestow."

"But he is content, my dear, with your esteem, with your friendship; and knows that, in such a heart as yours, love will follow his attachment to you; especially as you now surely cannot alledge that any other person possesses it."

Celestina, too conscious of all these circumstances that ought long since to have induced her to withdraw it from Willoughby, yet equally conscious that she could never feel for another that degree of affection of which she had been sensible for him, was silent a moment or two, and then said, "Dear Lady Horatia, why must I marry at all? while you afford me your protection can I be happier? and should I be unhappy enough to lose it, should I not be more likely to meet content even with my small and humble fortune, if I remained single, than if I gave my hand where I have no power to bestow my heart?"

"I am amazed," replied Lady Horatia, "that with such very good sense as you possess, you would accustom yourself to cherish these childish and girlish notions: what is this love, without feeling all the violence of which, you suppose it impossible to be happy?"

"Dear Madam," cried Celestina, interrupting her, "have I not heard you say, that you once was sensible of it yourself; and that having been compelled to quit the man of your choice, you considered such a necessity as a heavy affliction, and that it rendered most of the occurrence of your subsequent life indifferent to you?"

"Yes, you have heard me say so—I merely acknowledged a folly, a weakness, which I pretended not to defend in myself, and certainly not to encourage in you.—What has been the life of this man, whom I called, in the romantic simplicity of sixteen, my first love? When my father parted us, and I was compelled by his authority to give my hand to General Howard, he was a younger brother, with very little fortune. In a twelve-month afterwards, the death of his elder brother and an uncle gave him a very large fortune; and he quitted the navy, where he had, for so young a man, highly distinguished himself, and with his profession he seemed to resign his virtues. He married a woman towards whom he professed himself indifferent; and whose only recommendation was a fortune nearly as large as his own. To her he behaved with neglect, which she rewarded with scorn and infidelity. They seemed to agree in nothing but mutual extravagance; till at length they parted, and he now lives in France the greatest part of the year; at other times wanders about the world, to gratify his taste for variety, and fly from those corrosive reflections which must pursue him who has ruined his health and his fortune by debauchery. Can I, when I consider all this, help despising myself for the pain I felt at being separated from such a man; and ought I not rather to rejoice at what once appeared an insupportable misfortune?"

"Ah, Madam," said Celestina, "it is well if by these reflections you have been enabled to conquer those remains of useless regret which might otherwise have embittered your life: but give me leave to ask, since there is now no danger of renewing them, give me leave to ask, whether you sincerely believe that this gentleman, had he married you, would have passed a life as blameable? You have told me that he was passionately attached to you: you now say, that to the lady he married he was indifferent: surely to that may be imputed all his errors.—His mind became unhinged when he lost her to whom it was devoted, and he aggravated to himself the cruelty of his destiny. To you he might have been an excellent husband, because he loved you; but losing the possibility of being happy, he lost the wish to be respectable; and since he could not live with you, cared not with whom or how he lived."

"There may be some truth," said Lady Horatia, "in your remarks; but to be tolerably easy, Celestina, in this world, you must learn to be more of an Optimist; and to believe, that whatever happens, could not, nor ought not to have been otherwise.[1] Thus the interference of Lady Castlenorth, whatever might have been her motives, has saved you from a marriage that might have been a hideous crime; thus, not to enumerate other instances that must occur to your recollection; thus, the wild brutality of Vavasour, and even the wound of Montague, will all contribute finally to good, and produce that happiness for you with him, which I do not believe you would have found with any other person."

To this doctrine Celestina could not agree. But the fear and fatigue she had within the last twenty-four hours undergone, disqualified her for any farther discussion of the subject at present, or for the attempt she meant to make to prevail on Lady Horatia to allow her to go down to Jessy for a few weeks; her eyes were indeed so heavy, her complexion so pale in consequence of her long agitation, that now the immediate fears for Montague Thorold's life were over, Lady Horatia advised her to take some repose; a proposal which she gladly accepted; and in despite of the variety of uneasiness she still laboured under, exhausted nature obtained for her a few hours respite in sleep: though she was, in her previous contemplations, so far from assenting heartily to the resigned philosophy of Lady Horatia, that she thought with anguish of the fate of Willoughby, who might, she feared, by the same disappointments in the early part of

---

1 Lady Horatia refers to the philosophical doctrine of Optimism as propounded by the German physicist and philosopher Wilhelm Gottfried Leibniz (1646-1716), that whatever seems the result of chance or human error is a necessity of physics operating under the Divine Will, and could not have been otherwise, so that, as Alexander Pope says in his defence of Optimism in his *Essay on Man*, "Whatever is, is right." Voltaire parodied the philosopher and his contention that this is "the best of all possible worlds" in his portrait of Dr. Pangloss in *Candide*.

his life, became quite unlike what he once was; and from his cruel neglect of her since he had been in London, she already fancied she saw that this change had begun.

But could she for one moment have seen the real state of that mind whose virtues she believed to be tarnished, she would have found it as worthy as ever of her tenderness, and entitled to all her pity. Tormented by an affection which he could not indulge for one woman, and entangled by a series of perverse events in an engagement with another; embarrassed in his circumstances, and discontented with himself; his whole life passed in a continual tumult of contending passions; and whatever means he took to calm and mitigate them seemed only to irritate his sufferings.— Thus, when he left his own lodgings on the day of his interview with Miss Fitz-Hayman and his meeting Celestina, he went to the hotel where Vavasour usually lived when he was in town; and where it happened that a party of their mutual acquaintance that day dined: this prevented his having any conversation with Vavasour, which, though it might have contributed but little to relieve his vexation as to Montague Thorold, would have eased his heart by unburthening it to his friend; and Vavasour drank so much, that there was afterwards no hopes of his hearing him rationally. With him he was prevailed upon at a late hour, to go to Ranelagh;— where he saw Celestina again with the very man to whom he had been so repeatedly told she had engaged herself; and there, though Celestina happened not to see them together, he was compelled to take several turns with Lady Castlenorth, her daughter, and his sister; thus confirming, by his appearance in public with the two former, that it was indeed too late to retract, though he had already most bitterly repented it.

The quarrel between Vavasour and Montague Thorold, of which his suddenly quitting the place where he met Celestina was partly the occasion (for had he staid he might have prevented it), added to the conviction he now had that Thorold was very soon to be her husband; and increased his vexation, in despite of all that reason could say to counteract the effect of it. That reason repeatedly asked him—if Celestina had really been brought up and acknowledged as his sister, and had with so small a fortune been addressed by Thorold, and herself approved him, whether he could in such a case have made any reasonable objection? He was compelled to answer no! yet his heart revolted against the assent which common sense urged him to give to a marriage which differed in nothing from what would then have been the case, but in early prejudice. He never could learn to consider Celestina as related to him by blood; nor did all the pains he had taken to learn the truth convince him of it; though he dared not act as if he wholly disbelieved it. Yet so perverse is an heart under the influence of such passion as he felt, that while he had relinquished her, and agreed to marry another, lest that relationship should really exist, he detested Thorold for having, as he believed, possessed himself of those affections, which, otherwise than as her brother, he had owned he dared not claim.

When he left Celestina under the care of Mr. Howard at Ranelagh the preceding evening, he had gone, as he promised, in search of Vavasour; but not finding him any where about the room, or in the avenues to the Rotunda, he had gone to his lodgings, and waited there till near four in the morning.—He then left orders with his servant to send for him the moment his master came, but Vavasour, instead of returning to his lodgings at all that evening, slept somewhere else; and only called there in a hackney-coach at half past five o'clock to take his pistols; and his servant being ordered to attend him, with the surgeon, there was no possibility of his man giving Willoughby notice; and of course he could do nothing to stop a *rencontre* of which he did not hear till after it was over.

Vavasour, who then came to him, was not sober: and Willoughby saw, with more concern than surprise, that the habits his friend had acquired since his last absence were becoming inveterate, and were ruining alike his constitution, his fortune, and his understanding. Though he himself detested Montague Thorold, and cursed the hour when he had put Celestina under the protection of his father, and by that means thrown him in her way; he was too generous, even to an enemy, not to feel that Vavasour had behaved with unwarrantable brutality; and notwithstanding his long friendship for him, he felt too, that had he been as successful as he believed Thorold to be, all that friendship would have been cancelled.

He was vexed, however, at the conversation which this foolish business must occasion: and in which he knew the name of Celestina must be joined with that of Montague Thorold: and when Vavasour spoke with some triumph of his having chastised the young pedant, Willoughby, with a peevishness very unusual with him, said, he heartily wished he had let it alone.

From the little conversation he had with Lady Castlenorth the evening before, he found she expected him to wait on them the next day. Reluctantly, and with an aching heart, he had then given a sort of promise, and with still more regret he recollected it. The sun now never rose for him but to bring a renewal of misery; and his dejection never left him, but to give place to paroxysms of passion and fits of fruitless despair.

As the hour approached when he knew he was expected at the house of his uncle, his unwillingness to go increased. Farnham, who now anxiously watched all his looks, saw a deeper gloom come upon him: he saw him take out several letters, read them, replace them, then snatch up a pen, write a few lines, and hurry across the room as if undecided what to do. At length he wrote a few lines, sealed the note, and put it in his pocket. Farnham had heard a great deal of the duel that had happened the evening before, and knew it was about Miss de Mornay, and that a gentleman had been wounded dangerously. He had heard conversation between his master and Vavasour, and supposed, from their manner, that they parted in anger. This circumstance put it in his head, which was rather an honest than a clear one, that some other affair of honour, in which his master was concerned, was still in agitation; and he so thoroughly persuaded himself of this, that he determined to observe narrowly every thing that happened, and to take all possible precautions against his master's having such an accident befal him as had happened to Mr. Montague Thorold.

For this purpose he attached himself very closely to the hole in the door between the dining-room and the bed-chamber; and when he was summoned, by a furious ring, to attend him, he was under the necessity of first slipping softly down stairs, and then running up to ask his commands.

Willoughby gave him two notes, and asked if the groom was within. On hearing he was not: "Then go yourself," said he, "with these two notes: no answer is required to either: return as soon as you can." Farnham promising to be expeditious, left him; and reading the directions, found one to be, to Miss de Mornay, the other to Mr. Vavasour. This, with all he knew of his master's former attachment and embarrassing doubts about Celestina, and all that had happened that evening before, and that morning, convinced him beyond a doubt, that another duel would happen, which he imagined it to be his peculiar duty to prevent.—He was not very fertile in expedients: but it occurred to him that the best way would be to carry both these letters, and at the same time communicate his fears, to Sir Philip and Lady Molyneux. Sir Philip was not at home; but Lady Molyneux, on hearing he wanted to speak to her, ordered him up.

He opened his business with great gravity; detailed all the cause he had for apprehension from his master's behaviour, and produced the two notes. Lady Molyneux affected to agree with him as to the justice of his fears, and to commend his prudence and fidelity; she then told him she thought it would be the best way to open the letters, which as she happened to have a seal with the Willoughby arms, the same as her brother's, she could easily reseal; and send, if they contained nothing of what they suspected; and if they did, that it would be proper to destroy them.

Poor Farnham, trembling as he spoke, assented to all this, only entreating her to take care that his master might never know it. This she readily promised; and, taking all the blame upon herself, bade him retire while she opened the letters, and come up again when she rang. She then read them. That to Vavasour was merely to put off an appointment for the evening, which Willoughby found himself unable to attend. That to Celestina ran thus:

"I should have sent to you, Madam, immediately on my arrival in London: but illness for some days prevented my being able even to write, and in that interval I heard that you were on the point of putting yourself into the protection of one who might deem such an address improper, and render it needless.

"That you have come to this resolution without consulting any of those who were once honoured with your friendship, I can now no longer doubt. I, however, feel it in some measure incumbent upon me to offer you every service in my power; to say, that as soon as my own affairs are settled, I shall have the honour of troubling you on pecuniary matters; and if, in the mean time, you have any wish to see me as your friend, I will obey your summons: but leave it wholly to yourself.—I shall consider your silence as an acknowledgment that such an interview will be painful to you: and submit to offer, at a distance, those sincere wishes for your happiness, which must ever be felt by,
                    Dear Madam,
                              Your obedient, and most humble servant,
                              GEORGE WILLOUGHBY."
Bond Street,
May 17th 1789.

This letter, cold and unlike his former style to Celestina as it was, his sister immediately resolved to suppress. Her hatred to Celestina was increased to a degree of inveterate malignity of which it was difficult to conceive her haughty indolence was capable; and this arose chiefly from the admiration she every where saw her beauty excited, which was a point in which she could not bear to be excelled.

Convinced as she internally was, that Celestina was an orphan stranger, brought up on her mother's charity, she chose rather to leave the report of their relationship uncontradicted, than to see her united to her brother, and put on a footing with herself, to which that equivocal relationship could give her no claim; and since the suppression of her letter to Willoughby, which an interview now would explain, she was doubly solicitous to prevent it. Her pride could not bear that her brother should become the humble and reduced country gentleman that he must submit to be if he married a woman without fortune; and her avarice represented the possibility of his being, in such a case, a burthen on his affluent relations. All these considerations determined her to stifle it, and the sentence with which the letter concluded, assured her she might do it with impunity. She therefore called up Farnham, on whose simplicity it was very easy to impose, and told him that the letter to Mr. Vavasour was very immaterial, and that he might carry that; but that the other to Miss de Mornay, was of a nature to involve his master in great difficulties, and that therefore she would destroy it. She then put it in the fire; and bade him carry the other, which she had carefully re-sealed. This Farnham immediately did; but being unwilling to be guilty of a greater falsehood than there seemed to be occasion for, he actually went to Park-street that he might tell his master he had been there.

On his return, Willoughby questioned him who he saw at Lady Horatia's. For this question the poor fellow was not prepared. However he answered, "I saw John, Sir, my Lady's own footman."

"Well—and was Miss de Mornay at home?"

"No, Sir," replied Farnham, who had now acquired courage; "but you know you bade me not wait for an answer."

"Well, but had you not the sense to ask where she was?"

"No, Sir; to be sure I did not think of that: but, however, I fancy she was visiting, Sir, the wounded gentleman in Oxford-street."

Willoughby knew that Montague Thorold lodged there, and that it must be him alone who was described as the wounded gentleman.

"And why do you think so, Sir," said he, fiercely, as if poor Farnham had been accessary to it—"and what the devil have you to do to think about it?"

"Lord, Sir," cried Farnham, "only because as I came along I saw my lady's coach at the door where I knew young Mr. Thorold lodges, and just nodded to Sam, who was upon the box."

"Cursed fool!" exclaimed Willoughby—"could you not have asked whether she was there or no: yet why should I desire to know," added he, rising and walking about with his hands clenched together—"what it is to me? and why do I torment myself?—Go, Sir, and fetch my powdering gown[1] and my things to dress." Poor Farnham, convinced that Lady Molyneux was right in what she had done, yet rendered doubly timid by the consciousness of having committed a sort of fraud on his master, hastily obeyed.

Chapter VI

The situation of Celestina was rendered infinitely more uneasy to her by the transactions of the last two or three days; and her spirits could no longer support her. The certainty of meeting Willoughby wherever she went, and of meeting him only to be more and more convinced that he had ceased to feel any degree of affection for her, made the thoughts of continuing her present mode of life, which had no[2] charms in her opinion, quite insupportable to her. The conversation about the duel, the questions she should be asked, and the impertinence she must attend to, encreased the aversion with which she thought of appearing again in public; and she determined, at any hazard, to propose to Lady Horatia, that she might go into the country, and there wait, wherever she pleased, till she should herself quit London.

She took, therefore, the first moment they were alone together, to prefer and urge this request: and after making some objections, which, however, the altered looks and depressed spirits of Celestina very forcibly combated, Lady Horatia consented to her going; but as the house of Jessy was too near Alvestone, where it was supposed Willoughby and his bride were immediately to go after their marriage, it was settled that she should, with a maid to attend her, go to Cheltenham, and wait there till Lady Horatia could leave London, which she proposed doing in a fortnight or three weeks at farthest. This plan being once arranged, Celestina was impatient till it was executed; and so effectually set about the little preparations she had to make, that the next day she left London—and for the first time since her quitting the Hebrides, enjoyed the calm solitude she loved.

---

1 In lodgings where there was no purpose-built powdering room, fashionable people used a gown to protect their clothes during the hair-powdering.
2 The original has "any."

Wretched in the mean time was the state of Willoughby; he went to dine at Lord Castlenorth's, as he had been obliged to promise—where a large company were assembled, as if to receive him, for the first time, as the heir and acknowledged son-in-law of Lord Castlenorth. He had, however, no power to conceal, under the common forms of life, the misery of his internal feelings; his countenance refused to wear the forced smile of complaisance; his emotion when the duel was talked of, and the name of Celestina was introduced, was evident enough to all but those who did not chuse to see it.

Lord Castlenorth was, indeed, never very much celebrated for discernment; but his Lady, who highly piqued herself on her sagacity, on the facility with which she read characters, and penetrated the views of those with whom she conversed—her blindness therefore was evidently wilful. And that of her daughter, unless her love or her vanity intercepted her sight,[1] was equally strange. Certain it was, that they either could not, or would not, attend to the reluctant melancholy of Willoughby, under which he with difficulty concealed the bitter agonies of despair; and they appeared perfectly satisfied with him and with themselves.

There was one face, however, in the circle that, though it wore looks of festivity, yet was now and then seen to survey Willoughby with indignant scorn; and then, as if checked for indulging it, to resume the smile of approbation and complacency. Captain Cavanaugh indeed did not very frequently address himself to him; but conversed chiefly with the Ladies. But whenever he did speak to him, Willoughby himself, who had till now very little noticed him, could not help remarking that there was something peculiar in his manner.

When the Gentlemen were left together,[2] Lord Castlenorth, who could not drink, and whose health obliged him to retire early, called to his nephew, and bade him take his place. This Willoughby, who had been all day meditating how he might make an early escape, was compelled to do, though he observed, "that as Captain Cavanaugh usually took that seat when his Lordship retired, he wished him then to assume it." Lord Castlenorth, however, persisted; and Willoughby, willing to get rid of an irksome task as soon as possible, made the

---

1 The original has "right."
2 At dinner parties, formal or informal and in the middle as well as in the upper class, women left the dinner table after dessert and had tea or coffee in the drawing room, while the men remained behind to drink and talk freely, joining the women later.

wine circulate so quickly, that, as he was never in habits of drinking, he soon began to find himself losing his dejection in a kind of bewildering stupor: any thing seemed better to him than the task of entertaining Miss Fitz-Hayman for the rest of the evening; and as he felt he by degrees ceased to think of her, he found some satisfaction in drinking, and was very soon completely intoxicated.

He was no longer capable of judging for himself, or he would not have gone up stairs[1] in such a situation—he had just recollection enough left to stay, without committing any great extravagance, while tea was served; and then gladly followed a servant who whispered to him that Lord Castlenorth desired the favour of seeing him in his own apartment.

Thither he staggered with very little consciousness; and being seated where his uncle sat opposite to him, in a great chair, while several parchments lay open on a table, he heard, but without the least comprehension of what was said, a long harangue—on fortune and family, heraldry and genealogy, titles and successions;—the whole of which concluded, by his informing him that the money was ready to pay off all the incumbrances on his estate, which was to be immediately done; that the settlements were in hand, and to be finished in a week; and that, that day fortnight was fixed for the marriage. Willoughby, between the verbose confusion of his uncle's mode of delivery and his own incapacity of attention, heard it all, but understood nothing; he was not, however, so unconscious of pain and sickness. Mrs. Calder, who for the greater part of this conversation had sat reading a treatise on bilious concretions,[2] on the opposite side of the room, with her spectacles on, now finding Lord Castlenorth had done, and that Willoughby looked very likely to sink out of his chair, very wisely ended this conversation, by sending up Farnham to his master, who had him conveyed home in a chair.[3]

The next morning he was awakened to a perfect recollection of all that had passed the evening before; and became too certain, that the means he had taken to obtain a temporary release from his fetters, had served only to rivet them more closely. Alas! he remem-

---

1 The drawing room was situated on the first floor in a fashionable central London household, where the houses are tall and narrow, so as to be further from the kitchen in the basement. The dining room was usually on the ground floor.
2 Hard morbid formations in the body such as kidney or gall stones.
3 A sedan chair.

bered too—with poignant anguish remembered, that so many hours had elapsed since he had written to Celestina; and that it was now too certain she would not answer his letter, and wholly declined seeing him.

Though he had so often determined never to meet her again; so often persuaded himself not to wish it; this cruel conviction of her total estrangement from him, seemed to fall as heavily as if he had never dreamed of their separation—she might, however, be out of town; she might be engaged; something might have prevented her writing. To this slender hope he clung for some hours of the morning; but it insensibly became fainter as his impatience encreased, and at length he ordered Farnham to find the coachman of Lady Horatia, with whom he was acquainted, and try to discover any particulars he could.

Farnham, dreading lest his master should discover the imposition he had ventured to practice, dared not disobey him—he set out therefore for the stables, where, at that time in the morning, he was sure of finding his acquaintance; he found him indeed very busy in cleaning, with the aid of a postillion and a helper, two of his horses, which had been, "poor things!" he said, "the first stage to Cheltenham, with Miss de Mornay and Rebecca the maid, that my Lady sent with her." Farnham made him repeat this intelligence; to which he added, "Why, my Lady and all of us be going down to Gloucestershire, in about a fortnight; that is, as soon as young Mr. Thorold is well enough to be moved, which, the Doctor as tends him says, will be in that time or less. My Lady takes his illness sadly to heart, and so does Miss—and went out of town sadly down in the mouth; but, howsoever, 'tis well 'twas no worse, you know; and as he is like to do well—why there's no great harm, and Miss will be married all one."[1]

The minutest article of this account was remembered by Farnham, and punctually related by him to his master, who now thoroughly convinced that all hope was at an end of Celestina's retaining for him any affection; and a certainty so dreadful; the assurance of her being irrevocably engaged, and having gone into Gloucestershire, there to wait the recovery of Montague Thorold; the assurance that he should never see her more—all contributed, with his excess of the evening before, to inflame his blood, and by four o'clock he was in an high fever.

His indisposition was encreased by a visit from Vavasour, who

---

1 Just the same.

laughed at the vexation and disgust he expressed at what had happened in regard to Montague Thorold; but grew graver when he heard that, far from its having put an end to his pretensions to Celestina, it had served only to hasten their marriage. The wild and ill founded projects of Vavasour to prevent this, and to succeed himself, which to Willoughby would have been equally hateful, were but little calculated to appease his agitation, and quiet his boiling blood; before Vavasour went away, he became delirious, and Farnham, in a terrible fright, went for Lady Molyneux and a physician. Lady Molyneux was just stepping into her coach, when the affrighted face of Farnham appeared before her. She chid him for the needless alarm he had given her; and said, that she supposed it was nothing but a little return of the fever her brother was subject to. "I cannot," said she, "call now; but as I come home this evening, I will see him." The physician, for whom Farnham then went, directly attended; and found his patient, though not in so high a fever as he had seen him before, ill enough to require his immediate assistance, which he ordered with so happy an effect, that in a few hours the delirium entirely subsided, and Willoughby, though extremely languid, was at night almost free from his fever. Lady Molyneux who called on him, soon after midnight, for a few moments, again blamed Farnham for his officious apprehensions; and being well convinced that Willoughby would be glad of any excuse to keep back the preparations which were now going on, she endeavoured to persuade him that his illness was very trifling; and taking occasion to talk over what happened at Ranelagh, told her brother, laughingly, that she hoped he was now convinced of the attachment between young Thorold and Miss de Mornay—adding, "His brother, Captain Thorold, who is really an elegant and fashionable man, tells me they are to be married the moment Montague is able to leave London."

"Well, well," cried Willoughby, peevishly, "I know it; and I do not desire to hear any more about it. I thank you for calling on me; but it is very late, and my physician desires I will keep myself quiet."

Lady Molyneux then withdrew, and poor Willoughby, to whom she had administered a poison instead of a cordial, tried to find that repose which he so greatly wanted: but to him his estranged, his lost Celestina, on one hand, and on the other his intended bride, seemed to cry—"sleep no more."[1]

Farnham, who sat up by him to administer the medicines he was

---

1 Cf. *Macbeth* 2.2.34.

to take, heard him sigh the greater part of the night without ceasing; and whenever he thought he might venture, asked him how he did.—"Pr'ythee, Farnham," said he, after two or three of these questions, "do not ask me how I do—how should a man do, who is in a situation to envy every body but the fellow just going to be hanged—you know, that I am at this moment the most miserable fellow upon earth." "I am sure I am very sorry to hear it," answered his servant: "but if I might be so bold as to speak, I should say that I cannot think what cause you can have to be miserable—nor...."

He was going on, when Willoughby, eagerly catching aside the curtain,[1] said, "What cause!—Have I not lost an angel? And am I not, have I not condemned myself to marry a woman I cannot love?—no, never; never, by Heaven."

"To be sure, Sir," said Farnham, "to be crossed in love, as I may say, is very bad—as I have heard tell—but in this here matter—all things considered, I hope your honour's mind will be settled about it; and as for the two ladies, to be sure beauty is all fancy. Miss Celestina, for certain, is a fine young lady, and so good and gentle to servants, that it was always a pleasure to me to hear her speak to me, and to wait upon her; but then, for certain, Miss Fitz-Hayman, though she is higher and more stately, as she ought to be, being as she is a lady of title and quality—is a fine young lady too, and a very majestic grand person—and then her great riches—"

"Curse on her riches," exclaimed Willoughby. "Aye, Sir," said Farnham, who was not a little flattered by his confidence, and was now got into one of his prosing humours—"Aye Sir, it is very well for young gentlemen to cry curse on this, and that, and t'other—but as for riches—what can they do without them? Nobody is not respected the least in the world, if they don't make a shew, and a figure, and the like of that—and can it be done without money?—No—nor not without a pretty deal on't—and, for my part, I own—I don't love to see my master not able to vie with the best lord of the land—as to be sure he ought."

"Thou art a fool, Farnham," cried Willoughby. "Do have done with thy Lords of the land, and give me twenty drops more of the opiate."—"Yes, Sir," said Farnham; and prepared to obey him; but while he was counting out the drops, he could not forbear going on—"One, two—there are other people, Sir—three, four—about my Lord's house, who, it's my notion—five, six, seven—are not so apt

---

1 Bed curtain.

to cry, curse money—eight, nine, ten—there is Captain Cavanaugh—eleven, twelve, thirteen, fourteen"—"Captain Cavanaugh?" interrupted Willoughby—"What of Captain Cavanaugh?" "Nay, Sir,—only the Captain—as far as I can find—don't hate money, nor cry, curse it and damn it—he has been long enough living about the world, to know that nothing can be had without it, and—that is all, Sir."

"But that seems to me not to be all, Sir. Pray, tell me what Captain Cavanaugh has to do with what we were talking of—with Miss Fitz-Hayman?"

"Lord, nothing, Sir, I am sure, that I know of. Only, if the young Lady was not engaged, and in love with you, perhaps—the Captain, Sir, is reckoned, by the women, a very handsome man, Sir. And Miss Fitz-Hayman may think so, as well as another." "Why he is married, you booby, what stuff have you got into your head? And who has been talking to you of him and Miss Fitz-Hayman? Let him be reckoned as handsome as he will by the women—he can be nothing to Miss Fitz-Hayman, for I know he has been married some years."

"Aye, Sir, I dare say that may be—but there is such a thing as being un-married[1] again: not that I ever heard, I am sure, much about the Captain; only Justina was laughing one day, and saying, in her broken English—so that I can't say I quite right understand her—that if my Lord should die, and the Captain should ever be able to get rid of his wife, she should not be much surprised if he and my Lady was to make a match of it; for that never was such a favourite as the Captain."

"I should not be much surprised at that myself," answered Willoughby, "for I believe the Captain has a good deal of interest there. So, then, he has been trying to get rid of his wife?"

---

1 Incompatible couples usually lived apart if they could afford to, but divorce, though costly, rare and requiring the sanction of Parliament, was possible. A man could divorce his wife for adultery or even for "criminal conversation," that is, the likelihood that adultery had taken place. But a husband who left his wife to shift for herself and took no interest in her manner of life could not easily sue for divorce later because it happened to suit him, though this is what Captain Cavanaugh intends. A woman did not have the right to divorce her husband for adultery unless it was incestuous or unless he brought his mistress to live as one of the family and eat at the same table with his wife. Adultery with a servant living in the house was not therefore grounds for divorce.

"Justina told me, Sir, one day, as a great secret, that my Lady[1] had helped him to money, to try at it. But, Sir, if Justina should know I ever mentioned it, I should never be able to get a word out of her again." "I promise thee, she never shall, so tell me, Farnham, all thou hast heard from her about Lady Castlenorth and the Captain."

"Why, Sir, it was not much—but only Justina was laughing t'other day about my Lady's having such a great friendship for him, and there's no stopping her tongue when she begins—so she told me— Lord, Sir! a great many things that were odd enough to be sure—but only Ladies of quality, I reckon, don't much care what people says of them. She said, that my Lady knew well enough, that my Lord could not hold it[2] long—and that she was providing herself with a hand-some young husband, and making sure of him, as she thought, before the old one hobbled off—'but let her take care,' said Justina, 'that she marries her daughter first, or I know what will happen. The Captain knows well enough, that a young woman is better than an old one; and besides, that such a great fortune as my young lady will have, is better, twenty to one, than her mother's jointure.'"

This speech at once opened Willoughby's eyes, as to Lady Castlenorth's motives for the extreme haste and earnestness she had shewn to conclude her daughter's marriage; feeling as he did, in regard to Miss Fitz-Hayman, he was sensible neither of jealousy or mortification, at the idea of any preference she might entertain for Cavanaugh; but a hope, that, from this circumstance, something might happen to break off the connection for ever between him and his cousin involuntarily arose in his mind. In any event, it ought to be attended to; he bade Farnham therefore go the next day, and see if he could set Justina gossipping again. "I have a notion, Farnham," said he, "that you are very much in the good graces of the little Neapolitan."

"Oh, no, Sir; finer fellows than I am have all the chance there— and for my part, Sir, I don't much fancy her, though she is lively and smart, and when I get her by herself will tell the secrets of all the family."

"Which thus lovest to hear; therefore get her by herself as soon as thou canst, and make her tell thee all she knows."

Willoughby then again tried to compose himself, and by the help of the medicines he had taken, obtained four or five hours sleep. He

---

1   The original has "my Lord."
2   Hold out, live.

was a great deal better in the morning; as he breakfasted, a note was brought him from Lady Castlenorth, informing him that his uncle had been seized in the night with a violent return of that asthmatic complaint which so frequently had rendered his stay in England impossible: that the spring, though far advanced, was so cold and wet, that there was no chance of his being better while he remained there now; and that therefore he had, by the advice of his physicians, and by his own inclination, determined to set out that very day for the Continent. She added, "You will come to us, of course, instantly, and if you cannot go with us, settle when you will follow us; but your uncle wishes you to accompany us."

This intelligence was to Willoughby like a reprieve from what to him was worse than death; since the longer he considered of his marriage, the more dishonourable now, and the more certainly miserable hereafter, it appeared to him. He wrote an hasty note, saying how ill he had been the whole night, and how impossible he feared it would be for him to see his uncle that day; but that, if his physician, whom he every moment expected, gave him leave to go out, he would certainly wait upon him.

This answer had not been dispatched above an hour, and his medical friend had just left him, with a strict injunction not to stir out that day, when Lady Castlenorth and Mrs. Calder entered his room.

"So, my dear Sir," cried the former, "what is to be done! Lord Castlenorth will be wretched to leave you behind—and my poor girl too!—What is this sudden fever—you really look ill—I cannot imagine what is to be done. For my Lord to stay, he thinks it death."

Willoughby muttered something which he meant should express concern at his uncle's illness: but Mrs. Calder fortunately precluded the necessity of his being very distinct in his hypocrisy, by stepping up to him, and taking his hand, "Come, come," said she, "let me feel your pulse." She then, gravely counting its vibrations as she held her stop-watch, said, "Why, really now, here is much less fever than I expected from your appearance—let us see your tongue.—Humph—'tis white to be sure. Where are your medicines? I should think, if you were well wrapped up and put into a chair, you might go to your uncle without any danger—on such an emergency, you know, a little may be hazarded."

"No," said Lady Castlenorth, "by no means; nothing must be hazarded. And after all, my Lord may make himself easy, as I dare say you will be able to overtake us before we get to Paris; where, if my Lord is better, and finds that relief he generally does from a change of air, we will stop till you join us: I think you will be perfectly restored in a week: but, however, I will go myself to Dr. B——,[1] and hear what he says."

"Oh, I can tell you," interrupted Mrs. Calder, "that he'll be well, perfectly well, in less than a week.—I have been tasting his medicines, and understand clearly from them what Dr. B—— thinks of his fever. It was a mere ephemeris[2]—of that be assured."

"Well," said Lady Castlenorth, "my dear Willoughby, what shall we say?"

Willoughby was ready to answer, "Nothing more, good Madam," but sighing from a sense of pain and restraint, he only replied, "that he could only say that he was very sorry for his uncle's illness—and—"

"That you will hasten after us?—that, I think, I may venture to assure your uncle. He was settling this morning that you should be married in the English ambassador's chapel at Paris; and I really don't see myself that, upon the whole, these unlucky illnesses of my Lord's and of your's need impede the affair a single hour; all the difference will be, that you will be married at Paris, instead of at London, and we will pass the rest of the year in Italy instead of Castlenorth."

"But the dear young Lady," cried Mrs. Calder, "our sweet and lovely child, how will she bear even this transient separation?"

"Indeed, I don't know," said Lady Castlenorth, affecting to be quite sympathetic, "but she shall come, and bring the letter my Lord will have directed to be written with his last directions about the deeds and carriages; which our dear George must bring with him: and," added she, smiling, "I fancy, upon the footing they are now, there will be no great indecorum in her coming to his lodgings."

Willoughby found immediately his fever returning, and that he should have a terrible headach: he put up his hand to his temples. "I am obliged to your Ladyship," said he in a languid voice, "and I wish this most oppressive headach of mine would—"

"What it aches now, does it?" said Mrs. Calder, "I wish Dr. B—— was here, I am sure I could give him a hint or two on this case which might be of use to him."

"Let us go to him," interrupted Lady Castlenorth, "and talk to him about this ugly fever; and when we have found him, it will be

---

1 Smith employs a frequent narrative strategy of realism, leaving out the name to suggest that a well-known London doctor is meant.
2 A one-day illness.

time to return to my Lord, and to send my daughter hither; for we think to sleep at Rochester to-night."

Willoughby now blessing her for her haste, made his compliments in a low voice and still complaining of his head—the Ladies departed.

They were no sooner gone, than he tried to discover by what means he might best avoid receiving the favour of the visit Lady Castlenorth had promised him from her daughter. He was ashamed of the part he was acting, however ill and reluctantly he performed it. For the first time in his life his conduct was contrary to his sense of honour, and, he was conscious, altogether unworthy of him; and while he had thus betrayed himself, he was become the dupe of Lady Castlenorth, and perhaps was meant to be the dupe of Miss Fitz-Hayman and their mutual favourite. His pride, as well as his rectitude, revolted from the idea of carrying on this odious farce, which he now wondered what demon had tempted him, in the moment of passion and despair, to begin, and which he, however late, thought he should now act more honourably in ending at once, than in suffering it to proceed another day. He was, however, by no means able to determine, at once, how he should do this; and what he had most immediately to consider was, how he should escape the enquiry and adieu of the heiress, which he might now every moment expect.

He at length determined to go to bed, and sending again for his physician, who was very much his friend, acknowledged the truth to him, and got an absolute prohibition against his seeing any body. He told Farnham, therefore, that he again felt himself extremely ill; and bade him immediately run for Dr. B——. Fortunately he met him in the next street; and in less than ten minutes he had received Willoughby's confession, that all his illness, both before and since his return from abroad, had been owing to distress of mind, which he could now no longer hope would abate, by the necessity he had thought of putting himself under to conceal it. In short, he owned that his dislike to Miss Fitz-Hayman, as a wife, was unconquerable; and that as he was determined at all events to break the treaty off, however far it had gone, and therefore entreated his friend to find some reason for evading an interview so useless and so irksome, when it was impossible for him to continue acting a moment longer the part he had so rashly undertaken; and yet did not mean, and especially in the present condition of his uncle's health, abruptly and rudely to end it; but to soften, at least to him, a disappointment which he had thus rendered doubly heavy.

Dr. B—— entered at once into his meaning, and smiling, said, "It is a little unusual, my friend, for me to contrive an illness to separate a lady from her lover, though I have been often asked to make pretences for bringing them together. However, the fact is, that you really are unfit to entertain the lady, for your fever is considerably increased since I saw you in the morning; and we see very plainly that any agitation is hazardous while you continue in this irritable state. I will therefore wait here and see Miss Fitz-Hayman myself; and so contrive as to bring you off this time, and for the future you must manage it yourself."

"I am sure you despise me, Doctor," cried Willoughby, "for the part I have acted in this cursed affair."

"No," answered he, "not exactly so. But I own I think you wrong, inasmuch as any kind of dissimulation is unworthy of you; and above all, that which goes to rob a young woman of her heart under false pretences."

"But I hope I have not done that—for, upon my honour, I should never forgive myself, if I had."

"It looks very like it though, my friend, from your own account of the matter. And if it is so——"

"You think I ought, at all events, to marry her?"

"Indeed I do."

"Alas, my dear Sir," said Willoughby, "it is surely better for me, even more honourable, to decline her hand now, than to accept it and make her miserable."

"I don't believe you could make any woman miserable," answered Dr. B——, "because you have good nature, honour and generosity. But, my dear Sir, I did not mean to play the casuist in such an affair—and here—if I am not mistaken, is the lady herself at the door."

"Dear Doctor," cried Willoughby, "have the goodness to go down directly." He immediately obeyed, and returning in a few moments, said, "Well, I have sent away the disconsolate fair one—broken-hearted—for fear of losing her love."

"Don't rally me, my friend," answered Willoughby, "but, tell me, did my cousin appear very much concerned?"

"She endeavoured at least to appear so."

"Do you think then it was merely endeavour?"

"Would you not be mortified, now, if I said it seemed so to me?"

"No, upon my honour—I might perhaps be mortified to find that I was believed to be an easy subject of imposition, but for the rest—nothing would be a greater relief to me, than to be well assured that the partiality my cousin shewed for me was either never real, or, having been so, exists no longer."

"I don't know her enough," replied Dr. B——, "nor have I been long enough talking to her now to be a very good judge. The honestest of them, my friend, are not easily understood, and I am much mistaken if your fair relation comes under that description. I mean, when I say honestest—the most candid, the most sincere."

"Well! But what do you judge, from her behaviour just now, are Miss Fitz-Hayman's sentiments towards me?"

"She would have me believe, I think, that they are those of great attachment and trembling apprehension for your health. But, somehow, it was, I fancied, a sort of concern that had more stage effect for its object, than real concern ever thinks about, and I do believe, that if you do prove a perjured swain after all, the heiress of Castlenorth will not add to the sorrowful catalogue of damsels who have died for love."

Willoughby, glad to hear this, now readily promised a ready acquiescence with his friend's orders, which were to keep his mind as quiet as he could, and to see nobody till he had quite conquered his remaining indisposition; and the Doctor then took his leave.

In less than two hours, a large pacquet came to him from Lord Castlenorth—which Willoughby sent word down to the man who brought it, that he was then too ill to open. On Farnham's delivering this message, the servant said, that no answer then was required, for that his lord and lady, their daughter, Mrs. Calder, and Captain Cavanaugh, had all departed, with the servants who were immediately about them, the very moment he came away, and were then, in two post coaches and four, on their way to Rochester. Willoughby felt for a moment as much relieved by this intelligence, as if half his troubles had been removed by their departure. Too soon, however, this temporary respite ended, by his recollecting how much he must yet encounter before he could feel himself free; and that whatever freedom he might gain, Celestina would be another's.

Chapter VII

In the mean time Celestina was alone at Cheltenham, indulging that regret which arose from the certain loss of Willoughby's friendship, and the assurance that she should see him no more. Every day she expected to see in the newspapers, or to hear from Lady Horatia, that he was married, and though she tried to reason herself into a calm acquiescence with what was unavoidable, she never opened a paper or a letter without trembling.

But her own unhappiness prevented her not from feeling for the unhappiness of her friends. The letter she had received from Emily Cathcart had made a great impression upon her, though she knew not how it would be proper to act to answer the views of the writer.

At length she determined to write to Mrs. Elphinstone, and enclose the letter itself, and this she did a few days after she was settled at Cheltenham.

Almost every post brought her accounts of the amendment of Montague Thorold, from Lady Horatia, who visited him constantly, and in almost every letter she expressed, either plainly or by implication, her expectations that Celestina would attend to the wishes of all her friends, and give him her hand immediately on his recovery. This repeated importunity from a person to whose wishes, and for whose opinion she felt so much deference to be due, was infinitely painful to her; but how to escape from it she knew not. If she quitted Lady Horatia she had no proper protection—no home to receive her, and though her little income had hitherto more than sufficed to support her while with such a friend, and though she had received about an hundred pounds from Cathcart, paid her by the direction of Willoughby while he was abroad, which yet remained almost untouched, yet on such a sum, and on the interest of fifteen hundred pounds, she could not with any degree of prudence adopt the plan on which her imagination had lately dwelt with peculiar pleasure— that of setting out alone, or with only a female servant, and travelling through France. She fancied that there she might be enabled, though she had yet no clue to guide her, to find some traces of her family. An invincible inclination, which she sometimes took for the inspiration of heaven, had been for some weeks gaining on her imagination, and every thing seemed to encourage it; but reason and prudence, both of which were perhaps decidedly in favour of her accepting the proper establishment offered her, by a man who had not only given so many proofs of his sincere and tender affection for her, but who was the son of one of her best friends, and avowedly recommended to her by another, and whom she would have chosen had Willoughby never been in question.

For her it was very certain that he was in question no longer; he was in fact dead to her, and no probability remained of his ever feeling for her even the regret that the loss of an agreeable acquaintance might have given him. But still her heart and her imagination had been so long accustomed to consider him as their first object, that she found it impossible for her to transfer to another the same attachment; and without being sensible of love she could not promise it; she desired nothing but to be permitted to live single; and be mistress of her time and herself—and not to be importuned to undertake duties which her heart told her she could not conscientiously fulfil.

But she foresaw too evidently, that while she remained in her present situation, and Lady Horatia continued so eager for the match, her life must pass in a continual conflict between her wish to gratify her friend, and her disinclination to marriage. At her time of life, professions of a resolution to remain single were merely laughed at, and never believed; and Montague Thorold had never hitherto considered her gentle refusals and friendly admonitions to desist, but as being in reality as much encouragement as she could give him, while her situation in regard to Willoughby remained so aukwardly undecided—that while he might renounce the name of lover, he might still assume that of a near relation, and have the power of controlling, or at least of directing her.

Now that it was decided, beyond a doubt, that he neither meant to avail himself of either the one or the other, she saw that she had nothing to urge in support of her refusal which would be listened to; and while her mind dwelt on all the friendly but still irksome controversy in which she must of necessity be engaged when Lady Horatia and Thorold came down, it of course adverted to the means of relief, which could, she thought, be obtained only by her quitting England—and for her doing so, her natural desire to discover her parents was, she thought, a sufficient excuse.

In her present solitude she found so much to soothe and console her, that she longed for nothing so much as the power of enjoying it, and at the same time wandering through various countries, and particularly through that which she had been taught to consider as her own. The longer she thought of this plan, the more agreeable it became to her imagination; and she passed many hours every day in reading travels through France, Italy, and Switzerland, still humouring this visionary idea till it had acquired the force of a presentiment; a persuasion that could she go to the South of France she should find her family.

Of this she continually thought: of this she continually dreamed; and though one great motive that would have urged her to attempt it, the possibility of being restored to Willoughby, was at an end, she still determined to execute this plan before the summer elapsed.

She had indeed nothing but her gratitude and attachment to Lady Horatia to detain her in England; she could not go to Jessy, because it was so near Alvestone; nor enjoy the friendly and instructive conversation of Mr. Thorold, because of the unfortunate partiality of his son. The sole remaining friend of her childhood, Lady Molyneux, was not merely estranged from her, but had invariably treated her with negligence, scorn, and contempt. To England therefore she had at least no friends who attached her; the whole world was her country; and with that restlessness to which the unhappy are subject, she fancied that in any part of it she should find more satisfaction than in her present situation.

By her wandering continually alone in the pleasant country that surrounded the town where she resided, at a season too when the face of nature was every day growing more lovely, her talent for poetry, which sometimes remained for whole months unexercised, was again called forth; but whatever were the objects really before her, whatever were presented to her mind by books, Willoughby was ever the principal figure in the landscape. If she sat on the green hill, as she often did for hours together, lost in mournful yet not unpleasing reverie, it was only to recollect scenes that were passed; which the same sounds she had then heard, the simple sheep-bell, the early song of birds; the same scents of fresh turf and wild flowers, brought again most forcibly to her recollection.

If in her reading, she was by the traveller's lively description of the countries he had passed through, to fancy herself there, she reverted instantly to the delight she should have felt could she in a progress through such romantic scenes have been the companion of Willoughby; and it was in this disposition of mind, that after perusing an account of a cottage and its inhabitants overwhelmed by the fall of an avalanche, a great body of snow from the mountain above, she composed the following little lyric poem.

THE PEASANT OF THE ALPS.

WHERE cliffs arise by Winter crown'd,
And through dark groves of pine around,
Down the deep chasms, the snow-fed torrents foam,
Within some hollow, shelter'd from the storms,
The Peasant of the Alps his cottage forms,
And builds his humble, happy home.

Unenvied is the rich domain,
That far beneath him on the plain,
Waves its wide harvests and its olive groves;

More dear to him his hut, with plantain thatch'd,
Where long his unambitious heart attach'd,
Finds all he wishes, all he loves.

There dwells the mistress of his heart,
And *love*, who teaches every art,
Has bid him dress the spot with fondest care;
When borrowing from the vale its fertile soil,
He climbs the precipice with patient toil,
To plant her favorite flow'rets there.

With native shrubs, an hardy race,
There the green myrtle finds a place,
And roses there, the dewy leaves decline;
While from the cragg's abrupt and tangled steeps,
With bloom and fruit the Alpine berry peeps,
And blushing, mingles with the vine.

His garden's simple produce stored,
Prepar'd for him by hands adored,
Is all the little luxury he knows;
And by the same dear hands are softly spread,
The Chamois' velvet spoil that forms the bed
Where in her arms he finds repose.

But absent from the calm abode,
Dark thunder gathers round his road,
Wild raves the wind, the arrowy lightnings flash,
Returning quick the murmuring rocks among,
His faint heart trembling as he winds along;
Alarm'd!—he listens to the crash

Of rifted ice!—Oh, man of woe!
O'er his dear cot—a mass of snow,
By the storm sever'd from the cliff above,
Has fallen—and buried in its marble breast,
All that for him—lost wretch—the world possest,
His home, his happiness, his love!

Aghast the heart-struck mourner stands,
Glaz'd are his eyes—convuls'd his hands,
O'erwhelming anguish checks his labouring breath;

Crush'd by despair's intolerable weight,
Frantic he seeks the mountain's giddiest height,
And headlong seeks relief in death.

A fate too similar is mine,
But I—in lingering pain repine,
And still my lost felicity deplore;
Cold, cold to me is that dear breast become,
Where this poor heart had fondly fix'd its home,
And love and happiness are mine no more.[1]

While Celestina was thus, with more tenderness than discretion, cherishing the memory of the friend she had lost, Willoughby was very differently occupied from what her imagination suggested. Instead of being the gay and fortunate lover, on the eve of marrying one of the greatest heiresses in England, he was suffering in his personal health, from the anxiety of a mind at war with itself, and certain of nothing but that for him the world no longer contained any happiness. The intelligence, however vague, and like the common gossipping stories so usual among servants, that he had received from Farnham, had made a great impression, which what he afterwards gathered from the same quarter had increased. Justina had told Farnham, as a secret however of the first importance, that Captain Cavanaugh had been of late in the habit of being admitted to her young lady's dressing-room after Lady Castlenorth and the family were retired, however late the hour might be; that her young lady was obliged to entrust her with these visits, that they might be more securely concealed from the rest of the family; but that sometimes she had been dismissed to bed, and sometimes ordered to wait till he retired. That on some of those occasions she observed her young lady had been crying, by the redness of her eyes; and that then the Captain had always left her with the air of a man much offended. That she had sometimes heard them talk in voices as if they were arguing upon something, but could never distinctly understand what their conversation was about. "They were in sad fright always," said Justina, "that Miladi hear them. Miladi knows not at all what goes on in this house." "And my lady, I suppose," said Farnham, "would be in a horrible passion if she heard of it?" "Oh, for me," replied she, "I could not stay if she did find it out." "But why," enquired Farnham,

---

1   *The Poems of Charlotte Smith*, ed. Stuart Curran, 90.

"why, if your young lady likes the Captain so as to have him keep company with her in this manner, what does she mean by marrying my master?" Justina then, with an arch look, answered, "Oh, my good friend, the Captain has one wife already; and why should not my young lady have one husband? The Captain will be her Cecisbeo—cavalier servante."[1] "I don't understand your French out-of-the-way names," replied Farnham; "but I am sure, that if your lady marries my master only to play such pranks as some other fine ladies do, she will get into a bad scrape—for he is not a man to be quiet when such sort of doings are a-going on, that I can tell her—and if she don't love him better than any other man, I think she had much better say so."—"Oh, silly man," answered Justina—"as if my young lady could not have a regard for both of them—!" "Aye, aye," replied Farnham, "that may do well enough in your country—but it will never do here."

Justina now, afraid that Farnham's zeal for his master would perhaps urge him to reveal the dangerous secret with which she had thus entrusted him, began to soften the harshest features of it; by saying, that she believed there was no harm at all in the friendship between her young lady and Captain Cavanaugh—that to be sure, the Captain was a sweet handsome man, and very agreeable, and therefore her young lady liked to talk with him, which she never could do when her mother was by; as she never suffered him to speak hardly to any body else, and that it was natural enough for her lady to like the Captain, and have a regard for him, because she had known him so long. She ended her conversation with exacting from Farnham a promise that he would never mention a syllable to any body of what she had told him: a promise which he kept, however, only till he could reveal it all to his master.

Willoughby had, after receiving this information, no longer a doubt as to breaking off instantly his proposed alliance; but how, without plunging a dagger in the heart of his uncle, to do this, required some consideration. Lord Castlenorth had sent him full directions as to paying off all the incumbrances upon his estate, and deposited the money at a banker's, where he had also left a large sum for his own use; and expecting him to join the family at Paris, if he did not overtake them sooner; and was now pleasing himself with the

---

1 Admirer of, attendant on a married woman, more usually cicisbeo (Italian); attendant knight (French). Both terms could mean merely a "walker" or escort but often implied "lover."

idea, that in a very few days the favourite project of his life would be completed; and that in adopting the son of his sister, and uniting him with his daughter, he should transmit his name and his honours to posterity with little variation from lineal descent.[1] It was this hope, that seemed to have sustained his feeble existence to its present period, in spite of the numerous infirmities he laboured under, and even of the prescriptions and nursing of Mrs. Calder. And though it was impossible for Willoughby either to love or esteem such a man as Lord Castlenorth, yet he felt for him some regard, as his mother's brother, and some pity not only for his real but his imaginary sufferings, which he knew must be dreadfully increased, and perhaps become fatal, from so heavy a disappointment of all his expectations.

He hesitated, then, how to act; whether to write or go to him, or whether he should not rather address himself to Lady Castlenorth or her daughter; and for two days after their departure, had been unable to resolve on any thing, when a porter, who immediately disappeared, gave to the servant of the house a letter for him. It was evidently written in a foreign hand, and in a foreign idiom—though pains seemed to have been taken to disguise both. The contents were these:

"Sir,
"One who is and will be always a stranger to you, takes the liberty to approach you with this advice so important to you, and fearing it may be soon too late.
"You are, Sir, on the point of being married, as the report goes, to the daughter of Lord Castlenorth, Miss Fitz-Hayman, your relation. I have cause to know that her heart is belonging to another person, and only chagrin and inquietude will be the effect, if you execute this marriage, whatever may have seemed to the contrary. If there is any doubt of the truth of this, a little observation, or making enquiry among those near her, will explain what I would say: and if there is question of the person she has a great friendship for, you have only to think of those who are always with her. A word they say to the wise is enough for them to understand. I have the honour to be,
                    "With profound respect,
                              Sir,
                    Your devoted servant,
                              Unknown."

---

1 From the direct line, from father to son.

Willoughby had no sooner read this letter, than it struck him that it was written either by Cavanaugh himself, or by some person employed by him, and his motive evidently was to prevent a marriage he now saw so nearly concluded, and which would destroy all his hopes of securing to himself this opulent heiress, rather than her mother, whose lavish fondness for him had enabled him, by some means or other—it was probable they were not very justifiable means—to release himself from his former engagements,[1] engagements which, with far other views, she had assisted him to dissolve.

Many concurring circumstances strengthened the persuasion that this letter was fabricated, if not written, by Cavanaugh. It seemed to be the translation of a letter first written in French, and Willoughby heard that Cavanaugh could not write English with facility from long disuse. It was certainly Cavanaugh's interest, by any means, to stop the marriage between him and Miss Fitz-Hayman, which perhaps no means could have done more effectually; since from the tears she had frequently been observed by Justina to shed in their long conferences, it was probable his arguments had failed of their effect.

If Willoughby had before felt something like antipathy towards Miss Fitz-Hayman, which he never could wholly conquer, he now found it amounting to abhorrence and detestation. The love she had shewn towards him must either have been the effect of art or of vice—both were to him equally odious. That she could hope to impose upon him by the one, or think him a proper object for the indulgence of the other, were ideas equally hateful and equally humiliating; and under the first impulse of indignation, he was tempted to write to her, and, inclosing the letter from his anonymous correspondent, add to it all the circumstances Farnham had learned of Justina, as reasons why he renounced her with contempt.

But after a little reflection, his manly and generous spirit inspired him with far other designs. It was possible, that his cousin, whom he now considered with as much dislike, but with more compassion, might yet be saved from the artifices of a villain, and he thought himself bound to attempt it by every exertion, except the sacrifice of himself in marriage. It was possible that his uncle, though he could not make that sacrifice to gratify him, might yet be in some degree preserved from the dreadful shock which his daughter's conduct must give him, were it described to him in the horrid light he himself now saw it in; or revealed to him by any one less cautious

---

1 His marriage-vows.

than himself. Distressing, therefore, as the scenes must be that he should have to go through, when, instead of joining the family, to complete his marriage, he should meet them with those charges which put an end to it for ever; he determined to follow them immediately; and writing to Cathcart such instructions as were most requisite, as to the management of his affairs, and without hinting how different the purpose of his journey was from what it was supposed to be, he departed as soon as his physician dismissed him, for the Continent; which was in something more than a week after the Castlenorths had left London.

Every body concluded that he was gone to his bride; and every body's conjectures remained uncontradicted. Lady Horatia, in her letters to Celestina, told her that Lord Castlenorth's illness having obliged him to quit England, on a very short notice, Willoughby and Miss Fitz-Hayman had been privately married[1] the day before they set out; that some business, as to his estates, detained him afterwards five or six days in London; but that he was now gone to the Castlenorth family at Paris, and was to proceed with them to pass the summer in Italy. The same account found its way into the public prints, and was received without any doubt. Celestina shed many tears over the first information she received, and then accusing herself of folly, tried to dry them, and to detach her mind from thinking of Willoughby, but this no effort enabled her to do; and though all anxiety was now lost in the most painful certainty, she sunk from fruitless solicitude into hopeless dejection.

In such a frame of mind Lady Horatia found her, when after a separation of about three weeks, she rejoined her at Cheltenham. With her arrived Montague Thorold, quite recovered from his wound, deriving from it, and from thus being allowed to attend Celestina, more hope than ever; while his love seemed to have increased, if to increase were possible; and while his sufferings and his merit certainly rendered him interesting to Celestina, and combined to entitle him to her friendship, her pity, and esteem; she felt, and felt with regret, that, decided as she believed her fate now to be in regard to Willoughby, friendship, esteem, and pity, were yet all she could give to Montague Thorold.

---

1 The original has "warned."

Chapter VIII

Willoughby, with every sensation that could render such a journey unpleasant, proceeded to Paris, where he learned that his uncle impatiently waited for him; had he gone immediately to him, he must have crush'd at once, all the expectations his appearance raised: and the shock must have been too great and too cruel. He determined at first, therefore, to write to Lady Castlenorth—yet after some reflection, doubted whether it would not be better to give the letter he had received to Miss Fitz-Hayman; and leave it to her to find the means of dismissing him, without his being compelled to assign the true reason. It was still possible that the charges against her might be unfounded or exaggerated. It is possible, that were they neither, he might rescue her from the abyss to which she seemed to be devoting herself. But, from the pride and violence of her temper, and from that imperious spirit, which had never yet borne to be told of an error, he not only felt great uneasiness from the idea of the scene that was before him, but doubted whether the person for whose sake he was willing to encounter it, would not baffle all his endeavours to rescue her from evil, or conceal her errors by clamour and resentment.

After some deliberation, however, as it was necessary to fix on something, he wrote a short note to Miss Fitz-Hayman, desiring she would favour him with a few moments conversation; and entreating her, for reasons which he would then explain to her, not to inform Lord or Lady Castlenorth of his arrival at Paris, till he had seen her.

This note he sent by Farnham to Justina, to be delivered to her mistress; and received in a short time an answer, that she should be alone that evening at ten o'clock, and that Justina should conduct him to her, in her own dressing room.

He found her sitting alone; and, under the appearance of receiving him with pleasure, there was, he thought, a lurking apprehension of the occasion of this mysterious visit. He felt himself extremely distressed how to open such a conversation; but the consciousness of rectitude, and some degree of indignant resentment, immediately restored that calmness and resolution, which on his first entrance he feared he might fail of commanding.

He began by apologizing for the liberty he had taken in thus soliciting an interview with her, before he saw the other parts of the family. "But, I am persuaded, Madam," continued he, advancing towards her, with the letter open in his hand, "that whatever foundation there may be for the assertion which this letter contains, it will be less uneasy to you to read it yourself, than to have any appeal made on it to Lord and Lady Castlenorth." She took the letter with an air of mingled astonishment and indignation; but Willoughby saw it tremble in her hand. "A letter, sir, in which mention is made of me! I am really quite at a loss to know what there can be in it, that I should, in your opinion, wish to have it concealed." "It is not long, Madam," said Willoughby, fixing his eyes on her face; "and if you will have the goodness to read it—" "Oh, certainly, Sir." She ran her eyes over it, and as he attentively watched her countenance, he saw pride struggling to conquer fear and shame, and with some degree of success; for having read it, she paused a moment, and then assuming an air of haughty resentment, she threw the letter on the table that was between her and Willoughby, and said, contemptuously, "I know not whether most to despise, the Author of such a letter, or the man who—if indeed he is not included in both descriptions—can poorly make it a pretence for insulting a person, who has already been too much his victim." "Pardon me, Madam," said Willoughby, "for interrupting you; but I must take leave to say, that I am included in neither. A moment's reflection will convince you that I am incapable of the latter; and had the former been my object, I should not have chosen this method of shewing this extraordinary billet to you; nor thus put it in your power to detect the author, without any hazard to yourself of having his charges believed. Miss Fitz-Hayman, I will be very ingenuous with you: the person here alluded to, is Captain Cavanaugh. I know it: I know that the partiality, whether real or affected, with which you have appeared to favor me, has been superseded by his more eminent merit; and, though I am very willing to relinquish all prospect of an honor of which I am unworthy, I cannot feel much satisfaction, in reflecting on the idea you seemed to have entertained of my facility or blindness; nor, indeed, can I, without regret, see you likely to—"

"Say, rather, Sir," interrupted Miss Fitz-Hayman, "say, rather, that you rejoice in having found, or made, an excuse to break through the promises you have given, from which, however, Sir, you would have been released without degrading yourself, by this poor and unmanly artifice. The daughter of Lord Castlenorth need not, surely, solicit the hand of any man." Pride and anger now choaked her utterance; and Willoughby, taking advantage of her want of words, again seized the opportunity to speak; he took her hand, which she would have snatched from him, but he continued to detain it, while, in the gentlest accents of friendly remonstrance, he said, "Come, come, my dear cousin, if I am not your lover, at least, I can never be your enemy. For Heaven's sake, be not your own; confide in me, and believe that I will rather take the blame and inconvenience of our separation on myself, than suffer you to incur either with your father. You cannot suppose, I trust you do not even wish, I should proceed farther in forming the alliance that brought me hither, knowing what I know."

"And what do you know, Sir? and from whom have you obtained this knowledge?"

"From sources, which render it impossible that I should be mistaken—Captain Cavanaugh."

He was proceeding; but, either from the tone in which he spoke, or some other circumstance which at that moment struck her, she was suddenly impressed with a fear that he had been calling Cavanaugh himself to an account;[1] who, as it happened, had not that day dined with them. This idea threw her instantly off her guard; she turned pale, and asked in an altered and tremulous tone, "what he meant by these sources of information?"

Willoughby saw immediately what she believed, and the truth of the information he had received from Justina was evident beyond a doubt. Her fears for her own reputation, or of the anger of her father, she could conquer; but the moment she apprehended that the life of Cavanaugh either had been, or might be hazarded, her fortitude failed her. It was now the moment to pursue the truth, which Willoughby, by soothing her, while he kept the idea of her lover's danger in view, at length, with great difficulty, obtained, by her half indignant, half contrite avowal, that Cavanaugh had been a too successful candidate for her heart,[2] and that her father and her mother's eager wishes, together with some other motives,[3] which Willoughby discerned, through the confusions and agitation with which she attempted to palliate or conceal them, had prompted her to affect for

---

1 That he had met Cavanaugh in a duel that morning and that Cavanaugh was wounded or dead.
2 That they are already lovers.
3 A difficult passage, partly because Smith, like most contemporary novelists, was reluctant to refer explicitly to pregnancy. It may mean that Miss Fitz-Hayman fears she is pregnant, before Cavanaugh is free to marry her, and therefore has needed to keep Willoughby in reserve to marry her if necessary. Or she may be happy to marry Willoughby, since Cavanaugh may never get his divorce, and to keep Cavanaugh as her lover. This would not suit the latter, however, as his interest in her is mainly financial.

him a passion she had not felt since she had been in the habit of listening to Cavanaugh.

Willoughby looked back with terror to the danger he had escaped, and with infinite pity, mingled with less gentle emotions, cast his eyes again on his cousin: he found her so deeply entangled by the art of Cavanaugh, that to save her from him, was no longer in his power; but it was possible perhaps to take upon himself the anger and indignation of Lord and Lady Castlenorth, and give her time to arrange her own plans, by immediately withdrawing in silence; though, how any comfortable arrangement could be made for her, with a man who was understood to be already married, he knew not; nor how Lady Castlenorth would bear so cruel a blow, as the preference thus given to her daughter by a man whom she certainly had intended as successor to her present husband, whenever his infirmities should release her. When the first tumult of those passions, which fear, shame, and love, had excited in the bosom of Miss Fitz-Hayman, subsided, by the kind and considerate arguments of Willoughby, she became able to talk with some degree of calmness on the subject; and he found that from the last renewal of their acquaintance with Captain Cavanaugh, this design had been certainly entertained by Lady Castlenorth; but that, on his part, no other advantage had been taken of her extreme partiality toward him, than to obtain, by her means, money to enable him to prosecute a divorce from his wife, a young woman whom he had married some years before for the sake of some fortune, and a great deal of beauty, which she then possessed. Having in two or three years dissipated the former, he left her to make what advantage she could of the latter; and had never troubled himself about her since, till his reception in the family of Lord Castlenorth opened to him prospects of carrying off the rich heiress, and made him desirous of obtaining a dissolution of his marriage, for which his wife's ill conduct, though entirely owing to his desertion of her, gave him a very good pretence. Much of this Willoughby had learned from various little circumstances which escaped Miss Fitz-Hayman in this long conversation; for her representation of him was, that of the most amiable and unfortunate of men; married early in life to a woman insensible of his merit; and now rendered unhappy by a passion for another object, whom he had long seen on the point of being given to a rival, who saw her with very different eyes.

Willoughby could not, without astonishment, observe the blind infatuation of a woman, possessed of rather a good understanding: but he found that the art of Cavanaugh, to the success of which his very handsome figure had undoubtedly contributed, had so completely attained the government of Miss Fitz-Hayman's mind, that she no longer saw but with his eyes; and that while, to prevent any suspicion on the part of her mother, she had been suffered to affect a degree of affection for Willoughby, which had long since ceased, Cavanaugh trusted to his reluctance to delay a marriage, which it was easy to see he dreaded; and hoped that the divorce would be obtained before that reluctance would be conquered. He found, however, that Willoughby suddenly agreed to hasten it; and then it was that, in his conference with her, after the rest of the family were in bed, he urged her to find delays; and to procrastinate, herself, a period,[1] to the arrival of which Willoughby no longer seemed averse. Her tears, and the alarm in which Justina had observed her, were the effects of the earnestness and impetuosity with which Cavanaugh now pressed the necessity of her doing this; and the alternative he sometimes offered her, of declaring to Willoughby himself, the footing upon which he was with her. Her father's illness, fortunately for her, intervened; and now Cavanaugh was every hour in hopes that he should be set free from his matrimonial engagements and possess himself of the prize so long the object of his ambition, and the end of all his designs.

Miss Fitz-Hayman and Willoughby now were to discuss the means by which, with the least prejudice to her, their intended union could then be broken off. The lady, though she did not ingenuously own it, had many reasons for accepting, unconditionally, her cousin's generous offer, to take the whole burthen of their displeasure upon himself. She knew, not only the extravagant and furious passions which any suspicion of its real cause would excite in her mother, but she was aware of the increasing fondness of her father for his nephew; and apprehended, that if he appeared the injured and forsaken person, that fondness might urge him to make him amends, by giving him a part of the great sums and estates that were in his own power, and this, rich as she would still have been, she had not any disposition to promote.

After some debate, then, in what way Willoughby should excuse himself, and his rejection (on account of their falsehood) of some methods which Miss Fitz-Hayman proposed; he at length determined to write to Lady Castlenorth, stating simply, that he had

---

1 Put off the time of the marriage herself, since Willoughby was no longer doing so.

changed his mind, and found it impossible to fulfil his engagements: and leave it to her to break it to her Lord as she thought proper; for he imagined any letter from himself might be a still severer shock, unless he could assign better reasons than any it was possible for to offer.

This point being settled, Miss Fitz-Hayman retired to recover herself from the effects of the scene she had passed through; and to study her part in those that were to come. Willoughby returned, unseen by all but Justina, to his hotel; where he composed a short note to the purport they had agreed upon: and early the next morning he set out on horseback for Lyons, from whence he intended to proceed, along the coast of the Mediterranean, to the Pyrenees, and to pass some weeks among those mountains which he had never seen.

The recent and extraordinary events that had befallen him, gave his mind sufficient subject for contemplation, during the first part of his journey. It was now very certain that he was forever released, and that by means which left him nothing to reproach himself with, from his engagements with Miss Fitz-Hayman, and of course from that promise to his mother, in consequence of which those engagements were made. One great objection, then, to his union with Celestina was thus removed; and never did her image more tenderly occupy his thoughts than at this moment: but, alas! it was no longer cherished with delight. The mystery that clouded her birth, and which he despaired of ever removing, empoisoned the pleasure with which he would have thought of her; and with yet greater bitterness, he adverted to the probability there was that she was now the wife of another.

Very certain that he should now never find that happiness of which her loss had deprived him, the lesser evils—evils from which, a few years before, he would have shrunk with dismay—seemed to have lost their effect. It was almost impossible for him, without injustice to others and uneasiness to himself, to keep such a place as Alvestone, in the present shattered state of his fortune; and resolving to disembarrass himself from the necessity of returning to England, for some years, he wrote from Lyons, to Cathcart, giving him directions to put the estate to sale: and at the same time informed the banker, in whose hands Lord Castlenorth had left money for the discharge of all his incumbrances, that he should not avail himself of it; but that it must be replaced to his uncle's account.

Having thus loosened almost every tie that connected him with England, from which he did not wish even to hear, lest the information of Celestina's marriage should reach him,

"The World was all before him where to chuse;"[1]

and his utmost hope was, to obtain, by change of place, so much tranquillity of mind, as to allow him to feel some satisfaction in the variety of the scenes it offered.

He journeyed from Lyons to Avignon; and then proceeded along the coast, by Bezieres and Mirepoix, into Roussillon: interested by the grandeur and beauty of these remains of Roman antiquity[2] which he saw in his way; still more charmed by the sublime views, which, in this romantic line of country, every where offered themselves to his sight; and hearing, and *but* hearing, at a distance, the tumults, with which a noble struggle for freedom[3] at this time (the summer of 1789) agitated the capital, and many of the great towns of France, till, among the wild and stupendous scenes which he at length reached, even this faint murmur died away.

In one of the cottages scattered at the foot of Montlouis, he found a young mountaineer, acquainted with all the passes of the Pyrenees: he was there only a few days, on his way back from Perpignan to his home, in the Vallei de Douron; and on Willoughby proposing it to him, he most willingly undertook to be his guide through the mountains.

Willoughby had left his horses at Perpignan, and his present equipage consisted only of Farnham, carrying a light portmanteau, and a sort of havresac for provisions, which he took himself, strapped over his shoulders.

On the morning of his departure from the foot of Montlouis, he travelled towards the south east, always ascending, and was soon in the very heart of the Pyrenees. In scenes which had hardly ever been traversed but by the shepherds and goat-herds, and where no vestiges of man were seen, but here and there a solitary cabin, serving them for shelter, during a few weeks of summer, built of the rough

---

1 Cf. John Milton, *Paradise Lost*, Book XII, line 646.
2 The South of France, especially the eastern part nearest to Italy, was more urban and relatively peaceful under the administration of the Romans than the rest of Gaul, and its towns and cities remained Roman in character; excavations of classical remains were now of increasing interest to historians and travellers.
3 Smith refers to the debate about constitutional reform at the Estates General, that is, the convention on 1 May 1789 of representatives of the clergy, aristocracy and bourgeoisie, and the popular unrest throughout the first half of that year that led to the storming of the Bastille, the Paris prison-fortress that for many symbolised state tyranny.

branches of pine or chesnut, covered with turf, and lined with moss; in these huts, which were now some of them inhabited, Willoughby found a wild, but simple and benevolent people; always ready to supply him with such food as their flocks, among those desert regions, afforded to themselves; and in one of them, on a temporary bed, made of the skins of their sheep, whom accident had destroyed, after a deep sigh, which was drawn from him by the memory of Celestina, and with which every day concluded, he obtained a few hours of refreshing sleep, and with the dawn of the next day pursued his journey towards the summit of the mountain.

Amid these paths that wound among the almost perpendicular points of the cliffs, he often sat down; surveying with awe and admiration the stupendous works of the Divine Architect, before whose simplest creation, the laboured productions of the most intelligent of his creatures sink into insignificance. Huge masses of grey marble, or a dark granite, frowned above his head; whose crevices, here and there, afford a scanty subsistence to lichens and moss campion; while the desolate bareness of other parts, added to that threatening aspect with which they seemed to hang over the wandering traveller, and to bid him to fear, lest even the light steps of the Izard[1] (the Chamois of the Pyrenees), or the wild goats, who now and then appeared suspended amid the craggy fissures, should disunite them from the mountain itself, and bury him beneath their thundering ruins.

Dashing down amongst these immense piles of stone, the cataracts, formed by the melting of the snows, and the ice of the glacieres, in the bosom of the mountains, fell roaring into the dark and abyss-like chasms, whither the eye feared to follow them; yet, frequently, amidst the wildest horrors of these great objects, appeared some little green recess, shaded by immense pines, cedars, or mountain-ash; and the short turf beneath them appeared spangled with the Soldinella and fringed pink,[2] or blushing with the scented wreaths of the Daphne Cneorum[3]—while through the cracks and hollows of the surrounding wall of rock, were filtered small and clear streams, that crept away among the tufts of juniper, rosemary, and the Rhododendron of the Alps[4] that clothed the less-abrupt declivity;

---

1 A capriform (goat-like) antelope, a native of the Pyrenees.
2 Smith's note: Dianthus Superbus.
3 Also known as the garland flower, this is an evergreen, low-growing plant, a native of southern Europe.
4 Smith's note: Rhododendron Alpina; dwarf rosebay. This plant supplies firing to the shepherds of the Pyrenees.

where, uninterrupted by intervening crags, the mountain shelving gradually to its base, opened a bosom more smiling and fertile; through which the collected waters, no longer foaming from their fall, found their way towards the Mediterranean sea; their banks feathered with woods of cork trees, chesnuts, and evergreen oaks, while the eye, carried beyond them, was lost in the wide and luxuriant plains of Languedoc.

Never did such a spot offer itself to the eyes of Willoughby, but the figure of Celestina was instantly present to his imagination; he saw her sitting by him, enjoying the beautiful and romantic scenery; he heard her, in those accents which had long such power to enchant him, expatiate on its charms, with all that exquisite taste and feeling he knew her possessed of; and remembering a charming description given by Rousseau, in his *Julie*, of a spot of this sort among the rocks of Meillerie.—"*It sembloit que ce lieu désert, dût être l'asyle de deux amants; échappés seuls au bouleversement de la nature.*"[1]

For a moment or two he indulged such a delicious reverie, till the sudden recollection of the truth cruelly destroyed it. Celestina was not, never could be his, never could share with him the simple and sublime delight offered by the superb spectacle of nature, "with all her great works about her."[2] Whether he was among the rude mountains that she has raised as a barrier, to divide two powerful nations;[3] or gratified with the more mild beauties of his native country, never could she share in his satisfaction, or heighten his enjoyment, but her hours and her talents were all destined to make the happiness of Montague Thorold. At that idea he started up, and hardly conscious of the rugged precipices beneath him, renewed his wandering researches; and sought, by activity of body, to chase the fearful phantoms of lost happiness that haunted his mind.

He had now passed three weeks among the Pyrenees; had traversed several Glaciers, and descended on the Spanish side, and looked over part of Catalonia. Again he took his way to their

---

1 Jean-Jacques Rousseau's *Julie, ou la Nouvelle Heloise*, Part 4, Saint-Preux's Letter 17. As usual, Smith quotes from memory: the original lacks the internal punctuation and has "asile" and "amans." The mountain landscape description was one chosen by Rousseau for illustration. Smith's translation: "It seemed that this desart spot was designed as an asylum for two lovers, who had escaped the general wreck of nature."

2 Laurence Sterne, *Tristram Shandy*, Vol. VII, Ch. XXIX, first paragraph, in a section describing a tour through southern France.

3 France and Spain.

summits; again crossed deep vallies of ice, and wandered over regions where winter reigns in all its rigour, though under a sky of the deepest blue, illuminated by the ardent sun of July; a sky so clear, that not even a fleeting summer cloud, for a moment, diversifies its radiance. One of the tallest of these stupendous points is *Le pie du midi de Bagneus,*[1] which seems to be the sovereign of the inferior points around it; from its tall head he descended to Bagniers; and there meaning to close his researches, he rested some days, and then, by another route, returned towards the country of Roussillon, from whence he had first begun his journey.

But when he arrived there, he had nothing to do but to form some scheme of farther progress; and therefore, pleased as he was with the variety and novelty offered him by this long chain of immense mountains, he determined to lengthen his stay amongst them. His guide, who had by this time acquired an affection for him, delighted to carry him to every place that he thought might offer either novelty or amusement; and he now conversed with the smuggler, who conveyed, at the extremest peril, prohibited articles of commerce between France and Spain; now joined the solitary hunter of the Izard, or smaller Chamois; and now shared the more dangerous toils of those who sought the bear, the wild boar, or the wolf, among the deep woods that clothed the sides of the mountains.

It was in an excursion with an hunter of the Izard, that, Farnham having been left behind at the cabin of a shepherd where Willoughby intended to pass the night, he and Gaston, his guide, were, by an accident, separated; and he found himself alone, on one of the most savage spots of the whole chain; above him arose a point covered by eternal snow; beyond which a Glacier spread its desolate and frozen surface and barren rocks: on one side, fed by this magazine of ice and snow, a broad and thundering torrent threw itself, falling, with deafening noise, into a rocky cauldron, so far below that the eye could not fathom it. A dark and apparently inaccessible wood of firs was on the other side, where no tree or plant could find its abode, that was not equally able to endure the severity of those cold winds, that, passing over these immense magazines of ice, carry with them frost and desolation, even into the rich vineyards and luxuriant pastures of Gascony and Languedoc, and there assume the name of the Bize-wind.[2]

---

1   A volcanic eruption south of the city of Bagnes.
2   The bize or bise wind is the prevailing wind in winter in southern France.

Willoughby had lingered so long among these mountains, that it was now the second week of August. The evenings were, of course, somewhat shortening; and the sun was visible only by reflection from the snowy point above him, when he found himself lost on a place where he knew not his way to any human habitation, or was likely to hear the sound of a human voice. Little accustomed, however, to fear of any kind, he sat himself down on a piece of broken rock, to consider if, by any of those remarks[1] which Gaston had taught him to make, he could find his way before night-fall to rejoin his servant and his guide, or to find at least some place of shelter.

These observations, however, were impeded by the clouds that seemed to arise from the extensive plains below him, and to gather round the base of the mountains. These increased every moment, and at length surrounded him like waves; so that he no longer distinguished the objects beneath him, while immense volumes of white vapour were poured like a sea between him and the neighbouring precipices. He heard louder than ever, but he no longer saw the torrent that threw itself down within a few yards of him; and had apprehension ever been, under any circumstances, troublesome to him, he now might well have feared that, lost in this chaos of mist, he should at least remain all night where he was, and perhaps never regain his companions at all.

Life, however, had so few charms for him at this moment, that his indifference for it, added to his natural courage, when only himself was in question, made him perfectly calm and collected, though the thick clouds of mist continued to gather, and darken round the spot where he was now compelled to remain.

For a few moments the sighing of the wind which bore this floating vapour, the increased hollow murmurs of the rushing waters of the cataract, were interrupted only by the screaming vulture, and the deep hoarse raven, who seemed by their cries, as they sailed above the grey abyss of mist, to be warning their companions of some approaching danger: thunder was in fact gathered in the bosom of these clouds, and Willoughby, as he sat on his solitary rock, heard it muttering at his feet; and after some tremendous bursts, which seemed to shake the mountains to their foundations, accompanied by blue and vivid lightning, a violent wind arose, and dispersing the foggy clouds, drove them, with the storm generated in their bosom, to the country beneath.

---

1   Observations.

The last rays of the departed sun were now reflected from the summits of snow, the air became perfectly serene and Willoughby saw distinctly every object around him. He observed at some distance to the left a cross, in an elevated situation, but far below the extremest point of the cliffs; and he recollected, that the day before Gaston had shewn him that cross, and had told him that near it was the residence of a shepherd; and that not far from it a convent, near the foot of the mountain. Towards this, therefore, he now endeavoured to find his way; and by the help of a stick, with an iron fixed at the end of it, and by his own activity, he at length passed difficulties that to many people would have seemed insurmountable; and, attended only by a terrier which had followed him from England, and which had been the faithful companion of all his wanderings, he reached the pointed rock where the cross was erected.

It was now, however, so late, that he began to despair of finding the hut which Gaston had told him was situated something lower down. The moon, indeed, was rising in majestic beauty behind him; but her light, he feared, would hardly be sufficient to guide him among the woods and crags with which he was surrounded, to an object, perhaps, entirely concealed within them, and with which he was wholly unacquainted. He sat down, however, till she should afford him more benefit, and to consider what he should do, when, amidst the silence of the night, the sound of a human voice, in slow cadence, accompanied by some musical instrument, was borne on the faint breeze that arose from the low lands. He listened—it was not the illusion of fancy, as he had for a moment supposed; and he involuntarily exclaimed—

"O, it came o'er mine ear, like the sweet south,
That breathes upon a bank of violets—
Stealing and giving odour."[1]

His dog, too, gave evident signs of hearing something unusual, ran from his master to the brink of the precipice, then returned, jumping towards him, and seemed rejoiced that they were once more within reach of a human habitation. His sagacity assisted his master to follow the sound; and descending the mountain, by an entangled and almost overgrown sheep-path, that led from one pointed rock to another, he at length entered one of those woods of larch, pine, and

---

1 *Twelfth Night* 1.1.5-7. Smith's note: Shakespeare.

chesnut, that fill many of the hollow bosoms of the Pyrenees; and though the trees rendered it entirely dark, the music, which still continued at short intervals to float in the air, led him on, till, in a small glade, overshadowed by rocks clothed with brush-wood, he saw a small cabin, or rather cottage, where he had no doubt of finding an asylum for the night: his terrier now run gaily before him, and was presently saluted by the loud barking of those dogs which guard the Pyrenean flocks; but on meeting, the animals courteously saluted each other, and the shepherd's dog seemed glad to shew the strangers to his master.

Chapter VIII. Continued.[1]

The moon, though not yet risen above the trees, which on every side shaded the rocks surrounding this solitary glen, yet afforded general light enough for Willoughby to perceive a groupe of peasants assembled round the door of a cottage, superior in size to any of the cabins of the shepherds which he had yet visited. As he approached, the sounds which had guided him towards it ceased; and a man advanced to meet him, whose air and manner were very different from the native mountaineers whom he had been accustomed to see, though his dress was nearly the same. Willoughby accosted him in French, told him he was a stranger who had lost his guide, and desired to be permitted to remain in his cottage till the morning enabled him to find his companions. The man to whom he spoke hardly allowed him to finish the sentence, before, in language unadulterated with the Patois[2] which is spoken in that country, and is a coarse mixture of Spanish and French, he expressed the utmost solicitude for his accommodation, and leading him to the door of the cottage, presented him to his wife, to an old man her father, and to several young people whom his music had assembled round the cabin, and who were inhabitants of a little group of cottages, dispersed at short intervals among the woods on this part of the Vallée de Louson.

---

1   This is the only place where Smith gives the same number to two chapters; there seems no reason for it, unless she wanted to emphasise a continuity in the dreamlike or fairytale quality of Willoughby's journey of discovery, or unless she divided the chapter after most of the volume was typeset.
2   Dialect.

Every individual of this simple party was eager to shew civility and attention to the stranger. "Louison," said he, who appeared to be the master of the house, and who had met Willoughby—"Louison, go and prepare what our cottage affords, to refresh this gentleman, who may well have occasion for it, after such fatigue as he has gone through." Willoughby owned he was almost exhausted, and in a moment, milk, bread, and such other simple food as they themselves lived upon, were before him.

With the same hospitable simplicity, Louison went again, at her husband's request, to prepare him a bed, which one of the younger brothers of his host relinquished to him; saying, he could find a lodging that night at a neighbouring cottage. Le Laurier, which he found was the name of his host, then pressed him to retire to his bed, but Willoughby, refreshed by what he had eaten, found his curiosity so strongly excited, by the manners and language of this man, that it became more powerful than fatigue, and he could not help expressing a wish, to know how a man, who possessed such musical talents, and whose conversation was certainly not that of a mountaineer, should be found inhabiting a sequestered nook, in the bosom of the Pyrenees.

"I inhabit it, Sir," replied Le Laurier, "because I was born in it; but it is true, that I have also seen a great deal of other parts of the world, that it is not yet a month since I quitted the capital of France, to return hither, after a very long absence." "Long, indeed," said his wife, who had now rejoined them. "Alas! so long"—and she sighed deeply—"that I never expected, Sir, to have seen him again."

"Let me hear," said Willoughby, "not only what you have to relate of yourself, but what is now passing at Paris, which you say you have so lately left. I have been so long wandering among these mountains, that I am wholly ignorant of the consequences of that fermentation which was evident there among all ranks of men when I passed through it?"

"And I was in the midst of it all, Sir," replied Le Laurier, "for my master, Chevalier de Bellegarde, was among the prisoners who were released from the castle of Mont St. Michel; but our history is too long for this evening." He gave, however, a brief detail to Willoughby, of what had passed at Paris the preceding July [1]—and then, gaily turning the conversation, said, "Well, Sir, but here am I, after all this,

---

1   Among other events, the attack on the Bastille, the murder of its Governor and the release of the prisoners.

returned to my cottage in the Pyrenees, and here is Louison and my family. We are all happy together, and what is yet better, my dear master is restored to his home here below us." "And where is his home?" "Oh, Sir, the Chateau of Rochemarte, where his family have lived since the beginning of the world, I believe, is just down in the valley. Have you never seen it? To-morrow, please Heaven, you shall, and you shall see my master, who is now indeed the Count of Bellegarde, for his father and brother are dead—you shall see him, Sir; and see how a man enjoys liberty that has been a prisoner so many years. Not, indeed, that he is so happy as some people would be, because of the misfortunes in the beginning of his life, which always hang upon his mind. But now, I hope, in time, he will get over them. For my part, I think it folly to lament what we cannot help, or regret what cannot be recalled, and I wish the Chevalier was of my disposition."

"'Tis a very fortunate one, at least for yourself," replied Willoughby, "and has undoubtedly helped you gaily through the world." "No, sir, not gaily, but tolerably; amidst the severest of those misfortunes, which I shared with the Chevalier, I had always a persuasion that I should revisit my cottage, and my Louison." "Ah, thank Heaven, your persuasion was a just one, my friend," replied his wife—"and now that we may not part with melancholy impressions on our minds, let us have a little more music."

Le Laurier then began to play on the instrument Willoughby had before heard, and which was something between a lute and a Spanish guitar; he touched it with uncommon taste, and sang a simple rustic air; the cadence was solemn and pathetic, and at every close, the female part of his auditory joined their voices in unison. Willoughby had now time to observe the group before him by the clear light of the moon, which cast a mild and unclouded radience around them. The scene was simple and affecting: Le Laurier, a fine manly figure, sat on a seat of turf by the side of his door. His wife, a very handsome woman, stood leaning against the side of it, her head inclined towards him; a girl, twelve or thirteen years old, who was his eldest daughter, leaned on the turf, and looked up towards him, with a sort of innocent and affectionate admiration; while a boy of seven, the youngest of his children, had fallen asleep as he sat at her feet, and rested his head on her lap; two or three young peasants were behind, listening to the music, and gazing at the stranger; and, in a chair, before the door, the venerable father of the family, sat, contemplating the felicity so lately restored to them all, by the return of Le Laurier, with the mild resignation of reposing age.

A thousand fragrant smells floated in the air, after the rain; and the lightest wind whispered among the woods by which they were every way surrounded. Not a sound interrupted the plaintive pastoral air, which the performer now began to play, while his wife and daughter alternately sung a stanza. It was a kind of romance in Patois, but Willoughby understood it to be the complaint of a mountain shepherd, whose mistress had forsaken him for a richer establishment. There was nothing new in it, but it was the language of nature, and brought forcibly to the mind of Willoughby his own misfortunes.

★★★★★★★★★1

The soothing melancholy which every object around him seemed to breathe; the light of the moon trembling among the waving branches, of which Celestina had so often remarked the effect when they were wandering together; the simple cadence of rustic music, even the happiness which he saw on the countenances of his host and his family, combined to raise in his mind regret and languor. Never could he now hope to enjoy such a scene with Celestina; never was he likely to taste the delight of being restored to all he loved. Oh, no! Celestina was the wife of another, and the world had no happiness for him. As he indulged these melancholy thoughts, he sat almost motionless, and appeared to be attending to the music of Le Laurier; but on a sudden they quite overcame him, and striking his hands together, he started up, and walked suddenly away from the little assembly.

His host immediately ceased to play, and following him, enquired with unaffected solicitude, if he was ill. Willoughby immediately recovering himself, thanked him for his kindness; and assured him, that his emotion was occasioned merely by the song he had heard, which had brought some unpleasing recollections to his mind. The man, instead of attempting to console him by commonplace speech-

---

1 Eight lines of stars follow in the original, as the compositor notes where to place the lines of verse which should follow, though there is not enough room left for the narrative in stanzas referred to in the text. For some reason the poem was not inserted, and the compositor did not alter the text to eliminate reference to it. This, like the transposal of some chapters of *Desmond*, CS's next novel, into the wrong volume, is evidence of the haste and inadequate editorial support with which many popular authors of the time worked.

es, said, he would then leave him a moment; and hoped he would soon rejoin them, and allow them to wish him a goodnight. Willoughby walked on a little farther towards the wood; he looked up to the moon. "Even at this moment," said he, "perhaps the eyes of Celestina are fixed on thee, mild and beautiful planet. Those fine and expressive eyes, which I have seen fill with tears of admiration and delight, as they have contemplated the beauty of the universe, and the wisdom of its Creator. Ah, Celestina! Our hearts were made for each other, but yours—yours is perhaps changed, and to me is lost as well as your person." He dared not trust himself with this train of thought; but turning, walked slowly back towards the cottage door, where only Le Laurier, and his Louison, now waited to shew him to his bed. As he walked silently along, the bells of a convent below seemed to be calling its inhabitants to their evening prayers; and from an higher part of the mountain, which arose very suddenly beyond the woods, a small bell answered, and was re-echoed among the rocks. On his reaching Le Laurier, he enquired what these sounds meant. "The bells, below," said he, "are those of the convent of St Benoit,[1] about half a mile below us; and the smaller one is that of Father Anthony, a hermit,[2] who inhabits one of the rocks above—he has lived there many years."

"And where is the castle of Rochemarte?" enquired Willoughby.

"It is almost close to the convent," replied Le Laurier, "and if you wish to see them both I will wait upon you thither tomorrow."

Willoughby now repeated his acknowledgments for the courtesy he had received; and retired to his rustic bed, where fatigue, in despite of the depression of spirits, which his last reverie had brought upon him, gave him up to repose; and he, for a while, enjoyed that

"Sweet forgetfulness of human care,"[3]

without which the wretched would lose the power of enduring their wretchedness; and the happy, that of enjoying their good fortune.

---

1 Old form of St. Benedict; a Benedictine order. A convent could refer to an establishment of monks as well as of nuns.
2 A member of a religious order, who lived a solitary life of prayer and austerity.
3 Alexander Pope, translation of Homer's *Odyssey*, Book XII, 365–66: "... each in slumber shares/ A sweet forgetfulness of human cares."

Chapter IX

Willoughby had left his rustic couch, and joining his host and family, partook of their simple meal. He felt some concern, on reflecting on the panic poor Farnham must have been in, when the guide returned without him to the place of rendezvous, the preceding evening. He expressed his uneasiness on this head to Le Laurier, who said, he knew the place described, perfectly; and would immediately send thither the son of a neighbouring shepherd, who was then employed about his cottage, and bring his servant and the guide to him: in the mean time, he proposed to shew Willoughby the chateau of his master; a proposal which his guest readily accepted.

Louison, however, on their being about to depart, had, in her very expressive face, a look of concern; and in her manner, an appearance of inquietude, for which Willoughby wished to account. He was not long left in suspence: she took her husband's hand, and said, "My friend, you will not leave me long." "No, simpleton," replied he, and then turning to Willoughby, he gaily exclaimed, "Here is a woman, who is afraid of trusting her husband to go half a mile!"

"Ah, Monsieur," said Louison, "you would not blame me, if you knew how he once left me; he went away only for a few days, and he staid near three years."

"But not voluntarily, indeed," answered Le Laurier. "I met my master, my dear master, who had been so kind to me, in prison—in distress—in a state of mind bordering on insanity, and I could not leave him."

"I do not blame you for that, my friend," said Louison; "but I own I am afraid of its happening again."

"How happen again? The Chevalier, or rather the Count, my master, is not now as he was then?"

"Ah, no! But you have owned yourself, that he is restless and unhappy; and though he appears at times delighted with being restored to his liberty, his estate, and his daughter, yet, that at times his mind is unsettled, and his schemes wild and certain—and if he should take it into his head to travel again!"

"You fear that I may be tempted to travel with him?"

"Yes," said his wife, "indeed I do." Le Laurier then tried to laugh away her apprehensions, and then left her; while Willoughby felt his dialogue give new force to the curiosity he had to see the Count de Bellegarde.

As their way was down through the woody side of the mountain, they soon reached the domain of the chateau; in which, the first object that struck Willoughby, in a spot which had once been cleared of trees, but where the underwood, and a smaller growth of wood again, almost concealed it, was a pavilion, which had once been magnificent, but was now in ruins. It was built of various-coloured marbles, found in the Pyrenees; was of Grecian architecture, and seemed to have been a work of taste. The pillars of the portico, though broken, yet supported its roof; and behind it were three apartments, that had once been richly furnished: one, as a banqueting room; the other two as rooms for the Siesta,[1] which is usually taken here as in Spain. The canopies of yellow damask, were fallen, and the hangings of the rooms devoured by the moths, and decayed by the damps from the windows; which, having never been glazed, the shutters had long since dropped down. There was something particularly melancholy to the mind of Willoughby in contemplating this building, once the seat of gaiety, splendour, and luxurious repose, thus deserted, and he enquired of Le Laurier, if the present Count never intended to repair it. "Sir," replied he, "My Lord, the Count, has hardly had time to think about that yet; for he has been so little a while at his castle, that every thing there remains as it was—ruinous enough. But, as for this pavilion, I question if ever it will be put in order, though my lord has such an odd sort of a liking to it, that the moment almost he got home, he came down to look at it. It was quite late in the evening; but it was not dark, and he looked in at the window, for that night I could not open the door; the key was lost and the locks were all rusty, and by what he said, I am sure there is some story belongs to this place. The people of the castle, indeed, always had a notion of its being haunted ever since the death of my lord's sister, whose heart, they say, was broke by her father's ill usage. Certain it is, that the old Count caused this place to be shut up, and took away the fine glasses and pictures that were in it once—but what you see now he left to fall to pieces. There used to be large trees all around it; and all manner of flowers; and the stream, that now almost stagnates among those reeds and rushes, and with difficulty finds its way to the moat of the castle, was then brought into a bath, behind the banqueting-house, and into a bason, which is now grown over with weeds and grass, so that it can hardly be traced."

---

1   Smith's note: Siesta—reposing for an hour or two after dinner, during the extreme heat; as was usual in Spain, Portugal, Italy, and the West Indies.

Willoughby left this desolate spot with a sigh, and as his companion led him through the obscure paths of the woods that surrounded it, he enquired whether the castle itself had equally suffered from time. "Oh, yes, Sir," replied Le Laurier, "from time, and from war, too. It was formerly a place of great strength, and of great importance, as a pass into France, from the Spanish side of the Pyrenees; and held out a long siege when the famous Count of Bellegarde, my lord's ancestor, defended it for Henry the Fourth, our king; against the army of the League."[1] "Perhaps," said Willoughby, "your Lord may not like the intrusion of a stranger into his retirement?" "Oh," replied his conductor, "we may not happen to meet him; or, if we should, it will be a sufficient introduction and recommendation, for you, Sir, that you are an Englishman, for he loves the English."

Encouraged by this assurance, Willoughby proceeded, and in a few moments, the woods ascending a little, as they reached the extreme base of the mountain, opened into what could only be called a plain, when opposed to the surrounding hills, for the ground was rugged and uneven, scattered with masses of ruined buildings, that had formerly been part of the outward fortifications, but of which some were fallen into the fosse,[2] and others overgrown with alder, ash, and arbeal. The gate of the castle, and all beyond the moat, however, was yet entire, as were the walls within its circumference, bearing every where the marks of great antiquity, but of such ponderous strength, as time alone had not been able to destroy. Where breaches had been made by cannon, the walls had been repaired; but this work being of less durability than the original structure, had gone to decay; and the depredations of war were still very visible. The whole was composed of grey stone; the towers, at each end, rose in frowning grandeur, above the rest of the building; and having only loops,[3] and no windows, impressed ideas of darkness and imprisonment, while the moss and wall-flowers filled the interstices of the broken stones; and an infinite number of birds, made their nests

---

1   Henry IV, King of Navarre, was the first of the Bourbon French Kings. A Protestant, he was opposed by Spain and the Catholic League and there was fierce resistance to his accession to the French throne in 1593. He facilitated peace by converting to Catholicism, with the famous remark, "Paris is worth a mass."

2   Moat.

3   Narrow window-slits designed for shooting arrows, which exposed the archer to view as little as possible.

among the shattered cornices, and half-fallen battlements, filling the air with their shrill cries.

Over the moat, which was broad and deep, but now only half-full of water, which was almost hidden by aquatic plants, sheltering several sorts of water-fowls, that now lived there unmolested; a draw-bridge, with massive chains, led to the gate of the first court, under an high arched gate-way, defended by a double port-cullis: this court was where the castle guard were used to parade. It was spacious, and the buildings that surrounded it were gloomily magnificent; but now, no warlike footsteps wore away the grass which grew over the pavement; no martial music echoed among the arches and colon-ades. One solitary figure alone, appeared slowly walking with his arms crossed, on the terrace that led to the second court. "There is my Lord, the Count," said Le Laurier. "Speak to him, then," replied Willoughby, "and apologize for my intrusion." Le Laurier advanced, with his hat in his hand, and at the same moment, the Count, who then first perceived him and Willoughby, came towards them. His military air, and dignified figure, were tempered by the mild and courteous manner with which he moved forward to receive the stranger whom Le Laurier announced to him. He was greatly above the common height, thin, and a little bent, as if from depression of spirit, but his face pale, sallow, and emaciated, as it was, was marked with such peculiar expression, that all the adventures of his life seemed to have been written there. When he spoke, his dark eyes were full of fire and vivacity, yet at times they were wild; and at others, heavy and glazed; his brows were a little contracted, and hol-lowness about his temples and cheeks, and the strong muscular lines of his whole face, seemed to bear the harsh impressions of the hand of adversity, rather than of time: for though his hair was grey, and he looked much older than he really was, Willoughby did not think him above four or five-and-forty: at his breast was the cross of the order of St. Esprit;[1] and his dress, that of a captain of cavalry, was not mod-ern, and apparently neglected; his whole appearance instantly announced him to be a man of high rank.

If Willoughby was pleased with his manner and address, he seemed equally, or even more gratified by the curiosity expressed by an Englishman, to visit him. "You see me here, Sir," said he, "released

---

1 Order of the Holy Spirit. This French order of chivalry was created by Henry III in 1578, and has been, apparently, awarded to the Count for distinction in the American War of Independence.

only a few weeks ago from a long imprisonment, wondering at my freedom, and a stranger in my own house. To those only, who have been the victims of despotism, it would be easy to comprehend my sensations on such a sudden emancipation; and the triumph with which I reflect that I owe it to the same noble efforts which have given liberty to France, to my country."

"Ah!" continued he, pausing, and losing at once all the vivacity with which he had, a moment before, spoken, "Ah! what sensations of concern are mingled with this exultation. I regain my freedom, but where shall I regain my happiness?"

He now fell into a deep musing, which lasted only a moment, while Willoughby walked by his side, on the terrace; then suddenly awaking from it, he cried, "But it is too soon to trouble you with this sort of conversation. We shall have time enough, for I flatter myself, Sir, with a hope of your staying with me, as long as you remain in this country. You must have no other home. If you knew the pleasure I have in conversing with the English!" He paused again, as if forgetting what he meant to say, and then added, "I will introduce you to my daughter, to my little Anzoletta, for I have saved her; that one little gem is restored to me in all its lustre, amid the wreck of every thing else that was dear to me. We will find her now." He then entered through another arched way, the second court of the castle, and Willoughby accompanied him in silence, while Le Laurier, with his hat in his hand, followed, as the Count bade him.

They entered an immense hall; barbarously magnificent; it was roofed with beams of oak, and the sides covered with standards, and trophies of armour, the perishable parts of which were dropping to pieces. The narrow Gothic windows were filled, not with glass that admitted the light, but with glass painted with the achievements[1] of the family; mingled with the heads of saints and martyrs, whose names were now, no where to be found, but in the archives of the neighbouring convent. But, in contemplating the innumerable coats of arms that were blazoned on the windows, and on the banners that hung in faded majesty, between them, Willoughby could not help recollecting what food they would afford for the favourite speculations of his uncle, and his thoughts dwelt a moment on the scene that might have passed in consequence of his absence, in the family of Castlenorth.

These reflections, however, he had neither inclination nor time to indulge, for the Count ascending a broad, but steep stair-case of

---

1   Escutcheons; coats of arms.

stone, that led out of the hall, and wound within one of the turrets, entered a gallery, and at the end of it was his daughter's apartment, the door of which was open, and Willoughby was immediately introduced to a young person, who sat before a frame, working on a piece of embroidery: a woman between fifty and sixty, who seemed to be a kind of governess, was with her.

Willoughby was pleased by the graceful simplicity of her figure, and the beauty of her face; but when she spoke, in answer to the compliment he made her, this pleasure was converted into amazement. He fancied he heard the voice of Celestina!

So strikingly did its tones resemble those to which his heart had been always tremblingly responsive, that had he not seen who spoke, he should not have doubted of its being Celestina herself. He started, and felt the blood rush into his cheeks, nor could he immediately recollect himself enough to reply to what Anzoletta said; and again call forth those sounds, to which, the second time she spoke, he listened with increased astonishment and more painful delight; for, not only the similarity of her voice, to that of Celestina, was more evident, but he saw a resemblance to her in the air and manner of Anzoletta, that assisted the delusion.

Anzoletta seemed to be about the age of Celestina, but her figure was less: her hair and eyes were much darker, nor had she that dazzling and radiant complexion which made it always difficult to believe of Celestina, that she was a native of the South of Europe; the features of Anzoletta were, perhaps, more regular, and were not turned[1] like Celestina, so that the resemblance consisted in that sort of air of family, which we sometimes observe among relations—a kind of flying likeness, which we now detect, and now lose.

The Count seemed highly gratified by the notice Willoughby took of his daughter, to whom he now spoke, and bade her prepare herself for dinner, for that his guest was to remain with them. He then led Willoughby back to the room where he usually sat himself; and as they went, he said, "Is not my Anzoletta charming?" "She is indeed," replied Willoughby. "Perhaps," added the Count, "perhaps you would not believe that she is the child of the daughter of a man of inferior rank, one of my father's vassals." "Is she not *your* daughter, my Lord?" enquired Willoughby. "Yes," replied the Count, "she is my legitimate daughter; and as such, I glory to acknowledge her, but

---

1   A turner was a carver or potter, occasionally a garment-finisher who smoothed or completed the work: thus, not "finished" or refined like Celestina's.

her mother was *roturier*,[1] and, to my marrying her, she owed all her misfortunes; and I many of mine. But if ever you think it worth while to hear the incidents of a life, that has, I think, been marked with some singular occurrence, I shall have a melancholy pleasure in relating them."

"Nothing would oblige me so much," said Willoughby, whose curiosity had been every instant increasing, especially since he had seen Anzoletta. "May I, till I can be so gratified, enquire where is the mother of your lovely daughter?" "Yes," replied the Count; "and you will hear a fresh instance of the barbarous policy which despotism encourages and protects. Her mother! she was compelled by my father, the last Count of Bellegarde, to enter into a convent of Carmelites, at Bayonne, and there to take the vows. She was my wife, by the laws of God and man, but I was absent with my regiment, I was unable to protect her—and the power of the governor of the province, and of an enraged and tyrannic father, were united to tear her from me. Would to heaven, we had been the only victims, but there was yet another!—another, who is gone whence there is no return." Here he fell into one of those fits of silent musing, to which Willoughby had, even during their short acquaintance, observed him to be subject. It lasted, however, only a moment, and then recovering from it, he clasped his hands eagerly together, and cried, with energy, "But, for my wife, my Jacquelina—thanks to the generous, the glorious spirit of my country, I shall retrieve her.[2] She yet lives, I have seen her through the iron bars of her cloister, I have spoke to her! I have, in my bosom, a handkerchief which she gave me, bathed in her tears! She told me where to find our child, our little Anzoletta, and I go to Paris to demand and obtain her liberty: to claim her as my wife, and to be enabled to bring her hither, to a husband, who, changed as she is, by confinement, and affliction, still adores her—to a daughter, whose early excellence promises to reward us both for many, many years of separation and sorrow."

The eyes of the Count were filled with tears, as he ceased speaking; and Willoughby, whose heart was as tender as it was manly, was deeply affected. "Heaven grant you all your wishes, Sir!" cried he, "and that your private happiness may be one of the innumerable blessings attending on public felicity." The Count wrung his hands,

---

1 Commoner, not of a titled family.
2 As Smith was ending her novel, French legislation was preparing to enable those in religious orders to leave their institutions.

and cried, with yet increased vivacity, "It will—it will, my friend!" There was in his manner a something bordering on wildness, as he continued this discourse, which Willoughby remarked with some concern. He was not, therefore, sorry, when it was interrupted by the entrance of Le Laurier, who told him, that the messenger he had dispatched, had found his servant and the guide; and, relieving them from their fears for his safety, which had been cruelly severe upon poor Farnham, had brought them both to the castle, whither his wife had directed them.

Willoughby had been under a good deal of concern for Farnham, who, he knew, must have been dreadfully alarmed for the safety of his master; his arrival, therefore, was particularly welcome, and he was glad to change his clothes; for which purpose, he now begged leave to retire. The Count ordered Le Laurier to shew them to an apartment, and to take care he had every accommodation he desired. Willoughby, as he marched gravely along, through the long galleries, and across the gloomy hall, fancied himself a knight of romance; and, that some of the stories of enchanted castles, and wandering adventurers, of which he had been so fond, in his early youth, were here realized.

Chapter X

After a repast, rather hospitable than splendid, during which the looks of paternal admiration, and tenderness with which the Count observed every action of Anzoletta, and her innocent and agreeable vivacity, rendered them both more attractive to Willoughby: Monsieur de Bellegarde, finding that Willoughby rather wished to listen to the history he had promised, than to take any repose, during the heat of the day, proposed retiring to the north gallery, and there beginning this interesting account. Willoughby most readily agreed to the plan—and the Count, dismissing his daughter and her governess, led him hither.

This room extended far on the north side of the building and looked over the moat to a wood of fir and cypress, fringing the abrupt ascent of the mountain, which rose almost perpendicularly from the plain. As this acclivity commanded the castle, two strong redoubts were built on it, where, in hostile times, parties were stationed to keep the enemy from possessing posts, whence the castle might be annoyed. In the port-holes of these fortresses, now fast approaching to decay, the cannon yet remained, though rusty and useless, and the strong buttresses, and circular towers, mantled with ivy, were seen to aspire above the dark trees, on every side encompassing them, while, a little to the west, from a fractured rock, of yellow granite, which started out amid the trees, a boiling and rapid stream rushed with violence, and pouring down among the trees, was seen only at intervals, as they either crowded over it, or, receding, left its foaming current to flash in the rays of the sun.

It was altogether one of the most sublimely beautiful landscapes Willoughby had ever seen; and he contemplated the scenery with pensive pleasure, while the master of it thus addressed him:

"Perhaps you are so well read in the history of France, as to make it unnecessary for me to remark that my family is ancient and illustrious. My father, the Count of Bellegarde, was educated with every prejudice that could make him tenacious of his rank, and anxious to support it. He was married early by my grandfather to the heiress of the house of Ermenonville; and his eldest son, the only issue of that marriage, inherited from his mother the great property of that family.

"But ambition, of which my father possessed a great share, both from his temper and his education, saved him not entirely from the influence of softer passions. During the life of his first wife, an indigent relation of his own, was received into the family of one of his sisters, as a dependant. She was beautiful and interesting, and my father being released, by death, from an engagement, in which his heart had never any share, married her, and thought himself overpaid, by the felicity of his second marriage, for the little satisfaction he had found in the first.

"But though he had in one instance, suffered his inclinations to conquer that aspiring temper, which, under less-powerful influence, would have led him to seek for a second great heiress, he seemed determined to apply himself with more assiduity to the attainment of power and honour, by other means. He had some capacity for business; was daring in forming schemes, and obstinate in adhering to them—proud, vindictive, and violent; with such a portion of national pride, as made him hold every other nation but his own in the utmost contempt; and, whenever they seemed likely to dispute the superiority of France, he was tempted to wish, like Caligula,[1]

---

1   Gaius Caesar, nicknamed Caligula (Little Boot), succeeded Tiberius as Roman Emperor in AD 37, when his behaviour became increasingly mad and despotic.

that the people so presumptuous, had but one neck, that he might destroy them at a blow.

"With this disposition, you will easily imagine the inveteracy with which he regarded the English. He held a high post in the war-department of France, in 1755, when those hostilities[1] commenced, in which, for a series of years, the English had almost always the advantage; events that added to national hatred, or a kind of personal and peculiar malignity, for of many of the operations in which his country failed of success, the Count of Bellegarde was the projector.

"By a long course of defeat, however, his master, Louis the Fifteenth,[2] and his co-adjutors, grew weary of his influence; and, in 1759, after the loss of Quebec,[3] he was suddenly dismissed in disgrace.

"Nor was this mortification the only one he was at that period fated to sustain. A violent and infectious fever at the same time deprived him of his wife, and wounded thus deeply, by the public and domestic misfortune, he took the sudden resolution of quitting the world, and retiring to this castle, with my brother, my sister, and myself. Hither, then, he came, leaving, at Paris, his eldest son, who had been some time in possession of his mother's fortune, and had lived entirely independent of his father, and on no very friendly terms with him. To the young, gay, and dissipated D'Ermenonville (for he took the name of his mother) the austerity of a statesman, and conversation of a politician, were alike repulsive; and he had no feelings about him that disposed him to submit to the authority of a parent, from whom he had nothing to expect, for it was well understood, that of all the Count de Bellegarde either possessed from his ancestors, or acquired from his political advantages, D'Ermenonville would inherit only that share which, by its being entailed, his father could not deprive him.

"The error of which the Count thought he had been guilty, in allowing to this eldest son early independence, and boundless expence, made him determine to adopt, in regard to me and my

---

1 Afterwards known as the Seven Years' War. It was fought across a global theatre, in Canada, America, India and the West Indies as well as in Europe, the British success securing those areas as part of their Empire.

2 The grandfather of the French king at the time Smith was writing, Louis XVI, who succeeded him.

3 A famous victory for the British, in which General James Wolfe died after taking Quebec in 1759. Smith, then aged ten, wrote a poem in his praise which has not survived.

brother, a conduct altogether contrary. On his retirement from the world, my brother, who was the eldest of the two, and called the Baron de Rochemarte, was near fifteen, and I was only fourteen months younger; yet, though at that age, we should have been either pursuing our studies, or with the army, in which we had both commissions, my father took us away with him: and, with a governor whom he engaged, because he was the most rigid pedant he could find, he fixed us both in what we then thought the desolate solitude of Rochemarte, a place which he had fixed upon for his own residence; not only because it was so far from the scene of his former elevation; but because it was the only one of his capital houses that was not entailed on D'Ermenonville.

"The gloomy solitude in which he lived, the power of life and death which he possessed in his domain, and the proneness of his mind to superstition, which was encouraged by the Monks of the neighbouring convent, who soon found the advantage of having so liberal a benefactor, at once darkened and soured a temper, never very good. Accustomed to dictate and command, he could not now divest himself of the habit: and his vassals, and his sons, being the only persons over whom he could now exert it, were the victims of his harsh and imperious spirit, for in them he delighted to discover, or to fancy faults, only for the satisfaction of imposing punishment.

"It may be easily imagined, that to two lads of our ages, and who had from temper and constitution a keen relish for pleasures of every kind, the life we led was insupportable. The mild and soft-tempered Genevieve, our sister, who was then not more than twelve years old, though from her sex and disposition, more accustomed to, and able to endure solitude and confinement, began to feel the weight of those chains, of which, however, she did not complain; but endeavoured, by her soothing sweetness, to make ours sit more easy. She was my father's favourite, and her influence had, for some time, the power to assuage the harshness of his temper; but, by degrees, even that failed of its effect, and his mortified pride, his lost happiness, and his gloomy notions of religion, combined to increase his ferocity, and irritate his asperity, till, at length, his children, though the children of a woman he so fondly loved, seemed to afford him nothing but objects of anger and tyranny, and he was left alone to the influence of Father Ignatius, a Jesuit,[1] whom he took into his house as the

---

1 A member of the Society of Jesus, a Roman Catholic Order founded by
   St. Ignatius Loyola in 1533 to combat the spread of Protestantism in

director of his conscience; and whose purpose, it seemed to be, to estrange him from his family entirely.

"There is a point, beyond which, the endurance of the most patient sufferer cannot go. Genevieve, indeed, was not yet arrived at this point, but the Baron and I had long since passed it, and determined to break the fetters, which, in their present form, we did not think even paternal authority had a right to impose. The Baron, therefore, wrote to D'Ermenonville, representing our situation, and entreating his assistance to deliver us from it.

"The Marquis D'Ermenonville had, perhaps, no great affection for us; but he could not be totally indifferent to the representation of the Baron; and felt, perhaps, some pleasure, in being able to thwart his father, where it seemed to be a sort of duty to act in opposition to him. For this purpose, he immediately, and by a way which we had pointed out to him, sent us a considerable supply of money, and directed us both to quit the castle in the night, and find our way to Perpignan, where his servant and horses should attend to conduct us to Paris. He urged, not only the cruelty the Count de Bellegarde was guilty of, in thus obliging us to waste the best of our days in a desart; but the appearance it must have to the world, that when a war was carrying on, two young men, enlisted in their country's service, submitted to be confined, like monks, in a cloister. This remark would have been enough to have fired us with ambition and military ardor; but to the incitements of honour, he added the allurements of pleasure, and every scruple that remained (for I had still some as to leaving my father without his permission) gave way before their united influence.

"I could not, however, with equal success, conquer the regret I felt at leaving my beloved Genevieve, to whom, from our earliest infancy, I had been particularly attached. She would, we were well assured, be compelled to encounter all the fury and indignation of the Count, when our departure should be known; and when we saw her tremble with the mere apprehension of it, we would very fain have obviated every difficulty that seemed to forbid our taking her with us: but, child as she was, she answered with firmness and resolution, of which her gentle temper seemed little capable; 'No, my dear brothers,' said she, 'it is fit you should go, but that I should stay. No point of honour, no military duty calls me; and I will not desert

Europe. The Jesuits' reputation for influencing public events in secret made them feared in Protestant and sometimes also in Catholic countries.

my father; he is unhappy—he has need of me—he must not be deprived at once of all his children; and, if he treats me with rigour, the consciousness of not having deserved it, will enable me to sustain it with patience.'

"It was necessary, however, that she should appear wholly ignorant of our flight, and we dreaded that her resolution would give way, when she was charged with having been acquainted with it; insomuch, that we should now have repented having made her a party in our secret, could we have borne the thoughts of leaving, abruptly and unkindly, a sister, whom we both so fondly loved.

"At length, the hour came for this cruel parting. My father, who since his residence here, had affected all the state of a feudal baron, and even many of the precautions of a besieged chief, though he had no enemies to apprehend, but the wolves and bears of the Pyrenees; not only had the draw-bridge taken up every night, but had a sort of guard parade, at stated hours, the courts of the castle. Our desire of liberty, however, surmounted all the difficulties by which our escape seemed to be impeded; and, by means of our sister, and our own resolution, we descended in safety, from one of the lower windows; crossed the moat, which was then full, in our drawers, by swimming, and dressing ourselves on the opposite bank, we proceeded on foot to Perpignan; and with hearts exulting in our success, and the joy it gave us, allayed only by our apprehensions for Genevieve.

"Our tutor had taken a fancy to wine, and we took care liberally to supply him, in consequence of which, and of the increase of pleasure he found, from this easy indulgence of his favourite passion, he had insensibly abated of his former strictness; suffered us every evening to go to the apartment of Genevieve; and frequently took, in our absence, such plentiful potations, that he was in bed, and asleep, before we returned to our apartments, which were within his. Thus, we were not missed till the morning; and, as we left no traces on our way, and had not even entrusted a servant with our secret, the pursuit that was then made for us, was quite ineffectual. We arrived safely in Perpignan; in spirits too elevated to be affected with the fatigue of our long walk. We found that D'Ermenonville had punctually adhered to his promise; and, on his horses, and attended by his servants, we proceeded gaily to Paris.

"D'Ermenonville received us with more cordial friendship than I believed to be in his nature; he furnished us with money to equip us for joining our respective regiments, as became the sons of the Count of Bellegarde, and assured us of his continued assistance, till my father could be brought to reason. It is not, therefore, wonderful, that his friendship made us blind to his faults; and, that we saw not the dissolute libertine, in the kind and generous brother. In fact, he had many virtues; and it was to him we owed our support after the peace of 1763 restored us to the pleasures of Paris. Then, however, the Count of Bellegarde, though he resisted every argument which could be brought by the other parts of our family, to induce him to receive, and forgive us; yet was so far averse to our owing any farther obligation to D'Ermenonville, whom he held in abhorrence, and no longer acknowledged as his son, that he agreed to make us each an handsome allowance.

"Peace being made, my brother, the Baron de Rochemarte, went into Germany where, during the war, he had formed some attachments; and I was for several years in garrison with my regiment, hearing nothing of my family but what I learned from the letters my sister contrived, by stealth, to send me. After our elopement, she had been, for some years, more rigorously confined, and had suffered inconceivable harshness and cruelty from her father, but at the end of six years, though his temper was far from being softened by age, the death of the Jesuit, who had been his confessor, seemed to have procured some little alleviation to her sufferings. A younger, and less-austere director, of the same order, had succeeded to the government of his conscience; and Genevieve now informed me that, accustomed as she had been, almost from her infancy, to confinement, the moderate severity of that in which she now lived, was comparatively easy to her; that her father admitted of her services with more pleasure than he used to do; spoke to her with great kindness; sometimes allowed her to walk out, and had promised that the daughter of one of his vassals, for whom she had conceived a friendship, should be allowed to reside with her at the castle, as her companion: she always added her vexation, that his execution of this promise was, she knew not why, always delayed from time to time; though her old governess was become quite useless as a companion—but her greatest uneasiness seemed to arise from our long, and she began to fear, endless separation.

"This regret she repeatedly dwelt upon, with so much pathetic tenderness, that I at length determined to go in secret, and in disguise, to Rochmarte, and embrace once more, this beloved sister; for whom, long as we had been parted, I still felt the warmest affection. I was at Paris when I made this resolution, where, a short time before, I had formed an intimate acquaintance with a young Englishman, the second son of a nobleman; he was two or three years younger than I was: in person, remarkably handsome; and in manners, the most engaging man I ever met with. Our acquaintance soon became the sincerest friendship, and as he communicated to me every interesting circumstance that befel him, so my situation in regard to my father, and my increasing desire to see my sister, were no secrets to him. He entered into all my solicitude, and encouraged me to indulge the inclination I had to visit Rochemarte in disguise, for the pleasure of seeing Genevieve.

"A letter I at that period received from her, determined me to hesitate no longer. She intimated, that her situation was become extremely unpleasant, from the extraordinary behaviour of the Spanish Jesuit, who had succeeded old Ignatius; that this man seemed to have designs of the most improper nature, in regard to her; and, that it was he, who had hitherto opposed her having Jacquelina, the young person to whom she was attached, with her; because he foresaw, he should then have less frequent opportunities of entertaining her alone: finding, however, the Count disposed to indulge her, and being unable to form any longer pretences to prevent it, he had at last told her, that he would immediately influence the Count to oblige her, if she would consent to ask for the addition of another member to the family, and receive, as if at her own desire, a sister of his, who must be a superintendant over both her and her friend, and replace the superannuated governess, who was no longer capable of her charge. To this, my poor Genevieve told me she had consented, rather than not have the company of Jacquelina, to cheer her solitude; that Jacquelina was consequently arrived, and the other expected every day, but that, notwithstanding she now had a companion, the Jesuit continued to find but too many opportunities to entertain her with conversation which she could not misunderstand.

"My blood boiled with indignation, while I read this letter, and I instantly communicated the contents of it to my friend, Ormond. 'It is not possible,' said he, 'that you can hesitate, my dear Chevalier, how to act; let us set out instantly for Rochemarte—you see a friend ready, not only to attend you, but to lose his life in your service.' We departed the next day, followed only by two servants, and arriving at Perpignan, began to consult on the means of meeting Genevieve, without the knowledge of my father, or the inhabitants of the castle, and the properest expedient that occurred to us was, to disguise ourselves and our servants, as hunters, and to watch, in that dress, till chance should throw my sister in our way.

"I sometimes thought of going openly to my father, and making one effort to awaken his paternal feelings; to obtain my own pardon, and my sister's liberty; but after consulting with Ormond, we agreed, that it was better to endeavour to see her first; for a failure in the success of this scheme would probably occasion her to be so closely confined, that we might never have an opportunity of seeing her at all.

"Equipped, therefore, as Izard hunters, we reached this castle, and wandered about a whole day in its neighbourhood without any success; the weather was so intensely warm, for it was now autumn, that I believed my sister came out only early in the morning, or late in the evening, and that the best probability of meeting her, was at those hours. To take up our abode near the castle, therefore, was material, and I recollected the banqueting-house in the wood, which had then, I imagined, been long neglected, and where our residence could not be suspected. But, on entering, I was surprised to find it newly fitted up, and sumptuously furnished with every article that could contribute to luxury and repose. This had been done by the Jesuit's directions, and here he now and then made little entertainments for some favourite fathers of the convent and their female penitents, which Apicius[1] or Marc Anthony[2] might have beheld with envy.

"Dread of the Count's power and severity, effectually secured every part of his domain from the intrusion of any of the neighbouring peasants. The pavilion, therefore, furnished as it was, was never locked; and, as I imagined nobody had so good a right to it as myself, I took up my abode in it without much apprehension of being dislodged. My friend occupied the other room, and our servants found a lodging in the deserted cabin of a shepherd, on the other side of the castle; from whence they were ordered to watch for the appearance of the ladies we desired to see; and immediately, on perceiving them, to acquaint us.

"The whole of the second day passed as the first had done; we wandered about the woods that skirt the castle, but all about it appeared the desolate abode of sullen despotism. At night, when we had no longer any thing to fear from the observation of those who

---

1   Marcus Gavius Apicius was a Roman gourmet flourishing in the reign of the Emperor Tiberius (AD 14-47), some of whose recipes have been preserved.

2   Marcus Antonius (c. 82-30 BC), Roman general and politician, was one of the triumvirs, with Octavius and Lepidus, who defeated the Republicans Marcus Brutus and Gaius Longinus Cassius, and divided the then known world between them. The historian Plutarch records the extravagance of Antony's hospitality; his passion for Cleopatra is represented by Shakespeare.

might belong to it, we approached its walls more nearly, and watched the lights at the windows, hoping that Genevieve might pass with a candle; though even then it would have been very difficult, if not impossible, to have apprized her of our being so near.

"If my friend had been eager for the expedition, he was now more earnest for its success. The wild and mountainous country, around a castle such as is described as the habitation of enchanters, and monsters of fable, was exactly suited to inflame his ardent and romantic imagination; and when, to these circumstances, was added our purpose, to save a young woman from the harsh severity of a father, and the wicked hypocrisy of a Jesuit, he became an absolute enthusiast; and vowed, like a true knight errant, never to leave the spot till our adventure was successfully accomplished.

"The second night, however, we were slowly retiring to our pavilion, and had almost reached it, when we fancied that among the trees, on one side of us, which were then cut into alleys, we heard female voices talking low and plaintively. The evening was so profoundly still that we heard every leaf that quivered in the scarcely-perceptible air; and these voices we now lost, now heard more distinctly, till at length I was sure that one of them was the voice of Genevieve, though it was so long since I had heard it. I would have flown into her arms, but Ormond, for once more considerate than I was, withheld me, by representing to me, that if the person with her should be the Jesuit's sister, we should be ruined by our rashness. Instead, therefore, of shewing ourselves abruptly, we glided along on the other side of a treillage[1] of beech, which entirely concealed us, and, listening attentively, heard distinctly, that it was to her friend Jacquelina, that my sister addressed herself.

"I knew not whether my voice or the sight of me could alarm her least; but at length determined to walk from the banqueting-house, and meet her. We both, therefore, proceeded slowly down the walk in which she was, leaning on the arm of Jacquelina; but neither of them immediately perceived us, and I had time (for though it was evening, every object was yet distinct) to observe the wonderful alteration that time had made in the person of my sister.

"I had left her, a beautiful girl, of twelve years old; her fine hair hanging loose over her face and neck; and her features, though then lovely and expressive, not yet formed. She was now in her nineteenth year, with the figure of a nymph, and a countenance beaming with

---

1 Trellis or partition.

sensibility and sweetness, with a sensibility that seemed to have no object, and with sweetness that had something of patient acquiescence infinitely interesting. Her companion was so beautiful a woman, that at any other time, I should have been immediately struck with her charms; but at this moment, I had no eyes but for Genevieve; and Ormond, whose heart had been prepared for any impression, was so fascinated, that forgetting my injunctions of silence, he exclaimed, 'Heavens! Chevalier—you never told me that your sister was an angel!'

"At this exclamation, though not uttered in a loud voice, Genevieve, whose eyes were before fixed on the ground, raised them, when seeing two men approach, she was extremely alarmed, and taking Jacquelina by the arm, she cried, 'Here are strangers, my friend—let us hasten back to the castle.'

"'No,' cried I, 'no, Genevieve, it is no stranger, but your brother, who comes to defend and protect you.' 'My brother! my dear brother!' said she. 'What, both? Is it possible; can you be both so good?'

"I held her in my arms, for she was unable to support herself, while Ormond passionately exclaimed, 'Oh, would to Heaven I were your brother! but accept me, loveliest of women, as your friend; and be assured, that I will defend so glorious a title with my life.'

"She was soon so well recovered as to listen to what I related to her, and her beautiful eyes were turned towards Ormond, full of such expressions as charmed his very soul, while she thanked him for having accompanied her dear Chevalier. From her conversation, and from that of her amiable companion, I learned, that my infatuated father was not only entirely governed by his confessor, but had lately shewn so much attachment to the sister whom he had introduced, that there was every reason to apprehend the consequence of the increasing influence of both. Genevieve, however, spoke of her father's failings, and even of his unreasonable harshness towards her, with reluctant sweetness that was bewitchingly interesting; and Ormond, in this short conversation, was gone whole ages in love. His eyes watched every turn of her countenance, his ears drank the soft sounds of her plaintive voice.

"I saw that the beauty, the simplicity of Genevieve, aided by the singularity of her situation, and the scene in which he saw her, had effected an instance of what has often been denied, and often ridiculed: love at first sight. Neither Ormond, nor my sister, nor I, were conscious of the course of time; but Jacquelina at length reminded her, that it would be hazardous to be longer absent from the castle. She instantly recollected herself, and said with a sigh, 'My

Chevalier, we must part—when shall we meet again?' It was agreed, that by the earliest dawn of the following morning, we would wait for them in the wood, near the pavilion: we attended them as far as we dared, towards the approach to the castle, and then slowly and unwillingly bade them good-night.

"Ormond stood watching my sister as she passed among the trees, and when he could see her no longer, he turned[1] to me, and said, with an energy peculiarly his own, 'Bellegarde, I am in love with your sister to distraction!' 'I am sorry for it, my friend,' said I; 'And why sorry?' interrupted he, with an air of displeasure. 'Because,' replied I, 'this attachment, if it indeed becomes permanent, though very honourable to her, may be a source of misery to you both. My father has so great an antipathy to an Englishman and a Protestant, that were a man who is both, to possess the world, I am convinced he would refuse him his daughter.' 'Refuse,' cried Ormond. 'Do you think I would ask him? or do you, Chevalier, mean to leave your sister—such a sister—here in his power?' 'I hardly know what I mean yet, my dear friend. Let us, however, do nothing rashly, lest we injure the objects we wish to serve.' Alas! at this time, I was cool and collected, and could argue with the romantic enthusiasm of my friend; but in a few days I was as madly in love with Jacquelina, as Ormond was with my sister.

"The impediments between us, were as great as those between my friend and Genevieve; Jacquelina was of inferior birth, the daughter of one of my father's vassals; and to the sullen pride of the Count of Bellegarde nothing could be so repugnant as such an alliance. I was not yet of the age when sons were allowed to dispose of themselves;[2] and my allowance from my father would, I was well assured, be instantly withdrawn, if I offended him anew. All these considerations, however, weighed nothing against the violence of my passion, and determined as I was to marry Jacquelina, and to give Genevieve to my friend, the only difficulty seemed to be to find a Priest on whom we might depend; for, sensible of our affection as were the objects of our love, they refused to leave their home unless under the protection of their husbands.

"While I was studying how to find and secure the fidelity of such a man as we had occasion for, Genevieve endured from the insolence of the Jesuit, and the encroaching authority of Mademoiselle

---

1   The original has "hinted."
2   Under French law in the *ancien regime,* men and women under 30 need-
    ed parental consent to marry. In England the age of independent consent
    was 21.

D'Aucheterre, his sister, insults which she dared not avow to us in all their extent. But Jacquelina, when she was alone with me, spoke with less reserve, and told me she had no doubt that it was the plan of D'Aucheterre, the Jesuit, to marry his sister to the Count: and that so entirely was he governed by him, that there was no doubt of his falling into the snare. This was very unpleasant intelligence; but I forgot it when she added, that she dreaded every day lest the walks Genevieve was now allowed to take should be prohibited.

"It was necessary immediately to hazard something. I contrived to make an acquaintance with one of the younger Monks of the convent; he had never seen me as the Chevalier de Bellegarde, and believed, for some time, that I was an hunter, from Pau in Berne. As length, when I believed myself tolerably acquainted with him, I told him who I was, and with what view I had so long lingered about my father's abode, from whence I had been many years exiled. From the manner of his receiving this intelligence, I believed I could trust him. It was very hazardous; for the Fathers of the convent were for the most part decidedly in the interest of the Jesuit. But I offered to this Monk the means of gratifying some of those passions which his poverty and mode of life afforded him little opportunity of indulging, and he agreed to do whatever I pleased.

"The rising sun of the following morning saw my friend Ormond the enraptured husband of the lovely Genevieve; and gave me, in Jacquelina, the only woman who seemed to me worthy to be her friend. Trembling at every breath of air, at every whisper of the falling leaves, they hurried back to the castle, where an unusual degree of tranquillity seemed on that day to reign. The Count spoke kindly to his daughter, and she, encouraged by the certainty of now belonging to the man she loved, put a restraint upon herself, and behaved with more civility to D'Auchterre and his sister than she could generally command. In the evening they met us as usual; but our felicity was embittered by the apprehensions for our safety that had taken possession of Jacquelina. 'Though there is not a peasant, or a shepherd round the domains of the castle,' said she, 'that loves the Count well enough to do him any kindness on his own account, yet fear may have the influence which affection and gratitude have not. Some of them have been telling the servants that two strangers have been seen for many days among the mountains, who call themselves Izard hunters, though they have no dogs with them: that nobody knows where they sleep, or how they live; and that they are suspected to belong to a banditti[1]

---

1 Band of robbers.

who have for some time infested the Vallée d'Aran, about the source of the Garonne. This whisper,' continued Jacquelina, 'terrifies me. It was only to-day I heard it, and I have never had a tranquil moment since: I figure to myself that your lodging in the banqueting-house may be discovered; that you may be taken up—imprisoned—punished.' I endeavoured to appease the fears of my angelic wife, though I felt that they were too well founded. Ormond, intoxicated by love, and knowing less of the manners of the people than I did, treated them slightly. 'Let them come,' said he: 'are we not armed?' The reports among the servants gained ground; the Jesuit had heard of them, and had said to Genevieve and her friend, that if such men were lurking about the confines of the castle, their early and late walks would become very unsafe, and that he must speak to the Count to forbid them.

"To remain another night in the pavilion was not safe. Our little council deliberated what to do, and Love was the president. Under his auspices, the timid Genevieve learned courage to propose what appeared a more hazardous measure than to remain where we were. 'The eastern side of the castle,' said she, 'is never inhabited on that side: the guard-room, and the rooms above and under it, have not been opened for many years: in that quarter, you, my Chevalier, may recollect there was a considerable breach made in one of the sieges, and the windows are dismantled and broken still. As nobody ever goes near that range of rooms, would there be much danger in your remaining in them till we can depart?'

"'The danger,' cried Ormond, 'is no consideration, but why should we not depart immediately? why should you and Jacquelina ever return to the castle?'

"To this my sister answered, that unless precautions were taken, such as she feared we had not thought of, our flight would undo us. 'My father,' said she, 'by the death of that nobleman, who was the most powerful among his enemies, has obtained the government of Roussillon, and has even had offers of other advantages which may awaken his dormant and disappointed ambition. Thus armed with powers to detect our flight, consider what would be the consequence of our being missing, if we are not sure of getting out of his reach before he can exert that power. Secure, if possible, the means of an escape, and we will fly: in the mean time, you must think of your own safety till that can be done.'

"We were too much in love to raise any difficulties to a plan which brought us nearer the objects of our affections; and the remark Genevieve made as to the difficulty of our carrying her and

Jacquelina with us, without some quicker means of conveyance than their delicate limbs afforded them, was perfectly just. How to procure such conveyance was a matter that required more deliberation than the present moment afforded, and it was therefore agreed that at night, when all about the castle was quiet, Genevieve and Jacquelina should be at one of the lowest windows on the eastern side; and that we should cross the moat, and by their aid ascend to that window, which we considered as a very easy undertaking.

"As it was now late in the autumn, and there was no moon, it was dark enough for our purpose. We crossed the moat with ease, and found our lovely conductresses waiting for us; with almost equal ease ascended the broken wall, and I was thus in my father's house, unknown to him, and took possession of the paternal mansion of my ancestors as if I had been a robber and an assassin.

"Here, however, under such circumstances, I passed the most fortunate period of my life. Ah! short fleeting felicity, which never, never can return again!

"We were not, however, so intoxicated with our present happiness, as to neglect the means of its continuance; but nothing was so difficult as to carry them into execution. It was only of a night I could get out, for with such a commission I was unwilling to entrust the daring and impetuous Ormond; and the application I made for horses at two or three villages at hours so unreasonable, raised such suspicion of my intention, that I twice narrowly escaped being seized by the peasants as one of the banditti; and once, on my return to the castle, was watched and compelled, instead of entering it by the window, as usual, to plunge into the woods, and conceal myself till the following evening: while my wife, my sister, and Ormond suffered the most cruel anxiety and were almost dead with apprehension. After this unsuccessful sally, they entreated me not to venture out again, and we continued to live on some time longer in security. The immense extent of the castle made our abode in this uninhabited part of it attended with very little risk; for the passages were all stone, and our footsteps could not be heard, even if we had not taken all precautions against noise. The appearance of complaisance which Genevieve was compelled to assume towards D'Aucheterre, obtained for her any little favour she chose to ask of him: and he allowed her frequently to dine in her own apartment, while his sister was thus enabled to carry on, with more success, her plan of operations against the heart of the Count, in which indeed she had made a much greater progress than we apprehended. Thus we were supplied with food without raising any suspicion, and were so well content with our confinement, since it was the imprisonment of love, that could we have been sure of its continuance with safety to the objects of that love, we should never have regretted our loss of liberty.

"To this moment I am ignorant of the means by which we were discovered, though I can impute it only to the treachery of the Monk who married us. It was after midnight, near five weeks after our residence in the castle, that I was awaked by a loud shriek from Jacquelina, who at the same moment threw her arms about me. I started up, and flew to a cutlass which I usually placed in a chair near the bed; and with which I defended Jacquelina for some moments, till I was stunned by a blow which one of the ruffians who surrounded me aimed at the back of my head, and I recovered not my senses till many hours afterwards, when I awoke in a kind of litter,[1] in which two hideous figures guarded me, with their swords drawn. I was confined by heavy chains; and when I enquired why I was thus fettered like a malefactor, I was shewn a *Lettre de Cachet*,[2] which directed me to be conveyed to the Bastile[3]—and thither I was now travelling. Oh, sir, if you have ever loved! you may be enabled to judge what were my feelings! Yet, who was ever so cruelly outraged, who was ever torn from such a woman, unless it was my unhappy friend, Ormond! whose fate I had reason to fear was yet severer than my own, because I doubted whether my father, savage and inhuman as he was, could exercise on me exactly the same degree of cruelty, which he would feel himself disposed to inflict on one who, in addition to his being the husband of Genevieve, was an Englishman, and an heretic.

"The anxiety I felt for his fate, and for that of my sister, and the dread of what might have befallen Jacquelina, whose shrieks, as they endeavoured to tear her from me, yet vibrated in my ears, made me insensible of my own sufferings, notwithstanding my wounds and the inconveniences of my confinement. But my guards were obsti-

---

1   A framework supporting a bed for the transport of the sick or wounded, either on wheels or carried by porters.
2   Regarded as one of the worst abuses of the *ancien regime*, the *lettre de cachet* was a letter signed by the King or by someone to whom this power was deputed, that authorised the imprisonment of the victim named, without term and without trial.
3   A Bastile or, more usually, Bastille, could be any fortified tower, but usually refers, as here, to the prison-fortress built in Paris in the fourteenth century.

nately silent, and neither threats nor entreaties could procure for me the least intelligence of what was to be the fate of my beloved friends from whom they had divided me.

"While any hope remained, I retained some degree of composure and recollection: but at length despair took possession of me. I became delirious. Furious, frantic, I was only prevented by my chains from destroying, first my keepers, and then myself. I knew nothing of what happened for many days, during the disorder of my senses: when I recovered them, I was in a room in one of the towers of the Bastile, so much weakened with the loss of blood that they had taken from me during my frenzy, that I could not leave my bed. My head had been shaved, and I was under the regimen appointed for those who are decidedly insane. Pardon me, if I here ask your patience till to-morrow—the recollection of what I then suffered is too painful for me to dwell upon longer; and when I think that these sufferings were inflicted by a father!"

Here the Count put his hand on his heart, and sighed deeply. Willoughby remarked in his eyes that unsettled expression that still bore testimony of the state of mind into which the sufferings he had been relating had thrown him; and extremely affected himself by the Count's narrative, he was glad, powerfully as his curiosity was excited, to delay hearing the melancholy catastrophe, for melancholy he feared it must be, till the next day.

Chapter XI

When the Count de Bellegarde and Willoughby met the next morning, the former seemed perfectly composed, but pensive and melancholy. It was early—he proposed walking towards the convent. "And as we go," said he, "I will conclude, as briefly as I can, my mournful history. I will not dwell upon the nature of my sufferings in the Bastile: of much of the time I passed there I have no perfect recollection; and, for the rest, suffice it to say that, by the orders of my inflexible father, I endured all the rigours of imprisonment, in its most hideous form for several months, during which I made some attempts to escape. Attempts, the failure of which only served to convince me of the impossibility of effecting it; and, in the impotency of rage, I cursed my existence, and, I fear, reproached Heaven itself for permitting such horrors on earth. The idea of Jacquelina, abandoned to the inhuman vengeance of a man capable of acting with such malignity towards his own son; the thoughts of the misery in which I had probably been the means of involving Ormond and Genevieve, hardly suffered me to attend to my own wretchedness, when I was capable of feeling it; but many weeks past in wild ravings about them, and then for myself I felt nothing.

"I thus lost some of those miserable days, the course[1] of which, when I was sensible, I marked on the wall of my prison. I had now, though my reckoning was thus rendered defective, past near two years in my prison; when my barbarous father, at the intercession of my brother the Baron, sent a priest to offer me my release on certain conditions: one of which was, that I should immediately, on leaving my confinement, be conducted to my regiment, which was then in garrison at Lisle, and give my parole[2] that I would not quit it without the permission of the commanding officer. Though I saw that this restriction was intended to prevent my gaining any intelligence of Jacquelina, of Ormond, or of my sister, I gave the promise desired, as being released from my detested prison always seemed a step towards them; and two days afterwards the governor of the Bastile delivered me to the persons whom my father had sent for me; and I was thus conducted, like a prisoner, to join the regiment, where the colonel, a friend of the Count's, took care to take the parole in the strongest manner; and believing, perhaps, that under such circumstances I should not feel myself bound in honour to keep it, he continued to have me watched so strictly that I was still in fact a prisoner.

"And thus, at the age of twenty-nine, was I treated; my soul revolting against the tyranny, without the means of escaping from it, and consuming itself in vain projects, to see or to hear from the wife so adored, from friends so tenderly beloved.

"A few days, however, after my arrival at Lisle, my brothers, D'Ermenonville and the Baron De Rochemarte, came in disguise to find me. They hardly knew me, so greatly was I changed by despair and confinement; but without giving them time to express their concern, I enquired for Jacquelina—for Ormond, for our sister.

"Their countenances, particularly that of the Baron, told me that I had only tidings of sorrow to expect; and knowing the state in which my mind had been, he studied a moment how to soften them; but the impatience of my fear would not give him time. 'Tell me,' cried I, 'tell me, where is Jacquelina, where is Genevieve, where is my

---

1 The original has "cause."
2 Word of honour, promise.

friend Ormond? They are dead, I know they are; that inhuman man, who calls himself my father, has destroyed them all.'

"'No,' replied the Baron, 'Ormond lives, and is long since returned to England. Jacquelina lives; but lives not for you: she has taken the veil.[1] As for our unfortunate sister, she is, perhaps, happier; she has been dead some months.' This cruel intelligence—that of the three beings dearest to me on earth I should never again see either, was too much for me. Again I lost the sense of my misery in delirium; and it was many days before I could attend to the consolation offered me by the Baron, or the lighter arguments by which D'Ermenonville attempted to wean me from reflections which it could answer, he said, no purpose to indulge. The state I then fell into was only another species of madness. I no longer raved or vented my fury in cries and execrations; but I became silent and sullen: never spoke but to the Baron, who still attended me with fraternal[2] pity, and got leave of the commandant to do so; and whatever I said to him was only enquiries after some particulars relative to Jacquelina and my sister, in which he could not satisfy me—all that he knew being from my father, or Madame de Bellegarde; for the sister of the Jesuit, D'Aucheterre, had long since been raised to that title, and had brought the Count to Paris, where he was again admitted to such a share of power as had enabled him to execute more securely his unnatural vengeance.

"As I was no longer capable of duty, and my malady seemed to be incurably fixed: as Jacquelina had taken the vows, and was for ever out of my reach, the Baron obtained leave for me to go with him to a house he had in Normandy; where the patient pity with which he watched over me, gradually restored me to my senses! but I regained them only to feel with keener anguish all the horrors of my destiny. The Count de Bellegarde, now far advanced in life, and repenting, perhaps, whenever his new wife gave him leave to think, of his cruel treatment of his daughter, expressed some inclination to see and to forgive me; but I felt that it was I who had much to forgive: and, alas! I felt, too, that though he was my father I could not forgive him.

"The first moment in which I enjoyed both reason and liberty, I should have used in flying to Perpignan, where, with difficulty, I learned that Jacquelina was confined; but I had promised the Baron, that I could not yet attempt it, and to him I held my word to be

---

1 Become a nun.
2 The original has "paternal."

sacred, whatever it cost me to keep it. All my present satisfaction was in traversing the sea coast, near which my brother's house was situated, and looking towards England, whence I every day expected to hear of Ormond, to whom I had written. Impatiently I waited month after month for an answer. At length I recollected the name of an English gentleman, with whom Ormond lived in habits of intimacy while he was in France. I wrote to him, and my letter was immediately answered. He informed me, that Captain Ormond, who had returned to England about ten months before in a very bad state of health, had been ordered very soon afterwards to America, with his regiment, which was sent thither to quell the troubles which about that time broke out in the English colonies. Thus I had no longer any hope of seeing my dear friend, who was of a disposition to have joined me in my attempt, however hazardous, for the recovery of Jacquelina, which I was at all events determined to try at.

"Wild and impossible as the project was, it had taken such forcible hold of my imagination, that reason was no longer heard. I concealed my intentions, however, carefully from my brother, affected composure I was far from feeling; and, as he began to believe me reconciled to my destiny, he no longer refused to talk of Jacquelina, when I calmly led the discourse to that subject: and by degrees he told me all he knew, which was, indeed, little more than the name of the convent, where she had taken the veil, at Perpignan.

"Having gained all the instruction I could, I left a letter to the Baron, who had long ceased to insist upon any parole; and telling him that being now well enough to return to my duty, I should merely see Jacquelina, take an eternal adieu, and then rejoin my regiment. I set out alone in the night, and, taking bye-roads, arrived at Perpignan.

"I found a brother of Jacquelina's, who was settled there: he confirmed all I had heard of the compulsion that had been used by the Count to force my unhappy wife to take the veil. He had threatened the destruction of her whole family: he had imprisoned her father, and assured her that I was dead. If I shuddered at this relation, judge how my tenderness, my regret, my rage was encreased when this brother of my Jacquelina went on to speak of what he thought I had known. That she became a mother during this inhuman persecution; and that an infant daughter then existed. My sister, too, had given birth to a daughter; and died in consequence of the anguish of mind she suffered at having her child taken from her. 'Where are these children?' cried I, in an agony it is impossible to describe; 'Oh, carry me instantly where I may claim them!' 'Alas, Sir!' replied my wife's brother, 'my sister's child was taken by my mother, who, ill as she could afford it, would never part with it to the Count, who offered to provide for it; because she doubted what were his designs. She doubted, indeed, with reason, for the other baby was sent away to Bayonne, as was then said; but every thing relative to it was so secretly managed, that nobody knew for a long time what was become of it: and it was not till some time afterwards that my sister, who from her tender affection for Mademoiselle Bellegarde, was as anxious for it as for her own, persuaded me to enquire about it; for we all dreaded to hear that the Count, under the influence of the D'Aucheterres, had been very cruel indeed to it!'

"Oh! Sir, reflect a moment on my feelings at this detail. In the same breath, I bade my informer to go on with the account of all he knew of Ormond's child, and carry me to my own. The wildness of my impatience frightened him; he endeavoured to soothe me with assurances that my infant was living, and well, and then told me as gently as he could, that he had been guilty of a breach of promise in naming it, for that the Count had made the whole family enter into an agreement never to let me know any thing about the child. Irritated by this new instance of barbarity, I swore, in a transport of passion, that I would have my daughter restored to me, or perish in the attempt; and that I would find the child of my murdered sister if I traversed the world. 'Alas! my dear Chevalier,' said my wife's brother, 'there will be danger enough for you even in attempting to see your own daughter; for the Count has never ceased to have it watched: but for that of your sister, you will certainly never recover it. All my researches, which I assure you were not indolently nor feebly made, traced it no farther than into the house of a certain Madame de Pellatier at Bayonne, a friend of the present Madame de Bellegarde, who undertook—'"

"Madame de Pellatier!" cried Willoughby, "Oh! eternal Heaven, are you sure—Merciful God!—Are you sure it was Madame de Pellatier?"

Amazed at the vehemence and singular manner of Willoughby, for which he could so little account, the Count looked at him a moment, and then said, "Am I sure? Yes, very sure. Have you then any knowledge of Madame de Pellatier?" "Oh! if I could tell you," cried Willoughby, in agitation that deprived him of his breath, "but I cannot—'tis impossible. Yet thus much—did you recover the daughter of your sister?—was she ever restored to you?"

"No, never," answered the Count, "all the intelligence I was long afterwards to obtain was, that Madame de Pellatier had placed her in a convent at Hières; but her name was changed, and before I could obtain, after my last return to France, even this information, the people who had received her were dead, and I could only guess from some memorandums kept in the convent, that a child, whom I guessed to have been the same, was taken from thence by an English lady."

"It is Celestina," cried Willoughby, in the wildest transport, "it is my own Celestina. She is mine again—without a doubt, without any impediment, mine!" He was conscious that at that moment he was not in possession of his senses, so extravagant was his joy. The Count, accustomed as he had been to the impulse of violent passions himself, was astonished at this phrenzy, because he comprehended not what had produced it, nor could Willoughby, for some moments, command himself enough to explain it; till at length, from his proxysm of agonizing joy he sunk at once with as deep dejection, for the probability had occurred to him, that, at the very moment when he was exulting in having so wonderfully and so unexpectedly discovered the birth of Celestina, and thus recovered all his losses, she was, perhaps, married, and no longer interested for him, nor solicitous to enquire on his account to whom she belonged.

Then as every hour's delay might be fatal if this had not already happened, he determined to set out instantly for England. The wonder, however, with which he saw the Count survey him recalled his wandering and bewildered senses; and as well as he could, though very incoherently and inarticulately, he related his history to the Count.

Monsieur de Bellegarde had not a doubt but that the Celestina of Willoughby was his niece; every circumstance, as they became cool enough to compare them, answered exactly. Convinced of this, and becoming every instant more partial to his guest, the Count now entered with the warmest interest into all his apprehensions lest he should lose her; and approved of his hastening instantly back to England. Willoughby now intreated him to return to the castle, that he might not waste a moment, for on the event of a moment, perhaps, said he, my life depends. As they returned, however, the Count concluded his own history, and Willoughby, since Celestina was concerned in it, commanded that portion of attention which, perhaps, no other subject, however otherwise interesting, could at that moment have commanded.

"I was not deterred," said the Count de Bellegarde, "by any of the threats that my father had uttered; but I flew to the convent where Jacquelina was. It was guessed by my impatience and ardour who I was, and I was refused admittance to the grate.[1] I then had recourse to the disguise of a female dress; and, in despite of all the menaces that had been thrown out against their family, I prevailed on one of her sisters to accompany me.

"I saw her!—but she did not know me. Her eyes were cast down; she was pale and thin, resignation and patience seemed to have softened the horrors of her destiny, but they gave to her faded beauty an interest so powerful, that I never loved her so ardently as that moment. I would have forced myself through the grate, which was one of those that are so narrow as scarcely to admit an hand. I threw myself against it—I spoke to her—she then knew me, and caught hold of the bars to save herself from falling. I kissed her hand in the wildest transports, I besought her to remember, that her vows were not—could not be binding, either in the sight of God or man! That she was my wife; and that against the infamous tyranny that had divided us, all nature revolted. Thus I raved, while tears, such as angels shed, fell from her lovely eyes. 'Oh! Bellegarde,' said she, when she was able to speak, 'This is all vain and frantic rage! Learn, my dear, dear friend, to submit, as I do, to a fate, which, cruel as it is, is inevitable. I am dead to you!—for from hence, no power, no force, can now release me. Ah! they told me you were no more, or never, never would I have taken those vows, which my heart refused! But it is done!—and this short moment is the last we shall ever have!' At this instant the superior of the convent, and several nuns appeared, and severely reproaching her, forced her from the grate. 'Inhuman,' said she, 'even this last moment is denied me! Farewell, my dear Bellegarde, farewell for ever—believe I am dead; and transfer the tenderness you felt for your Jacquelina, to her little Anzoletta. In her I still live.' This sentence was hardly articulate, amid the efforts her persecutors made to force her away. When I lost sight of her, again I threw myself frantically against the grate that divided us, I beat my head against it, fury and despair possessed me anew, and I became, for some days, again insensible—or sensible to nothing but the sight of my little girl, whose innocent smiles appeased my rage, and made me recollect that there was yet a being in the world for whom I ought to live.

"Every calm interval was employed in projects, more wild, perhaps, than my wildest ravings, to force Jacquelina from her accursed imprisonment. I talked about it continually to her brothers, and

---

1 The iron grille that separates the nuns from their visitors, but through which they may walk.

persuaded myself that nothing was impossible to a man so injured, and so attached as I was. My father, however, was too powerful in a province, where he was governor, and in a community into which he had influence to get Jacquelina received,[1] notwithstanding her reluctance, and even her marriage. At this time, power did every thing in France, and nature and justice were silenced. Thank God it is so no longer!"

In this ejaculation, Willoughby most sincerely joined, and the Count proceeded:

"My father, as I was about to observe, was too well served to leave me any probability of success in this mad project; far from being able to procure the liberty of my wife, I could not preserve my own, but was, under pretence of my insanity, carried away a prisoner from Perpignan; and the only favor the Baron could obtain for me was, that I might be confined in his house in Normandy. Here I remained only a short time, sunk again into the impotent sullenness of despair, when the regiment, to which I belonged, was ordered to America,[2] and my father desired I might go. I wished for death, and had I had any motives to desire life, my honour compelled me not to hesitate. For America then I embarked; and on my arrival, my first care was to enquire for the English regiment, in which my friend Ormond had a company. I heard, from deserters, that it had suffered greatly in the beginning of the war, and was ordered back to England. Even the mournful satisfaction which I had promised myself in embracing my friend, the husband of my beloved unfortunate Genevieve, seemed thus to be denied me; and every circumstance contributed to promote that desperation, that impatience of life, which is the effect of incurable calamity.

"Before I left France, I had recommended my infant Anzoletta to the care of the Baron, in case of my death, and secured to her all the property that would be at my disposal, on the death of my father. I thought, that were Jacquelina dead, I should think of her with less painful regret, than I did now; languishing within the walls of a monastery; of my natural friends, only the Baron, and D'Ermenonville, affected to feel any interest in my fate: the former was now deeply engaged in the duties of his profession as a soldier; and for the latter, he was decidedly a disciple of Epicurus, and made it a rule of his life to enjoy every possible pleasure, and avoid every pos-

---

1 Into the convent as a nun.
2 France contributed troops and naval support to the colonists in the American War of Independence.

sible pain. Of course, my loss would be but slightly felt by either of my brothers, and my father—for so many years my persecutor and tyrant—would rejoice at it. I continually sought death as my only refuge against the evils he had inflicted upon me; and what was called bravery, was, in fact, despair.

"In one of the rencontres which our troops and the revolted Americans had with the English army, it was my chance to be stationed to defend a small post on the borders of an immense wood, with a small detachment of French. The engagement was warm between the main bodies; but the troops, under my command, were not called into the action. Impatient to be thus idle, I sent one of my aid-de-camps to the general, representing, that we were absolutely useless where we were, and entreating his leave to advance; when he returned and told me, that the battle was over with disputed success; that the English had suffered greatly, particularly in their officers; while the Americans and French, hardly in a better condition, were making their retreat, which I was directed to cover with my fresh troops. I advanced, therefore, through the wood by the way I was directed; and after proceeding half a mile, I met a party of Indians, in the interest of the colonists, carrying with them an English officer, who was, they said, mortally wounded. By his uniform, he appeared to be of rank. I approached him, and spoke to him in French. Judge of my sensations, when I saw in this dying prisoner my friend, my Ormond! Not even the calls of duty were so pressing as those of friendship. I even deliberated a moment, whether I should not hazard every thing to attend him myself, but when I expressed this, though he could hardly speak, he conjured me to go on, and merely to take him out of the hands of the Indians. 'I know I must die,' said the gallant fellow, 'but I would die in your hands, if you can, without injury to your honour, grant me such an indulgence.' I ordered a guard to convey him, with the utmost care, to the nearest French quarters; and then hastening to obey the orders I had received, I had the happiness, successfully, to execute them; and having done so, hurried to my friend.

"I found he had received every assistance which in the situation we then were, could be given him: he was easy, and though his wounds were mortal, his death was not likely to happen immediately.

"He thanked me, as soon as he again saw me, for my attention to him, and then eagerly asked me after his wife and his child. 'But she is dead,' cried he, 'my Genevieve is dead; I was but too certain of that before I left Europe.' My silence, my tears, confirmed the sad truth. 'Well, my dear Chevalier,' cried he, clinging to my hand, 'I am following her fast. I know what you would tell me of my infant, of that dear pledge of my Genevieve's affection. Your inhuman father has eluded your search, as he did mine. Oh! I could curse him!—but I will not, because he is your father. If ever your friendly solicitude for the offspring of your sister, and your friend, should enable you to discover her, give her these pictures—they are those of her father, of his favourite sister, of her mother. See,' added he, 'this resemblance of Genevieve which she gave me, when I received the dear avowal of her love, never till now has it left my bosom, and I conjure you, Bellegarde, never to part with it, till you place it on that of my daughter.'

"My noble friend lingered a few days longer, not in great pain, however, and perfectly sensible, and then, in my arms, he resigned his gallant spirit to his God.

"This loss added strength to the gloomy resolution I had before made to die. Among my friend's papers, which, by his order, his servant delivered to me, after his death, I found a narrative of all he had done, after his release from imprisonment in the Bastile, at the demand of the English ambassador (for he was there part of the time that I was, though we never saw each other), to gain admittance to his wife, and to have his child restored to him; and such an abhorrence did this add to that I had already conceived against my father, that I could not bear the name of Bellegarde; nor endure to think of returning to breathe the same air with a man whom I considered as a monster.

"To France, however, I returned, without even a wound in all the hazards to which I had voluntarily exposed myself. This inhuman father was still living, but my brother, the Baron de Rochemarte, had fallen at the head of his regiment, at the attack made on the island of Jersey,[1] and I succeeded to his fortune, a fortune which, ample as it was, could make me no amends for the excellent kind brother I had lost.

"Alas! I had lost two brothers, and two friends equally dear to me; they were not to be recalled, but I still found a gloomy kind of satisfaction in complying with their last requests. That of my brother de Rochemarte was, that I would take his name; and most willingly I quitted that of Bellegarde. The dying request of my beloved friend I endeavoured—ah! how vainly endeavoured—to fulfil. I never could discover his daughter till this fortunate day!

---

1   The French attacked the island of Jersey, one of the (British) Channel Islands, in 1779 and 1781.

"But my residence among the Americans, had awakened in my mind a spirit of freedom. The miseries, the irreparable injuries I had received from ill-placed and exorbitant power, prompted me to assert it. I was now possessed of considerable property useless to me, because Jacquelina could not share it. Though comparatively free myself, I was wretched. In this disposition, it may easily be imagined, that if I possessed the power, I was not without inclination to add fewel to that fire, which immediately after the end of the war in America, was kindled, though it yet burnt but feebly in France. I wrote, I acted upon my newly-acquired principles, with the energy of a sufferer, and with the resolution of a martyr. I was already the martyr of despotism, and ruined in my happiness for ever. I knew that all the vengeance I could excite could injure me no farther.

"I now saw Jacquelina, but she was still pining within her convent. I saw my child, I held her to the grate while her mother bedewed her little hands with tears, which I kissed off! It was a scene to move every heart but such as inhabited the breast of my father! Again, the hopelessness of rescuing my wife from her cruel bonds, gave him occasion to put other fetters on me. In the rashness of my desperation, I said, I wrote, I acted such things as made me be considered by government as a dangerous person. My father took advantage of my rashness—he represented me as being disordered in my senses, and obtained an order for shutting me up in the fortress of Mont St. Michel.[1]

"Between four and five years had I been a captive in that gloomy prison, when the glorious flame of liberty, of which I only saw the first feeble rays, burst forth. I regained my personal freedom, when my country became free. I found my father dead! Every thing he could give away, his wife possessed; but this, and some other of his estates, were mine—and D'Ermenonville gave me the lands which then gave the title of Bellegarde, the name which I abhor; and which, though it is yet given me by the people, who have been accustomed to give it to the head of my family, I will not keep, but take that of Montignac,[2] which is my *untitled* name, the original designation of our family.

"The first use I made now of the general and particular freedom, in which I rejoiced, was to fly to Perpignan, but the moment is not

---

1   Mont-Saint-Michel is a half-mile-wide island off the south-west coast of France, with a medieval Abbey and a fortress at times used as a prison.
2   Titles were abolished in France on 19 June 1790: the Chevalier is anticipating the change in the law.

yet come, when I can deliver my imprisoned Jacquelina. I am, however, assured, that she will very soon be restored to me;[1] in that hope I came hither to attend to my long-neglected affairs, and to enjoy the society of my daughter. Even greater happiness has been the consequence of my abode here than I dared to hope; for by you, my friend, towards whom, the moment I saw you, I was impelled by an invincible propensity, I shall, I trust, recover the dear orphan child of Genevieve and Ormond.

"In a few days I shall go back to Perpignan; leave Anzoletta again in the care of her mother's family, and then hasten to assist in the glorious business of securing the liberty of France—yes!—the immortal work of defending myriads yet unborn from ever suffering the oppressions, under which I have groaned."

Here the Count de Bellegarde ended his narrative; and Willoughby, with an inexpressible contrariety of sensations—joy and hope—fear and apprehension, being furnished with every assurance he could wish, of the real parents of Celestina, took a tender leave of the Count and Anzoletta, whose voice was to him as the voice of a seraph, promising him felicity to come, and he then departed, as had been agreed upon between him and the Count, for Perpignan: where he delivered, at the grate, a letter to Jacquelina, of whom the Count had desired that she would describe to Willoughby any particulars of the person of his niece[2] which she recollected, for in her care, the infant Celestina had been left a few weeks.

With trembling impatience Willoughby waited while the interesting, and still lovely nun perused this letter, and heard her, while his heart sunk with apprehension, thus describe the child of her unfortunate friend—"She was," said Jacquelina, "fairer than my child, and her features greatly resembled those of her father. On her neck, a little on the left side, were three remarkable, though diminutive, moles." "It is enough," said Willoughby, "those moles are on the lovely neck of Celestina—a thousand times have I kissed them as we played together in our infancy, and here on this portrait of her, drawn when she was about twelve years old, they are described."

1　After the declaration of the new *Constitution Civile du Clerge* (civil constitution of the clergy) on 12 July 1790, some convents and monasteries were closed and monastic clergy enabled to disperse. These events were already anticipated in late 1789 and early 1790, however, allowing Smith to work them into her narrative, which ends in early 1790.

2　The original has "wife."

Jacquelina kissed the picture. "Little as can be judged from a likeness done so many years afterwards, I feel an assurance," said she, "that this is the picture of my Genevieve's child. May heaven grant her those blessings which, in its unsearchable decrees, it refused to my lovely, luckless friend." Willoughby, who would not have been a moment detained by any interview less interesting, or less necessary, now took his leave, and with the utmost expedition, though all he could make, answered but ill to his impatience, he hastened on towards England.

Chapter XII

While these things passed at Rochemarte, Celestina, no longer doubting of Willoughby's marriage, and entire desertion of her, was trying to acquire once more that calm resignation, which she had so often determined to adopt, and so often lost. Montague Thorold accompanied Lady Horatia to Cheltenham; where, as Celestina foresaw, his ardent entreaties, and the wishes of her friend so strongly enforcing them, gave her so much pain, that she grew hourly more fond of travelling. If she found it difficult to evade the importunities of her lover, and her benefactress, she dreaded yet more the arrival of the elder Mr. Thorold; who, about six weeks after Montague's recovery, came with him (after a short visit he had paid at home) to Cheltenham.

He soon found an opportunity of speaking to Celestina, alone, and then she became more than ever conscious of the influence that his solid understanding, his excellent principles, and his tender regard for her, gave him over her ingenuous mind. Though he never complained, she well knew, that he was not happy in the other branches of his family, and that his hopes were particularly fixed on his younger son, whose attachment to Celestina, which, had it been successful, might have secured, in one point, the felicity of his father, had hitherto produced for him only anxiety and solicitude.

He had seen his life once more in imminent hazard, from the fierce and impetuous Vavasour, and from his own rashness, which he could not but condemn; he had seen, for many months, all his talents, and almost all his affections, lost and absorbed in this one predominant passion, and he knew not what the effect might be on his intellects, and on his health, should he finally be refused: yet, while Willoughby was uncertain as to his own situation, or unmarried, the elder Mr. Thorold had been withheld from making any efforts with

Celestina, on behalf of his son; now those impediments were removed, he no longer thought himself restrained from applying to her himself. So mildly and rationally, however, he entered on this conversation, that Celestina retained more courage, while she heard him, than she, at its commencement, had dared to expect; and when he had recapitulated all the advantages which might, he thought, be derived, from her union with a man so passionately devoted to her, of suitable age; of easy fortune—one whose taste was congenial to her own; whose temper was remarkably good, and who had a heart uncorrupted by vice, and unexhausted by a long course of intrigue; and a family who would consider her admission into it, as the greatest blessing that they could receive; Celestina acknowledged it was all very true.

"I own too, Sir," said she, "that to many people, and perhaps to you, I may have appeared to give your son such encouragement, as never ought to be given, unless it is meant to end in marriage. I have felt, without having it in my power to avoid, this seeming impropriety—yet he will do me the justice to say, I have always told him, that whatever were my sentiments in his favour, and however I wished to encourage those sentiments, because I was persuaded he deserved them, yet, that my heart never felt for him that decided preference, without which, I cannot believe, he could be happy, were I to give him my hand. I was too sure, that from an unfortunate prepossession, in favour of another, I never could feel this preference; and that, therefore, though I should always be happy to be considered as his friend, I never would be his wife. Allow me, dear Sir, to repeat to you, a resolution from which I do not believe I shall ever recede. You know how true a love and veneration I have for you; there is not on earth, a man whom I would so soon chuse to supply to me that sacred and tender relationship I have never known! but I cannot, indeed I cannot marry. I know not why, but some invincible persuasion hangs over me, that if I do, I shall be miserable, and render my husband miserable, whatever may be his merit or affection, and can I, ought I, under such a conviction, to wish it? Be assured, that if time and reason conquer this weakness—for perhaps it may be only weakness—if ever I feel that I can give your son a heart, weaned from every other attachment, and worthy of his, I will say so, as candidly, as I declare the impossibility of my doing so now. And you are so liberal, that you will forgive my weakness, and save me, I am sure, from importunity, which is the more distressing, as it comes from those I so much esteem, and whose wishes it would be, on any other subject, my pride and my pleasure to obey."

Mr. Thorold, after this conversation, and some other of the same nature, was convinced, that Celestina acted from motives of the most delicate honour. The more he saw of her heart and disposition, the more fondly he became attached to her; and the more ardently desired that she might become the wife of his son. He saw, that though her ideas were what would be generally called romantic, they were not cherished merely because they were so; but that a high sense of the tender duty she wished to pay to the man with whom she was to pass her life, made it impossible for her to enter into such engagements till she was sure of fulfilling them according to her own ideas; and he hoped, that her entire separation from Willoughby; his unkindness and neglect on one hand; and on the other, the acknowledged merit of his son, would though almost insensibly, yet not slowly, produce that change which she allowed herself to be possible, though at present it did not seem probable. In this hope he was contented to rest; and promising Celestina, that if she would still allow Montague to see her frequently, he should not teize her by importunity, he threw himself entirely on her generosity and sincerity; and after a visit of near a week, he left Montague at Cheltenham, by the desire of Lady Horatia, and returned home.

In a few days after his departure, Celestina had another and more painful scene to encounter. Cathcart arrived early one morning, and eagerly asked to speak to her. She went down to him immediately, but when she saw him, she dared not ask the purpose of a visit so little expected. He was pale—he trembled and hesitated—he looked fatigued and dejected. Willoughby instantly recurred to her, for he was always the first object of her thoughts. "Is any thing the matter, dear Cathcart," said she, "with Willoughby?" "Oh, no," replied he; "nothing new; I have not heard of him since he went, which I think strange."

Celestina sighed, and thought she was able too well to account for it. "But is Jessy well?" "Yes, thank Heaven," replied he: "but my sister—" "What, Mrs. Elphinstone?" "No, my other, my unfortunate sister Emily—I have been sent for to her at Bristol, where, you know I went to her some time since, at your entreaty: she has now, I think, only a few days to live. My sister Elphinstone is with her. Poor Emily wishes to see you. I know not how to ask such a favour of you; but you are *so* good—will you—can you oblige a family who already owe to you all the happiness they possess?"

"What will I not do to give any part of it satisfaction?" said Celestina. "But do you, can you guess the reason of your sister's wishes to see me? Surely Vavasour is not there?" "He was not, when

I left her; but a few days before he had been at Bristol, raving like a madman at the fatal intelligence he had then had confirmed, that Emily could not live. If, however, he should come, you can have nothing to fear, for I will not leave you a moment; and I know you so well, that I am persuaded, there were few disagreeable circumstances, which would not, to you, be compensated, by the reflection of having given comfort to the last moments of my dying Emily."

This plea Celestina could not resist: she went, therefore, by the consent of Lady Horatia, with Cathcart, to Bristol; where a scene awaited her, that for some time almost suspended even her thoughts of Willoughby himself.

The lovely, unhappy victim to early seduction was in the last stage of a Consumption,[1] and, unlike many of those who are cut off by that distemper, was perfectly aware, and perfectly reconciled to her fate. Her earnest wishes had been to be forgiven by Cathcart, and to die in the arms of her sister; they both now attended her with the tenderest affection, and had even yielded to her request, to be allowed to see Vavasour, towards whom all her anxiety was now turned, and for his happiness she felt that concern, which she no longer was sensible of for herself.

Her exhausted heart was, from gratitude and habit attached to Vavasour; and she saw that her death would take away the only tie that had been some restraint on his ungovernable licentiousness; that his disappointment in regard to Celestina, had embittered his temper; and given him a sort of excuse for the libertinism in which he seemed resolute to persevere; and while his good qualities, his generosity, and his candour, as well as his attentive tenderness towards her, had made her affection for him the last sentiment she was capable of feeling: she fancied it yet possible, young as she was, Celestina might be induced to save a man who appeared so well worth the attempt: and that, interesting as he appeared to her, he could not fail of having some interest with others, and particularly with one who had learned from Willoughby an early prejudice in his favour, which she hoped all his subsequent rashness had not yet wholly destroyed.

Such were the views of Emily Cathcart, in requesting this visit; and her beautiful eyes, lit up with the fire that was consuming her became yet more dazzlingly bright when her lovely visitor was led into the room by her brother.

Celestina entered trembling; and fearing the sight of Vavasour,

---

1 The term usually meant tuberculosis.

whom she had never met since the terrifying night at Ranelagh; but the moment she beheld Emily, she no longer thought of any thing but the affecting object before her.

Emily sat in a great chair, supported by pillows. The extreme beauty that had been so fatal to its possessor, still remained, though its lustre was gone. Emaciated, and of a delicate fairness, her hands and her face had a transparency that gave an idea of an unembodied spirit, and her dress was such as favoured the deception. The blood might almost be seen to circulate in her veins, so plainly did they appear; and her eyes had the dazzling radiance of ethereal fire, to which the hectic heat of her glowing, though wasted countenance, still added. A few locks of her fine light hair had escaped from her head-dress; and played like broken rays from a receding planet, round a face, which only those who had hearts unhappily rigid, could behold, without feeling the sense of her errors suspended or over-whelmed by strong emotions of the tenderest pity.

She held out her hand to Celestina, as she entered, and in a voice faint and interrupted, from the difficulty with which she breathed, said, "Ah! dearest madam, how good this is; how worthy that tender and sensible heart, of which I have heard so much." She stopped, as if unable to speak more at that moment, and rested her head against the chair. Celestina affected to tears, sat silently down near her. Cath-cart left the room.

After a short pause, she recovered strength to say, "But a moment will be allowed me, perhaps; let me then hasten to thank you for this condescension, and to say, how earnestly it is my hope, that it will not be made in vain; but that it will afford me an opportunity of suc-cessfully pleading for another penitent—for poor Vavasour."

"I forgive him most willingly," cried Celestina, "and most sin-cerely wish him happy."

"Ah, Madam!" said Emily, "you must then carry your generosity farther, for you only can make him so. I dared to represent this in a letter to you. I now repeat it. Victim as I am, even in the morning of my days, I should, however, die in peace, for I hope my peace is made with Heaven, if I could see any prospect of Vavasour's being happy; reclaimed from that wild career where he is now wasting his time, his fortune, and his life. I owe him so many obligations! I know him to have so good a heart! that it is terrible to me to see him devoted[1] as he is, and plunging into an abyss of misery, from whence it will

---

1 Doomed to destruction.

soon be no longer in his power to return. It has been a great consolation to me, that I have had some little influence in stemming the progress of the evil; but it is you only who can save him from himself effectually; and how worthy would it be of goodness, of compassion like yours!"

Celestina knew not what to answer. To promise what she never could perform, was little in her nature; yet did she not love to check the disinterested hope that thus animated the soft heart of the fair pleader. "I believe," said she, after a short pause, "I believe you are mistaken: and that I have no such power as you impute to me; be assured that, though Mr. Vavasour's conduct has been to me a source of the most poignant uneasiness, I not only will forget it, but shall rejoice in seeing him happy, for his own sake, and for the sake of that dear friend through whose means we first became acquainted: a friend"—her voice trembled, and she dared not attempt to name Willoughby, lest it should wholly fail her—"a friend who is still, and who I dare believe will ever be truly attached to him: and who, on his return to England, will, I am sure, use all the influence that friendship gives him over Mr. Vavasour, to recall him from a way of life you so much apprehend." She was proceeding to evade, as tenderly as she could, the pathetic prayer she had just heard, when Emily was seized with one of those spasms which announced her approaching death. Celestina, terrified, called for Mrs. Elphinstone; and unable to bear a scene in which she could be of no use, she retired to another room, where she passed with Cathcart, two melancholy hours, at the end of which, they heard that the fair unhappy Emily was no more.

Vavasour, who was in another lodging at the Hot-wells, no sooner heard of this sad event, than the wildest frenzy possessed him: nor did his having so long expected it, at all mitigate the blow. He ran to the house, and regardless of Cathcart and Mrs. Elphinstone, who would have opposed these frantic expressions of useless regret, he threw himself on his knees by the bedside, called to her, as if she were still living, was sure she should not die—and now reproached Heaven that she was dead. From this state of temporary insanity, nothing had the power to recall him, till Cathcart, reproaching him very warmly, for the impropriety of his conduct, asked him, whether it was thus he meant to promote the last wishes of his sister, and obtain the pardon of Miss de Mornay? That name had still all its influence on the heart of Vavasour: by a strange, though, perhaps, not uncommon division of his affections, he at once vehemently loved the woman he had lost, and the woman he hoped to gain. Starting from his knees, he asked where Celestina was? for Cathcart had not yet told him of her arrival, and had promised to prevent his distressing her. "Miss de Mornay is below, Sir; but you must not go to her." "Not go to her! who shall prevent it?" was his answer, and he hastily went down stairs.

When he entered the room where Celestina sat weeping with Mrs. Elphinstone, he had every appearance of a man out of his senses: but, at the sight of her, he seemed subdued in a moment; and while she dreaded some wild and frantic speech, he threw himself on his knees before her, and burst into tears.

His convulsive sobs, as he eagerly caught her hands, and pressed them to his heart; and the broken voice in which he attempted to speak, disarmed her at once of all the resentment which she had, till then, felt for his unwarrantable behaviour, when they last met; and so tenderly, in a voice of such soothing pity did she speak to him, that he soon became reasonable; thanked her for her generous attention; even blessing her, and calling her the restorer of his reason, while Celestina availed herself of this disposition of his mind, to prevail on him to retire; which he did, on her promise, that she would see him again the next day.

After a mournful night, of which more was passed in comforting and consoling Mrs. Elphinstone than in sleep, that day arrived, on which Celestina was not only bound by the promise which in the agitation of mind she was in the night before, she had made to Vavasour, to see him; but induced to declare to him again, how totally he was mistaken in supposing her engaged to Montague Thorold. Again he cherished the hope which she never meant to revive; and at once to do, what he knew would gratify her, while he acquitted himself of the promise he had given to his regretted Emily, he had a deed drawn up and executed, by which he gave to Mrs. Elphinstone, and her children, two hundred a year; and settled them at the house he had in Devonshire. On the moment of her departure, he gave this deed to Celestina, beseeching her not to open it till her arrival at Cheltenham. "And whither are you going, Mr. Vavasour?" said Celestina, who felt her pity revive for him, now that she saw him so dejected and subdued. "Ah," replied he, "I am careless whither. I cannot, however, go back to my Staffordshire house in the state of mind I am in now; for I should infallibly hang myself; I believe I shall go to London, for even at this time of year, a wretched dog, such as I am, may find somebody or other to help them to get rid of themselves; and the gaming houses are always open." "The gaming houses!" said Celestina. "Aye," replied he, "I have been there always of late when I have been cursedly miserable, and play has a momentary effect on me, in making me forget other things. Perhaps, in wandering about London, I may meet with some unsettled, unhappy fellow, like myself, who may like to go abroad for six or eight months: we may go find Willoughby, perhaps, and my return may be the more welcome to *you*, if I bring you an account of *him*."

"Alas!" thought Celestina, "what account of *him* can I now hear with pleasure; unless indeed that he is well; that I always wish to hear! And I *think*," added she, her heart swelling as she said it, "I think I should *sincerely* rejoice to hear, that in his new situation, he is happy with his *wife*!"

Vavasour, again feeling the renewal of that hope which had almost escaped him, saw Celestina depart with more calmness than he expected. Cathcart saw her safe in the protection of Lady Horatia, at Cheltenham; and then returned to Bristol, to perform the last sad offices to his lost Emily; Vavasour, at his and Mrs. Elphinstone's request, leaving the place before her remains were consigned to their early grave.

The scenes which, during this period, passed in the family of Lord Castlenorth, were more turbulent, and to some of the parties equally melancholy.

The anxious peer, whose health was, as usual, a little amended by change of country, waited at Paris the promised arrival of Willoughby, with extreme impatience: impatience which had such an effect upon his feeble frame, that death, which had so long been lying in wait for him, now seized him, and at a period, when the blow saved him from knowing what could not have been concealed from him many hours. Lady Castlenorth having enacted with great dignity all that a mournful relict [1] must do on such an occasion: and Miss Fitz-Hayman having also performed her part admirably, the will was opened in due form, of which Lady Castlenorth thought herself perfectly sure of the contents; and she had indeed secured to herself a great deal of money, and a splendid income, besides her settlement. The property descending to Miss Fitz-Hayman, immediately, was about eight thousand a year; but, in a codicil (made in the immediate pleasure he received when Willoughby first declared himself resolved to marry his cousin) he had given him an estate of five-and-twenty hundred a year; and ten thousand pounds in money, as a nuptial present; without, however, affixing any conditions to the gift.

---

1 Widow.

The short ceremony of reading the will being over, another was to be gone through less easy to Miss Fitz-Hayman; which was, announcing to her mother her actual marriage with Captain Cavanaugh, which she thought must otherwise be revealed by somebody else.

The dialogue was short, but decisive. Miss Fitz-Hayman, or rather Mrs. Cavanaugh, had more courage than tenderness; and having now nothing to fear from her mother's influence with her father; and secure of her fortune, both at present and in reversion, she assumed rather an air of triumph than of contrition. Lady Castlenorth would be but faintly described by the strongest of those representations that have been given of an enraged woman, when she has been compared to a tygress robbed of her young. Cavanaugh had possessed the art to make her believe, that his admiration of her mental perfections was the foundation of that attachment he felt for her; yet, that while he adored her beautiful mind, her fine person was an object of tender admiration. To find that he cared for neither the one nor the other; but had availed himself of her credulity to obtain a footing in the family; and money to get his matrimonial fetters broken, that he might marry her daughter, were convictions so extremely mortifying to her pride, that they, for a while, suspended the power of expressing her rage. When, however, that power returned, she raved like a lunatic, gave way to the most extravagant sallies of passion, and though her Lord was yet unburied, protested that the same house should no longer hold her and her "pelican daughter."[1] Mrs. Cavanaugh was more calm, and retired to her room: where Mrs. Calder, at length, persuaded Lady Castlenorth to let her stay till after the remains of her father were sent forward to England, which they were in a few days; and then Mrs. Cavanaugh set out, by the way of Rouen, to England also, with her husband, who was impatient to take possession of his great acquisitions, the price of so much patient perfidy. Though he would willingly have been excused giving to Willoughby even the small share of the ample property which his uncle had assigned to him; yet he knew he must see the will, and finally obtain it. He thought it better, therefore, to continue with him the appearance of honour; and therefore wrote to him, informing him of Lord Castlenorth's death; of his own marriage; and the

---

1 Cf. *The Tragedy of King Lear* 3.4.70: "twas this flesh begot/ Those pelican daughters." The pelican was (wrongly) believed to feed its young with its own blood.

codicil in favour of Mr. Willoughby. But not knowing whither to direct this letter; for Willoughby had left no intimation of the route he meant to pursue, when he quitted Paris; he addressed it to Alvestone; where, with one on the same business from Lady Castlenorth, it lay, while Willoughby was wandering among the Pyrenean mountains, and while he pursued his impatient way towards England.

Chapter XIII

Unconscious of the good that awaited him, and dreading the evil that might be irreparable, Willoughby landed at Brighthelmstone[1] from Dieppe. Though it was eleven o'clock when he got on shore, he ordered post-horses to be instantly ready; and used the moment he waited for them to take a slight refreshment. On the table of the room he was in, a newspaper lay. It was long since he had seen an English newspaper, and he took it up, where the first article that struck him was an account of the funeral of Lord Castlenorth, after his having laid in state at his house in town.

Willoughby felt an immediate impression of concern for his uncle, and feared lest disappointment should have hastened his death. On himself, or any advantage he might derive from the event, he never bestowed a thought; but as the mind, under the influence of any predominant passion, returns immediately to its bias, however temporarily diverted from it, it almost instantly occurred to him that if his uncle had been so long dead without his knowing it, Celestina might possibly have been as long married. Trembling, he looked among the marriages, but there were no names there at all resembling those which he dreaded to see united. His chaise was ready, and he departed for London; for it was there only that he was likely to gain intelligence of Lady Horatia Howard, and he knew of no other clue to guide him to Celestina.

Celestina had left Cheltenham with her friend, and was now at Exmouth, where Montague Thorold was continually with them. Whether he was present or absent, Celestina was equally pensive and melancholy; but it was only in the latter case, that she attempted to indulge those sensations in the solitary walks which the sea-shore afforded her: for she avoided as much as possible being quite alone with him, because her heart every day confirmed her in the opinion

---

1 Brighton.

that she never could love another man as she had loved Willoughby, and it was distressing to her to be frequently under the necessity of repeating, what it inflicted such pain on her impassioned and indefatigable lover to hear. It was now late in September: the evenings soon shut in; and, when there happened not to be a supply of new books, Lady Horatia often engaged Montague Thorold at piquet,[1] while Celestina sat by them at work; or, if she could be sure he was so occupied as not to be able to follow her, she walked out alone, and as the moon trembled on the waves, recollected the nights when, with Willoughby and Matilda, in the early days of their innocent friendship, they used to mark and admire together this beautiful appearance of the sea illuminated by the moon. Here, on this very spot, she had with him beheld it. The waves had now the same trembling brilliancy; the surrounding objects were the same; but Willoughby was changed: and happiness and Celestina were, she thought, parted for ever.

Such were her contemplations one evening, when, towards the end of the month, and of Lady Horatia's intended stay at the place, she left the company who were assembled at the lodgings; and who happened to be the elder Mr. Thorold, his wife, their son Montague, and Mr. and Mrs. Bettenson, who being on a visit to the elder Mr. Thorold, when he was ordered to the sea for his health, had accompanied him all together to Exmouth, and were shewn every attention by Lady Horatia, as the relations of her favourite Montague.

They were at cards; and Celestina, who never played, took the opportunity of her admirer's being engaged at a whist table, from which she knew he could not immediately escape, to go out. The wind was high, and the sea boisterous; it was growing dark, and she fancied a particular gloom hung over every object. Still, however, it was luxury to her to be alone; she was particularly wearied by the conversation of Mrs. Thorold; and found nothing in that of Mrs. Bettenson to make her amends: Bettenson was ignorant inspidity itself; and time, instead of adding to the number of his ideas, seemed to have rendered him, if possible, more stupid. Amid such society, she could derive no pleasure from the conversation of Mr. Thorold and Lady Horatia; and the unusual weight she felt on her spirits seemed lessened, when she could sigh at liberty, and hear nothing around her but the wind, or the sea breaking against the shore.

---

1 A game played by two people with 32 cards (low cards excluded) in which points are scored for various groups or sequences of cards.

She had not, however, been out long, before the chill and gloomy appearance increased; and darkness coming on, she slowly and reluctantly returned to the house. She heard, a little before she quitted the road, horses behind her; but not attending to them, she did not even distinguish whether they were the horses of the people of the place, or those of travellers. She entered the parlour, and sat down by the card table, where Montague Thorold, having performed his evening's task, had just resigned his place to Mr. Bettenson. Suddenly a voice was heard in the passage, enquiring for Lady Horatia Howard of her servant. "My lady is within, Sir," replied the man. "And who are with her?" "Mr. and Mrs. Thorold, and—" The servant was going on, when the enquirer said vehemently, "It is enough—let me however see them." Celestina, at the first sound of this voice, had started from her chair. The second sentence it uttered affected her still more; but she had no time to answer the eager enquiry of Montague Thorold—"What is the matter?"—before the parlour door opened; and pale, breathless, with an expression to which only the pencil can do justice, she saw before her the figure of Willoughby.

There was agony and desperation in his looks. He gasped, he would have spoken, but could not. The company all rose in silence. Lady Horatia, who hardly knew him even by sight, looked at Celestina for an explanation, which she was unable to give. At length Willoughby, as if by an effort of passionate phrenzy, approached Celestina, and said, in a hurried and inarticulate way, "I would speak to you, Madam—though to this gentleman, I suppose," and he turned to Montague Thorold, "I must apply for permission."

His manner, his look, as wildly he cast his eyes around and saw all the family of the Thorolds assembled, which confirmed his idea of her being married, contributed to overwhelm Celestina with terror and amazement. She no more doubted of his marriage with his cousin, than he did of hers; and could not conjecture why he came, or why he looked so little in his senses. She sat down, for her limbs refused to support her, and faintly said, or rather tried to say, "I hope I see Mr. Willoughby well."

Lady Horatia then addressed herself to him, desired him to take a chair, and to do her the honour of staying supper with her. He heard or heeded her not, but with fixed eyes, gazing on Celestina, he struck his hands together, and cried, while the violence of his emotion choked him, "It is all over then—I have lost her, and have nothing to do here. No, by heaven, I cannot bear it." He then turned away, and left the room as hastily as he had entered it.

"My dear Celestina," cried Lady Horatia, "what does all this mean? Do, Mr. Montague, for Miss de Mornay is, I see, much alarmed, do, speak to Mr. Willoughby. I am really concerned to see him in such a situation."

"No:" said Celestina, who would not for the world have had Montague Thorold follow him. "No; I will go myself after him." Her fears now gave her resolution, and without heeding Montague Thorold, who would have prevented her, she hurried after Willoughby, and overtook him just as he was quitting the house.

"Dear Sir," said she, "dear Willoughby!" At those well known sounds, once so precious to him, he turned round. She took his hand. "I am very sorry to see you," continued she, "in such agitations of spirits. I greatly fear—perhaps—" Some misery between him and his supposed wife occurred to her. "I am afraid something is wrong—"

"Wrong!" cried he; "Wrong!—and do you, Celestina, inhuman Celestina, insult me with such an enquiry? Wrong! Am I not the most cursed of human beings?"

"I hope not," interrupted she, "for your happiness—" She knew no longer what she meant to say; nor did he give her time to recollect; for, eagerly rivetting his eyes on her face, and grasping her hands between his, he cried, "My happiness!—and what of my happiness? Is it not gone, lost for ever. Have you not destroyed it? Damnation and distraction, why do I linger here?" He then plunged away, and rushed out of the door, where Farnham waited with two post-horses. Celestina, trembling, and attempting to stop him, followed.

He tried, however, to mount his horse, but could not; he desisted, leaned against it, with his arm over the saddle, and resting his head on his arm. Farnham spoke, and Celestina immediately recollected him. "What is the matter with your master, Farnham?" said she. "Indeed he terrifies me to death!" "Oh, Ma'am," replied the honest fellow, sorrowfully, "my poor master! Come, Sir," added he, interrupted by a look of anguish and horror from Willoughby, "come, dear Sir! You cannot ride any farther, I am persuaded, tonight; let me lead you to the inn." Willoughby, without resistance, suffered Farnham to lead him a step or two; but he waved with his hand for Celestina to leave him, and faintly said, "Go! Go! Madam! I wish you well! I wish you well!" "Which is the way to the inn?" cried Farnham.

"Not to the inn, do not go to the inn," exclaimed Celestina; "you are very ill, dear Willoughby; let us take care of you here: Lady Horatia requests it." Farnham led him towards the door again; he leaned upon him, and sighed loudly and deeply. At length he said, "I am a fool! I came hither knowing all I know now, and ought to have been better prepared for it. But I am better: let me then execute my last resolution, and bid her one long, one eternal adieu."

There was a little vacant parlour near the door; there Willoughby sat down. The servants, who were assembled, brought candles: Celestina stood silently by the table on which they were placed; and Willoughby bid Farnham leave the room.

A short silence ensued. Willoughby seemed to be ashamed of his weakness, and trying to collect fortitude to bear like a man the cruellest moment he had ever past, he arose and approached Celestina, saying in a low, grave, and tremulous tone, "I have no right, Madam, to distress you. I have no just cause of complaint against you. I am very miserable. I deserve your pity, your prayers. I have been deceived—you, I hope will never have so much cause to regret it, as I must have. You, I hope, are happy, will be happy." He could say no more, but put his hand on his heart, and looked at Celestina with eyes so expressive of despair and grief, that all the exquisite tenderness she had ever felt for him returned at once; she forgot that he was (as she believed) the husband of Miss Fitz-Hayman; but he was in a moment the beloved Willoughby, the first and only possessor of her heart. She threw her arms around him, and, sobbing on his bosom, became almost senseless from the violence and variety of emotions that overwhelmed her.

He shrank, however, from her. "Who is it," said he, "gracious Heaven! that I thus hold in my arms? Not my Celestina, my own Celestina; but the wife of another. Go, Madam, I entreat you leave me. Go, or phrenzy may overtake me, and I may attempt impossibilities—to tear you from your husband."

"Husband!" cried Celestina, "I have no husband." "Are you not married then? Not married to Montague Thorold?" "No, indeed—indeed, I am not." "Not married—nor intending to be married?" "Neither, indeed." "And you are at liberty, then, to be mine?" "I am, if you know that we ought not to be divided."

Those only who have loved like Willoughby, and who, by a sudden transition, are raised from the abyss of despair to the height of felicity, can imagine what he felt at that moment. If the fear of Celestina's being married, had, for a moment, bereft him of reason; the certainty of her being not only free, but as passionately attached to him as ever, had, for a little time, an equally violent effect. Amidst her own transports, the extravagance of his terrified her. There was a wildness in his joy which made her tremble for his intellects. But, after a moment, her soft melting voice; the tender assurances she gave him, that she lived only for him; that her heart had never been estranged from him, soothed and subdued the tumult of his beating heart. As his arms fondly encompassed her; as he rested his head on her bosom, he shed tears of tender gratitude; his spirits became calmer, and the native serene dignity of his mind returned.

He was not, however, quite tranquil enough to relate that night to Celestina the extraordinary series of events, which had led to the enchanting certainty he now possessed that she was not his sister, but the daughter of Lady Horatia's brother; that regretted brother, to whose picture she had so great a resemblance. The information, however, such as in his present agitated state he was able to give, convinced her, not only that the fatal supposition of her being too nearly related to Willoughby was for ever removed; but, that she was born of parents to whom it was honourable to belong: and that she was nearly allied by blood to her kind protectress.

She desired Lady Horatia might be acquainted with this. "Not to night," said Willoughby. "I would to-night see nobody but you, my Celestina; hear no voice but yours. To-morrow I will explain it all. But now I feel my unexpected felicity too forcibly to be able to talk about it."

He could not, however, determine to quit Celestina; nor were either of them conscious of the course of time, till Lady Horatia sent to let Celestina know supper was ready, and to beg the honour of Mr. Willoughby's company.

It was then that Celestina prevailed upon him to go from her, promising to be ready to walk with him by the dawn of the next morning. "And you must go with me," said he, "immediately to Alvestone; for I will not live another week without you." He then recollected that Alvestone might be sold; for he had never heard from Cathcart since he had given directions to have it disposed of. He paused a moment, and felt some uneasiness in the reflection: but the happiness he possessed was too great to allow him to feel any concern long. He smiled, and added, "If indeed Alvestone is still mine; and, if it is not, my Celestina will create for me a paradise wherever she is."

"And wherever you are," replied she, while tears of tenderness filled her eyes, "Celestina will find a paradise."

He then once more bade her good night—again returned—and again bade her adieu. "You are going now to rejoin the company," said he, "and there is Montague Thorold, of whom, I know it is a weakness, I do not love to think—"

"It is indeed, Willoughby, a weakness unworthy of your generous heart; and, I hope, what I can never have deserved that you should indulge." "Well, well, my angel! I will not indulge it. But must you sup with them? They will fatigue you with questions—they will distress you by enquiries." "No; I had determined to send an excuse; for, indeed, my heart, yet wondering at its unexpected felicity, beats fearfully, and my trembling nerves have unfitted me for conversation."

At length Willoughby withdrew; and Celestina, with a pencil, told Lady Horatia, who waited the event of this extraordinary interview in the most uneasy suspense, that some extraordinary conversation with Mr. Willoughby had agitated her so much, that she could not return to the company, but must retire to her bed.

Montague Thorold, who was the most interested of the party, had suffered all the tortures of anxious jealousy while Celestina was absent. Every noise he heard in the passage, every time the door opened, he hoped she was coming. She came not. He went out, not to listen, but in hopes of meeting her. He heard a low murmur of voices. The tones were those of tenderness—Willoughby then was come to claim her: he was forgiven, and he himself had lost all hope. He returned to the parlour, pale and dejected; his lips trembled; his eyes were still eagerly turned to the door. He heard nothing that was said to him; but unable to remain in his seat, again arose, went out, and returned. At length he heard the door of the parlour open, where Willoughby and Celestina were. He listened attentively; he heard her say, "Good night, dear Willoughby," Willoughby seemed, as he answered, to kiss her hand. Poor Thorold could not bear it; but became more restless—again went to the door—came back—opened it to see if Celestina was coming, then helped the servant to put the chairs round the supper table, without knowing what he was doing, and sat down himself in one next to that which he had placed for her. The supper was announced, but no Celestina appeared. At length the servant brought in the note she had written. Lady Horatia read it, while poor Montague anxiously followed her eyes. She gave it to him across the table: he ran it over, and his solicitude becoming insupportable: he complained of being ill with the headach, and desired permission to go to his lodgings.

The eyes of his father were turned mournfully towards him, as he went out of the room. Mr. Thorold, however, did not speak, but he sighed, and Lady Horatia understood him. As for his wife, though she had been extremely averse to the thoughts of her son's marrying Celestina, while Celestina seemed to be no more than a rejected dependent on the Willoughby family; yet now, since Lady Horatia

Howard had adopted her, she appeared to be altogether as fond of the connection, so easily are minds like her's changed by adventitious circumstances, and influenced by sounds. The notice Lady Horatia took of her, and her daughter Bettenson, delighted and elated her; rending her so disgustingly civil, that only the regard Lady Horatia felt for Mr. Thorold and Montague, would have induced her to support the awkward and offensive adulation of Mrs. Thorold.

The lady of the house was so anxious about Celestina, that only her general politeness, or what is usually termed *l'usage du monde*,[1] enabled her to acquit herself in the usual forms towards her guests.

The supper was short and dull, the conversation being divided between Captain Bettenson, who related a long story of a duel between Jack Marsham, of his regiment, and one Mr. Abbersley, an ensign[2] in the seventeenth; the merits of which nobody understood, and for the event of which, nobody cared; and Mrs. Thorold, who described a dinner and ball given at Exeter, the week before, by a banker of that place, on occasion of his daughter's marriage. With the termination of these dissertations, the supper ended; and Mr. Thorold, who had long been uneasy and impatient, withdrew with his family.

Lady Horatia then hastened to the chamber of Celestina; she was just in bed, but knowing who it was tapped at the door, begged her to come in.

"Well, my dear child," said Lady Horatia, "and what is all this? I am impatient to know." "And I, Madam, impatient to relate, though this evening I am quite unable to undertake it, all the extraordinary circumstances recounted to me by Willoughby."

"You are then related to him?" "No, thank Heaven, I am not. I thank Heaven too, that I am related to you." "To me?" Celestina then gave a brief account of her birth, and the way by which Willoughby had learnt those particulars he had recounted: Lady Horatia embraced her with tears of rapture. Every circumstance she recollected of her brother's visits to France, confirmed the truth of Willoughby's story; and she very perfectly recollected the desponding state of mind in which he went to America, after his last return from thence. His imprisonment for a few weeks in the Bastile, which was imputed to some indiscretion, and that he himself never otherwise explained, exactly corresponded with what the Count de Bellegarde had related. But while every concurrent tes-

---

1 Literally, the custom of the world; accepted social behaviour, good manners.
2 The flag-bearer.

timony evinced the truth of that narrative, Lady Horatia could not account for her brother's never having mentioned his marriage, or his daughter. "Perhaps, however," said she, "he might have reasons for this, which I cannot penetrate. My father was harsh, obstinate, and avaricious; and always expected Ormond would marry as his elder brother did, to aggrandize his family. This he used frequently to be teazed to do, but always refused, and for some years, his disposition retained nothing of its former vivacity, but an ardour for war, in which he seemed, I often told him, desirous rather of death than of promotion: and he answered me more than once, 'that I guessed right, for he was weary of life.' I own, I not unfrequently suspected, that some unfortunate attachment had so shaded his natural gay and vigorous mind, with gloomy depression. I have told him so, and he has replied, 'that whatever might have been the case, he had no attachment then.'"

At length, as Celestina extremely needed repose, Lady Horatia left her, reflecting, with infinite delight, on the kindness she had shewn her, as an orphan and a stranger, while she had, in fact, been protecting the daughter of her beloved brother. With pleasure too she now thought of Willoughby, since Celestina's happiness was to be restored by her union with him. But poor Montague Thorold, dejected and in despair, relinquishing all those charming hopes, which, with more pity than prudence, she had herself encouraged him to cherish, presented himself to her imagination, and greatly abated the satisfaction, with which she thought of the approaching felicity of Willoughby and her niece.

She determined, however, to mitigate, as much as she could, the force of this cruel blow, and early the next morning, while Celestina was walking with the happy and enraptured Willoughby, she sent for the elder Mr. Thorold, and related to him all she had learned from Celestina the evening before.

"I now blame myself, my good friend," said she, "for the part I have taken, but who could foresee this? Yet, I own, I fear the consequences, and heartily wish I had never given so many opportunities to your son, of contemplating those perfections of mind and person, which he will never, I fear, be able to forget."

Mr. Thorold knew too well that this observation was just, and dreaded, lest the loss even of reason itself should be the consequence of Celestina's marriage. He returned home, however, immediately, to relate to Montague the probability there was, that this event would immediately happen. But, however tenderly he communicated such fatal intelligence, he found his son more affected by it, than even his paternal fears had represented.

A silent and heavy despondence took possession of him. He neither complained of, nor reproached any one, but persisted in saying, that he would see Celestina, take a last leave of her, and then try to reconcile himself to his fate.

But in his manner of saying this, there was something more distressing to his father, than he would have felt from the wildest ravings of despair. He entreated him to relinquish his project of seeing Celestina. "Why should you see her, Montague," said he; "to what purpose? You own, that while Willoughby was in question, you entertained no hope. That Celestina has never afforded you any since; but that in spite of her assurances that she could never feel a second attachment, that you have persevered, and *taken* that hope which she refused to give. You have no one, therefore, to blame; and if you have sought pain, you must learn to bear it. But after all that has passed, I cannot consent to your inflicting it on Celestina, or hazarding the possibility of giving uneasiness to her husband."

"Husband!" cried Montague Thorold. "He is not her husband yet, but if he were, can my humble adoration offend him, when I mean to bid her an everlasting adieu? She will console my sick heart by tender pity, she will bid me be at peace, and I may try then to obey her. The sound of her voice is to me so soothing, that if she does not refuse it, I must hear it once more speak to me in accents of kindness."

Mr. Thorold, finding every thing he could say to dissuade Montague from indulging this unhappy inclination quite ineffectual, became extremely uneasy; and dreaded, lest some alarming consequences should arise from an interview, which he thought Willoughby could not approve, even if it were reasonable or proper in his son to ask it.

But Willoughby, now perfectly secure of the affections of Celestina, was too generous, and too noble-minded, not to feel pity for his unfortunate rival. His own happiness, great as it was, would have been more complete, if he could have believed Montague Thorold less unhappy. "Would to Heaven," said he, as he spoke of him to Celestina, "would to Heaven that he could see Anzoletta, and transfer to her that affection, which, while it is fixed on you, can serve only to render him miserable." Celestina joined most cordially in this wish. "He deserves to be happy, I believe," said she; "and the desire you express to see him so, is worthy of the heart of my Willoughby."

But however liberal and reasonable Willoughby was in regard to a competitor, from whom, though he had suffered much, he had now nothing to fear; he was not so patient under any circumstance that was likely to impede his union with Celestina. All that she or

Lady Horatia could urge to him on the propriety and necessity of a short delay, for preparations and forms, he treated as ridiculous, and so vehemently insisted on the necessity of fulfilling the promise he had made to the Count de Bellegarde, at parting with him, to return to him immediately with Celestina as his wife, that their opposition was to little purpose. So totally engrossed, however, had Willoughby been by his fears lest Celestina might be lost to him, that he did not even know whether he had a house to take her to. But, as with him, all places were alike to her, he sent an express that morning to Cathcart, informing him, that he should be at Exeter the next day with Celestina, desiring him to meet him there with Jessy, and to go with them to Alvestone, if Alvestone was yet in his possession.

He dispatched another messenger to London for a special licence to be married at Alvestone, or Exeter, and obviating every remaining scruple, he prevailed on Celestina to set out with him that evening for the latter place, with the consent of Lady Horatia, who promised to follow them in a few days.

The distance was so short, that though it was late in the day, after Willoughby's arrival at Exmouth, before this was determined upon, they were at Exeter by seven in the evening; and in an hour afterwards, Cathcart and Jessy arrived also.

Cathcart not only informed Willoughby that his estate was still his, but put into his hands those letters that brought the intelligence of that acquisition of fortune which came by the death of Lord Castlenorth. The satisfaction of this intelligence, the pleasure of meeting Cathcart and Jessy, who were overwhelmed with joy to see them, the certainty of returning together to a place they both so fondly loved, seemed to complete the happiness of the long divided lovers. Early the next morning they reached Alvestone, where, in the absence of Mr. Thorold, his curate joined the hands of Willoughby and Celestina, above eighteen months after that period, when they believed themselves separated for ever.

In three days Lady Horatia arrived at Alvestone; and the additional pleasure her company gave them, was checked only by the account she gave of the situation of Montague Thorold, who not having been allowed to see Celestina, the time of whose departure from Exmouth had been industriously concealed from him, had sunk into such a state of despondence, as made his father tremble for his reason, if not for his life.

For Vavasour too, whom Willoughby had always loved, he could not help feeling concern. He knew not whither to direct to him; but from all the accounts he was able to gain, he feared that all the good qualities of his heart and understanding were obscured, if not destroyed, by the dissolute style of life into which he had plunged with such avidity, since their last parting. He endeavoured, however, to counteract the impressions of these only alloys to supreme happiness, by reflecting on the probable felicity of other friends, and particularly of the Count of Bellegarde; from whom, ten days after his marriage, he received a letter, informing him, that he was then going to Perpignan; empowered to release his wife from her convent, and that they should go, together with their Anzoletta, immediately to Rochemarte, where he besought Willoughby to rejoin him, with Celestina; promising, that if he would do so, they would return with him, and pass the winter all together in England.

Though it was now late in the year, and though Celestina would have preferred remaining at Alvestone, where she had fixed all her ideas of happiness, yet the wishes of her uncle, and the melancholy satisfaction of visiting the place where her mother had lived, and where she died a victim to parental harshness, and maternal grief; together with the inclination Willoughby showed to gratify the Count, and introduce his wife to him and Anzoletta, determined her to make no objection to their immediate departure. There was, indeed, no time to lose; as the winter was so near. Lady Horatia too, who awaited impatiently an interview with Monsieur de Bellegarde, though she had not health to undertake such a journey, hastened them as much as possible; and in something less than a month after Willoughby called Celestina his, he presented her, at Rochemarte, to her uncle de Bellegarde, to Jacquelina, and Anzoletta. To the two former she appeared the precious representative of their two beloved and regretted friends; the tender recollection of whom, added to her own merit, made her to him an object almost of adoration; while Anzoletta loved her as a sister, to whom she became more tenderly attached, from taste and affection, than even that near tie of blood alone could have attached her.

With what melancholy pleasure did the Count tie round the neck of Celestina that picture of her mother, which her father, as he was dying, had taken from his own bosom, with an injunction, never to part with it, but to his daughter. And how many tears did Celestina shed, as, leaning on the arm of Willoughby, he pointed out to her the spot, which the Count had shewn him, as the grave of Genevieve. Willoughby kissed those tears away, as they filled her eyes, and bade her turn from the too frequent recollection of the past, to those scenes of future happiness, which love, friendship, and fortune, seemed to be preparing for them.

In the romantic and magnificent scenes round the castle the poetical taste of Celestina was highly gratified. Willoughby took her to the spot where he had been lost in the fortunate night that eventually led him to the residence of the Count of Bellegarde. They visited together the humble cottage of Le Laurier, whose family they loaded with kindness; and traced with her the scenes which were so many years before witness to the clandestine marriages of Genevieve and Jacquelina.

Winter, however, put an end to these excursions in the mountains; and the Count de Bellegarde, having completed the settlement of his affairs, agreed, at the earnest request of Willoughby and Celestina, to go with his wife and daughter to England.

On their journey thither, they met at Paris Captain and Mrs. Cavanaugh. They found the former become a man of the utmost importance, and arrogantly enjoying the splendour of his new situation, in a country where he had appeared in one so very different. Mrs. Cavanaugh seemed to affect being happy, and to disdain all she had relinquished to obtain that happiness her own way. But, from some strange caprice, she now appeared so fond of Willoughby, that had Celestina been liable to jealousy, or had Cavanaugh really cared for his wife, they might both, in her manner, have found sufficient cause of discontent. Mrs. Cavanaugh related to Willoughby all the artifices her mother had used to break off his marriage with Celestina; and when he expressed his wonder that Lady Castlenorth should go to such lengths in an affair in which her interest did not appear to be immediately or particularly concerned, she answered, in her usual sneering way, "If you could know my mother so well as I do—but it is impossible by words to do her justice—you would no longer wonder. Her scheme lay much deeper than you were aware of."

Lady Castlenorth, to console herself for the defection of Captain Cavanaugh, had taken, as her travelling companion, a young Abbé, who, discontented with the prevailing politics of his country, found in her at once an admirer of his person and character, and a strenuous supporter of his aristocratic principles—and, what was yet better than either, he found himself sharing a fortune beyond what he had ever dreamed of possessing. This well assorted pair were at Brussels, and Mrs. Cavanaugh diverted herself with some sarcastic remarks on the Director chosen by her mother, of whom she always spoke with a degree of rancour which made Celestina tremble, while Willoughby shuddered to recollect how near he once was becoming the husband of one who could thus express herself towards her mother.

Captain and Mrs. Cavanaugh were going to Italy. The happy party, who took leave of them, hastened to England, where, on their arrival in London, Lady Horatia joined them, and they were soon fixed at Alvestone, in such perfect felicity as is seldom enjoyed, and still more rarely deserved. The first enquiry of Celestina was for Mr. Thorold and his family. She learned that Captain Thorold was the great friend and favourite of Lady Molyneux, with whom he was gone to Ireland, to the displeasure of his father, who had however no influence over him, and whose disappointment in his eldest son was embittered by the condition into which a hopeless and incurable passion had thrown the youngest.

Celestina, who could not reflect, without great pain, on the unhappiness with which the days of her excellent friend were thus over-clouded, took an early opportunity, after her being settled at Alvestone, to desire an interview with the elder Mr. Thorold. He came, and she saw with redoubled concern, the ravage which anxiety had made on his manly face and figure, even in a few short months. He related to her, hardly refraining from tears, the sad change that had happened in the temper and talents of his son. "I have sometimes thought," said he, "that you, my dear Madam, and you only, can rouse him from these alienations of mind. I was averse to his seeing you before you went abroad, but now I wish it: your reason may recon-cile him to his fate, your pity soothe him. Or, be the event of your meeting what it may, no change can, I think, be for the worse." Celestina promised to see him, and his father contrived, with her, the means of procuring this interview; for Montague now shunned every body, and very frequently would not appear, even to his own family.

Celestina did not, however, mean to meet him alone; but to shew him, in Anzoletta, beauty, understanding, and sweetness, with a heart untouched by any passion, and worthy of his. Her generous inten-tions succeeded. Montague Thorold, struck with the resemblance between them, and particularly with the voice of Anzoletta, was soon as passionately attached to her, as a man could be, who had once loved Celestina herself. The Count of Bellegarde, who intend-ed to bestow her, with her ample fortune, on an Englishman, and a Protestant, hesitated not a moment, in consenting to an union which would, he found, make his daughter happy; and eight months after the marriage of Willoughby and Celestina, Anzoletta gave her hand, in the chapel of Alvestone, to Montague Thorold.

Willoughby had now but one wish unfulfilled, for every pecu-niary difficulty, the munificence of the Count de Bellegarde, and the legacy of Lord Castlenorth, had removed; and this one wish was, to see Vavasour such as a reasonable being, with every reasonable means of happiness in his power, ought to be. But in this, as he had no second Anzoletta to give him, and should have feared his want of steadiness if he had, he almost despaired of being gratified.

Vavasour, however, sometimes visited at Alvestone; and, unlike Montague Thorold, he seemed to have conquered his extravagant passion for Celestina, since it was become hopeless. He had, unluckily for him, taken up no permanent affection in its place; but lost his health, and his fortune in pursuits which could not afford him even a temporary possession of that happiness for which he still declared himself to be in search.

When Celestina reflected on his kindness to Mrs. Elphinstone and her children, who now lived in comfort on the provision he had made for them, and on many other generous and noble actions; she could not but lament, with Willoughby, that infelicity of which he continually complained, even amid his wildest and most determined perseverance in the career of dissolute pleasure. But for this source of regret, as there seemed to be no remedy within her power, she did not suffer it to embitter the satisfaction she derived from almost every other friend.

Lady Horatia no longer complained of that tedium which, at the beginning of their acquaintance, seemed to have rendered life indifferent to her. She had now, in Willoughby, and his lovely wife, objects of her affection; and hoped to grow old amidst their children. Monsieur and Madame de Bellegarde, were most acutely sensible of their present happiness, from the poignancy of their past afflictions; and their daughter, the object of their tender solicitude, made the felicity of a worthy man, who deserved the affection she felt for him. In Cathcart and Jessy, Celestina beheld the earliest objects of her beneficence, enjoying all that affluence and mutual tenderness could bestow. And the widowed heart of Mrs. Elphinstone was at ease, not only by her own present independence, but from the assurances Willoughby had given her, of providing for her boys, as soon as they were of the age when they could be put to professions. The elder Mr. Thorold, too, her venerable and respectable friend, was restored to happiness, in contemplating that of his son: and above all, Celestina beheld in Willoughby, the best and most affectionate of husbands, whose whole life was dedicated to the purpose of making her happy, and whose only apprehension seemed to be, that with all he could do, he must fall infinitely short of that degree of merit towards either heaven or earth, which that fortunate being ought to possess, who was blessed with so lovely and perfect a creature as Celestina.

THE END.

Appendix A: The Reception and Influence of Celestina

[Like Smith's previous two novels, *Celestina* was on the whole well received, especially for its landscape description, and influenced Ann Radcliffe and Jane Austen among others. In *Celestina*, George Willoughby's envelopment by the clouds among the Pyrenees was imitated, and surpassed, by Emily's crossing the Alps among the clouds in Radcliffe's *The Mysteries of Udolpho*. Along with other episodes of Smith's narrative, George Willoughby's encounter with Celestina at a London party is revisioned in John Willoughby's encounter with Marianne Dashwood in Austen's *Sense and Sensibility*.]

1. **Mary Wollstonecraft [signed "M."], *The Analytical Review* (August 1791), in *The Works of Mary Wollstonecraft*, Vol. 7, ed. Janet Todd and Marilyn Butler (London: Pickering, 1989) 388–89**

This ingenious writer's invention appears to be inexhaustible; yet we are sorry to observe that it is still fettered by her respect for some popular modern novels. For in the easy, elegant volumes before us, she too frequently, and not very happily, copies, we can scarcely say imitates, some of the distressing encounters and ludicrous embarrassments, which in Evelina,[1] etc. lose their effect by breaking the interest.

As a whole, Mrs Smith's amusing production is certainly very defective and unnatural; but many lucid parts are scattered with negligent grace, and amidst the entanglement of wearisome episodes, interesting scenes, and prospects, seen with a poetic eye, start to relieve the reader, who would turn, knowing something of the human heart, with disgust from the romantic adventures, and artificial passions, that novel reading has suggested to the author. It were

---

1 In *Evelina*, Frances Burney's first novel of 1778, the heroine is frightened at Marybone Gardens by drunken young men and prostitutes. *Celestina* also has scenes resembling the Vauxhall scenes in *Cecilia*, Burney's second novel. This is not necessarily plagiarism, however, since the way different heroes and heroines coped with stock novelistic situations, as well as differing accounts of London resorts that readers themselves knew, formed part of the interest a new novel had to offer.

indeed to be wished, that with Mrs S.'s abilities, she had sufficient courage to think for herself, and not view life through the medium of books: sometimes, it is true, she has given us portraits forcibly sketched from nature; we shall only particularize Mr and Mrs Elphinstone.[1] The extracts that we mean to give, display the easy flow of her style, and render praise superfluous; and after seeing them, it is almost impertinent to add, that there is a degree of sentiment in some of her delicate tints, that steals on the heart, and made us *feel* the exquisite taste of the hand that guided the pencil.

[Here Wollstonecraft quotes the passage where Willoughby is lost among the Pyrenees when the clouds come down, then follows the sound of music down the mountain; and the passage where Willoughby reaches the pavilion near Rochemarte, visits the castle and encounters its owner. She concludes:]

Many of the Scotch landscapes deserved to be selected; but our quotations already far exceed our limits.

2. Anonymous, *The European Magazine and London Review* 20 (October 1791): 278-79

If to delight the imagination by correct and brilliant descriptions of picturesque scenery, and to awaken the finest sympathies of the heart by well-formed representations of soft distress, be a test of excellence in novel-writing, the pen of Mrs. Smith unquestionably deserves the warmest praise. The faculty, indeed, of exhibiting the charms of rural nature, in all their beautiful and sublime varieties, seems peculiar to *the pen*, or rather *the pencil*, of Mrs. Smith; for her descriptions frequently present to the mind more perfect pictures than even painting could express. To afford our readers, however, an opportunity of judging of the truth of this observation, we shall extract, from among a number of others, a short description of part of the Pyrenees ... as a proof of the art with which the authoress touches those springs that are most likely to excite emotions in the heart. To render this extract the more intelligible, it may be necessary to premise, that Willoughby, the lover of Celestina, a supposed orphan, on receiving doubtful

---

1 Wollstonecraft implies that the couple are representative of Smith and her husband.

information that she was probably his own sister, had quitted her abruptly, on the evening preceding the day of their intended nuptials, in order to learn her history and origin from the Principal of a Convent in which she had been placed in the south of France.

[The reviewer then quotes from Volume IV, Chapter VIII, where Willoughby leaves Perpignan and travels into the Pyrenees, observing the rock formations, wildlife, glaciers and vegetation.]

3. Anonymous, *The Critical Review* 3 (November 1791): 318-23

In the modern school of novel-writers, Mrs. Smith holds a very distinguished rank; and, if not the first, she is so near as scarcely to be styled an inferior. Perhaps with miss Burney she may be allowed to hold 'a divided sway;' and, though on some occasions below her sister-queen, yet, from the greater number of her works, she seems to possess a more luxuriant imagination, and a more fertile invention. Let not miss Burney be angry at this remark; or, if she is, we will bear with pleasure the whole weight of her indignation, if it arouses her sleeping genius, and urges her to show that, in these respects also, she can excel.—But this is from the purpose of our present design.

We had lately occasion to observe that Ethelinde, less splendid than Emmeline, shining with a mellower, less obtrusive light, possessed a peculiar merit, and was, on the whole, highly pleasing and interesting. Celestina, perhaps, is of a similar kind, inferior in some respects to Emmeline, and less varied in characters than Ethelinde, yet scarcely less interesting or entertaining. We had heard by accident the outline of the story, and thought it trite and artificial; but we were agreeably disappointed by finding the mystery so artfully involved, that a common incident appeared in a light so important, as to show greater ingenuity than a less hackneyed plot. The conduct of the story, through the whole of the first volume, is excellent; and the doubts which, in her last moments, Mrs. Willoughby left, the obscurity that hung over the story of Celestina, give force and probability to the fabricated tale of Lady Castlenorth. In the second and third volume the error that we observed in Ethelinde is conspicuous: the story hangs suspended. But for the suspense in Celestina some apology occurs. To preserve the heroine from a suspicion of change, and at the same time affording Willoughby room for suspicion to aggravate the distress, it was necessary to bring Montague

Thorold's numerous, quiet attentions forward, and give Celestina's[1] gratitude the appearance of a softer passion. If this was Mrs. Smith's intention she has succeeded very well, by introducing the journey to the Highlands, and judiciously varying the stiller scenes, by the impetuous and irregular wildness of Vavasor. In the last volume, the distress is very artfully raised to its highest pitch; but perhaps the catastrophe is not very dextrously unravelled. An experienced novel-reader knows, that a long story is not introduced at the conclusion of a work without a particular design: the object therefore is too obvious; and it is even more improperly anticipated by noticing the resemblance of Anzoletta to Celestina. If the count de Bellegarde had not been introduced so formally, if Anzoletta had been kept out of sight; if his story had been told with the numerous interruptions of a disturbed mind, the orphan left at the convent of Hieres, and taken by an English lady, abruptly mentioned, the effect would have been much greater. The mind of the reader would have been at once diverted from the attention bestowed on the count to the subject most interesting, and would have returned with an elasticity proportioned to the pain it had felt from being so long absent from the heroine. At present, the whole is foreseen, and curiosity is only excited, by the method of introducing it to Willoughby. The real denouement, or rather the part of it most affecting, is the scene at Exmouth.—We know not how the ladies will forgive Mrs. Smith for making her heroine so very condescending, after such numerous *apparent* insults. Though fastidious criticism may point out these little errors, the feeling heart will, on various occasions, acknowledge our Author's power of affecting it by frequent tears. We have been induced, more than once, to take off our spectacles, and wipe our eyes, "of drops that sacred pity had engendered."[2]

To notice all the characters would be superfluous. The hero and heroine must be of course faultless; and the delicacy of the drawing, the skill in distinguishing the minuter features of the mind, are generally displayed in the subordinate characters. The newest and most striking is that of Vavasor, the friend of Willoughby. He is described as an impetuous young man, the slave of his passions, but not devoid of better principles, of honour, generosity and courage. Though attached to Willoughby, he loves Celestina; and, unused to controul, his violence often breaks out, when Willoughby has left Celestina,

---

1 The original has "Cecilia's."
2 *As You Like It* 2.7.122.

on the supposition that she was his sister; a tale founded on the obscurity of her birth, the fond partiality of his mother, and fabricated by his aunt lady Castlenorth, a woman of obscure family, who wishes to secure Willoughby for her daughter. This union, or rather this contrast of different qualities in Vavasor, rendered the representation of his conduct a difficult task. We watched him with care, for we feared he might prove the fatal rock on which the character of the author would at last be endangered. Sometimes she trembled on the verge of error, sometimes we thought the danger inevitable; but we can add, that she has not once failed, nor has she shunned the most trying situations. Vavasor, in every part, is supported with great skill and propriety. Lord Castlenorth's character has often appeared; he is the man of quality, vain of his titles and his pedigree. Lady Castlenorth, the vain, intriguing, low-bred woman, is well drawn, and accurately supported: her daughter, Miss Fitzhayman, is not particularly discriminated. The first introduction of Cathcart resembles a little the first appearance of Macartney in Evelina; but the resemblance is momentary only. Montague Thorold, the susceptible scholar; the indolent man and listless woman of fashion in Sir Philip and lady Molyneux; the artless affectionate Jessey; the volatile, lively, scheming Elphingston, the dupe of his own sanguine temper and good heart, are very well discriminated. The last character reminded us of Stafford—Has our author copied from her own work, or again taken a portrait—a more pleasing sketch from real life?

The situations are generally interesting, and generally well chosen: the descriptions display all Mrs. Smith's usual fancy and glow of colouring. The sonnets are pleasing and poetical. But, while we admire the park scene at Alvestone, when Celestina, left by Willoughby, and in suspence respecting the cause, leaves the seat to which she had been so much attached, during the life of her patroness, we cannot admit of the propriety of introducing a sonnet. Poetry is the production of a mind that has regained some share of ease; it is incompatible with deep distress, and more so with anxious uneasy suspense. Even that introduced during her residence on the isle of Skie, though elegant and beautiful, speaks rather too warm a language.

We ought not to conclude without adding a few specimens; and, as the descriptive parts are more easily separated from the rest, we shall prefer those sketched in the Hebrides. The following description of the approaching storm is excellent.

[The reviewer then quotes from Volume III, Chapter 1, where the season is changing from summer to autumn, and Celestina sits on the sea-shore mourning Willoughby's loss; and from Chapter 3, where she walks out at night and sees the Northern Lights and the storm coming that will drive Elphinstone's boat on to the rocks. These scenes recall Thomas Stothard's illustration of Sensibility in the fifth edition of Smith's *Elegiac Sonnets*. The reviewer concludes with a long extract from near the end of the novel when Willoughby and Celestina meet again at Exmouth and learn that there is no barrier to their marriage.]

4. From Ann Radcliffe, *The Mysteries of Udolpho* (1794), ed. Bonamy Dobree (Oxford: Oxford UP, 1966) 163-66

[Leaving her lover Valancourt in France, Emily travels south with her aunt and her uncle Montoni, crossing the Alps from France into Italy.]

With what emotions of sublimity, softened by tenderness, did she meet Valancourt in thought, at the customary hour of sun-set, when, wandering among the Alps, she watched the glorious orb sink amid their summits, his last tints die away on their snowy points, and a solemn obscurity steal over the scene! And when the last gleam had faded, she turned her eyes from the west with somewhat of the melancholy regret that is experienced after the departure of a beloved friend; while these lonely feelings were heightened by the spreading gloom, and by the low sounds, heard only when darkness confines attention, which makes the general stillness more impressive—leaves shook by the air, the last sigh of the breeze that lingers after sun-set, or the murmur of distant streams.

During the first days of this journey among the Alps, the scenery exhibited a wonderful mixture of solitude and inhabitation, of cultivation and barrenness. On the edge of tremendous precipices, and within the hollow of the cliffs, below which the clouds often floated, were seen villages, spires, and convent towers; while green pastures and vineyards spread their hues at the feet of perpendicular rocks of marble, or of granite, whose points, tufted with alpine shrubs, or exhibiting only massive crags, rose above each other, till they terminated in the snow-topt mountain, whence the torrent fell, that thundered along the valley.

The snow was not yet melted on the summit of Mount Cenis, over which the travellers passed; but Emily, as she looked upon its clear lake and extended plain, surrounded by broken cliffs, saw, in imagination, the verdant beauty it would exhibit when the snows should be gone, and the shepherds, leading up the midsummer flocks from Piedmont, to pasture on its flowery summit, should add Arcadian figures to Arcadian landscape.

As she descended on the Italian side, the precipices became still more tremendous, and the prospects still more wild and majestic, over which the shifting lights threw all the pomp of colouring. Emily delighted to observe the snowy tops of the mountains under the passing influence of the day, blushing with morning, glowing with the brightness of noon, or just tinted with the purple evening. The haunt of man could now only be discovered by the simple hut of the shepherd and the hunter, or by the rough pine bridge thrown across the torrent, to assist the latter in his chase of the chamois over crags where, but for this vestige of men, it would have been believed only the chamois or the wolf dared to venture. As Emily gazed upon one of these perilous bridges, with the cataract foaming beneath it, some images came to her mind, which she afterwards combined in the following

Storied Sonnet[1]

The weary traveller, who, all night long,
Has climb'd among the Alps' tremendous steeps,
Skirting the pathless precipice, where throng
Wild forms of danger; as he onward creeps,
If, chance, his anxious eye at distance sees
The mountain-shepherd's solitary home,
Peeping from forth the moon-illumined trees,
What sudden transports to his bosom come!
But, if between some hideous chasm yawn,
Where the cleft pine a doubtful bridge displays,
In dreadful silence, on the brink, forlorn
He stands, and views in the faint rays
Far, far below, the torrent's rising surge,
And listens to the wild impetuous roar;
Still eyes the depth, still shudders on the verge,
Fears to return, nor dares to venture o'er.
Desperate, at length the tottering plank he tries,
His weak steps slide, he shrieks, he sinks—he dies!

---

1   A sonnet with a narrative.

Emily, often as she travelled among the clouds, watched in silent awe their billowy surges rolling below; sometimes, wholly closing upon the scene, they appeared like a world of chaos, and, at others, spreading thinly, they opened and admitted partial catches of the landscape—the torrent, whose astounding roar had never failed, tumbling down the rocky chasm, huge cliffs white with snow, or the dark summits of the pine forests, that stretched midway down the mountains. But who may describe her rapture, when, having passed through a sea of vapour, she caught a first view of Italy; when, from the ridge of one of those tremendous precipices that hang upon Mount Cenis and guard the entrance of that enchanting country, she looked down through the lower clouds, and, as they floated away, saw the grassy vales of Piedmont at her feet, and, beyond, the plains of Lombardy extending to the farthest distance, at which appeared, on the faint horizon, the doubtful towers of Turin?

The solitary grandeur of the objects that immediately surrounded her, the mountain-region towering above, the deep precipices that fell beneath, the waving blackness of the forests of pine and oak, which skirted their feet, or hung within their recesses, the headlong torrents that, dashing among their cliffs, sometimes appeared like a cloud of mist, at others like a sheet of ice—these were features that received a higher character of sublimity from the reposing beauty of the Italian landscape below, stretching to the wide horizon, where the same melting blue tint seemed to unite earth and sky.

Madame Montoni only shuddered as she looked down precipices near whose edge the chairmen trotted lightly and swiftly, almost, as the chamois bounded, and from which Emily too recoiled; but with her fears were mingled such various emotions of delight, such admiration, astonishment and awe, as she had never experienced before.

Meanwhile the carriers, having come to a landing-place, stopped to rest, and the travellers being seated on the point of a cliff, Montoni and Cavigni renewed a dispute concerning Hannibal's passage over the Alps, Montoni contending that he entered Italy by way of Mount Cenis, and Cavigni, that he passed over Mount St. Bernard. The subject brought to Emily's imagination the disasters he had suffered in this bold and perilous adventure. She saw his vast armies winding among the defiles, and over the tremendous cliffs of the mountains, which at night were lighted up by his fires, or by the torches which he caused to be carried while he pursued his indefatigable march. In the eye of fancy, she perceived the gleam of arms through the duskiness of night, the glitter of spears and helmets, and the banners floating dimly on the twilight; while now and then the blast of a distant trumpet echoed along the defile, and the signal was answered by a momentary clash of arms. She looked with horror upon the mountaineers, perched on the higher cliffs, assailing the troops below with the broken fragments of the mountain; on soldiers and elephants tumbling headlong down the lower precipices; and, as she listened to the rebounding rocks, that followed their fall, the terrors of fancy yielded to those of reality, and she shuddered to behold herself on the dizzy height, whence she had pictured the descent of others.

5. From Jane Austen, *Sense and Sensibility* (1811), in *The Novels of Jane Austen*, Vol. 1, ed. R.W. Chapman (Oxford: Clarendon, 1933) 175–78

[*Sense and Sensibility* was published in 1811 but begun in the 1790s, then revised. In Devonshire, the impoverished seventeen-year-old Marianne Dashwood falls deeply in love with a romantic stranger, John Willoughby, who seems to return her feelings, but he leaves Devonshire suddenly without proposing to her, and she hears no more from him. When she goes to London with her elder sister Elinor, she sees him again at a party to which the sisters are chaperoned by their relation Lady Middleton.]

They arrived in due time at the place of destination, and as soon as the string of carriages before them would allow, alighted, ascended the stairs, heard their names announced from one landing-place to another in an audible voice, and entered a room splendidly lit up, quite full of company, and insufferably hot. When they had paid their tribute of politeness by curtsying to the lady of the house, they were permitted to mingle in the croud, and take their share of the heat and inconvenience to which their arrival must necessarily add. After some time spent in saying little and doing less, Lady Middleton sat down to Cassino,[1] and as Marianne was not in spirits for moving about, she and Elinor luckily succeeding to chairs, placed themselves at no great distance from the table.

They had not remained in this manner long, before Elinor

---

1   A card game where eleven points constituted a win, in which the ten of diamonds (great cass) counted as two points and the two of spades (little cass) counted as one.

perceived Willoughby, standing within a few yards of them, in earnest conversation with a very fashionable-looking young woman. She soon caught his eye, and he immediately bowed, but without attempting to speak to her, or to approach Marianne, though he could not but see her; and then continued his discourse with the same lady. Elinor turned involuntarily to Marianne, to see whether it could be unobserved by her. At that moment she first perceived him, and her whole countenance glowing with sudden delight, she would have moved towards him instantly, had not her sister caught hold of her.

"Good heavens!" she exclaimed, "he is there—he is there—Oh! Why does he not look at me? Why cannot I speak to him?"

"Pray, pray be composed," cried Elinor, "and do not betray everything you feel to every body present. Perhaps he has not observed you yet."

This however was more than she could believe herself; and to be composed at such a moment was not only beyond the reach of Marianne, it was beyond her wish. She sat in an agony of impatience, which affected every feature.

At last he turned round again, and regarded them both; she started up, and pronouncing his name in a tone of affection, held out her hand to him. He approached, and addressing himself rather to Elinor than Marianne, as if wishing to avoid her eye, and determined not to observe her attitude, inquired in a hurried manner after Mrs Dashwood, and asked how long they had been in town. Elinor was robbed of all presence of mind by such an address, and was unable to say a word. But the feelings of her sister were instantly expressed. Her face was crimsoned over, and she exclaimed in a voice of the greatest emotion, "Good God! Willoughby, what is the meaning of this? Have you not received my letters? Will you not shake hands with me?"

He could not then avoid it, but her touch seemed painful, and he held her hand only for a moment. During all this time, he was evidently struggling for composure. Elinor watched his countenance and saw its expression becoming more tranquil. After a moment's pause, he spoke with calmness.

"I did myself the honour of calling in Berkeley-street last Tuesday, and very much regretted that I was not fortunate enough to find yourselves and Mrs Jennings at home. My card was not lost, I hope?"

"But have you not received my notes?" cried Marianne in the wildest anxiety. "Here is some mistake I am sure—some dreadful mistake. What can be the meaning of it? Tell me, Willoughby, for heaven's sake tell me, what is the matter?"

He made no reply; his complexion changed and all his embarrassment returned; but as if, on catching the eye of the young lady with whom he had been previously talking, he felt the necessity of instant exertion, he recovered himself again, and after saying, "Yes, I had the pleasure of receiving the information of your arrival in town, which you were so good as to send me," turned away hastily with a slight bow and joined his friend.

Marianne, now looking dreadfully white, and unable to stand, sunk into her chair, and Elinor, expecting every moment to see her faint, tried to screen her from the observation of others, while reviving her with lavender water.

"Go to him, Elinor," she cried, as soon as she could speak, "and force him to come to me. Tell him I must see him again—must speak to him instantly.—I cannot rest—I shall not have a moment's peace till this is explained—some dreadful misapprehension or other.—Oh go to him this moment."

"How can that be done? No, my dearest Marianne, you must wait. This is not a place for explanations. Wait only till tomorrow."

With difficulty however could she prevent her from following him herself; and to persuade her to check her agitation, to wait, at least, with the appearance of composure, till she might speak to him with more privacy and more effect, was impossible; for Marianne continued to give way in a low voice to the misery of her feelings, by exclamations of wretchedness. In a short time Elinor saw Willoughby quit the room by the door towards the staircase, and telling Marianne that he was gone, urged the impossibility of speaking to him again that evening, as a fresh argument to her to be calm. She instantly begged her sister would intreat Lady Middleton to take them home, as she was too miserable to stay a minute longer.

Lady Middleton, though in the middle of a rubber, on being informed that Marianne was unwell, was too polite to object for a moment to her wish of going away, and making over her cards to a friend, they departed as soon as the carriage could be found.

Appendix B: The Political Context

[Unrest in France from 1788 onward, the meeting of the Estates-General and creation of a National Assembly in May and June 1789, and especially the storming of the Bastille on 14 July 1789, sparked off widespread debate in England. The published sermon of the Unitarian clergyman Richard Price—friend of Benjamin Franklin and mentor of Wollstonecraft—alarmed traditionalists. Edmund Burke was the most eloquent; his *Reflections on the Revolution in France* was influential. However, in 1790 and 1791, many English people welcomed the Revolution as a possible model for Europe. Tom Paine, a supporter of the American War of Independence, was one of Burke's strongest opponents, reaching a wide readership in his *Rights of Man*. But by 1791 the Revolution was proving difficult to reconcile with persistent feudal and religious loyalties, as the *Patriote François* passage shows.]

1. **Reverend Richard Price, "A Discourse on the Love of Our Country" (4 November 1789), in *Political Writings of Richard Price*, ed. D.O. Thomas (Cambridge: Cambridge UP, 1991) 191-92, 195-96**

[This sermon was delivered on 4 November 1789, and published shortly afterwards.]

But the most important instance of the imperfect state in which the Revolution[1] left our constitution, is the inequality of our representation.[2] I think, indeed, this defect in our constitution is so gross and

---

1 Price refers to the English "Glorious Revolution" of 1688, which bloodlessly deposed the Catholic monarch James II, replacing him with his daughter Mary and her husband William of Orange, Protestants who undertook to rule with the consent of Parliament. Price's sermon was addressed to a society that met to celebrate the anniversary of that event.
2 At this time the right to vote for a Member of Parliament was limited to men with a minimum property qualification which was usually, in the country, a rateable value of two pounds per annum, in other words, men of at least middle class status. In urban boroughs the qualification varied greatly. Overall, a fraction of men had the franchise, since most did not own sufficiently valuable housing or land. Voting rights could be sold,

[continued on page 556]

so palpable, as to make it excellent chiefly in form and theory. You should remember that a representation in the legislature of a kingdom is the basis of constitutional liberty in it, and of all legitimate government; and that without it a government is nothing but an usurpation. When the representation is fair and equal, and at the same time vested with such powers as our House of Commons possesses, a kingdom may be said to govern itself, and consequently to possess a true liberty. When the representation is partial, a kingdom possesses liberty only partially; and if extremely partial, it only gives a semblance of liberty; but if not only extremely partial, but corruptly chosen, and under corrupt influence after being chosen, it becomes a nuisance, and produces the worst of all forms of government—a government by corruption—a government carried on and supported by spreading venality and profligacy through a kingdom. May heaven preserve this kingdom from a calamity so dreadful! It is the point of depravity to which abuses under such a government as ours naturally tend, and the last stage of national unhappiness. We are, at present, I hope, at a great distance from it. But it cannot be pretended that there are no advances towards it....

What an eventful period is this! I am thankful that I have lived to see it; and I could almost say, *Lord now lettest thou thy servant depart in peace, for mine eyes have seen thy salvation.*[1] I have lived to see a diffusion of knowledge, which has undermined superstition and error— I have lived to see the rights of men better understood than ever; and nations panting for liberty, which seemed to have lost the idea of it.—I have lived to see thirty millions of people, indignant and resolute, spurning at slavery, and demanding liberty with an irresistible voice; their king led in triumph, and an arbitrary monarch surren-

---

and votes had to be cast publicly. There was also a property qualification for MPs, and most were owners of estates, or successful merchants or lawyers. Members of the House of Commons had less influence on public affairs than the non-elected members of the House of Lords. Thus the interests of a great proportion of citizens were unrepresented in Parliament.

1 Known as the Nunc Dimittis, the prayer comes from Simeon's words on Christ's presentation in the Temple, Luke 2.29-32, beginning: "Lord, now lettest thou thy servant depart in peace, according to thy word, for mine eyes have seen thy salvation." Already in ill health, Price died eighteen months after delivering this sermon. For Dissenters especially, reform of social injustice was seen as an aspect of religious practice.

dering himself to his subjects.—After sharing in the benefits of one Revolution, I have been spared to be a witness to two other Revolutions,[1] both glorious.—And now methinks, I see the ardour for liberty catching and spreading; a general amendment beginning in human affairs; the dominion of kings changed for the dominion of laws, and the dominion of priests giving way to the dominion of reason and conscience.

Be encouraged all ye friends of freedom, and writers in its defence! The times are auspicious. Your labours have not been in vain. Behold kingdoms, admonished by you, starting from sleep, breaking their fetters, and claiming justice from their oppressors! Behold, the light you have struck out, after setting America free, reflected to France, and there kindled into a blaze that lays despotism in ashes, and warms and illuminates Europe!

Tremble all ye oppressors of the world! Take warning all ye supporters of slavish governments and slavish hierarchies! Call no more (absurdly and wickedly) reformation innovation. You cannot now hold the world in darkness. Struggle no longer against increasing light and liberality. Restore to mankind their rights and consent to the correction of abuses, before they and you are destroyed together.

2. From Edmund Burke, *Reflections on the Revolution in France, and on the Proceedings in Certain Societies in London Relative to that Event* (1 November 1790), in *Select Works*, Vol. 2, ed. E.J. Payne (Oxford: Clarendon, 1887) 39–42

This policy [inheritance of property and titles] appears to me to be the result of profound reflection; or rather the happy effect of following nature, which is wisdom without reflection, and above it. A spirit of innovation is generally the result of a selfish temper and confined views. People will not look forward to posterity who will not look backward to their ancestors. Besides, the people of England well know, that the idea of inheritance furnishes a sure principle of conservation, and a sure principle of transmission; without at all excluding a principle of improvement. It leaves acquisition free, but it secures what it acquires. Whatever advantages are obtained by a state proceeding on these maxims, are locked fast as in a sort of

---

1   The American and the French.

family settlement; grasped as in a kind of mortmain[1] forever. By a constitutional policy,[2] working after the pattern of nature, we [the British] receive, we hold, we transmit our government and our privileges, in the same manner in which we enjoy and transmit our property and our lives. The institutions of policy, the goods of fortune, the gifts of Providence, are handed down, to us and from us, in the same course and order. Our political system is placed in a just correspondence and symmetry with the order of the world, and with the mode of existence decreed to a permanent body composed of transitory parts; wherein, by the disposition of a stupendous wisdom, moulding together the mysterious incorporation of the human race, the whole, at one time, is never old, or middle-aged, or young, but in a condition of unchangeable constancy moves on through the varied tenour of perpetual decay, fall, renovation and progression. Thus, by preserving the method of nature in the conduct of the state, in what we improve we are never wholly new; in what we retain we are never wholly obsolete. By adhering in this manner and on those principles to our forefathers, we are guided not by the superstition of antiquarians, but by the spirit of philosophical analogy. In this choice of inheritance we have given to our frame of polity[3] the image of a relation in blood; binding up the constitution of our country with our dearest domestic ties; adopting our fundamental laws into the bosom of our family affections; keeping inseparable, and cherishing with the warmth of all their combined and mutually reflected charities, our state, our hearths, our sepulchres and our altars.

Through the same plan of a conformity to nature in our artificial[4] institutions, and by calling in the aid of her unerring and powerful instincts, to fortify the fallible and feeble contrivances of our reason, we have derived several other, and those no small benefits, from considering our liberties[5] in the light of an inheritance. Always

---

1 The condition of lands or buildings held inalienably by an institution such as the monarchy or the church, which therefore cannot be sold or willed out of the direct line of inheritance by those who enjoy possession. Burke uses mortmain as a metaphor for stability.
2 Government; administration.
3 The meanings of this word are very close to the meanings of "policy," but Burke perhaps intends by it something more comprehensive, "nation" or "commonwealth" rather than merely "administration."
4 Social or man-made.
5 Rights.

acting as if in the presence of canonized[1] forefathers, the spirit of freedom, leading in itself to misrule and excess, is tempered with an awful gravity. This idea of a liberal descent inspires us with a sense of habitual native dignity, which prevents that upstart insolence almost inevitably adhering to and disgracing those who are the first acquirers of any distinction. By this means our liberty becomes a noble freedom. It carries an imposing and majestic aspect. It has a pedigree and illustrating ancestors. It has its bearings and ensigns armorials.[2] It has its gallery of portraits; its monumental inscriptions; its records, evidences and titles. We procure reverence to our civil institutions on the principle upon which nature teaches us to revere individual men; on account of their age; and on account of those from whom they are descended. All your sophisters[3] cannot produce any thing better to preserve a rational and manly freedom than the course that we have pursued, who have chosen our nature rather than our speculations, our breasts rather than our inventions, for the great conservatories and magazines[4] of our rights and privileges.

You [the French] might, if you pleased, have profited of our example, and have given to your recovered freedom[5] a correspondent dignity. Your privileges, though discontinued, were not lost to memory. Your constitution, it is true, while you were out of possession, suffered waste and dilapidation; but you possessed in some parts the walls, and in all the foundations of a noble and venerable castle. You might have repaired those walls; you might have built on those old foundations. Your constitution was suspended before it was perfected; but you had the elements of a constitution very nearly as good as could be wished. In your old states you possessed that variety of parts corresponding with the various descriptions[6] of which your community was happily composed; you had all that combination, and all that opposition of interests, you had that action and counteraction which, in the natural and in the political world, from

---

1   Revered; held as saintly in the national memory.
2   Coats of arms.
3   Clever but specious reasoners. Burke probably refers to the '*philosophes*,' the French radical thinkers such as Jean-Jacques Rousseau and Voltaire who were credited with advancing the ideas that led to the Revolution.
4   Safes and storehouses.
5   Burke implies that the French monarchy, which was absolute, that is, ruling without need of consent from a French Parliament, needed curbing, but that reform is now going too far..
6   Types or classes of people.

the reciprocal struggle of discordant powers, draws out the harmony of the universe. These opposed and conflicting interests, which you considered as so great a blemish in your old and in our present constitution, interpose a salutary check to all precipitate resolutions. They render deliberation a matter not of choice, but of necessity; they make all change a subject of *compromise*, which naturally begets moderation; they produce *temperaments*,[1] preventing the sore evil of harsh, crude, unqualified reformations; and rendering all the headlong exertions of arbitrary power, in the few or in the many, forever impracticable. Through that diversity of members and interests, general liberty had as many securities as there were separate views in the several orders; whilst by pressing down the whole with the weight of a real monarchy, the separate parts would have been prevented from warping and starting from their allotted places.

You had all these advantages in your antient states; but you chose to act as if you had never been moulded into civil society, and had every thing to begin anew. You began ill, because you began by despising every thing that belonged to you. You set up your trade without a capital. If the last generations of your country appeared without much lustre in your eyes, you might have passed them by, and derived your claims from a more early race of ancestors. Under a pious predilection for those ancestors, your imaginations would have realised in them a standard of virtue and of wisdom, beyond the vulgar practice of the hour: and you would have risen with the example to whose imitation you aspired. Respecting your forefathers, you would have been taught to respect yourselves. You would not have chosen to consider the French as a people of yesterday, as a nation of low-born servile wretches until the emancipating year of 1789. In order to furnish, at the expense of your honour, an excuse for your apologists here for several enormities of yours, you would not have been content to be represented as a gang of Maroon slaves,[2] suddenly broke loose from the house of bondage, and therefore to be pardoned for your abuse of the liberty to which you were not accustomed and ill fitted.

---

1   The adjustments made to a musical instrument so as to fit the scale for use in all keys, a metaphor for harmony among all the various groups and classes in a nation.
2   Escaped West Indian slaves, or their descendants.

3. From Mary Wollstonecraft, *A Vindication of the Rights of Men, in a Letter to the Right Honourable Edmund Burke; occasioned by his "Reflections on the Revolution in France"* (December 1790), in *The Works of Mary Wollstonecraft*, Vol. 5, ed. Janet Todd and Marilyn Butler (London: Pickering, 1989) 41–42

But, in settling a constitution that involved the happiness of millions, that stretch beyond the computation of science, it was, perhaps, necessary to have a higher model in view than the *imagined* virtues of their forefathers, and wise to deduce their respect for themselves from the only legitimate source, respect for justice. Why was it a duty to repair an ancient castle, built in barbarous ages, of Gothic materials? Or why were they obliged to rake amongst heterogeneous ruins; or rebuild old walls, whose foundations could scarcely be explored, when a simple structure might be raised on the foundation of experience, the only valuable inheritance our forefathers can bequeath? But of this bequest we can make little use till we have gained a stock of our own; and, even then, the inherited experience would rather serve as lighthouses, to warn us against dangerous rocks or sand-banks, than as posts that stand at every turning, to point out the right road.

Nor was it absolutely necessary that they should be diffident of themselves when they could not discern, or were not at the trouble to seek for themselves the *almost obliterated* constitution of their ancestors. They should first have been convinced that our constitution was not only the best modern, but the best possible one; and that our social compact was the surest foundation of all the *possible* liberty a mass of men could enjoy, that the human understanding could form. They should have been certain that our representation answered all the purposes of representation; and that an established inequality of rank and property secured the liberty of the whole community, instead of rendering it a sounding epithet of subjection, when applied to the nation at large. They should have had the same respect for our House of Commons that you, vauntingly, intrude on us, though your conduct throughout life has spoken a very different language.

That the British House of Commons is filled with everything illustrious in rank, in descent, in hereditary and acquired opulence, may be true,—but that it contains every thing respectable in talents, in military, civil, naval, and political distinction, is very problematical. Arguing from natural causes, the very contrary would appear to the speculatist to be the fact; and let experience say whether these speculations are built on sure ground.

It is true that you lay great stress on the effects produced by the idea of a liberal descent; but from the conduct of men of rank, men of discernment would rather be led to conclude, that this idea obliterated instead of inspiring native dignity, and substituted a factitious pride that disemboweled the man. The liberty of the rich has its ensigns armorial to puff the individual out with unsubstantial honours; but where are blazoned the struggles of virtuous poverty? Who, indeed, would dare to blazon what would blur the pompous monumental inscription, and make us view with horror, as monsters in human shape, the superb gallery of portraits thus set in battle array.

But to examine the subject more closely. Is it among the list of possibilities that a man of rank and fortune *can* have received a good education? How can he discover that he is a man, when all his wants are instantly supplied, and invention is never sharpened by necessity? Will he labour, for every thing valuable must be the fruit of laborious exertions, to attain knowledge and virtue, in order to merit the affection of his equals, when the flattering attention of sycophants is a more luxurious cordial?

Health can only be secured by temperance; but is it easy to persuade a man to live on plain food even to recover his health, who has been accustomed to fare sumptuously every day? Can a man relish the simple food of friendship, who has been habitually pampered by flattery? And when the blood boils, and the senses meet allurements on every side, will knowledge be pursued on account of its abstract beauty? No; it is well known that talents are only to be unfolded by industry, and that we must have made some advances, led by an inferior motive, before we discover that they are their own reward.

But *full blown* talents *may*, according to your system, be hereditary, and as independent of ripening judgment, as the inbred feelings that, rising above reason, naturally guard Englishmen from error. Noble franchises! What a grovelling mind must that man have, who can pardon his step-dame nature for not having made him at least a lord!

4. From Thomas Paine, *The Rights of Man; being an Answer to Mr. Burke's Attack on the French Revolution, Part 1* (February 1791), ed. Henry Collins (Harmondsworth: Penguin, 1969) 70-71, 109

... there are many points of view in which this revolution can be considered. When despotism has established itself for ages in a country, as in France, it is not in the person of the king only that it resides.

It has the appearance of being so in show, and in nominal authority; but it is not so in practice, and in fact. It has its standard everywhere. Every office and department has its despotism, founded upon custom and usage. Every place has its Bastille, and every Bastille its despot. The original hereditary despotism resident in the person of the King, divides and subdivides itself into a thousand shapes and forms, till at last the whole of it is acted by deputation. This was the case in France; and against this species of despotism, proceeding on through an endless labyrinth of office till the source of it is scarcely perceptible, there is no mode of redress. It strengthens itself by assuming the appearance of duty, and tyrannizes under the pretence of obeying.

When a man reflects on the condition which France was in from the nature of her government, he will see other causes for revolt than those which immediately connect themselves with the person or character of Louis XVI. There were, if I may so express it, a thousand despotisms to be reformed in France, which had grown up under the hereditary despotism of the monarchy, and became so rooted as to be in real measure independent of it. Between the monarchy, the parliament, and the church, there was a *rivalship* of despotism, besides the feudal despotism operating locally, and the ministerial despotism operating everywhere. But Mr. Burke, by considering the King as the only possible object of a revolt, speaks as if France was a village, in which everything that passed must be known to its commanding officer, and no oppression could be acted but what he could immediately control. Mr. Burke might have been in the Bastille his whole life, as well under Louis XVI as Louis XIV and neither the one nor the other have known that such a man as Mr. Burke existed. The despotic principles of the government were the same in both reigns, though the dispositions of the men were as remote as tyranny and benevolence.[1]

What Mr. Burke considers a reproach to the French Revolution, (that of bringing it forward under a reign more mild than the preceding one), is one of its highest honours. The revolutions that have taken place in other European countries, have been excited by personal hatred. The rage was against the man, and he became the victim. But, in the instance of France, we see a revolution generated in

---

1 Louis XIV, the "Sun King," was considered profligate and despotic, while Louis XVI was aware of the need for reform in France and was beginning to move towards it when overtaken by events.

the rational contemplation of the rights of man, and distinguishing from the beginning between persons and principles....

One of the continual choruses of Mr. Burke's book is, 'Church and State.' He does not mean some one particular church, or some one particular state, but any church and state; and he uses the term as a general figure to hold forth the political doctrine of always uniting the church with the state in every country, and he censures the National Assembly for not having done this in France.—Let us bestow a few thoughts on this subject.

All religions are in their nature kind and benign, and united with principles of morality. They could not have made proselytes at first, by professing anything that was vicious, cruel, persecuting, or immoral. Like everything else, they had their beginning; and they proceeded by persuasion, exhortation, and example. How then is it that they lose their native mildness, and become morose and intolerant?

It proceeds from the connexion which Mr. Burke recommends. By engendering the church with the state, a sort of mule-animal, capable only of destroying, and not of breeding up, is produced, called *The Church established by Law*. It is a stranger, even from its birth, to any parent mother on which it is begotten, and whom in time it kicks out and destroys.

The inquisition[1] in Spain does not proceed from the religion originally professed, but from this mule-animal, engendered between the church and the state. The burnings in Smithfield[2] proceeded from the same heterogeneous production; and it was the regeneration of this strange animal in England afterwards, that renewed rancour and irreligion among the inhabitants, and that drove the people called Quakers and Dissenters to America. Persecution is not an original feature in any religion; but it is always the strongly marked feature of all law-religions, or religions established by law. Take away the law-establishment, and every religion reassumes its original benignity. In America, a Catholic priest is a good citizen, a good

---

1   The roots of the Inquisition went back a long way, but it was formally instituted by Pope Gregory IX in 1231 to punish heretics and unbelievers. It grew and spread through the later Middle Ages and was particularly oppressive in Spain under the authority of the Dominican monk, Thomas de Torquemada, in the 1480s. In France the last heretic was executed in 1766.

2   The London site for the burning of Protestants by the Catholic Queen, Mary Tudor, who reintroduced the Inquisition to England after a period of Protestantism.

character, and a good neighbour; an Episcopalian Minister is of the same description: and this proceeds, independently of the men, from there being no law-establishment in America.

5. Joseph Antoine Cerruti,[1] *Feuille Villageoise*,[2] reprinted in *Le Patriote François*,[3] ed. Jean-Pierre Brissot de Warville, No. 18 (8 January 1791): 30-31 [my translation]

[Jean-Pierre Brissot introduces Cerruti's attempt to reassure committed Catholics that the previous July's decree enforcing reorganisation of the church and the November decree ordering clerical recognition of the new regime by oath is not an attack on religion itself.]

On the National Reorganisation of the Clergy.

It seems to us so important to reassure nervous souls on this subject, to enlighten those in genuine error, and to confirm our enlightened readers in their adherence to the new decrees, that we think we should transcribe in its entirety for the general instruction, the excellent commentary that M. Cerruti has made in his *Feuille Villageoise*. We especially ask pious people to read it carefully:

My dear fellow citizens, you know that there are a great number of clergy in this country crying sacrilege against the National Assembly and its decrees. To listen to them one would think that those willing to take the oath to maintain and faithfully uphold the national reorganisation of the clergy are heretics and cowards. That would be true, if this law actually did attack religion. That's what I want to consider with you; as it would be a double misfortune to be mistrusted in this world and damned in the next.

First, don't you believe, from the fuss that's made about it, that this national reorganisation is an irreligious change, a heathen revolution

---

1 Joseph-Antoine Joachim Cerruti (1738-92) was a former Jesuit turned journalist, and a friend of Mirabeau, one of the early leaders of the Revolution.
2 *Countrywide News*.
3 *The French Patriot*, appearing just after the outbreak of the Revolution, was edited and largely written by Jean-Pierre Brissot, a Girondin, who wanted government by general consent and by the rule of law.

in the faith and in religious observance? Don't you believe that the sacraments will be abolished, that mass or at least evening prayers will be forbidden? Nothing of the sort. Not one religious procession, not one celebration of the mass will be abolished. This new law is not about religion, but about priests; it's not even about saying what priests should do, but only about the structure of their organisation.

Judges are not justice; similarly, priests are not religion. The people's representatives who regulate all the administrative districts ought also to regulate those clergy in charge of religious observance; they ought to decide in what places, and through what persons, ecclesiastical functions are fulfilled. That is all they are doing.

First, who are the clergy now? The bishops, the parish priests, the priests-in-charge, the curates, are in fact all the working ecclesiastics who are recognised. The new constitution does not recognise others. The religious offices of canons, private chaplains, priors, abbots, and all sorts of beneficiaries enjoying multiple livings are now abolished along with their useless and luxurious sinecures. The reorganisation of the church and the oath of loyalty only concern us, as citizens, and those priests who serve the nation and who earn their pay. What is the point then of all the redundant clergy defending themselves against a law which is not made for them, and against an oath which nobody will ask them to take? Where is the irreligion of saying to a hornet, you will no longer take the name of a worker bee? Yet it's the hornets of the church who are buzzing the loudest.

The regime now forbids every church and every clergyman to recognise the authority of any foreign bishop or any foreign power.[1] That is merely forbidding a Frenchman to be a German or an Italian. How can something so reasonable be impious?

Just as the regime has appointed revolutionary courts of justice and inaugurated new departments,[2] it will regulate ecclesiastical livings and ecclesiastical councils. Each department will form a diocese and have a bishop appointed. There will be no more archbishops, but ten new regional divisions (*arrondissements*) will be created, under the name of '*metropolitains*'; there will be ten principal bishops, each of whom will serve in one of them with a number of ordinary bishops, and exercise their higher authority over whatever pertains to ecclesiastical matters. Thus, far from being in the least an attack on the

---

1 This was, of course, an attack on the supremacy of the Pope and intolerable to most priests.
2 The main administrative divisions of France.

church, the law leaves the church her own internal and specific law-enforcement. That is the prerogative of ecclesiastical government. And here is the way that government will be set up.

The bishop will name twelve or fifteen vicars who will help him in his ministry. Furthermore, he will have at his seat a seminary, destined for the instruction of young clergy, of which the directors will be priests. This numerous clergy will add to the grandeur of ceremonial, enhance the splendour of religious observance and maintain the dignity of the bishopric. All the vicars of the bishop will together form his council or synod; for he will have the government of his diocese. But he will not make any other decisions on the advice of the synod, except in his Visits,[1] when he has the right to make provisional rulings. The judgements of the diocesan synods may be amended by the metropolitan synod, even when taken by the bishop's vicars. Finally the law requires that the cathedral church of each parish will be at one and the same time the parish church and the seat of the bishopric, and that church will have no regular officiating clergyman other than the bishop.

Such is the church's reorganisation. I estimate that instead of five hundred bishops, France will have only eighty three. But do you think a country would be all the more Catholic the more mitres and croziers there were? It's true, our bishops will no longer be able to gild their carriages, maintain a retinue of servants and cover their tables with unhealthy and expensive meat; since their pay is only twenty thousand livres in the largest districts, and only twelve in the others. It's true too that a bishop will no longer be able to parade his crozier and his ambition around in the middle of the excesses of a court; for all ecclesiastics in active employment will be obliged to remain in residence in their dioceses. Also, indeed, a bishop will no longer be able to insult with his arrogance the humility of a poor pastor; he will no longer be able to contradict him arbitrarily, to send him to a seminary or even send him into exile or embastille him with a restraining order.[2] But is that really a Catholic privilege? And does religion absolutely require that a bishop be a tyrant over his clergy, and the Grand Turk of his diocese? I can believe that our courtesan bishops are appalled at the thought of living like hermits

---

1 To the ecclesiastical courts, to settle ecclesiastical grievances and problems.

2 Cause him to be imprisoned for an indeterminate time by a *lettre de cachet* or restraining order.

and evangelicals. No doubt they find this new law alarming, and so they may; but that they should find it heretical and impious, that I can't understand at all.

Appendix C: Charlotte Smith's Life

[Smith's day-to-day life as a writer struggling to support—at this time—seven children (two older sons were in India with the East India company by now) is vividly documented in her letters. When she wrote *Celestina* she was living in Brighton, where she met fashionable people on holiday and radical thinkers who supported the Revolution. Her sister Catherine Dorset's memoir, though affectionate, shows a certain disapproval of this phase of Smith's life, but it also records her determination and hard work.]

1. **Charlotte Smith to Dr Joseph Warton, Brighthelmstone [Brighton], 31 August 1791, in** *The Letters of Charlotte Smith*, **ed. Judith Stanton (Indiana: Indiana UP, 2003)**

[Warton was a clergyman, brother of the laureate, and principal of Winchester College where her son Lionel was at school.]

Dear *Sir*,

When your very obliging letter reach'd this place, I was in London, or I should not have so long delay'd my acknowledgements. The information you have the goodness to give me about Lionel[1] gives me some concern, but if his slow progress is solely owing to inattention and not to a defect of ability, I trust that as he acquires more reason, this neglect will no longer exist. In better hands he cannot be, and I own I have fondly flatter'd myself that one of my boys at least would be found to answer the kind wishes my partial friends have express'd for them, merely because they were mine. Lionel has a very good heart and is really I believe solicitous to gratify me in this hope, for, when on my taking leave of him on Wednesday, I represented to him the complaint that you and Mr Goddard[2] had made of his want of proper exertion, he defended himself some

---

1 Her seventh surviving child.
2 William Goddard (1757-1845), Lionel's housemaster, was Second Master at Winchester, and unlike Warton a disciplinarian. He became Head in 1796, and in his philosophy of education influenced the Victorian reformist Head of Rugby, Thomas Arnold, who was also one of his pupils.

time on the ground that he was sometimes put upon a task utterly beyond his powers: I told him that he should consider that as a compliment from his Masters, & that instead of shrinking from such a task because it was difficult, he should exert his powers to conquer it & justify the opinion of his capacity which from their assigning him difficulties to execute, it was evident they entertain'd. At length he burst into tears and said, "Good God, Mamma, what a worthless fellow you must think me, if you believe I do not do all I can at my books, when I know that you have so much uneasiness and trouble for us all and that you pay so much money for me." There was *heart* in this which pleased me very much, and I am persuaded that my son will finally be a comfort to me & no discredit to those who are so good as to be interested in his education.[1]

I am afraid your partial opinion in regard to the powers I possess has received no additional strength from the entire perusal of Celestina, for many parts of it are weak, and none, except perhaps the close, of equal strength to the former Novels. I wrote it indeed under much oppression of Spirit from the long and frequently hopeless difficulties in which my children's affairs continue to be involved—Difficulties that my time and perseverance as well as the generous interposition of many friends of superior abilities in the Law have been vainly applied to conquer. For two three or four years, the burthen of so large a family whose support depends entirely upon me (while I have not even the interest of my own fortune to do it with) might be undertaken in the hope that at the end of that period their property might be restored to them. But when above seven years have

---

1   See *Dictionary of National Biography*. Lionel was thirteen at this time. He was expelled at fifteen in the summer of 1793 for leading a school rebellion, and that October brought his elder brother Charles home from field hospital in France after Charles' leg was amputated following a battle between French patriots and the Bedfordshires near Dunkirk. Smith wanted Lionel to become a clergyman, but he refused and joined the army, where his career was active and distinguished. Initially based in Canada, then in the West Indies, he took maroons to Sierra Leone and was badly injured on the Northwest frontier of India, but recovered and in 1809 led a successful expedition against pirates in the Persian Gulf. He was appointed Governor of Barbados, then of Jamaica when slaves throughout the Empire were officially freed in the 1830s, coming into conflict with the white West Indian planters because of his sympathy with the black population. He rose to the rank of Colonel of the 40th Regiment, and was made a baronet when Victoria became Queen in 1837.

pass'd in such circumstances, that sickness of the Soul which arises from Hope long delay'd[1] will inevitably be felt. The worn out pen falls from the tired hand, and the real calamities of life press too heavily to allow of the power of evading them by fictitious detail. Another year however is coming when I must by the same motives be compelled to a renewal of the same sort of task. A Tragedy would most undoubtedly be more honourable and more profitable. But it still appears to me an effort in which I should fail. And it is a very discouraging circumstance that the taste of the Modern World is not for Tragedy. I cannot however but be highly flatter'd by having in my favor an opinion to which I must ever pay the highest deference. And should I be able to obtain, what indeed I have little reason to expect, an interval of quiet and peace of mind this Winter, I will make an attempt such as your encouragement should urge me to make.

I am, Dear Sir, with great esteem,
     Your most oblig'd, and obed't ser't,
          Charlotte Smith

My Friend Mrs O'Niell[2] of Shanes Castle in Ireland is coming over in October to place her two sons at a Public School. They have been educated under Private Tutors. And she represents the eldest who is about fourteen as a very good Scholar. So good indeed that it is rather to introduce him into the World than to carry him forward in learning that Mr O'Niell intends to put him to one of the great English seminaries. He is himself much disposed to fix on Winchester. Mrs O'Niell rather prefers Eaton [sic], but they have with their usual partial opinion of my judgement referred the matter to my decision, whose wishes and best opinion certainly must be

---

1   Proverbs 13.12: "... hope deferred maketh the heart sick."
2   Henrietta Boyle was the daughter of Charles Boyle, Viscount Dungarvon, granddaughter of John Boyle, Earl of Orrery, a friend of Pope and Swift, of whom he wrote a memoir. On her mother's side she was the granddaughter of Henry Hoare, aesthete and antiquarian, the owner and designer (with William Kent) of the gardens at Stourhead. She married John O'Neill (the accepted spelling) of Shanes Castle, descendant of a dynasty that ruled Ireland until 1603. Stourhead was within a day's drive of the Smiths' Lys Farm, but it is not known when the two women became friends. Smith was nine years older.

for Winton.[1] My Friend, who was a Boyle, and whose talents are very extraordinary, is willing to believe that her eldest son inherits all the splendid abilities of her family. He is heir to a very Princely fortune, & these two boys are the only descendants in a direct line from Shan O'Niell.[2] Of course the debates where to place them are long and frequent. In her last Letter which I received the moment I had concluded this, she desires me to let her know what Young Men of rank are at Winchester and whether there are any objections made by the Masters to a private Tutor & a private boarding House? I could wish to be able to answer these questions from the best Authority. Yet do not mean to give you the trouble of writing about them. Only, as I have not at this moment the draft for Lionel's bills ready for Mr Goddard, nor time to write, I take the liberty of mentioning it here, and as my answer to Ireland is immediately required, wd intreat you to commission some person to furnish me by the Post's return with this information. Here is a Postscript longer than any letter.

2. Charlotte Smith to Mrs Thomas Lowes, Brighton, 27 November 1791, in *The Letters of Charlotte Smith*, ed. Judith Stanton (Indiana: Indiana UP, 2003)

Madam,

I intended to have done myself the honor of waiting on you yesterday, but Augusta told me at one period of the morning that you were out, and I was afterwards detained by Mr Wordsworth[3] (whom I could not take leave of, till he embarked) till it was too late to have

---

1 A contraction of the Latin for Winchester; another form is Wykeham.
2 Shane O'Neill, second Earl of Tyrone (?1530-67), ruled much of Ireland, refusing to acknowledge the authority of Elizabeth I and her representative, Sir Henry Sidney.
3 Wordsworth, then 21, was distantly related to Smith. He first read her *Elegiac Sonnets and Other Essays* while still a schoolboy at Hawkshead, and they shared an enthusiasm for the current reforms in France, which Wordsworth was on his way to see for himself. Smith gave him letters of introduction to Helen Maria Williams and probably to Jacques-Pierre Brissot. During that visit, they discussed Smith's poetry, and she showed him some of her work in manuscript. He had not yet published anything.

the pleasure I intended. This morning I am summoned to London & thus deprived of an opportunity of paying my respects to you here, but if you will allow me to wait on you in Town where I am likely to be in a fortnight, I will avail myself of that permission with great pleasure. My abode during that time is at 'The Hon'ble Mrs O'Niells, Henrietta Street, Cavendish Square' where, if you favor me with intelligence of your being at your London residence, I will take the earliest opportunity of assuring you personally that I am,

Madam
   Your most obed't and oblig ser't
     Charlotte Smith

[Mrs Lowes' husband Thomas Lowes added later, at the bottom of the letter:]

I saw a great deal of Charlotte Smith one Autumn [i.e., 1791] at Brighthelmstone & bating[1] a democratic twist (which I think detestable in a woman) I liked her well enough for some time, but she disgusted me completely, on the acc't arriving of the Massacre of the Swiss Guards at the Tuileries[2] by saying that they richly deserved it: I observed that they did merely their duty, & if they had not done what they did they w'd have been guilty of Treason & that I thought they deserved the pity of every person who reasoned and felt properly. After this I never w'd see Charlotte, but she and Mrs L[owes] sometimes met. Not long after this Augusta (mentioned in the note) married an emigrant French nobleman,[3] & I understand that her style both in her conversation and novels altered considerably. TL.

---

1 Excepting.
2 The French royal family had been prisoners almost from the start of the Revolution; their failed attempt to escape and a threatened invasion by Austria and Prussia to re-establish the old regime identified them as traitors, from the patriot point of view. On 10 August 1792 the patriots, including *gards français* and civilians, entered the Tuileries and killed about 600 of Louis XVI's personal guard, his Swiss, as they were called, although only about a third were Swiss nationals. It was the last day of even nominal monarchy for Louis.
3 Smith's second daughter, Anna Augusta, married Alexandre de Foville, a French aristocrat *émigré*, in July 1793. Smith's attitude to events in France was changing before the marriage, however.

3. Catherine (Turner) Dorset, "Charlotte Smith" from Walter Scott's *Lives of the Novelists* (1821), in Scott's *Miscellaneous Prose Works*, Vol. 4 (Edinburgh: Cadell, 1834) 20–42, 47–58

Charlotte Smith

This tribute of affection to one of our most distinguished Novelists, is not from the pen of the Author of the Biographical Sketches in the preceding volume [that is, the writer of this note, Walter Scott]. It was communicated to him in the most obliging manner by Mrs Dorset, sister of the subject of the Memoir, and not more nearly allied to her in blood than in genius.[1] The publication which it is intended to accompany, being discontinued,[2] as mentioned in the preliminary advertisement, vol iii., the following paper was never before in print. But, on collecting the Biographical Sketches in the present form, the author [Walter Scott] could not abandon the claim so kindly permitted him, to add this to the number.

———

Mrs Charlotte Smith was the eldest daughter of Nicholas Turner, Esq. of Stoke House, in Surrey, and of Bignor Park, in Sussex, by Anna Towers, his first wife. She was born in King Street, St James's Square, on the 4th May, 1749. Before she had accomplished her fourth year, she was deprived of a mother as distinguished by her superior understanding as for her uncommon beauty. The charge of her education devolved on her aunt, who, with unwearied zeal devoted the best years of her life to the duty she had undertaken. Accomplishments seem to have been the objects of her ambition, and no time was lost in their attainment; for her little charge was attended by an eminent dancing-master, and when such a mere infant, that she was taught her first steps on a dining-table. She never recollected the time when she could not read, and was in the habit of reading every book that fell in her way, even before she went to school, which was at six years old, when she was placed in a respectable establishment in Chichester.

---

1 Dorset was a successful author of children's books, and contributed some poems to her sister's *Conversations, Introducing Poetry*.
2 There is evidently some delay between the writing of Dorset's Memoir and its publication in Scott's work.

Her father, desirous of cultivating her talent for drawing, engaged George Smith, a celebrated artist, and a native and inhabitant of that city, to instruct her in the rudiments of his art, and she was taken two or three times a week to his house to receive lessons.

From Chichester she was removed in her eighth year to a school at Kensington, at that time in high repute, and where the daughters of the most distinguished families received their education. Of her progress at that time I am tempted to give the following account from the pen of a lady who was her schoolfellow:—

"In answer to your enquiry whether Mrs Smith was during our intimacy at school superior to other young persons of her age, my recollection enables me to tell you, that she excelled most of us in writing and drawing. She was reckoned by far the finest dancer, and was always brought forward for exhibition whenever company was assembled to see our performances; and she would have excelled all her competitors had her application borne any proportion to her talents; but she was always thought *too great a genius* to study. She had a great taste for music, and a correct ear, but never applied it with sufficient steadiness to ensure success. But however she might be inferior to others in some points, she was far above them in intellect, and the general improvement of the mind. She had read more than anyone in the school, and was continually composing verses; she was considered romantic;[1] and though I was not of that turn myself, I neither loved nor admired her the less for it. In my opinion, her ideas were always original, full of wit and imagination, and her conversation singularly pleasing; and so I have continued to think, since a greater intercourse with society, and a more perfect knowledge of the world, has better qualified me to estimate her character."

In this seminary it was the custom for the pupils to perform both French and English plays, and on these occasions the talents of Miss Turner were always put in requisition, as she was considered by far the best actress of the little troop; and her theatrical talents were much applauded both at school and at home, where she was freely called on to exhibit her powers to whatever company happened to be assembled at her father's. I do not think this early, and certainly injudicious display, produced the unfavourable effect upon her man-

1   Imaginative, fanciful.

ners which might have been expected. It induced no boldness or undue confidence, for she was rather of a retiring than an assuming disposition; yet it probably had an unfavourable influence on her character, and contributed to foster that romantic turn of mind that distinguished her even in childhood. It was at this school she first began to compose verses;—they were shown and praised among the friends of the family as proofs of early genius; but none of them have been preserved. I have an imperfect recollection that the subject of one of these early effusions was the death of General Wolfe,[1] when she must have been in her tenth year—though she speaks in one of her works of earlier compositions.

At twelve years of age she quitted school, and her father, then residing part of the year in London, engaged masters to attend her at home; but very little advantage could have been derived from their instructions, for she was at that early age introduced into society, frequented all public places with her family, and her appearance and manners were so much beyond her years, that at fourteen her father received proposals for her from a gentleman of suitable station and fortune, which were rejected on account of her extreme youth. Happy would it have been if reasons of such weight had continued in force a few years longer!

With so many objects to engage her attention, and the late hours incident to a life of dissipation, her studies (if they could be so called) were not prosecuted with any degree of diligence or success. As if foreseeing how short would be the period of her youthful pleasures, she pursued them with the avidity natural to her lively character; and though her father was sometimes disposed to check her love of dissipation, he always suffered himself to be disarmed by a few sighs or tears. Her passion for books continued unabated, though her reading was indiscriminate, and chiefly confined to poetry and works of fiction. At this time she sent several of her compositions to the editors of the Lady's Magazine, unknown to her aunt.

It is evident that Mrs Smith's education, though very expensive, was superficial, and not calculated to give her any peculiar advantages. Her father's unbounded indulgence, and that of an aunt who almost idolized her, were ill calculated to prepare her mind to contend with the calamities of her future life; she often regretted that her attention had not been directed to more useful reading, and the

---

1   General James Wolfe was killed in the capture of Quebec in 1759, during the Seven Years' War with France.

study of languages. If she had any advantage over other young persons, it must have been in the society of her father, who was himself not only an elegant poet and a scholar, but a man of infinite wit and imagination, and it was scarce possible to live with him without catching some sparks of that brilliant fire which enlivened his conversation, and rendered him one of the most delightful of companions of his time; yet when the short period is considered between the time of her leaving school and her marriage, and that his convivial talents made his company so generally courted, that he had little leisure to bestow on his family, she must rather have inherited than acquired the playful wit and humour which distinguished her conversation.

In 1764, Mr Turner decided on a second marriage, and his sister-in-law contemplated this event with the most painful apprehension for that being who was the object of her dearest affections, and who, having hitherto been indulged in every wish, and almost in every caprice, was ill prepared to submit to the control of a mother-in-law.[1] Without reflecting that the evil she anticipated with such feelings of dread would probably exist only for a short period (for it was unlikely a young lady who was so generally admired would long remain single,) she endeavoured, with a precipitation she had afterwards great reason to deplore, to establish her by an advantageous marriage, and her wishes were seconded by some officious and short-sighted relations, by whose means her introduction to Mr Smith was contrived, after having properly prepared him, by their representations and excessive praises, to fall in love at first sight. The event justified their expectations—he did fall in love; care was taken to keep alive the flame by frequent parties of pleasure, and meetings at public places. He was just twenty-one, and she was not quite fifteen, when the acquaintance first took place, and it was no difficult task to talk her into an acquiescence with her aunt's views. Proposals were made, and accepted without much enquiry into the young man's disposition or character. He was the second son of Richard Smith, Esq. a West India Merchant, and Director of the East India Company, who had realized a large fortune, and his younger son had been admitted a partner in his lucrative business. The choice of his son did not at first meet with his approbation—he would have been better pleased had he selected the daughter of some thrifty citizen, than that of a gay man of the world, whom he concluded (and just-

---

1   Stepmother.

ly enough) had not been brought up in those economical habits which he considered the most desirable qualifications in a wife; but the first interview with his future daughter-in-law overcame all his objections, and he ever after distinguished her with peculiar affection and partiality. This ill-assorted marriage took place on the 23d of February, 1765;[1] and after a residence of some months with Mr Smith's sister, the widow of William Berney, Esq., Mrs Smith found herself established in the house that had been prepared for her in one of the narrowest and most dirty lanes in the city. It was a large, dull habitation, into which the cheering beams of the sun had never penetrated. It was impossible to enter it without experiencing a chilling sensation and depression of spirits, which induced a longing desire to escape from its gloom, which not all the taste and expense with which it had been fitted up could dispel.

The habits to which its young mistress was expected to conform, were little congenial to her feelings. The lower part of the house was appropriated to the business, and hither the elder Mr Smith came every morning to superintend his commercial concerns, and usually took his chocolate in his daughter-in-law's dressing room. He was a worthy, and even a good-natured man, but he had mixed very little in general society—his ideas were confined, and his manners and habits were not calculated to inspire affection, however he might be entitled to respect and gratitude. He had no taste for literature, and the elegant amusements of his daughter-in-law appeared to him as so many sources of expense, and as encroachments on time, which he thought should be exclusively dedicated to domestic occupations; he had a quiet, petulant way of speaking, and a pair of keen black eyes, which, darting from under his bushy black eyebrows the most

---

1 Scott supplies footnotes to Dorset's account. He quotes Richard Phillips: "From this fatal marriage, which had been brought about by the officiousness of friends, and which was by no means the effect of attachment on either side, as both appeared to have been talked into it by the intermeddling of those short-sighted politicians, all the future misfortunes of the subject of these pages originated. An uncle of Mrs Smith was the only person of the family who seemed to have common sense on this occasion: he saw and foretold all the misery that would infallibly result from a union in which neither the habits nor the temper of the parties had been considered; when neither were arrived at a time of life to ascertain or appreciate the character of the other; but most unfortunately he had not sufficient weight to induce those, who saw this connection in a different view, to break off the negotiation."—*The Monthly Magazine*.

inquisitive of glances, always appeared to be in search of something to find fault with; so that whenever the creaking of his "youthful shoes well saved"[1] gave notice that one of his domiciliary visits was about to take place, it was the signal for hurrying away whatever was likely to be the subject of his displeasure, or the object of his curiosity. If any of her friends or acquaintances happened to call on her, he would examine them with a suspicious curiosity, which usually compelled them to shorten their visits, and took from them the desire of repeating them. His lady, who was at that time in very ill health, exacted the constant attendance of the family, and a more irksome task could hardly have been imposed on a young person.

"I pass almost every day," says Mrs Smith, in a letter to one of her early friends, "with the poor sick old lady,[2] with whom, however, I am no great favourite; somebody has told her I have not been notably[3] brought up, (which I am afraid is true enough,) and she asks me questions which, to say the truth, I am not very well able to answer. There are no women, she says, so well qualified for mistresses of families as the ladies of Barbadoes, whose knowledge of house-wifery she is perpetually contrasting with my ignorance, and, very unfortunately, those subjects on which I am informed, give me very little credit with her; on the contrary, are rather a disadvantage to me; yet I have not seen any of their paragons whom I am at all disposed to envy."

The stately formality of this lady, her tall meagre figure, languid air, and sallow complexion, with the monotonous drawl and pronunciation peculiar to the natives of the West Indies, rendered her one of the most wearisome persons that can be imagined, and I fear her economical lectures had very little attraction for a girl who had never been required to pay much attention to household cares, and were listened to with apathy and disgust. This lady did not live long enough to effect the reformation she was so anxious for; her death, however, produced no great relief from this bondage. Mrs Smith's attendance on her father-in-law was more than ever required, and a heavier duty never fell to the lot of youth and beauty. The poor old man was afflicted with a complication of disorders. From long

---

1 Cf. *As You Like It* 2.7.159-60: "His youthful hose, well saved, a world too wide/ For his shrunk shank."

2 The phrase might suggest that the lady is Richard Smith's second wife, rather than Benjamin's mother, which is confirmed by Mary Hays' account.

3 Practically; with domestic skills.

residence in the West Indies he was so sensible of cold that he shrunk from the slightest breeze—no air was permitted to refresh his apartment, in which he sat in the hottest days of summer wrapped in his red roquelaure,[1] surrounded with all the apparatus of sickness; she was expected to accompany him in his airings, on the dusty turnpike roads, with just enough of the carriage windows let down to admit the smell of brick kilns, or the stagnant green ditches in the environs of Islington.

In the intervals of this recreation she had to assist at the lectures of an old governante,[2] part of whose business it was to lull her master to sleep, by reading devotional books of the most gloomy tendency, with a broad Cumberland accent. Never did religion wear a garb so unalluring as in this house.

The comfort of her own family was not improved by the accession of four or five wild, ungovernable, West Indian boys, (sons of the correspondents of the house,)[3] who, during the Eton and Harrow vacations, were its inmates.

Though she could occasionally give way to the sportiveness of her fancy, and describe these scenes of *ennui*[4] and discomfort in the most humorous manner, yet the aversion she entertained for every thing connected with this period of her life, and its contrast with her previous gay and cheerful habits, seems to have made the deepest impression, and to have reverted to her mind latterly in the most forcible manner; and her feelings are beautifully depicted in her unfinished Poem of *Beachy Head*. The lines are quoted by the elegant author of the *Censura Literaria*.[5]

The following little poem, in which melancholy and humour are not unpleasingly blended, appears, from the feebleness of the handwriting, to have been composed a very short time before her death.

---

1 Dressing-gown.
2 Governess.
3 Sons of British employees stationed abroad.
4 Boredom.
5 Sir Egerton Brydges, who quotes lines 282-378 of "Beachy Head" in his *Censura Literaria, containing Titles, Abstracts and Opinions of Old English Books* (1815). Scott's note: see the first number of the *Censura Literaria*, in which Sir Egerton Brydges has given an elegant and eloquent criticism on Mrs Charlotte Smith's works.

To My Lyre

Such as thou art, my faithful Lyre,
For all the great and wise admire,
Believe me, I would not exchange thee,
Since e'en adversity could never
Thee from my anguished bosom sever
Or time or sorrow e'er estrange thee.

Far from my native fields removed,
From all I valued, all I loved;
By early sorrows soon beset,
Annoyed and wearied past endurance,
With drawbacks, bottomry, insurance,
With samples drawn, and tare, and tret;

With Scrip, and Omnium, and Consols,
With City Feasts and Lord Mayors' Balls,
Scenes that to me no joy afforded;
For all the anxious Sons of Care,
From Bishopsgate to Temple Bar,
To my young eyes seemed gross and sordid.

Proud city dames, with loud shrill clacks,
('The wealth of nations on their backs')[1]
Their clumsy daughters and their nieces,
Good sort of People! And well meaners,
But they could not be my congenors,
For I was of a different species.

Long were thy gentle accents drown'd,
Till from Bow-bells' detested sound
I bore thee far, my darling treasure;
And unrepining left for thee
Both calepash and callipee,[2]
And sought green fields, pure air, and leisure.

---

1   Smith alludes to Adam Smith's book on economics, *An Enquiry into the
    Nature and Causes of the Wealth of Nations* (1776).
2   The meat of the turtle, the former from the part nearest to the upper
    shell or carapace, the latter nearest to the undershell or plastron. Turtle
    was traditionally served at Lord Mayors' and City dinners.

Who that has heard thy silver tones—
Who that the Muse's influence owns,
Can at my fond attachment wonder,
That still my heart should own thy power?
Thou—who has soothed each adverse hour,
So thou and I will never sunder.

In cheerless solitude, bereft
Of youth and health, thou still art left,
When hope and fortune have deceived me;
Thou, far unlike the summer friend,
Did still my falt'ring steps attend,
And with thy plaintive voice relieved me.

And as the time ere long must come
When I lie silent in the tomb,
Thou wilt preserve these mournful pages;
For gentle minds will love my verse,
And Pity shall my strains rehearse,
And tell my name to distant ages.

The death of her first child,[1] which took place when she was confined with her second, had nearly proved fatal to her, from the excess of her affliction.[2] Change of air and scene were recommended, and a small house in the pleasant village of Southgate[3] was engaged for her, and in a few months she regained her health. Hither she retired as much as was in her power, and here she enjoyed more liberty and tranquillity than had hitherto fallen to her lot. Her aunt had for some time ceased to reside with her, and was afterwards

---

1   For records of her children, see the Chronology.
2   Scott quotes Mary Hays: "The disorder that robbed her of this child was of a nature so malignant and infectious, that, of all her household, only herself and her new-born infant escaped it; and that infant, though he survived ten years, suffered so much in this early state of his existence, for want of the care which is then indispensably necessary, that his feeble and declining health embittered with the most cruel solicitude the life of his mother, who loved him with more than ordinary fondness."—*British Public Characters*, vol. iii. 46. In "the care which is then indispensably necessary," Hays probably refers to breast feeding, adversely affected by the shock of the elder child's death.
3   Then outside London, now a suburb.

induced to become the wife of the elder Mr Smith, which, of course, rendered her personal attendance on him unnecessary; and as her husband usually went to London every day, she became mistress of her own time, and was enabled to employ it in the cultivation of her mind. She possessed a considerable collection of books, and read indiscriminately, without having any friend to direct her studies or form her judgment.[1]

The result of her mental improvement was not favourable to her happiness. She began to trace that indefinable restlessness and impatience, of which she had long been conscious without comprehending, to its source, to discriminate characters, to detect ignorance, to compare her own mind with those of the persons by whom she was surrounded.

The consciousness of her own superiority, the mortifying conviction that she was subjected to one so infinitely her inferior, presented itself every day more forcibly to her mind, and she justly considered herself "as a pearl that had been basely thrown away."[2]

"No disadvantage," she observes in one of her letters, "could equal those I sustained; the more my mind expanded, the more I became sensible of personal slavery; the more I improved and cultivated my understanding, the farther I was removed from those with whom I was condemned to pass my life; and the more clearly I saw by those newly-acquired lights the horror of the abyss into which I had unconsciously plunged."

Impressed with this fatal truth, nothing could be more meritorious than the line of conduct she pursued. Whatever were her opinions or her feelings, she confined them to her own bosom, and never to her most confidential friends suffered a complaint or a severe remark to escape her lips.

---

1 Scott quotes Mary Hays: "Mrs Smith, detesting more than ever the residence in the city, and being indeed unable to exist in it, had then a small house at some distance, where, as her husband was a good deal in town, and her sister not always with her, she lived very much alone, occupied solely by her family, now increased to three children. It was then her taste for reading revived, and she had a small library, which was her greatest resource. Her studies, however, did not interfere with the care of her children; she nursed them all herself, and usually read while she rocked the cradle of one, and had, perhaps, another sleeping on her lap."—*British Public Characters*, vol. iii., 46.
2 Cf. *Othello* 5.2.356-57: "Like the base Indian, threw a pearl away/ Richer than all his tribe."

During her residence at Southgate, her family had been considerably increased, and a larger house was become necessary; and it was hoped that by removing nearer to London, Mr Smith would be induced to pay a stricter attention on his business than he had hitherto done; and with this view his father purchased for him a handsome residence in Tottenham,[1] where it was hoped he would retrieve his lost time. But his habits were fixed, he had no turn for business, and could never be prevailed on to bestow more than a small proportion of that time on it, which nevertheless hung so heavy on his hands, that he was obliged to have recourse to a variety of expedients to get rid of it. Hence fancies became occupations, and were followed up with boundless expense, till they were relinquished for some newer fancy equally frivolous and equally costly.

Mrs Smith unfortunately disliked her situation at Tottenham, and the more so, from its having failed in the object proposed. She had little or no society, and her mind languished for want of congenial conversation, and her natural vivacity seemed extinguished by the monotony of her life.

Her father-in-law was in the habit of confiding to her all his anxieties, and frequently employed her pen in matters of business. On one occasion, she was called on to vindicate his character from some illiberal attack, and she acquitted herself of the task in a very able manner. This little tract was published, but not being of any general interest, has not been preserved. The elder Mr Smith has frequently declared, that such was the readiness of her pen, that she could expedite more business in an hour from his dictation, than any one of his clerks could perform in a day: and he even offered her a considerable annual allowance, if she would reside in London and assist him in his business, which he foresaw would be lost to his family after his death. Obvious reasons prevented her acceptance of this proposal, which, singular as it was, affords a strong instance of the compass of her mind, which could adapt itself with equal facility to the charms of literature, and the dry details of commerce.

Mrs Smith had long been endeavouring to obtain her father-in-law's consent to the removal of her family entirely into the country; and such was her influence over him, that she prevailed, in opposition to his better judgment, and in 1774 an estate in Hants, called

---

1   A little east of the City.

Lys Farm,[1] was purchased, and in a new and untried situation, she fondly imagined she could escape from existing evils; but she was soon awakened from her dream of happiness.[2]

In removing her husband from his father's eye, she had taken off the only check which could restrain his conduct, and accordingly he plunged into expenses more serious than any he had hitherto ventured upon. In other respects her situation was improved; and if she had not more actual happiness, she had occasional enjoyment; she had better and more frequent society; she was better appreciated, both on account of her talents and her personal attractions. Though she was at that time the mother of seven children, and had lost much of the lightness of her figure, she was in the meridian of her beauty—

> "In the sober charms and dignity
> Of womanhood, mature, not verging yet
> Upon decay, in gesture like a queen:
> Such inborn and habitual majesty ennobled all her steps."[3]

It was natural that she should take pleasure in society, where she was sure to be well received, and that she should seek, in such dissipation as the neighbourhood afforded, a temporary relief from the unremitting vexations which embittered her domestic hours. In 1776 she lost her best friend in her husband's father, who, if not an

---

1 "Hants" is the abbreviation for the county of Hampshire, in Southern England. Richard Smith already owned Lys Farm, which is beautifully situated, and had been used as a centre for cattle-breeding. Very little of the original building remains; a house on the same site is now a school.

2 Scott quotes Hays: "In consequence of so many cares, and a large establishment, (for Mr Smith launched into farming with more avidity than judgment, and purchased other parcels of land,) her time was so much occupied, that but little leisure was left her for those pursuits she most delighted in. Surrounding circumstances, however, and ill-judged expenses, which she had no power to prevent, rendered her extremely unhappy; and when a few hours of the solitude she had learned to love were allowed her, her thoughts and feelings were expressed in some of those little poems, which she has since called sonnets; but so far were they from being intended for the public eye, that her most intimate friends never saw them till many years afterwards."—*British Public Characters*, vol iii., 47.

3 Robert Southey, "Roderick, the Last of the Goths: a Tragic Poem," Part XVI, "Covadonga," 4109-13.

agreeable person to live with, had many estimable qualities, and had the discernment to appreciate hers. From his death may be dated the long course of calamities which marked her subsequent life. Mr Smith, whether from conceit of his own knowledge of the law, or from the mistaken economy of a narrow mind, that would risk thousands to save a few pounds, thought proper to make his own will. A most voluminous document! Which, from its utter want of perspicuity, from its innumerable incomprehensible and contradictory clauses, no two lawyers ever understood in the same sense. It was a tangled skein, which neither patience nor skill could unravel. He had appointed his widow, his son, and his son's wife, joint executors, intending to restrain his son's power, without excluding him; but the measure defeated itself. The widow, weak and infirm, was easily overruled by cajolery, or some less gentle means; and the appointment of the wife was (as to immediate power) completely nugatory; so that the entire power over the property fell into the hands least fit to be entrusted with it. Endless disputes arose among the parties interested, or rather their agents, for many of Mr Smith's grandchildren were orphans and minors; and, I believe, though Mrs C. Smith considered herself and her children as the victims of these unhappy dissentions, the other branches of the family were more or less sufferers. Besides what was expended in law, and what was wasted by improvidence, the sum of £20,000 was lost to the family, by the old gentleman having suffered himself, with all his caution, to be overreached by his solicitor, who persuaded him to lend that sum to a distressed baronet on mortgage. But the security was bad; and I believe the family never received any compensation. Mrs Smith had long foreseen the storm that was gathering round her, but had no power to avert it. A lucrative contract, which the interest of Mr Robinson[1] (then Secretary to the Treasury, and who had married a sister of Mr B. Smith's) procured for him, warded off the blow for a time, and he went on with his accustomed thoughtlessness. About this time he took an active part in a contested election for the county of Southampton, between Sir Richard Worsley[2] and ———.[3] As the brother-in-law of Mr

---

1   John Robinson, lawyer and politician, married Mary Crowe, Benjamin Smith's stepsister.
2   Sir Richard Worsley (1751-1805) was a traveller and antiquarian, MP for Newport on the Isle of Wight from 1774-84. He was a monarchist and member of the ruling party, a Tory rather than a Whig or reforming candidate.
3   Scott's note: name not recollected.

Robinson, his exertions were of course in favour of the Ministerial candidate. Mrs Smith had not at that time caught the contagion[1] which spread so widely a few years afterwards, and very willingly lent her pen in support of the cause; and among the many efforts which were made on both sides to unite wit with politics, hers were reckoned the most successful; but as she was not known to have been the author of them, her vanity could not have been much gratified.

In the spring of 1777 she lost her eldest son in his eleventh year.[2] His delicate health from his birth had particularly endeared him to his mother, and she felt this affliction in proportion to her extreme affection for him. She had looked to him as a future friend and companion; and it was observed by some of her intimates, that a visible change in her character took place after this event. To divert her mind from this irremediable calamity, and from the contemplation of the many anxieties that oppressed her, she amused herself by composing her first Sonnets, which were never intended for publication. I believe it was the late Bryan Edwards, Esq., author of the History of the West Indies, and some poems of great elegance,[3] who, by his warm and gratifying praises, first gave her an opinion of their merit, to which she had not before considered them entitled, and she was encouraged to add them to her little collection.

The peace of 1782[4] deprived Mr Smith of his contract. The legatees became importunate for the settlement of their various claims, and, wearied by incessant delay, at length took those strong measures which are detailed in the third volume of *Public Characters*.[5] The

---

1   The contagion of liberal and reformist views, Dorset means.
2   Her eldest surviving son, Benjamin Berney Smith.
3   Probably those mentioned in *Celestina* as models for the heroine's sonnet, "O, thou who sleeps't where hazle bands entwine."
4   The end of the American War of Independence: Benjamin's contract had been for supplying provisions to the army.
5   Scott quotes Hays: "On a subject of so much delicacy it would be improper to dwell: those who witnessed Mrs Smith's conduct, both while she apprehended the evils which now overtook her, or while she suffered under them, can alone do her justice, or can judge, at least as far as a single instance goes, whether the mind that feels the enthusiasm of poetry, and can indulge in the visionary regions of romance, is always so enervated as to be unfitted for the more arduous tasks and severe trials of human life. Neither the fears of entering into scenes of calamity, nor of suffering in her health, already weakened, prevented her from partaking

[continued on page 588]

estate in Hampshire was now sold. Mrs Smith never deserted her husband for a moment during the melancholy period of his misfortunes, and perhaps her conduct never was so deserving of admiration as at this time. When suffering from the calamities he had brought on himself, and in which he had inextricably involved her and her childen, she exerted herself with as much zeal and energy as if his conduct had been unexceptionable—made herself mistress of his affairs—submitted to many humiliating applications, and encountered the most unfeeling repulses. Perhaps the severest of her tasks, as well as the most difficult, was that of employing her superior abilities in defending a conduct she could not have approved. To a mind so ingenuous as hers, there could not have been a more painful sacrifice of talents at the shrine of duty. The estates were at length placed in the hands of trustees, and Mr and Mrs Smith were at liberty to return to their house in Sussex, which they had taken when Lys Farm was sold.[1]

---

the lot of her husband, with whom she passed the greater part of seven months in legal confinement, and whose release was at the end of that time obtained chiefly by her indefatigable exertions. But during this seven months some of her hours were passed at the house in Hampshire, which was now sold, under such circumstances as those who, in that sad hour, deserted her, are now as unwilling to hear of as she is to relate them. What were then her sentiments in regard to her summer friends, who so little a time before had courted her acquaintance, and delighted in her company! Of her relations, her brother only never for a moment relaxed in his tenderness and attention towards her, or in such acts of friendship as he had the power of performing towards her husband. It was the experience she acquired, during these seven months, *of the chicanery of law, and the turpitude of many of its professors, that, were it proper to enter into the detail, would fully justify those indignant feelings, which, on various occasions, she has not hesitated to express."*—British Public Characters, vol iii., 48-9.

1 Scott quotes Hays: "After a day of excessive fatigue, which had succeeded to the most cruel solicitudes, Mrs Smith at length experienced the satisfaction (the deed of trust having been signed) of beholding her husband freed from his confinement, and accompanied him immediately into Sussex, where their family remained under the care of their maternal uncle. Her sensations on this occasion are thus described in a letter to a friend: 'It was on the 2d day of July that we commenced our journey. For more than a month I had shared the restraint of my husband in a prison, amidst scenes of misery, of vice, and even of terror. Two attempts had, since my last residence among them, been made by the prisoners to procure their liberation, by blowing up the walls of the house. Throughout

The first edition of the Sonnets was published this year; the circumstances relating to them have already been amply detailed in the volume of the *Public Characters* already referred to; they were dedicated to Mr Hayley,[1] but I believe her personal introduction to him did not take place until some time afterwards. Mr Smith found it expedient to retire to the Continent, and as he was entirely ignorant of the French language, his wife accompanied him to Dieppe, and having made such arrangements for his comfort as the time admitted of, she returned in the same packet which had taken her over, with the hope of surmounting the fresh difficulties which had arisen; but this not being practicable, she soon rejoined him with all her family. Mr Smith had in the mean time been induced, with his usual indiscretion, to engage a large chateau[2] twelve Norman miles[3] from Dieppe. The inconvenience of the situation, so far from a market—the dreariness of the house, extremely out of repair—the excessive scarcity of fuel, and the almost brutal manners of the peasantry in that insulated part of the country, rendered her situation most melancholy. Yet here she was condemned to pass the peculiarly severe winter of 1783;[4] and here, without proper assistance or accommodation, she was confined with her youngest son; and, in

---

the night appointed for this enterprise, I remained dressed, watching at the window, and expecting every moment to witness contention and bloodshed, or perhaps be overwhelmed by the projected explosion. After such scenes and such apprehensions, how deliciously soothing to my wearied spirits was the soft pure air of the summer's morning, breathing over the dewy grass, as (having slept one night on the road) we passed over the heaths of Surrey! My native hills at length burst upon my view. I beheld once more the fields where I had passed my happiest days, and, amidst the perfumed turf with which one of those fields was strewn, perceived with delight the beloved group, from whom I had been so long divided, and for whose fate my affections were ever anxious. The transports of this meeting were too much for my exhausted spirits. After all my sufferings, I began to hope I might taste content, or experience at least a respite from calamity."—*British Public Characters*, vol. iii., 53.

1 Smith's friend and patron William Hayley, poet, playwright, biographer and essayist.
2 A chateau could mean a large country house as well as a castle.
3 The original Roman measure of 1000 paces has varied at different times and places; a Norman mile at this time has been computed at 2000 yards.
4 This is a misprint or an error: Smith was in France from October 1784 to Spring, 1785.

spite of her forebodings that she should not survive the birth of her child, she recovered her health more speedily than on former occasions, when surrounded with every sort of indulgence and comfort.[1]

A few days afterwards, she was astonished by the entrance of a procession of priests into her bedroom, who, in defiance of her intreaties and tears, forcibly carried off the infant to be baptised in the parish church, though the snow was deep on the ground, and the cold intense. As not one of her children had ever been exposed to the external air at so early a period of their existence, she concluded her boy could never survive this cruel act of the authority of the church: he was, however, soon restored to her, without having sustained the slightest ill consequence. It was during her seclusion in this forlorn residence, and when she had no power of selection, that, for the amusement of herself and some friends, (exiles like herself,) she translated the novel called *Manon L'Escaut*, written about fifty years before by the Abbe Prevost; and soon after her return to England, which took place in the summer of 1785, (for she had been convinced of the fallacy of her plan of living cheaply in France,) this translation was published, and she was severely censured for her choice as immoral; but I believe it was the want of the power of selection which induced her to employ a mind qualified for worthier purposes on such a work.

[Omitted here is Dorset's long discussion of the attack on Smith's translation of *Manon L'Escaut* by the scholar and editor of Shakespeare, George Steevens, the withdrawal of the novel by Smith's publisher, Thomas Cadell, at Smith's own suggestion, as it might damage his reputation, and Dorset's comments on Steevens. Though Dorset does not mention it, Cadell issued Smith's *Manon Lescaut* [sic] anonymously and in one volume in the following year, 1786.]

Mrs Smith was at this time employed in translating some of the most remarkable trials, from *Les Causes Celebres*,[2] which were published under the title of *The Romance of Real Life*, which, with the great difficulty attending it, helped to complete her disgust, and determined her to rely in future on her own resources, and to employ herself in original composition.

---

1 Scott's note: see *Public Characters*.
2 By Gayot (or as Smith spelt it, Guyot) de Pitaval, and first published in 1735.

In the spring of 1786, her eldest son was appointed to a writer-ship[1] in Bengal, and though he went out with more than usual advantages, it was a severe trial to a most tender and anxious mother; but an affliction yet more poignant awaited her in the same year, when her second son[2] was carried off, after only thirty-six hours' illness, by a fever of the most malignant nature, which, spreading through the family, reduced several of the children and servants to the brink of the grave; but by her personal exertions they were restored, and she escaped the infection.

They were at this time residing at Woolbeding House, near Midhurst, which they had engaged after their return from France in 1785; but Mrs Smith was not destined to be stationary in any residence. An increasing incompatibility of temper, which had rendered her union a source of misery for twenty-three[3] years, determined her on separating from her husband; and, after an ineffectual appeal to one of the members of the family to assist her in the adjustments of the terms, but with the entire approbation of her most dispassionate and judicious friends, she withdrew from Woolbeding House, accompanied by all her children, some of them of an age to judge for themselves, and who all decided on following the fortunes of their mother.

She settled in a small house in the environs of Chichester, and her husband, soon afterwards finding himself involved in fresh difficulties, again retired to the Continent, after having made some ineffectual efforts to induce her to return to him. They sometimes met after this period, and constantly corresponded, Mrs Smith never relaxing in her endeavours to afford him every assistance, and bring the family affairs to a final arrangement; but they never afterward resided together. Though the decisive step she had taken in quitting her husband's house, was perhaps, under the then existing circumstances, unavoidable, yet I have been told, the manner was injudicious, and that she should have insisted on previous legal arrangements, and secured to herself the enjoyment of her own fortune. That she was liable to much unmerited censure, was a matter of course; but those who knew the *dessous des cartes*[4] could only regret that the measure had not been adopted years before.

---

1   A "writer" is one who keeps the records, in the army, in the navy, in a large business or legal department, or here, in the Bengal branch of the East India Company.
2   Braithwaite.
3   In fact 22.
4   Literally, the undersides of playing cards, concealed from the other players; the real truth.

The summer of 1787 saw Mrs Smith established at her cottage at Wyhe,[1] pursuing her literary occupations with much assiduity and delight, supplying to her children the duties of both parents. It was here that she began and completed, in the space of eight months, her first, and perhaps most pleasing, novel of *Emmeline*, and its success was very general. It was published in the spring of 1788, and the whole of the first edition, 1500, sold so rapidly, that a second was immediately called for; and the late Mr Cadell[2] found his profits so considerable, that he had the liberality, voluntarily, to augment the price he had agreed to give for it. The success of her volume of Sonnets[3] was equally gratifying, and, exclusive of profit and reputation, procured her many valuable friends and estimable acquaintances, and some in the most exalted ranks of life; and it was not the least pleasing circumstance to a mother's heart, that her son in Bengal[4] owed his promotion in the civil service to her talents.

The novel of *Ethelinde* was published in 1789; *Celestina* in 1791.

She had quitted her cottage near Chichester, and lived sometimes in or near London, but chiefly at Brighthelmstone,[5] where she formed acquaintances with some of the most violent advocates of the French Revolution, and unfortunately caught the contagion, though in direct opposition to the principles she had formerly professed, and to those of her family.

It was during this paroxysm of political fever that she wrote the novel of *Desmond*; a work which has been greatly condemned, not only on account of its politics, but of its immoral tendency. I leave

---

1 Near Guildford in Surrey, now Wyke. A "cottage" might be considered a substantial house now.

2 Thomas Cadell's firm in the Strand was long-established and respected: he had published, for example, Samuel Johnson's *Lives of the Poets* and Edward Gibbon's *The Decline and Fall of the Roman Empire*. He became Smith's friend and mentor while publishing her early work, including her first three courtship novels, and the continually expanded volumes of her *Elegiac Sonnets*. But he disliked her pro-revolutionary tendency, first observable in *Celestina*, and refused her next two novels, *Desmond* and *The Old Manor House*. From the mid-1790s the firm was run by his son, also Thomas, and William Davies, with neither of whom she got on so well, though they published her last novel, *The Young Philosopher*.

3 First published in 1784 and reprinted in expanded forms throughout her lifetime.

4 William Towers Smith.

5 Brighton.

its defense to an abler pen, and content myself with regretting its consequences. It lost her some friends, and furnished others with an excuse for witholding their interest in favour of her family, and brought a host of *literary ladies* in array against her, armed with all the malignity which envy could inspire!

She had been in habits of intimacy for the last two or three years with Mr Hayley, (as well as with his lady,) then at the height of his poetical reputation, but this was a distinction not to be enjoyed with impunity. His praise was considered an encroachment on the rights of other muses,[1] (as he was accustomed to call his poetical female friends,) each of whom claimed the monopoly of his adulation. In the present day the prize would hardly be thought worth contending for. In 1792, Mrs Smith made one of the party at Eartham,[2] when Cowper[3] visited that spot. In 1793, her third son,[4] who was serving as an ensign in the 14th regiment of infantry, lost his leg at Dunkirk; and her own health began to sink under the pressure of so many afflictions, and continual harassing circumstances in which the family property was involved, in the arrangements of which her exertions were incessant. She removed to Bath, but received no benefit from the use of the waters. An imperfect[5] gout had fixed itself on her hands, probably increased by the constant use of her pen, which nevertheless she continued to employ, though some of her fingers were becoming contracted. Her second daughter[6] had been married to a gentleman of Normandy, (the Chevalier de Foville,) who had emigrated at the beginning of the Revolution. She fell into a decline after her first confinement, and died at Clifton in the spring of 1794. It would be impossible to describe the affliction Mrs Smith experienced on this occasion. Mothers only can comprehend

---

1　Dorset may refer particularly to Anna Seward's hostility to Smith.
2　Hayley's house in South Sussex.
3　William Cowper (1731-1800), author of *The Task* and other poems on religious and social subjects, admired by Smith.
4　Charles Dyer Smith, ensign in the Bedfordshires, had his leg amputated after fighting against French patriot forces, when the British government committed troops to support French counter-Revolutionary measures following the execution of Louis XVI.
5　Probably in the now obsolete sense of "cruel."
6　Anna Augusta.

it![1] From this time she became more than ever unsettled, moving from place to place in search of that tranquillity she was never to enjoy, yet continuing her literary occupation with astonishing application.

The dates of her different works are recorded in the Censura Literaria,[2] with the omission of a History of England for the use of young persons, which, I believe, was incomplete, and finished by some other person;[3] and Natural History of Birds, which was published in 1807.

The delay in the settlement of the property, which was equally embarrassing to all parties, at length induced one of them[4] to propose a compromise; and, by the assistance of a noble friend,[5] an adjustment of the respective claims was effected, but not without considerable loss on all sides. Still she derived great satisfaction that her family would be relieved from the difficulties she had so long contended with, although she was personally but little benefitted by it. So many years of mental anxiety and exertion had completely undermined a constitution, which nature seemed to have formed to endure unimpaired to old age; and convinced that her exhausted frame was sinking under increasing infirmity, she determined on removing into Surrey, from a desire that her mortal remains might be laid with those of her mother, and many of her father's family, in Stoke Church, near Guildford. In 1803, she removed from Frant,[6] near Tunbridge, to the village of Elsted, in the neighbourhood of Godalming. In the winter of 1804, I spent some time with her, when she was occupied in composing her charming little work for the use

---

1   Scott quotes from Hays' account: "'How lovely and how beloved she was,' says her afflicted mother in a letter to a friend, 'only those who knew her can tell. In the midst of perplexity and distress, till the loss of my child, which fell like the hand of death upon me, I could yet exert my faculties; and, in the consciousness of resource which they afforded to me, experience a sentiment not dissimilar to the Medea of Corneille, who replied to the enquiry of her confidant—"Where are now your resources?"—"In myself!"'"—*British Public Characters*, vol. iii., 62.

2   *Censura Literaria, containing Titles, Abstracts and Opinions of Old English Books* (1815), by Sir Egerton Brydges.

3   This was Mary Hays; the work was published in 1806.

4   Thomas Dyer, who married Benjamin Smith's widowed step-sister, Mary Berney.

5   George Wyndham, Earl of Egremont.

6   The original has "Frans."

of young persons, entitled '*Conversations*,'[1] which she occasionally wrote in the common sitting-room of the family, with two or three lively grandchildren playing about her, and conversing with great cheerfulness and pleasantry, though nearly confined to her sofa, in great bodily pain, and in a mortifying state of dependence on the services of others, but in full possession of all her faculties; a blessing of which she was most justly sensible, and for which she frequently expressed her gratitude to the Almighty.

In the following year she moved to Tilford, near Farnham, where her long sufferings were finally closed, on the 28th of October, 1806, in her 58th year. Mr Smith's death took place the preceding March. She was buried at Stoke, in compliance with her wishes, where a neat monument, executed by Bacon,[2] is erected to her memory, and that of two of her sons, Charles and George, both of whom perished in the West Indies, in the service of their country.[3]

To this sketch of the life of this admirable and much-injured woman, I am induced to attempt a delineation of her character, which, I think, has been as much misunderstood by her admirers, as

---

1   *Conversations, Introducing Poetry* (1804) is mainly by Smith but with some poems by Dorset.
2   John Bacon (1777-1859) R.A., also sculpted monuments for St. Paul's and Westminster Abbey.
3   Both were in the army, though Charles was in a non-combatant post because of his injury, but both were on family trust business at the times of their death. Scott quotes from *The Monthly Magazine*: "Of a family of twelve children, six only are living—three sons and three daughters. In her then surviving sons she was particularly happy—having lived to see the two elder ones advanced to honourable and lucrative appointments in the civil service of India, and both as high in character as in situation; their conduct towards their mother, to whom so much was due, and whom they loved so sincerely, was uniformly every thing that gratitude could dictate, and affection inspire. Her two other sons were in the army—the eldest of them a lieutenant-colonel, now on service with his regiment, whose conduct as a son, a gentleman, and a soldier, has ever been most truly gratifying to the feelings of a mother. The youngest son, who, with such a brother to excite his emulation, was advancing with credit and success in his military career, fell a second victim to the fatal fever at Surinam, the 16th of September, 1806, in his twenty-second year. His mother, who was particularly attached to him, was fortunate in being spared the misery of knowing he had preceded her to the grave— the sad tidings not having reached England till after her decease."—*The Monthly Magazine*, April, 1807.

it has been misrepresented by her enemies. Those who have formed their ideas of her from her works, and even from what she says, in her moments of despondency, about herself, have naturally concluded that she was of a melancholy disposition; but nothing could be more erroneous. Cheerfulness and gaiety were the natural characteristics of her mind; and though circumstances of the most depressing nature at times weighed down her spirit to the earth, yet such was its buoyancy that it quickly returned to its level. Even in the darkest periods of her life, she possessed the power of abstracting herself from her cares; and, giving play to the sportiveness of her imagination, could make even the difficulties she was labouring under subjects of merriment, placing both persons and things in such ridiculous points of view, and throwing out such sallies of pleasantry, that it was impossible not to be delighted with her wit, even while deploring the circumstances that excited it. It was said, by the confessor of the celebrated Madame de Coulanges,[1] that her sins were all epigrams: the observation might have been applied with equal propriety to Mrs Smith, who frequently gave her troubles a truly epigrammatic turn; she particularly excelled in little pieces of humorous poetry, in which she introduces so much fancy and elegance, that one cannot but regret, that, though some of them still exist, they are unintelligible except to the very few survivors who may yet recollect, with a melancholy pleasure, the circumstances that gave rise to them. She was very successful in parodies, and did not spare even her own poetry. In the society of persons she liked, and with whom she was under no restraint, with those who understood, and could enjoy her particular vein of humour, nothing could be more spirited, more racy, than her conversation: every sentence had its point, the effect of which was increased by the uncommon rapidity with which she spoke, as if her ideas flowed too fast for utterance; but among strangers, and with persons with whom she could not, or fancied she could not, assimilate, she was cold, silent and abstracted, disappointing those who had sought her society in the expectation of entertainment.

Notwithstanding her constant literary occupations, she never adopted the affectations, the inflated language, and exaggerated expressions, which literary ladies are often distinguished by, but

---

1 Marie-Angelique, Marquise de Coulanges (1641-1723), wit and commentator on the manners of her time; some of her correspondence was published.

always expressed herself with the utmost simplicity. She composed with greater facility than others could transcribe, and never would avail herself of an amanuensis, always asserting that it was more trouble to find them in comprehension[1] than to execute the business herself; in fact, the quickness of her conception was such, that she made no allowance for the slower faculties of others, and her impetuosity seldom allowed her to explain herself with the precision required by less ardent minds. This hastiness of temper was one of the greatest shades in her character, and one of her greatest misfortunes. As her feelings were acute, she expressed her resentments with an asperity, the imprudence of which she was not aware till it was too late, though perhaps she had forgotten the offense, and forgiven the offender, in ten minutes; but those who smarted under the severity of her lash were not so easily appeased, and she certainly created many enemies, from acting too frequently from the impulse of the moment.

She was always the friend of the unfortunate, and spared neither her time, her talents, or even her purse, in the cause of those she endeavoured to serve; and with a heart so warm, it may easily be believed she was frequently the dupe of her benevolence. The poor always found in her a kind protectress, and she never left any place of residence without bearing with her their prayers and regrets.

No woman had greater trials as a wife; very few could have acquitted themselves so well! But her conduct for twenty-three years speaks for itself. She was a most tender and anxious mother, and if she carried her indulgence to her children too far, it is an error too general to be very severely reprobated. To shield them as much as possible from the mortifying consequences of loss of fortune, was the object of her indefatigable exertions. Her reward was in their affection and gratitude, and in the approval of her own heart. If she derived a high degree of gratification in the homage paid to her talents, it was embittered by the envenomed shafts of envy and bigotry, and by the calumnies of anonymous defamers. By some she has been censured, because there is no religion in her works, though I believe there is not a line which implies a want of it in herself; and I am of opinion that Mrs Smith would have considered it as a subject much too sacred to be needlessly and irreverently brought forward in a work of fiction adapted for the hours of relaxation, not for those of serious reflection. Nor was it then the fashion of the day, as it has

---

1   To supply them with understanding.

become since. No one then took up a novel in the expectation of finding a sermon. 'Religious Courtships'[1] had not been revived, nor had Coelebs commenced his peregrinations in Search of a Wife.[2] In introducing politics in one of her works,[3] she incurred equal censure, and with greater reason; it was sinning against good taste in a female writer—perhaps there was a little personal spleen mixed up with her patriotism.[4]

Mrs Smith's reputation as an author, rests less on her prose works, (which were frequently hastily written, in sickness and in sorrow,) than on her poetry. Her Sonnets and other Poems have passed through eleven editions, and have been translated into French and Italian; and so highly were her talents estimated, that, on the death of Dr Warton,[5] she was requested to supply his epitaph, which she declined, though she could not but feel the value of such a compliment, from the members of a society so fertile in poets as Winchester College.

Mrs Smith left no *posthumous* works whatever. The sweepings of her closet were, without exception, committed to the flames. The novel published about three years ago,[6] with her name affixed to it, with an intention of imposing it on the public as her work, is a fraud

---

1   *Religious Courtship: Historical Discourses on the Necessity of Marrying Religious Husbands and Wives Only*, by Daniel Defoe, was first published in 1722, but as Dorset implies, the Evangelical Movement was growing in the last quarter of the eighteenth century. This supplied a larger readership for didactic texts in the nineteenth.

2   Hannah More's novel, *Coelebs in Search of a Wife* (1809), recommends piety as the most important quality a man should look for in a prospective wife.

3   *Desmond* (1792), Smith's most pro-Revolutionary novel.

4   As often, following the American Revolution, patriotism meant sympathy with the revolutionaries, here the French.

5   Joseph Warton, brother of the Laureate Thomas Warton, and First Master of Winchester College.

6   A three-volume novel called *The Republican's Mistress* appeared under Smith's name in 1821, too late to be the one intended here. *D'Arcy*, by a Charlotte Smith, was published in Dublin in 1793. Of this Smith said in a letter of 20 January 1794, "It is quite enough Heaven knows to answer for the nonsense one writes oneself.... Perhaps this D'Arcy may have been written by a Charlotte Smith, for one of that name was divorced not long ago, and another hang'd. If I were to indulge a *jeu de mots* [word-play], I should say I am neither so *fortunate* or so *unfortunate* as to be either of those ladies." She asked for a disclaimer of authorship to be published in the Dublin papers. Dorset may refer to a later edition of that novel.

which, it seems, the law affords no redress for. Those who have looked into it, assure me there is sufficient evidence in the work itself to defeat the intention, and that no person of common sense can be deceived by it; but a more public exposure of such an imposition is required, in justice to Mrs Smith's memory.

In closing this melancholy retrospection of a life so peculiarly and invariably marked by adversity, it is impossible not to experience the keenest regret, that a being with a mind so highly gifted, a heart so alive to every warm and generous feeling; with beauty to delight, and virtues to attach all hearts; so formed herself for happiness, and so eminently qualified to dispense it to others, should have been, from her early youth, the devoted[1] victim of folly, vice, and injustice! Who but must contrast her miserable destiny with the brilliant station she would have held in the world under happier circumstances? But her guardian angel slept!

[Catherine Dorset's memoir is followed by Scott's appreciative comment on Smith's work, first appearing in his *Lives of the Novelists* of 1821, some of which is extracted in the Broadview edition of Smith's *Emmeline*.]

---

1 Doomed.

Select Bibliography

Bermingham, Ann. "The Picturesque and Ready-To-Wear Femininity." *The Politics of the Picturesque: Literature, Landscape and Aesthetics Since 1770*. Ed. Stephen Copley and Peter Garside. Cambridge: Cambridge UP, 1994. 81-119.

Bray, Matthew. "Removing the Anglo-Saxon Yoke: The Francocentric Vision of Charlotte Smith's Later Works." *The Wordsworth Circle* 24 (1993): 155-58.

Butler, Marilyn. *Burke, Paine, Godwin and the Revolution Controversy*. Cambridge: Cambridge UP, 1984.

Brooks, Stella. "The Sonnets of Charlotte Smith." *The Critical Survey* 4.1 (1992): 9-21.

Copeland, Edward. *Women Writing about Money: Women's Fiction in England 1790-1820*. Cambridge: Cambridge UP, 1995.

Curran, Stuart. "Romantic Poetry: the I Altered." *Romanticism and Feminism*. Ed. Anne K. Mellor. Bloomington: Indiana UP, 1988. 185-207.

Doody, Margaret. "English Women Novelists and the French Revolution." *La Femme en Angleterre et dans les Colonies Americaines aux XVIIe et XVIIIe Siecles*. Lille: Pub. De l'Univ. de Lille III, 1976. 176-98.

Ellis, Kate Ferguson. *The Contested Castle: Gothic Novels and the Subversion of Domestic Ideology*. Urbana: Illinois UP, 1989.

Fletcher, Loraine. *Charlotte Smith: A Critical Biography*. Basingstoke: Macmillan, 1998.

Foster, James R. "Charlotte Smith, Pre-Romantic Novelist." *PMLA* 43 (1928): 463-75.

Fry, Carrol Lee. *Charlotte Smith*. New York: Twayne, 1996.

Hays, Mary. "Mrs. Charlotte Smith." *British Public Characters* 3 (1800-01): 44-67.

Hilbish, Florence M.A. *Charlotte Smith, Poet and Novelist (1749-1806)*. Philadelphia: Pennsylvania UP, 1941.

Howells, Coral Ann. *Love, Mystery and Misery: Feeling in Gothic Fiction*. London: Athlone, 1978.

Hunt, Bishop C. "Wordsworth and Charlotte Smith." *The Wordsworth Circle* 1 (1970): 85-103.

Mei Huang. *Transforming the Cinderella Dream: From Frances Burney to Charlotte Bronte*. New Brunswick: Rutgers UP, 1990.

Jones, Chris. *Radical Sensibility: Literature and Ideas in the 1790s*. London: Routledge, 1993.

Kelly, Gary. *The English Jacobin Novel*. Oxford: Clarendon, 1976.

Kennedy, Deborah. "Thorns and Roses: The Sonnets of Charlotte Smith." *Women's Writing* 2.1(1995): 43-53.

Labbe, Jacqueline M. "Selling One's Sorrows: Charlotte Smith, Mary Robinson and the Marketing of Poetry." *The Wordsworth Circle* 25.2 (1994): 68-71.

———. *Charlotte Smith: Romanticism, Poetry and the Culture of Gender.* Manchester: Manchester UP, 2003.

Maniquis, Robert M., ed. *British Radical Culture of the 1790s*. California: Huntington, 2002.

Martin, S.R. "Charlotte Smith, 1749-1806, a Critical Survey of her Works and Place in English Literary History." Diss. U of Sheffield, 1980.

Mullan, John. *Sentiment and Sociability: The Language of Feeling in the Eighteenth-Century Novel*. Oxford: Clarendon, 1998.

Pascoe, Judith. "Female Botanists and the Poetry of Charlotte Smith." *Re-Visioning Romanticism: British Women Writers, 1776-1837*. Ed. Carol Shiner Wilson and Joel Haefner. Philadelphia: Pennsylvania UP, 1994. 193-209.

———. *Romantic Theatricality: Gender, Poetry and Spectatorship*. Ithaca: Cornell UP, 1997.

Rogers, Katherine M. "Romantic Aspirations, Restricted Possibilities: the Novels of Charlotte Smith." *Re-Visioning Romanticism: British Women Writers 1776-1837*. Ed. Carol Shiner Wilson and Joel Haefner. Philadelphia: Pennsylvania UP, 1994. 72-88.

Schofield, Mary Anne. "The Witchery of Fiction: Charlotte Smith, Novelist." *Living by the Pen: Early British Women Writers*. Ed. Dale Spender. New York: Teachers College Press, 1992. 177-87.

Smith, Charlotte. *Emmeline*. Ed. Loraine Fletcher. Peterborough, ON: Broadview, 2003.

———. *Desmond*. Ed. Janet Todd and Antje Blank. Peterborough, ON: Broadview, 2001.

———. *Letters*. Ed. Judith Phillips Stanton. Bloomington: Indiana UP, 2003.

———. *Poems*. Ed. Stuart Curran. Oxford: Oxford UP, 1993.

———. *The Old Manor House*. Ed. Jacqueline M. Labbe. Peterborough, ON: Broadview, 2002.

———. *The Young Philosopher*. Ed. Elizabeth Kraft. Lexington: Kentucky UP, 1999.

[For other works by Smith, see Chronology.]

Spencer, Jane. *The Rise of the Woman Novelist: From Aphra Behn to Jane Austen*. Oxford: Blackwell, 1986.

Stanton, Judith Phillips. "Charlotte Smith's Literary Business: Income, Patronage and Indigence." *The Age of Johnson* 1 (1987): 375-401.

Turner, Rufus Paul. "Charlotte Smith (1749-1806): New Light on her Life and Literary Career." Diss. U of Southern California, 1966.

White, Daniel. "Autobiography and Elegy: The Early Romantic Poetics of Thomas Gray and Charlotte Smith." *Early Romantics: Perspectives in British Poetry from Pope to Wordsworth*. Basingstoke: Macmillan, 1998. 57-69.

Wright, Walter Francis. *Sensibility in English Prose Fiction: A Reinterpretation*. London: Russell and Russell, 1937.

Zimmerman, Sarah Mackenzie. "Charlotte Smith's Letters and the Practice of Self-Presentation." *The Princeton University Library Chronicle* 53.1 (1991): 50-77.

———. *Romanticism, Lyricism and History*. Albany: NYU, 1999.